Catherine Cooks daughter of a p believed to be her eventually move married Tom Co the age of forty she began writing about the lives of the working-class people with whom she had grown up, using the place of her birth as the background to many of her novels.

Although originally acclaimed as a regional writer – her novel *The Round Tower* won the Winifred Holtby award for the best regional novel of 1968 – her readership soon began to spread throughout the world. Her novels have been translated into more than a dozen languages and more than 50,000,000 copies of her books have been sold in Corgi alone. Many of her novels have been made into successful television dramas, and more are planned.

Catherine Cookson's many bestselling novels established her as one of the most popular of contemporary women novelists. After receiving an OBE in 1985, Catherine Cookson was created a Dame of the British Empire in 1993. She was appointed an Honorary Fellow of St Hilda's College, Oxford in 1997. For many years she lived near Newcastle-upon-Tyne. She died shortly before her ninety-second birthday in June 1998 having completed 104 works, nine of which are being published posthumously.

'Catherine Cookson's novels are about hardship, the intractability of life and of individuals, the struggle first to survive and next to make sense of one's survival. Humour, toughness, resolution and generosity are Cookson virtues, in a world which she often depicts as cold and violent. Her novels are weighted and driven by her own early experiences of illegitimacy and poverty. This is what gives them power. In the specialised world of women's popular fiction, Cookson has created her own territory'
Helen Dunmore, *The Times*

BOOKS BY CATHERINE COOKSON

NOVELS

Kate Hannigan
The Fifteen Streets
Colour Blind
Maggie Rowan
Rooney
The Menagerie
Slinky Jane
Fanny Mcbride
Fenwick Houses
Heritage of Folly
The Garment
The Fen Tiger
The Blind Miller
House of Men
Hannah Massey
The Long Corridor
The Unbaited Trap
Katie Mulholland
The Round Tower
The Nice Bloke
The Glass Virgin
The Invitation
The Dwelling Place
Feathers in the Fire
Pure as the Lily
The Mallen Streak
The Mallen Girl
The Mallen Litter
The Invisible Cord
The Gambling Man
The Tide of Life
The Slow Awakening
The Iron Façade
The Girl
The Cinder Path
Miss Martha Mary Crawford
The Man Who Cried
Tilly Trotter
Tilly Trotter Wed
Tilly Trotter Widowed

The Whip
Hamilton
The Black Velvet Gown
Goodbye Hamilton
A Dinner of Herbs
Harold
The Moth
Bill Bailey
The Parson's Daughter
Bill Bailey's Lot
The Cultured Handmaiden
Bill Bailey's Daughter
The Harrogate Secret
The Black Candle
The Wingless Bird
The Gillyvors
My Beloved Son
The Rag Nymph
The House of Women
The Maltese Angel
The Year of the Virgins
The Golden Straw
Justice is a Woman
The Tinker's Girl
A Ruthless Need
The Obsession
The Upstart
The Branded Man
The Bonny Dawn
The Bondage of Love
The Desert Crop
The Lady on My Left
The Solace of Sin
Riley
The Blind Years
The Thursday Friend
A House Divided
Kate Hannigan's Girl
Rosie of the River

THE MARY ANN STORIES

A Grand Man
The Lord and Mary Ann
The Devil and Mary Ann
Love and Mary Ann

Life and Mary Ann
Marriage and Mary Ann
Mary Ann's Angels
Mary Ann and Bill

FOR CHILDREN

Matty Doolin
Joe and the Gladiator
The Nipper
Rory's Fortune
Our John Willie

Mrs Flannagan's Trumpet
Go Tell It To Mrs Golightly
Lanky Jones
Nancy Nutall and the Mongrel
Bill and the Mary Ann Shaughnessy

AUTOBIOGRAPHY

Our Kate
Catherine Cookson Country

Let Me Make Myself Plain
Plainer Still

The Mary Ann Novels
Volume 2

Including
LIFE AND MARY ANN
MARRIAGE AND MARY ANN
MARY ANN'S ANGELS
MARY ANN AND BILL

Catherine Cookson

CORGI BOOKS

THE MARY ANN NOVELS VOLUME 2
A CORGI BOOK : 0552148016
9780552148016

First publication in Great Britain

PRINTING HISTORY
This Corgi collection first published 2000
Copyright © The Trustees of the Catherine Cookson Charitable Trusts 2000

3 5 7 9 10 8 6 4 2

including

LIFE AND MARY ANN
Originally published in Great Britain by Macdonald & Co. (Publishers) Ltd
Copyright © Catherine Cookson 1962

MARRIAGE AND MARY ANN
Originally published in Great Britain by Macdonald & Co. (Publishers) Ltd
Copyright © Catherine Cookson 1964

MARY ANN'S ANGELS
Originally published in Great Britain by Macdonald & Co. (Publishers) Ltd
Copyright © Catherine Cookson 1965

MARY ANN AND BILL
Originally published in Great Britain by Macdonald & Co. (Publishers) Ltd
Copyright © Catherine Cookson 1967

Set in 11/12pt Sabon by
Kestrel Data, Exeter, Devon.

Corgi Books are published by Transworld Publishers,
61–63 Uxbridge Road, London W5 5SA,
a division of The Random House Group Ltd,
in Australia by Random House Australia (Pty) Ltd,
20 Alfred Street, Milsons Point, Sydney, NSW 2061, Australia,
in New Zealand by Random House New Zealand Ltd,
18 Poland Road, Glenfield, Auckland 10, New Zealand
and in South Africa by Random House (Pty) Ltd,
Isle of Houghton, Corner of Boundary Road & Carse O'Gowrie,
Houghton 2198, South Africa.

Printed and bound in Great Britain by
Cox & Wyman Ltd, Reading, Berkshire.

Papers used by Transworld Publishers are natural, recyclable
products made from wood grown in sustainable forests.
The manufacturing processes conform to the environmental
regulations of the country of origin.

LIFE AND
MARY ANN

Catherine Cookson

CORGI BOOKS

PART ONE

GROWING PAINS

1

I wish I'd never clapped eyes on him. I wish he had left us alone.

What! In Mulhattan's Hall?

Mary Ann hunched her shoulders as indication that she was ignoring the voice of gratitude that usually played no small part as a component of her character. Well, he made you sick, he did. Who did he think he was, anyway? Playing God. Directing all their lives. He certainly tried to live up to his name . . . Mr Lord, indeed! Well, he could think he was the Lord, and act like him, but he wasn't going to get the better of her in this latest fight . . . But he had, he had already got the better of her, hadn't he?

Mary Ann unclenched her hands and rose slowly from the side of the bed and walked towards the window. There had been a black frost in the night, there would soon be snow. The cutting air came from the window-pane and chilled her nose and lips. So cold was her mouth that she did not feel her teeth biting into the flesh. But she felt the trembling of her chin in its fight, not against the cold, but against the rising storm of tears.

Although she was gazing across the farmyard

towards the house on the hill, Mr Lord's house, she was seeing none of these things. The width of the farmyard had taken on the shape of a face. The buildings at each side were cheeks, high-boned, prominent cheeks, and Mr Lord's house on the hill was a deep brow, half covered with tumbled black hair. Somewhere, in the distance between the farm and the house on the hill, were the eyes of Corny. They were deep-set, and dark. She couldn't see if they were merry, or sad, or held that spark of fighting fire that made him stand up to people . . . Stand up to Mr Lord.

For over three years Corny had stood up to Mr Lord. From the very day he had come to her thirteenth birthday party, a belated, awkward, aggressive, grotesquely dressed guest, he had stood up to him. His appearance on that day had thrown the whole party out of joint. But he had made an impression on Mr Lord, for the old man had recognised in the gangling fifteen-year-old a worthy opponent, worthy to fight, worthy of many things . . . in fact, of anything in the world, but herself. Corny, in a subtle, even cunning way, had stood firm against all Mr Lord's tactics, and had got the better of him time and time again where she herself was concerned. And in the end he would have won. She knew this, she felt it. But what does he do? What does Corny do? Of a startling sudden, he gives in to Mr Lord. He accepts the offer that the old man has been dangling like a golden carrot under his nose for years.

When she had gone for him last night, almost reaching five feet in her wild indignation, he had remained utterly calm. The only time he had raised his voice was when he said, 'Look, I'm tellin' you, he's got nowt to do with it.'

She knew that he had used nowt to vex her, because he could speak as well as anybody now, even as good as their Michael. Had she not coached him month after month from that thirteenth birthday when she had given him his first lesson in English? Northern English, for although her grammar was correct, the inflexion of the dialect was still thick on her. But so convincing had been his denial that Mr Lord had any hand in his decision to go to America, that she had asked, with pain-touched docility, 'Is it because they are always ragging you about me being so little?' He gave a scornful, hard laugh before saying quietly, 'Don't be daft.' And then he had added, with a touch of the quiet, sly humour that she loved, 'It's just as well you're no bigger, else you'd aim to wear the pants all the time. Not that you don't have a go, even now.'

She had not laughed for her mind was looking at the saying literally. The waist of his trousers would reach up to her bust, and her head came far below his thick shoulder. Over the last few years she had done everything possible to put on inches. During one period, she had measured herself every day for three months, until the disheartening result had begun to affect her. Her mother had said, 'If you worry, it will stop you growing.' Her da had said, comfortingly, 'You'll sprout all at once, you'll see. One of these mornings you'll wake up and find your feet sticking through the bed rails. Anyway,' he had added, with his arm about her shoulder, 'you've got more in your little finger than most people have got in their great boast bodies.' But that comfort did not make up for such silly remarks as, 'You two are like Mutt and Jeff,' or, 'Here comes the long and the short of it.'

She had tried wearing very high heels. The first pair of stiletto shoes she had worn had caused her da and Corny to fall against each other with laughing. Somehow she didn't suit high heels, and so she had been unable to take advantage of such helpful accessories. But what did it matter? High heels, the long and the short of it, Mutt and Jeff, that wasn't the reason he was going. He was going because Mr Lord had won.

At this point in her thinking the bedroom door clicked and her mother came in. At thirty-eight Elizabeth Shaughnessy appeared like a woman bordering on thirty. Her face was without lines, her long blonde hair resting in a bun on the nape of her neck still retained its natural sheen. Her bearing was dignified. During the last three years, with the lessening of worry, life had seemed to stand still for her. Only during these last years had she taken the comfort of the farmhouse and the security of Mike's position as a natural sequence of events. Mike no longer drank – at least he no longer got drunk – and this fact alone would have spelt security no matter where they had lived. But in the comparative opulence of the farmhouse – comparative when thinking of their early beginnings, in the slum in Burton Street, known as Mulhattan's Hall – the fact that he was steady had paid dividends far surpassing anything she had ever dreamed of. Not that she had been entirely free from worry over the last three years; she experienced the usual worries of a mother concerning her son and daughter. But, as from the very beginning, it was the daughter who gave her cause for most concern. Somehow, Michael's life had always seemed cut and dried. Right from when he was a child, even before he ever saw a farm, he had wanted, like his father, to be a farmer. In times past she had thought this was the only thing father and son had in common. Now, all that was changed. But with Mary Ann it had been different. Perhaps it was the fact of Mr Lord coming into her life that had made Mary Ann more of a trial. And yet she knew she shouldn't think of her daughter in that sense. Mary Ann had been the saviour of them all. But for Mary Ann they would be rotting in Mulhattan's Hall at this moment. She had no illusion about the strength of her husband. Without this environment, brought about by his daughter's strategy, Mike would still be fighting a losing battle with the drink and the shipyard.

Lizzie knew that everything in life must be paid for, and Mary Ann was expected to pay Mr Lord in the kind of payment he most desired. By becoming the wife of his grandson she would be tied to him for life. He would then have claims on her far outreaching those of the present. And it was a glorious prospect, Lizzie knew, when looked at unemotionally: Mary Ann Shaughnessy, a child from the slums of Jarrow, lifted into the family, the élite family of the Lords, where money and power went hand in hand.

Three years ago, when the old man's plans had been made known to her, Lizzie's first reaction had been one of shock and disgust. Mary Ann was only a child, a child of thirteen . . . not thirteen.

And Mr Lord was actually voicing his plans to marry her to Tony his grandson. Tony was then twenty-four and seemed already a very adult man. But the shock and disgust had not lasted long, for when Lizzie thought about it calmly she became excited, even elated, almost overcome with the idea of this wonderful future for her child. That was until she realised that Mary Ann's interest in Corny Boyle was no passing childish fancy. Her daughter, she knew, took strong likes and dislikes, and where she liked she almost nearly loved. She loved her father more than she did God. She loved, yes, she loved the old man, there was no doubt about that. She loved him, she stood up to him, she fought with him but she loved him. And she also loved Corny Boyle. That was the trouble, that was the worry now in Lizzie's life. Or it had been up till yesterday when Corny had sprung his decision on them all. He had walked into the kitchen, unannounced, and with a coolness that set Lizzie wondering, he had told them he was going to America. She wondered if this big, raw-boned fellow was calculating the benefits to be derived from submitting to Mr Lord, or if he was being super-humanly unselfish and leaving the road clear for her daughter. Whichever way it was, she thanked God from the bottom of her heart that Corny Boyle had decided to go to America. But now before her lay the task of comforting Mary Ann.

'Come on downstairs, lass, you're froze up here.'

Mary Ann remained gazing out of the window. And her voice was flat-sounding as she replied, 'I'm all right. I'm not cold.' Her mother had called her 'lass'. She only called her that when she was deeply touched. She usually called her Mary Ann or 'My dear', and she had insisted some time ago that she be called 'Mother' and not 'Ma'. Mary Ann's lips moved tightly over one another. That was Mr Lord again. She could hear his voice now, saying to her mother, 'You must make her drop this "Ma" way of addressing you, Mrs Shaughnessy. Make her adopt Mother. It is a much nicer term, don't you think?' When her da had found out about this – and he had found out, because her mother kept insisting that she did not call her 'Ma' – he had cried out indignantly, 'To hell! If you are Ma to her, then you are Ma to her . . . And let me tell you this. You'll lose something by being more Mother than Ma. I'm tellin' you! As for the old boy. If he approaches me with the idea of turning me into Father, I'll spit in his eye. So help me God, I will.'

Her mother had had to do a lot of talking to calm her father down that time.

'Come on down.' Lizzie's voice was soft and coaxing. 'The tea's all set, and Michael and Sarah will be here any minute. Come on.'

Mary Ann turned and looked at her mother, and her voice held no bitterness as she said, 'You're glad he's going, aren't you?'

'Oh no, I'm not. What makes you say that? Oh no, I'm not.' Lizzie's reply was too quick. There was too much emphasis on her words. Mary Ann lowered her lids, covering her great brown eyes from her mother's gaze. Her mother couldn't lie very well. She turned her head away and looked out of the window again before saying, 'Why is it you don't mind our Michael going with Sarah, but you have always minded me and Corny?'

Lizzie could find no words, no false words with which to answer this statement. If she had spoken the truth she would have said, 'It's a man's position that matters. Michael's future is set. At the end of this year, when he finishes his probation on the farm, he will go to the Agricultural College. His future is mapped out. He'll be a farmer. If there wasn't a job waiting for him here, he could get set on anywhere. Perhaps I would have liked someone better than Sarah Flannagan for him, because, as you know, none of us can stand her mother. But I must admit that Sarah's turned out to be a nice lass. And moreover she's Michael's choice.' Perhaps her son had one more thing in common with his father. There'd only ever be one woman for him. There were men like that. They were few and far between, God knew, but there were still some left; and she had the feeling in her heart that Sarah Flannagan was the only one for Michael and he for her, strange as it seemed, for only a few years ago Sarah hated the sight of Mary Ann, and Michael into the bargain. But then, like a child, she was taking the pattern from her mother.

Mary Ann said into the silence, 'You're supposed to like Mrs McBride, and she's his grandmother.'

'Of course, I like Fanny. I could almost say I love her. But there's a great distance between a woman and her grandson. Not that I don't like Corny. I've told you, I do like Corny. Why do you keep on?'

Mary Ann nodded to the icy window-pane. 'But

16

you don't like him for me, because there's Tony, isn't there? And Mr Lord. Mr Lord's little plan. Oh, I know all about it. But listen to me, Mother.' She pulled herself away from Lizzie's side. She even stepped back a pace to widen the distance between them, before saying, 'I'll never marry Tony. Not to please you, or him, or anybody else.'

'Who's talking about Tony?'

'You are. You're thinking about him all the time. That's why you've never been able to take to Corny. Corny hadn't a big house. He hadn't a splendid job. He hadn't a grandfather rolling in the money. But let me tell you, Mother, Corny will make his name with either one thing or the other. With either cars or his cornet. Oh, yes. That's been a laugh in the house for a long time now. Corny, with his cars and his cornet. The three Cs. Well! You wait and see . . .'

As Mary Ann's head drooped forward and the tears began to roll down her cheeks, Lizzie cried, 'Aw! lass, lass. Aw! don't cry like that.' And she enfolded her daughter in her arms and rocked her gently back and forwards as if she were still the elfin-faced child. The endearing, maddening, precocious, beguiling child. And she was still a child. She would always remain a child to Lizzie. And she wanted her child to be looked after; and like every mother, she felt that half the battle would be won if there was money at hand to help with the looking after.

Saturday tea was still a function, a time when Lizzie had her family all around her. It was usually a meal of leisure with no-one dashing to catch a bus to the secretarial school in Newcastle

– that was Mary Ann; or golloping the meal to attend to this, that, or the other on the farm – that was Mike; or, if not following his father's pattern and dashing outside, reading, reading, reading – that was Michael, always reading, and not eating. There were more books in the house concerning the diseases that animals were prone to than in the Public Library, so Lizzie thought. But Saturday was different.

All Saturday morning Lizzie baked for the tea. Besides the old standbys, egg-and-bacon pie, fruit tarts and scones, there was always something new. She liked to try a new recipe each week. On Tuesday she would look forward to the coming of her magazine. Not for the stories, but for the recipes, and each Saturday they would tease her, 'What's it, the day, another stomach binder? By! I'll sue that paper afore long.' Mike would generally start in this way, and the others would follow suit. However, they nearly always ate the last crumb of her new recipe. But today things hadn't gone according to plan. Mike made no reference whatever to the table. His large, heavy, handsome face looked dark as he took his seat at the head, and immediately he gave signs of his inward mood by running his hands through his thick red hair, and this after combing it only a few minutes earlier.

Lizzie felt a rising irritation in her as she gauged her husband's mood. He wasn't going to start and take up the cudgels again. Talk about like father, like son. It had never been like that in this family, it had always been like father, like daughter. Mike was also, she knew, blaming Mr Lord for Corny's decision. Although the boy had stated flatly that no-one had influenced him, Mike was as furious at this moment against the old man as Mary Ann herself. It was quite some time now since any major issue had occurred to make Mike take sides against Mr Lord. As Lizzie looked sharply between her husband and her daughter, she thought she could almost feel the emotions flowing between them, as if they were linked by actual blood vessels. Talk about Siamese twins. As was her wont when worried, she muttered a little prayer to herself. It was, as usual, in the nature of a demanding plea, and in this particular case she asked that Mike might not lose his temper with the old man. 'Let him go for anyone else, but not for Mr Lord, dear God.'

Trying to bring normality into the proceedings, Lizzie now addressed herself to Sarah. 'How's business been this week, Sarah?' she asked with a smile.

'Oh, not too good at all. The roads have been so slippery. It's been hard enough to exercise them. And nobody seems inclined to ride. I don't blame them. I nearly stuck to the saddle yesterday morning.'

'I don't know how you do it. I think you're wonderful.'

Sarah Flannagan remained smiling across the table at Lizzie. But she made no answer. She would have been glad had this woman thought she was wonderful, but she felt it was merely a phase. She knew there was tension in the house and that Elizabeth Shaughnessy was trying to smooth things over. Some day she hoped, and from the depth of her being, that this woman would be her mother-in-law, and yet she was a little afraid of her. Yes, the truth was, she was a little afraid of her. She thought she wasn't quite good enough for Michael. All mothers felt like that about daughters-in-law, so she understood, and so she felt sure that Elizabeth Shaughnessy would finally accept her into the family, whereas she would never reconcile herself to accept Corny Boyle. This thought brought her eyes flicking towards Mary Ann. It was hard at this moment to think that Mary Ann and herself had been bitter enemies from the day they first met until just a short while ago. She did not delude herself that the first day she came to this house, when she led the dapple, Mary Ann's thirteenth birthday present from Mr Lord, up the road, and was asked to stay to tea, that it was from that day that she and Mary Ann had become friends. No, on that day Mary Ann had tolerated her because her mind was taken up with other important things. Corny Boyle, for instance, and her pony, and her posh friends from Newcastle, to mention a few. Even in the days that followed Mary Ann's acceptance was touched with condescension, although she gave her back with good measure everything she dealt out . . . In a way, they had still been at war. It was only in the last few months Mary Ann had been different. But then she herself had been different. They both seemed to have grown up over night, and recognising this they had come together and talked. They had talked about Michael and they had talked about Corny. So now at this moment she could understand what Mary Ann was going through. She also knew that because his daughter was unhappy Mr Shaughnessy was in a tearing rage. She had never seen him look so thundery. She could remember back to the times when he used to come home roaring drunk to Mulhattan's Hall. She could remember the day he had danced and sang in the road; and Mary Ann had come and taken him home and she had gibed at her: 'Your da is a no-good drunk,' she had shouted. And mimicked Mary Ann's oft-repeated phrase, 'Me da's a grand man.' And yet now there was nothing more she wanted in life than to be a member of this family, and to call Mike Shaughnessy 'Da'. In a way, although she loved her own father, there was something greatly attractive, greatly endearing about Mike Shaughnessy, and it would be an added happiness the day he became her father-in-law.

'What are you dreaming about?' The gentle dig in the ribs from Michael turned her face towards him, and she laughed and said, 'Horses.'

Michael let his eyes rest on her. He loved to look at her. He knew she hadn't been thinking of horses; he had come to know all the flowing movement and expression of her vivacious dark face. Sarah was beautiful, she was more than beautiful. To him she was everything a fellow could dream of. She had a lot of sense in her, which was strange when he thought of her father and mother, though he must say he liked Mr Flannagan; he liked him much better than he liked her mother. But Sarah was like neither of them. She had a sort of deep wisdom about her. If he was going off the deep end about this, that, or the other, she would come out with something that astounded him with its profundity. He who had attended the Grammar School up to a year ago could not think to the depth that Sarah's mind took her. He wondered how his mother would take it if he wanted to get married before he started college. Likely she would go mad.

'Michael, you're not eating anything.' Lizzie brought his eyes from Sarah, and he said, 'Well, what do you expect after all that dinner?'

'I've never known your dinner stop you eating your Saturday tea.' Lizzie now turned to Mary Ann and said, quietly, 'Shall I fill your cup again?'

'No, Mother, no, thanks. I've had enough.' As she turned her glance from her mother, she met the full penetrating force of Mike's eyes on her. They were looking into her, probing the hurt, and feeling it almost as much as herself. In his eyes was a reflection of her own anger, and she thought in the idiom that no convent-school training, no English mistress who had selected her for personal torture while dealing with clauses had been able to erase: 'Eee! there'll be ructions if I don't stop him. But he's not to go for Mr Lord. I'll tell him what I think, meself.' She knew she could tell Mr Lord what she thought, she knew that she could show her temper to him, answer his own arrogant manner with what her mother would term 'cheek' and get away with it, but, not so, her da. Mr Lord liked her da. She felt that although she in the first place had to point out to Mr Lord, and emphatically, the qualities that made up her father, he had come to respect and like him from his own judgement. But that wasn't saying that he would stand her father accusing him of sending Corny off to America, and that is what Mike would do if she didn't stop him. She was thankful that Mr Lord wouldn't be back on the farm until Tuesday. In the meantime she must get at her da. But she knew she wouldn't have much weight with him unless she could prove to him that she wasn't all that much affected. This would be nigh impossible if she continued to go around looking as if the end of the world had come. But it had for her. Her world seemed to have been sliced in two, so that she was faced with a gulf over which she must either jump or remain in a state of pain for ever. She made an attempt at the jump by looking at Sarah and asking in a voice which she strove with great effort to make ordinary, 'What are you wearing for the wedding?'

Sarah, looking back at her with the threaded intuition of youth, immediately played up by raising a laugh. 'If this weather keeps up, black stockings, woollen undies, and a wind-cheater.'

Lizzie laughed, louder than she would have done on another occasion. Michael laughed, his head back in the same attitude that his father used when his laughter was running free. Mike only allowed a quirk to appear at the corner of his mouth, but he nodded towards Sarah as he said, 'Sensible idea.'

'Fancy having a white wedding at this time of year. And those two, with a nuptial mass!' Michael bowed his head and shook it from side to side as he chuckled to himself, and then added, 'I shouldn't have been surprised if Len had said he was going up to the altar in tails.'

Mary Ann too wanted to laugh at the thought of Len, the cowman, going up to the altar in tails. Len was dim – they all knew that Len was dim – and Cissie, his girl, was even lower down in the mental grade. She was round and placid, and ever smiling; and she had a stock phrase, with which she punctuated every question and answer. She could hear her now, 'Well now, Mrs Shaughnessy, I've always wanted a white weddin'.' 'And well now, with Mr Lord showing his appreciation of Len so, standing the spread for us, and givin' Len a rise and all that, well now, I thought we should do things fittin' like.' Part of Mary Ann felt sorry for Cissie but she didn't really know why. Sometimes she thought it was because, as she said to herself, Cissie had never had a chance, there had never been a Mr Lord in Cissie's life. Yet at the same time she recognised that all the Mr Lords in the world couldn't have made much difference to Cissie. Cissie, like Len, was dim. But that didn't say they shouldn't have a nuptial mass . . .

This point was as good as any other on which to start an argument with Michael. She knew she had to do something, and quickly, to switch her thoughts from weddings in general to a wedding in particular, which of late had been finding a prominent place in her thinking. So, as she had done from as far back as she could remember, she attacked Michael in her usual way. 'What's funny about a nuptial mass, about their having a nuptial mass? They've as much right to have a nuptial mass as you or anybody else!'

'Oh! here we go again!' Michael rolled his eyes towards the ceiling before bringing his head down and bouncing it towards Mary Ann, emphasising each word as he said, 'I didn't say they hadn't the right to have a nuptial mass. But those two won't have a clue what it's all about. They'll sit through the service without a clue. Do you think they will be affected by the spirituality of the whole thing? Can you imagine Len thinking?'

'How do you know if they'll be affected spiritually or not? Because Len has never been to a grammar school it doesn't say that his spiritual awareness isn't as alive as yours!'

'Aw . . . Bulls, heifers, cows and calves!' Michael always managed to impregnate this saying with the same quality that another would give to strident blasphemy and it affected Lizzie in this way; she often thought she would rather hear Michael swear than say that. It wasn't the words themselves but the stringing of them together, and the inflexion of his voice as he said them. 'Now, that's enough, Michael. And you too, Mary Ann! The pair of you stop it.'

'Well, Mother, I ask you.' Michael knew he was being pulled up and why. But he smiled at Lizzie and said pityingly, 'Well, I ask you. Len and Cissie in a nuptial mass! If one of them had been a little different, a bit bright, it mightn't have appeared so bad, but they are a pair . . .'

'Yes, you've said it there, they're a pair.' Mike was speaking now and they all looked towards him. But he was looking at Michael only. 'And they're paired properly. What do you think Len's life would be like if he was marrying a more intelligent girl? . . . Hell, that's what it would be. There's something in nature, if let alone, that helps us with our picking. We're not always aware of it at the time, sometimes not for years. Len's marriage won't break up, because he's picked according to the level of his mind. He doesn't know it, he never will, and he'll be all the more content. It sometimes comes about that you don't get the one to fit both your mind and your body, then things happen . . . Take it on a lower plane, so to speak. Take it in the breeding of stock . . .'

'Mike!' Lizzie's back was very straight; and Mike turned his face full to her and lifted his hands in a flapping motion, as if wiping away his name, before saying, 'Look, Liz. There's neither of them at school any more. They're no longer bairns! And all right, Sarah's here, but Sarah deals with animals.'

'Well, it's no conversation for the tea-table, and I'm not having it. I know where it will lead. We'll have the stockyard on our plates before many more minutes are over. Likening people to animals!'

'There's not a lot of difference that I can see.' Mike's voice was suddenly quiet; and there was a tinge of sadness in his tone as he went on, 'I've a sick cow in the barn now. Nobody will have it, nobody will believe that it's because Brewster's gone. But from the day she watched him mounting the ramp into that van, she's gone back . . . Cows are women . . .'

'Mike!' Lizzie had risen to her feet.

'All right, you won't have it.' Mike had scraped his chair back on the floor and was looking up at her. 'You won't have it, but nevertheless it's true . . . You know, your mother did everything under God's sun to prevent you and me coming together, didn't she? Well, if she had succeeded it would have been a bad thing, a loss to both of us, and you know it. The same thing is happening now and you're glad. You're glad, Liz. That's what hurts me, you're glad.'

Mike was on his feet now glaring at Lizzie, and

she put her fingers to her lips as she stared back at him, muttering, 'It isn't true, it isn't true. You know it isn't true.'

'Aw, I know you, Liz. I can read you like a book. Only remember this, you can't push big houses and money into a heart. A heart's only made for feeling.'

Mike's voice had come from deep in his chest on the last words, and they all watched him walking down the long farm kitchen towards the door. And when it closed on him Lizzie turned towards Mary Ann, her voice breaking as she said, 'He's blaming me. He's blaming me for it all! What had I to do with Corny going to America? I had nothing to do with it.' She was appealing to Mary Ann, seeming to have forgotten Michael and Sarah. 'You believe that, don't you?'

Mary Ann got to her feet. She too seemed to have forgotten the couple sitting opposite, their heads bent in embarrassment; and she put her arms about Lizzie as she said, 'Don't cry, Mother. Don't cry. Yes, I believe you. There, there, don't cry.' She pressed her mother into her chair again, and going to the teapot, poured her a fresh cup of tea; and as she handed it to her she said again, 'There, now, don't worry. I know you had nothing to do with it.'

But even as she said this, she was thinking along the lines of Mike. She knew her mother was glad and relieved, even happy, at the way things had turned out. She also knew that she must talk to her da before he met Mr Lord, or the place would blow up.

2

'How d'you think it's gone, Mary Ann?'

'Wonderfully, wonderfully, Len. It was a wonderful wedding.'

'Aye. Aa feel it was.'

Mary Ann smiled at Len, and her smile was as sincere as her words had been. For to her mind it had been a wonderful wedding, surprisingly wonderful. The nuptial mass had not been ludicrous, as Michael had foretold. In fact, as she had looked at the white-robed Cissie and the unusually spruce Len, she had felt that they were deeply threaded with the spirituality of the moment, as very likely they were. Cissie had even looked pretty. She was detached from all dimness in this moment. Cissie was a bride, and Mary Ann had wanted to cry.

She said to Len, 'You'll like Harrogate.' At the same time she wondered why on earth they had chosen Harrogate. Harrogate was stuffy – snobbish and stuffy. Cissie had said it was because there were things to do; it had a winter season. That was funny, if you came to think about it. The Spanish City in Whitley Bay would be more in their line.

'You know, Aa wish we weren't goin' away . . . Well, you know what Aa mean.' Len laughed. 'Aa mean not so soon like. Aa would uv liked to stay for the dance later on. Aa bet it's the first time there's ever been a dance in this old barn. Anyway, for many a long year.' Len looked along the length of the barn to where Lizzie was supervising the clearing of the tables, and added, 'By, your mother made a splendid turn-out, didn't she? With Cissie's folk not being up to anything like this, it's made her feel . . . well, you know what I mean.'

Mary Ann nodded. Yes, she knew what he meant. As well as all the bought cakes, her mother had cooked nearly all the week for the wedding spread. Hams, tongues . . . the lot.

'An' the old man's all right at bottom; curses you up hill and down dale one minute, then stands your weddin' expenses. He's all right, he is, if you understand him like. Look, there he is now. He's laughin'. Look, he's laughin' with that Mrs Schofield. By, she's a nice woman, that. She's got no side, has she?' He looked at Mary Ann. And she, looking to where Mr Lord was being entertained by Mrs Schofield, nodded before saying, 'Yes, she's nice.'

Lettice Schofield was the mother of Mary Ann's school friend. She had first come to the farm on Mary Ann's thirteenth birthday, and had since then not infrequently looked them up. Everybody liked Mrs Schofield, but everybody thought her a bit dizzy. Perhaps they liked her for that reason. At least everybody but Mike. Mike didn't think Mrs Schofield was dizzy, he never had. From that birthday party he had said, 'There's depth in that one. All this Mrs Feathering is just a barricade against something.' And over the past three years there had been times when Mary Ann thought her father was right, and others, when she listened to Mrs Schofield's light brittle chatter and her high tinkling laugh, when she had been inclined to think with Janice that her mother acted silly, like a girl . . . and she nearly thirty-four years old. Another thing that made Mary Ann wonder at times about Mrs Schofield was the fact that Mr Lord was always entertained by her, and she knew only too well that Mr Lord could not suffer fools gladly. So, on the whole she was inclined to think that her da's opinion of Mrs Schofield was correct. But whether she was thinking along the lines of her da, or her friend Janice, there always remained in her a liking for Mrs Schofield, a funny kind of liking, a sort of protective liking. It was a bit crazy when she came to analyse it, for it made her feel as if she were older than the mother of her friend. But the main trend of her thinking at this moment was not on Mrs Schofield, but on Mr Lord, and she thought bitterly as she looked at him, 'Yes, he can laugh and be amused. He's got his own way again.'

'Come on, me lad.' Mary Ann turned her head to where Mike was pushing his way through the crowd of guests towards Len. Her da stood head and shoulders above everybody in the barn. Dressed in his best, he brought a thrill of pride to Mary Ann, that for a moment obliterated thoughts of Mr Lord.

'Come on, lad. Do you want to miss that train?' He beckoned with his one arm above the heads of the gathering, and Len, laughingly jostled from all sides, pushed towards him.

Mary Ann, left alone for a moment in a little island of space, watched Mrs Schofield leave Mr Lord to go and say goodbye to the bride. Then to her consternation she saw Mr Lord rise slowly and come towards her.

It was the first time they had met face to face since his return, which had not been on Tuesday as expected, but yesterday morning, which was Friday, and since then he had, she felt sure, kept out of her way. In fact, out of everybody's way, until two hours ago when the wedding party had returned from the church. From which time he had allowed himself to be entertained by Mrs Schofield.

Mr Lord was standing close to her now and he looked at her for a long moment before speaking, and then he took the wind completely out of her sails by saying, 'You're wrong, you know, Mary Ann.'

As always when stumped, she blinked, but she continued to stare up at him.

'You have been blaming me for Cornelius's decision regarding America.' He always gave Corny his full name when speaking of him. 'Well, I want you to know I had nothing whatever to do with making up his mind. Oh, yes.' He raised his hand. 'I'm not going to deny that I have pointed out the advantages that would attend his taking up a position in America, and I have gone as far as to tell him I could secure him a post. Oh yes, I have done all that. But that was some time ago. More recently, I gave up the idea of trying to persuade him because I realised he was a very determined young man and would not be influenced by me, or anyone else, but would go his way. So I was surprised, as no doubt you were, when his decision was made known to me. He was the last person I expected to see in my office, and our meeting was brief, for in accordance with his character he came straight to the point. He told me what he wanted, and asked some questions . . . Usually I am the one who asks the questions, and I don't take kindly to cross examinations.' He smiled his tight smile down on her. Then finished abruptly. 'Cornelius Boyle knows exactly what he wants. I should say he will go far . . .

'Now, now, now, Mary Ann, don't be silly. You're not going to cry. This is a wedding, remember.' He took her arm in a firm grip and she allowed him to walk her towards the barn door.

She hated him, she did. Well, he could make all the excuses he liked, but she would never marry Tony just to please him. That was what he was after . . . Oh, she knew, she knew what his subtle game was. And played so smoothly, you couldn't get at him.

'If you start crying everyone will blame me.'

'I'm not crying.'

'Very well, you're not crying, not yet. But if you do start I will get the blame. Especially from your father, because he, too, thinks like you, doesn't he?'

They had reached the left side corner of the barn when he pulled her to a stop. And looking at her with gentleness that always managed to break her down, he said softly, 'Whether you believe it or not, Mary Ann, anything I do, I do for your own good. Out of the essence of knowledge garnered through a long and trying life, I can see what is right for you . . . I know what is right for you, and I want you to have what is right for you . . . You believe me?'

She was not crying, but her large brown eyes were so misted she couldn't see his face as she gazed up at him. He had done it again. She hated him no longer. What he said was right. Whatever he did was for her good. If only he would do something for Corny to stop him from going away. Her love gave her courage to say, 'I like Corny, Mr Lord.'

'Yes.' He nodded at her. 'Yes, of course, you like Cornelius. I know you like Cornelius. Anyone would be blind, or stupid, if he didn't realise you like him. And go on liking him, there's no reason why you shouldn't. And you should be proud that he wants to go to America and make a position for himself, so that when . . . when the time comes, he will have something to offer you. He would have nothing to offer you if he stayed in England.'

'He was getting on well at the garage. He's had a rise.'

Mr Lord turned his head with a quick jerk to the side as if he was straining to look up into the sky, and it was into the sky that he sent his words: 'Had a rise!' The scorn in them made Mary Ann stiffen, and she made to pull her hand from his grasp when he brought his gaze once more to bear on her and again softened his scathing comment by saying, 'What is a rise in that work? A few shillings a week! You give Cornelius a year in America and he will be making twice as much as the manager of that garage. Believe me . . .

Well. Well, now.' He had turned his head quickly towards the gate of the farmhouse, where a car was backing in, and he ended abruptly, 'No more of this now. Here's Tony.'

Mr Lord did not go towards his grandson but waited for him to come up to them. And although he kept his gaze fixed on the approaching figure, the expression in his eyes, which could have been taken for pride, was veiled with a mask of impatient arrogance.

Tony was tall and thin. A faint replica of Mr Lord himself. Perhaps he was better looking than Mr Lord had been at his age. His skin, even in the winter, kept a bronzed tinge as if he had just returned from a southern beach. In some measure, too, he had about him a touch of his grandfather's aloofness, which at the age of twenty-seven added to his attractiveness.

From a child Mary Ann had been conscious of this attractiveness, and in a childish way had looked upon Tony as hers. She had begun by liking him, then she had loved him . . . That was until she met Corny. But she still liked Tony very, very much, and was aware of his attraction, as were most of the girls who came into contact with him. His charm and natural ease of manner were part and parcel of his character. But he also had a vile temper, which could rip the charm off him like a skin, to disclose stubbornness and cold arrogance for which one hadn't to look far to find the source. And it was mainly when he was fighting with that source that these two facets came into evidence.

As Mary Ann watched him approach them now, she said to herself, 'He's wild about something.' She knew Tony as well as she did her da, or ma, or Mr Lord.

'Hello, there, you're late. The wedding's nearly over.' Mr Lord's tone was clipped.

'Yes, I'm sorry. I couldn't make it. I told you I might be late.' Tony nodded to his grandfather while looking him straight in the face. He did not look at Mary Ann, although he asked, 'Where's Mike?'

Was he mad at her? Why was he pointedly ignoring her? She had done nothing. She said to him, 'My father's gone to the house with Len.' She always gave Mike the title of father when speaking of him in front of Mr Lord.

'Thanks.' Still Tony did not turn his gaze on her, not even in a sweeping glance.

As she watched him stride away, she looked sharply at Mr Lord, saying, 'He's wild about something.'

The old man dusted his hands as if they had been soiled, and then he said, 'Young men are always wild about something. That's why they are young men. Once they stop being wild they are no longer young men.'

Mary Ann, looking at him for a moment longer, saw that he was not worried about Tony being wild. He was not coldly questioning why his grandson's manner was so abrupt, and this was unusual. And why he was not questioning was because he already knew.

She looked hard at the old man, who was looking to where Tony was now hurrying across the yard, not towards the farmhouse, but towards the gate that led up to the house on the hill. And she realised, as she had done so many times in the past, that this old man was clever, clever and cunning. He was like the devil himself. He could make you believe in him, in the goodness of his intentions, even while he plotted against you. And, as she had done in the past, she knew that she would hate him at intervals, but during the longer periods, and in spite of everything, she would always love him. And then she asked herself: What could he have done to upset Tony?

Corny arrived at six o'clock in Bert Stanhope's old car. Bert Stanhope was the chief mechanic in the garage. He was also the leader of the 'Light Fantastics', a suitably fantastic name for the four members of his band. For Bert himself was short and stubby, while Joe Ridley was as thin as a rake, and possessed a club-foot. Arthur Hunt, on the other hand, was of middle height with muscles straining from his coat sleeves. He had come by these, he proclaimed, through playing the mandoline. Topping them all by a clear head and shoulders was Corny.

Corny now eased his long legs out of the front seat of the car, and after raising his hand quickly in a salute to Mike, who was coming out of the barn, he turned his head in the direction of Bert, to ask, 'What did you say?'

'Aa said, "Is that the place we're doin' it?" '

'Yes, that's the barn.'

'Coo, lor! It'll be like the Albert Hall, only barer.'

Joe Ridley, surrounded by what looked like an entire band of wind instruments, remarked caustically, 'We'll have to blow wor brains oot to put anything ower in there. The sound'll all come oot through them slats up top.'

'You'll get them blown oot if we don't put it over, me lad.'

They were all laughing at their leader's reply when Mike reached them.

'Hello, there. You all set.' He looked around the four young men, but addressed himself to Corny.

'Aye. Yes, Mr Shaughnessy.' Corny had always given Mike his full title, and perhaps this was another reason why Mike was wholeheartedly for him. 'This is Bert Stanhope. It's his band, and this is Joe Ridley; and Arthur Hunt.'

Mike nodded with each introduction, and then looking at the paraphernalia spread round their feet, he asked seriously, 'Where are the others?'

'The others?' Bert flicked an inquiring and puzzled glance towards Corny before finishing, 'What others?'

'Well, with all this lot, I thought it must be the Hallé Orchestra that had come!'

There was more laughter, louder now, as the young fellows picked up the instruments and made for the barn. Corny, about to follow them, was stopped by a light touch on his arm, and Mike, his face serious now, said, 'I want a word with you.'

'Now?' Corny was looking straight at Mike. Their eyes were on a level.

'No, it needn't be now. Perhaps when you have an interval.'

'All right.' As Corny turned away, Mike said quietly, 'Mary Ann's just gone over to the house, if you want to see her.'

Corny did not turn to meet Mike's gaze now, but answered evenly, 'They want to start right away. We're a bit late. I'll see her later.'

Mike said nothing to this but watched Corny stride towards the barn, before turning and making his way to the house.

And there he banged the back door after him as he went into the scullery. But when he entered the kitchen he stopped just outside the door and looked across to the fireplace where Tony was standing, one foot on the fender, his elbow resting on the mantelpiece and his face set in a stiffness that spoke of inner turmoil.

'Oh, you all alone?' Mike attempted to be casual.

Tony moved from the fireplace and stood on the edge of the mat, rubbing his left shoulder with his right hand, a characteristic action of his when worked up about anything.

'Where's Mary Ann?'

'I think she's upstairs. I've heard someone moving about, and Lizzie's still in the barn. Look, Mike, I didn't intend to say anything to her. I was going to ignore the whole affair, but I've just got to tell her that I'm not in on this business of Corny's deportation.'

'Deportation is right!' Mike nodded at him. 'That's the must suitable word I've heard for it yet. But don't worry, I don't think she would believe for a moment you had a hand in it.'

'Oh, I don't know so much, Mike. She said the other day, over some little thing that I did, she said I was as wily as my grandfather. She might be thinking that, although I'm opposing the old man on the surface, I'm glad that Corny is going.'

'And are you?' The question was flat sounding.

'Aw, Mike, no. No.'

'But you like her?'

'Yes, of course I do. You know that, Mike.'

'Do you more than like her? I've got the right to ask this, Tony. Do you more than like her? Do you love her?'

Tony turned his head quickly and looked towards the fire, then bringing his eyes back to Mike he said slowly, 'Yes. Yes, Mike, in a way, I suppose I do. I always have done. But it's an odd kind of love. I don't understand it quite myself. I'm always fighting against her inside myself. I suppose this is the result of the Old Man's plans. If he hadn't pushed it but let it take a natural course, things might have been different; at least on my side. But no matter what I had felt it wouldn't have made very much difference as long as Corny was in the picture. And you know, Mike—'

'And when he's out of the picture?' Mike cut in. 'What then? On your side, I mean.'

'I don't know, Mike. I've got to wait and see. The odd thing is I've never met anyone I like better. I was brought up, so to speak, on her personality.' He smiled now, before adding, 'And as you know, it'll take some beating.'

Mike turned from Tony and, pulling a chair from under the table, straddled it. And with his one hand he thumped the top with his closed fist as he said, 'I'm mad over this business, Tony, flaming mad. I know the old boy, he's worked on that lad for years.' He looked up at Tony. 'You know this is the kind of situation that always makes me want to get drunk.' He gave a little jerk to his head. 'I'd better not let Lizzie hear me say that. But at this moment I'd like to get blind drunk. You see, all my early married life, and occasionally even now, I've had to fight against Lizzie's mother. You know the old girl. Well, I see in the old man a male replica of Madam McMullen. He's aiming to direct and ruin Mary Ann's life as surely as Lizzie's mother tried to ruin ours. And I tell you, Tony it boils me up inside . . . Ssh!' Mike got to his feet quickly. 'Here she's coming. Look, Tony. I wouldn't say anything now. Let it pass off, for the night at any rate. Talk to her later. Let her dance the night and have a bit of carry on, and forget it if you can. Although she'll be hard put to it with Corny up there blowing his heart out through that cornet, and nothing will convince me but he'll go on doing that where she's concerned, America or no . . . Ssh!'

Although it was Mike who had been doing the talking he admonished Tony to silence with his last Ssh! and when the door opened and Mary Ann came into the kitchen he flung his arm up over his eyes and cried, 'Oh, Lord, what a dazzle!'

'Don't be silly, Da.' Although Mary Ann's voice was chiding, she smiled at Mike but did not look toward Tony, until he said, 'A new dress, is it?'

'Yes.' She nodded her head once.

'It's nice. Red suits you.'

'It's not red, it's cyclamen.'

'Oh . . . oh. Cyclamen, is it? Well, anyway, it's very charming. Although, mind, I think it makes you look older.'

The last was a covered compliment and would have at any other time pleased Mary Ann, for next to wishing to be taller she longed to appear older. Although she would soon be seventeen, she sometimes, because of her height, looked no more than fifteen years old.

'The band's come,' said Mike, his back half towards her now. 'Listen, they've started. Come on, wrap yourself well up. Wait, I'll get my big coat and put it around you; your top looks half-naked, you'll catch your death.'

When Mike went out into the hall, Tony, moving towards Mary Ann, said, 'May I have the first dance, Miss Shaughnessy?' His smile was kind, and she returned it. But she did not enter into his playful mood.

Mike, coming into the room again, put his coat about her and they all laughed at the picture she presented; then, one on each side of her, they went out of the house down the road to the farm gate, and across the yard to the barn. And when they were inside the doorway, Mike took his coat from her, and she turned to Tony, and they danced . . .

Lizzie was standing in the far corner of the barn behind the refreshment table, which also served as the bar. And it was the bar at this moment that was worrying Lizzie. Mr Coot was attending to the bar and also to himself. In her estimation he'd already had too much, and the night was young yet. The bride's father had not been satisfied with the amount of wine and beer Mr Lord had provided, but had had to bring his own quota. Instead of spending so much on drink, Lizzie thought to herself, they could have bought something different for the young couple instead of that clarty cheap tea-set. Or provided some of the eatables. Thriftless lot. She had better see Mike and tell him to keep an eye on Mr Coot and his personal friends.

She was looking here and there in between the dancers for Mike when she saw Mary Ann and Tony dancing together. At the sight of her daughter's dress, all thought of Mr Coot left her mind for the moment. Oh, that dress! Why on earth had she picked a red dress? It wasn't her colour and the style was all wrong. It was the first dress she had let her buy on her own, and she had to pick red! It looked cheap, and it didn't suit her; it made her look older. She could be eighteen . . . nineteen. She kept her eye on her daughter as she waltzed nearer. And as the couple passed the table, Lizzie smiled at them. Anyway, Mary Ann was dancing nicely. It was the first time she had seen her dance except in the kitchen at the Christmas do's. Her steps and Tony's seemed to match. Somehow, she didn't look out of place with Tony, not like she did with . . . Lizzie's eyes flicked towards the temporary platform where the band was arrayed. Corny, his legs apart, his elbows level with his shoulders, his head back, was blowing his heart into his cornet. She could see the full meaning of Mike's phrase now. He was cornet mad, that boy. And, yes, yes, from the bottom of her heart she was glad he was going to America. And she prayed God that he would go soon and Mary Ann would have a chance to settle down with . . . She turned her eyes to Tony and Mary Ann again. Then she brought her gaze to the right of her, where Mr Lord was sitting, once again being entertained by Mrs Schofield. Let him scheme, let him plan, she was with him every inch of the way. Although she would not be able to open her mouth to him about the matter, she knew that the day her daughter married his grandson would be one of the happiest in both their lives.

She saw Mike now and she came round from behind the table and threaded her way towards him, and when she reached him she turned and stood by his side, letting her gaze follow his as he looked at the merry-making. But under her breath she said, 'You'd better keep your eye on that Mr Coot. He's going it some with the bottle.'

When Mike did not answer or turn his eyes towards her she was forced to look at him, and she said, still in a whisper, but with an edge to it, 'I'm saying something, did you hear me?'

'Yes, I heard you, Liz, but it happens to be a weddin'.'

'But you don't want it broken up, do you, with a drunken brawl?'

'Who says there's going to be a drunken brawl?'

'The night's young, and I'm telling you he's pretty well loaded now.'

'And he mightn't be the only one afore the night's out.'

Something jumped within Lizzie's chest. It was a frightening feeling. But one that was familiar – at least had been familiar up to those last few years. And now the feeling attacked the muscles of her stomach, bringing with it a slight nausea and she was back in the past, when each weekend had been a dread, and she didn't know from one day to another how they were going to get by. She was staring through glazed sight at the dancers while she cried out wildly inside herself, 'It's not fair, it's not fair, he's taking it out on me.' Then

43

her vision clearing, she turned her eyes without moving her head towards the seat of state, in which Mr Lord still sat; and she ended her thinking with, 'Well, far better he take it out on me than on the old man. But if he gets one too many himself it will be on both of us.' On this she was swamped with apprehensive fear, and the fear made her bold. With her eyes still directed towards the swirling couples, and her voice almost drowned by the noise and laughter, she said, 'If you do anything to spoil this night, Mike, I'll walk out . . . I'm telling you, I'll walk out.'

'Will you, Liz?' Mike too had his eyes fixed on the dancers, and his tone was deceptively even as he went on, 'I should have thought you knew better than that, Liz. Threats have always been as effective on me as water on a duck's back.'

The band stopped. The dancers clapped and called for more. The band started again and Mike, without any further words, walked from Lizzie's side and along to where Mr Lord was seated. As Lizzie watched him go her hand went instinctively to her lips. Then slowly it dropped away and her shoulders went back, and her chin moved up just a little as she watched her husband bending over Mrs Schofield. She watched him put his arm around Mrs Schofield's slender waist while she rested both her hands on his shoulders. She watched for a moment longer as he laughed down into Mrs Schofield's pretty face, and she watched Mrs Schofield laugh up at him; and then she turned abruptly away.

She had, up to this minute, liked Mrs Schofield, even though she thought her a bit dizzy. He had always maintained there was another side to her . . . Oh, she wished it was tomorrow and the wedding well behind them. She wished it was next week or the week after, or whenever it was Corny Boyle was leaving. Once he was gone Mary Ann would settle down. She would do everything in her power to see that she did settle down. But, oh, she did wish this night was over, and she wished that Mrs Schofield hadn't come.

When the band stopped for a break, Mary Ann was standing waiting to the side of the platform for Corny. She had no pride left. During the hour and a half the band had been playing, Corny hadn't looked at her; at least, when she was looking at him. It was as if she didn't exist for him; or, once having existed, he had decided to forget her. She knew that her father would try to get at him during the interval. And if not, her mother would insist that he had something to eat. Or Mr Lord would raise an authoritative finger to beckon him to his side. And then the interval would be over, and when the dance finished he would pack up and go back with the other lads, and she didn't know whether he was coming tomorrow or not. She just had to talk to him.

As he stepped down off the wobbling planks, she looked up into his big face, which was redeemed from ugliness only by the mould of his mouth. This feature, taken separately, could be described as beautiful, yet it almost went unnoticed in the ruggedness of the whole. 'Hello,' she said. It was as if they had just encountered each other.

'Hello.' After looking down at her for a moment he thrust his head upwards, and gazing towards the refreshment table he exclaimed, 'Lord, but I'm starvin'.'

'I'll get you some sandwiches . . . stay here, and I'll get them. Look, there's a seat.' Her voice was rushed, eager, and he looked down on her again. Then jerking his head, he said abruptly, 'I can get it.'

'Corny, I've got to talk to you.'

'Aw, Mary Ann . . .'

'You'll go with the others as soon as the dance is finished, won't you.'

'Aye, it's the only way of gettin' back. I can't do anything else.'

'Well, I've got to talk to you now.'

'Leave it till the morrer.'

'Are you coming tomorrow?' Her eyes were wide and fixed hard on him now.

He looked anywhere but at her as he said, 'No. No, I wasn't. I promised to take our Stan's motor-bike to bits.'

As she stood gazing up at him she made a great effort to use the pride that was in her and turn from this gangling individual and march away, her head in the air and her step firm. But, as with her da, she could bring no pride to her aid when dealing with Corny, at least not as yet. In the past she had sold her soul to the devil over and over again in her own small way to defend her father. And she would do the same for this boy. She did not question why she should love Corny, she only knew that she did. And it was a love that could not be killed by ridicule or parting. Or even a statement from his own lips to the fact that he did not love her. That was a strange thing. And she had dwelt upon it quite a bit these past few hours.

Corny had never said in words that he loved her; but in every possible way his actions had spoken for him. He had never even paid her a compliment that she could remember, and he had certainly never said, 'Oh, Mary Ann, I love you.' And his desertion now was not to be verbal either. He spoke, as usual, in actions, and his actions, like the proverb, spoke louder than words.

'Comin' for some grub?' Bert was calling to him from the far side of the stage. And Corny, looking over his shoulder, answered in an over-loud voice, 'Be with you in a tick,' and then, walking towards the seat that Mary Ann had proffered, he said quietly now, 'Sit down, I'll get you something.'

She remained standing looking at him. 'I don't want anything . . . When are you going away?'

'Aw, Mary Ann, man.' He tossed his big head from side to side. 'Let's forget it.'

'When are you going away?'

'All right, all right, if that's how you want it.' Again his head was tossing. But it had ceased its moving before he said, 'The fourteenth.' His voice had dropped and his head with it. His eyes were not looking at her, but were shaded by the wide lids, and they flickered once when her voice, cracking with surprise, cried, 'The fourteenth! That's just over a week . . . Oh, Corny!'

'Look, Mary Ann, don't go on. I'll come over the morrer . . . Yes, I will, and talk about it . . . Look, I'll go and get something to eat. Sit there, I'll be back.'

He did not wait for more protestations but hurried from her and threaded his way towards the far corner and the refreshment table.

Mary Ann sat down. She felt lost, sick, and she

47

wanted above all things to lay her head on her arms and cry.

Up to a moment ago this corner of the barn had been comparatively empty, but now people were making their way back to the forms that lined the walls, carrying plates balanced on the tops of cups of coffee or glasses of beer. And as she was forced to answer, and even smile when she was spoken to, she was thinking, 'There's no place for him to sit now. And it's too cold outside, and he won't come over to the house.' She looked around now, not for Corny, but for Mike. Just to stand near her da would be a comfort. Moreover, she realised that she should be sitting close to her father from now on; because when she last saw him there had been a glint in his eye that told her he was well past his restricted number of whiskies.

Corny had pushed his way to her with a dinner-sized plate full of food, but his attention was not on her, for he kept looking towards the stage. And then he brought out under his breath, 'Lordy, I hope they don't play about with the instruments. Bert will go crackers if anything's busted up.'

Mary Ann, following his perturbed gaze, saw Mrs Schofield, her head back, her mouth wide with laughter, holding a trombone, and Tony, who was sitting at the piano – which incidentally had been brought down from the house but had not so far been played – calling to her: 'One . . . Two . . . Three.'

The sound that issued from the stage now caught the whole attention of the barn. And everybody was laughing as they looked towards Mrs Schofield. It was evident that she had some

48

knowledge of the trombone but was laughing so much herself that she could not keep in time with Tony, but the guests, catching the theme of 'The Old Bull and Bush', began to sing.

Mary Ann didn't join in, nor did Corny, but he whispered to her in reluctant admiration, 'She could play that, you know. With a little practice she could be good.'

Mary Ann looked at Mrs Schofield, who was consumed with laughter and only intermittently keeping in time, and thought, 'This is what Janice means when she says her mother is dizzy.' And she felt a little ashamed of Mrs Schofield. Ashamed of her, and ashamed for her. She was too old to act the goat like that. Mary Ann at this moment gave thanks that her mother would never do anything like that.

But it would appear that Mary Ann was alone with her feeling concerning Mrs Schofield, for the rest of the company were enjoying her with high delight. And when one song was finished there was a call for another, and another.

Then Mike was on the stage, standing by Tony, and he let his deep rich voice soar through the barn as he led the singing. That was all right; Mary Ann liked to hear her da sing. And as long as he was singing he wouldn't be drinking. Yes, it was all right until Mrs Schofield put down the trombone and went and joined him. And then Mary Ann watched her da put his arm around Mrs Schofield's shoulder and lead her to the front of the stage, and with their heads together they sang duets to the great amusement of the company, with the exception of herself and her mother. For Mary Ann caught sight of her

mother's face, and she knew that she was upset.
She also knew that her da was letting rip like this
on purpose because he was vexed, not only with
Mr Lord but with her ma. And it was all on
account of her and Corny. As Lizzie had said a
short while ago, now Mary Ann also said to
herself, 'Oh, I wish this night was well over.'

There was just one other who was not pleased
with the spectacle. And that was Mr Lord. He
had found Mrs Schofield a very entertaining companion; when you got past the frivolity of her
veneer there was a serious side to the woman.
He had found her intelligent and observant, and
possessed of a quality that, in his opinion, was
rare in most women – wit. Many of them had a
sense of humour, but humour and wit were on
two different planes. Yes, indeed, he had liked
Mrs Schofield and he did not relish seeing her
making a spectacle of herself with Shaughnessy,
and his grandson. Shaughnessy, too, he noted,
had taken on more than was good for him, and in
a very short while his good humour would turn
to surliness, and from that . . . Well, he wasn't
going to be present when Shaughnessy brought up
the subject of why young Cornelius Boyle had
decided to go to America. He was well aware of
Shaughnessy's championship of the boy. And it
was not only because of Mary Ann's affection for
the fellow, but because Shaughnessy saw in the
big, bony unlovely Cornelius a replica of himself
as he was at that age. And in championing his
daughter's choice, he was also pandering to the
vanity in himself. Oh, he knew Shaughnessy, he
could read Shaughnessy.

'Well, I must be making my way up the hill,

Mrs Shaughnessy.' Mr Lord was facing Lizzie now, bending towards her to make himself heard. And she only just managed to keep the relief out of her voice as she answered, 'You must be tired, it's been a long day . . . Thank you very much, indeed, for all you have done.'

The old man raised his bushy brows into his white hair, and brought his chin into his neck as he said with a rare twinkle in his eye, 'We're never thanked for the right things by the right people, Mrs Shaughnessy. The ones who should be thanking me are past thinking of anything at this moment but the next drink. I have done nothing to deserve your thanks, but there it is. That is life.' He nodded his head slowly. 'And I am grateful for your thanks, Mrs Shaughnessy.'

They looked at each other for a long moment.

'Good night, Mr Lord.'

'Good night, Mrs Shaughnessy. And don't worry. Everything will turn out all right.' He did not explain to what he was referring, there was no need. Lizzie looked back into his pale eyes as she said, 'I'm sure it will, Mr Lord. I sincerely hope so from the bottom of my heart.' The last words were merely a whisper.

Again he nodded. 'We understand each other, Mrs Shaughnessy. It's a very good thing when two people understand each other. Good night, Mrs Shaughnessy.'

'Good night, Mr Lord. Good night, Mr Lord. You'll be able to manage?' She pulled the barn door open for him.

'Yes, quite well, Mrs Shaughnessy, quite well; there's a moon.'

He paused for a moment and looked up into the

sky, then turning his head towards Lizzie he said, 'Don't let her stay up too late. Young girls should get their rest.'

Lizzie did not answer but inclined her head towards him, and stood for a moment watching him walk across the moonlit farmyard. He was telling her to protect Mary Ann from the moonlight, the moonlight and Corny. For a moment, just for a fleeting moment, Lizzie experienced a feeling that she thought could be akin to that which was eating up Mike. Why should Mary Ann be kept from the moonlight and Corny? The moon was made for the young. But as she closed the barn door again, the feeling passed. He was right; moonlight was dangerous. A dose of it created a madness that some people had to pay for all their lives. She was not going to stand by and see Mary Ann paying such a price . . .

The dance ended at eleven o'clock, but long before this time Tony and Mrs Schofield were running a shuttle service taking people home. Tony's first car-load had contained the prostrate form of Mr Coot, who, true to Lizzie's prophecy, had become blind drunk very early in the evening. But not aggressively so as she had feared. Whereas Mike, who was not as drunk as he could have been, was tinder dry for a row. Mr Lord's disappearance had brought forth his caustic comments, and Mr Coot's recumbency had aroused his scorn. Tony he frowned on more and more as the evening advanced, and it would appear the only person who pleased him was Mrs Schofield. But it seemed that as Mike's boisterousness increased, Mrs Schofield's merriment went the other way, until, towards the end of the evening, although still smiling, her gaiety had diminished. Perhaps this was because Mrs Schofield did not drink. Even a natural gaiety is hard to sustain hour after hour on lemonade. Or perhaps it was because Mrs Schofield was really a nice woman, an understanding woman.

Yet Lizzie's liking for Mrs Schofield did not return, not even when she witnessed her persuading Mike from getting into the car and accompanying her in her taxi-ing. You can't like a woman who is trying to prevent your husband from making a fool of himself even when you know that she is in sympathy with you . . .

The barn was almost deserted when the band finally packed up. And Mike, swaying just the slightest, stood with his arm around Corny's shoulder, and he grinned widely at him as he muttered thickly, 'Cum on, me young buck, cum on. You and me 'ave got some talkin' ta do.'

'I've got to go, Mr Shaughnessy. They're waitin'.'

'Waitin'? What for? Let them get themselves away, you're comin' in with me. Why, the night's young, lad.'

'I'll come in the morrer.'

'You'll cum in the night!'

'Da!'

Mike turned to look at his daughter, saying, 'Ah, there you are. I was just tellin' Corny here the night's young.'

'Da. Come on indoors, please.'

'We're all goin' indoors, me dear.'

'Listen, Da.' Mary Ann gave a rough tug at Mike's arm, pulling him to attention. 'Listen. Corny wants to go home; they're waiting for him.'

She inclined her head backwards. 'Let him go! Do you hear me, Da? Let him go!'

Not only did the tone of her voice catch Mike's attention, but it brought Corny's eyes hard on her. His neck jerked up out of his collar as if he had been suddenly prodded with a sharp instrument, and he looked down on her with a wide, startled expression as she went on, 'You go now, Corny.' Her words were spaced, her voice level. 'Go on. And don't come back tomorrow, or any other time. Go to America, and I wish you luck . . . Come on, Da.'

As she had done so often in her young life, she tugged at Mike's arm and guided him away, and this time unprotestingly away, leaving Corny in a wilderness of words he could not voice. And as she went, she clung on desperately to the fringe of her old courage, which she had dragged from its retreat to save her from utter desolation after an evening of torment, an evening of being rejected, overlooked by the only one that mattered. Just a short while ago she had rehearsed a plea she would make to Corny when she had him to herself. For somehow she would get him to herself, at least that is what she had thought.

Mary Ann had never yet in her life recognised total defeat. Her agile mind had always supplied her with a plan. But in this telling moment if it had presented her with a plan that would keep Corny at her feet for life, she would have rejected it.

As they entered the garden Mike's docility vanished and he pulled them to a stop, exclaiming, 'Why the hell! I'm not havin' this. Where is he?' He flung round, only to be dragged back again by Mary Ann, and, her voice as stern as Lizzie's ever could be, she said to him, 'Look, Da, listen to me. I'm telling you, I don't want to see him.'

'Aa . . . ah! So you're playing the old fellow's game, eh?' He swayed slightly towards her.

'I'm playing nobody's game. Come on in.' Suddenly her tone changed and she was the little girl again, pleading with him. 'Aw, Da. Come on. Come on to bed . . . I've had enough for one night.'

He peered at her through the moonlight, and then without further words he put his arm about her, and together they went up into the house.

3

'What are you goin' to be when you leave your typin' school . . . a secretary?'

'Yes, I suppose so, Mrs McBride.'

'Do you want to be a secretary?'

'No, not really.'

'Then what did you go in for it for?'

'Oh, well.' Mary Ann gave a faint smile and, looking down, said, 'I fancy I'll be able to write.'

'Write?'

'Yes, stories and things, you know. I've always been able to make up poetry.'

'Well! well!' Fanny stopped basting the joint and gazed down on Mary Ann where she sat at the corner of the kitchen table. 'Now, that's an idea, a good idea, for you were always the one for tellin' a tale. Oh, you were that . . . Remember the things you used to spin around, about all the cars, and the horses your da had, and the big house you lived in?'

Mary Ann nodded, and she kept smiling up at this old friend of hers as she listened to her recalling the escapades she got up to in the days when they lived in the attics at the top of this grim house. But she knew, as Mrs McBride kept prattling on in her loud, strident voice, that they were both just marking time, waiting for the moment when Corny's name would be mentioned. She was bitter in her heart against Corny. Although she had dismissed him with a cold finality the night of the wedding, she hadn't imagined for a single moment that that would be the last she would see of him. When he hadn't come on the Sunday, she had known he would turn up one night during the week. But as the days ticked off towards the fourteenth of November, her pride sank into oblivion once more, and she paid earnest, even frantic, attention to her praying, beseeching Our Lady to bring him before he sailed. But her prayers weren't answered. And the day of his departure came without a word or a note from him.

Her da was still mad, and part of his temper now was directed towards Corny himself. Even her mother was annoyed at Corny's cavalier treatment. And she had overheard her saying to Michael in the kitchen, 'After the way he's been welcomed in this house. Every weekend for years he's been here. And never once was she invited back!'

Michael had answered, 'Well, you can understand that. The fellow wouldn't want to take her to the set-up in Howdon.'

'Well,' her mother said, 'I hope it shows her she's well rid of him.'

When their Michael had answered, 'I wouldn't count on it doing that, Ma,' she had wanted to fly into the kitchen and cry, 'Well, it has! Me ma's right. Me ma's right. I never want to set eyes on him again.'

That was a week ago. And now here she was, drawn to Mrs McBride's, waiting, as each minute passed – glossed over with topics that didn't matter – for her to speak about her grandson.

Fanny pushed the dripping-tin back into the oven, and threw the coarse sacking oven-towel on to a chair. Then going back to the table, she sat down opposite Mary Ann. Heaving a sigh that hardly disturbed the huge sagging mountain of her breasts, she put her head on one side and looked at Mary Ann with compassion in her glance. 'Well!' she said abruptly.

Mary Ann, staring at her old friend, bit on her lip, looked downwards, then back into the wrinkled face, and muttered, 'Oh, Mrs McBride, I feel awful.'

'You do, hinny?'

Mary Ann nodded and blinked, but the blinking could not check her crying, and the tears welled from her eyes.

'Aw! there now, there now, don't cry. It had to be like this, lass. It had to be like this.'

'He . . . he went off and never even said goodbye to me. He needn't have gone off like that and . . . and after him coming to us every week. He . . . he never missed, and then to go off . . .'

'Now wait a minute.' Fanny held up her hand. 'There was a reason for him goin' off like that. And you know it.'

'I don't, Mrs McBride. I don't.' She was shaking her head desperately.

'Aw, come on, come on. Face up to facts. If he had come to say goodbye to you, he would have never seen America.'

Mary Ann's mouth was open and she moved

her head in a slow painful motion, her tears still running down her face.

'It's a fact,' said Fanny. 'He stood in this kitchen . . . Stood? No, I'm tellin' you a damned lie. Stand, he didn't do, he raged about the room until I threatened to hit him with the frying-pan if he didn't let up. And talk. I never heard that lad talk so much in all me born days. All mixed up, seemingly without sense or reason, until I shouted at him, "If you don't want to go, don't go," I said. "Blast Mr Lord. You'll get other chances." "Where?" he said. "If I was even managing that garage I wouldn't be able to make much more than fifteen quid a week, and what can you do on that?" "What can you do on that?" I said to him. "I wish to God I had the half of it, that's all." '

Fanny paused now, and after nodding towards Mary Ann she went on more slowly. 'It was after I said that, that he held his head in his hands and said, quiet like, in a way that made him sound like a settled man, "Gran, you don't know what you're talkin' about. I'm not askin' her until I have enough to start off decent, and if I don't get goin' now, it'll be too late. Unless I start doing things on the side with the cars to make a bit like the rest of them. And I don't want to get mixed up in anything, I've seen where that can lead . . ." '

'Oh! Mrs McBride. If he had only told me . . .'

'Wait a minute, wait a minute. I haven't finished yet,' said Fanny. 'You know how I like your mother, don't you? I think of Liz with more affection than any of me own. But apparently she doesn't see me grandson in the same light. She's got ideas for you, Mary Ann, and—' Fanny spread her arms wide. 'It's natural, isn't it? She's your mother. But my Corny is no fool. Perhaps I say it as shouldn't, but he's a big chip, a great big chip of meself, and he read through Liz right from the beginnin'. The same as he knew what old Lord was up to all the time. Old Lord wants you for Mr Tony, lass, and you know, I can see his point an' all. And I'm not blaming your mother for wantin' to fall in with his little scheme. For it would be a wonderful thing if her daughter, her Mary Ann, could marry the old man's grandson . . . Now, now, don't take on so, I'm just statin' facts, and there's no hard feelin's atween Liz and me, and never atween you and me. We know each other too well, don't we now?' She reached forward and patted Mary Ann's hand.

It was all too much for Mary Ann. Turning on a loud sob, she buried her face in her arms on the table, and Mrs McBride, pulling herself to her feet, stood over her, tapping her shoulder and saying, 'Come on, now. Come on.' Then after a moment she said, 'Stop now, an' I'll give you somethin'. He left it to me for to do with what I thought best. "If you think she needs it, Gran, let her have it," he said. "If you don't, put it in the fire." '

Mary Ann raised her tear-stained face and watched Fanny take her wobbling body to the fireplace, where she reached up and extracted a letter from behind the clock. When she placed it in her hand, Mary Ann looked down on it. There was no name on the envelope, no writing of any kind; and when automatically she turned it over, she knew from the condition of the flap that it had been steamed open. This did not affect her, it did not bring any feeling of resentment against her friend. Fanny had likely wanted to know what her grandson had said, and whether she should pass it on or not.

Slowly Mary Ann slit open the envelope and read the very short letter it contained.

If you read this it'll be because you have been upset at me going and you didn't really mean what you said the other night. I'm going to stay in America for a year. If I know I can make a go of it I'll come back then and tell you. If I feel I can't – that is make a go of it – then don't wait but do what they want you to. Perhaps in a year's time you'll want to do that anyway because you always liked him.

Corny.

Would you come and see me Gran now and again? She gets lonely for a bit of a crack.

'Oh! why couldn't he tell me this?' Mary Ann shook the letter in her hand as she looked up into Mrs McBride's face. 'Why couldn't he say it?'

'Well, he was never very ready with his tongue, especially when it was about anything that really mattered.'

'I'll wait. Oh, I'll wait, Mrs McBride.'

'Well, now, hinny.' Fanny put her hand heavily on Mary Ann's shoulder. 'Make no rash promises. You're only sixteen, you know. You're very young yet.'

'I'm getting on seventeen, Mrs McBride.'

'Well, aye, you might be, but you know you still look such a bairn. And a lot of things can happen in a year, God knows that.'

'Nothing will ever happen to change me, Mrs McBride.'

'Aw, well, we'll wait and see. But now you feel a bit better, don't you?'

Mary Ann nodded.

'Would you like a bite of dinner?'

'No thanks, Mrs McBride.'

'A bit of bread dipped in the gravy?'

Mary Ann gave an involuntary shudder when she thought of the black fat surrounding the meat. But she smiled and said, 'Thanks, all the same, but I'll have to be off. You know what me ma is if I'm not there on time . . . Goodbye, Mrs McBride, and thanks.' Impulsively she reached up and kissed the wrinkled cheek. And Fanny held her tightly for a moment, and as she did so she whispered, 'You're not the only one who'll miss him, you know, lass.'

'I know that, Mrs McBride . . . and, and I'll come and see you more often.'

'Do that. Do that, hinny. You're always more than welcome.'

'Goodbye, Mrs McBride.'

'Goodbye, lass. Give me love to Lizzie, and don't forget Mike. Tell them I'll drop in one of these days.'

'Oh, do, do, they'd love to see you.'

After more repeated goodbyes, Mary Ann went down the steps of Mulhattan's Hall with a lighter tread than she had ascended them, and as she hurried through the quiet Sunday-stripped streets towards the bus stop, she gripped the letter in her hand inside her coat pockets. She had no experience of love letters with which to judge this, her first one; but even so she knew it was lacking in the niceties that went to make up such a letter.

Yet every line had brought Corny closer to her. The terse, taciturn, blunt individual was near her once again. There had been no sign in the letter of his lessons in English. Corny could, she knew, speak all right when there was nothing to deflect his attention from the rocks and pitfalls of grammar. But when he was angry, or disturbed in any way, he fell immediately back into the natural idiom. But what did she care how he talked? He could talk broad Geordie for the remainder of his life if only he was here with her now. But she had his letter, and his promise, and to this she would hang on for the coming year. And longer, yes, longer, if necessary. As long as ever he wanted.

4

The farm had fallen under a spell of peace. It was like an enchanted place because everybody was happy. Mike sang and joked once more. Lizzie bustled about her house. She cooked more than ever. She took an interest in books that went in for pictures of big houses, and she laughed quite a bit. And Mr Lord seemed to be very pleased with himself these days. He appeared to be floating on a firm cloud of achievement. As for Tony, Tony smiled and laughed and teased Mary Ann; and on occasions took her out for a run in the car. This was a new departure and might account for Mr Lord's cloud of achievement . . . Then Michael and Sarah; they were living in a world of their own and enjoying a separate happiness – they were not involved with Corny Boyle.

This change in atmosphere as far as Mary Ann and Mike were concerned had been brought about simply by Corny's letter. Mary Ann had, on the quiet, shown the letter to her da, and Mike had grinned widely and said, 'Stick to your guns. Don't let on. Let them go on thinking and planning what they like.' He had not intimated who 'they' were, but she knew he was referring to her mother and Mr Lord. He had added, with a warning lift of his finger, 'Don't show that to your mother, mind.' And looking back at him she had said, 'As if I would.' And they had laughed together. But some time later Mike had said to her, 'I would show that letter to Tony if I was you.'

'To Tony?'

'Yes. It would put things straight in his mind, and he won't start walking up any garden path.'

So she had shown the letter to Tony, with the result that after a long moment of looking down at her, with perhaps just a trace of sadness in his expression, he had suddenly punched her playfully, saying, 'What do you say to playing them at their own game?' And she knew that here, too, Tony was referring not only to his grandfather but also to her mother, Lizzie, with whom he was on very good terms. But she had asked, 'What do you mean?' He didn't explain fully what he did mean, but said, 'Well, we needn't fight, need we, and give them cause for worry? I'll have to take you out for a run now and again, and to a show. It'll make the year pass quicker. What about it?' She had laughed freely for the first time in weeks. Her da was happy again, so was her mother. What did it matter if it was for different reasons. And Tony was nice. She had always liked Tony. As Corny had said, she had always liked Tony. But that wasn't loving. There was all the difference in the world.

So everyone, with the exception of Michael and Sarah, began putting on an act.

*　　*　　*

It was on the Thursday morning that Mary Ann received a letter from Janice Schofield, asking if she could come up and see her on the Friday evening. During working hours Mary Ann, escaping the keen eyes of Miss Thompson and wishing to show off her typing prowess, wrote Janice a sketchy reply, the gist of which was: Of course, she could come up on Friday evening.

Mary Ann had been rather surprised to receive a letter from Janice. At one time during her school days, they had been good friends; but Janice had never been close to her like Beatrice Willoughby. Beatrice, to use schoolgirl jargon, was her best friend, and Janice her second best. Janice was nine months older than Mary Ann and had been left school for more than a year, while Mary Ann had just finished in the summer term. Beatrice, on the other hand, was still at school making her way to college . . . Years ago Mary Ann had thought she, too, would like to go to college, but Corny had changed her mind about this matter, and strangely, when she had put forward her idea about taking up shorthand and typing, there had been little or no objection from any quarter. This, she had reasoned, was because her da had Corny in mind and further education was going to serve no purpose. In fact, it might do Corny a disservice. Her mother's reaction, she knew, was patterned on Mr Lord's, and this is where the word 'strangely' applied most. For Mr Lord had not gone off the deep end about her proposal to become a secretary.

Two more years at school and three at college would not have helped Mr Lord's scheme at all.

Five years is a long time when a man is over seventy.

Mary Ann wondered what Janice wanted to see her about, and she hurried home on the Friday night and changed into her new loose sweater and pleated skirt so as to look her best when Janice arrived. For Mary Ann knew that she would come all dressed up – 'killingly smart', as their Michael termed it, 'and smellin' like a poke of devils'. Janice worked on the cosmetic counter in a large store in Newcastle and undoubtedly this had a lot to do with her choice of perfume.

Lizzie lit the fire in the sitting-room, and at ten minutes to seven, Mary Ann and Michael went down the road to the bus stop. Michael to meet Sarah, and Mary Ann to meet Janice. But only Sarah alighted from the bus.

At eight o'clock Mary Ann, accompanied this time by Mike, met the bus again, but still there was no sign of Janice.

'You'd better phone her up,' said Mike, 'and find out why she hasn't put in an appearance.'

They now had an extension of the phone in the house, and the operator, after trying several times to get Janice's number, informed Mary Ann that there was no reply. So there was nothing for it but to wait until the next morning and see if there was a letter from her.

But on the Saturday morning there was no letter from Janice. As always, Mary Ann was in a tear to get to the bus, and she did not phone the Schofields' until she returned at lunch time, when once again she was told there was no reply.

Lizzie said now, 'Likely their phone's out of

order; you should take a trip over there this afternoon and see her. It's a lovely day, it will do you good.'

'But it's such a long way. It's right outside the town, Mother.'

'Well, it's just as long for her to come here . . . Why don't you ask Tony to run you over? He's nearly sure to be going into Newcastle this afternoon.'

Lizzie had her face turned away from Mary Ann when she made this proposal, and Mary Ann allowed herself the reaction of raising her eyebrows slightly, but that was all.

Not for a long time had she asked Tony to take her anywhere, even from the night he had proposed that they, too, should put on an act she had left the invitations to him. But today, when she did ask him, he expressed delight at the opportunity of running her into Newcastle. He would do more than that, he said. He would take her to the Schofields. He would very much like to see his theatrical partner again. Oh, yes, Mrs S. and he should team up.

He repeated much of this when he called for her, and Mike and Lizzie and he all laughed together, but Mary Ann thought he was overdoing it a bit.

Lizzie smiled warmly down on Mary Ann as she watched Tony reach over and tuck the car rug around her; she even waved them off as if it was a special occasion.

They were out on the road going past the cottages when Tony gave Mary Ann a sidelong quizzical glance as he remarked, 'Everybody's happy . . . everybody. For the Lord himself gave his blessing on our excursion before I came out.'

Tony was referring to his grandfather. And now her laughter joined his. Oh, Tony was nice, he was. He was good fun. She liked him ever so much. For a fleeting second she even wished that she didn't know Corny. But it was just for a second.

Mary Ann had not been to the Schofields more than three times during her acquaintance with Janice. But Mrs Schofield had been to the farm many times; in fact, Mary Ann had lost count of Mrs Schofield's visits during the past few years. The Schofields' residence, one would be right in calling it that, was an imposing house standing on a piece of land unusually large even for such houses in that select district. You entered the grounds through a long drive, which was bordered by larches. Although the trees were bare they were entwined with the dark, shining green of canes. These, in turn, were laced with dead bramble. The effect was the same as entering a tunnel, although not quite so dark. The gravel of the drive was covered with matted grass and, except for two deep car ruts, appeared like a field track. The front of the house, too, when they came upon it, had the appearance of being buried under masses of undergrowth. It looked as if it was fighting the clematis, climbing roses, and virginia creeper hanging in dead profusion, even from its tiles.

Perhaps it was the unexpected condition of the house that made Tony bring the car to a stop before he reached the front door. He sat with his head bent forward, staring upwards through the windscreen for a moment, before saying, 'Great Scott! There hasn't been much work done here for some time, I should say.'

'It wasn't as bad as this the last time I was here.' Mary Ann was speaking in a whisper. 'But that's nearly two years ago. It was rather nice then. It was summer. Mrs Schofield used to do the garden herself. There's a beautiful rose garden at the back . . . Will you wait until I see if they're in?'

'Of course, of course.' Tony brought his gaze round to her. 'I'll come in with you for a moment. I meant what I said, I'd like to see her . . . not Janice.' He nipped his nose, and they both laughed. Then he added, 'She's not a patch on her mother.'

'She's all right.' Mary Ann felt bound to defend her friend. 'You've just got to know her.'

'I don't want to, thank you very much.'

They were out of the car now and walking towards the front door, which was covered by a glass porch, quite a large porch. They stood for a moment, as people do, hesitating just that second before ringing the bell, and it was as Tony's hand was uplifted that the yell came to them. Bawl would be more appropriate in describing the sound of the man's voice. It came from the right, from inside the room to the right of the front door. This room had a large high window, which protruded into the drive with squared sides. Looking through the glass of the porch they were right opposite one side of the window, which was a pane wide but half-covered by a twist of dead stems. The bawl had been in the form of a curse. It was a word that Mary Ann hadn't heard before, although Mike at times swore freely. And its effect on Tony was to make him bring his startled glance down on her, and then to take her arm and move her quickly back towards the drive. But before they reached the entrance to the porch they had stopped again, and were once more looking towards the window. And there to be seen quite plainly was Mrs Schofield. She was walking backwards into the far corner of the recess, and advancing on her was a man. When Mrs Schofield could go no further the man, too, stopped, and his voice came clear and penetrating to them. 'You would bloody well put up with it and like it, and if you make any more of your highfalutin' shows I'll bring her here . . . You're always on about needing help, aren't you?'

'You can't do this to me, I'll . . . I'll leave you.'

The man threw his head back and laughed. 'That's what I've been wanting you to do for years, but you won't will you? You're afraid of what your dear, dear friends would say! That wonderful, charming Lettice couldn't hold her man! You wouldn't like that, would you? Oh, no!'

'I'll go when I'm ready.' Mrs Schofield's voice came to them in trembling tones like those of an old woman; and immediately there followed the man's voice, saying, 'You'll go when . . . I'm . . . ready. You'll stay here until Jan is married. And then I'll have the great pleasure of escorting you to the door with my foot in your backside . . . You stuck-up bitch, you!'

Mary Ann was standing with her hand pressed tightly to her mouth, and as she saw the man's arm come up she closed her eyes and turned her face towards Tony's chest. Automatically Tony's

71

arms went round her shoulders, but he did not look at her, and when the sound of the second blow came to Mary Ann she felt his body jerking as if the man's fist was hitting him.

There were footsteps sounding inside the house now, and Tony, loosing his hold on Mary Ann, turned and faced the front door.

Her fingers still tightly pressed to her mouth, Mary Ann stood looking apprehensively at Tony. She had often seen him in tempers, but she had never seen him look like this. There was not a vestige of colour in his face, it had a bleached look. Even his eyes appeared to be drained of all pigment. She was as frightened at this moment for Tony as ever she had been for Mike. There was going to be a fight. She knew there was going to be a fight; and it would be a terrible fight. Mr Schofield was a big man, as big as her da. She had only met him once and she hadn't liked him. Tony was tall, but he had no bulk with which to match Mr Schofield. Yet he had something else that perhaps might kill Mr Schofield; it stemmed from the livid passion showing on his face.

The footsteps had gone, and the door hadn't opened. A full minute passed before Tony turned his neck stiffly and looked towards her. Then his gaze lifted almost reluctantly towards the window again.

Mary Ann, too, looked through the window. Mrs Schofield was now sitting in a chair, her face turned into the corner, and she was crying, but no sound reached them. What they did hear was the whirr of a car engine starting up. The next second there shot from the side of the house a Humber Snipe with Mr Schofield at the wheel.

If Tony's car had been opposite the front door the man must surely have seen it, but from where it was standing on the far side of the drive underneath the overhanging trees, it must have escaped his notice, for he did not stop. Within seconds, the loud grinding of changing gears told them that he was on the main road.

Mary Ann was feeling sick. She always felt sick when there was fighting. But this was a different kind of sickness. She was puzzled, bewildered, and absolutely out of her depth. Mrs Schofield was bright and gay, and had a lovely life. That's what people thought about Mrs Schofield. She was light as thistledown, she was amusing . . . she amused Mr Lord. This couldn't be Mrs Schofield; this woman who had backed away across the room and almost whimpered when she talked. Mary Ann had lived in the slums of Jarrow and yet she had never seen a man actually strike a woman. She had heard of Mr and Mrs So-and-So having rows and going for each other, but she had never actually seen them fight; and never once in her life had she seen her da raise his hand to her ma, not even when he was paralytic drunk.

'What are we going to do?' She was whispering up to Tony. 'Oh, poor Mrs Schofield.' She shook her head and swallowed against the threatening tears.

When Tony did not answer but kept staring through the window, she asked softly, 'Shall I ring?'

'No.' His voice was sharp. 'She won't answer.' He moved from her, out of the porch, on to the drive; and she followed him. And when he stood on the overgrown flower-bed before the window and tapped gently on the pane, she herself was startled, so quick was the jump Mrs Schofield gave from the chair. She watched her stand for some minutes staring in painful amazement through the window at Tony, before screwing her face up, and then burying it in her hands.

'Open the door.' Tony's voice was quiet. And when Mrs Schofield only shook her head slowly from side to side, he called louder, 'Open the door.'

A few seconds later the front door opened, and Mary Ann, following Tony, saw Mrs Schofield's back disappearing down the dim hall.

They were in the room now, and Mrs Schofield was standing looking through the window, and Tony was standing behind her talking to her back. Quietly he said, 'We saw what happened, so it doesn't matter. Let me look at your face.'

'No, no, please . . . and please go away.'

'I'm not going away.'

Mary Ann noticed he did not say we. And then he went on, 'How long have you put up with this?'

'Oh, please.' It was a low, beseeching cry. And when Mrs Schofield's head dropped, Tony took her gently by the shoulders and turned her around.

Mary Ann gave a sharp gasp before going to the side of this woman who to her had been the personification of frivolity and lightness. 'Oh! Mrs Schofield . . . Oh! I'm sorry. Your poor mouth. Will . . . shall I get some water?'

Mrs Schofield's head was held level now, and although the tears were running down her swelling cheekbone and over her bruised lip, she managed a faint smile as she said, 'Don't worry, Mary Ann. It's all right, it's all right. Come and sit down.'

Tony, with his fingers just touching her elbow, led Mrs Schofield to the couch, and when he had seated himself on the edge beside her, with his body turned fully to her, he asked pointedly, 'Why do you stand it?'

As Mary Ann watched Mrs Schofield's mouth quiver she wanted to say to Tony, 'Don't ask questions. Can't you see she's upset enough,' but she continued to look at this surprising woman as she moved her eyes slowly about her drawing-room. It was as if she were looking at the articles about her with surprise, as if seeing them after a long time. And then she answered him absently with, 'Why? Yes, why?' Her head continued to make small pathetic jerks until her eyes came to rest on Tony, and then she said, in that voice that held a peculiar charm for all who heard it, 'I suppose it's because I was born here. I was brought up in this house. My whole life has been spent here.'

'Is it worth it?'

'No! No! Oh, no.'

There was vehemence in the tone now, and as Mrs Schofield went to cover her face once again with her hands, she stopped, and seeming to be becoming fully aware of Mary Ann's presence, she swallowed and drew in a deep breath, before turning and looking at her and saying, 'You've come to see Janice, I suppose, Mary Ann?'

'Yes, Mrs Schofield. She was going to come last night, and she didn't, and I couldn't get through. I tried several times.'

'No, you wouldn't. The line's broken.' She didn't go on to explain how the line was broken, but added, 'Janice is upstairs.'

Before Mary Ann could make any reply to this, Tony brought out in an amazed tone, 'Upstairs! and all this going on?'

Mrs Schofield did not answer Tony, but, turning to Mary Ann, asked, 'Would you like to go up to her, Mary Ann? It's the second door at the top of the landing, on the right-hand side.'

'Yes. Yes, Mrs Schofield.' Mary Ann glanced towards Tony, but Tony was looking at Mrs Schofield.

Out in the hall she stood for a moment gazing about her. The house inside was clean, tidy and clean, not bright like their house was bright, but not dirty. She did not go immediately up the stairs, for she was overwhelmed with pity not untouched with shock. She had just experienced the first great surprise of her life. She had been shown in one swift swoop the meaning of . . . putting a face on it. Mrs Schofield must have spent all her married life putting a face on it. She could see her now on the night of Len's wedding, standing on the platform playing the trombone when she could stop herself laughing. And later that night she would have gone home to perhaps a similar scene to that which had just taken place . . . Ee! it was awful. Poor Mrs Schofield. She went slowly up the stairs and knocked on the second door to the right. And when it was opened, Janice said, 'Oh, you.' Then looking past her and toward the stairs, she asked, 'How long have you been here?'

'Not very long. I tried to phone you, but

couldn't get through. I thought something was wrong when you didn't come last night, after saying you would.'

Janice turned her back completely on Mary Ann and walked back into the bedroom; then after she had sat down on the side of the bed, she said, 'Well, come in, don't stand there.'

Mary Ann went into the room, closing the door behind her. She felt rather gauche in Janice's presence, and very, very young. Janice was sitting with her hands nipped between her knees, and she looked at her hands as she asked, 'Did you hear anything going on?'

'Yes, we did.'

'We?' Janice's head came up.

'Tony's with me.'

'Oh, my God!' Although Janice said this in a very swanky tone, it sounded much more of a blasphemy than if, say, Mrs McBride had said it.

'Well, he would get an earful.'

'I think you should come down. Your mother's lip's all swollen.'

Janice looked down at her hands once more and began to rock herself, before she said, 'Oh, it won't be the first time. And anyway, she asks for it.'

'Asks for it?' Mary Ann's voice was high and sharp. 'She's nice. I've always said that.'

'If that's the kind of niceness you want, yes. But she's always got on his nerves. She should never have married him. She should have taken some-one polished, and re-feened. Someone who liked to go to concerts, yet someone who would laugh at her jokes when she was being funny ha-ha. But most of all somebody who would keep up this damn mausoleum.' She released her hands from between her knees and flung them sidewards. 'Oh, she gets on my goat too.'

'But he hit her, Janice . . . twice!'

'He was drunk and worried about me.'

'About you?'

'Yes. It all came out last night. That is what I wanted to see you about. I was in a blue funk yesterday, but now all the beans are spilt it doesn't matter . . . I'm going to have a baby.'

Mary Ann's mouth dropped into a large 'O', before she brought her lips together again, saying, 'Janice!'

'Oh! For God's sake, don't look like that, Mary Ann. You look like the Virgin Mary, only more damned good.'

Although Janice had attended the Convent she wasn't a Catholic, and Mary Ann had always resented her digs at the Virgin Mary. But now all she could say was, 'Are you . . . are you married?'

'Oh, be your age . . . Why I thought of coming to see you I don't know. Of course I'm not married. What do you think all this hoo-ha is about? And I'm telling you, I don't care much if I do or I don't. But Father's going to play the gigantic square and make him do . . . the right thing. Oh, my God!' Janice jerked herself from the bed. 'The right thing! And live a life like theirs! I wouldn't have believed it, but Daddy's taken it worse than she has. You get surprises if you've got anything left to feel surprise with. She didn't blink an eyelid, yet Daddy, he nearly went through the roof. And him running one in Newcastle and another in Pelaw.'

It must have been Mary Ann's puckered expression that made Janice close her eyes and fling her head back as she cried defiantly, by way of exclamation, 'A woman . . . he's always had a woman, but now he's got two.'

Mary Ann knew that she should sit down. She had a frightened feeling. It was like the time she had thought that Mr Quinton wanted her mother. She wasn't as green as Janice thought she was. It wasn't Janice's knowledge that was shocking her, but the open flaunting of it. She herself would rather have died than talk like this about her parents. Then Janice surprised her still further by turning on the bed and flinging herself face downwards.

'Oh, don't, Janice, don't.' Mary Ann grasped Janice's hand which was pounding into the pillow, and when she began to cry with a hard, tearing sound, Mary Ann knelt on the floor and put her arms around her and her face on the pillow as she murmured over and over, 'Oh, don't, Janice, don't. Don't cry, don't cry so.'

When Janice finally stopped crying she seemed to have washed away the hard covering of her personality, for, sitting once again on the side of the bed, one hand only now nipped between her knees, she looked at Mary Ann and said quietly, 'I won't have a life like theirs, I'd rather take something and finish it.'

'Oh, Janice! Don't say such things, don't. And you needn't have a life like theirs . . . Is . . . is this boy nice?'

'No. No, he's not. He's as far removed from me as Daddy is from . . . from her.' Janice now turned her head to the side and said, 'I've got a lot of my father in me so that's why I know that if I marry Freddie I won't be able to stick it. I think that's why I grew to dislike her . . . my mother. Because she had the power to stick it. To put a face on it. She should have left him years ago. And she might have, too, if it hadn't been for Grandpa. He died only three years ago. They were both barmy about this house and garden. There's something to be said on both sides, because it was Daddy's money that was keeping it going. That is until he turned nasty . . . and he can be nasty, hellish. He cut out the gardener, and the maids . . . and, oh . . . oh, lots of things. And the more things he did the more face she put on, and that drove him almost round the bend . . . But I won't marry Freddie, I won't.'

'He can't make you if you don't want to.' Mary Ann was holding Janice's hands tightly between hers now. 'Look, come and stay with us for a while.'

Janice turned and stared into Mary Ann's face. 'Would your mother let me?'

'Yes. Yes, of course she would.' Mary Ann hadn't stopped to consider whether Lizzie would fall in with this arrangement or not. She only knew she wanted to help Janice.

'I'd be glad to get away from here. If only for a few days. But I'm beginning to show . . . and there's, there's your Michael.'

Yes, there was Michael, and Sarah. But Mary Ann, overriding this as well, said casually, 'What does it matter? They're not to know.'

'Oh, they'll know. Everybody will know shortly. It would be better in the long run, I suppose, to do what I'm told.'

'Does he . . . Freddie, want . . . want to get married?'

'Oh, yes. He would jump in feet first at the idea. He's only in the dock office and he'll know when he's on a good thing; Daddy would set him up. Oh, I know exactly what'll happen. He'll set him up, and he'll buy us a house and a car. He's rotten with money, and he'll spend it on anything or anybody outside this house.'

The bitterness was creeping back into Janice's tone, and Mary Ann shook her hand and said, 'Well, wait and see. And think about coming to us. You needn't worry about phoning or anything, just come. My mother will love to have you.'

Janice, now looking down into Mary Ann's upturned face, smiled and said, 'You're sweet, you know, Mary Ann. I used to be jealous of you and Beatrice being close pals. I always wanted you for a friend, a complete friend. Because you were different somehow. I suppose it was because you had nothing in your family life to hide.'

'O . . . oh!' Mary Ann's head went back on a little laugh now. 'Oh, Janice, you don't know the half of it. I'm beginning to think we all have something to hide. I've been fighting for me da since . . . oh, I can't remember the time when I wasn't putting him over as somebody wonderful; when I wasn't covering up his drinking bouts. It isn't like that now, but things still happen and I always seem to be covering up for him. You do things like that when you love someone . . . Nothing to hide! Do you know, I've always envied you.'

'Envied me? God! Envied me? The times I've been going to run away, or commit suicide; or throw myself over the banisters to stop them havin' a row . . . Envy me!'

The two girls sat looking at each other on the side of the bed. And their hands held tightly for a moment, before Mary Ann said through a break in her voice, 'I'd better be going down now, Janice; Tony will want to be getting away. But remember what I said. Come any time . . . any time. Goodbye, now.'

'Goodbye, Mary Ann, and thanks. But I'll let you know if I'm coming. I'll drop you a line, or phone. Goodbye. I feel better now. Goodbye.'

In the drawing-room Tony was no longer sitting on the couch but on a chair some distance from Mrs Schofield, and as Mary Ann entered the room it did not seem as if she had interrupted their talking, it was as if they had been sitting quiet for some time. She stood in front of Mrs Schofield when she said, 'I've asked Janice to come and stay with us for a while, Mrs Schofield.'

'That's nice of you, Mary Ann. But hadn't you better ask your mother first?'

'Oh, my mother won't mind . . . she won't.'

Mrs Schofield did not speak, she only moved her head slightly. And then Mary Ann added, 'I'll have to be going now.' She turned sharply and looked towards Tony, and he rose from the chair but made no comment.

Mrs Schofield, too, rose to her feet, but she did not accompany them from the room, and Mary Ann was slightly puzzled when Tony took leave of her with just a single goodbye; a rather curt-sounding goodbye.

As the car went through the tunnel of the drive, Mary Ann said softly, 'It's awful, awful.'

Tony made no response to this. He slowed the car up as he neared the end of the drive, then, when he had swung into the main road, he quickly changed gears and they went roaring towards the city.

Mary Ann realised that Tony was quiet because, like her, he was upset. He, too, must have seen Mrs Schofield as a gay creature. And she supposed that men could be shocked as much about such things as women could. She said now, as if they were continuing a conversation, 'I hope she doesn't marry that Freddie.'

'Who? Who are you talking about?'

'Janice.'

'Is she going to be married?'

'Well.' She glanced at him. Did he, or didn't he know? She said softly, 'Well, you know she's going to have a baby.'

'Good God!' The car almost jerked to a stop, then went on again. 'So that's it.' He was not speaking to her but answering some question of his own. She did not take it up for he did not look in the mood to talk. He looked like her da did at times, but more so like Mr Lord when he was very angry inside. So they didn't speak again until they reached the farmyard. And there he turned the car before stopping. Then reaching over to open the door for her, he said, 'Are you going to tell your mother?'

'Yes.' Mary Ann hesitated. 'I'll have to if Janice is coming.'

'Yes.' He nodded his head without looking at her, and said again, 'Yes.'

83

She closed the car door, then watched him speeding back along the road down which they had just come.

Mike had been going in the direction of the byres, and he turned on the sound of the car leaving the yard again and, coming to her, said, 'My! you're soon back. Where's he gone?'

Mary Ann looking up at Mike, meant to say, 'I don't know,' but instead she bowed her head and burst out crying.

'What's the matter? What's happened?' Mike's voice was deep.

'Nothing. Nothing.'

'Tony said somethin' to you?'

'Oh, no, no. Come in a minute, will you? I've . . . I've got to tell me ma.'

In the kitchen, with Mike sitting at her side and Lizzie sitting in front of her, she held their silence with her story. And when it was finished she looked from one to the other, and they returned her gaze, still without speaking. Then Mike, getting up and walking to the pipe rack, lifted a wire cleaner from the top of it and rammed it down the stem of his pipe before shaking his head and saying, 'I think this is one of the biggest surprises of me life.'

'Yes, that's how I felt, Da. I couldn't take it in.'

'Poor soul! Look at her the night of the wedding. Who could have been more full of fun?' Lizzie had forgotten her irritation towards Mrs Schofield on that particular night, and her sympathy at this moment was very genuine. 'Did you actually see him hit her?'

'Yes, Ma.' Mary Ann reverted to the old form of address. At moments such as this Ma seemed more fitting, for the three of them were joined in their pity. 'I didn't see him do it the second time; I hid my face.'

'You never know, do you?' They both looked towards Mike as he went on pushing the cleaner down the stem of the pipe. 'I would have staked me last shilling that she was the happiest woman alive. Mind you' – he wagged the pipe towards Lizzie – 'I've said, haven't I, that she wasn't as dizzy as she made out. I knew from the minute I first clapped eyes on her there was a depth there. But it never struck me that all this light fantastic was just a cover . . . did it you? Did you ever have an inkling?'

'No. No. Like you, I would have sworn she was happy.' Again Lizzie added, 'Poor soul.'

'You don't mind me asking Janice here?' Mary Ann now asked of Lizzie.

'No, no. It will be better if she's away from that set-up for a time. But with a man like that, it looks as if he'll get his own way, and make her marry the fellow. Which, I suppose, will be all for the best. At least best for the child . . . Oh, dear God, it's awful, when you think of it. I've never liked Janice very much, but now I'm sorry to the heart for her. And it's not a bit of wonder she's gone wrong, not a bit.'

'Oh, I'm not as sorry for her as I am for the mother.' Mike put the pipe into his mouth. 'That young un's got a tough core, she'll get by . . . But you see, don't you, Liz, money isn't everything.' Mike now thrust out his arm and wagged his finger at Lizzie. It was as if money, and its value, had been under discussion. 'Schofield's rotten with money. I understand he's got his fingers in all sorts of pies. Real estate, shipping, the lot. He's as bad as the old man. And where's his money got him? What has it done for him? Except help him to run three homes!'

'Mike!'

'Oh, don't get on your high horse, Liz. She's told us all about it, hasn't she? It's herself that's told us.' He flapped his hand towards Mary Ann. 'Her education's been advanced this afternoon. But as I was sayin' about money . . . see what it does?' Mike bounced his head once, then turning on his heel, went out, and Lizzie, sitting straight in her chair, remarked in hurt tones, 'Why has he to go off the deep end like that? Who was talking about money?' She looked at Mary Ann and shook her head. Mary Ann said nothing. She knew that her da had been pointing out to her ma that people who married for money were not always happy. And she knew that her mother was being purposely blind to the parable.

The sound of Michael coming in the back way at this moment brought Mary Ann to her feet, and she said hastily, 'I'll go upstairs and do my face. Don't tell him about Janice, will you not? He doesn't like her very much and if she's comin' here it will make things awkward.'

'Go along. All right. Don't worry.'

Mary Ann had not reached the hall door when Michael entered from the scullery, and as he watched her disappearing back he remarked, in a brotherly fashion, 'What's up with her? Has she been crying? Why did they come back so quickly?'

'Oh . . . Janice wasn't very well.'

'What's she been crying for?'

'She's upset. Just a little upset about something.'

'What?'

'Oh, Michael, don't ask so many questions.'

'Oh, all right, if it's private. Only if I started to howl my eyes out, there'd be a reason for it.'

Lizzie turned and looked at her son and smiled fondly at him as she said, 'There would, if you howled your eyes out; that would be the day when you howled your eyes out.'

Lizzie was to remember these words and to think, 'Isn't it strange the things we say? It's as if we have a premonition of what's going to happen.' But at this moment she had no feeling of premonition. She just said to her son, 'It's time you were getting yourself changed as Sarah will be here and you not ready.'

'Mother.'

'Yes, what is it?' Lizzie had gone to the sideboard and taken out the teacloth.

'I want to ask you something.'

She turned and glanced at him. 'Well, I'm listening, go on.'

'It's about my holiday.'

'Your holiday? It's late in the year to start talking of holidays.'

'Father owes me a week. He said I could have it any time. You remember?'

'Yes. But we'll soon be on Christmas. And you don't want your holiday with snow on the ground, surely?'

'Yes, that's just it, I do.'

'Where are you going?'

Michael turned from her penetrating gaze

and walked towards the fire. 'I want to go to Switzerland.'

'Switzerland?'

He swung round sharply to her. 'Yes, Mother, Switzerland.'

'But that'll cost a penny, won't it?'

'Well, I've never had a real holiday in my life. South Shields, Whitley Bay, Sea Houses. But now I want to go abroad. It will only be for a week.'

'Well, well. If you want to go, I suppose you'll go. What does Sarah say to this?'

Michael now looked down towards the mat. Then without raising his head, he cast his eyes up towards Lizzie as he said, 'That's it. We want to go together.'

Lizzie's lips closed with a light pressure; the line in between her brows deepened, and then she said quietly, 'Together? You and Sarah away in Switzerland?'

'I'm nearly twenty, Mother.'

'Yes, I know that. And don't tell me that Sarah's eighteen. I know that too, and I'm going to tell you right away I don't hold with young people going on holiday together. And there's your father. Just think what he'll say to this.'

'I've asked him.'

'You've asked him . . . well! . . . What did he say then?'

'Do you want to know word for word?'

Lizzie made no reply. But her shoulders went back a little, and she drew her chin in.

'He said it's my own life; nobody can answer my conscience but myself. He said, "If you ever intend to marry a girl never take her down first if you can help it . . ."'

88

'Michael!' Lizzie's voice seemed to hit the back of her throat and check her breathing. Twice in the matter of minutes life in the raw had been let loose in her kitchen.

'Well, I'm only telling you what he said, and I know he's right. And I'm just repeating it to put your mind at rest . . . You understand?'

Lizzie understood all right; but it didn't alter the fact that she didn't want her son to go on holiday alone with Sarah Flannagan or any other girl. She knew men, even the best of them were what she called human. Well, he'd certainly had his say. Lizzie wiped her lips. 'Is there anything more you have to tell me?'

'What father said? Well, he said there were worse things than a man getting drunk; and I'm beginning to believe him . . .'

'No, I didn't mean I wanted to hear anything more your father said. He'd said enough, I should imagine. As for worse things than getting drunk, there's two opinions on that point. And I should have thought you knew that.'

'Yes, I do, Mother.' Michael's tone was soft now and he came towards her, and putting his arm about her shoulders he said, 'Don't worry, we'll do nothing we shouldn't do, let me tell you.' He smiled at her now. 'Sarah will see to that.'

Lizzie pulled herself away from Michael's hold. She didn't like this kind of talk; not from her son, her Michael. She knew that one day, and not in the far distant future, she would have to give up this boy of hers, but until that day came he would remain her boy. Not someone who discussed the possibilities of intimacy on holiday. What were young people coming to! She knew that young people went away on holidays together even when they weren't engaged, and she was also well aware of what happened; but she didn't want that kind of thing in her family. And Michael having a good deal of his father in him was bound to be . . . human. Oh dear, oh dear, one thing on top of another. She had thought she would have no more worries when she left Mulhattan's Hall. It just showed you. The word Mulhattan's Hall conjured up first Mrs McBride, and then Mrs Flannagan, and she turned swiftly towards Michael and said, 'What about her mother? What does she say to this?'

'I don't know.' Michael held out his hand with a sort of hopeless gesture. 'I won't know until Sarah comes. She's asking her this afternoon.'

They continued to look at each other for a moment longer, then Lizzie, with a deep flick, spread the cloth over the table, and Michael, with an equally deep sigh, went upstairs to change.

It was after dinner on the Sunday and the family were relaxing in the front room. Mike was asleep in the deep chair, his long legs stretched out towards the fire. Lizzie sat opposite to him at the other side of the hearth. She was pursuing her favorite hobby of looking at antique furniture and big houses. Michael was sitting at one end of the couch reading *The Farmers' Weekly*; and Mary Ann, with her legs tucked under her, was sitting at the other end. She had two books on her lap. One was *The Art of the Short Story* and the other was Fowler's *Modern English Usage*. But she was reading neither at present. She was staring across the hearth rug into the fire. Her thoughts darting from Corny to Mrs Schofield then back to Corny again, then on to Janice and back to Corny again. Then to Tony, and strangely not to Corny now but to Mrs Schofield. For she was seeing them wrapped in that strange silence when she entered the drawing-room of that unhappy house yesterday. Then once again she was thinking of Corny; hearing Mrs McBride talk of him; seeing Mrs McBride give her his letter. Her mind dwelt on the letter. She had read it countless times in the past few weeks. She could, without any exaggeration, have quoted it word for word backwards. But the thought of it at this moment brought her legs from under her, and in order not to disturb her da nor yet her mother nor Michael, she went quietly out of the room and upstairs to her bedroom.

After the heat of the sitting-room the chill of the bedroom made her shiver, and she swiftly went to the top drawer of the dressing chest, and there, from the box in which she kept her handkerchiefs and the flute which Corny had given her for her thirteenth birthday, and which, in spite of her promise, she had never learned to play, she took out the letter. To read it she had to stand by the window, for the sky was dark with coming snow, and her heart quickened as it always did when she came to . . . 'If I know I can make a go of it, I'll come back and tell you.' There was a statue of Our Lady on a little shelf above the head of her bed and she turned her eyes up to it as she did night and morning, and now she prayed: 'Make the time go quickly, dear Mother . . . please.'

When she folded the letter again she held it to her cheek for a moment as she looked out of the window. One minute her eyes were dreamy, lost in the promise of a year ahead. The next minute she was bending forward towards the window pane, her mouth open and her eyes screwed up. It couldn't be! But it was; yes, it was. She stared one moment longer at the figure walking primly towards the house gate, and then she thrust the letter into her handkerchief box, banged the drawer closed, and went belting down the stairs. As she thrust the sitting-room door open, all concern for her father's afternoon nap was gone as she cried, 'Mrs Flannagan! . . . It's Mrs . . . It's Mrs Flannagan . . . Mrs Flannagan's coming.'

'What! Who?' Lizzie and Michael had turned towards her, and Mike, shaking his head and blinking rapidly, pulled himself into a sitting position. 'Good God! Flannagan? The old 'un? You said her . . . Mrs?'

Before Mary Ann could make any further retort, Michael cried, 'Oh Lord!' And Lizzie, turning on him, hissed under her breath, 'This is you and this Switzerland business. Good gracious, on a Sunday afternoon, and me looking like this!'

'Let me get out.'

As the knock came on the front door, Mike, buttoning up his shirt neck, pushed past Mary Ann and made for the stairs. And Michael, about to follow, was checked when Lizzie hissed, 'Now, Michael, you're not going to leave this to me, you've got to face it.'

'Oh, Mother! . . . Well, let her get in, I'll come back in a minute . . . it mightn't be about that at all.'

'Michael!' Lizzie was whispering hoarsely to Michael's disappearing back as Mary Ann, on the second knock, went towards the door.

'Oh, hello, Mrs Flannagan.' The feigned surprise, and even pleasure, in Mary Ann's voice, said a lot for her advancement from the days when, next to the justifiable hate she had for Sarah, she considered Mrs Flannagan not only an enemy of her . . . ma and da, but someone in close association with the devil himself.

Mrs Flannagan was dressed very nicely. She had always attended to her person with the same meticulous care she gave to her house. These qualities of cleanliness were considered by Mrs Flannagan offsprings of virtue and as such had been enough to arouse Fanny McBride's hate, and Mary Ann, always a staunch ally of Mrs McBride, would have hated Mrs Flannagan if for no other reason but that Mrs McBride couldn't stand . . . the upstart.

'I hope you don't mind me comin' like this, Mary Ann?' Mrs Flannagan's tone held none of the old condescension.

'No, no. Come in, Mrs Flannagan. You must be frozen. Isn't it cold?' Mary Ann closed the door behind the visitor. 'Will I take your hat and coat?' She was playing for time to allow her mother to compose herself, and perhaps tidy her hair; but at this moment Lizzie came to the sitting-room door.

Lizzie couldn't be blamed for the slight tilt to her chin as she looked at this woman who for many years had been the bane of her existence. Life was strange. But she had no time to delve into this deep problem now, she would keep that for when she lay in bed awake tonight. She was glad, oh she was, that she had insisted on having the new square carpet for the hall. In spite of Mike's saying 'It's madness, lass. It's madness, with all the feet tramping in and out.' But she had always wanted a proper carpet in the hall, with a matching colour going up the stairs. Mike had said, 'Why pick on a mustard colour?' And she had informed him that dark mustard would go with the old furniture, the pieces that her flair had guided her to bid for at the auction sales. And now on one of these pieces, a small hall table, stood a wrought-iron basket showing off a beautiful plant of pink cyclamen. Oh, she was glad her hall looked nice. If only she'd had a chance to change into something decent. But her skirt and blouse were really all right, and what was more, oh, of much more significance, she was mistress of this fine home . . . Yes, life was funny.

Lizzie fell into the part of the hostess. With only a slight touch of reserve to her manner she held out her hand to Mrs Flannagan, saying, 'If I'd known you were coming, I would have had Michael meet the bus.' The censure wasn't too tactfully covered, it wasn't meant to be. But Mrs Flannagan was, today, out to placate, and she answered, 'Well, I know I should have phoned, Mrs Shaughnessy. But it was the way Sarah sprung it on me. And it made me rather vexed.' She smiled. 'So I said, "Well, I'll go myself and see what Mr and Mrs Shaughnessy have to say about it." . . . But very likely you don't know what I'm talking about?'

'Yes. Yes, I think I do.' Lizzie inclined her head. 'But come in and sit down; it is cold today, isn't it?'

Mary Ann followed Mrs Flannagan into the sitting-room. She had a great desire to laugh. Laugh loudly . . . Go and see Mr and Mrs

Shaughnessy. Oh! Mr Shaughnessy would have a laugh about this for weeks ahead. The times Mrs Flannagan had called her da a drunken no-good . . . All of a sudden she was glad Mrs Flannagan had made this unexpected visit. After yesterday, she needed light relief, she felt they were all in need of a little light relief. She sat down opposite Mrs Flannagan and watched her look around the sitting-room with open amazement. And she found herself even liking her when she said generously, 'What a beautiful room, Mrs Shaughnessy, what a beautiful room. Did you do it yourself?'

'We all helped, Mrs Flannagan. Mike's very good at papering and painting.' Lizzie's chin, still high, moved a little to the side.

'But my mother chose the furniture,' Mary Ann put in. 'She's always picking up nice pieces.' She looked with pride towards Lizzie, and Lizzie smiled back at her. And then inclining her head towards her guest, she said, 'Would you like a cup of tea?'

'That's very kind of you, Mrs Shaughnessy . . . Yes, I would. I'd be obliged.'

'I'll make it, Mother.'

Mary Ann jumped up and left the room. And as she went laughing into the kitchen, Michael, standing to the side of the door, pulled at her arm.

'What has she said?'

'Nothing, nothing. We've only reached the polite exchange stage so far. You've got all that to come, me lad.' She dug her brother in the chest.

'Oh! They get you down.' Michael put his hand to his head.

'Who?'

'Oh, mothers. The lot of them.'

'Me ma's right about this.' Mary Ann's face took on a straight pattern as she nodded solemnly at Michael. She had only heard that morning about the proposed holiday in Switzerland, and her first reaction had been one of shock. And then she had thought . . . well, it would be all right, they were Catholics. But this statement had been countered by a cynical voice that was making itself heard in her mind quite a lot of late, and it said, with a little smear of a laugh, 'What difference will that make when it comes to . . .' She had shut the door of her mind on the voice before it had dared to go into forbidden topics. But she found now that she was vexed with Michael's attitude towards her ma, because her ma, she knew, put Michael first, and always had done, the same as her da had put her first and would always do so. And Michael knew this, and up to now he and her ma had been very close. If she hadn't had her da's unstinted love she would have at times been jealous of Michael. She said again, 'Me ma's right.' And he turned on her, whispering fiercely, 'What do you know about it? Your ideas are so infantile, you should still be in white socks.'

'Well!' She drew herself up. Then with sisterly affection she finished, 'I hope you get it in the neck.'

At this moment the kitchen door opened quietly and Mike entered, and at the sight of him both Mary Ann and Michael were forced to laugh.

'Oh, Da! She must have you frightened at last.' Mary Ann was spluttering through her fingers.

Mike, unloosening the button on the coat of his

best suit, and hunching his shoulders upwards, said, 'All right, laugh. I'm on me own ground; but I still feel I need some armour against that one.' Then looking at Michael he said kindly, 'I've always had the idea that Sarah was adopted.'

'I don't think I'll hang anything on to that hope.' Michael returned his father's grin. 'She takes after her mother in some ways . . . she's finicky about her clothes.'

'Well, I wouldn't stand there, both of you,' Mary Ann thrust at them. 'I'd go on in and get it over.'

'After you.' Michael held out his hand with an exaggerated gesture to his father. And Mike, following suit, replied, 'No, after you. This visit, don't forget, is for the benefit of your soul.'

'Ha!' On this telling exclamation Michael led the way out of the kitchen, and Mary Ann, in case she missed much, flung the things on to the tea-tray and only a few minutes later carried it into the sitting-room, there to see her da ensconced in the big armchair with his legs crossed, his pipe in his mouth and his whole attitude proclaiming the master of the house, and to hear Mrs Flannagan repeat an earlier statement, 'It's a beautiful room, Mr Shaughnessy.'

'My wife has taste, Mrs Flannagan.'

Mrs Flannagan lifted her watery smile up to Lizzie's face, and Lizzie, slightly embarrassed, and praying inwardly that Mike was not all set to have his own back on this she-cat-turned-dove, said, in a smooth tone that tempered the abrupt plunge into essentials, 'It's about Sarah and the holiday you've come, Mrs Flannagan?'

'Yes, yes, Mrs Shaughnessy, you're right. You

see, I would never have dreamed of coming without an invitation.' She flickered her eyes around the company asking them all to bear witness to her knowledge of propriety. 'But this, I felt, was an emergency. You know what I mean.' She eased herself to the edge of the chair. And as she did so Michael coughed, and Mike made a funny sound down the stem of his pipe that brought Lizzie's sharp warning glance on him. 'Now as I said to Sarah, this thing has to be talked over; not that I don't trust you, Michael.' Mrs Flannagan's head now went into a deep abeyance. She had lost her nervousness; she had forgotten for the moment that she was in the enemy's camp, so to speak. For Mrs Flannagan, at rock bottom, was no fool; she knew that Mike Shaughnessy's memory was long. And although she didn't want to do anything to put a spanner in the works of the match, she wasn't going to let her daughter appear as a . . . light piece, her own phraseology for any female who gave to a man her company in the first hours of the day. 'I do trust you, I do, Michael, but . . .' Mrs Flannagan seemed to be stumped for words with which to make her meaning plain, but this obstacle was overcome for her by Mike.

'But taking into account human nature, Mrs Flannagan?'

Was Mike Shaughnessy laughing at her? Mrs Flannagan stared back into the straight countenance of the big red-headed man. There was no sign of laughter on his face, but that was nothing to go by when dealing with him. She knew this from experience, but now she clutched at his explanation, which was really what she had wanted to say but had found a little indelicate.

Now however she affirmed, 'Yes. Yes, you're right, Mr Shaughnessy. Human nature has got to be taken into account. And . . . and the look of the thing, it's the look of the thing, and what people will say. And once give a dog a bad name, you know . . .'

'Yer . . . ss, I know. I know, Mrs Flannagan.' Mike was nodding at their guest. 'Don't I know, Mrs Flannagan.'

Oh my. Mary Ann had a little uneasy fluttering inside her chest. This could lead to anything. Her da was going to rib Mrs Flannagan. He was going to lead her on, and on, and then knock her flat. She knew the tactics. In the hope that it might divert the topic, she put in quickly, 'You haven't drunk your tea, Mrs Flannagan.'

'No. Oh, no.' Mrs Flannagan smiled at Mary Ann and took two very ladylike sips from her cup. It was as she took the second sip that she gulped slightly, for Michael was speaking, and with no prelude.

'I hope some day to marry Sarah, Mrs Flannagan.' His voice was quiet, his tone very level, and his air not that of a boy not yet twenty, but of a man who knew his own mind.

Mrs Flannagan's head made a half-moon turn as she took them, one by one, into her glance again. Then after a gulp that had nothing lady-like about it whatever, she addressed Michael pointedly. 'There, that's what I said to her. I said, "It would be different altogether if you were engaged or something." That's what I pointed out to her. I said, "If there was an understanding or something." '

Oh, Lord. Mary Ann's head dropped. This was

enough to break up any romance. Poor Michael. Poor Sarah.

'Michael will do what he thinks is right in his own time, Mrs Flannagan.'

'Yes, yes, I'm sure he will, Mrs Shaughnessy.'

'You might as well know I don't hold with this business of holidaying together any more than you do.'

'Oh, it isn't that, Mrs Shaughnessy.'

'No, no, it isn't that.' Mike's voice was a deep bass as he repeated Mrs Flannagan's words. And it was evident he meant to go on, when Michael cut in sharply on them all, and he was on his feet when he spoke. 'Leave this to me, Father . . . and you, Mother.' And now he looked straight at Mrs Flannagan while he said, 'Sarah and I have the same ideas about an engagement. We've talked it over. In the meantime we want to go away together . . . We don't intend to sleep together . . .'

'Michael!' Lizzie, too, was on her feet, and Mike, sitting up straight in his chair, said quietly, 'It's all right, it's all right. It happens, don't be so shocked. Nor you, Mrs Flannagan. Go on, son.'

Michael swallowed before saying, 'What we do want is to go away for a time and enjoy ourselves, and be together all day. And see different places . . . together. On our own. And you know' – he was now not looking at Mrs Flannagan but casting his glance sideways at Lizzie as he went on – 'It's not held as a sin any longer when a fellow and a girl go off holidaying together. It might be frowned on but—'

At this point Michael stopped and jerked his head round towards the sitting-room door. Mary

Ann, too, was looking towards the door. Her attention had been drawn to it before Michael had stopped talking, and now Lizzie said, 'What is it?' and following Mary Ann's gaze she asked abruptly, 'See if anyone's there. It might be Tony.'

Mary Ann was at the door before her mother had finished speaking, and when, pulling it open with a quick tug, she almost fell on to the high breast of her granny, she let out a scream.

Her granny. Of all days her granny had to come today. Of all times her granny had to come precisely at this time, when Mrs Flannagan was here. She had always considered her granny a form of witch who went round smelling out mischief for the sole purpose of enlarging it. As far back as she could remember she had hated her granny. There was no alteration in her feelings at this moment. In the presence of her granny she lost all her girlish charm. Mrs McMullen had the power to bring out the very worst in Mary Ann, and she always put this power into motion as soon as her eyes alighted on her grand-daughter.

'Well, knock me over. That's it, knock me over.'

'Oh, no!' Mary Ann heard her mother's stifled murmur, and above it came Michael's audible groan. Mike alone made no sound. But Mary Ann knew that of all of them her father would be the most affected by her granny's visit. Whereas he would only have chipped Mrs Flannagan, and revelled, no doubt, in the superiority of his family's position now that the tables were almost completely turned, the afternoon, nevertheless, would have gone off with a veneer of smoothness, but when her da came up against her granny veneers were useless. For her granny hated her da, and would do until the last breath was dragged from her.

'What are you gaping at? Standing there looking like a mental defective.'

'I'm not then . . .' Whether Mary Ann was denying that she was standing gaping, or that she was a mental defective was not plain. The only thing that was plain was the aggressive note in her voice.

'Well, there's one thing I can always be sure of when I visit my daughter, and that's an all-round welcome.'

Mrs McMullen was now in the room, and her chin went up and her abundantly covered head, both of hair and hat, were slightly to the side as she feigned surprise at the sight of Mrs Flannagan.

'Well! well! And who would have expected to see you here! . . . Good afternoon, Mrs Flannagan.'

'Good afternoon, Mrs McMullen.' Mrs Flannagan was smiling her thin smile but it was evident that she was more uneasy now than she had been before Mrs McMullen's entry.

'Well, Lizzie.' Mrs McMullen looked at her daughter.

'Hello, Mother . . . I wasn't expecting you.'

'Are you ever?'

'Well, you rarely come on a Sunday. I've never known—'

'All right! All right! I rarely come on a Sunday. But I live alone, don't forget, and people do forget that old people are living alone and without company. So I felt that I would visit my daughter, and have a look at my grandchildren.' She made no mention of her son-in-law who was now sitting, legs uncrossed, his spine tightly pressed against the back of the chair.

'Sit down. Give me your hat . . . Will you have a cup of tea?'

'Well, I won't say no. I'm practically frozen to the bone.'

'Pour your granny out a cup of tea, Mary Ann.'

'Why does she have to look so gormless?' Mrs McMullen had turned her gimlet eyes on her grand-daughter, and Mary Ann, rearing up now well above the side table and Mrs McMullen's seated figure, spat out, 'Do you make a list of all the sweet things you're going to say before you—'

'That's enough!' Lizzie was not only speaking to Mary Ann as she extended her one hand towards her, but was already addressing Mike with a warning look, for Mike had pulled himself to the edge of the chair – his face dark with temper.

It was at this point that Mrs Flannagan, seeing herself in the light of peacemaker, turned to Mrs McMullen and remarked, 'I was just saying to Mr Shaughnessy, what a delightful room this is.'

Mrs McMullen's head moved in a series of short waves as she calmly and aggravatingly surveyed the room; then her verdict came. 'It's too light.' There followed a pause when no-one spoke, and she went on, 'Never put good pieces of dark furniture against light wallpaper. I've told her.' She looked towards Lizzie. 'I was picking up things in antique shops long before she was born and I've always said dark paper, dark furniture . . . haven't I?'

Lizzie did not answer her mother. And Mrs

McMullen took a sip from her tea, only to comment, 'No sugar.'

'I did sugar it.'

'Well, I should say that in this case the sugar is about as sweet as the donor.'

It was evident to all that Mrs McMullen was in a temper. She was usually in a temper. It seemed to be her natural state. But she generally waited until she could diplomatically fire her darts. Unfortunately, whatever had upset her today had robbed her of her finesse. And then she gave evidence of the source of her annoyance by turning to Michael for the first time.

'What you want is a visit from the priest.'

'WHAT!'

'You heard what I said.'

There was a wrinkled query spreading over the faces of them all as they looked towards the old woman, ageless in her vitality. 'You heard what I said. A priest . . . going away with a young lass for a week!'

The comments to this remark seemed to come simultaneously from all directions of the room.

'Mother!' This was Lizzie.

'Look here, Gran.' This was Michael.

'Really, Mrs McMullen!' This was Mrs Flannagan.

'Well, I'll be damned! Your cuddy's lugs got working quick, didn't they? Did you find it draughty standing in the hall?' This from her beloved son-in-law.

Only Mary Ann made no comment, for she was thinking rapidly. She would have to get her da away out of here else there would be a row. This would have to happen when Mrs Flannagan was here, wouldn't it?

Mrs McMullen, it would appear, had not heard her son-in-law's remarks, for she turned now to Mrs Flannagan, and her tone was sympathetic as she said, 'I can well understand how you feel, I would be the same in your shoes. And you're right to put your foot down and forbid such a carry on . . .'

'But . . . Mrs McMullen, it . . . it isn't like that.' Mrs Flannagan was definitely floundering. She held out a wavering hand towards Mike, who looked livid enough to explode, and he cut in on her in deep, deep tones.

'If my son wants to take Sarah away, then he has my permission and my blessing on the trip . . . Are you listening?'

'Mike . . . Look, wait a moment.'

'I'm not waitin' any moment, Liz. I'm making this clear once and for all. My son is not a boy, he's a man.' This was the second time Mike had spoken of Michael as my son, not our son, and he had stressed the 'my' this time.

'You know my opinion, Mrs Flannagan.' Mrs McMullen was entirely ignoring Mike, and doing it in such a way that a saint would have been forgiven for springing on her and putting a finish to her mischief-making existence. 'You must be very worried, and you're quite right to put a stop to it . . .'

'But, Mrs McMullen, wait . . .' Mrs Flannagan was leaning towards the old woman now with her hands raised in an agitated flutter. 'You've got me slightly wrong. I trust Michael with Sarah.' She glanced with her thin smile towards Michael's stiff countenance. 'Mr Flannagan and myself think very highly of Michael, and now that, well . . . they're going to be engaged, I can't, as I was saying to Mr Shaughnessy a moment ago, see any harm in them having a holiday together, now they're going to be engaged . . . You see, Mrs McMullen?'

Mary Ann had never liked Mrs Flannagan, and she had imagined that she never could, but at this minute she had a strong desire to fling her arms around her neck and hug her. True, she had precipitated an engagement, but that's what she had come for. Still, no matter how she had accomplished it she had got one over on her granny. But, what was much more significant, she had sided with her da against her granny. This was indeed a change of front and a blow to her granny, because Mrs Flannagan and her granny had been on very polite speaking terms simply because they both had a joint enemy in her da. And now Mrs Flannagan had blatantly left her granny's ranks and come over to their side. Oh, if only her da would use this turn in the situation and play up. And her da, being her da, did just that.

Undoubtedly Mrs Flannagan's statement came as a surprise to Mike, and that is putting it mildly. Perhaps before the end of her visit she might have indicated that if the couple were engaged, they would have her blessing to take a trip together. Whether she had cunningly grasped at the situation to use a little motherly blackmail didn't matter. She, Mrs Flannagan, the thorn that had been in Mike's side for years, had openly flouted his mother-in-law, and had openly agreed with him. Whatever he had thought of her in the past, this afternoon he would be for her. He reached for his pipe and once more lay back in his chair and crossed his legs, before saying with a smile, which he directed upon Mrs Flannagan, 'Yes, you're right. An engagement makes all the difference. You can trust your daughter as I can trust my son. And I don't think there'll be any need for a priest. Do you, Mrs Flannagan?'

Mrs Flannagan blinked, she preened, she returned Mike's smile in the face of Mrs McMullen's thunderous countenance as she replied banteringly, 'Well, not just yet awhile, Mr Shaughnessy.' And she continued to smile across the hearth-rug towards this big rugged, red-headed man, who had more than once threatened to throw her down the stairs if she didn't mind her own so-and-so business. But those things were in the past. For now she was delighted that her Sarah would marry into such a family. Into a family that would soon be connected with Mr Lord, and him owning a shipyard. She knew why Corny Boyle had been sent packing. She couldn't get much out of Sarah these days, but some time ago she had let slip that old Lord had his grandson all lined up for Mary Ann.

'What do you say to this?' Mrs McMullen had turned her whole body towards Lizzie, and her attitude would have intimidated anyone less strong. From anyone less used to the subtleties of this woman it would have brought forth the truth. And if Lizzie had spoken the truth at this moment she would have said, 'I'm as against it as you are.' But she could never desert Mike openly in the face of her mother. Nor could she stand on one side

while Mike was taking sides with Mrs Flannagan.
Where Mike stood in this she must be also. She
looked down into her mother's face and said, with
just a little side dig of censure at Mrs Flannagan,
'I think we are all concerning ourselves far
too much about something which isn't entirely
our business. Michael and Sarah will do what
they want in the long run, with or without our
consent.'

'You've gone soft, me girl.'

A silence followed this remark, and Mrs
McMullen moved her body slowly round again
and surveyed the company. And when her eyes
came to rest on Michael, his dropped away,
and he tried his best at this juncture not to laugh
. . . Talk about manoeuvring and counter-
manoeuvring. They had settled his life between
them. He was already engaged; if they only but
knew it, he had been engaged to Sarah from the
first moment he set eyes on her, and she to him.
But let them have their say, let them think they
were fixing everything. There would be no harm
done.

He looked towards his father, and Mike, catching his eye, gave the faintest of winks. As Michael
grew older he found he liked his father more and
more. It hadn't always been like that. He knew
now that Mike was enjoying the situation, he had
got one up on the old girl, even if it meant joining
forces with Mrs F. It was as good as a play, the
whole set-up.

Lizzie broke the awkward silence now by saying, 'I think I'd better set the tea.'

'I'll help you, Mother.' Mary Ann, glad of the
chance to escape, was about to move from behind

the table when Mrs McMullen, turning her cold fish eyes on her, remarked, 'Nice goings on among your friends, eh?'

'What?'

'Is that all you two can say?' Mrs McMullen flicked her eyes between Michael and Mary Ann: 'WHAT!'

'No, it isn't all I can say.' Mary Ann defended herself, standing squarely in front of her grandmother now. 'And what do you mean about my friends?'

'That Schofield piece, no better than should be expected.'

At the name of Schofield, a swift glance passed between Lizzie, Mike and Mary Ann. Then Mary Ann's eye came to rest on her granny again. It was true what she had always maintained, her granny was in league with the devil. Father Owen had told her many years ago that the devil walked the earth in different guises, and for a certainty, she would maintain, he had taken on the guise of a bitter, envious, hateful, cantankerous old woman. How else would her granny know of Janice's trouble? But now Mrs McMullen gave her the answer.

'A come-down for the Schofields, I'd say, wouldn't you, them having their daughter tied up compulsorily with the Smyths?'

'Which Smyths are you talking about?' Lizzie, now, not Mary Ann, snapped the inquiry at her mother.

'The Smyths above me, you know them well enough. Two doors up. It's their Freddie she's got mixed up with. And there was her dear papa yesterday afternoon in his car as big as a house, and May Smyth in tears after. But they weren't too salt, for there's money there.'

'What do you know about it?' Mike's voice was harsh. 'You're just surmising, as always. Putting two and two together, a putrid two and two.'

Mrs McMullen did not turn her superior expression on her son-in-law, but looked up at her daughter as she said, 'Mrs Smyth told me the whole story after Mass this morning.'

'She's a blasted fool then.'

Mrs McMullen continued to ignore Mike as she went on, still looking at Lizzie. 'Of course it didn't surprise me, with a mother like she's got gallivanting here, there, and everywhere. Never in, I should say. Every bazaar and flower opening, there she is, with that Mrs Willoughby and Bob Quinton's wife. They have nothing better to do, the three of them, but going around showing themselves off on platforms and not attending to their families. It will be the Willoughby one next . . . and you, me gel.' Now Mrs McMullen brought her face sharply round to Mary Ann's dark countenance. 'You should go on your bended knees every night and thank God you haven't got a mother who gallivants—'

'When I go on my bended knees every night, it isn't to thank God but to ask Him—'

'Mary Ann!' Lizzie had to shake Mary Ann by the arm to bring her riveted attention from her granny.

'Oh, leave her alone, leave her alone.' Mrs McMullen flapped her hand at her daughter. 'I suppose it shows some good quality when she tries to defend her friends. And they need some defending is all I can say . . . With the girl in a packet of trouble, and the mother joy-riding up the country lanes with that young fellow.'

Mrs McMullen did not go on to give the name of the young fellow, but she looked around her silent audience, waiting for one of them to prompt her disclosure. But when no-one spoke, she wagged her head before ending, 'I wonder what the almighty Mr Lord will say to his grandson running round with a married woman?'

'Oh, you! you wicked old . . . ! You always were a wicked creature, you . . . !'

'Stop that.' It was Mike speaking now, his voice low and steely. 'Let your granny go on, she came to give us this news. She won't rest until she tells us.'

But Mary Ann didn't allow her grandmother to go on. She was quivering with rage as she blurted out, 'You're lying. Tony never saw Mrs Schofield until yesterday.'

Mrs McMullen's eyebrows went up just the slightest at this new piece of information and she replied coolly, 'Yesterday? I'm not talking about yesterday. I'm talking about today, not an hour gone. The police were holding the traffic up, there'd been an accident, and as I sat in the bus I happened, like any ordinary person, to look at the passing cars. He was letting them pass one by one as the lorries were half over the road, and there, sitting side by side, was your Mr Tony and the Schofield woman. And something else I'll tell you, she had her head down, but that didn't prevent me from seeing one of the best black eyes I've spied for a long time.'

'It's a pity someone hadn't the guts to give you—'

'Please, Mike, please!' As Lizzie appealed to Mike she had her eyes closed, and looking up into her white face he obeyed her plea. But, pulling himself to his feet, he remarked, 'Let me out of this. I'm in need of fresh air.'

As Mike reached the sitting-room door, Mary Ann was behind him, and as they went into the hall Michael came on their heels.

All three stood in the kitchen and looked at each other, and then Michael asked quietly, 'Is it true, do you think, about . . . about Janice Schofield?'

'Yes, it's true enough, more's the pity.' Mike took in a deep breath.

'And about . . . Tony?'

'No, it isn't. That part isn't true. Mr Schofield hit Mrs Schofield yesterday, and Tony and I saw him. Tony was taking me to see Janice. That's all there was to it.' Mary Ann stopped gabbling and again they looked from one to the other, but not one of them said, 'Why is he with her today though?' Yet Mary Ann knew that both Michael and her father were asking themselves the same question. She sensed Michael's bewilderment at the situation, but she more than sensed her father's real reaction to this latest piece of news. He would welcome the idea of Tony having an affair . . . And she herself, how did she feel about it? If Corny had been here, perhaps she would have just shown a friendly interest, mixed with a little wonder that Tony should take out a woman so much older than himself, for Mrs Schofield must be nearly thirty-five . . . But Corny wasn't here. And she was amazed at the feeling of resentment that had whirled up in her quite suddenly against Mrs Schofield. She liked Mrs Schofield. Yesterday, she had loved her. If pity is akin to love, then she had loved her. But this afternoon she was out with Tony!

She turned her eyes from her father's penetrating gaze and said aloud, with the fervour of the younger Mary Ann who had cared nothing about self-discipline, decorum, and putting a face on things, 'I could kill me granny! And you know, one of these days I feel sure I will, I won't be able to help it.'

5

Janice neither wrote or phoned during the following week to say that she was coming, and Lizzie, her sympathy now ebbing, said testily, 'She might have at least let us know. I suppose she doesn't think there's a room to be got ready, and other things.' She had gone to some pains to make the spare room attractive, and she had added, 'Only three weeks to Christmas and everything to do. People don't seem to have any consideration at all these days.'

Mary Ann did not in her usual way make any defensive retort. She understood how her mother felt. She was feeling slightly annoyed herself. Janice might have phoned. Moreover, she was curious to know what was happening. She had been tempted twice already this week to bring up the subject with Tony, but strangely enough she had found herself shy of broaching it! For Tony, from the time he had said, 'Are you going to tell your mother?' had, it would seem, dismissed the Schofields from his mind, for he had made no reference whatever to them. This would have seemed strange enough if Mary Ann had not known he had met Mrs Schofield since the incident at the house, but now that she knew he had taken Mrs Schofield out on the Sunday it was more than odd. His silence, she felt, put upon the situation a cloak of secrecy that wasn't . . . nice. And it was this cloak that prevented her from inquiring about Janice.

Yet when he called into the house he laughed and talked with her ma and da, and seemed in very good spirits. And she asked herself on these occasions, didn't he himself think it was odd, knowing that she had told them about Mrs Schofield, that he shouldn't mention the matter?

Then there was her mother's attitude towards this business. The fact that Lizzie hadn't referred to her granny's denouncement added another cloak of secrecy to the affair, and strengthened this feeling of the situation being beyond the pale of . . . nice.

Her mother had said last night that everything happened around Christmas time and that she wished it was over. She knew that her mother was worried about Michael going to Switzerland with Sarah, for it was now settled that they would have their holiday together. And in bed last night she herself had felt a keen jealousy against the two of them. It did not last long and she went to sleep on the thought: 'When Corny comes back I shall have my holiday with him. Me ma won't be able to say anything, she can't after this . . .'

When yet another week had passed and still no word had come from Janice, Lizzie dismissed the subject with the emphatic statement, 'That's the last bottle I'm putting up in that bed.'

It was a week before Christmas and on a Friday night that Mary Ann brought home news of

Janice. Lizzie was in the kitchen and anxiously looking towards the clock – Mary Ann was half an hour late, which was unusual. Lizzie got worried when she was five minutes late – you heard of such dreadful things happening to girls these days.

The sound of Mike scraping his boots on the scraper outside the scullery door brought her hurrying through the kitchen, and as he opened the door she said, 'She's not in yet.'

'No! What's keeping her, I wonder? She phoned or anything?'

'No.' Lizzie shook her head. 'Would I be like this if she had? Hadn't you better go down and meet the next bus?'

'Aye. Yes, I'll do that.' He rebuttoned the top of his greatcoat, saying as he did so, 'The buses will likely be late, the roads are icy.' Then as he was about to turn from her he laughed as he cocked his head upwards. 'Listen, that's her running. All your worry for nothing again.' He pushed past her and, taking off his coat, sat down on the cracket in the scullery. He was unlacing his boots when Mary Ann came in.

'What's kept you?' Lizzie's tone was sharp and indicative of her anxiety.

'I lost my bus. I came on the one on the top road.'

'What's the matter?' Mike lifted his head from its bent position, and his fingers came to a halt where they were entwined in his laces. Mary Ann stood looking down at him for a moment, and her voice shook just the slightest as she said, 'Janice phoned just after I'd finished.'

'Oh? Well . . . go into the kitchen, you look

froze. Get something to eat before you go any further.'

Mary Ann went into the kitchen, and she turned her white, peaked face towards her mother as she said, 'I don't want anything to eat, not yet, just a drink.'

'What's the matter?' Lizzie's voice was now quiet.

'It's Janice. She's married.'

'Married? Oh.' Mike, coming into the room, picked up her words. 'Well, she could have let you know sooner, couldn't she?' He sat down in his chair, and Mary Ann looking from him to her mother, said, 'No.'

'You're upset about something.' Lizzie put her hand around her daughter's shoulders. 'Sit down and I'll get you a cup of tea.'

Mary Ann sat down, but immediately turned her face into her mother's waist. It was an action that she had not indulged in for a long time. But at this moment she had a frightened feeling. Life could be terrible. Life, she knew, was hard and painful. She had been educated in that kind of life all during her early childhood, but there were other things in life, terrifying things. She drew her head from the shelter of her mother's flesh and looked up at her as she whispered, 'She tried to kill herself!'

'Oh, my God!'

'Did she tell you this?' Mike was leaning towards her now, his hand outstretched holding hers.

'Yes, Da. I had just finished work and Miss Thompson told me I was wanted on the phone. It was Janice. She sounded just as if . . . well, as if

117

she was drunk. She was laughing most of the time, except at the end. She kept talking and talking. She said she was married last Friday and her father was going to set Freddie up in business. He had bought them a car and a bungalow on the Fells Road. And then she stopped laughing and carrying on and said she was sorry about not letting me know she wasn't coming, but she hadn't expected to go anywhere for she had taken some stuff and locked herself in her room.' Mary Ann's lips began to tremble. 'From what she said I think she would have died but her mother climbed up the trellis and got in through the window – the house is covered with creeper – and after her doing that she . . . she said, Ma, Janice said that she hated her mother, that she should have left her alone . . . Poor Janice. She must have been in an awful state.'

'Poor mother, I should say.' Mike now hitched himself up to Mary Ann and, patting her hand, said, 'Don't be upset, lass. Madam Janice will come through all right, you'll see. I wish I could say the same for her mother.'

'Where was she married?' asked Lizzie. 'Newcastle or Shields?'

'Newcastle, Ma. At the Registry Office.'

'But she couldn't . . . he's a Catholic.'

'Oh, my God! Liz.' Mike shook his head.

'All right, all right. There's no need to use that tone.'

Mary Ann rose from her chair, saying now, 'I'll get washed, Ma.'

'Will I set your tea on a tray and have it in the front room? Michael and Sarah are there.'

'No, Ma. I'll have it here.'

Almost before she had closed the door behind her, she heard her da speak. It was the bitterness of his tone that made her pause for a second to listen, as he said, 'If the old man gets his way, what about it then? Tony's no Catholic and I'm damned sure you'll not get him to turn. He's as stubborn as they come, and no blame to him.'

'I'll meet that obstacle when it arises. And what's the matter with you going for me like this?'

'Because it makes me flaming mad, Liz, when you put a second-class label on people who aren't Catholics.'

'Oh! How can you say such a thing? What about us, eh?'

'I'd be a better man in your eyes if I changed me coat.'

'Oh, that's unfair, Mike. That's unfair. Oh, it is.'

As her mother's voice trailed away in sadness, Mary Ann went slowly up the stairs. Why was it that nothing was going right inside or outside of the house lately?

Some minutes later when Mary Ann descended the stairs into the hall again, she approached the sitting-room door with a discreet cough. She would say Hello before she had her tea. But when she opened the door – without knocking, of course – such action would have slapped diplomacy in the face – she did not find Michael and Sarah sitting on the couch, but Michael sitting on his hunkers in front of Sarah, and he looked up quickly at Mary Ann, saying, 'She's off colour.'

'Are you feeling bad?' Mary Ann bent over the back of the couch.

'No, not really bad. I just can't explain it.' Sarah dropped her head backwards and looked up into Mary Ann's face. 'A bit head-achey, a bit sick . . . achey. Just like when you're going to get the flu; but I don't feel as if I've got a cold. Oh!' She smiled up at Mary Ann. 'I think the real truth is I'm after a few days in bed. As much as I love those horses, it's been pretty stiff going in more ways than one these last few mornings. I had to break the ice on the trough with a hammer this morning.'

'I know,' said Mary Ann. 'Prince's water was the same. Me da's kept him inside for days, he doesn't like the cold. And I haven't ridden him for nearly three weeks.'

'But look here,' Michael drew Sarah's attention to him again with a tug at her hand, 'you don't want to take this lightly. And don't try to be brave and laugh it off. I think it's as you said, you want a few days in bed, you're under the weather.'

'Yes, sir.' Sarah's voice was demure, and she laughed now, and Michael, getting to his feet, his face straight, passed off his concern by saying, 'Now look, don't you go and get anything serious. After all the schemozzle there's been about our holiday, you're going to go on it if I have to take you in a box!'

Twenty-four hours later, Michael, remembering these words, was to droop his head and press his chin into his neck with the horror of them. But now he looked at Mary Ann and said, 'She hasn't had a bite of anything to eat all day.'

'Does me ma know?'

'No, but I'm going to tell her. You stay there.'

He dug his fingers down towards Sarah, and added, 'You'll eat what I fetch in.'

When the door had closed behind him, Sarah, looking at Mary Ann, who was sitting beside her on the couch now, said, 'I won't, you know, I just couldn't.'

'Perhaps your stomach is upset.' Mary Ann nodded knowingly. 'Whenever there is trouble of any kind it always goes to my stomach.' She laughed. 'Even if I get into a temper, I'm sick. Oh! Last Sunday night I felt like death after dear grandmam's visit . . . Oh, Sarah, I do hate that woman.'

Sarah, nodding sympathetically, said, 'I'm not very fond of her myself. Never was.'

'That needn't worry you, for she's no relation of yours, but she's my granny, and the only one I've got. And oh, I hate the thought of her being my granny. Do you know, I felt so hateful on Sunday that I could have killed her. I could, I'm not just kidding, I could. I've always prayed, as far back as I can remember, that she would die. But on Sunday I actually felt that I could have killed her. It was a dreadful feeling, Sarah. I felt awful after and, as I said, I was sick.'

'Talking of killing' – Sarah's head fell back on to the couch again – 'it doesn't seem so very long ago since I felt that way about you, and you about me, remember?'

Mary Ann, her face straight now, nodded her head, and bit on her lip before she said, 'Seems daft now, doesn't it?'

Sarah did not answer this, but staring up towards the ceiling, she said slowly and quietly,

'I'll die if anything separates me from Michael . . . I'll die.'

'Oh, Sarah, don't talk like that. Why are you talking like that? Don't be silly, what can separate you from Michael?' As Mary Ann looked at Sarah's face, her eyes staring upwards, she was amazed to see two large tears roll down in the direction of her nose. Leaning swiftly forwards she touched Sarah's cheek, saying under her breath, 'What is it? What is it, Sarah?'

'Nothing.' Sarah lifted her head with a heavy movement from the back of the couch, and groping for her handkerchief, she remarked, 'I feel altogether odd, I can't remember ever feeling like this before, sort of depressed.' Then after blowing her nose, she lifted her eyes to Mary Ann, saying, 'I know how you feel about Corny, and I think you've been marvellous. I should have gone round looking like . . . well, as your da would say, a sick cow. Do you still miss him?'

The conversation wasn't keeping to pattern, but Mary Ann said, 'Yes, awfully. I just seem to be passing the time towards the end of the year . . . not this year but what I think of as this year. I get terrified when I think he won't come back.'

'You could never like Tony?'

'Not that way.'

'He'd be a catch.'

'Could you give up Michael for someone similar to Tony . . . a catch?'

Sarah shook her head, and then clapped her hands swiftly over her mouth and muttered through her fingers, 'I'm – I'm going to be sick.'

Mary Ann, leading Sarah into the kitchen,

exclaimed to her mother and Michael, 'Sarah's sick . . . she wants to be sick.'

'Oh! my dear.' Lizzie, taking up a position on the other side of Sarah, hurried her towards the scullery. And that was the first of a number of trips between the front room and the scullery during the next hour. At half-past eight, Lizzie, standing in the kitchen looking at Mike, said, 'She's in no fit state to go home. We'll have to get word to her mother in some way.'

'I'll phone the house and see if Tony's in.'

Tony was in, but on the point of going out, and when, a few minutes later, he came into the farm kitchen after a brief word with Sarah, who was now lying on the sitting-room couch, he looked from Lizzie to Mike and said, 'I would get a doctor.'

'What are you thinking it is?' Mike narrowed his eyes towards Tony. And when Tony said what he thought might be the matter with Sarah, Lizzie cried out, 'Oh no! no! Not that.'

'I hope it isn't. I may be wrong. But those symptoms look pretty familiar, I've seen someone with them before. I'd phone the doctor if I were you, and I'll slip into Jarrow and take a message to her mother.'

The kitchen became very quiet, the house became very quiet, and the quietness was heavy with fear.

Mike phoned the doctor. He came within half an hour, and within a few minutes of his arrival the life of the house changed.

It was suspected that Sarah had polio.

*　　*　　*

The waiting-room was quiet. It had coloured pictures on the wall, and modern low tables and comfortable chairs. Michael, sitting on the edge of a chair, had his elbows on his knees, his hands clasped between them, and he kept his gaze fixed on his hands, except when the waiting-room door opened. It hadn't opened for some time now. Mary Ann sat next to him. She kept going round the edge of her handkerchief with the finger and thumb of her right hand, while she smoothed the small piece of cambric material with the other. Opposite to them, across the low table, sat her mother and Mrs Flannagan. They had all ceased to talk. From time to time her da would push the waiting-room door open. Or Mr Flannagan or Tony. And then they would go out again and sit in the car.

At a quarter to twelve a grey-uniformed sister entered the waiting-room, followed by a doctor. The sister remained silent as the doctor talked. He was very, very sorry, yes, the young girl had polio. How serious it was, was yet to be seen. He advised them to go home. They'd be kept informed. No, it wasn't advisable for any of them to see her. Perhaps tomorrow. Everything that possibly could be done would be done, they could be sure of that.

'I'm staying,' said Michael.

'I wouldn't,' said the doctor. 'You can do no good. Come in first thing in the morning and see how things are going then.'

'I'm staying,' said Michael again.

The doctor nodded.

The doctor now looked at Mrs Flannagan and said, 'You are the mother?'

'Yes.' Mrs Flannagan had lost her spruceness. For the first time that she could remember, Mary Ann saw her other than neat. Her face was tear-stained; her hair, like thin wire, stuck out from each side of her hat. She seemed to have shrunk and was now no bigger than Mr Flannagan. It seemed odd, too, to see her sitting there with one hand clasped in the tight grip of her mother's hand.

Mike and Mr Flannagan came into the room, and the doctor said again, 'It would be better if you all went home, for you can do nothing, nothing at all.'

He was passing Mary Ann now, and he put his hand on her head as if she was a child, as indeed she looked at this moment. And he seemed to be addressing her solely when he said, 'The only thing now is to pray and leave the rest to God . . .' And it was with a sort of gentle inquiry that he added 'Eh?' to his words.

Michael, not to be deterred, stayed in the waiting-room and Mr Flannagan stayed with him. Mrs Flannagan went back to the farm with Lizzie and the rest . . .

Three days later Sarah was fighting for her life, kept alive only by the miracle of the iron lung. On the seventh day it was known that she would live, but without the use of her legs, and Michael sat at the kitchen table, his head buried in his arms and cried. And Lizzie cried, and Mary Ann cried and Mike went out to the cowshed.

Lizzie stood by Michael's side, her hand on his head, but she could say nothing. She could not find words adequate for comfort, until some minutes elapsed, and Michael, lifting his head slowly from his arms and shaking it from side to side in a despairing movement, muttered, 'And I said I would take her on that holiday if I had to take her in a box . . . Oh! God.' And Lizzie, remembering the time not long ago when she herself had said, 'That'll be the day when you howl your eyes out,' whispered brokenly, 'We say things in joke, take no notice of that. She's alive, and they can do wonderful things these days.'

Mary Ann's throat was swollen with the pressure of tears as she stood at the other side of the table and looked towards Michael. Poor Michael. But more so, poor Sarah. She was feeling for Sarah, at this moment, anguish equal to that which she would have felt if they had been sisters. It was impossible to remember that they had ever been enemies. She thought, 'Her poor legs, and she loved to ride. Oh, what will she do?'

It was as if Michael had heard her thinking, for he stood up and, brushing the back of his hand across his eyes and around his face, he said, 'As soon as she comes out we'll get married.'

'Michael.'

Lizzie had just spoken his name, there was no indication of shock or censure, but he turned on her sharply, saying, 'You can do what you like, Mother, say what you like, put all the obstacles on earth up, but as soon as she's out of that place we're getting married.'

'Yes, yes. All right, Michael, all right.'

'Don't say it like that, Mother.' He was yelling at her. 'As if I'd get over it and change my mind, and by the time she's out I'll be seeing things differently. I won't, I won't ever.'

'Don't shout, Michael.' Lizzie's voice was very low. 'I understand all you feel at this minute, believe me . . .'

'But you wouldn't want me to marry Sarah, crippled like that, would you? She would handicap me, wouldn't she? What would happen to my career?'

'Now, now, now.' This was neither Lizzie nor Mary Ann, and they all turned to see Mike standing in the kitchen doorway. His face looked pale-ish, his eyes were bright, and his voice and manner were quiet. How much he had heard of the conversation Mary Ann didn't know. But little or much she knew he had got the gist of it, for looking at Michael, he said, 'Don't worry at this stage. Just go on praying that she'll get better quickly, and then do what your heart tells you you've got to do.'

Mary Ann watched Michael looking towards her da. She watched their eyes holding for a long while before Michael turned away and went out of the kitchen and up the stairs. It was strange, she thought, Michael was her ma's, her ma and Michael were like that – metaphorically, she crossed her fingers – yet lately it had been her da who had seen eye to eye with him, while her mother seemed to cross him at every point. Perhaps, like all mothers, she was afraid of losing him, and he knew it, and this was bringing a slight rift between them.

Lizzie had the palms of her hands pressed tightly together. If her fingers had been lifted upwards, they would have indicated her praying, but they were pointing towards the floor, and she rasped her palms together as she said under her breath, 'He says they're going to be married as soon as she comes out.'

'I heard.' Mike nodded his head. 'Well, you'll have to face that, Liz.'

'But how will he manage? He's just starting out, Mike.' Lizzie's voice was soft. There was no tone of opposition in it, just helpless inquiry.

'People have managed like that afore, they're shown a way.'

'But if she can't walk. If she's in a chair . . .'

'Liz!' Mike walked over to her and put his arm around her shoulder. 'Listen to me. Things'll pan out. Just remember that. Whatever you think or do, things'll pan out one way or the other. But this much I think you'd better get into your head and accept it. Whatever condition Sarah comes out in, she'll be the only one for him . . . Now it's no use saying he'd get over it. Don't start to think along those lines, because I know this . . . he'd rather have his life a hell of a grind with Sarah than be on velvet with anybody else . . . Now don't cry.'

But Lizzie did cry. She turned her head into Mike's shoulder, and as he held her and spoke softly to her, he looked across the room at Mary Ann, but she herself could hardly see him, her vision was so blurred. She felt a weight of sadness on her that she had never before experienced. It sprung, she supposed, from Sarah's condition. Yet she knew that not all her feelings were due to Sarah. Vaguely she realised that life was opening her eyes wide, stretching them with knowledge, painful knowledge, such as the fact that her mother was crying, not so much because Sarah was crippled for life, but because her son was determined to take on a burden that to her mind would cripple him too.

It was the worst Christmas Mary Ann had ever known. No-one felt like jollification. Presents were given and received without much enthusiasm. Mr Lord bought Mary Ann a portable typewriter for her Christmas box, and although she was pleased with the gift, she simulated delight that she didn't altogether feel. But Mr Lord was very thoughtful and kind during this period. And she wanted to please him.

The old man had shown great concern over Sarah. Twice a week he sent her gifts of flowers, he had looked at Lizzie and said, 'There's no need to inquire if the boy will stand by Sarah. I feel that Michael knows his own mind, and it's a very good thing. Perhaps it will be very good for both of them. And he can rely on all the help he needs when the time comes.'

Lizzie had said nothing, but Mary Ann had wanted to fling her arms about the old man's neck, as she had done years ago, by way of thanks.

Corny did not send Mary Ann a Christmas box, but he sent her a letter which was of much more value in her eyes. Although the letter was brief, she read volumes between the lines. He liked it in America. He liked the people he was staying with, they were very good to him. He liked his job. The boss was very good to him. He had been put into another department which meant more money. He could get a car if he liked, but he wasn't going to. He was saving. It was funny not being at home for Christmas but everybody was nice to him.

Mary Ann felt a stir of jealousy against this oft-repeated niceness. But she told herself he hadn't known what to say, he was no hand at letter-writing. His writing was as terse as his speech. Her Corny was a doer, not a sayer. She liked that idea, and she told herself a number of times: Corny was a doer not a sayer. The letter ended with the same request as had his first one: Would she go and see his granny?

The only other thing of note that happened over the Christmas was an announcement in the paper to the effect that Mrs Lettice Schofield of The Burrows, Woodlea End, Newcastle, was seeking a divorce from her husband.

PART TWO

THE YEAR PASSES

6

'Look,' said Mike, as he leant towards Michael across the little table in his office, 'I know the old fellow means well, at least I want to keep on thinking that. But I'd rather you didn't start your life, your real life along with Sarah, beholden to him.'

Michael with one elbow raised high resting on the top of the small window, rapped his ear with his fingers as he stared out across the farmyard towards the chimneys of the house, where they reared up above the roof of the byres. 'I know, I know what you mean.' His voice was deep and very similar to Mike's now, except for the inflexion garnered from the Grammar School. 'I don't want to take the place, for the very reason you've just stated, but another reason is that Sarah's cut off enough where she is now. Although she's with her mother, she's cut off. She feels lost, they don't speak the same language. She's closer to her father, but he's out all day. And then there's not a blade of grass to be seen, looking out from that window on to the street. It drives me mad when I'm sitting with her. I can't imagine that we ever lived opposite. The only good thing in taking the bungalow is that she would see a tree or two, and the fields. But then it's a good two miles away, and although there's houses round about, Sarah doesn't want other people.' He brought his eyes from the window towards his father. 'She's already one of us. She's always seemed to have been one of us. She hasn't said this, but I know that she looks upon us as . . . her people. As I said, she likes her da, but I can tell you this, she likes you ten times more.'

Mike dropped his eyes away from his son as he said, 'That's good to hear, anyway.'

There was silence in the little office until Mike said, 'There's a way out of this.' He cast his eyes on the open ledger as he spoke, and Michael kept his eyes on the view across the farmyard as he replied, 'Yes, I know. But who's going to put it to her?'

He did not say put it to Mother . . . but to 'her', and this phrase hurt Mike. Although it meant that he and his boy were closer than ever before in their lives, it also meant that Michael had moved farther away from Lizzie during the last few months. Somehow, he would rather that the situation were the same as it had been years ago . . . yet not quite. He did not want his son to hate him and he had, at one time, done just that. No, he didn't want that again, and please God he would never deserve it, but he didn't want Lizzie to be hurt. Michael was Lizzie's, at least she had always considered him so. It was as if years ago she had said to him, 'You have got Mary Ann, Michael is mine.'

At this moment the door was pushed open and Mary Ann, coming round it, said, 'Oh, there you are.' She looked at Michael. 'I'm going in to Sarah's, Tony's running me down. Is there anything you want to go?'

'No.' He shook his head. 'Tell her I'll be there round about six.'

'What's the matter?' Mary Ann looked from one to the other. 'Anything wrong?'

'No, no.' Mike got to his feet. 'We're just talking about the bungalow.'

'Oh, the bungalow.' Mary Ann nodded her head, and looking again at Michael she said, 'Are you going to take it?'

'I don't want to.'

Again she nodded her head. 'Then why don't you ask her?'

Again, the 'her' was referring to Lizzie, and Michael, moving out into the yard, said, 'I couldn't stand a row. And if she did consent, having Sarah on sufferance would be worse than anything so far.'

Mike and Mary Ann, left together, looked at each other, and when Mike's eyes dropped from hers she said to him under her breath, 'Something should be done, Da. What's going to happen to Sarah up there by herself all day? It won't work. He just couldn't take that place.' She looked at Michael's broadening back as he went across the yard, then her gaze lifted up the hill towards Mr Lord's house, and her tone indignant now, she commented, 'If he's going to advance him the money for a bungalow why couldn't he have one built here? He's got piles of land.'

'There's such a thing as laws about building on agricultural ground.'

'Poloney!'

'Not so much poloney as you think.' Mike nodded solemnly at her. 'Once you start that, it's like a bush fire, one house goes up and then the place is covered.'

Mary Ann looked her disbelief, then after sighing she remarked, 'Well, I'm off, Da. See you later . . . Goodbye.'

His goodbye followed her as she went across the yard towards the road that led up to Mr Lord's house. She knew that he was watching her.

In the far distance she could see the hood of Tony's car. She glanced at her watch. He had said half-past two on the dot, and now it was twenty-five to three. She walked slowly up the hill, through the gate, over the back courtyard to where the car was standing. There was no sign of Tony and, going to the back door, she knocked as she opened it, a courtesy she still afforded Ben.

'Hello, there.' The old man's tone was gruff, and he hardly raised his eyes from the occupation of silver cleaning to look at her. But Mary Ann, over the years, had come to know Ben, and a 'Hello there' she had come to consider a very affectionate term.

'Lovely day, isn't it, Ben? How's your hip?'

'Same as afore.'

'Well, it's your own fault.' She stubbed her finger at him. 'You should have taken it easy these last few weeks while Mr Lord was away. It's your own fault.'

'And have him come back finding fault in every corner, like an old fish woman.'

'You should let Mrs Rouse do it.'

'Ugh! Ugh! I have to go behind her all the time now.'

Mary Ann smiled, then said, 'Is Tony upstairs?'

'No. In the study . . . on the phone.'

'Oh.' Mary Ann went out of the kitchen and across the large hall towards the study. There was no sound of anyone speaking on the phone, and she stood outside the door for a second before saying, 'Are you there, Tony?'

'Yes. Come in.'

When she entered the room she saw him sitting at the desk, and he turned his head towards her, saying quickly, 'I won't be a minute, I want to get this off.'

She sat down in the hide chair to the side of the fireplace, and her small frame seemed lost in its vastness. She liked this room: the brown of the suite, the soft blue of the deep carpet; the low, ranging bookcases set against the panelled walls. She looked towards Tony, his head bent over the letter. He looked nice . . . he always looked nice, but today she seemed to be seeing him in a different light. She realised with a kind of pleasant shock that he was very handsome, in a thin, chiselled kind of way. She supposed Mr Lord had once looked like this. Her gaze was intent on him when he turned his head quickly and looked at her. 'I'm glad you came up,' he said. 'I hoped you would, I want to talk to you.'

As she watched him turn to the desk again and quickly push the letter into an envelope, she experienced a quiver of apprehension. It went through her body like a slight electric shock, and felt as unpleasant. Tony and she had exchanged nothing but polite pleasantries for months. He had continued to take her into town on a Saturday, and sometimes he picked her up later, but where he went in the meantime he did not say. Nor did he ask where she spent her time. He no longer seemed interested in anything she did, but she knew that Mr Lord was under the impression that they were together during these Saturday afternoon jaunts. She had an idea now, in fact she knew, what he was going to talk about. And when he came towards her, and pulled a small chair close to the big one before sitting down and leaning forward, she could not meet his eyes.

'Mary Ann.'

'Yes.' She still did not raise her eyes.

'If Corny had not come on the scene, would you have liked me enough to have married me?'

She lifted her head with a jerk, and her eyes flicked over his face for a moment before she looked away towards the window beyond the desk, and she seemed to consider for quite a while before she answered.

'I don't know . . . I suppose I might, and yet I don't know.' She paused again. 'There might have been someone else. You just don't know, do you?' Now she was looking at him full in the face.

'No, you just don't know. But as things stand you want Corny, don't you? Tell me . . . please.'

'Yes . . . yes, I want Corny.' She felt she was blushing right into the depths of her stomach.

'Yes, I knew you did. But I wanted to hear you say it. I don't want you on my conscience. I have enough to face up to without that . . . I'm going to marry Mrs Schofield, Mary Ann.'

Although Mary Ann had known that he had wanted to talk about Mrs Schofield, that he might say to her, 'I'm friendly with Mrs Schofield . . . I like Mrs Schofield,' she had not expected him to say, slap bang, that he was going to marry her. This statement suggested an intimacy between him and Mrs Schofield that deepened the blush. She could have said she was going to marry Corny, and Michael could say he was going to marry Sarah, but in either case it would not have been the same as Tony marrying Mrs Schofield. Mrs Schofield was a married woman. And then there was Mr Lord. Mr Lord would go mad, she knew he would go mad. She said as much.

'What will he say? He'll go for you, he won't stand for it. He'll go mad.'

'I know that. But whether he will or no, I'm marrying Lettice as soon as the decree nisi is through.'

Mary Ann put her fingers over her lips and swayed a little. She felt some part of her was in pain, and it was for Mr Lord. At this moment she would gladly have fallen in with his wishes and married Tony if that had been possible, just to save him the pain that she knew the failure of his cherished plans would bring him. And the pain would not be alone. There would be with it anger and bitterness. Once before she had seen what extreme anger and bitterness did to him. That was the time when he had discovered that Tony was his grandson. And what had been the result? He had a heart attack and nearly died. She clasped her hands tightly now between her knees and asked, 'How are you going to tell him?'

'I don't know. Lettice wanted to come and tell him herself. But I wouldn't have that.'

It was funny hearing him speak of Mrs Schofield as Lettice. She hated Mrs Schofield at this moment, yet remembering back to the time when she liked her, she also remembered that Mr Lord liked her too. Here was a ray of hope. She said to Tony, 'You should have let her come. He liked her. She could get it over better than you, I'm sure of that. There'll only be a row if you tell him, and that's putting it mildly. Don't forget what happens when he gets worked up.' She leant further forward. 'Do you realise this might . . . it might kill him.'

'I've thought of all that. It's been hellish this last few months. In fact since that day . . . you remember, that Saturday when I saw him hit her, I knew then what was going to happen to me. I think I knew before. You see, Mary Ann' – his voice dropped almost to a whisper – 'I was attracted to her long before that day. When she used to come up here, to your house, I always made a point of being there. Perhaps no-one noticed. They wouldn't, would they?' He smiled a sad smile at her. 'But that day when I saw that pig of a man – and he is a pig of a man, Mary Ann, and that's putting it mildly – when I saw him hit her, I knew it was all up with me. It was as if the blow that struck her had sprung my mind wide open, and I saw the fix I was in. And I'm not going to say at this juncture that I tried to fight it and make a brave stand against it. Oh, no. Although I knew what it would mean to the old man in the end I went ahead, and I still count myself lucky that I did. She is a grand person, Mary Ann. A very, very sweet person.'

Mary Ann dismissed the unique qualities of Mrs Schofield, and said, 'He'll cut you off.'

'Yes, I expect that. But I've got quarter shares in Turnbulls. He signed those over to me two years ago. They'll give me a start somewhere, and Lettice doesn't want much . . . It seems odd though to think that those very shares were the first thing he allowed me to put my name to, although I was supposed to be his heir. And he only gave them to me as an inducement to fall in with his plans concerning his . . . protégée.' Tony's hand came out and grasped Mary Ann's. 'I could wish at this moment for him that his plan had worked out, because, you know, I like his protégée very much.' He squeezed her fingers.

Mary Ann swallowed and blinked her eyes, the tears were welling in her throat, and as she pulled her hands from his she said with a touch of the cheeky asperity he knew so well, 'I'm not crying because of you, don't think that.'

'I wouldn't for a moment, Mary Ann.'

'I just don't know what's going to happen to him when he finds this out.' She sniffed twice, blew her nose, then asked, 'When is he coming back? It was next Tuesday, wasn't it?'

'As always he's changed his plans. You know his old trick of dropping in when he thinks nobody is expecting him, that's likely what will happen this time. I had a wire this morning to say he was staying on another week. But I shouldn't be surprised if he came in tonight, or tomorrow night, or then, on the other hand, not for another month. We should know by now, shouldn't we?'

'But he'll come.' She bounced her head at him. 'And you'll have to tell him . . . When are you—' she paused and her voice sunk again as she ended, 'getting married?'

'It could be in three weeks' time.'

'But if he shouldn't be back by then you won't

leave, will you? You won't leave and get married before he gets back?'

'No, Mary Ann, I won't do that.'

She turned her eyes from him, and feeling again that she was going to give way to tears, she jumped up from the chair, saying, 'It's awful. He'll die.'

'No, he won't.' Tony had his arm around her shoulders now. 'He's tougher than you think.'

'If he gets into a paddy, he'll have a heart attack, you'll see.'

'Oh, Mary Ann, don't make it worse for me, please.'

'I don't want to.' Her voice was soft now. 'But I'm frightened for him, Tony.' She looked up. 'And you won't make matters any better because you'll lose your temper and there'll be a pair of you. You know you can't keep your temper with him. I don't think you should tell him. I think you should leave a letter for him, something like that . . . Oh, I don't know what to suggest.'

'I won't leave a letter for him, Mary Ann. What I've got to say, I'll say to him.'

'And kill him!'

'Don't!' He swung away from her. 'Don't keep suggesting that. It's got to be done.' His voice had risen now. 'And I'll have to stand the consequences, but don't keep saying that.' They stared at each other in hostility, and then Tony, taking his breath in on a deep sigh, said, 'Come on. We had better be going. Sufficient unto the day.' He opened the door for her and she went past him, through the hall and into the kitchen. And she did not say goodbye to Ben, where he sat still rubbing away with his rheumaticky hands at the silver, and this caused him to stop his work, and even rise to his feet and go towards the door from where he watched her getting into the car.

When a few minutes later Ben returned to the table, he looked at his work for a moment before touching it, and remarked, 'What now, eh?'

Mrs Flannagan's front room was fourteen feet by twelve feet. In it was a three-piece suite, a small sideboard, a corner cabinet, besides two small tables and an ornamental coal scuttle. The floor was covered by a small carpet and a surround of highly polished check-patterned linoleum.

Sarah was sitting on the couch, her legs painfully immobile beneath the rug. Her back appeared bent as if she was leaning towards them, and her complexion, which had been a thick cream tan, had now a bleached look. The only thing about her appearance that remained untouched by her illness was her hair. It was still black and shiny. She held out a half-finished nylon petticoat towards Mary Ann, saying rather hopelessly, 'Look at those stitches, I'll never be able to sew.'

Mary Ann looked at the stitches. 'You're doing fine; they're only half an inch long now, they were an inch on Wednesday.'

They both laughed, and Sarah moved her shoulders into the cushion. Then the smile disappeared from her face when, looking at Mary Ann, she said below her breath, 'Oh, I wish I had that chair. I want to get out. I want to get out. I'll go mad with much more of this.'

'They said next week, didn't they?' Mary Ann's voice was low also. 'But Tony would come and take you out tomorrow. He's offered time and time again. Why won't you go?'

'Oh.' Sarah moved her head wearily on the pillow. 'To be carried into a car and all the street out. It's bad enough in the ambulance going to the hospital. I don't want to be carried and lifted for the rest of my life. And I'm not going to.' She pulled her body forward now until her face was close to Mary Ann's, and then she whispered fiercely, 'I've been praying and praying and praying. I'm going to use my legs again, I am. I don't care how long it takes – ten years, twenty years.' Her voice was becoming louder now, and Mary Ann, getting up and putting her arms around her, said, 'That's the spirit. You feel like that and you will. Oh, I'm glad to hear you say that. It's like an answer to my prayers. In fact, I'm sure it is. Every night after I've left work I slip into church and say a decade of the rosary for you, just for that, that you'd get the urge to use your legs . . . Isn't it funny?' Her voice was high with excitement.

'Oh, Mary Ann.' Sarah leant her head wearily between Mary Ann's small firm breasts. 'You've been so good, always coming in. People stop after a while, you know. They used to come in a lot at first, but not now. And I'm seeing too much of me mother. Oh, I know I shouldn't say this because she's been so good, but she keeps on, she keeps on, finicking about, polishing, dusting, tidying up, all the time, all the time . . . Mary Ann?' It was a question.

And Mary Ann said, 'Yes, Sarah?'

'Do you think that Michael really wants to marry me?'

Mary Ann drew away from Sarah and actually

gaped at her as she repeated, 'Really wants to marry you. He'll go round the bend if he doesn't. What's put that into your head?'

'Oh, I think people are saying things. I know they are. I hear that Mrs Foster in the kitchen with me mother. It's not what she says, it what she leaves unsaid . . . the pauses. They don't think it right that I should marry Michael, not like this, I know they don't. But if I don't, Mary Ann' – she looked into Mary Ann's eyes now and repeated – 'if I don't, I'll do meself in, I will.'

Another one talking about doing herself in. Janice, and now Sarah. Was this what sorrow did to you, took away all desire for life. She couldn't see anything bad enough happening to her to take away the desire for living. She loved life, she loved breathing. She used to stop sometimes, on the road from the bus to the farm, and say to herself, 'I'm breathing.' It wasn't silly for she knew within herself, deep within herself, that it meant a great deal, something she couldn't as yet explain. She was breathing, she was alive. She felt at times that no matter what happened she wanted to live . . . To know all about living and then write about it. She dreamed of writing about living. Yet two girls that she had known intimately talked about dying, about killing themselves, and one had already tried. She shuddered and grasped hold of Sarah's hands as she said, 'Don't say such things, Sarah. And now get this into your head, there's only one person in the world for Michael and that's you. And if you don't know it by now, you never will. He's driving us all crazy about you.'

Sarah's smile spread across her face. It was a sweet smile, and it made her beautiful, more beautiful than when she had been the outdoor, hard-riding, youth-filled girl. But the smile faded, and on its going she said, 'Your mother's not pleased, and I can't blame her. I can understand how she feels.'

'What's got into you all of a sudden? Don't be silly. Of course mother's pleased, she'd rather have you for Michael than anybody else.'

'Has she said so?'

'No, but there's no need. I know.'

'You're just being kind as usual, Mary Ann. You're always trying to fix people's lives. I used to laugh about it at one time, but I give you leave to fix mine right now.' She shook her head. 'But if your mother wanted me for Michael she would have asked me to go there, to live with you. I wouldn't have been a burden, I wouldn't. I feel that if I could go and live with you all I would get better. When I was in hospital, Michael sort of said that we'd have . . . the front room. It was like a dream that I hung on to. I thought your mother must have suggested that we could, and I thought it was wonderful of her, because it's a beautiful front room, and you can see the farm from the window. I dreamed of that front room. Then when I came home Michael said Mr Lord was going to put up the money for the bungalow. There was no more mention of the front room, and I knew somehow that your mother had never said anything about it . . . I don't want that bungalow, Mary Ann. I don't want to go and live all that way off. I want to live close to Michael, where his work is. And with your da near abouts. You da infuses strength into people, Mary Ann. It's funny that, isn't it? For me to say that, I mean.

But he does. I always feel that I could get up and walk when he's talking to me. Not that I don't like your mother, I do. I think she's a fine woman . . . sort of a lady. I've always thought of her as a lady . . .'

'Oh, Sarah, Sarah! Look, don't worry. Everything'll come out all right. And you will live with us, I promise you will.'

Sarah smiled through very bright eyes now at Mary Ann, and it was doubtful if she was seeing her as she said, 'You've always made rash promises, you're the Holy Family rolled into one, not that they make rash promises . . . You know what I mean. You were always going to the side altar praying to them, weren't you?' She laughed now, a sharp loud laugh to stop herself from crying as she said, 'I remember I stopped going to their altar because I didn't want to do the same thing as you.'

'Oh, Sarah.' Mary Ann could not cap this with any amusing reply. She felt she couldn't bear much more today. There had been Tony just an hour ago, and now Sarah in this state. It was awful, awful. Everything was awful.

She stood up and looked towards the window merely to turn her face from Sarah's for a moment, and as she did so she saw coming down the steps of Mulhattan's Hall, right opposite, the great wobbling figure of Fanny McBride. The sight of her old friend brought a smile to her face and she turned round to Sarah and explained excitedly, 'Look, bend over, there's Mrs McBride coming down the steps. I'll pull the curtain and you can wave to her.'

Mary Ann dared to pull Mrs Flannagan's stiffly

arranged curtains to one side, and she went even further, she dared to tap gently on the pane to attract Fanny's attention. And when Fanny, her eyes darting across the road, caught sight of Mary Ann, she waved her great arm in the air. Mary Ann now acting on the assumption 'In for a penny, in for a pound', ran to the couch and pushed the head towards the window . . . and now Sarah waved. The two girls watched Fanny hesitate a moment at the bottom of the steps, undecided to risk the journey across the road to the portals of her enemy. But the habit of years was too strong. Mary Ann knew that Fanny was indeed sorry for Sarah, but she also knew that she still held Mrs Flannagan in lip-curling disdain. But the sight of the old woman did them both good, for they laughed as they watched her wobbling away down the street to the corner shop. And when her figure had disappeared, Mary Ann said, 'Well, there's one thing you should be thankful for: you're in this room and not in Fanny's.' Yet as she said this she wondered if Sarah would not be better, in both health and spirits, were she in the untidy, smelly, lumber-filled room on the ground floor of Mulhattan's Hall.

Later that evening, as Mary Ann neared home, her depression deepened, which was unusual, for the mere sight of the farm had the power to bring a feeling of security to her and to lessen the day-to-day irritations, which were multiplying, she was finding, as she was growing older. But this evening she didn't want to reach home, she didn't want to face her mother, for she knew she wouldn't be able to resist bringing up the question of . . . the front room. It was funny about the front room. Her da had thought the front room was a grand idea for Michael and Sarah. Michael had thought the front room was a grand idea for himself and Sarah. She had thought the front room was a grand idea for the pair of them. Yet to her knowledge not one of them had mentioned the subject to her mother, and yet she knew that her mother was well aware of what they were all after. She also knew that the front room was her mother's pride. It was the only room in the house in which she had been able to let her ideas have scope. The front room was really hers. A place where she could invite people without making any excuses about the upset, or the untidiness. None of them left magazines, or books, or sweet papers lying about in the front room. It was an unspoken agreement that they cleared up their stuff each night before they left the room. The kitchen could look – as Lizzie sometimes said – like a paddencan, but never her front room.

And now Mary Ann knew the time had come when the room must be brought into the open. Not only to relieve the tension in the house, but the tension in Sarah. She was very worried about Sarah.

She had hardly got in the door before Lizzie said, 'How is she?' and she answered, 'Oh, she's very depressed, Ma. I'm worried.'

'Why? What is she depressed over? I mean more than usual.'

Mary Ann looked at her mother. She was sitting in the easy chair in her front room. She fitted into the room. The subdued colour of her dress, the calmness of her face – she had her eyes cast down – all seemed to be part of the atmosphere of the room. She was busy copying some recipes from a weekly magazine into her cookery book.

Mary Ann stood in front of her, their knees were so close they almost touched. She knew it was no use leading up to this subject. She was feeling so keenly about the matter at the moment that she would only make a mess of any strategic approach, so she said, straight out, 'Ma?'

Lizzie gave a little lift to her head, and said, 'Well?'

'Sarah doesn't want to go and live in the bungalow.'

'No?' There was a sound running through the syllable as sharp and hard as the pointed end of a carving knife.

'It would be as bad there as it is in Burton Street. And she's nearly going off her head there . . . Ma . . . Ma . . . She wants to come and live with us.'

As Lizzie stared back into her daughter's face she had the strong desire to lift her hand and slap it. It would have to be her who would bring this thing into the open, this thing that had hung around them for weeks. Hidden under quick tempers and sharp retorts. Under sullen silences and pathetic looks. She had resisted them all. Because it wasn't as if Sarah was homeless, she was going to have a lovely bungalow built. She was going to marry Michael; yes, she was going to marry Michael. Was she not having her son? Wasn't that enough? But no . . . she wanted . . . they all wanted to take this room from her. There had been no suggestion of Sarah having one of the rooms upstairs, because that was an impossibility. No, the idea, which she knew was a flame behind the asbestos curtain of all their minds, was that she should give up this room to Sarah and Michael.

'Get out of my way.'

'But, Ma.'

'I said, get out of my way, I want to get up.'

When Mary Ann was slow in obeying, Lizzie, jerking herself to her feet, almost thrust her on to her back. The little table to the side of the chair, which had held the magazine and her notebook, jumped from the floor as if it had a life of its own. Lizzie put out no hand to steady it. She marched towards the door. But before opening it, she turned to Mary Ann and demanded, 'Did they pick you as spokesman for them all?'

'No! No, Ma. I haven't talked about it to anyone. It was just what Sarah said.'

'Are you sure?'

'Yes, Ma.'

Mary Ann was speaking the truth, she hadn't discussed it openly with her da and Michael, but she knew that from the time Michael had heartened Sarah with the thought that she was coming to live here, the idea had been prominent in all their minds.

Lizzie, turning from the door, made one step back into the room, and, looking intently at her daughter, she said in an almost threatening tone, 'Well, if it hasn't been discussed, don't you start now, do you hear me? I forbid you to say anything about it.'

'All right, Ma.' Mary Ann's voice was very low.

'And furthermore . . . listen to me.'

'I'm listening, Ma.' Her voice was still low.

'Well, do then. And remember what I'm saying. Don't you tell either your father, or Michael, that you mentioned this to me . . . Do you understand?'

Yes, Mary Ann understood. If the matter wasn't brought into the open by either Michael or her da, the room was safe. In as quickly as it takes lightning to strike, a strange feeling assailed her, a fearful feeling. Out of nowhere came a hate for this room, and, more terrible still, a dislike of her mother. As she looked at Lizzie's tight, straight countenance, she knew she disliked her. 'Oh . . . !' She groaned aloud with the fear of this feeling, and turning away she cupped her face in her hands. Then, sitting down, she dropped her head into the corner of the chair. But she did not cry, she was too frozen with fear of this dreadful thing that had come upon her – she didn't like her mother.

After one long look at the back of Mary Ann's head, Lizzie turned sharply away and went out of the room and up the stairs. When she entered her own room she stood in the darkness with her back to the door. She knew that she had reached a crisis in her life, not a crisis brought about by the desertion of her husband for another woman, not a crisis brought about by Mike's drinking, as had often happened during the early years of their marriage, or yet by her son walking out on her and picking a girl that she did not like. Nor yet a crisis where her daughter had got herself into trouble, but a crisis caused by the fact that she wanted to hang on to her way of life. And her way of life was personified by her sitting-room. The sitting-room that everyone remarked on. The sitting-room that she loved, that she had made part of herself. For months now she had been warding off this moment, daring them by her silence to approach her and mention this room. And now she knew that the matter could no longer be shelved, because Mary Ann had dared, with her usual foolhardiness, to bring it into the open. If Sarah came here to live, the life of the house would be changed. It wasn't that she disliked Sarah, she liked her. She liked the girl very much, she could even say she liked her next to Mary Ann. She could say in all truth that she liked her better than any of the friends Mary Ann had picked up for herself at school, much better. And she knew, crippled though she was, that she was the right one for Michael. She also knew something else . . . She stared into the blackness of the room, and in its depths she faced up to a fact that she had not permitted herself to look at these past weeks, although it had been thrusting itself at her almost daily from the direction of her son and her husband, and within the last few minutes it had stared out of the face of her daughter, the fact was that if she kept her room she would lose them all. She might live with them for years and years, but things would never be the same again. If Michael took Sarah to the bungalow he would never come back into this house as her son . . . her Michael. She had felt him drifting away from her lately, but she knew now that by making this sacrifice she could pin him to her for life. But there was another reason why she hadn't wanted Michael and Sarah to start their married life in this house. She must be fair to herself, it wasn't only the room. As much as she liked Sarah, she knew she could not bear to see another woman — a girl, in this case — ruling his life. Being all in all to him. Filling her place entirely. Only if she hadn't to witness it, would it be bearable. This had been more than half the reason for her conduct. But now the decision had to be faced. Did she want to lose Mike, too, through this business? Not that he would ever leave her. But he could go from her without leaving the house . . . And, Mary Ann? . . . Yes, and Mary Ann. Look how she had glared at her before she had turned her face away into the chair. She had never seen her daughter look at her like that before . . . never.

Lizzie groped in the darkness towards the bed. She did not switch on the light, nor turn down the cover. But flinging herself on to the bed she thrust her face in the pillow and cried . . .

An hour later, when Mike came in, he found Mary Ann in the kitchen. 'All alone?' he said.

'No, Da.'

'Where's your mother? In the front room?'

'No, she's upstairs, Da.'

Mike looked intently at his daughter before asking quietly, 'What's the matter?'

'Nothing, Da. I think she's got a bad head. I think she's lying down.'

'You think, you're not sure. Haven't you been up?'

'No, Da.'

'What's happened?' He took her by the shoulder and turned her towards him. As she looked back at him she said, 'Nothing, Da.'

'How long has your mother been upstairs?'
Mike's voice was quiet and even.

'Just over an hour, I think.'

'And there's nothing the matter?'

'No, Da . . . Do you want a drink?'

'Yes. Yes, I want a drink. But it isn't tea or cocoa.'

The old anxiety leapt within her to join the fear that had sprung on her in the front room. If her da went out in this mood he would likely come back drunk, and he hadn't been drunk for a long time. She said to him, in the little-girl voice she had used to coax him years ago, 'You're not going out now, Da, are you?'

'What do you think?'

'I wouldn't. I would have some tea, strong tea.'

'Aye . . . well.' He sat on the edge of the chair undecided. And as she stood before him the anxiety made her tremble, and he thrust out his arm and pulled her towards him, saying, 'All right, all right, come on, don't worry. Stop that.' He punched her gently in the chest. 'Where's that tea?'

Mary Ann made him a strong pot of tea. She cut him a shive of meat pie. She watched him as he ate, and when a few minutes later she watched him settle himself in the big chair towards the side of the stove, she felt sick. He wasn't showing any signs of going upstairs to see what was wrong with her mother. This in a way was worse than him getting drunk and coming back roaring out all the things that were troubling him. Her ma, she knew, would suffer more from this attitude than from the drink. She felt, as she had done years ago in Mulhattan's Hall, torn asunder with

155

anguish for them. She could stand anything, anything as long as they were close. The feeling of dislike for her mother had fled as swiftly as it had come. All she wanted now was to see her ma and her da close once again, laughing and chaffing, and that meant loving. And they hadn't been like that for weeks.

7

During the weekend that followed the tense atmosphere of the house did not lessen, and at the beginning of the week Lizzie began to behave peculiarly. Rain, hail or snow, she washed on a Monday, but not this Monday. On this Monday she declared to her family that she was going to do no more heavy washing. She was going to send all the sheets, towels and pillow-cases to the bag-wash. She'd had enough of heavy washing to last a lifetime. It was as she served breakfast that she made this revolutionary statement.

Under ordinary circumstances there is no doubt that the family would have shot comments at her. Why? Hadn't she said, time and again, that the laundries poisoned the clothes, they were never the same again if sent to the laundry? But this morning they did not bombard her with whys, and if she thought their reactions were peculiar she made no comment.

There was really very little she could comment on, for neither Mary Ann nor Michael said anything. And Mike, merely raising his glance from his plate, remarked, 'You feeling like that? Well, it's Monday mornin'.'

That was all.

On Monday evening, when she stated she was going into Newcastle the following day to do some shopping, Mary Ann was the only one who reacted. Without a great deal of enthusiasm she said, 'Do you want me to meet you?'

'No, I don't think so,' said Lizzie, in a tone that could be considered airy. 'I'll see how I feel, but I might go to the pictures in the afternoon.'

Mike was doing his accounts at the edge of the kitchen table – it was warmer in the kitchen than in the office – and he brought his head round to look at Lizzie, but Lizzie was bending over the stove. And as his eyes returned to his work they met Mary Ann's for a second, and widened slightly. Still he did not say anything.

But Mary Ann knew that, like herself, he had been surprised. Her mother never went to the pictures, she didn't care for the pictures. They had talked about getting television ages ago, but she had said, 'I don't care for the pictures, so I don't suppose I'll care for that.' And now she had stated she was going to spend the afternoon at the pictures . . .

By Friday of that week Lizzie had been out on her own three times, and it came as a surprise to no-one except perhaps herself, when Mike stated, in a casual, even off-hand manner, which however did not disguise that his statement was one of retaliation, 'I think I'll have a day out the morrow meself. I'm long overdue for a trip.'

Michael's eyes darted towards his father, but Mary Ann did not look at him. She knew what the trip forbode, and she thought sadly to herself, 'Well, me ma has asked for it this time. She may never have done before, but she's asked for it this time.'

Lizzie had been on her way to the scullery with a tray of dishes as Mike spoke, and when she reached the table she slowly put the tray down, but without releasing her hold on it she bent forward over it and bit tightly on her lip. That was all for the moment.

Mike went out to do his round, and Michael, as usual after changing, got on his bike and rode to Jarrow and Sarah, and no sooner had the door closed on him than Lizzie's cold, calm front dropped away. Coming to Mary Ann, where she sat before the fire, working assiduously at her shorthand, she said quickly, 'Leave that a minute and listen to me. Your da will be back at any time . . . Put it down, I say.' She flicked the book from Mary Ann's hand, and this caused Mary Ann's face to tighten.

'Don't look like that. I'm telling you don't look at me like that. And listen to me . . . If your father goes out tomorrow you must go with him.'

'He won't want me with him.'

'I don't care if he wants you with him or not . . . Look.' Suddenly Lizzie knelt down by Mary Ann's side, and as she caught hold of her daughter's hand her whole expression changed. Mary Ann was now looking at her old ma, the ma she knew and loved. And when she saw the tears come into Lizzie's eyes her face and body relaxed, and the resentment she was feeling at the moment against her mother died away. She asked under her breath, 'What is it, Ma? What's the matter?'

'Nothing, nothing. I only want you to do this for me. Please do this for me, keep with him tomorrow. He mustn't get anything into him tomorrow. Will you do it? You can. You know you can.'

'But if he says I haven't got to go with him. If he says no, what about it then?'

Lizzie turned her eyes away and looked towards the fire, and after a moment she pulled herself to her feet and said in a dead tone, 'Well, if he won't let you go with him, I'll . . .' Her voice trailed away. 'I'll only have to tell him . . .'

'Tell him what?' Mary Ann was on her feet.

Lizzie shook her head. 'Oh, it doesn't matter . . . it doesn't matter. I just didn't want him to break out tomorrow, that's all. Go on, get on with your work, it doesn't matter.'

Mary Ann stared at Lizzie as she went towards the scullery again. What was the matter with her mother? What was up anyway? Where had she been those other times this week? On Monday she had gone to the pictures. But she was out on Wednesday, and yesterday again, and she looked all worked up, and she sounded worked up. Mary Ann went back to her seat, and as she picked up her notebook she looked down at the last words she had written in shorthand. They read, 'Me da says he's going out tomorrow. He sounds just like he used to years ago when he was going on the beer . . . Will things never straighten out?' She looked up from the book. Would things never straighten out?

There was a wind blowing over the fields. It was like a gigantic scythe whipping across the frozen earth. It bit into Mary Ann's ankles causing her to comment, 'I wish I'd put my boots on.'

Mike, walking by her side up the road towards the bus stop, did not pick up her remark, and it was the third such she had made about the weather since leaving the house. But when she slipped on an icy patch in the road his hand came out swiftly and steadied her, and as he released her he said, 'Your mother told you to come along of me, didn't she?'

'No, Da.'

'All right, don't tell me if you don't want to. But I know me own know. After last night she was frightened I was goin' to get bottled, and she had reason, for that's just what I intended to do.'

'No, Da.'

Mary Ann was looking up at him, but Mike kept his eyes ahead as he asked abruptly, 'Do you know where your ma's been this week?'

'No, Da.'

His eyes were hard on her and there was a sharpness in his tone as he said, 'Now look, Mary Ann. This could be serious. I might do just what she fears, and in spite of you go and get a skin full. I feel like it. By God! I do at this minute. So if you know what she's been up to on these jaunts, tell me.'

'But I don't, Da.' Of one accord they drew to a halt, and Mary Ann looked at him as she went on, 'I only know she's upset about something, sort of worked up.' Her eyes flicked away. 'She did say to me to come with you today. For some reason or other . . . well, she doesn't want you to do anything . . .' Her voice trailed off.

Mike continued to look down on her for a moment, then with a deep intake of breath he walked on, and she had to hurry her step to keep up with him.

Mike did not speak again until they reached the crossroads and then he said, as if to himself, 'If the old fellow were here I'd feel there was something hatching, but I can't blame him for this.'

Mary Ann, picking up his words, said, 'No, Da, you can't. And talking of him, I'm scared of him coming back an' all, for there's going to be trouble.'

A moment ago she'd had no intention of telling him about Tony, but it now appeared like a heaven-sent diversion, a subject that would interest him and keep him, at least for a while, from thinking, and not kindly, of her mother.

'Trouble?'

'Yes, about Tony . . . He told me yesterday that he's going . . .' She lowered her head, and finished in a soft-toned rush, 'He's going to marry Mrs Schofield, da.'

Mike was silent so long that she looked up at him.

'He told you that himself?'

'Yes, Da.'

'Well, my God!' Mike pushed his trilby back from his brow. 'That'll be news that'll knock the old man over. Although it's really no surprise, not to me, it isn't, but it will be to him, because he hasn't got the vestige of an inkling. I know that . . . And what about you?' His head came down to her. 'How did you feel when he shot that at you?'

Mary Ann raised her eyebrows, then turned her gaze away over the fields as she said, 'A bit odd for a moment.'

'You're still keen on Corny though?'

'Yes, Da.'

'If there hadn't been Corny would you've had Tony?'

She brought her eyes back to him again. 'That's what Tony asked me. How can I say? I don't know. I like Tony, I always have.'

'Do you think your mother knows and this is what's been upsetting her?'

'No, da. No. He told me first, I feel sure of that.'

'Well, there's one thing for certain.' Mike drew in another long breath. 'When your mother does know it's not going to make her any happier. She didn't take much notice of that tale your grannie brought that Sunday, about seeing them together. She remarked at the time on Mrs Schofield being so much older than him and she dismissed the idea as ridiculous, because she wanted to go on thinking about the nice cushy future all planned out for you. For, like the old fellow, she had set her heart on this business and believed in the tag that time would tell. But you know, when he first mentioned it she went off the deep end. Can you believe that? She was actually shocked. Ah well, time has told, hasn't it?' He put his hand out and touched her cheek. 'Life's funny. But don't worry. Tony wasn't for you. He's a fine fellow, but not for you. He's not your type of man . . . don't worry.'

'But I'm not worrying about that, Da. Not about Tony and me, but I am worrying about Mr Lord coming back. You remember the last time him and Tony went at it?'

Again Mike took in a deep breath before

163

saying, 'We'll wait until he does come and see what happens then. I think the best thing that you and me can do is to both get drunk . . . eh?' He was bending down towards her, and they both laughed now. With a sudden impulsive movement she tucked her hand into his arm, and for no other reason but that she was with her da and he wasn't going to go on the beer, she felt a momentary wave of happiness.

As was usual on his visits to the city, Mike did some business for the farm. Then he and Mary Ann had lunch together. Following this, he pleased her mightily by taking her to the pictures.

It was turned four o'clock and nearly dark when the bus dropped them at the crossroads again. They were quiet now as they went down the road, and neither of them spoke until, through the dusk, the farm came in sight, when Mary Ann exclaimed, 'Look, da. Is that our Michael on the road?'

Mike screwed up his eyes. 'Aye, it is. I wonder what's up. He's waitin' . . . he seems as if he's on the look-out for us . . .'

Before Mike had finished speaking, Michael came towards them at a run, and Mary Ann's heart began to pound with painful intensity. Something had happened to her ma. She knew it had. That was the feeling that had been with her all day. In spite of the joy of her father's company, and the brief happiness she had experienced this morning, there had been a heaviness around her, and Mike endorsed this feeling in himself when he muttered under his breath, 'I've been waitin' for this.'

But when Michael's face loomed up through the dusk and he came panting to their side, both their expressions took on a similar glint to his own, for Mary Ann was smiling, and Mike's eyebrows were raised in pleasant inquiry.

It was Mike who spoke first, saying, 'It can't be the sweep, the results won't be through yet . . . What are you looking so happy about?'

'It's me ma.' Michael, in this moment of high excitement, had dropped what was to him the familiar use of mother. 'You'll never believe it. But come on . . . come on, hurry up. I've been on the look-out for you on and off for the last couple of hours. Where've you been?'

'To the pictures. But what is it?' Mary Ann tried to catch hold of his coat as they now hurried on. 'What's me ma done?'

'Wait and see.' Michael was one step ahead of them, practically at a trot.

'Here, hold your hand a minute.' Mike gripped his son's arm. 'What's happened? It's something nice for a change anyway to make you look like that.'

'Just you wait and see . . . just wait and see. No, don't go in the back way.' He turned and pulled at Mary Ann as she was about to enter the farm gate. 'Come on in the front.'

'With our slushy boots on? Do you want us to get murdered?' Mike was still following Michael, and Michael threw over his shoulder, 'You won't get murdered this time.'

When they reached the front door, he stopped and, looking from one to the other, he said, 'Shut your eyes.'

'Shut me eyes!' Mike pulled his chin into the

side of his neck, and slanted his eyes at his son. 'What's the game?'

'Go on, Da. Shut your eyes.'

Mary Ann didn't need a double bidding to shut her eyes. She screwed them up, anticipating as she did so a happiness streaked with wonder. It must be something wonderful that Michael had to show them because his face was portraying a look that she had never seen on it before. It radiated a feeling of deep, deep happiness.

After opening the door she felt Michael grip her hands, and her da joggled her as they tried to get through the framework together. She wanted to giggle, but it was not the moment for giggling, she knew that. When she felt Michael turning them in the direction of the front room she sensed immediately what she would see. Yet the surprise was so great that she was for the moment struck speechless. She was looking at what had been her ma's room. Now, as if a giant hand had swept the house, mixing up the furniture, she was gazing wide-eyed at a complete bed-sitting-room, and there, sitting propped up in bed, looking almost like her old self, was Sarah.

Michael, standing near the head of the bed gripping Sarah's hand, looked at them, saying softly, 'Would you believe it?'

'No, no, I wouldn't.' Mike came slowly across the room, and when he was standing at the foot of the bed he looked down at Sarah and said, with what might have been a break in his voice, 'Hello, lass . . . you got here then.' It sounded as if he knew she had been coming. So much so that Michael exclaimed in a surprised whisper, 'You didn't know, did you, Father?'

'No, I didn't know. Not an inkling.'

'Nor me.' Michael gave a series of quick shakes to his head. 'It's amazing.'

Mary Ann came and stood by Michael's side, and putting her hand out she touched Sarah's face, and there was no disguising the cracking of her voice as she said, 'This is what me ma's been up to all week, isn't it?'

Sarah nodded. She was unable to speak.

Mike now said, 'I'll be seeing you, lass,' and turning quietly from the bed, went out of the room.

Sarah, looking from Michael towards Mary Ann, brought out brokenly, 'I'll love her all me life.'

It was too much emotion for Mary Ann to cope with without openly breaking down, and she too went hastily from the room, thinking as she made her way towards the kitchen, 'An' I will an' all.' In moments of great stress she always dropped into the old vernacular.

As she pushed open the kitchen door it was to see her mother held tight in her da's arm, and to hear him saying over and over again, 'Oh! Liz. Liz.' And as her mother raised her head quickly from his shoulder, he finished, 'You won't regret it, we'll all see to that.'

Lizzie braced herself against Mary Ann's rushing onslaught. It was indeed as if they had all slipped back three or four years. And as Lizzie's arms went round her daughter, she said, 'There now, there now, stop it, and let me get on.'

'Oh, Ma, I think you're wonderful.'

Lizzie made no open comment on this but a

section of her mind, speaking with a touch of sadness, said: 'All my married life I've done what one or the other wanted and they never thought to say I was wonderful, until now.' The feeling she thought she had conquered during the early part of the week returned, and for a moment she felt the bitterness rise in her again. She had created a beautiful room – it was the symbol of her personal success – worthy in its taste of the finest house, and then they had succeeded, with their innuendoes of silence and suggestion, to bulldoze the ultimatum at her . . . the room or us . . . Either you let Sarah have the room or you keep it . . . just to yourself, for we'll have none of it.

'But how did you manage it?' Mike was following her round like a kitten – a better description would have been a huge cat – purring on her, and when his arm, coming swiftly out and round her waist, almost lifted her off her feet as he pulled her to him again, the action seemed to slam the door shut on her self-pity. She had been right. Oh, yes, she knew she had been right. Sarah was happy and would likely get better much quicker here. And although she had only been in the house a matter of three hours, her gratitude had been so touching that it didn't seem to matter any more about the room. There would be times, she told herself, being a level-headed woman, when she would want her room to herself, but they would be few and far between. The main thing was she had her family with her again going her way. How, she wondered now, had she ever let them go so far from her? She must have been mad. She pushed off Mike's arm, saying, 'And you stop it, an' all. I've got to think of the tea, nobody else seems to be going to bother.'

'But how did you do it, Liz? I want to hear.'

'I went out three times this week, didn't I?'

'You did, Mrs Shaughnessy!' He nodded his head deeply at her.

'I went off jaunting to the pictures!'

'You did, Mrs Shaughnessy.' His head was moving slower and deeper now, and Mary Ann began to laugh. The laugh was high and thin. It spun upwards in a spiral of sound ending almost on a squeak, and the next minute Mary Ann had her head resting in the crook of her elbow on top of the sideboard and Mike was saying, 'Ah, there now, there now, give over. It's no time for crying.' With his one good arm he swung her up and carried her like a child towards the chair, then, sitting down, dumped her on his knee, and as he stroked the back of her head he muttered into her hair, 'You're always the one for enjoyment, aren't you? It's like old times; when anything nice happened you always had to bubble.' Mike looked to where Lizzie was now flicking the cloth across the table and their gaze met and held. They were both thinking back to the ending of many of their rows and disagreements, and they couldn't think of one where Mary Ann had not howled her eyes out with happiness. Or was it just relief?

'Now that's all right, Mr Flannagan.' Mike laid his heavy hand on the small man's shoulder. 'She would have been coming into the family soon in any case.'

'Yes, yes, I know that. They would have got married, yes, I know that, Mr Shaughnessy.' Mr

Flannagan had always addressed Mike as Mr Shaughnessy. From that far-away day of the peace tea, when the little man had rebelled openly against his wife's tyranny and had marched down the street with Mike to get blind drunk for the first time in many years. From that day, whenever he had spoken to him since, he had always given Mike his full title, and Mike had returned the compliment.

Mike liked the little bloke, and in a way admired him, for he had showed his missus he was no worm, although she had treated him as one for years.

'That room was so pokey.' Mr Flannagan moved his head from side to side. 'I'd think about her at odd times of the day stuck in there and her loving the open air, but here it's so wide looking, so free. And the view from that window does your heart good. I'm not being hoodwinked by what you're sayin', Mr Shaughnessy. It's the goodness of yourself and your wife's heart that have brought this about. And if she gets better, I mean if she gets her legs back, then it'll be thanks to the pair of you.'

'Now, now, let's forget it. What about a little wet on the side . . . I've no hard.' He winked at the smaller man. 'It's not allowed in the house, except at Christmas, and births and deaths, and we haven't had any of them for a long while.' They both laughed. 'Of course, beer's a different thing. Liz tells me that the beer hasn't been brewed yet that could make me drunk!' Their laughter rose, then Mike, jerking his head towards the front room, said, 'Hark to 'em. They're going at it in there, aren't they?'

'It sounds like a party. It does that, Mr Shaughnessy. And listen there a minute . . . I believe I can hear her laughing above the rest.' The *her* referred to his wife, and Mr Flannagan's face was definitely stretched with amazement. There came a deep twinkle into his eye now as he looked up at Mike. 'The age of miracles isn't passed, is it, Mr Shaughnessy?' Mike's head was going back to let out a bellow of laughter when he checked it, saying, 'I think that's someone knocking, but I can't hear for the noise.'

He handed Mr Flannagan a glass of beer, then went hurriedly through the scullery towards the back door, and when he opened it he exclaimed in almost startled surprise, 'Good God!'

'No, just me, Shaughnessy. I always turn up like the proverbial bad penny.'

'You're . . . you're welcome, sir.'

'Yes, but you didn't expect me, you never do. May I come in?'

'Yes, sir. By all means.' Mike pulled the door wide.

'Oh, you've got company?' The sound of the laughter penetrated to the scullery, and Mike answered, 'Only the family, and Sarah and her parents.'

'Sarah?' Mr Lord nodded at Mike. 'She's here then? Oh, that's good, she's getting out and about, I'm very pleased to hear that.'

Mike did not at this moment go into any particulars. The old boy wasn't going to like it when he heard that Michael was turning down the bungalow. He mightn't be greatly distressed about it, but nevertheless he didn't like any of his suggestions to be flaunted, and it would be in that light he would take this business.

In the kitchen, Mike said, 'This is Sarah's father. This is Mr Lord, Mr Flannagan.'

'Good evening.'

'Good evening, sir.'

Mr Lord did not know Mr Flannagan, but Mr Flannagan knew Mr Lord. He received his pay packet from him every week, for he worked in his yard. It was funny when you came to think about it, Mr Flannagan's mind told him, but if things worked out the way Mrs Flannagan said they were going to, Mr Lord here and himself would, in a way, be connected . . . Very distantly, admitted, but still connected. Life was indeed funny, Mr Flannagan commented.

'You're Sarah's father?'

'Yes, I am, sir; I am that, sir.'

'Very nice girl, very nice. A great pity about this business. But still, wonderful things are done these days . . . We'll see, we'll see.'

'Did you have a good trip, sir?' Mike was speaking now.

'Yes, Shaughnessy. A very, very good trip. I enjoyed every moment of it. I only wish I could have made it longer.'

Mike was thinking . . . 'Well, why didn't you then, things go on just the same,' when Mr Lord said, 'Is Tony here?'

'Tony? No, sir.'

'Do you know where he is?'

'No. No, I don't, sir. He doesn't usually tell me where he's going.' Mike gave a small smile.

'He hasn't been out with Mary Ann today?'

Mike's eyes dropped away. 'No, no, not today. I took Mary Ann into Newcastle . . . Won't you sit down a minute?' He turned the chair towards the old man, then added generously, 'I'll tell Mary Ann you're here. She'll be pleased to see you.'

'Thank you, Shaughnessy. I'll be pleased to see her, too. Yes, yes, I will indeed. Thank you.'

Mike left the kitchen and went into the front room, and held up a sharp warning finger to stop the laughter and chattering. Making sure that the door was closed behind him before he spoke, he said under his breath, 'He's come home. The old boy.'

'What, Mr Lord?' He looked towards Lizzie, who had risen to her feet.

'But I thought Tony said another week or so,' Michael put in.

Mike now nodded at Michael as he whispered, 'Well, you know him.'

Mary Ann hadn't moved from her position on the side of the bed near Sarah. Part of her wanted to dash into the kitchen and throw her arms around the old man's neck in welcome, but there was a larger part that was filled with anxious fear. It was just like him, as Tony said, to do the unpredictable. They had all been so happy . . . happy and laughing. It had been like old times. She had felt during the last hour or so that life was going to run smoothly again. She had forgotten for the moment what Tony had told her about him and Mrs Schofield. She had forgotten what that would mean to the old man who had just come back. Her da was looking at her and speaking again, still in a whisper, 'Come on. Get off that.' He pointed to the bed. 'He wants to see you.'

'What's the matter with you?' Lizzie's voice

was soft but sharp. 'Don't go in looking like that. He'll think he's as welcome as a snake in paradise.'

Lizzie did not often make these quips, and there was a low rumble of suppressed laughter. Mary Ann did not laugh. She pulled herself off the bed and went slowly round the foot, excusing herself as she stepped over Mrs Flannagan's feet, and made her way towards her da who was now opening the door. There was nothing to laugh about, nothing to smile about any more. They weren't to know that perhaps in a short time – the distance was determined on how long it would take Mr Lord and Tony to come together – he would be dead. He could not stand shocks, great shocks, at his age, with his heart in the bad state it was already.

When she reached Mike, he stopped her passing him by saying quickly, 'Hold your hand a minute till I bring Mr Flannagan in here, it'll be better that way . . . Stay a minute.'

Within a matter of seconds Mike came from the kitchen accompanied by Mr Flannagan, and nodding to Mary Ann he held the kitchen door open for her, and she went in to greet Mr Lord.

'What's the matter with you?' said Lizzie some time later, as they piled sandwiches on to plates ready for transporting into the front room.

'Nothing,' said Mary Ann.

'Now don't be silly . . . nothing. You know there is something. You were all right until Mr Lord put in an appearance.' She stopped her arranging of the sandwiches, and, turning Mary Ann towards her, she said, 'You haven't been up to anything, have you?'

'Me, Ma?'

'Yes, you. And don't look so wide-eyed.' Lizzie was smiling now. Smiling down on her daughter. She was relaxed and happy, it was as if she'd had a drink, like at Christmas. But the strongest drink she had taken tonight was coffee.

Mary Ann could have told her mother what was troubling her, but she did not want to spoil this night, and if she said to her, 'Tony is going to marry Mrs Schofield,' the night would indeed be spoilt for her. She would have to know sooner or later, but not tonight, because she was happy in the sacrifice she had made. Everybody was full of praise for her, and all their gratitude flowed round her in a heart-warming wave. She could not spoil it.

'Well then, if you've been up to nothing' – Lizzie moved her head gently – 'stop looking like that. To say the least, you don't seem very glad to see him back. And as usual he's been more than kind. Fancy him thinking about a camera for Michael, and such a camera. And a projector to go with it. The two must have cost sixty pounds if they cost a penny. And he's going to get a television for Sarah. You know, he couldn't be kinder.'

She lifted three plates now, and balancing two on one hand and one in the other, she went towards the hall, saying, 'I'm looking forward to seeing his American pictures. You know he's a marvellous old man really, going around taking pictures at his age. You remember the ones from his last holiday . . . Oh, that's them now.' She half turned. 'They've got back. Bring the coffee.'

Mary Ann picked up the tray with the percolator and milk jug, and turned from the sound of her father's and Mr Lord's voices coming from the scullery.

Mary Ann, at this moment, was not interested in seeing the pictures of where Mr Lord had been. She was feeling very down and apprehensive. She wished that Mr and Mrs Flannagan would go home, and the house was quiet and they were all in bed. She wanted to think, and you couldn't think in this chattering racket . . .

The big chair was pulled up to the side of Sarah's bed and Mr Lord directed to it.

Michael had arranged a portable screen at the far end of the room and fixed the table for the projector. This took a little time as he had to arrange a number of books to bring it to the required height. And then all was ready.

'We'll have the lights out now,' said Mr Lord. Then with a little lightness that for him amounted to high gaiety, he said, 'The show is about to begin.' There was a murmur of laughter before silence took over in the room. Silence but for the warm burr of the projector.

There were six magazines of slides, and Michael, after slipping in the first set, worked the handle that clicked each picture into focus on the screen, and on each one Mr Lord commented. This was the aeroplane with which he did the trip to New York. That was the hotel in which he stayed . . . Oh, yes, that Negro had been a porter in the hotel and had proved himself very helpful. On and on it went, thirty-six pictures in the first magazine, thirty-six pictures in the second magazine. And when Michael was about to slip in the third set, Mr Lord stopped him by saying, 'We won't have that one as arranged, Michael, let me have the end one next . . . Yes, the end one.'

There was a few minutes of anticipatory silence while Michael made the changeover, then came the first click. Hardly had the picture lit up the screen but there burst from everyone in the room, perhaps with the exception of Mrs Flannagan and Mr Lord, one name . . . Corny! For it was Corny. A full-length picture of Corny in a red sweater, tight cream jeans, and a grin on his face that almost split it in two.

Mary Ann's hands were cupping her face, pressing her cheeks in and her lips out. Her eyes were riveted on the screen. Corny was looking straight at her, smiling his wide grin. Michael did not click away Corny's face for some minutes. When he did, she recovered her breath and turned with the sound of a laugh in her voice as she cried to the old man, 'You said you wouldn't be able to see him . . . You said it was too far . . . thousands of miles down the country . . . Oh, Mr Lord! . . .'

'Wait a moment, wait a moment.' He checked her impetuous thanks with a quick pat on her knee. 'There are many, many more. Wait a moment.'

The click came again, and there was Corny once more. His figure was shorter now. He was in a sort of gigantic showroom, where cars stretched, it appeared, for miles. It seemed to hold all the cars in the world, and there was Corny standing by one of them, pointing out something to a man. Mr Lord's voice penetrated Mary Ann's mind now saying, 'He sold that car to that client. He's doing very well in that department, although he's only been there a month. Yes, he's doing very well indeed. We'll have the next one, Michael.'

They had the next one, and the next, and the next. Corny with this car, and that car. Corny in a great glass office. Corny sitting at the wheel of a car. Then the pictures changed abruptly. First, there was a picture of a house. It was a beautiful house with an open garden. There were two cars standing in the roadway, each looked as big as two English cars put together. There were a number of people sitting on the lawn of the house having tea, and Corny was one of them.

The next picture was of a tennis court. Corny was playing tennis. Mary Ann's eyes narrowed at the stationary figure on the screen, the racket held ready for a back-hand drive. She had never imagined Corny playing tennis. The picture changed again. And there was the blue sea, it was very, very blue, and the edge was trimmed with a high frothy breaker. On the beach there were a number of people, and Corny was among them. They were having a picnic.

'They are a great family for picnics.' Mr Lord's voice broke in on Mary Ann's thoughts again. 'They're always eating out of doors. They have taken to Cornelius and like him very much. America has done him good. He seems to have opened out quite a lot . . . not so tongue-tied as I remember him . . . at least, that's a mistake, I wouldn't say tongue-tied, brusque would be a better term. Yes . . . he is not so brusque as he used to be.'

Mary Ann's fingers were holding the neck of her jumper now. She was looking at Corny in the water. His head was close to that of a girl, the girl she had seen in the front garden of the house. And also on the same side of the net on the tennis court. Although then she had her back to the camera, Mary Ann knew it was the same girl, for she had blonde hair, and although it was tied back it still reached below her waist. Suddenly she hated that hair. Her own hair, although a lovely dark chestnut with a deep shine, only came below her shoulders. She not only hated the fair hair, she hated its owner, but more so in this moment she hated Corny Boyle. And she thought of him as Corny Boyle, not just the familiar Corny.

'He seems to be having the time of his life.' This was Mrs Flannagan's voice coming out of the darkness.

'Yes, I think he is.' Mr Lord's voice was pleasant, and he seemed to be speaking to Mrs Flannagan alone. 'At least he is getting a broader view of life. His years in America will certainly not be wasted.'

His years . . . Mary Ann gulped and tried to make it noiseless.

The machine clicked again, and there was Corny playing his beloved instrument. Elbows up, head back, it was as if he was standing in the room before them. But he wasn't in the room, he was standing on the steps of that house, and there, squatting all round, were that family again. Only there seemed to be more of them this time, for protruding from the edge of the picture were numerous arms and legs. It looked like another party.

'This was one of their usual get-togethers. Corny and his playing are in great demand.'

There was no answer to Mr Lord's remark.

The machine clicked yet again, sharply this time, and there was Corny in a close-up, sitting on the top of a gate, and next to him was the girl with the long fair hair. She was very bonny, beautiful they would call her out there . . . And Corny and her had their arms round each other.

It was the end of that particular magazine and no-one made any comment whatever until Mr Lord spoke, and directly to Sarah now. 'Would you like to see more pictures, Sarah?'

It was a few seconds before Sarah said, 'Yes. Yes, I would . . . please.' But there was no enthusiasm in her voice. Sarah was now one of the family and through her own feelings for Michael she could gauge at this moment how Mary Ann felt, and she knew, as surely as did Mary Ann, that the pictures of Corny had been shown for a purpose.

The set of pictures now flicking on and off the screen were dealing with the scenery, and as Mr Flannagan said in a respectful tone, 'Aye, it's a grand-lookin' country. I've always had an idea I'd like to go there,' Mary Ann slid quietly from her chair and went out of the room, and no-one said, 'Where are you going?'

But it was only a matter of minutes before Mike joined her in the kitchen. He came straight to her where she was standing looking down into the fire. She wasn't crying, but she nearly did when Mike put his arm around her shoulders, and, pulling her tightly to his side, said, 'The old swine. He's a bloody scheming old swine, and I've got to say it.'

Mary Ann said nothing. And Mike went on, 'Take no notice of pictures like that. Ten to one he was told to pose for them. Things are done like that, you know. Come on, they'll say. Come on, huddle up together there, I'm going to take your picture . . . You know what it's like, don't you? We've done it ourselves in the garden. You remember when Michael took me and Mrs Schofield and we were laughing our heads off, remember that tea-time? Well, anybody seeing that would get the wrong idea, wouldn't they?'

Still Mary Ann did not answer. She had been hating Mr Lord, she was still hating him. She knew, and her da knew, that he had deliberately brought these snaps to show her that Corny was no longer remembering the North or anyone in it . . . was no longer remembering her. And the name of Mrs Schofield did not for a moment soften her feelings towards the old man. But as though Mike had picked up her thinking, he said after a moment's silence, 'I could have one great big bloody row with him at this minute if it wasn't for the fact that he'll have enough to think about in a very short while when Tony spills the beans . . . Look.' He turned her round, gripping her with his one hand. 'I tell you, take no notice of them pictures. You know the old fellow's always scheming. When he took them he didn't know that his plans were already down the drain. And if I know Corny Boyle, and I think I know him, he's not the kind of lad to be swept off his feet by a bunch of golden locks and two goo-goo eyes.' Mike gave a little laugh. 'She had goo-goo eyes, hadn't she? Not forgetting a big sloppy mouth. Come on . . . come on, laugh at it. What do you bet? I bet Corny's back here within the next few months.'

Within the next few months, her da had said. Within the next few months, not this month, or next. The year was nearly up, and next month it would be Christmas again, and Corny had said he would give it a year. But when he said that he hadn't realised the temptation of promotion, of big money, of a car . . . if he wanted one . . . of a girl with long blonde hair whose eyes weren't goo-goo, nor whose mouth was not big and sloppy. Mary Ann didn't hide the fact from herself that the girl with the long blonde hair was beautiful, by any standards she was beautiful.

'Look, come on back into the room, and don't let him see it's affected you. Keep the old boy guessing, that's the best way with him. Come on . . . laugh, smile.' He stretched her mouth gently with his middle finger and thumb, and when she didn't respond, he said urgently, 'Listen to me. Apart from what you feel, what we both feel about this, for it's made me as mad as a hatter, we don't want to spoil this day for your mother, do we? . . . and Sarah. Because Sarah is as near content now as she'll get until she's on her legs again. We don't want to do anything to bust up this day, eh? Come on.'

Side by side they went out of the kitchen, across the hall and quietly into the room again to hear the end of Mrs Flannagan's comment, 'He's a very lucky young man.' Which told them that there had been more pictures of Corny.

'I'll have to put the light on a minute, this one's stuck,' said Michael.

As the light went up in the room, and caused them all to blink, Mary Ann found that Mr Lord was looking at her, but his eyes were not blinking. With their penetrating blueness they peered out at her from the wrinkled lids, and there was a question in their depth and Mary Ann, looking back at him, found she could not play up to her father's request and smile. And the old man, reading the hurt he had dealt her, looked sad for a moment. But only for a moment.

They were all late going to bed. Mary Ann heard the clock strike twelve as her father came up the stairs and made his way to his room. She had been lying for the last half-hour staring at the sloping ceiling, her eyes dry and burning. She hadn't cried and she told herself she wasn't going to. She was angry not only with Mr Lord, she was angry with Corny Boyle. She did not believe what her da had said, that Corny had been pushed into posing for these pictures. He might have been the first time, but there had been a dozen or more of him with those people . . . and that girl was always near him. If he wanted to stay in America then he could; nothing apparently she could say or do could stop him now. He was too far away for her to have any impression on him. But she hated him for wanting to stay in America.

As the muttered, companionable sound of her da, talking to her ma, came to her from their room across the landing, she was enveloped in a wave of self-pity. Of a sudden she felt utterly alone, quite lost, friendless. She had neither Corny Boyle nor Tony. The term 'falling between two stools' was certainly right in her case. The burning in her eyes became moist, and now she no longer tried to prevent the hot tears flooding down her face. Turning swiftly, she buried her head in the pillow.

She must have cried for about half an hour, for she felt weary and sick when she turned on to her back again, and continued, through blinking wet lids, to look towards the ceiling. It was at the point where sleep was about to carry her away from her misery that the sound of the telephone bell jangled through the house.

Mary Ann brought her head up from the pillow and listened. She expected to hear the door of her parents' room being pulled open. After some seconds, when the telephone bell, ringing again, seeming determined to disturb the quiet of the house, she threw back the bedclothes and, getting out of bed, pulled on her dressing-gown. She was on the landing when Michael's door opened, and she whispered across to him, 'It's the phone.'

As they went softly, and hurriedly, down the stairs together Michael whispered back at her, 'I'll bet something's happened to me grannie.'

Mary Ann felt not a trace of sympathy at the thought of anything happening to her grannie, and whispered back, 'She would pick this time of night. It's just like her.'

So sure were they both that they would hear some news of Mrs McMullen that, after switching on the hall light, they exchanged knowing glances as Michael lifted the mouthpiece from the stand on the hall table.

'Hello?'

The voice that came over the phone was no stranger's telling them that grannie had been taken ill, but the voice of Mr Lord. He was saying, 'Oh, is that you, Michael? I thought it might be your father.'

Again they exhanged glances.

'Is anything the matter, Mr Lord?'

'No, no, nothing I hope . . . I just wanted to inquire if your father knew where Tony was going this evening . . . or last evening. It is now after one o'clock and he's not in.'

Again the exchange of glances.

'Your father is not awake, I suppose?'

'No, no, Mr Lord, or he would have been down. I suppose he's in a deep sleep, and my mother too, they had rather a hectic day.' Michael said nothing about his own hectic day, and the excitement that was still depriving him of sleep. He said now, 'Very likely Tony's gone to a dance.'

'To my knowledge, he doesn't go to dances.'

Michael's eyebrows went up as his eyes slanted towards Mary Ann's again, and his lips pressed themselves into a tight line and his expression interpreted the words coming over the wire.

'Would Mary Ann know where he was likely to be?'

Mary Ann bit on her lip and shook her head at Michael.

'I don't think so, Mr Lord.'

'Haven't they been going out on a Saturday as usual?'

Again Mary Ann motioned towards Michael, nodding her head this time.

'Yes . . . yes, I think so, Mr Lord.'

'You think so? You're not sure?' The voice was loud and the words clipped, and Mary Ann took more of her lower lip into her mouth.

'Did Tony not tell Ben how late he might be, Mr Lord?'

'As far as I can gather, no. From the information I have screwed from Ben, it would appear that he hasn't even seen my grandson since I left the house three weeks ago. I have long suspected Ben to be an idiot, now I have proof of it.'

From this heated remark, Mary Ann knew that Ben was within ear-shot of the old man. Poor Ben. He'd likely got it in the neck because he hadn't been able to tell Mr Lord where Tony was. Very likely if he knew about Mrs Schofield he still wouldn't have told on Tony. The main reason being not so much to protect Tony from the old man's wrath, but to protect his master from the consequences of that wrath.

'I shouldn't worry, Mr Lord. He's likely gone to a dinner or something.'

There followed a pause so long it would have indicated that Mr Lord had left the phone but for the fact that there hadn't been the usual click at the other end of the line. The old man's voice came now, thick and muffled, saying curtly, 'Thank you. I'm sorry to have got you out of bed. Thank you.' Now came the click. And Michael put the receiver back on to its rest.

'Lord! There'll be a shindy. I wonder what Tony's up to. He doesn't dance, does he?'

Mary Ann did not give a reply to this but said, 'We'd better look in on Sarah and tell her it's all right.' Michael nodded and moved towards the front-room door, and after opening it gently and putting his head round, he said, 'You awake, Sarah?'

He closed the door quietly before turning to

Mary Ann. 'She's dead to the world. Relief, I suppose.' And going towards the stairs again he whispered, 'I wonder what Tony's up to. Likely he's got in at a party or something. But I didn't think parties were in his line.'

'He's with Mrs Schofield.'

'What!' Michael stopped dead on the stairs. 'How do you make that out?'

'They're going to be married.' There was a trace of bitterness in Mary Ann's tone.

'Him and Mrs Schofield. You're kiddin'?'

'No, I'm not kidding.'

'How long have you known this?'

'Since Friday.'

'I didn't even know he was seeing her.'

'Well, you and me ma and Mr Lord must be the only three people on the Tyne who didn't know about it.'

Michael watched Mary Ann ascend the stairs in front of him. Then, moving slowly, he followed her. For a moment he felt a deep brotherly concern for her. She was a tantalising, aggravating little madam at times, but she was also an engaging little madam. And she was kind. Look at her with Sarah. And she had indeed been given enough tonight to try the temper of the best, with those pictures of Corny and that blonde. And this, on top of knowing that Tony was going to marry Mrs Schofield . . . Mrs Schofield, of all people. She seemed old enough to be his mother. Well, perhaps not quite, but too old for him.

On the landing he paused as Mary Ann's door closed on her, then his eyes were drawn towards his mother's room. Lord, this was going to be a blow for her. She had set her heart on Tony for

Mary Ann as much as the old man had done. There was a balloon going to burst shortly.

Mary Ann, sitting on the edge of her bed, tried not to think of where Tony was at this present moment. He could not have married Mrs Schofield, as the decree had not yet been made absolute, but there was no other place she could think of where he could be, except with her. The young Mary Ann told herself he was wicked, wicked. And she was answered by the Mary Ann against whom life had been thrust wholesalely these past few months, saying, 'Be your age, it happens . . . it happens every day. Is he any different?'

Yes, Tony was different. He should be different. Like Corny. Corny was different . . . He should be different. It appeared to her that because she liked both Corny and Tony, they should be different. When her mind, still clinging to the black and white theory of her upbringing, asked her why peopled did bad things, she said to herself, and impatiently now, 'Oh, go to sleep and forget it.'

But she couldn't go to sleep and forget it. It must have been around four o'clock in the morning that her fitful dozing overbalanced into sleep. Then it seemed as if she was only in this beautiful oblivion for a matter of seconds when a hand dragged her upwards out of it. She woke to her father's voice, saying, 'Mary Ann!' and his hand gently rocking her shoulder.

'Yes, Da?' She was sitting straight up blinking at him.

'Don't look so worried, it's all right. There's nothing wrong.' He bent towards her. 'I had to get up a short while ago, I heard Prudence bellowing her head off. She got her horns fixed in between those boards again, and when I was out I saw the light on up in the house, downstairs, and I was just wondering what was wrong when I caught sight of the old man walking up the hill. I could see him plainly . . . the moon's full.'

'What time is it?'

'About twenty past five now, but this was before five, I've just had a word with Michael. He's had a sleepless night it appears, too much excitement over Sarah I think in that quarter, but he tells me that the old man rang about one o'clock. Tony wasn't in then, and it looks as if he's still not in. I've got a feeling that I should go up and have a word with him. What do you think?'

'You mean tell him about Tony and – and Mrs Schofield?'

'What do you think?'

Mary Ann looked down at the rumpled bed-clothes, and she pulled her legs up under her and shook her head before answering, 'I don't know. When Tony does come in there'll be a dreadful row, because now, having to explain . . . well, he'll likely blurt it out.'

'Yes, that's what I was thinking. I was thinking an' all it wouldn't be a bad idea if it was to come from you.'

'Me, Da! Me tell him about them?'

'Yes. I don't think the shock would be half as great. You see, Tony will lose his temper, but you won't, not on this occasion.' He smiled at her. 'And although the old man will be worked up he won't be aggravated, and by the time Tony does get in he'll likely have got the matter settled in his own mind. He won't be less furious. I'm not looking forward to seeing him when he hears the news from either you or Tony but I think it's likely to have less of a bad effect if you tell him.'

Mary Ann looked towards the window as she said, 'When, Da?'

'Well, what about now? Do you feel like getting up?'

'Yes, Da. I'll be down in five minutes.'

'Don't make a noise. I don't want your mother disturbed. She won't take this matter much lighter than the old man, you know.'

'I know, Da.'

Bending swiftly, Mike kissed Mary Ann on the side of the cheek. It was an unusual gesture. Their deep love and understanding for each other did not show itself in demonstration, other than the clasping of hands. And when the door had closed on her father, Mary Ann had a desire to start to cry all over again, even more heart-brokenly than she had done last night, but instead she grabbed angrily at each garment as she got into her clothes . . .

Ben let them in, it was as if he had been waiting for them. 'He's in the drawing-room,' he said.

If the business of coming to the house at this hour wasn't odd enough, Mr Lord too seemed to be expecting them, for he showed not the least surprise when Mike, gently pushing Mary Ann before him, went past Ben, who was holding open the door, and into the room.

Mary Ann looked towards Mr Lord sitting in a chair to the side of the big open fireplace, with the fire roaring away up the chimney. And for all the heat of the room, she felt as cold as Mr Lord looked.

'Sit down, Shaughnessy.'

Mr Lord did not appear to notice Mary Ann as he addressed himself to Mike. 'Do you happen to know where my grandson spent the night? Don't tell me, please.' The old man lifted up a tired-looking hand. 'Don't tell me that you think he has been to a party, or a dance. He is no dancer, and not given to all-night parties. I happen to know the friends he has do not go in for all-night parties.'

'It's a pity, sir. Perhaps it would have been better if he had picked friends who did go in for all-night parties.' Mike did not end as he was thinking, 'You've made a rod for your own back.'

'What are you telling me, Shaughnessy? That he has gone off the rails and that it is my fault? . . . And I think it would have been better had you come alone.' Mr Lord was still ignoring Mary Ann's presence even as he spoke of her.

'I don't think so, sir. Mary Ann, we all seem to forget, is no longer a little girl, and this business concerns her more than any of us. Next to you, she, I should imagine, is the most concerned.' Mike knew he wasn't actually speaking the truth here. Next to the old man it would be Lizzie who would be most concerned about the failure of the plans for Mary Ann's future. And he ended, 'And as she's known what has been going on while all the rest of us were in the dark, I think it had better come from her.'

For the first time since she came into the room, Mr Lord looked at Mary Ann. He looked so frail, so tired, that pity for him mounting in her obliterated all other feeling at the moment. Only his eyes indicated the vitality still in him.

'Well! What have you to tell me, Mary Ann?'

She did not know how to start. There seemed no way to lead up to this business. Even as she searched frantically in her mind, none came to her.

Mike gave her arm a gentle squeeze, saying, 'Go on, tell it in your own way.'

Someone began to talk. Mary Ann didn't feel it was her voice. It had a cracked sound, yet was unhesitant, and she heard it say, 'You like Mrs Schofield, Mr Lord?'

'Mrs Schofield? Yes. Yes, I like Mrs Schofield. What about her?'

'Only that Tony and Mrs Schofield have been seeing a lot of each other this past year.'

Mr Lord's face seemed to close. It had looked tight and drawn before, but now the wrinkled flesh converged towards the point of his nose and became white. The whiteness spread over the nostrils and around the blue-lipped mouth.

The voice that still didn't sound like her own, went on, 'It was one Saturday when I went to see Janice . . . Janice Schofield, and as we knocked on the door there was shouting, and we saw through the window Mr Schofield hitting Mrs Schofield . . . It was from then.'

She watched the tremor pass over the old man's body, right from the lips, over his shoulders, down the legs right into the hand-made shoes. But whatever emotion Mr Lord was feeling he was going to great lengths at this moment to control it. Now his lower jaw began to move slowly back and forward, and she could hear the sound of his dentures grinding against each other in passing. Her father's voice broke in quietly, 'These things happen, sir, unavoidably . . . unaccountably . . . for no reason whatever. People don't want them to happen, but they happen . . . Mrs Schofield's a nice woman.'

'Mrs Schofield is a married woman.'

The words came from Mr Lord's closed lips as if they were indented on a thin strip of steel.

'She got her divorce a few weeks ago, sir.'

'She is still a married woman.'

My God! Mike closed his eyes for a moment. The old man wasn't speaking from any religious bias. He had no God, not to Mike's knowledge anyway, yet in this day and age he could be narrow enough still to discredit divorce.

'Moreover she is a woman years his senior.'

'She doesn't look it, sir.'

'He won't marry her, I'll see to that.' With what seemed a great effort the old man pulled himself up in the chair until his spine was pressed tightly against the back.

'You can't stop him.' It was Mary Ann speaking now. 'He loves her. He loves her very much.'

'What are you talking about, child? What do you know about love?'

'I know that Tony loves Mrs Schofield.' Mary Ann had stepped a small step away from Mike and towards Mr Lord as she spoke. She could recognise her own voice now. She felt that the worst was over, he wasn't going to have a heart attack, not yet anyway. 'Mrs Schofield's a nice woman. She'll be better for him than I would have been. Tony never loved me and I didn't love him, not in that way.'

'She's a silly, feather-brained woman.'

'Now, sir.' Mike was smiling. 'You know that isn't true. You know yourself you found a depth in her that couldn't be hidden by that airy-fairy manner. If I might suggest, sir, it would be a good thing if you would accept the situa—'

'Be quiet, Shaughnessy! I will accept no such situation.' Now Mr Lord did look as if he could be on the point of a heart attack. His turkey-like neck was stretching out of his collar and his head was wagging with such speed that it looked as if it could spiral itself up and off. 'Accept the situation! I tell you this much. He will come into this house just once more, and that to get the little that belongs to him, and that will be the end. I want to see him, or hear of him, no more . . . Accept the situation! What do you think I am? He has been out all night . . .' Mr Lord flicked his eyes towards Mary Ann then back to Mike. 'I want to speak to you alone for a few minutes.'

Mary Ann looked at her da, and when he gave a nod of his head she went slowly from the room and into the hall, there to see Ben standing.

'He's all right? He's not bad?'

'No.'

'He didn't have an attack of any sort?'

'Only temper, Ben.' Mary Ann touched Ben's sleeve. 'Don't worry, he's all right. At least until Tony comes. What will happen then . . .' She shook her head.

'Is it true what you said in there about Master Tony and Mrs Schofield?'

'Yes, Ben.'

'God above! I knew there was something on. I felt once or twice that he wanted to speak to me but was afraid to in case I told the Master. He needn't have worried . . . I wouldn't be the one to kill him off.'

'Well, it hasn't killed him off, Ben. We can be thankful for that.'

'Yes, but as you said, not yet. Wait until the young one comes in . . . I'll make some strong coffee and lace it.'

He turned like a busy old woman and shambled towards the kitchen, and Mary Ann went towards the long window that looked on to the garden. The curtains had not been drawn and she looked up into the still dark, deep, frost-laden sky. Well, part of it was over. She knew why Mr Lord wanted her out of the room, he wanted to talk about Tony, and where he had been all night. He needn't have worried about shocking her. She knew Tony had been with Mrs Schofield. Married or not, they had been together. As she turned from the window and walked across the hall towards the kitchen she felt old, very old. She seemed in this moment to know all about life, and it wasn't a nice feeling. She had thought that no matter what happened to her in her life, whatever sadness came into it, she would still have the desire to go on breathing . . . living. And oddly enough it wasn't the fact that she had lost Corny . . . and Tony, that made her for a moment lose this desire but the cause of her having been sent out of the room. This was what momentarily dampened the desire for existence. This thing wasn't nice. This thing that you read about in the papers. This thing that the girls at the Typing School nattered over, and giggled over. This thing that made you turn on yourself at times and say,

'Be your age. Remember Janice Schofield had to get married because she was going to have a baby. And there are girls at the school who don't go home until four o'clock in the morning. And another is going with a man nearly fifty; and people think nothing of it.'

In the kitchen Ben was pouring a glass of brandy into a cup of black coffee. It was as he picked the cup up that they heard the car come into the courtyard, and at the moment Tony entered the kitchen Mike came in from the hallway.

Tony stood with the door in his hand looking from one to the other. Then in a voice that sounded remarkably like Mr Lord's when about to mount his high horse, he said, 'He's back then?'

This wasn't a question, it was a statement, but Mike answered, 'Yes, last night, early evening.'

'Trust him . . . And now I'm to be chastised like a naughty little boy for being out all night. Is that it, eh?'

'I think it's a bit more than that, Tony.' Mike's voice was low. 'Mary Ann, on my advice I might say, broke the news to him. I thought it would come easier on him from her than from you.'

Now there was a stong resemblance to Mr Lord as Tony looked at Mike and said, 'You shouldn't have done that, Mike, that was my business.'

'Aye, it might have been, but I know what the pair of you are like when you get going. I didn't want you to have anything more on your conscience.' Mike's voice too had taken on a cold note. 'If he had collapsed on you I doubt whether you would have felt so determined to go through with this business of yours.'

'Nothing would have stopped me going through with . . . this business of mine, as you call it. And it's because it happens to be my business that I prefer to look after it.'

Mary Ann's eyes, dark and large, were flicking now between her father and Tony. Things were taking a tangent she had never imagined possible. Her da and Tony were on the verge of a row. Her da liked Tony, and Tony liked her da, but there was a bitterness between them now, she could feel it. Her da might subdue himself to Mr Lord out of respect for the old man's age and because, deep down, he was grateful to him, but she was sure he did not have the same feeling towards Tony. Tony had come to the farm as a boy, a student, out to learn. That he was Mr Lord's grandson made no difference, he was still an ordinary young fellow in her da's eyes. There were very few people whom her da would knuckle under to, and Tony was taking the wrong tack if he was going to try to put her da in his place. To deflect their attention from each other, she said sharply, 'I had made up my mind, Tony, to tell him in any case, because, what you seem to forget at this moment is that I am concerned in this affair. Not that I want to be. And I don't think I was minding anyone else's business but my own when I explained to him that his plans hadn't worked out. What's more, I didn't want to see him drop down dead when you blurted this—'

'Don't worry, Mary Ann.' The voice came from the half-closed door in front of which Mike was standing, and they all swung round as

Mr Lord came through into the kitchen.

'. . . don't worry, I've no intention of dropping down dead.'

Mary Ann looked at the tight face. The skin had that awful bluish hue, right from the white hair line to where his neck disappeared into his collar.

The old man turned his gaze now from Mary Ann, and although his eyes were directed towards his grandson they did not look at him, but at some point above the top of his head, as he said, 'I'm not expecting any explanation from you, nor have I any intention of listening to one. I would be obliged if you would make your departure as quick as possible.'

Tony's chin was up and out, but nevertheless it was trembling. 'You needn't worry, this is one time I'll be pleased to obey you. But whether you want any explanation or not, I'm going to tell you that I haven't spent the night with Mrs Schofield. She happens to be in London. You can confirm that if you like.'

'I'm not interested in your activities, nor in the people you choose to share them with.' Mr Lord's eyes came down from the space above Tony's head, and looking at Ben he said, 'As soon as our visitors have gone you might lock up. I think we need a little rest.'

As his thin body turned stiffly towards the hall door again, his glance came to rest on Mike. His expression did not alter, nor yet his tone, as he said, 'Thank you, Shaughnessy.' He did not look at Mary Ann.

When the door closed on him, Mary Ann, Mike and Ben turned towards Tony. Whereas Mr

Lord's face had been of a blue hue, Tony's was scarlet. He was shaking, and this was evident to them all when he turned to Mary Ann and there was deep bitterness in his voice as he said, 'You see, it'll take a lot to make him drop down dead. He's tough, and he glories in it. You have to live with him just to know how tough he is. He's—'

Ben's quivering lips were open to make a protest when Mike put in sharply, 'Don't say anything you'll be sorry for later, Tony, because then you'll remember he's always been good to you . . . I would say more than good. You can't blame him for wanting his own way. We all do. You particularly. And you've gone your way, so don't blame him.'

'You definitely know which side you're on, don't you?' Tony's voice was as furious as his glance.

Mike's tone threatened fire too, with the retort, 'Look here! I'm only being fair. You know my feeling about the old fellow, and I damn well toady to no-one, so be careful. But if you want my opinion – and you don't – I'll say you've got off pretty lightly with this business. What did you expect him to do? Greet you and her with open arms?'

For a moment longer Tony returned Mike's glare, then with a swift movement his head drooped sideways and, his teeth digging into his lower lip, he stared at the floor. Then with a muttered, 'Oh, hell!' he thrust himself out of the room.

Mike walked to where Mary Ann stood near the table, and turning her about, he led her to the door, saying grimly, 'So long, Ben.'

'Goodbye, Mr Shaughnessy.'

Mary Ann did not speak. She did not speak as they went down the hill and across the farmyard. Nor did she speak when she entered the kitchen, but she flung herself into a chair and, burying her face in her arms, burst into a storm of weeping.

As the sound of Tony's car breaknecking down the lane into the main road came to them, Lizzie pushed open the kitchen door, her eyes blinking with sleep, as she exclaimed, 'What on earth's the matter?'

'You'll know soon enough,' said Mike. 'But I think we'd all better have a strong cup of tea first.' On this, he lifted up the kettle from the hob and went into the scullery. And Lizzie, bending over Mary Ann, said, 'Stop it, stop that crying and tell me what's the matter now, and at this time in the morning. What is it?'

'Tony . . . Tony's lea . . . ving. He's going to marry Mrs Schofield.'

Lizzie straightened her back. Her mouth was open and her gaze directed to where Mike was coming in from the scullery, but she could only stare at him, she could not speak.

8

The Typing School term had ended and Mary Ann
had received a diploma for her speed at typing
and a certificate for her shorthand. Moreover, she
had written her first short story, but she knew
that no magazine would print it, because it was
much too sad, and too long. Also she realised,
from what she had read about short-story writing,
that it lacked two main essentials: a plot and a
twist. Her story was just about people and the sad
things they did. She could not write about the
reverse side of life, for at the moment she could
not see it.

There had been no word at all from Corny since
Mr Lord had come back. Mrs McBride would
undoubtedly have heard from him. But in spite of
her promise to go and visit his grannie, Mary Ann
had not been near Burton Street for some weeks.
Mrs McBride, she knew, would have been kind.
She would likely have laughed the whole thing
off, and the louder she laughed the more awful,
Mary Ann knew, it would have been. She couldn't
risk it. Nor had Lizzie been near her old friend,
but she had sent a parcel now and again and
had received a card in Fanny's almost illegible

handwriting to say, thank you. Neither of the women mentioned Corny . . . or Mary Ann.

So many things were adding to the sadness of life for Mary Ann at the present moment. Her mother, for instance. Her mother had taken the news of Tony much better than she had expected. At least, that was, at the time, that early morning in the kitchen. But as the days went on there seemed to settle on her the lassitude of defeat, and this quietness spoke of her disappointment louder than any words. Mary Ann thought that if it hadn't been for Sarah's presence in the house, which strangely enough had a brightening effect on them all, the place would have been more dismal than a cemetery.

If Mary Ann could have measured her own feelings, she would have found that her sadness, which was balanced between Corny and Mr Lord, tipped not a little towards Mr Lord. Although the shindy on that particular early morning had not caused him to have a heart attack, it seemed to have brought him up-to-date with his age, for suddenly he was a very old man. The vitality that had suggested youthful vigour was gone. So much so, that he had been into town only twice during the last month. As Mike had said macabrely, 'The house was like an open grave, with him lying in it just waiting to be covered up.'

Mary Ann left the warmth of the kitchen and the Christmas smell. She left Sarah sitting in her wheel-chair close up to the table, happily helping Lizzie with the Christmas cooking. Getting her hand in, as she laughingly said, for when she would have to do it herself. Sarah had become very close to Lizzie during these past few weeks and this had aroused just a tiny bit of jealousy in Mary Ann, although she saw that the urge to be close came from Sarah. Lizzie made no effusive return of affection, but Mary Ann knew that her mother was pleased with Sarah's gratitude; moreover, she liked Sarah. With the wisdom that was an integral part of her, Mary Ann realised, despite her own feelings, that this state of affairs was really all to the good, because Sarah was going to need her mother in the future, more than she herself would.

She pulled the coat collar around her ears as she went up the hill towards the house. It would snow before the morning, she could feel it. Like most northerners, she could smell snow coming.

Her breath was rising before her face in clouds when she entered Ben's kitchen. Ben was setting the tea-tray with old-fashioned silver that was polished to reflection standard. Mary Ann smiled at him as she took off her coat, saying, 'There'll be snow before morning.'

'We don't want that.'

Mary Ann looked towards the Aga cooker and said, 'Is the tea made? I'll take it in.'

'You'll do no such thing.' Ben hadn't even looked at her. He was going about his duties as if she wasn't there. But that didn't affect her, for she knew he was always glad when she came up. One day lately she hadn't paid her usual visit and he had trudged all the way down the hill to find out why. He hadn't seemed satisfied that having a tooth out was sufficient reason for her not coming up to see his master. Ben, too, seemed to have aged in the past few weeks. He had always appeared to Mary Ann as a very old man, half as old again as Mr Lord, but now the word ancient was more appropriate to him. She said impetuously, 'Don't be silly. I'll carry it in.'

'When I'm not able to carry the tea-tray in, then you can do so with pleasure. And I won't mind, for I won't be here.'

She gave in and said, 'How is he?'

'Just the same. Very cold. I doubt if that coal will see us over the holidays. We should have had another ton in.'

'Oh, there's plenty of wood down in the shed. I'll get Len to bring some up.'

She tapped on the drawing-room door and without waiting for an answer went into the room. In contrast to the outside atmosphere the room was stifling. There, before the fire, almost lost in the huge armchair, sat Mr Lord. He turned his face towards her as she came across the room, but did not speak. She sat down in the chair at the other side of the fireplace. She did not say 'How are you?' or 'We'll have snow by the morning,' but sighed and leant back in the depth of the chair. Then after a few moments she said, 'I've just finished a short story.'

He nodded his head at her. 'What about?' His voice was just a mumble.

'Oh, I don't know . . .'

For a moment he seemed to come out of his cocoon, and a tiny spark of the old irritability was visible as he said, 'Don't say such silly things. You say you have written a story, so you are bound to know what it is about.'

She said, 'Well, I meant to say that it wasn't the right way to write a short story, there are too many people in it doing too many things.'

He said now with a show of interest that caused

her to move in the chair, 'You must bring it and read it to me.'

'Oh, I couldn't do that.'

'Why? . . . Is it about me?'

'No. Oh, no.' Her denial was too emphatic, and he lifted his hand wearily as if to check any further protest. Now leaning his head back against the wing of the chair and closing his eyes he said, 'What would you like for Christmas?'

What would she like! She knew what she would like. He had taken from her the person she had liked best in the world, apart from her da, and he could give him back to her. For it was in his power to bring Corny tearing across the Atlantic. But she wouldn't want Corny that way, she wouldn't want Corny as a gift from Mr Lord. She didn't want anyone who hadn't a mind of his own. She was going to answer him, 'I don't know,' when Ben entered the room following a tap of the door. But he was not carrying a tea-tray. He came right up to the side of his master's chair and, bending his already stooped back further down, he said gently, 'There's some-one to see you, sir.'

'Who is it?' Mr Lord had not opened his eyes.

'It's a lady, sir.'

'A lady! Which lady? What's her name?'

'She did not give me her name, sir.' This had been quite correct, there was no need for the visitor to give Ben her name. If he hadn't already known it, he would have surely guessed it.

Mr Lord now opened his eyes, and his wrinkled lips flickered as he said, 'I don't have to tell you that I'm not seeing anyone, lady or gentleman. Why have you . . . ?'

There was a movement in the room, and as Mary Ann brought her head from the cover of the wing, she almost gasped to see Mrs Schofield standing well inside the drawing-room. With a wriggle and a lift, she was on her feet, apprehension showing in every part of her.

Mr Lord had his eyes on Mary Ann, and now he slowly moved his body in the chair, bringing it round so that he was looking squarely at Ben. Then his eyes, flicking to the side, came to rest on Mrs Schofield, where they stayed a moment before returning to Ben. His voice was louder than Mary Ann had heard it for a long time when he said, 'I have no desire to see this lady, Ben. Kindly show her out.'

'I know you don't want to see me, Mr Lord, but I must see you.' Mrs Schofield's voice was low, but her words came slow and distinct.

'You heard what I said, Ben.'

Ben turned away, but he did not go to the door and hold it open for Mrs Schofield. He passed her and went out and closed the door after him, and the action brought a flow of blood to Mr Lord's deathly complexion.

Mary Ann now brought a chair towards Mrs Schofield, and Mrs Schofield looked at her, and thanked her, as if she had brought her some precious gift.

'I do not wish you to sit down, madam.' Mr Lord was not looking at Mrs Schofield but directly ahead, and now Mary Ann, coming to the side of the chair, surprised even herself, with not only her tone, but her words as she said, 'Don't be so silly.'

Mr Lord's Adam's apple moved up into the

hollow under his chin, stayed there for a second, then slid down to the deeper hollow at the base of his neck.

Mary Ann said, 'I'm going now . . . Listen to her . . . listen to Mrs Schofield. There can be no harm in listening.'

'Sit down.'

'But I'm—'

'I said sit down.'

Mary Ann, turning from the chair, sent an apologetic glance towards Mrs Schofield, then sat down.

After a moment of an uneasy silence she looked towards the older woman, and her first thought was, 'By, she's beautiful!' and then, 'She's not old.'

Mrs Schofield was staring at the averted profile of the old man, and her lip was trembling, just the slightest as she began to speak.

'I – I haven't come to plead my cause. I am not going to marry your grandson, Mr Lord.'

Mary Ann's eyebrows sprang upwards, drawing the contours of her face with them. She transferred her wide gaze to Mr Lord, but his expression had not altered in the slightest.

'I – I intended to marry him when my divorce was made absolute, but since he left you I have realised that should I marry him I would have to combat you for the remainder of my life.'

Now there was a movement in the old man's face. For a moment Mary Ann felt he was going to turn his glance on Mrs Schofield and it would have been one of inquiry. But when his nostrils stopped twitching he remained immobile.

'My married history will, I am sure, be of no

concern to you, but I have been combating forces, seen and unseen, for the past seventeen years. And I am tired, Mr Lord, very tired. I am tired of putting on a front. I have acquired a deep feeling for Tony, but it isn't strong enough to enable me to take up my life with him, knowing that you will be always there in the background of his mind, and whether he would believe it or not, he would be blaming me for having separated him from you. I have started by telling you this, but it isn't the only reason for my visit. Nor is it, I think, the real reason, for I didn't come with any hope that you would relent and give us your blessing. I came . . . I came because Tony has had an offer from Brent and Hapwood. Since they heard about his break with you they have been after him. They have even offered him a place on the board, so badly do they want him.'

Even before Mrs Schofield had finished speaking, Mr Lord's body had turned towards her. Slowly, as if on an oiled pivot, he brought himself round to face her. And then he spoke. 'Hapwood,' he said under his breath. 'Hapwood? Why do you think they want him? Do you know why they want him? . . . They want him because they imagine I will relent and leave him everything. There is nobody else I can leave the yard to, is there? And so I will relent . . . Old Lord wouldn't leave his money to a Dogs' Home or Spastic Children. No of course he wouldn't. He's only got one kin and he's too fond of him not to relent. That's the idea, isn't it? And when I'm gone – which won't be long they hope – they will be able to amalgamate Lord's yard with their fiddling, little-finger-in-every-pie industry. Well, you can tell him and them that I have no intention whatever of relenting. So if they are going to employ him it better be for his work alone.'

There was a pause before Mrs Schofield said, 'It may be difficult for you to believe, Mr Lord, but I am convinced that Tony does not want your money. But he must live, he must work. He doesn't want to go to Brents, he – he wants to come back to you.'

Her voice had sunk to a whisper and Mr Lord continued to stare at her for a long moment before saying, 'Then why, madam, may I ask, had he to send you as his advocate?'

'He didn't send me. He doesn't know I'm here. Nor would he admit to me that he wanted to come back. But I happen to know him.'

'Your acquaintance has ripened in a very short time.'

'I think you can live with some people for twenty years and know nothing at all about them. Well, there it is, Mr Lord, if I drop out of his life will you have him back? Make – make the first gesture.'

'Make the first gesture!' Mr Lord's eyes looked like small pale-blue beads. 'No, madam, I will make no gestures whatever. I didn't bring about this state of affairs, it was he who did that. Whatever gestures are to take place they must come from him. If he is sorry for deceiving me, and is man enough to say so, then I hope I will be man enough to listen.'

On this pompous statement Mary Ann closed her eyes. Tony was too much of his grandfather ever to admit openly that he was in the wrong. She could not envisage him coming to this house and saying, 'I am sorry, please forgive me.' But it was not so much Tony she was concerned about at the moment, it was Mrs Schofield. She wanted to cry for Mrs Schofield. With the impetuousness of her emotional make-up she wanted to fly the few steps to her and comfort her, to put her arms around her, and bring her head down to rest on her shoulder. She felt that if anyone needed comfort at this moment it was Mrs Schofield. She was sitting there, looking so humble, sad, sweet and painfully humble. If she went to her she knew she would say, 'Oh, don't look like that, he won't thank you for it. He knows nothing of humility, you've got to stand up to him.'

In the next momement Mr Lord brought her attention away from Mrs Schofield, and, listening to him, it seemed that he had regained a spark of his old self, for picking up a point that Mrs Schofield had made earlier he said, 'You decided before you came here that you weren't going to marry my grandson?'

'Yes. Yes, I came to that decision.'

'Because you thought his conscience would be an irritant to you?'

'If you like to put it like that.' Her voice was so low her words were scarcely audible.

'Taking the supposition that he might some day return, what then?'

'I'll give you my word, I won't marry him.'

Mary Ann was sitting right on the edge of the chair. With intent concentration she was watching Mr Lord. She could almost see his mind at work. Tony back in the fold, Mrs Schofield's promise to which she would hold, making the way clear – Tony would be in the market for herself again.

'No. No.' The protest was so loud in her head that it burst from her mouth, startling both Mr Lord and Mrs Schofield. But it was to the old man that she addressed herself, and without any finesse. 'I'll never marry Tony. Don't think that if he were to come back things would go as you want, because if there had never been Corny I wouldn't have married Tony, because I don't like him enough to marry him. Nor he me. He never wanted to marry me, so don't get that into your head.'

'Mary Ann.'

Definitely it was the tone of the old Mr Lord, the Mr Lord who would brook little or no interference. But for the moment she was past caring. She was standing up now and their heads were on a level. She had regained her breath and her next words caused him to close his eyes, for she was speaking in the idiom that was natural to her, and claimed no connection with her convent education. 'Now look here, an' I'm tellin' you, if Tony comes back an' he doesn't marry Mrs Schofield, then I'll leave home. I can, you know . . . if I made up me mind. If there's a good enough reason me ma or da wouldn't stop me, I know that. Not if I went to live with Mrs McBride, an' that's where I would go, an' . . .'

'Be quiet!' Mr Lord still had his eyes closed, and he repeated in what was nearly a growl, 'Be quiet!'

Mary Ann became quiet. The room became quiet. There was no sound, not even of hissing from the fire, until a knock came on the door and, following it, Ben entered, pushing a trolley noiselessly over the thick carpet. As Mary Ann turned towards him she knew that he had been standing outside the door listening, and must have felt that this was the strategical point at which to make his entry.

Mr Lord looked towards Ben and the moving trolley, but he made no comment. Slowly he turned his body away from both Mary Ann and Mrs Schofield, and sinking back into the big chair he directed his gaze towards the fire.

Ben now moved the trolley close to the side of Mrs Schofield's chair, and his action, and words, startled not only her, but Mary Ann, so much so that she waited for Mr Lord's thunderous countenance to be turned on his servant and to hear his voice blasting him out of the room. For Ben said, 'Would you care to pour out, madam?'

Ben's voice was not low, nor was it loud. It was just clear enough to make sure that his master heard it, and in hearing, would know his servant's opinion on this delicate matter.

And Ben's opinion, Mary Ann knew, was conveyed to Mr Lord as clearly as if he had shouted 'I'm for her.' And not only that, Mary Ann saw that Ben's deferential attitude, as he arranged cups to Mrs Schofield's hand, also said clearly that she was a woman he wouldn't mind having about the house. Mrs Schofield might not be able to read this from the old man's attentiveness but she could, and, what was more, Mr Lord could.

When the door closed on Ben, Mrs Schofield looked appealingly at Mary Ann, then flicked her eyes towards the figure in the big wing chair. All Mary Ann did was to nod. It was an encouraging nod which said, Get on with it.

The cups rattled slightly as Mrs Schofield

poured out the tea. Mary Ann took Mr Lord's cup, putting in the required amount of sugar, before placing it on the little table to the side of him.

It could not be said that any one of them enjoyed the tea, and no-one partook of the hot buttered scones.

Mrs Schofield had scarcely finished her tea before she gathered her gloves and bag towards her and, standing up abruptly, said, 'Goodbye, Mr Lord.'

It was evident to Mary Ann that her quick departure had nonplussed him, for she saw his lower jaw working agitatedly. But he did not answer Mrs Schofield until he heard the door open, and then moving only his head, he said, 'Madam.'

'Yes?' She had the door in her hand and she turned and looked at him.

'Thank you for coming.'

Mrs Schofield made no answer to this, she merely inclined her head just the slightest, then went out and closed the door softly behind her.

Mary Ann could not see the door because the tears were full in her eyes. She could not even see Mr Lord, but she spoke to him, saying quietly, 'She's nice. Tony will never get anyone nicer than her. You're being very wrong in stopping them.'

'I am not stopping them.'

'You can say that, but you know you are. She'll make Tony come back, she'll promise him this, that, and the other, so that he'll come back. As soon as he does, she'll go off where he can't find her.'

The tears cleared from her blinking eyes for

a second as his voice came to her with the old cutting quality, saying, 'I would keep your romantic fiction for the books you intend to write.' For a moment she could have laughed, but only for a moment.

He said, now, 'Stop crying and come here.'

She went to him and stood by the arm of his chair, and his thin, mottled-skinned, bony fingers touched hers lightly as he said, 'Were you telling me the truth when you said that you didn't care enough for Tony to marry him?'

'Yes, the absolute truth. Nothing would make me marry Tony. You sent Corny away because you thought if I didn't see him, I would turn to Tony, didn't you?' She didn't wait for an answer but went on, 'You see, you cannot make people like people . . . or love people, or turn liking into love. Tony and I . . . well, we like each other, but that's all, we'd never be able to love each other. But he loves Mrs Schofield, and if you don't let him have her, he'll likely marry somebody eventually who's entirely opposite to him and who'll drive him round the bend.' She just restrained herself from adding, 'Like you were when you married somebody who didn't suit you.'

'Mary Ann.' His voice cut in on her.

'Yes?'

'I'm very tired.' He withdrew his hand from hers and slumped back into the chair. Then looking at her, he said, 'Would you like to tell Ben I want him?'

This was dismissal, and she nodded at him. Then bending forward she laid her lips against the blue cheek. When she straightened up his eyes were closed again, and she put her fingers gently on to his brow and lifted to the side a wisp of thin white hair, saying, 'You'll sleep better tonight. I'll be over first thing in the morning.'

When she reached the hall Ben was waiting, and she said to him, 'He's tired, Ben.'

'I guess he would be.' He moved past her towards the drawing-room door, then turning his bent shoulders round towards her, and beckoning her with a finger as bony as his master's, he whispered, 'Here, a minute.' And when she came to his side his head nodded with each word, as he muttered, 'If you see Master Tony tell him Ben says he liked madam.' And then he gave her the reason for his swift and open championing of Mrs Schofield. 'There's no telling, I might go before he does, and what then?'

'Oh, Ben! You're going to live a long time yet.' She smiled at him. 'But I'll tell him what you said, Ben. I know it will please him.'

But as she went out of the house she thought dully, 'How can I? I don't even know where he is, or even where Mrs Schofield is staying.' And as she went down the hill she chided herself for her lack of inquisitiveness in this particular case by saying, 'You are a mutt. Why didn't you go after her and ask her?'

9

Early in the morning of Christmas Eve Mary Ann brought her mother to a dead stop as she was crossing the kitchen. She said to her, 'Ma, what am I going to do with me life?'

'What?' Lizzie had heard what her daughter had said. But this was Christmas Eve, and a mountain of work staring her in the face. It was no time to discuss life, particularly Mary Ann's life.

Mary Ann, aware that her mother had heard her remark, went on, 'I'll never be able to write, not to make anything of it. Everything I do reads like rubbish, and I don't want to go into an office . . . not stuck indoors all day.'

'Look,' said Lizzie slowly, 'it's Christmas, and me up to my eyes.'

'Well, I don't feel it's Christmas,' said Mary Ann bluntly.

'You mightn't,' said Lizzie. 'It may surprise you that I don't feel it's Christmas either. But there are other people to consider; and when you are grumbling about your future life just remember you've still got the use of your legs.'

'Oh, Ma, that isn't fair.'

Lizzie, coming towards her daughter, now said softly, 'Look, Mary Ann, you've got to snap out of this; what can't be cured must be endured.'

'It isn't only me, Ma.' Mary Ann was looking at her feet. 'It's everybody. Nobody seems right.'

'That's life, and you'll find you've got to accept it. You never used to go on like this. What's really the matter with you?'

Mary Ann lifted her head and stared back at her mother, until Lizzie turned away sharply, saying, 'Well, I've just got no time to bother with you and your fads.' But as she neared the hall door she looked over her shoulder, and said quietly and patiently, 'Why don't you go down and see Mrs McBride. We can't get at the decorating until after tea, and Sarah is going to help with the last bit of baking this afternoon.'

'I'm not going to Mrs McBride's.'

'Very well.' Lizzie closed her eyes and lowered her head in a deep abeyance, and the irritation was back in her voice as she said, 'Do what you want to, only don't go round with a face like that, because when you're like that, he's not far behind.'

Mary Ann looked at the closed door. It was true what her mother said. Her da too wasn't particularly joyful these days. Although he didn't say so, she felt that he was concerned about Mr Lord, and not only him, but Tony. He had parted in anger from Tony, and her da wasn't the one to hold his anger. But he had been unable to do anything about it, because from the morning Tony left the house no-one had seen or heard of him since.

With what she felt was righteous indignation,

Mary Ann asked herself now how her mother expected her to go about grinning from ear to ear when everybody was at sixes and sevens. And anyway, if the rest of the family were falling on each other's necks, she would still feel the same. She had not had the scribe of a pen from Corny, and threaded through her longing, and hurt, was a strong feeling of bitterness against him. He could have written her, couldn't he, and told her he wasn't coming back, not left it to those pictures, which he knew Mr Lord would show her. It was a cowardly way out, and she had no use for cowards of any sort . . . But oh! oh, she wished . . .

She heard the telephone ringing in the hall and her mother answering it. Then the kitchen door opened and Lizzie, her tone lowered and slightly puzzled, said, 'It's Ben, he says Mr Lord's asking for you . . . But you've just come down, haven't you.'

'Asking for me? Yes, Ma. I've just come down because he wasn't awake. Ben said he was dozing. He had been on the prowl about the house half the night again.'

'Well, he wants you, so you'd better go right away.'

'Did he say he was bad or anything?'

'No. No, he didn't sound worried. He just said that Mr Lord wanted you.' Lizzie smiled now. 'Very likely he's going to give you your Christmas box.'

Mary Ann raised her eyebrows and widened her eyes as she shook her head. It was as if she had never heard of Christmas boxes. And truth to tell, she was not interested in Christmas boxes, not the ordinary ones anyway. She pulled on her coat and went out, and she didn't slide on the thin patches of ice covering the flagstones, along the path, nor yet scrape the sprinkling of frosted snow into a ball and pelt it into the air. The joy of breathing, of being alive, had slipped its hold; she felt very old. And she had once imagined that nothing could happen to her to make her want to die. How wrong could you get?

Ben said, 'Go up. He's still in bed.'

'Is he all right?'

'No different from what he was yesterday, or the day before, as I can see.'

She mounted the thick carpeted stairs, crossed the wide landing and tapped on Mr Lord's bedroom door, and was immediately bidden to enter. He was sitting, as she had so often seen him before, propped up in bed, his white nightshirt buttoned up to his chin, his face, like a blue-pencilled etching, above it.

She said immediately, 'Are you all right?'

'Yes. Yes, I'm all right. Sit down.'

'Did you have a good night?'

'I have had some sleep.'

'I think we'll have more snow, it's enough to freeze you.'

'We won't waste words talking about the weather. You're wondering why I sent for you.'

'Yes, I am.' She could be as blunt as himself.

'I'm very tired, Mary Ann.'

Although she was looking at him she jerked her body now more squarely to him. 'You're not feeling . . . bad, or anything?'

'I'm no worse, or no better, than usual. I've just said that I am very tired. Tired of fighting, tired of wanting, tired of desiring, tired of hoping. I am very tired of life, Mary Ann.'

'Oh.' It was a small sound and again it came, 'Oh.' She knew how he felt but she said, 'Don't say that.' She reached out and grasped his hand between her own, and he looked down at them, and placing the long thin fingers of his right hand on top of hers he actually smiled as he asked, 'Are you happy, Mary Ann?'

She stared into the pale-blue eyes for a moment before saying, 'Not very.'

'I have been rather cruel to you. What I did, I did with the best intention in the world . . . Selfish men always use that phrase, and I can't think of a better one to replace it . . . Yes, I have been cruel to you.' His fingers tapped hers. 'And now I doubt whether I shall be able to rectify my mistake. You know what I mean?'

She knew what he meant. He had sent Corny to America. He had had him housed with a charming family, and the charming family had a daughter. Oh, she knew what he meant. But she said now soothingly, 'It's all right, it's all right. Don't worry.'

His fingers patted her hand again and he lay back on his pillows and closed his eyes, and after a space he said, 'You have a big heart, Mary Ann. It was bigger than your body when you were a child. It hasn't grown any less, that is why I love you.'

She nipped at her lip and blinked her eyes but kept looking at him. Never before had he said outright that he loved her. She had the desire to drop her head on to his knees, but she refrained because he wasn't finished, there was something more he wanted to say. And after a short space, during which he kept moistening his lips, he said it.

'I want to see my grandson, Mary Ann. I have waited for him coming, forgetting that he is so much a part of me he won't give in. If there had been only himself to consider perhaps he might have come back . . . But there . . . there . . . Will you tell him, Mary Ann?'

'Yes, oh yes.' The words had to leap over the lump wedging her gullet, and now she dared to say, 'And Mrs Schofield?'

'With or without her.'

The words were so low she could scarcely catch them, but she squeezed his hand tightly, and getting immediately to her feet she bent towards him, saying, 'I'll bring him.'

He did not open his eyes. She felt he dare not. He was not Mr Lord at this moment, not THE MR LORD. He was just an old man, a lonely old man, and he was weak as old men are weak.

She managed to pause in her rush through the kitchen and cry to Ben, 'He wants me to get Tony.'

'Thanks be to God.'

'Yes . . . yes, thanks be to God.' She was out of the door and running down the hill – she actually slid on a stretch of ice – and her running did not stop until she came to the cowshed and heard Mike's voice calling to Michael at the far end. And then she herself called, 'Da! Da!'

'What is it?' Mike turned about and, seeing her bright face, added, 'Hello, what's happened this time?'

'He . . . he wants to see Tony. He told me to fetch him . . . and Mrs Schofield . . . and Mrs Schofield, Da.'

'No!'

'Yes, yes, it's a fact. He said, Da' – she shook her head – 'he said he was tired.'

'Poor old boy.'

'What's this?' Michael came up and joined them, and Mary Ann said, 'He wants to see Tony. He wants me to go and fetch him. And Mrs Schofield an' all.'

'No kidding?'

'No kidding, that's what he said.'

'Well, what's holding you?'

Mary Ann didn't move, the smile slid from her face. She looked from Mike to Michael then back to Mike again. Her first finger and thumb were jointly tapping at her teeth as she exclaimed on a high note, 'But, Da, where will I look? I've no idea where he is.'

'You've hit something now.' Mike nodded his head at her.

'You could try phoning places, that would be a start,' Michael said. 'Try some of the yards first, he's bound to have a job of some sort.'

'Can I use the office phone, Da?'

'Go ahead.'

Mike pushed her, and she ran out of the byre.

It could be a Dickens Christmas Eve. She did not like to think of Mr Lord as a Scrooge, but part of her mind was commenting, 'It's funny what Christmas does to people.'

By five o'clock Mary Ann had not only made thirteen phone calls, she had been into Newcastle as well. Michael had been going in to pick up some goods from the station, and he had run her out to Mrs Schofield's old home, only to find it completely empty. So empty that it looked as if it hadn't been inhabited for years. They even visited Mr Lord's yard, but the chief clerk in the office could give them no help. He hadn't seen Mr Brown for weeks, but he said that Mr Connelly might be able to help them. Mr Connelly was works manager, and they went to his house, but without success . . .

And now Mary Ann was tired, and Lizzie said to her, 'Sit down there and get your tea, you're not going out again unless you have something to eat. The next thing I know I'll have you in bed.'

It was Sarah who said, 'Have you thought of going to Father Owen?'

'Father Owen?' Mike screwed up his face. 'It isn't likely that Tony would go to the priest; he's not a Catholic, you know, Sarah.'

'I know that, but you did say that Mr Lord and Father Owen used to be friends in their young days. It was just a thought, and Mary Ann seems to have been every place else.'

Mary Ann, jumping at this pleasant possibility, gulped at her tea and said, 'It's an idea, Sarah, there are very few people around that Father Owen doesn't know.'

'That might be in Jarrow and thereabouts' – Lizzie moved her head slowly – 'but don't forget Tony is more likely to be living in Newcastle.' She did not add 'because Mrs Schofield will be there'.

'And don't you think Father Owen would have said something when he was up to see Mr Lord last week?' Lizzie again was using her reason.

'No, Liz. I don't think he would have,' Mike put in. 'He knew how the old boy felt, and he wasn't likely to talk about Tony, even mention his name. He knew that one thing might lead to another, and before you could say Jack Robinson something would be said that would be better unsaid. For he's not without his share of temper, is Father Owen, and whatever some people might imagine to be the reverse, priests are not infallible.'

On this remark Lizzie's expression became prim, and she was just about to make some sharp comment when Mary Ann startled her by jumping up from the table, saying, 'Well, look, I'm going to see him anyway.'

'Sit down and have your tea first.'

'Oh, Ma, the time's getting on and he's been waiting all day . . . Will you run me in, Michael?'

'OK.'

'It will be a wild-goose chase, if you ask me.' Lizzie looked around at the tea – hardly anything had been touched – and Mike, following her gaze, leant towards her and, patting her on the shoulder, said, 'Don't worry, it'll all have disappeared afore the night's out . . . Go on.' He turned towards Mary Ann and Michael, and pushed at them with his hand, saying, 'Get yourselves away. And don't come back without him.'

As Mary Ann ran to the hall once again to scramble into her coat, Lizzie exclaimed on an indignant sigh, 'I get sick to death of this family and the things they get up to . . . always something happening, Christmas Eve and everybody going mad.'

'You want the old boy to go on living, don't you? Or do you?'

'Mike! The things you say.'

'Well then, hold your whisht.'

Michael with head reverently bowed, spoke out of the corner of his mouth, saying, 'We'll be here all night, there's half of Jarrow waiting to go in.'

Mary Ann turned her head slightly on her clasped hands and answered in a whisper, 'I'll go to confession and ask him there.'

Michael made no comment on this. Trust her to do something that other people wouldn't even dream about. Using the corner of his mouth again, he said, 'You'll be a good hour, I'll slip home and come in again.'

She made a slight motion of assent with her head, and when Michael left her side she too rose, and crossing over from the aisle that fronted the altar of the Holy Family, she went and joined the sombre throng waiting to go into Confession.

Father Owen sat in the candlelit gloom of his section of the confessional and waited. Mrs Weir had bad feet, it always took her a long time to shuffle out of the box, and once outside she always meticulously closed the door after her. That it would be pulled open almost instantly seemingly did not occur to her, she must finish the job properly. So she obstructed the next penitent with her overflowing hips. As Father Owen listened to her fumbling with the door, he wondered, rather wearily, how many more were out there. He would like a little quiet and rest before midnight mass, and he was feeling rather cold. Either that boiler chimney was blocked up or Jimmy Snell had gone off again without banking down properly. It was either one or the other. Or perhaps it wasn't, it was more likely the system. He had felt the church cold more than once lately, and it wasn't all due to his old bones. He rested his head on the palm of his hand and wondered if in the beginning of the year he could encourage somebody to start off a subscription jaunt to get a new water system in. If only Father Bailey would come off his high horse about tombola, the thing would be as good as done. But there, he had a very pious bee in his bonnet. If only the bee didn't split hairs. What was the difference in tombola and running raffles at every function he could . . . Oh there, what was the use. Anyway, sooner or later there would be a burst, and if it took place in the pipes under the grid the consequences could be both disastrous and amusing. He had an irreverent picture of one of a number of his more tiresome parishioners being sent heavenwards on a spurting jet of hot water.

'Please, Father, give me your blessing for I have sinned. It is three days since my last confession.'

In the name of God it was Mary Ann. Well! well! well! It was some time since she had been to him for confession. She took herself to Newcastle or Gateshead more often than not now, because they were nearer. Well! well! Christmas Eve and Mary Ann. He felt a spark of gaiety ascending up his cold body, but this was followed immediately by what could only be described as a long question mark which covered him from head to toe, and the question mark said, 'What brought her in? Something's wrong.' Three days since her last confession and here she was again! She was after something . . . oh, he knew Mary Ann.

'Is that you, Mary Ann?'

'Yes, Father.' It was a haloed whisper.

'How are you?'

'I'm not too bad, Father.'

Not too bad. He knew it, he knew there was something wrong. 'How's your da?'

'Oh, he's fine, Father.'

Well, that was the biggest obstacle out of the way. It was usually her da who brought her helter-skelter to the church. At least in the past it was Mike who could have been given the credit for her ardent piety. 'And your mother?'

'She's very well, Father.'

That disposed of the two main factors in her life. Michael and Sarah were all right, at least they were up to a few days ago when he had visited the farm. He hadn't seen Mary Ann on that occasion, in fact, he hadn't seen her for quite this long while. Was it her grannie? He said now, 'Don't tell me, Mary Ann, that you've come to confess to murdering your grannie.' Aw, it was Christmas Eve and the Good Lord would forgive him for a joke even in the confessional.

On her side of the box Mary Ann suppressed a giggle. And her lips were quite near the wire mesh as she whispered, 'No, Father, but it's likely that some day I will.'

There was many a true word spoken in jest. He metaphorically crossed himself and said, 'Go on, my child. I will hear your confession.'

And Mary Ann had enough sins on her mind to make a confession, even though her conscience had been cleared three days previously. She laid aside her main reason for coming to see Father Owen and said, 'My heart is full of bitterness, Father, against someone, and I don't want it to be like that – I want to forgive. And there is Sarah, Father. There are times when I give way to jealousy. I like Sarah, Father, I like her very much. But my mother has become very fond of her and I get jealous. It is wrong of me but I can't help it. It would be different if—' She stopped, she couldn't go on and say, 'If I had anyone of my own.' Because she had someone of her own. Hadn't she her da? But that wasn't what she meant.

'Go on, my child.'

'I miss my morning prayers very often, Father, and I have started . . .' There followed another long pause, and the priest prompted her, saying, 'Yes? yes?' 'I have started to criticise my religion, Father.'

There was silence behind the grid. She'd had no intention in the world of confessing that sin, it had just slipped out. And she didn't really criticise, she only tried to work things out in her own mind.

On the other side of the grid Father Owen suddenly knew he was an old man. He had known Mary Ann since she had first toddled up to the side altar and made her bargains with the Holy Family, and now she had reached the age when she was thinking for herself, and when you started thinking for yourself you couldn't help but criticise. It was a phase of life. He said to her gently, 'You are growing up, Mary Ann. Don't worry. Your religion will bear your criticism. A thing that cannot bear criticism is built on sand and will soon be washed away by the tongues of men. Come and have a talk with me sometime and tell me what you think. We'll have a long crack on the subject, eh?'

Oh, he was lovely was Father Owen, he was always lovely. He made things so easy.

'Make a good act of contrition.'

'Oh, my God, I am very sorry that I have sinned against thee, because thou art so good, and by the help of thy Holy Grace, I will not sin again.'

He said the absolution.

'Amen.'

'A happy Christmas, Mary Ann.'

'A happy Christmas, Father.'

'Father.' She could, in this moment, have cast off nine or ten years and be hissing her petitions through the grid once more.

'Yes, Mary Ann?'

'Do you remember Tony?'

'Do I remember Tony? Of course, I remember Tony. Why?'

'Do you know where he is?'

Ah, so that was it. He said, 'No, I don't, Mary Ann. Why? Do you want to find him?'

'Mr Lord has been asking for him.'

'Oh!' So he had been asking for him. When he saw him the other day the name of Tony was not mentioned between them. He had hoped it would be because he felt that Peter Lord's burden needed lightening if he were to go on living. He was a man without hope. He whispered now, 'I wish I could help you, Mary Ann, but I can't.'

'Thank you, Father.'

'Wait a minute.' Father Owen took his hand away from the side of his face that sheltered it from the penitent, and he brought his fingers over his lips as he thought, Young Lettice Schofield! He had known her father, Brian Trenchard, as a young man, and many were the times that Brian had dined him well. It was hard to think that she, whose life story had been filling the papers of late, was the same young Lettice he had teased when he was a guest in her father's house. He had seen little of her since her marriage, and it had come as shocking news to him the life she had led. For he felt she must have suffered nothing less than refined torture to keep up the façade of respectability. God knew that she was to be pitied, yet it was she who had caused the rift between Peter Lord and his grandson. Unintentionally perhaps, for he could not imagine there being any vice in Lettice. He had run into her quite unexpectedly about three weeks ago and they had talked about this and that without touching on anything personal. But he did remember now that she had mentioned that she was staying with her uncle, and if he remembered rightly Brian Trenchard had only one brother, and his name was Harold. He said now, 'Mrs Schofield might help you. She was staying with her uncle. His name is Harold Trenchard. Look in the telephone directory and go on from there.'

'Thank you, Father . . . Oh, thank you, Father.'

'God bless you, my child.'

'Good night, Father.'

'Good night . . . A minute, Mary Ann. How many do you think are waiting?'

'I should say over twenty Father.'

Father Owen closed his eyes. Over twenty! 'And at Father Bailey's box?'

'About ten, Father.'

Father Owen sighed. 'Thank you. Good night.'

'Good night, Father.'

Self-consciously Mary Ann went down the aisle,

past the patient penitents. They would, she thought, be thinking that she hadn't been to confession for a year, she had been in so long.

Kneeling before the crib she said her penance, one Our Father, and three Hail Marys. It was a stock penance of Father Owen's. She didn't know what other people got, but she had never got anything worse than that. Even when she had tried to empty the candle money box behind the altar. She looked at the Holy Family, not the real Holy Family that stood up on the altar, larger than life size, but the little Holy Family staged among the straw with the animals around them. And she prayed for each member of her family, and for Father Owen. And then, still being Mary Ann, she had to ask for something. She said, 'This being Christmas Eve, please help me to find Tony, and I'll—' She just stopped herself from making some outrageous promise in return for their guidance. In the past she had always promised them to stop hating her grannie, or to tell no more lies, or to resist getting one over on her enemy, Sarah Flannagan. This thought coming into her mind made her smile, and, looking up from the small statues towards the group that had been the focal point of her spiritual life, she knew that the power of God was wonderful, for there was in her heart now not the smallest trace of jealousy towards Sarah. In this moment when the sacrament of penance was washing her conscience she could even see the funny side of her grannie. This feeling wouldn't last, she knew it wouldn't, but while it did she thanked God. She did not mention the name of Corny Boyle to them. It would have been difficult to explain about the part of her that didn't care, and the part of her that cared too much. And then about the part of her that was bitter and full of resentment. Oh, she couldn't go into all that.

And now she went out of the church, and there was Michael waiting in the sloping passage to greet her; as he had done once many years ago. He said, 'Where on earth have you been?'

'You know where I've been.'

'Well, you've taken long enough about it. I've nearly froze waiting for you. What did he say?'

'He doesn't know where Tony is, but he thinks Mrs Schofield's staying with her uncle . . . I want a telephone directory.'

'Where for?'

'It'll be in Newcastle.'

'Oh, good Lord. We're not tearing off there now, are we?'

'If there's a Harold Trenchard, we are.' She looked at him and smiled, and then with an unusual gesture she tucked her arm in his.

Mr Harold Trenchard's name was in the telephone directory. Michael suggested, before dashing off to Newcastle, why not phone and find out if Mr Trenchard were there. And this she did.

It was a woman's voice who answered the phone, and she said she was a Mrs Trenchard. Mary Ann politely made her inquiries, and the woman at the other end said, 'Who's speaking?'

'My name is Mary Ann Shaughnessy.'

'Oh, Mary Ann Shaughnessy. Oh yes, I've heard of you . . . Well, Lettice . . . Mrs Schofield is not with us now.'

'Oh.'

'But I can give you her address.'

'Thank you. Thank you very much.' Mary Ann repeated the address and Michael wrote it down in his pocket book. And then Mary Ann said, 'Goodbye and thank you.' And she added, 'A Merry Christmas.'

Mary Ann had hardly put down the phone before she started to gabble. 'Look, it's not in Newcastle, it's in Shields. She's in Shields, Sunderland Road!'

'Well, come on, don't stand gaping.' With brotherly courtesy Michael pushed her out of the box, and when she almost slipped on the frost on the pavement he grabbed at her, saying, 'That's it, break your neck. We only want that now.' They were both laughing when they got into the van.

Within a quarter of an hour they had reached Sunderland Road, and after some searching they found the house. There was a plate to the side of the door that held three cards, and the bottom one which said Flat 3 had the name Lettice Trenchard written on it. They rang the bell twice before there was any response, and then a man opened the door. Without waiting to question them he said, 'I thought I heard someone there. Is it the top flat you want, because the bell's out of order? But just go on up.'

'Thank you.' They went past him and up the two flights of stairs. And when they came opposite the door they exchanged glances before Mary Ann tapped gently.

When the door opened there stood Mrs Schofield, her lips apart with surprise. No-one spoke until Mary Ann, after what seemed a long moment, said quietly, 'Hello, Mrs Schofield.'

Mrs Schofield, after wetting her lips and

looking from one to the other, smiled and said, 'Mary Ann!' Then she half-turned her head over her shoulder and looked behind her, before saying, 'Won't you come in?'

Mary Ann walked slowly past Mrs Schofield into a tiny hall, and Mrs Schofield said, 'Will I take your coat?'

'We won't be staying, Mrs Schofield. We just came to . . . to ask you something.'

'Well, you'll sit down for a while. Let me have your coat . . . and yours, Michael.'

She took their coats and hung them on the hallstand. Then going towards one of the three doors leading out of the hall, she opened it. And when they entered the room, there, standing on the hearth-rug before a small fireplace, was Tony.

The sight of him was as much a surprise to Mary Ann as her and Michael's arrival had been to Mrs Schofield. She hadn't really expected to find Tony here. Somehow, she thought Mrs Schofield would have cut adrift from him in order to make it easier for him to return to Mr Lord.

Mrs Schofield must have sensed something of what Mary Ann was thinking, for after she had seated them she looked at her and said, 'You may not believe it but Tony has only been here a short while; a matter of minutes, in fact. I'm being discovered all in a bunch it would seem.'

Tony had not spoken to Mary Ann, and his greeting to Michael had been merely an abrupt nod of the head. Now all his attention was on Mrs Schofield, and Mary Ann's attention was on him. He did not, she noticed, look his usual spruce self, anything but, in fact – he looked rather ill. Her sympathy aroused, she said now,

'Well, hello, Tony.' And when he turned towards her he gave her a smile as he answered, 'Hello, Mary Ann.' Then looking towards Michael he added hastily, 'How's it going, Michael?'

'Oh, not so bad, Tony. How's it with you?'

'Oh fine . . .'

'It isn't fine, don't tell lies.' Both Mrs Schofield's glance and voice were soft as she looked at Tony. Then glancing between Mary Ann and Michael, she said, 'He's been ill, he's had flu. I knew nothing about it.'

'Have you been on your own?' Mary Ann's tone was full of concern as she gazed at him, and now he replied in a slightly mocking tone, 'Yes, entirely, but I don't want you to cry about it.'

'Who's going to cry about it?' Mary Ann's chin jerked up, and on this they all laughed. The tension was broken, and Mary Ann, becoming her natural self, exclaimed as she looked him straight in the eye, 'You're a fool.'

'I wouldn't for the moment dream of contradicting you. Now tell me, what have you come for? What are you after?'

'Well, if you're going to use that tone, I've a good mind not to open my mouth.'

'That'll be the day.'

This retort came almost simultaneously from Tony and Michael, and again there was laughter.

'Take no notice of them, Mary Ann . . . Come here.' Mrs Schofield was holding out her hand to Tony. 'Come and sit down.'

As Mary Ann watched Tony, with willing docility do as he was bid, she thought, and not without a slight pang, 'She could do anything with him, anything.'

'Tell us what brought you, Mary Ann.' Mrs Schofield was now looking at her, and Mary Ann answered her as if Tony was not sitting beside her, saying, 'Mr Lord wants him back. He asked me to fetch him . . .'

'On conditions that I—'

Mary Ann, turning sharply on Tony, cut him off with, 'Oh no conditions attached whatever! You don't give me time to finish.' Her voice dropped. 'He's very low and tired . . . and lonely, and he said to tell you to come back, with or without . . .' She turned her eyes from him now to Mrs Schofield as she ended, 'With or without you. But I do believe he would rather it were with you.'

There followed an embarrassing silence, during which they all seemed to be staring at each other, until Mrs Schofield whispered, 'Oh, Mary Ann.' Her face began to twitch and she lowered her head and bit hard on her lip.

When Tony's arms went about her and he drew her tightly into his embrace as if quite oblivious of either Michael or herself, Mary Ann experienced embarrassment that brought her to her feet, and she blurted to no-one in particular, 'We'd better be getting back. If you like, we can all go together.'

Again Mrs Schofield said, 'Oh, Mary Ann.' Then pulling herself away from Tony's clasp and looking up through wet eyes, she exclaimed on a broken laugh, 'That's all I seem able to say . . . Oh, Mary Ann. But I must add: Thank you. Thank you, my dear.'

'And me too, Mary Ann. That's all I can say too: Thank you.' Tony was on his feet now looking down on her. 'You were always the one for getting things done, for getting your own way. And from the bottom of my heart I can say at this moment, I'm glad you're made like that. Because – because I want to see him. It's been pretty awful these last few weeks . . .' When Mary Ann, finding it impossible for once to say anything, remained mute, Tony turned abruptly from her and, looking at Michael, said in a lighter tone, 'How's Mike?'

'Oh, the same as usual, you know.'

'Yes. But I don't suppose he'll be the same with me though . . . I'll have to do a bit of apologising in that quarter.'

'Oh, forget it. I'm sure he has, he's not the one to remember rows, he's had too many of them.'

'Well, come on, get your coat on.' Tony had turned to Mrs Schofield, but now she looked back at him and shook her head, saying, 'No, you go alone. I'll come tomorrow. You can come and fetch me.'

'I'm not going without you.'

'Now don't be silly, Tony.'

'He's right, it's Christmas Eve and we're not going to leave you here.' Mary Ann bounced her head. 'And if you won't come now we'll just sit down and wait until you change your mind, won't we, Michael?'

'We will that.'

Mrs Schofield looked from one to the other, then she turned swiftly from them and went into the bedroom.

Tony went into the hall and collected their coats, and as he handed Mary Ann hers, he said under his breath, 'I woke up this morning feeling like death and wishing it would come quickly. I was in digs, awful digs, and I thought: Oh, my God, Christmas Eve . . . But I never dreamt it would turn out like this.' A quiet smile spread over his white features as he ended, 'It wouldn't take much to make me believe that your . . . Holy Family had been at work, Mary Ann.'

'You can laugh.' Her voice was prim. 'But if it hadn't been for Father Owen, we wouldn't be here would we, Michael? So you can say that the Holy Family had a hand in it.'

'I'm not laughing, Mary Ann, far from it. I don't feel like it at this moment. Oh, no, I'm not laughing, not when I've just been handed two good reasons for living. And the Holy Family apart . . . thank you, Mary Ann.'

When Tony put out his hand and gently touched her cheek she had a sudden desire to howl her eyes out there and then, for the excitement was over, the good deed had been accomplished. Tony had Mrs Schofield, Mr Lord would have Tony. Sarah had Michael, and her ma had her da. And who was there for her? Nobody. She hated Corny Boyle.

10

'Well!' Mike let out a long-drawn breath that expanded his chest and pressed his ribs against his shirt. 'It's been a night and a half.'

Lizzie, making no pretence to stifle the yawn, said, 'Night? It's day again. It's half-past one on Christmas Morning. Come on, let's get upstairs or I'll sleep until dinner-time tomorrow.' She turned towards Mike who was now standing staring pensively at the two bulging stockings hanging from the brass rail. On Christmas Eve two stockings had always hung in front of the fireplace, no matter where they lived or how little money they had. But this year they were not Mary Ann's and Michael's, they were Mary Ann's and Sarah's, Michael having thankfully relinquished the childish habit kept up by Lizzie.

Mike had his hand in his pocket and his shoulders were hunched, and after looking at him for a moment longer in silence she said softly, 'What is it now?'

'Oh, I was just thinking.' He raised his head and looked across the high mantelpiece which was covered with a galaxy of Christmas cards, then up to the strings looped to the picture rail which were carrying the overflow, and he remarked, 'Every-body happy but her.'

'Now, now. Oh, don't let's start that, not at this time.'

Mike turned slowly towards her, and putting his hand out he softly turned her chin, and his voice held a deep and gentle note as he said, 'You're the best in the world, Liz, and I know it, but there are times when I think you've got a hard spot in you towards her.'

'Oh, Mike, that isn't right, and it's unfair of you to say it. Just because I don't go around dribbling, it doesn't say that I don't feel for her. I do.'

'Yes, perhaps you do. I'm sorry.' His fingers rubbed against her soft flesh.

Lizzie was very tired. Her eyes began to smart and her voice broke as she said, 'You shouldn't have said that to me, Mike. Not at this time. Bringing up things like that at an hour when we should all be in bed.'

'Well, it was in me mind, and you know me. I said I'm sorry, and I am. But I'd mortgage me life at this minute to see her happy. She's run off her feet all day to put things right for the old man and Tony, and she's as happy about Mrs Schofield as if she was you. And then the night, at supper, did you see her face when Sarah named the wedding day?' He now slipped his arm around Lizzie's shoulder as he said, 'Our girl is very human, Liz. She's all emotion, all feelings, and she's seventeen and a half and she hasn't got a lad. You know, I feel in two minds about Corny Boyle at this minute. If he was standing afore me now, I don't know whether I'd punch him on the jaw or shake him by the hand . . . What would you do, Liz?'

Mike had shot the last question at Lizzie, and he felt her start under his hand. And then she said, 'You think I didn't like Corny. It wasn't that at all. Corny was a nice enough lad. Being part of Fanny he was bound to have good in him. I had nothing against Corny, not as a lad. But somehow I wanted somebody different for her, somebody who could give her things. It is understandable, isn't it?' She turned her head and looked up at him.

'Aye, Liz, I suppose it is. Her mother didn't do very well for herself, did she?'

'Aw, Mike.' She dropped her head now against the strong muscles of his neck. 'What do you want me to say?'

'Nothing, nothing.'

'Well, I can tell you this.' Her voice was smothered against him. 'If I had to pick again this minute I would make the same choice.' As his arm pressed her tighter to him she straightened up, saying, 'Come on, we'd better get up, and quietly, or we'll be wakening the house.'

When he released her she did not move away from him, but looking into his weathered, ruggedly handsome face, she said simply, 'I love you, Mike.'

'An' I love you.' Slowly now their heads came together, and the kiss they exchanged was gentle.

'Happy Christmas, Liz.'

'Happy Christmas, Mike.'

Their arms around each other, they went out of the room, Lizzie switching off the light as they went through the door.

It was as they went, still linked together, to mount the stairs, that the unmistakable sound of a motor-bike being pulled up in the road outside the house brought them to a halt.

'That's a motor-bike, and stopping here.' Lizzie was whispering.

Mike's ear was cocked. 'Likely somebody looking for Len and didn't see the cottages.'

'They're not having a do, are they?'

'I didn't think so, not till the New Year.'

Simultaneously, they turned from the foot of the stairs and went into the hall again. And although they were both expecting a knock, they were visibly startled when the rat-tat came on the door.

Mike went forward, leaving Lizzie in the centre of the hall, and when he opened the door the exclamation he let out was high. 'Well, my God!'

Lizzie repeated this phrase to herself when Mike, moving aside, said, 'Look, Liz. Look what the wind's blown in.'

As Corny Boyle stepped slowly into the hall, Lizzie gaped at him with open mouth, and her gaping was caused by a number of reasons, not the least was that here stood a different Corny Boyle from the lad she knew. Here, enveloped in a great coat, his big head actually on a level with Mike's, was a man, not the boy she remembered.

Corny Boyle cast his glance between them as he said quietly, 'I'm sorry I'm so late, but I'm glad I caught you up, I thought I might. I was held up here and there, or I'd have been over sooner.'

'Well! well! well!' Mike was gazing at Corny. He too was surprised at the change he saw in him. It was only a few minutes since he had said that if he were confronted by this lad he wouldn't know whether to shake him by the hand or punch him on the jaw. But he knew now what to do, for his hand went out as he said airily, 'Don't worry your head about the time, the day's young. I'm right glad to see you, Corny. You're a better sight than Santa Claus . . . Mary Ann!' This last was a bellow up the stairs.

'Mike! You'll have the whole house awake.' Lizzie's lids were blinking rapidly.

'And why not?'

'MARY ANN! Do you hear? MARY ANN!' His voice was even louder this time.

'Are they all in bed?' Corny looked at Lizzie, and Lizzie, not quite sure of her feeling at this moment, almost answered, 'What do you expect, going on two o'clock in the morning?' But she managed to be gracious and say, 'Well, they haven't been up all that long, but we have Mrs Schofield with us. You remember Mrs Schofield?'

Corny's smile was the old wide remembered grin, and he nodded his head as he said, 'I should say I do. Is she staying over Christmas?'

'Yes.' Lizzie paused and then added, 'Yes, she's staying with us over Christmas.' It was evident that Corny knew nothing about Mrs Schofield's affair. Lizzie still thought of the situation as an affair but Corny disillusioned her the next moment by saying, 'Is Tony with her?'

Lizzie's eyebrows moved just the slightest. 'No, not here, he's up at the house with Mr Lord.'

'Mary Ann! . . .' Mike was at the beginning of another bellow when Michael appeared at the top of the stairs. He was pulling his dressing-gown on as he exclaimed, 'What is it? What are you bawling for?'

'I'm not bawling for you, anyway. Give a rap on her door or else I'll be up there.'

But there was no need now to give a rap on Mary Ann's door, for even as Mike spoke she came on to the landing, and looking down the stairs, she too asked, 'What is it?'

'What do you think?' Mike had pushed Corny towards the wall out of her line of sight, and his face was one large grin as he looked up at her saying, 'What would you like in your stockin'?'

If Mary Ann hadn't been sure that she had left her da solid and sober in the kitchen somewhere about an hour ago, she would have sworn he was tight.

Michael had gone down the stairs, and was now standing in the hall under the pressure of Mike's hand, which warned him to make no comment on what his eyes were seeing, and then Mary Ann came within three stairs of the bottom and she looked from her da to Michael standing side by side, then behind them to her mother. Following this her eyes lifted to the side and saw, standing near the wall between the kitchen door and the sitting-room, a man who looked like Corny Boyle. Her fingers went to the top button of her dressing-gown and pulled on it so sharply that she gulped.

'Hello.' The man that looked like Corny Boyle had stepped away from the wall and was speaking to her. She felt slightly dizzy. All the faces rolled together, and before they separated her da's voice came to her saying, 'Well, open your mouth. Here he's come all the way from America on a motor-bike.' Mike laughed at his own joke and went on, 'And you can only stand and stare. Didn't you ask Santa for something in your stockin'? . . . Well . . .'

'Be quiet, Mike.' Lizzie now took the situation in hand. 'Come on into Sarah's room. She's bound to be awake and it's warmer in there.' Lizzie pushed open the door exclaiming, 'Are you awake, Sarah?'

'I'd have to be dead, Mam, not to hear the cafupple.'

'It's Corny.' Lizzie was talking into the room.

'Yes, I've guessed as much.'

During this Michael had moved past his mother into the sitting-room, and Mary Ann had moved down the stairs and was now standing opposite Corny Boyle.

Corny Boyle . . . Corny Boyle . . . But a different Corny Boyle. This was not the boy she remembered, he was almost a stranger. So much so that she felt she didn't know him.

'Well, this is a nice welcome. What's the matter, have you lost your tongue?'

Mary Ann jerked her head from Corny and looked at her da. She stared at him for a moment before turning towards Corny again. And now she did speak. 'Did Mr Lord send for you?' she said.

'No, he didn't. Nobody sent for me. I COME on me own.'

The answer had come so quickly it startled her, and for the first time in the last surprise-filled minutes she recognised in this unfamiliar man the boy she knew.

A laugh now came from the sitting-room, and Michael's voice cried, 'They've started.'

At this Corny too laughed and, turning completely away from Mary Ann, said to Mike, 'It's as if I'd never been away, isn't it? Oh, Mr Shaughnessy, you don't know what it's like, this feeling of being back.'

Mary Ann, still looking at him, but at his back now, was thinking two things. He had come on his own after all. That was one. And the other, that although he looked different, and sounded different, for he didn't talk like he used to, he still called her da Mr Shaughnessy. As she allowed her da to push her into the sitting-room, she remembered that for years she had tried to make Corny speak differently, with little success. Yet here he had been gone just over a year, and besides looking like anybody else but Corny Boyle, he was speaking like anybody else but Corny Boyle. There was only one explanation . . . somebody had worked on him. This thought pulled her round to look at him as he went across to Sarah and took hold of her outstretched hands. Nothing could make him beautiful, nor handsome, yet he looked . . . She searched for a word, and might have found it, but Mike's voice cut across her thinking as he yelled up the stairs again, 'Mrs Schofield!'

'Oh, Mike, have you taken leave of your senses?' Lizzie was dashing out of the room, and Mike answered her, 'We can't leave her up there and all this going on.'

It only seemed a matter of seconds before Mrs Schofield's voice came across the landing, saying, 'Nothing could stop me coming down. I heard who it was. Oh, I am glad.'

In the sitting-room, Mary Ann, seeming to

stand apart as if watching a play being acted, saw Mrs Schofield and Corny greeting each other, holding hands and laughing as if they had been lifelong friends.

'Where is it?' Mrs Schofield made a pretence of looking behind him.

'Where's what? . . . Oh, I've left it in me grip, but I'll bring it over tomorrow and serenade you.'

Indeed here was a different Corny. His grip . . . and he would serenade Mrs Schofield. The other Corny would never have talked like that. If this time yesterday someone had said to her, 'How would you feel if Corny were suddenly to drop out of the sky and into the house, how would you feel?' she would have drawn a long breath and clasped her hands together, and answered truthfully, 'Oh, wonderful. It would be the most wonderful thing on earth that could happen.' And now here he was, larger than life, and she was quite numb. She was even asking herself at this point: Had she ever been mad about Corny Boyle? The Corny Boyle that she had known . . . and loved . . . was a reticent person; brusque, Mr Lord had said. But Mr Lord had also said that America was bringing him out . . . America had certainly brought him out, you could say that again. Sarah turned Mary Ann's attention away from her questioning thoughts by saying, 'Oh, Mary Ann, isn't this wonderful! I'm so happy for you.'

She was holding Sarah's hand now, and looking down into her great dark eyes. She was envying her again, jealous of her in a funny way. Sarah was happy . . . she loved Michael, and Michael adored her. Somehow it didn't seem to matter about her legs. Sarah had said, 'Oh, I'm happy for you.' For what? Why was she feeling like this? Things weren't right.

Mike's eyes were tight on his daughter now, and the tie between them that had always been stronger than any umbilical cord transferred to him in some measure what the effect of Corny's appearance was having on her, and so he cried, 'Look! We want something to celebrate with. It's either got to be tea, or beer.'

'We'll make it tea.' This was Lizzie.

'Good enough. Hi! there, Mary Ann, get yourself into the kitchen and get busy.'

'I'll—'

The pressure of Mike's hand on Lizzie's arm cut off her words, and he cried again, 'Did you hear what I said? Get that kettle on, me girl. The sooner you get your hand in the better.'

Mary Ann, relinquishing her hold on Sarah's hand, went round the bed and out of the room, without once looking in the direction of Corny. And when she closed the kitchen door behind her, she stood with her back to it and with the fingers of both her hands pressed over her mouth. She stood in this way for some seconds gazing, but unseeingly, at the stockings hanging from the rod, before going to the fire. The kettle was on the hob, but the fire had been banked down and would take too long to bring up again, so she took the kettle into the scullery and put it on the gas stove. Then she returned to the kitchen and put the cups on the tray, and after picking up the teapot she went into the scullery again. She was measuring out the tea when she heard the kitchen door open, and her hand became still as the footsteps came nearer. Then there he was, as she knew her da had planned. And when he spoke there was a faint resemblance to the old Corny by his straightforward approach to the subject.

'You don't seem overjoyed to see me.'

She turned and looked at him. 'Should I be?'

'Well, what do you think I'm here for?' His face was straight. 'It isn't like getting a bus from Jarrow, popping over from America!'

'No, no, it isn't.'

'Why didn't you go and see me grannie?'

'Why should I?' She rounded on him now, her tone sharp. 'You know, Corny Boyle, you've got a cheek. I never hear a word from you for months, and you expect me to be sitting waiting for you coming . . . to drop in, as me da says, like Santa Claus!'

'You know that I don't like writin' letters, I'm no hand at them.'

'There's lots of things I don't like doing that I've got to do . . . Anyway, you were going to come back when the year was up, but you didn't. And you didn't even write to tell me that. No . . . you had to send some fancy photographs through Mr Lord.'

'I didn't send any fancy photographs through Mr Lord. What are you gettin' at?'

'Well' – she shook her head slowly as she gazed at him – 'surely you haven't got a double in America, and Mr Lord was taking the wrong Corny Boyle at picnics, parties, swimming and tennis.'

'No. It wasn't a double. I'm the same bloke. People live like that out there. Everybody mixes up together, it's a different world. It took me some time to get used to it, but—'

'But when you did, you lapped it up, didn't you?'

Corny's head had dropped slightly to the side, and now the corner of his mouth came up and there spread across his face the grin she remembered. But she could have slapped it off when in the next moment he said, 'I was beginning to worry, I thought you had stopped likin' me . . . coo! I was sweatin'.'

'You needn't start any of your glib American chat here. Not on me. You can keep that for – for—'

'Good-looking girls with blonde hair?'

Her lips came together, her chin went up, and her eyes flashed danger at him. But apparently he was not unduly disturbed, for his grin widened, and he dared to go on and say in a voice that was almost a drawl, 'They called her Priscilla, but she wasn't a bit like her name. And she was tall, taller than most girls, five foot eight, and one of the best lookers over there, I should say . . . But it was no use . . .' The smile suddenly slid from his face and he went on, rapidly now, 'Everybody was nice, more than nice. They had my life planned until I was ninety, and the more cushions they kept padding around me, the more I was seeing you. I told meself that I could live with you until I was ninety; even if we fought every day I could still live with you . . . But those over there . . .' He shook his head slowly. 'I couldn't make them out. I couldn't explain if I tried, I only know why they have two or three wives. But even then I might have stayed, because although I told you I'd be back when the year was up, I'd no intention of comin'. I knew what your mother wanted for you, I knew what Mr Lord wanted for you. I could never, not in a month of Sundays, hope to compete against Tony and what he stood for. And as me grannie said, it was better to leave the way open to you, there'd be less recrimination in later years if it was your own choice. Then she wrote me a letter, me grannie, not a fortnight since. She said that you hadn't been near the door but she had heard that there was an affair going on between Tony and' – his voice dropped – 'Mrs Schofield. That Mrs Schofield was divorced and Tony had left old Mr Lord. Well, that decided me. I couldn't come on the minute, I had to work a bit of notice. But I finished yesterday, or was it the day afore. Anyway, I didn't arrive in Howden until ten o'clock last night. Well, there it is, Miss Mary Ann Shaughnessy, so what about it? Your mother isn't pleased I've come back, I know that, but what about you?'

'Oh, Corny! . . . Corny!'

As his arms came out and lifted her off her feet she cried again, 'Oh, Corny!'

They had kissed before, fumbling, shy, self-conscious kissing. This was different. Corny was no longer a gauche lad, and Mary Ann was no longer a little girl. When he released her they stood, their arms holding tight, staring into each other's eyes for a long while. And then he said thickly, in a voice that sounded oddly like Mike's, 'I've fetched you a Christmas box.' And putting his hand into his pocket he brought out a small box and handed it to her.

She knew before she opened it what to expect.

But the sight of her first ring swamped her with joy. He said, 'Do you like it? I got it through the Customs. It was Christmas Eve and they were kind to me.' She raised her eyes from the ring. 'It's wonderful, Corny, wonderful.' Swiftly she put her arms round his neck again and once more they were lost in each other.

When next she looked at the ring she started to sniff, and said, 'I'd better make this tea. They're all waiting.'

'There's no hurry. Your da's a very astute man, Mary Ann.'

'Me da's a lovely man.' She looked up at him. 'I'm glad you like him, and he likes you.'

'I feel he does. I wish your ma did though.' He was once again speaking in the tongue of the old Corny, and as he ran his fingers through her hair she replied in the idiom of the real Mary Ann, 'Ee! I must mash the tea, leave over.' And they both laughed together.

In the kitchen she pointed to the tray of cups saying, 'Fetch it in.' And then she went before him into the room.

The conversation stopped as soon as the door opened. All eyes were on her, and as Corny put down the tray next to Lizzie, Mary Ann held out the box before her mother and said, 'Look. Corny's brought me a Christmas box.'

'Oh, isn't that beautiful!' The exclamations came from both Mrs Schofield and Sarah. Michael said nothing, nor did Mike. And Lizzie just looked at the ring that Mary Ann was holding in front of her. Then she almost ricked her back, so quickly did she twist about when Corny made a casual-sounding remark, as he turned from the table. 'We're going to be married next year,' was what he had said.

'Well, my God!' said Mike, on a deep note.

'Fast work,' said Michael.

'Oh, how lovely, Mary Ann,' said Sarah.

'Congratulations, my dear.' This was Mrs Schofield.

Lizzie said nothing, she just gaped. And Mary Ann gaped too, she gaped at the audacity of this big fellow who was again behaving unlike Corny Boyle. And without thinking about the rest of them she cried at him, 'What do you mean, next year? You haven't even asked me.'

'No?' Corny was looking straight at her, the quizzical lift was at the corner of his mouth again. 'I'm just tellin' you now. I'll ask you the morrow, or later on the day, that is.'

The bellow that Mike let out filled the room, and set them all off laughing, all except Lizzie. Lizzie was still gaping. Married next year, indeed! Married! Mary Ann? She was still . . . The word child was ripped from her mind. No, she would never be a child again. She would soon be eighteen. In another year she would be nineteen . . . But married. She turned again, as Corny spoke and directly to her now, looking her straight in the eye as he said, 'If her mother will have me in the family?'

What could she say? What could she do? There was only one thing she was thankful for at present: this Corny Boyle was different from the Corny Boyle that went to America. Certainly the year abroad had not been wasted. And after all, she supposed, the main thing was that Mary Ann should be happy. She must remember the hell on earth her own mother had caused her when she married Mike. She mustn't be a pattern of her mother. She'd faced up to the problem of Sarah and that had turned out a hundred per cent to the good. Well, if this worked out properly, perhaps it would have the same result. She prayed to God it would anyway. She smiled now at Corny as she answered him, 'I can't see that you've left me much say in the matter, Corny. But there's one thing very evident. You would never have learnt to be such a fast worker had you stayed in England.'

'I don't know so much about being a fast worker.' Corny was slightly red in the face now, but showing a relieved grin. 'It was that way or going on shilly-shallying for weeks. It's no use talking to her.' He thumbed in the direction of Mary Ann. 'She'd only argue, you know what she's like.'

In her own mind Lizzie confirmed her previous statement. Yes, indeed, Corny Boyle had learned a lot in America. The person whom it was no use talking to and who would argue, had not been Mary Ann . . . but herself. She had to admire him for his adroitness. In a way she felt pleased.

Mike was roaring, and as he hugged Mary Ann to him he cried down at her, 'Well, me lass, you've met your match this time.' And he turned to Mrs Schofield, who was seated at his side, and drawing her into the family, said, 'What's your opinion of all this?'

Mrs Schofield, looking between Corny and Mary Ann, said softly, 'I think it will be a wonderful match. I hope they have all the happiness they both deserve.' She looked at Mary Ann and said, 'Do you remember your thirteenth birth-day?'

Mary Ann nodded. Tears were misting her vision and she had no words to fit this occasion. Mrs Schofield now looked towards Corny and said, 'Do you remember it?'

'Could I ever forget it? Me and me shrunken suit!' He extended his long arms to demonstrate how his coat cuffs had at one time receded.

'Oh, I don't mean that. Don't be silly. I meant you and your cornet. You remember how you played, and we all sat on the lawn and sang. Oh, I've thought about that day often, and often. And that song: "He stands at the corner".'

'Oh, aye.' Mike's head went back. 'He stands at the corner and whistles me out. By! It's a long time since we sang that one. Come on . . . come on, all of you. Come on, all together. Come on, Liz.' He grabbed her hand and held it in a comforting grip. 'Come on now. One, two, three.

> *He stands at the corner*
> *And whistles me out,*
> *With his hands in his pockets*
> *And his shirt hanging out.*
> *But still I love him—*
> *Can't deny it—*
> *I'll be with him*
> *Wherever he goes.*

Mary Ann was singing. She was looking at Corny and his eyes were hard on her. There were only the two of them in the entire world, and they were singing to each other. And when the chorus was finished for a second time the last line echoed loud in the large territory of her heart.

I'll be with him wherever he goes,
I'll be with him wherever he goes,
I'll be with him wherever he goes,
I'll be with him . . . WHEREVER HE GOES.

Yes, Corny was the one for her and she would be with him – come hail or shine.

MARRIAGE AND MARY ANN

Catherine Cookson

CORGI BOOKS

To Muriel Baker
An unusual friend, who from the beginning
not only liked my books, but bought them

1

'And all this has come about because they went on a holiday.' Fanny McBride thrust out her thick arm and pulled the blue sugar bag towards her, and after ladling three spoonfuls into an outsize cup of tea she added, 'But you're sure you're not enlargin' on everything, Mary Ann?'

'No, Mrs McBride. I wish I was. But it isn't imagination, it isn't.'

'Well, I was just thinkin' you have a lot on your mind at the present moment, with Michael and Sarah's wedding in the offing, and your own looming up ahead. By the way, I must tell you, I was glad when you and Corny decided not to make it a double-do. I think you want your own glory on a day like that.' Fanny smiled broadly at Mary Ann. 'Aw – she shook her head – 'the day I see you and Corny married I think my heart'll burst for joy. I've known you since you were that high' – she measured a short distance with her hand – 'and I've watched you grow up to great things.'

'Aw, Mrs McBride.' Mary Ann was shaking her head as she stared down towards the table. 'I've done nothing with me life, nothing as yet.'

'Not for yourself you haven't, me dear, except to take me grandson for your husband, but you've done it for others. Where would your da be the day without you and your schemes, eh?' She poked her broad face towards that of the heart-shaped, elfin face of Mary Ann. 'Would Mike be managing a farm with a grand house, an' be the right hand of Mr Lord, if it be his only hand?'

'It was through me he lost his hand, don't forget that, Mrs McBride.'

'Do I forget that God works in strange ways, child? If Mike hadn't lost his hand he wouldn't be where he is the day.'

'I know that.'

'Well then, you've no need to bother your head about the things you haven't done, for to my mind you've achieved almost the impossible where your da's concerned. As you know, I'm very fond of Mike, an' I know him inside out, his strength and his one weakness, an' that being the drink. But he's conquered that, thanks be to God. Well, knowing him as I do, I wouldn't have said that he had a weakness for the women, although I could say that some women might have a weakness for himself, for the older he gets the more fetchin' he gets.'

'That's the trouble.'

Mary Ann was looking solemnly at this big, voluptuous old woman, who, as she had said, had known her from a small child. And from a small child Mary Ann had looked upon Fanny McBride as her friend and comforter. From the day they had first come to live in the attic of Mulhattan's Hall – which place her mother had considered the very end of the downward trail – from that day she had been comforted and helped by the tenant on the first floor, Mrs Fanny McBride. There was no-one else in the world she could talk to freely about her da, except to this woman, because, as Fanny had also stated, she knew Mike Shaughnessy inside out.

Mary Ann said now, 'It seems sad to think that it was my mother's first real holiday, and she had been looking forward to it so much; and we all had fun and carry-on before they went saying what would happen to them at a holiday camp. The awful thing is that it was herself who plumped to go to a holiday camp; me da wasn't for it at all, he just went to please her.'

'How old did you say the girl was?'

'Nineteen.'

'And she has red hair?'

'Yes, and my mother says that's how it started. They were at the same table and her mother – the girl's mother, Mrs Radley – pointed out that me da's hair was almost the same shade as her daughter's. Then he danced with her, and after that they were in the swimming pool together. My mother can't swim and she just had to sit and look on. At first she didn't think anything about it, until Mrs Radley and her – Yvonne, they call her – tacked on to them everywhere they went . . . and me da seemed to like it.'

'And your mother told you all this?'

'Yes.'

Fanny shook her head again. 'Lizzie must be upset in her mind to speak of it so plainly, because she was ever so close about some things was Lizzie, reserved like, about the private things in her life, even when she was upstairs here. She must be taking this very badly, and it's hitting her at the wrong time of life. But then, that always happens; these things always hit women at the wrong time of life. I think men were built to cause it to be so, just to make things harder for us.'

'She can't set her mind to the wedding because they're coming.'

'Who was it asked them?'

'It must have been me da because she says that she never did.'

'Well, it needn't have been him, you know, Mary Ann. People, clever people, have a way of gettin' themselves invited – aye! begod, even into me house here.' She laughed. 'They put you on a spot. Perhaps your da was put on a spot; I wouldn't lay that at his door.'

Mary Ann rose from the table and walked to the window, and, looking out through the narrow aperture of the curtains down into the dull, sunless street, she turned her gaze towards the top end from where she hoped to see Corny coming, and then she fingered the curtains before saying, 'He must have known that if she came to the wedding me mother would be upset, and if he didn't ask them outright he could have done something to put them off. That's what's in me mind all the time. I hate to think of him deliberately hurting me mother.'

Fanny, pulling herself to her feet by gripping the worn, wooden arms of her chair, shambled towards the open fire, and there, lifting up the long rake, she pulled some pieces of coal from the back of the grate down into the dulling embers. Then, placing the rake back on the fender, she said, 'Tell me, was he pleased to see them when they came on the hop last Sunday?'

'Yes . . . yes, he was. He seemed a bit taken aback at first, but then he started to act like a young lad, skittish. I . . . oh, Mrs McBride . . .' Mary Ann turned from the window and looked across the cluttered, dusty room to the old woman, and she bit on her lip before she ended, 'He made me so ashamed. I . . . I never thought I would feel like that about him . . . ashamed of him. It was . . . it was a different kind of feeling to when he used to get roaring drunk. I wasn't really ashamed of him then, only sorry for him, pitying him, sort of; but last Sunday I . . . I knew I was ashamed of him. Oh . . . oh, Mrs McBride, it was awful. I . . . I can say this to you, can't I, because I've always been able to talk to you, haven't I?'

'Aye, hinny, you have that,' said Fanny in a low tone. 'It's another thing I've thanked God for. Go on.'

Mary Ann came and took her seat at the table again, and, moving the spoon round in the empty cup, she concentrated her gaze on it as she said, 'Well, there was a time when I began to dislike me mother for certain things she did, for her attitude towards the front room . . . Remember, when she didn't want Sarah to have it. And then the way she used to go for me da at times. But I could never imagine me ever disliking me da, because you know . . .' She lifted her eyes to those of Mrs McBride and said very softly, 'I worship him, I really do. At least I did. He was like God to me, but when I saw him actually put his arm round that beastly, scheming cat's waist' – her lips were now squared from her teeth – 'I felt that I hated him.'

'Where did this happen?'

'It was in the kitchen, but me mother was there.'

'Aw well, that's not so bad. It would have meant something much worse if she hadn't been there.'

'I don't see it like that, Mrs McBride, for if he'll do that in front of her what'll he do when she isn't there? That's how I see it. And . . . and he's started sprucing up. He never used to get changed in the evening unless he was going out, because sometimes he's got to see to the cattle late on, but now after tea he goes upstairs and gets into a good suit, collar and tie and everything.'

'Does he take himself out?'

'One night last week he did.'

'Did you know where he went?'

'No. He didn't say, and me mother didn't ask him, and I wouldn't. But on other nights he just strolled round the fields all dressed up like that.'

Returning to her chair, Fanny lowered herself slowly down, her head wagging the while. She sucked in her lips, closed her eyes, and, joining her hands together, moved these too in a wagging movement; then simultaneously all these actions ceased and she looked straight ahead towards the fire as she said, 'Within a few months you'll be married, Mary Ann, an' life will open out for you, an' you'll learn lots of things. But they all won't come at once, an' let's thank God for it, but it'll be some time afore you come really aware of the fact that there comes a period in life when women are not themselves. You'll have likely heard without understanding much about it that the middle years are very trying to a woman, but nobody's likely told you, for nobody seems to think along the same lines regarding men, but . . .' Now Fanny swung her head round towards Mary Ann, and, pointing her finger at her, she said solemnly, 'But now, let me tell you, because I know, havin' reared a number of the specimens, that men are tested much more sorely than women during the middle years, maybe not along the same lines, but nevertheless they are tested. There's something stirs in them, aggravatin' them, seeming to say "Come on, lad, you're not dead yet. Show them that you're as young as ever you were." An' there, Mary Ann, you've got the core of the whole matter . . . as young as ever they were. Now a woman doesn't like growin' old, it hurts her vanity; even if she's as ugly as sin it hurts her vanity. But, begod, a man likes growin' old less, for it not only hurts his vanity, it threatens his manhood. He is torn to shreds in that way much more than a woman is. Men, you know, Mary Ann, are merely grown-up lads. They may look old, and act old, but under their skins they're just lads, an', as I've said, there comes a time when they want to prove to the world they're still lads, so what do they do? Well, they take up with a lass young enough to be their daughter, some young enough to be a granddaughter. Now as I see it, this is what's happening to your da, an' your mother should know all about this. There's no doubt she does, but she's troubled in herself, an' in me own opinion Lizzie's no fit person to handle this situation at all. No, as I see it she's not; but you, Mary Ann, you with all your experience of your da, you're the one best able to talk to him.'

'Oh no. Oh no.' Mary Ann was again on her feet. 'I couldn't Mrs McBride, not about this.'

'But you've done it on other occasions, you've talked him round from other things than drink.'

'Yes, well . . . but I haven't so much talked to him as did things . . . Oh, I can't explain.'

'There's no need to, I know. As I said afore, you've schemed and manoeuvred . . . Well, why not use the same tactics now?'

'I couldn't, Mrs McBride; I tell you, I just couldn't, not over this. Him going mad over this girl, this young girl. I've thought about it but I just couldn't. I . . . I can't even speak to him ordinarily.'

'You mean you're not speaking to Mike at all?'

'No, I haven't for the past three weeks.'

'Aw, God in heaven! Now you are askin' for trouble.'

'Well, I can't help it.'

'Well now, Mary Ann' – the fat, not too clean, finger was wagging at her again – 'you'll just have to help it, for that's the worst thing you could do, not be speakin' to him . . . Tell me, how's Lizzie treatin' him?'

'She hardly speaks to him either.'

'Name of God! I thought you both had more sense, at least you. If you want to drive him away that's the way to do it. Go on not speakin' to him, push him out, and that girl, with the help of her mother, will have him in her arms afore you can say Jimmy McGregor. Now look . . . Aw' – Fanny turned her head towards the door – 'if I know that step, this is the Lado himself, so we'll take this matter up another time. But think on what I've said.'

Mary Ann, too, was looking towards the door, and when it opened she managed a smile for the young man entering.

Corny Boyle was now six foot two and broad with it. He had a fine physique, and if he'd had a matching face he might have been billed as a modern Apollo, but Corny could lay no claim to good looks. His best feature was his eyes; for the rest, his face gave the impression of a piece of granite that had been hacked by a would-be sculptor. He looked older than his twenty-three years, in fact he could at times have passed for thirty; this was when his face was in repose, for when he smiled he looked youthful. It could be said that to Corny's one good feature you could add his smile, for it was an impish, irresistible smile, and it infected those it fell upon, it even at times gave some people the impression that he was handsome. It had this latter effect on Mary Ann.

'Hello, Gran.' He took three strides across the room to Fanny's side, and, bending over her, he kissed her cheek, while she placed her hand on his thick hair. Then, looking towards Mary Ann, he said, 'Hello, you.'

'Hello yourself. You've been some time. You said four o'clock.'

'I know I did but I'm only half-an-hour out and I knew you'd be here, sitting gossiping' – he glanced towards Fanny – 'and so . . .'

At this point Mary Ann, bouncing her head, took up his words, and together they chanted, 'And so I went and had a look at Meyer's garage.'

Fanny's head was back now and her laugh was filling the room. 'Aw, begod, you're startin' early!

Well, as long as he wasn't in Flanagan's bar, or at the bettin' shop waitin' the result of the last race, it isn't too bad, eh?' She put her hand out towards Mary Ann, and Mary Ann, laughing, replied, 'That's all he can talk about, cars, cars, cars.'

'Well, as I'll have to support you on cars for the rest of your life what better subject could I talk about?' Corny bent his long length above her and they stared at each other for a moment, their faces becoming solemn; then, doubling his fist, he twice punched her gently on the side of the chin before saying, 'Well, if you want to go to that dance and go home first, you'll have to get a move on.'

'Oh! A move on! We're nowt all bustle and hurry.' Mary Ann inclined her head towards Fanny's broadly smiling face, and as Corny exclaimed, 'Who is it wants to go to the dance, anyway?' she put on her coat and hat and, turning to Fanny, said softly, 'Bye-bye, Mrs McBride, and thanks . . . for the tea and everything.'

'Thank you, hinny, for comin' in.'

'Bye-bye, Gran.' Again Corny kissed the networked skin, but before he straightened up he cast his glance towards Mary Ann, saying, 'Don't you think it's time you called this old faggot Gran, instead of Mrs McBride?'

Fanny and Mary Ann looked at each other, then with a small smile Mary Ann said, 'I suppose so, but somehow . . . well, I always think of you as Mrs McBride and it's got the same feeling as me saying ma, or da . . . You understand?'

'I understand, hinny, an' I'll remain Mrs McBride. An' you know, I like it that way, it's got a dignified ring, don't you think . . . Mrs McBride?'

'Dignified!' Corny now took the flat of his hand and pushed the big broad face to one side, exclaiming, 'You, dignified! . . . You're in your dotage, woman.'

'Get out of it, an' this minute, or I'll let you see who's in their dotage . . . or an old faggot at least.'

Fanny pulled herself up and brandished her fist at him, and Corny, pushing Mary Ann into the passage and about to follow her, looked back into the room and said softly, 'Go on with you, fat old Fan. Dignified, indeed!'

Her grandson's words could have been a compliment, for they brought a warm tender smile to Fanny's face, and when the door closed on him she sat down again, and the smile remained with her as she looked about her with eyes that did not take in the muddle and dust amidst which she sat; for what was muddle she would have said if she had thought about it, and what was dust when your heart was happy knowing that your favourite grandson had had the good sense to pick himself the nicest little lass in the world?

In the street, the nicest little lass walked sedately by Corny's side. She always felt slightly self-conscious when with him in the street, for she remembered experiences when children had shouted after them, 'De ya want a step-ladder, miss?' and, 'Aa'll bunk you up to him for thruppence.' Then there was the day when the woman behind them in the bus said, 'That's the long an' the short of it, isn't it?' And so she resisted her desire to link arms with him, for in her mind's eye she could see how ludicrous it would look. Even when they held hands it must appear to other people as if he was taking a child for a walk. She was five foot tall and, try as she might, she couldn't add a fraction of an inch to this. Her height wasn't noticeable when she was on her own, only when she was with Corny, for besides being small she was slightly built, and this didn't help matters.

'You're quiet,' he said, 'what's the matter?'

'Nothing.'

'Well, it couldn't be much less, could it?' They turned their eyes towards each other and smiled, and the smiles brought a humorous twist to their faces.

'Want to go to that dance?'

Mary Ann moved one shoulder, 'I'm not really particular, I'd just as soon go to the pictures or the bowling alley. What about you?'

'Anything'll suit me. I tell you what though . . .' He moved nearer to her and, his voice dropping to a whisper, he went on, 'I've got some new car catalogues. We could have a smashing time just sitting looking at them.'

Forcing herself not to laugh, she pushed at him with her elbow as she replied, 'That would be wonderful. You wouldn't like us to sit on that seat outside Meyer's garage, would you?'

'Aw.' He moved his head as if in wonder. 'Aw, that would be simply marvellous, just to sit all the night looking at Meyer's garage and them cars.'

'You're barmy. Cars, cars, cars.'

Now her tone had an edge to it, and he mimicked it, saying, 'Cars, cars, cars.' Then went on, 'Yes, I'm barmy about them all right, an' before you're finished you'll be glad I'm barmy about them, because cars, cars, cars, are going to get you all you want . . . In the end they will, anyway.'

'How do you know what I want? For all you know I might want you to go round the streets playing your cornet.'

He slanted his eyes down at her for a moment, then said quietly, 'Look, what's up with you? You're ratty about something. Anything happened in me grannie's?'

'Of course not. What could happen in there?'

'Only talk . . . What were you talking about?'

'Oh, nothing. Look, there's the bus.' She pointed. 'If we miss it, it'll be another half-an-hour.'

Grabbing her arm, he ran with her, almost lifting her off the ground, and he actually hoisted her on to the platform of the bus just as it was about to move away.

Half-an-hour later they were in the country, walking up the lane towards the farm. Although it was a dull day the field to the right of them seemed lit by sunshine, for, with the breeze passing over them, the full heads of barley were making waves of light and shade.

Mary Ann's eyes, following the waves, were lifted into the far distance to the big house on the hill, Mr Lord's house . . . and now Tony's house . . . and Lettice's house. It was strange to think of Tony married to Lettice and then both living with Mr Lord . . . and he liking it. Why was it, she asked herself now, that in spite of her good intentions she always felt the slightest bit of jealousy when she thought of Mr Lord liking Lettice living with him? Although she herself had had a hand in Mr Lord's acceptance of his grandson's wife, she still couldn't help the feeling that she didn't want him to be too happy about it . . . But she really knew what caused this feeling. It was the fear that if he became too engrossed in Tony and his wife he would forget all about her.

'You're not listening to me.'

'What? What did you say?'

Pulling her to a stop, Corny placed his hands on her shoulders and surveyed her through narrowed eyes before saying, 'I said, if they make that branch road off the Newcastle road and come up by Meyer's garage, and if we get the garage, we're made. That's what I said. I've been talking since we got off the bus and you haven't heard a word.'

'You're always talking.' She smiled tenderly up at him. 'But you don't talk to the right people.'

'Oh, don't I?' He raised his brows. 'Well, I'll have to find the right people, won't I? But for the present I'll keep practising on you, to get me fit for the real thing . . . And that's another thing, I was talking about the real thing a minute ago, but you weren't with me. We are going to have a wedding, aren't we?'

'Yes.' She blinked her eyes. The smile was still on her face, but when he snapped his body upwards away from her, exclaiming harshly, 'You're as interested in what I'm saying as if I was talking about a Methodist Sunday School treat,' she cried: 'All right! All right! Don't go on like that.' She swung away, her voice cracking now. 'I might as well tell you I can't think of the wedding . . . so there. I can't think of anything but me da at the present moment.'

'God in Heaven!' Corny put his fist to his brow. 'Don't start on that again – it'll work out. Men go through these phases . . . It'll work out.'

As she stared at him she thought, That's what Mrs McBride said. It's a phase and it'll work out. But what if it doesn't work out?

'How do you know it'll work out?' she demanded now. 'Have you been through the phase?'

'I don't happen to be in me forties.' The impatient note in his voice caused her to respond with, 'Oh, it happens in the forties, does it? Then you've got something to look forward to, haven't you?'

'Aye, yes.' He put on a false smile and his tone was harsh now as he went on, 'I hadn't thought about it in that way. You've got a point there. And, by gad, by the time I've lived with you until I'm forty I imagine I'll be damned glad of a little variety . . . that is, if I manage to stick it out that long.'

'Manage-to-stick-it-out-that-long!' She spaced his words. 'Well, I can tell you here and now, Mr Cornelius Boyle, there'll be no need to endure any purgatory through me.'

They were off again. Their association had always taken this pattern: sunshine, then sudden storm, then sunshine again.

'Good . . . good.' He was towering over her, glaring down at her. 'So we're breaking up. That's it, isn't it?'

'Yes, that's it.'

They stood for a long moment exchanging their momentary animosity, then with a swiftness that startled her his hands were under her oxters and

275

he had lifted her off her feet, and he was kissing her, a hard, rough kiss. Then still holding her to him, he said softly, 'I had to have that for the road, seeing that I'll be on my own for the next forty years.' Now both their bodies began to shake and melt into each other. Her arms were around his neck as she repeated, 'Oh, Corny! Corny! I'm daft I am. I'm daft.'

'I know you are.'

'I mean about me da.'

'That's what I mean an' all; but I tell you he'll get over it.'

'But me mother's worried sick, Corny. And it's the disgrace, and with a young girl. Do you know she's months younger than me?'

'She looks ten years older, and I'm not kiddin'.'

'That's as may be, but she's younger, and when I see her with me da . . . oh, it makes me sick, and I just can't believe it. I can't believe he can be so silly, so nauseatingly silly.'

'Has it happened like this afore?'

They were walking slowly up the lane now, their arms about each other.

'No, not like this, but there have been women who have fallen for him. But then, as I say, they were women, not girls.'

'Did he have affairs with them – I mean the women?'

'No, no, never; he just laughed at them, and laughed about them to me ma. Not that she wasn't worried once or twice, like the time she thought he was gone on Mrs Quinton.'

'Mrs Quinton? Bob Quinton's wife? She's a smasher.'

'There you go . . . smasher. Well, perhaps she is

a smasher but she liked me da.' She nodded her head up at him. 'But this present business is different; it's – it's nasty, and it's keeping on.'

'It's just because he's flattered. Look, do as I say, let things rest and take their course.'

'I can't, Corny, because I'm frightened, really I am. I know it's as you say, it's because she flatters him. And her mother and all, she's as bad, and he laps it up . . . All the more so now because me mother doesn't let on he's there . . . Well, you know what I mean? But she hasn't made much of him for a long time, because she hasn't been feeling too good herself.' She stopped in the road and, twisting round, looked up at him, saying, 'Do you know, I can see both their minds working, both that sly cat's and her mother's. They've got it all set between them. I'll be out of the way when I get married; Michael and Sarah will be in the bungalow; so there will be only me mother and me da left, and now that it's open knowledge that the farm will be me da's one day they think they're on to a good thing. Miss Yvonne's just got to have an affair with me da . . . get herself a baby, and then me mother's out . . .'

'Mary Ann!' As Corny loosened his hold on her he drew his chin into his neck, and the action seemed to pull his voice up from deep down in his chest. 'Don't talk like that,' he said. 'I'm tellin' you, don't talk like that.'

Mary Ann stared at him. Both in voice and manner he could have been her da at this moment. Her lips trembled; she felt alone, lost. Mr Lord no longer required her company, and her da had gone from her, and now Corny turning on her. Well, she wasn't going to put up with it, she wasn't. She cried at him, 'Why shouldn't I talk like that? It's the truth.'

'It may be, but I don't like to hear you taking that tack.'

'You don't, do you? . . . Well, for your information, I'd better remind you we're in nineteen-sixty-four, and I would also remind you that you're supposed to have been around a bit . . . America and all over the . . .'

'I don't care if it's twenty-and-sixty-four.' His voice had a rasping edge to it. 'And yes, I've been around a bit, scoff as much as you like, but I've been around more than you have, and when I was . . . around America I didn't hear the girls, at least not the ones I mixed with, saying things like that. If you were still living in Mullhattan's Hall, or over our way in Howden, and you hadn't had your fancy education, it would be understandable.'

Mary Ann's neck and face were scarlet. Her wide eyes were smarting, and her trembling lips moved with soundless words, a number of times before she whimpered, 'You can think what you like about me, I don't care, I don't care, only I know it's true what I've said; it could happen. As for the girls in America not talking like that, don't . . . don't make me la . . . laugh.' Choking on the last words, she gave a demonstration of laughter by bursting into tears. And when he caught her close, crying, 'There! There! Give over.' 'I'm sorry,' she gabbled, 'I'm worried. I'm frightened. I know it could happen. I do, I do. And you . . . you going for me and making me out to be something nasty just because I said what . . . what I know she's trying to . . .'

'There! There! All right, all right. Come on, don't cry. And you're right. Listen . . . listen to me.' He lifted her face upwards. 'I know you're right, but somehow . . . well!' he moved his head slowly – 'I hate to hear you talk like that. Let everybody else in the world say what they want to say, and how they want to say it, but you . . . aw.' He hunched his shoulders. 'Here, dry your face.'

Clumsily he wiped the tears from her face, then said, 'Come on, smile. You don't want to go in and give your mother something else to worry about, do you? She's got enough on her plate at present. Come on.' His mouth twisted sideways as he ended, sanctimoniously, 'Let us be a comfort to her in her old age, anyway.'

Mary Ann hiccoughed; the tears were still rolling from her eyes but she wanted to laugh, and she actually did laugh when, bending down to her, he whispered, 'About the American girls, that was a pack of lies. Coo! The things that some of them used to say, they made you sizzle, like water on a hot frying pan.'

'Oh, Corny, Corny, you're daft. Oh, you are daft.'

They were hurrying up the road now, close once again, and as they neared the farm the dull clouds parted and the sun shone, picking out the newly pink-cement-dashed farmhouse, with its two ornamental red-bricked chimneys straining upwards towards an overhanging branch of a mighty oak tree whose base boarded the road some yards away. It picked out the farm building, white-washed and neat, forming three sides of a square. It showed two farm cottages with their long gardens patterned with vegetables and early chrysanthemums.

As they entered the farm gates there was a murmuring of cattle from the byres, the sharp bark of the dog, and the distant thud of a galloping horse sporting in the field beyond the buildings.

This, her home, had always been a form of heaven to Mary Ann, but now she was experiencing the knowledge that surroundings only become significant when the people close to you are at peace. But there was no peace either in or between those close to her, and the reason for that state was now coming across the courtyard.

Mary Ann did not call to Mike or hurry to greet him, or he to her. As she took in the fact that he was hesitating in the middle of the yard she felt Corny's swift decision, almost as if he had said aloud, 'Well, somebody's got to stand by him.' 'I'll be with you in a minute,' was what he said to her, and as he went towards her father she made her way slowly towards the house.

2

Mary Ann woke up with the sun streaming on to her face, and she blinked into it; then, turning completely over on to her stomach, she stretched one leg after the other and lay supine for some moments. Her mind not yet disturbed by thoughts, she felt relaxed and warm . . . and nice, but the more she tried to hold the feeling the faster she was becoming awake. As she wondered what time it was, she raised her head and looked at the bedside clock. Half-past seven. She twisted round and pulled herself upwards by putting her hands behind her head and gripping the bed rail, then, leaning back and staring into the sun once more, she began to pick up the sounds from below her. She heard the even note of her mother's voice, then the deeper tone of Michael's, then came a short, thick spray of words, the tone of which she had not heard before rising from the kitchen at this time of the morning. It brought her upright in the bed; she had forgotten for the moment that Corny had slept here last night. They had all, except her father, stayed up late talking about the wedding, and when Corny was ready to go it was blowing a gale. It was her mother who had said,

'You can't go out in this, you'll get soaked.' As usual, Corny had his motor-bike with him but he hadn't a cape. He hadn't taken much persuading to stay and he had phoned a fish-and-chip shop that was three doors away from his home and asked a neighbour to tell his mother that he was staying the night.

Mary Ann smiled to herself; it would be funny going down and seeing Corny at breakfast. She had better get up. She threw the clothes back and sat on the edge of the bed and again she stretched – she hadn't to go to the office today. She had taken the day off to help get things ready for the morrow, and Sarah's wedding. That's why she had felt so nice, she supposed, when she woke up, not having to go into work. But the niceness hadn't lasted very long, had it, because now she was feeling as she had done for weeks, worried. Well, she sighed, she wasn't the only one, everyone in the house was worried . . . And yet that wasn't true. Michael wasn't really worried about what was going on; nor was Sarah. They both seemed already to be living separate lives, a joint separate life. And they were chary about discussing the business of her da and Yvonne Radley. Sarah, because she had become very fond of Mike, and Michael, Mary Ann knew, because he wanted to preserve the picture of her da that he had built up around him these last few years. He didn't want to go back to his childhood and the feeling of hate he'd had for the man who couldn't stop drinking. Michael and her da had become very close during the last few years, and now he was shutting his eyes to anything that would show up her da in an unfavourable light . . . She wished that she, too, could shut her eyes to it.

A few minutes later, when she went into the bathroom, she found all the towels wet. That was their Michael; he not only used his own towel but everybody else's. She felt she wanted to rush to the stair-head and cry, as she sometimes did, 'Not a dry towel again! You leave my towel alone, our Michael.' But as she looked in the mirror she said to herself, 'Stop it, there's enough trouble.' Yet she still asked her reflection, 'But why does he want to use so many towels?'

Ten minutes later, as she descended the stairs, she paused for a second when she saw Mike crossing the hall. He was going out the front way and he had his big boots on . . . He was just doing it to aggravate her mother, for her mother took pride in the hall and it always looked lovely.

When she reached the bottom stair Mike had pulled the front door open, and he turned towards her, and after a second, during which he looked hard at her, he said, 'Mornin'.'

'Good morning, Da.'

'Mary Ann.' His voice was low.

'Yes, Da?'

He jerked his head and beckoned her to him, and when she stood before him he looked straight at her as he said, 'I should be down in the bottom field around ten, do you think you could spare me a few minutes?'

Her eyes dropped from his. 'I . . . I don't know; me mother's got so many things she wants doing and—'

'All right, all right.' He stood stiffly, holding up his hand in a checking movement. 'Don't come if you don't want to; I understand it's a very busy day for everybody.' His tone was sarcastic. 'But just suppose you have a minute or so to spare, I would—' he paused, 'I would be grateful for a word with you.'

She looked up at him. Her da had never talked like this to her in his life, sarcastically, nor had he ever had to ask her to go and have a word with him. He'd always had to push her from him, stop her from having too many words with him. 'I'll be there,' she said.

'Thank you.' The sarcasm was heavy in his tone.

She turned away and went into the kitchen, there to meet her mother's inquiring glance. It was just the flick of Lizzie's eye but it said plainly, 'What did he say? What did he want?'

Mary Ann answered it with, 'I don't want any bacon, Mother, just some cereal.'

'You'd better get a breakfast into you.'

'I don't feel like it.'

Mary Ann now turned her head towards the table and looked at Corny. His eyes were waiting for her. 'Hello,' she said. 'Did you sleep all right?'

Corny grinned as he replied, 'Like a man with a clear conscience.'

'Huh! Aren't we self-righteous.' She sat down opposite to him, and Corny, looking now at Lizzie and his grin widening, said, 'This is the first time I've seen her first thing in the mornin'. Lord, doesn't she look miserable!'

Lizzie smiled faintly at this boy, at this young man, at this big fellow whom she had tried so hard to dislike – this boy who was the last person on earth she would have wanted Mary Ann to marry; this young man who was too big altogether for Mary Ann and whose prospects, on the other hand, were too small for what she wanted for her daughter; this big fellow who was the cause of Mary Ann not marrying Tony. For years she had set her heart on her daughter becoming the wife of Mr Lord's grandson and having all the things that that marriage would entail. But apparently it wasn't to be. How many more disappointments in life could she put up with? How much more could she stand and keep sane? Her mind on the last thought had moved away from Mary Ann, and now she was saying to herself, What were they talking about at the front door? . . . And fancy him going out the front way in his dirty boots. He just did that to work me up after last night. As she picked up the teapot she thought, Perhaps I should have let him talk. Yet, listening to him making excuses and giving reasons for his madness would only have made things worse. I couldn't have bore it.

Mary Ann's raised voice brought her attention to the table. 'What's the matter now?' she asked.

'Well, I'm just saying I'm right.' Mary Ann looked up at Lizzie as she pointed a finger of toast across the table in the direction of Corny. 'He said, why do I want to cut up the toast like this and put finicky bits of marmalade on it, and I said it was the right way. And it is, isn't it? Not to butter and marmalade a slice all at once, I mean.'

'Oh, Mary Ann!' Lizzie shook her head at her daughter with a despairing movement. 'Why must you start on such things?'

'But I didn't, Mother, it was him.' She nodded at Corny.

'Huh!' said Corny. 'She was talking as if I didn't know the right way to eat. I know all about fingers of toast and dabbing bits of this, that, and the other on it, but you only do that when you're in hotels, or out with posh company, don't you, Mam?' He addressed Lizzie with the familiar term he had always used since he had become engaged to Mary Ann; and his attitude now towards her was as if she was his mother and arbitrator in a family dispute.

And now Lizzie smiled at him. You couldn't help but like Corny; however much you tried not to, you couldn't help but like him. She nodded at him, saying, 'Yes, you're right, Corny.'

'He's not, Mother. And don't stick up for him about such things, it only makes him worse . . . big-headed.'

'Whose going to stick up for whose big head?' The door from the scullery opened and Michael came in. He looked a younger edition of his father, and as he walked down the long room to the table he could have been Mike himself twenty years earlier. When he picked up a slice of toast from the rack and started to butter it, Lizzie said, 'You've had your breakfast not half-an-hour ago.'

'Was it only half-an-hour? It seems I've never had a bite since yesterday.'

'Well, tomorrow's not affecting your appetite, that's something.' Lizzie smiled tenderly at her son, and Michael, reaching out for the marmalade, stopped with his hand in mid air and inquired of Corny, 'What's the matter?'

'Nothing . . . nothing.' Corny's voice was rapid. 'Go on, marmalade your toast.'

'Aw you!' Mary Ann, her lips tight now, was

shaking her head at the aggravating individual, and when Michael had finished spreading his slice of toast thickly with marmalade, Corny looked at her and gave one wide grin as he let out a deep chest full of air and said, 'There now.'

'There now, what? What's this all about? What's the matter with you two first thing in the morning?'

'She says it ain't—' Corny stressed the ain't, 'she says it ain't refeened to eat toast like that, Michael. We should cut it into refeened little fingers, like so.' He demonstrated.

'Oh, we should, should we?' Michael was returning Corny's grin. 'Oh, what it is to be a lady; it must be painful.' And leaning towards Corny, Michael pityingly added, 'Boy, I don't envy you . . . Poor blighter . . .'

'Aw, there's a pair of you.' Mary Ann tossed her head disdainfully. 'You eat like pigs, clagging everything up . . .'

'HA!' A high derisive hoot came from Michael. 'Listen to her. Listen to her. Listen to her. Ooh! Miss Shaughnessy, how can you let yourself down to such a low level? Did you hear what she said, Corny?' He turned wide eyes in Corny's direction again. ' "Clag," she said. Did you hear her? . . . Clag.'

'Now, now, stop it, or it'll end up in words, hot words, if not in tears.' Lizzie, addressing the two young men and bringing their eyes towards her, motioned with a jerk of her head towards Mary Ann's back.

'Tears.' Mary Ann rounded on her mother. 'They won't reduce me to tears, not that pair.'

As she bounced up from the table, Lizzie placed

a hand on her shoulder and said, 'Sit down and have something to eat. Now you're not going to start doing anything until you have your breakfast.' As she pressed her daughter into the chair again she could have added, as she might have done some weeks earlier, 'What's put you in this tear so early in the morning?' But she had no need to question her daughter's state of mind, she knew the reason only too well.

Although Lizzie's own nerves were near to breaking point, and her heart was sore, and her feelings towards her husband were almost verging on hate at this moment, she wished Mary Ann had not taken a stand against her father, for her attitude towards the man she had always adored seemed to Lizzie to put a finality on the whole thing. Nothing Mike had ever done in his life had made Mary Ann stop speaking to him, until now, and Lizzie found her feelings entwining round her daughter, loving her as she had not done for some time, in fact, since she was a baby, because since Mary Ann had come to the use of reason she had always taken her father's part. Be he in the right or wrong – and he was more often in the wrong than not – Mary Ann had always stood valiantly by him. But Mary Ann was no longer a child, she was almost twenty and she was soon to be married, and in her father's present madness she was seeing him for the first time as he really was. Yet in spite of all this Lizzie wanted to say to her: 'Go and talk to him; be kind to him, because I can't.' And, knowing her husband, she knew that he needed somebody . . . he always needed somebody to be kind to him.

At this moment there came the sound of

fumbling with the handle of the door leading from the hall, and although all their eyes turned in the direction of the door no-one got up to open it, and it was seconds later before it was pushed wide, and there entered Sarah Flannagan.

Sarah was supporting herself on two elbow crutches, and while her right foot tentatively touched the ground she dragged the whole of her left leg from the hip downwards as if it was part of a dead carcass that had been tied to her. From the waist up she was well formed, and above the long neck was a radiant face.

This was the Sarah Flannagan who had lived opposite to Mary Ann in Mulhattan's Hall for years. This was the girl who had been Mary Ann's enemy, who had fought with her daily, playing on her weak point, her affection for her drunken father. This was the girl who had written things about Mike Shaughnessy on walls and had driven Mary Ann to a frenzy of retaliation. This was the girl who had found, at an early age, that she loved horses and wanted to work with them, and had worked with them until two years ago when she had been struck with polio. But above all, this was the girl who loved Michael Shaughnessy and whom Michael Shaughnessy adored. There was no resemblance between this wise, tender, beautiful cripple, and the girl who had been brought up in Burton Street.

No-one in the room moved to help her until she almost reached the table; then Michael went quietly to her side and pulled out a chair for her, and when she was seated they looked at each other for a moment. It was the look that always brought an odd feeling into Mary Ann's body.

Mary Ann, it could be said now, also loved Sarah as much as she had once hated her. And although they had scrapped all their lives, she also loved Michael. Yet when she saw Sarah and Michael together there emanated a feeling from them that created in her a sense of want, and of loss. For what exactly, she didn't know; she told herself it was because they never fought, but seemed always at peace in each other's company, whereas she and Corny rarely met unless they went for each other in some way.

'Sleep well?' Michael was asking Sarah; and she answered with a shake of her head. 'No, hardly at all . . .' She paused, then asked, 'Did you?'

Michael, bowing his head as if in shame, tried to suppress a smile as he confessed, 'Like a top.'

'They have no finer feelings, that's why they can sleep.' Mary Ann was looking at Sarah, and Sarah answered, 'Perhaps you're right. Or no nerves.' She cast a swift glance again towards Michael, and he, bending and kissing her quite unselfconsciously, said softly, 'I'll move my coarse presence from you to the cow sheds.'

As Michael went to leave the kitchen Corny asked, 'Give you a hand or anything, Michael?' And Michael, turning from the doorway, answered, 'We never say no to an extra hand, Corny, but I thought you'd have to be at the garage.'

'No, I took a couple of days off,' said Corny. 'And for no other reason, mind you' – he was nodding his head now at Michael – 'but that Miss Shaughnessy had done the same and she'd be lonely without me . . . Wouldn't know what to do with herself, in fact.'

Michael was laughing, Sarah was laughing, but Mary Ann, refusing to smile, was giving Corny a straight stare as he, rising from the table, bent towards her and chucked her under the chin, saying with tenderness that was more real than make-believe, 'Good-bye, sugar.'

When the door had closed on the two young men Mary Ann let her face slide into a smile, and when she looked at Sarah they both began to laugh.

Lizzie sat down at the table, poured herself out a cup of tea, and, looking at her daughter, remarked, 'Your breakfasts, in the future, should be very entertaining.'

'Well, he's so aggravating.'

'And you're not, of course.' Lizzie's remark was softened by the tilt of her lips. 'In some ways I think he's very patient with you.'

'Patient! Huh!' Mary Ann tossed her head, while at the same time feeling pleased that her mother was taking Corny's part. She wanted her mother to like Corny, for she felt that even after all this long time of knowing him, and accepting him as her future son-in-law, she was still in two minds about him.

But her attention was drawn to Sarah, who was saying, 'Breakfasts in the future are going to be different for me; I'll miss all this . . . the talk . . . the bustle.' She looked at Lizzie as she spoke, and Lizzie replied softly, 'I'll miss you, too. It won't be the same without you, Sarah.'

As her mother and her future sister-in-law exchanged warm glances there was wafted to Mary Ann that feeling of want, of loss. Her mother liked Sarah, and this fact alone said a great deal, because Lizzie adored her son, and Sarah was marrying that son . . . taking him away.

Sarah was now saying, 'It's funny how your opinions change. A year ago I was dead against going into the bungalow, wasn't I? And so was Michael, although his reasons were different from mine. He didn't want to be beholden to Mr Lord, whereas I didn't want to be stuck helpless in a house away from you all. But now—' her smile widened and lit up the whole of her face, 'now I can get about, it's different . . . And fancy me being able to drive a car. You would never have believed it a year ago, would you?'

'No,' said Lizzie. 'You never would, Sarah. It's like a miracle.'

Yes, thought Mary Ann, what had happened to Sarah was like a miracle. When she came to take up the front room here it was with the idea of her and Michael marrying almost straight away, and then one day she announced, and quite calmly, that she wasn't going to marry Michael until she could walk. Her decision had caused a bit of an unheaval at the time and a great number of shaking heads. But tomorrow Sarah would achieve the goal she had aimed at, she would go up to the altar rails on her feet. In a white wedding gown that would cover her trailing limb, she would stand by Michael's side while they were married.

Remembering the work, the patience, yes, and the tears that Sarah had endured to achieve her object, there now attached itself to that odd feeling in Mary Ann one of inadequacy. She felt useless, utterly useless. She had never done anything. When Mrs McBride's words of yesterday came to her, she said to herself, Aw, what's that? Mrs McBride was just trying to be nice. And as she rose abruptly from the table she wished that something awful would happen so that she could prove herself like Sarah had.

'Where you off to in a rush?' Lizzie looked at her sharply.

'Nowhere. I just wanted to make a start . . . Shall I do the dishes and clear the scullery?'

'Yes. Yes, you could do that.'

As she stood at the sink washing the dishes and the murmur of her mother's and Sarah's voices came to her, she thought, Why don't they get up and get going? She said there was so much to do – that's why I stayed off the day . . . When her hands became still in the soapy water she looked down at them and said to herself, I don't feel nice inside, I don't . . . It's awful, awful feeling like this.

At half-past nine Mary Ann was wondering what excuse she could make in order to leave the house and go down to the bottom field. And then her mother made it plain sailing for her by saying, 'Will you take the tea out to them?' She did not say to your da. 'They're in the bottom field I think.'

Taking the basket loaded with three lidded cans of tea and a cellophane bag of substantial cheese sandwiches, she left the house by the back door, then cut across the farmyard, calling to Simon as she did so. She touched the Labrador's head as he took up his position close to her side, and when they went through the gate and on to the field path a long-haired black cat jumped from a low hayrick and joined them. The cat mewed and she stooped and patted it, saying, 'All right, Tigger.' Then they moved on, the dog close to her side and the cat trotting behind them.

When they reached the low wall that bordered the south meadow Sarah's horse – which she was determined to ride one day – threw up its head and came galloping towards them, and when, neighing as it went, it trotted at the other side of the wall, Mary Ann called to him, 'When I come back, Dusty, when I come back.' When they reached the end of the wall the horse, unable to go further, neighed loudly as they went down a steep cart track towards a large field, where, in the far distance, she could see the binder, driven by Michael, turning in the direction of Corny, who was at the other end of the line. But she couldn't see her da. She walked towards where the ground rose before drooping into a miniature valley, and as she neared it Mike came into view.

On the sight of him the dog gave one staccato bark, and Mike turned his head, then straightened his back, and as they approached the dog left Mary Ann's side and went quietly forward and nuzzled him.

'I've brought your break.' She was looking down into the basket.

'I'm ready for it.' He held out his hand, and she handed him one of the cans.

'Come and sit down a minute.' He pointed to a hillock of ground, but she answered quickly, 'I've got to take theirs; it'll . . . it'll get cold.'

'It can wait a few minutes.' His gaze, fixed on her face, brought her eyes up to his and she went and sat down.

When Mike lowered himself to the ground, but not too near her, the dog lay down against his side, while the cat, thinking it was about time to show some remnants of her independence, strolled, delicate-pawed, over the stubbly grass along the hedgerow.

Taking the lid off the can, Mike drank thirstily. After replacing the lid and setting the can on the ground, he wiped his broad mouth with the pad of his thumb; then, pulling up his knees, he rested his forearm on them, and, his head going slightly back, he looked up into the wide, high sky before saying gruffly, 'What's come over you and me, Mary Ann?'

When she made no answer, except to lower her head, he, with his eyes still turned skywards, went on, 'I thought nothin' on God's earth could come atween us. I would have sworn that if I'd committed a murder you would have stood by me.'

'And I would.' Her words were scarcely audible to him. 'You know I would . . . But this isn't a murder, it's something different . . . something . . .' She paused for a long while before adding in a thin whisper, 'Nasty.'

'Aw, my God, Mary Ann!' He was no longer looking skywards; his head had drooped and his brow was resting on his clenched fist, and his face became contorted as he ground his strong teeth. Then, raising his head slightly from his hands, he muttered, 'You don't know. And how should you? You can't understand; things happen. You don't ask for them to happen, you don't want them to happen, they happen in little episodes. Aye, that's how they happen, in little episodes. And I can tell you this . . .' He turned his head slightly in her direction. 'They would stay little episodes if people would leave them alone, if they would stop making issues out of them; stop keeping on, if they would forget them, or just take them as part and parcel of life. Then they wouldn't grow. You understand what I'm saying now?' His head was fully turned towards her, waiting for her answer, and she turned hers and looked at him. She understood what he was saying. The people he was referring to were simply her mother; but she didn't blame her mother for the attitude she had taken, how could she? Very likely she would react in the same way herself if Corny were to carry on with another girl . . . Oh, she would go on worse than her mother, she knew that. Her mother could be cool, and distant, staving off words . . . She paused here in her thinking. Perhaps that attitude was worse than having it out, having a row. Yes, she knew it was.

'Look, Mary Ann, I've done nothing wrong.' Mike's voice was quiet and level now. 'You understand what I mean, don't you?'

'Yes, Da.' She gave a small nod. 'Yes, I understand. But how long will you be able to say that?' She was amazed at herself for asking such a question, of her da of all people.

'Mary Ann.' Mike closed his eyes now and rocked his big head in wide, slow movements. 'It's a passing phase, it'll blow over.'

'Why did you start it?'

'Why does a man breathe? You don't know . . . it's one of those things.' He turned and looked over the wide field to where the binder was now coming towards them, and he said, as if to himself, 'Life gallops on, and the quicker it gallops the more set it gets. And sometimes in the night you get frightened – aye, frightened; you're done for, finished, you're old. And then along comes somebody who makes you feel a lad again, and you like it. You get a new lease of life, it's like a drug. And you've got enough sense in the back of your mind to recognise it as just that, an' you know damn well that its effects will wear off. But for the time being you're living like you thought you would never live again . . . Aw, it's all too complicated . . .'

Mary Ann, her own hands clasped tightly now, was thinking, Mrs McBride, that's what Mrs McBride had said. At least, her words had meant the same thing. She was wise, was Mrs McBride. But then she was very old; whereas her mother wasn't old enough to be wise in that way yet, and her da was being cruel to her. He was indulging in a second childhood. Well, anyway, a second youth, and not thinking about the effects on her mother . . . or the effect on herself. This thought forced from her mouth the words, 'She's younger than me, Da.'

As Mike began to beat his brow with his clenched fist, Mary Ann rose slowly to her feet, and when she went to pass him his hand shot out and pulled her close to him. Her face just above his, they stared at each other. Looking at him, Mary Ann did not think as she had done from a child, He's handsome, me da, and there's something about him. Years ago she had been flattered when women like Mrs Quinton had liked her da, but not any more. Her eyes now took in his neck. It was thick, and brown, and had lines on it; and there was hair sprouting from within his ears. Her da was no longer a young man, he was in his forties. Never before had she thought like this about him, she had always seen him young.

'Are you listening to me?'

She blinked twice. 'Yes, Da.'

'I said, it would be over the morrow.'

'What?'

'You weren't listening . . . I said it'll be finished the morrow.'

'Oh, Da.' Slowly she smiled at him. 'You'll tell them . . . ?' She did not think of the girl alone in this matter; her mother was a force to be contended with also, and she was fully aware of this. 'When they come to the wedding, you'll tell them?'

'Well . . .' He moved his full lips one over the other and lowered his gaze for a moment, before saying, 'There . . . there won't be any need to tell them, but it'll be finished, you'll see.'

'But, Da . . .'

'Believe me.' He cupped her cheek with his hand. 'Don't worry any more; it'll be over the morrow night, you'll see. I promise you that.'

She believed him. She knew he meant it. She wanted to burst into tears and fall against him, burying her head in the beloved neck. She gulped and, lowering her head, turned from him, saying, 'All right, Da, all right.'

Mike made no further move to detain her, but as she hurried across the field Corny's voice hailed her, shouting, 'Hi there!' But it did not turn her round. For answer, she began to run, the tears raining unchecked now down her face. Her feet slipping on the stubbles, she ran until she reached the car track, and it was as she was crossing this that another voice came to her from where the track joined the road leading to the farm. And there she saw Tony's car, and Tony himself waving to her.

Aw, what was she to do? If she didn't go down to him he would turn back to the house and find out what was wrong with her. She rubbed her face hastily with her handkerchief and, walking slowly now, went down the slope towards the car.

As Tony came to meet her she could see Lettice leaning from the car window, and as she answered Lettice's salute with a lift of her hands, Tony came up to her, saying, 'What's the matter? What are you crying for?'

'Leave me alone.' She could talk like this to Tony.

'Well—' he smiled ruefully, 'to use your own phraseology, Miss, nobody's touching you.'

'Aw, don't be clever or facetious, I can't stand it this morning.' She had for a long while now stopped thinking, with regard to Tony, I could have married him if I'd liked, because she knew that Tony wasn't for her, or she for him. Lettice was the right one for Tony. She might be a bit older but she was what he needed.

'Hello, Mary Ann.' Lettice opened the door and stepped into the road.

'Hello, Lettice.'

Lettice now bent towards her, saying softly, 'What's the matter?'

'Oh . . .' Mary Ann shook her head. 'You know what it is.'

As Lettice remained silent, Tony put in, 'You're still worrying about Mike?'

'Wouldn't you? If you were in my place . . . or me mother's?'

As Tony raised his brows, Lettice put in, 'Of course he would, but at the same time, Mary Ann, I can't imagine your father doing anything really stupid. He's flattered by the girl; men are made like that.'

If anybody had experience about men being flattered by girls it was Lettice. She had suffered from it for years, putting a face on things to keep her first marriage together, and what had happened in the end?

'Some men', went on Lettice, with a knowing quality in her voice, 'would let it go to their heads, but not Mike.'

In the pause that followed, Tony put in, lightly, 'I saw Michael earlier on this morning. He appeared as calm as a cucumber, quite un-concerned.'

Mary Ann gave a little smile at this, saying, 'Our Michael doesn't give much away. I heard him moving about in his room at two o'clock this morning. Yet he told Sarah he slept like a top, and made her believe it.'

Lettice and Tony laughed, then Tony said, 'I've got a message for you . . . he wants to see you.'

There was no need for Mary Ann to question the 'he'; there was only one he . . . Mr Lord. 'What does he want?' she asked.

Tony shook his head. 'I don't know.'

Mary Ann stared up into the thin face that was so like Mr Lord's, and she said, 'Of course you know; there's nothing you don't know . . . He does know, doesn't he, Lettice?'

Confronted with the question, the older woman

said, 'Leave me out of this, Mary Ann. But I can tell you this, he's in good spirits this morning.'

'That's a change,' said Mary Ann. 'What's brought it on?'

'Oh . . .' Lettice looked from Mary Ann to her husband, then back to Mary Ann as she said, 'He had a bit of news last night that seemed to please him. He's . . . he's hoping for a great-grandson.'

Mary Ann's mouth dropped open as she turned her gaze towards Tony, but Tony was looking at Lettice. Lettice was going to have a baby, but she was old . . . Oh well, not really . . . but old to have a baby. She was over thirty-six. Well, people had babies up to forty and after, didn't they? She supposed so, but somehow . . . well, it didn't seem quite right. Lettice herself was a grandmother. Her only daughter, whom she rarely saw, had had a baby last year.

Both Lettice and Tony were looking at her now, and she made her smile broad as she said, 'Oh, that'll be lovely for you. Fancy you going to have a baby . . . Do you want a baby?'

Lettice's attractive face puckered as if in doubt; and then she said, 'Not . . . not particularly, Mary Ann, but I have two men to please, and both of them seem bent on it. The old one more than the young one, I must confess.' She now lent her head gently towards Tony, and he put his arm around her and pressed her to him. And Mary Ann thought, I wish they wouldn't do that. And this was strange, because never had she witnessed affection between her da and her mother without finding joy in it. When they were happy she wanted the whole world to be happy, but when, as now, they weren't happy she supposed she resented other people's happiness. And yet she'd had a large hand in bringing happiness to Tony and Lettice, so she shouldn't feel like this.

She said quickly, 'Eeh! I'll have to be going, there's so much to do . . . But I'm glad for you, I am, I am . . . Will you call it Mary Ann if it's a girl?'

'Not on your life. Fancy another like you!' Tony pushed at her with the flat of his hand as he laughed, then added seriously, 'You will go up, won't you?'

'Yes, I'll go up . . . Imagine what would happen if I disobeyed the order.'

'Yes, imagine.'

'And you won't tell me what it's about?'

'I told you, I don't know.' He was grinning at her now.

'Oh, go on.' She turned from him, then turned back again, saying swiftly, 'Bye-bye, Lettice.'

'Bye-bye, Mary Ann.'

Mary Ann did not give her mother Lettice's news, because she felt that Lizzie would consider it should be her to whom this news should apply, and so would cry. What she did say to Lizzie was, 'I saw Tony and Lettice going out in the car. Tony said Mr Lord wants me.'

'What for? Did he say?'

'He said he didn't know, but I'm sure he does.'

'Well, you'd better get yourself off, hadn't you?'

'But there's all those cakes to ice.'

'Never mind about them, get yourself away up.'

Her mother always saw to it that Mr Lord's orders were obeyed, at least as far as it lay within her power, and she added now, 'Don't dawdle, you don't know what he might want to see you about.'

'Well, it can't be anything that's going to go bad for an hour or so, can it?'

'Mary Ann!'

'All right, all right, I'll go now.'

Once again Mary Ann went through the farmyard, but this time she turned up the hill towards the big house that stood on the brow. She went through the paved courtyard, with its ornamental urns of flowers, to the back door, and, after knocking, she opened the door and entered the kitchen.

A middle-aged woman, turning from the Aga stove, said brightly, 'Good morning, miss.'

'Good morning, Eva . . . Ben about?'

'I think he's with the master, miss.'

The advent of a woman servant in Mr Lord's house, and in Ben's kitchen, in itself spoke volumes for Lettice's power.

As she left the kitchen, Ben, his old head sunk into his hollowed shoulders, came shambling across the hall. He had a small tray in his hand, on which was an empty glass and plate, and on the sight of Mary Ann he put the tray on the side table and, turning to her, said in a hoarse whisper, 'He's waiting for you. He's in high fettle this morning.' His wrinkled face moved into what for him was a smile, and Mary Ann, bending towards him, whispered, 'What does he want, do you know, Ben?'

It wasn't strange that Mary Ann should ask Ben this question, because Ben knew everything. Ben had lived with the taciturn Mr Lord for as far back as he cared to remember, and although his master treated him at times as a numskull, to Ben he was God, all the God he needed.

The small smile still on his face, Ben said, 'You'll know soon enough. Go on, don't keep him waiting.'

When Mary Ann entered the drawing-room, Mr Lord was sitting in his favourite position before the tall windows, looking out on to the terraced gardens. He was a tall man, thin as a rake, with skin wizened almost as much as that of his servant, but his pale-blue eyes held a brightness and vitality that denied his age.

'You've taken your time.' The voice was stern, the face unsmiling, and to this greeting Mary Ann said, 'Well, Tony only told me not more than fifteen minutes ago; I can't fly.'

A quiver passed over the wrinkled skin, and the eyes, from under lowered lids, looked keenly at her as he said, 'In a bad mood this morning, aren't you?'

'Me in a bad mood?' Her eyes stretched wide, and on this he held up his hand, saying, 'All right, all right, we won't go into it . . . Everybody very busy, I suppose?' His voice held a quiet note now.

'Yes.' She sat down in front of him. He always demanded that she sit in front of him, where he could look fully at her.

'And everybody on edge?'

She nodded at him, then said, 'All except Sarah and Michael.'

He smiled, and the wrinkles on his face converged together. And then his head nodding slowly, he said, 'They'll be happy, those two. Although he's taken on a burden, it'll become lighter, not heavier, with the years, and as she works at her miracle she'll weave wonder into their lives . . . Don't you think so?'

The pale, steely gaze was tight on her face, and she answered abruptly, 'I don't know.' And she didn't know, because she wasn't thinking of Michael or Sarah. But she knew this old man, she knew that his mind was really not on Sarah and Michael's future, but was working in another direction.

His eyes still hard on her, his lips moving as if he were sucking on a sweet, he stared at her for a full minute before inquiring, 'What's the matter with you? You're upset.'

If Mary Ann knew her Mr Lord, Mr Lord knew his Mary Ann.

'I'm not. What makes you think that?'

'You always were a big liar, my dear, but you were also a bad liar. What's troubling you? I ask you, what's troubling you?'

'I tell you, nothing. But we're all in a rush down there.' She motioned her head backwards towards the window, indicating the farmhouse. 'We . . . we don't have a wedding every day.'

Again the pale-blue eyes were holding hers. And now Mr Lord said, 'It's Mike, isn't it? . . . Oh! oh! don't get on your high horse.' He now bent his stiff body towards her and said softly, 'I know that look in your face, and only your father can put it there. He's done so before and he's doing it now, and I've no doubt but he'll do it again many times before you die.'

'I tell you . . .'

'You can go on telling me, but what I want to hear is what he has been up to now.'

'Nothing, nothing.' That would be the last

straw if Mr Lord heard about Yvonne Radley. Oh, Holy Mother – a section of her mind was praying now – don't let him find out about that.

'If you don't tell me I can find out. I have my ways and means.' He was nodding quickly at her. 'Tony and Lettice just tell me what they think is good for me, but if I want to know anything I have my ways and means.' His head was moving slower now, and Mary Ann thought, Yes, he has his ways and means. Ben was his ways and means. She liked Ben, and Ben, she knew, liked her; surprisingly, because Ben had no thought but for this old man here, and that his days should be spent in peace and free from worry. But to achieve this she knew that Ben, even in his doddering old age, would take on the task of the CID to find out anything his master needed to know. But Mary Ann thought none the less of Ben for this, she only feared what his probing might do to her da, because, besides trying to rule her life, Mr Lord had also tried to rule Mike's, and her father wasn't as easy under the reins as she was. Not that she was really easy.

'Well, have it your own way.' Mr Lord leaned back and rested his head against the wing of the chair, and, after drawing in a long thin breath and placing his bony fingertips together, he said, 'How would you like me to do something for that big fellow of yours?'

Mary Ann's eyes were completely round now, and, knowing the other thing he had done for Corny, which had transported him to the other side of the world, she was wary in her answer. 'It all depends on what it is,' she said.

'Yes, that's a good answer: it all depends on

what it is. Well . . . how would you like to see him set up in a garage, a real garage?'

'But . . . but he's after the one in Moor Lane.'

Mr Lord jerked his head disdainfully. 'That isn't a garage, that's a broken-down repair shop, and on a side road at that. What business can he expect there?'

'They're thinking of opening it up, making it a main . . .'

'Yes, yes, in twenty years' time. I know all about that . . . But there's a place going now, at least shortly, on the main road . . . Baxter's.'

'Baxter's!' Her mouth now formed an elongated O, and when she closed it she swallowed before repeating, 'Baxter's! But it's a show place.'

'I grant you it's a show place. But it also does a very good business.'

'Oh.' She was smiling. 'You'd really set him up in that?'

He nodded. 'Yes, I would. I feel I owe him something for that little trip he made on my suggestion. Baxter's will be in the market in three months' time. I intend to buy it and lease it to him, and if he shows progress I'll give him a share in it, in a year or so. I think that is a fair enough deal, don't you?'

'Oh, yes . . . yes.' Her words were slow. It was wonderful. She said now, 'He's got quite a bit of his own saved up, over four hundred.'

'Four hundred! Huh!' Mr Lord's tone was now derisive. 'What do you think can be done with four hundred, Mary Ann, when you want to buy a business of this kind? Baxter's will go for nothing less than thirty thousand . . . thirty thousand pounds!'

Her face was straight. She couldn't visualise the enormous sum of thirty thousand pounds and the potentialities therein, but she could see the great achievement, and what could be done with four hundred pounds because she had helped in the gathering of it. When Corny would say on a Saturday night, 'Shall we go down to the bowling alley in Jarrow?' she would think for a moment: if they went to the bowling alley it would mean anything up to two pounds spent in the evening. So time and time again she had said, 'Oh, let's just go for a run on the bike.' And sitting on the pillion, clinging tightly to him, she had spent wind-torn, chilling hours, to enable them to add to the growing sum on which their future was to be built.

'You must be realistic, Mary Ann. Businesses are not bought in hundreds today, it takes thousands, tens of thousands to get a start, that is if you want to make real money and not peddle your life away in a backwater.'

The backwater he was referring to was, she knew, Meyer's garage in Moor Lane.

'You're pleased, aren't you?' It was a question, and she forced herself to smile as she answered, 'Oh, yes, yes. And it's kind of you.'

'Don't be a hypocrite.' He was sitting upright again. 'You don't think it's kind of me at all. You don't like the idea that your Cornelius can't buy a motor concern with his four hundred . . . Am I right?'

She did not reply for a moment, but her head wagged just the slightest. And then, getting to her feet, she said, 'Yes, you are right, because he's worked hard to save it and—'

'Doubtless, doubtless. And I like to hear it, it's a promising trait in him; it could get him far, the saving trait, but not four hundred, not in the car business, not in this day and age. The days of the Morris miracles are over. But your future husband, Mary Ann, has, I think, a head on his shoulders and he won't be so foolish as to look a gift horse in the mouth . . . Now will you go and tell him that I would like to see him? I understand he is on the farm, and' – he raised a finger to her – 'I would like to think that his reception of my offer will be a little more enthusiastic than yours.'

'I'm sorry . . . I know it's good of you and I'm grateful, I really am.' She moved towards the chair and placed her hand on his, to find it immediately gripped, and she was almost brought to tears for the second time that morning when, his face softening, he said, 'I want to do things for you, Mary Ann. I want to see you settled with all the comforts and amenities which would have been yours if you had come into this house. I have grown very fond of Lettice . . . yes, I have, which is just as well, for it helps to oil the wheels of living together, but Lettice will never be you, my dear . . . I've thought recently that you might have imagined that you were being shut out, but no, no. And I thought I must do something to prove to you that that'll never happen. And then, when I learned yesterday that I may in the near future be presented with a great-grandchild, I was pleased, and when one is pleased one thinks about other people, and as you, my dear, are never very far from my mind, I thought, I'll celebrate.' He squeezed her hand. 'And what better way to celebrate than by acquiring a garage.'

There was a lump wedged tightly in her gullet. Oh, he was good, good, he always had been; aggravating, dominating, an old devil at times, but good. Swiftly, she bent forward and pressed her face to his while holding his other cheek with her hand. When, turning quickly from him, she went to leave the room, he checked her quietly, saying, 'Tell Cornelius I want to see him.'

She hurried through the kitchen with her face averted from both Ben and Eva, and then she was running down the hill. When she came to the low stone wall she mounted its broad top and, looking over the fields to where, in the far distance, she saw the figures of Michael and Corny, and her da, she put her fingers into her mouth and blew a sharp high whistle that could have been the envy of many a boy, and when she saw the faces turn towards her she cupped her mouth in her hands and called, 'Cor-NY! Here . . . here!' When she felt she had his attention, she beckoned him with a wide wave of her arm.

She saw Corny break away at a trot and take the field in long, loping strides. She saw him jump the other end of the stone wall, and then he was coming up the steep incline, still running, towards her.

When he reached her he stood for a moment, panting; then exclaimed, laughingly, 'Coo! That would get you in training . . . You want me?' His face wore a broad grin, and before she had time to reply, he added, 'A whistling woman and a crowing hen is neither good for God nor man . . . that's what me mother says.'

'Perhaps your mother's right.'

He narrowed his eyes at her as he stooped

down and, looking searchingly into her face, asked, 'What's up? You been crying?'

'No.' She jerked her chin to the side. 'You've got to go and see Mr Lord.'

'Who, me? What for?'

'Because he wants you to . . . that's all.' The downward movement of her chin now lent emphasis to the words.

'When he wants me it doesn't mean good. I don't trust that old boy, and never will.' He straightened up and pushed his shoulders back.

'Now, Corny, stop it. It is for your good . . . for our good.'

'Ah . . . ah. Here we go . . . Well, what is it?' His expression changed.

As she stared up into his stiff, straight face she decided that if he was to obey Mr Lord's command she'd better keep Mr Lord's proposal to herself. She knew her Corny. His mind was full of odd values, odd ideas. You never knew but that he might turn down the offer if it wasn't put to him right. She lied unblinkingly as she said, 'If I knew what he wanted you for wouldn't I tell you? He just said he wanted to see you.'

Corny wrinkled his big nose. 'I don't like it. He's hardly spoken to me since I came back from America.'

'Can you blame him? You shut him up before he started by telling him that you wanted help from nobody and that you were going to join the band.'

'Aye, yes, I did.' At the memory, a smile twisted Corny's lips. 'And I remember he said that all I'd have to live on would be the hot air that was left over from blowing my cornet. He's sharp, is the old boy.'

'And he was right. That's all you would have had to live on if you'd taken up with the band again. They went flat . . . in more ways than one.'

'That's because they hadn't me with them.' As he brought his fist along the point of her chin, she said softly, 'Go on, Corny. And don't aggravate him.' She caught at his hand. 'He's old.'

'All right.' He gripped both her hands now and went to pull her towards him, but Mary Ann, noting the deep, tender look in his eyes, protested swiftly, 'Eeh! no, Corny. Now stop it, there's Jonesy down in that field.'

'He won't mind.'

'Don't be daft . . . Now give over. Ooh!'

She tried vainly to push off his long arms as they went around her, but when her feet left the ground and she was held tightly to him, and his mouth touched hers, she relaxed against him for a moment. And she still leant against him when he released her and she was on her feet again. Then, as was often the case, they turned from each other without a word, for words would only have diminished the depths of feeling between them.

'You're mad . . . daft . . . up the pole.' Mary Ann seemed to grow as she stood facing Corny; and now she twisted her head around and addressed her mother, where Lizzie was toying with her half-finished dinner. 'Isn't he, Ma? Tell him, isn't he mad?'

Lizzie was vitally aware of Mike sitting at the far end of the table, his head bowed over his plate, eating solidly as if all that was going on was no concern of his. But Mary Ann had asked her a question – she had not, as usual, asked it of her da, she had asked her. She turned her head slowly to where Corny stood, seemingly isolated on the edge of the hearth rug, and she forced herself to say what was in her mind, yet the translation of her thoughts was mild, for all she said was, 'I think you're being very foolish, Corny; it's a wonderful offer.'

'Wonderful offer be damned!'

Mike had risen from the table, almost over-turning the chair as he did so, and although he had taken up, and repeated, Lizzie's words, it was to Mary Ann that he looked as he barked, 'He's right. And he's told you why he's right; the old man is not doing this for him, he's doing it for you so that when you're married he can still keep the reins on you . . . You're being foolish!' He was again quoting Lizzie's words, and it was her he was yelling at, her he was getting at, not at Mary Ann, although he levelled his spleen towards her. 'Let him go his own road, make his own decisions. He's made one the day; instead of going for him stand by him. You mightn't have so much ham on it but what you do have will be what he's earned and worked for, it won't come from the backhander that's buying your affections.'

As Mike grabbed up his pipe from the mantel-piece and stalked from the room Lizzie rose slowly from her seat, and she stood, her hands gripping the edge of the table, looking to where Sarah sat with bowed head, and Michael opposite to her chewed on his lower lip.

'See what you've done?' Mary Ann's voice, cracking with temper, turned on Corny, and before he could answer her Michael's clear tone cut in. 'He's done what he thinks is right.'

Michael was also on his feet now, and, looking towards Corny, he said, 'I know how you feel. I felt the same when he first offered us the bungalow . . .'

'But you took the bungalow, didn't you?' Mary Ann bent her body aggressively towards her brother, and he, his voice rising now, shouted back at her, 'But only on my own terms, not as a gift.'

There was a moment of tense silence when no-one moved, but in it Mary Ann noticed the slight quiver attacking Sarah's shoulders, and, contrition swamping her, she bowed her head and murmured, 'I'm sorry . . . I'm sorry, Sarah, I . . . I didn't mean anything.'

'I know, I know.' Sarah's hand moved out in Mary Ann's direction, and Mary Ann, going towards her, said, 'All this carry-on and your wedding the morrow.'

'That makes no difference . . . Would you hold the chair?'

Mary Ann held the back of the chair firmly while Sarah gripped the table and pulled herself to her feet; then looking towards Michael, she said softly, 'Have you a minute? I've packed that case but I can't close it.'

Without a word Michael went towards the door leading into the hall, and holding it open, waited until Sarah had passed, before following her into the front room.

And now Lizzie gathered up an armful of dishes and went into the scullery; a minute later the door clicked shut, and Corny and Mary Ann were alone together. Mary Ann stood with her back to him, a stiff, defiant, angry back, and she almost thought it was her da speaking when Corny's voice came at her, saying too quietly, 'You've got to make up your mind, and soon, if it's me you want or a big house and a lush life, because I can tell you here and now it'll have to be one or the other for a good many years because I can't see me getting rich quick, I'm not built that way. If I was I would have jumped at his offer and become a yes man, and I would have risen to manager, but the business would never have been mine . . . Oh, aye . . .' Although Mary Ann wasn't looking at him she knew he was wagging his head in wide sweeps. 'Oh, I know I was to be given a share, enough to enable me wife to live as he thinks she should live, as she would have lived if she had married Tony . . .' She swung round on him now but she didn't get a chance to speak, for his look stilled her tongue. Slowly he turned his gaze from her, and, picking up his cap from the chair, he went towards the scullery door, saying, still quietly, 'There it is. I'll give you time to think it over one way or the other. I'm going home now, but tell Michael I'll be back in the morning in plenty of time.'

As the door closed on him she put out her hand towards it, but she didn't move from where she was. Then, as if her legs had suddenly become tired with running, she found she had to sit down. She didn't want to cry; nor was she in a temper any longer; but filling her small body now was a feeling of fear. It said to her, 'You'd better go careful, you could lose him. You can't please both of them. And if you lose him you'll never get anybody to love you as he does, for in a way he loves you like your da does.' This was true, she knew, and the ingredients in her love for him were similar to those in her love for her father. She had loved Corny from when he was a gangling boy, but she loved him more deeply when she recognised traits in him similar to those in Mike. She had a desire now to fly after him, and fling her arms about him, and cry, 'Corny . . . Corny, have it any way you like, your way will suit me.'

At this moment Lizzie re-entered the kitchen. She did not look at Mary Ann as she gathered up the remainder of the dishes, but just as she was about to return to the scullery she said, 'He said he told you you've got to think about what you want, he's going to give you time.'

Mary Ann, looking up into Lizzie's face, knew that deep down in her, her mother would be glad if Corny and she were to break up. 'I won't need any time, I've done all the thinking I'm going to,' she said under her breath.

Lizzie paused as she was turning from the table, and her eyes asked, 'Well, and what are you going to do?'

'Whatever he wants will suit me in the long run.'

Lizzie did not immediately turn away, and when she did she sighed, and her lids drooped, and as she crossed the kitchen she remarked, as if to herself, 'That's the way it always works out.'

3

Taking up the two front pews at the left-hand side of the church were Sarah's people – her aunts, her uncles, her cousins, but dominating them, the figure of her mother. Mrs Flannagan was seated near the aisle. Her back was straight, her head was high; her thin face – which, to use Mrs McBride's description, was snipy – was at this moment aglow with satisfaction. God was just. She had demanded that He would be so to her, for hadn't she struggled all her life against the environment of Burton Street, and what help had she got? . . . for he – meaning her husband – had done nothing in his life but disappoint her. And then for her only child to be afflicted with polio; she had thought that would be the end. But God's ways were strange; He had used the affliction as an instrument, and He had given her daughter courage to fight, and this had not gone unnoticed by Mr Lord. Mrs Flannagan did not think of Michael at this moment. Michael was just another one of God's instruments placed in Sarah's path to bring her to the notice of the influential owner of a shipping firm, a dock – even if it was only a small one – a farm, and a splendid house. Mary Ann Shaughnessy was not now alone the recipient of all good things.

The thought of Mary Ann brought Mrs Flannagan's eyes to where Mary Ann herself was kneeling behind the bride and bridegroom, and if Mrs Flannagan had ever given way to the weakness of gratitude she did so now, for she was thankful, she told herself, that Mary Ann had decided against making this a double wedding, for this was her daughter's day . . . and her own day, the day she would shine as the mother of the bride, the beautiful bride, for her daughter did look beautiful in spite of everything; but it would have been difficult to shine if she had been one of the mothers of the brides, the other mother being Lizzie Shaughnessy. Yes . . . yes, she was grateful to Mary Ann for this.

At the other side of the aisle there sat in stronger force the friends and relations of the bridegroom, and Lizzie Shaughnessy was thinking much the same thing. Oh, she was glad that Mary Ann had decided against a double wedding, for with her heart so sore the strain of Mary Ann going at this particular time would have been too much – Mary Ann, she knew, was on her side, wholly and completely. The thought in itself was of some comfort, for she was a good ally to have, was Mary Ann; that was why, she supposed, she had at times been jealous of her whole-hearted affection for her da. At this point Lizzie became conscious of Mike standing by her side, almost touching her, yet they were poles apart; all that closeness that had been between them was gone, never to return. Nothing would ever be the same again. She wondered what he was thinking as he watched his only son being married. Was he remembering his own wedding day and the starvation years that followed, she wondered.

Mike wasn't remembering his own wedding day, or the starvation years that followed, but as he stared at the stright back of his son he thought, It'll pass him by, the torment, the hell; he'll hold to her through life, and if his love ever fades there'll be compassion. But he doubted if his love would fade. Sarah had a habit of working at things; because of her handicap she would work at marriage, not just accept it. No, there was no need to worry about that pair. And they were starting off well, with a fine little house, and Michael with a sure job ahead of him for the rest of his life. And what was more, people all around him were kindly and sympathetic to them both . . . And what had he himself started with? Kindness and sympathy? No. Censure all his life; from his upbringing in the cottage home which was part of the workhouse, until he met Liz. Then there were a couple of golden years, poor but golden, and although the gold dimmed as time went on it had never really tarnished, until these last few weeks. Mike's head moved downwards and his glance took in the black-gloved hand of his mother-in-law and the thought that took the feeling of guilt away was, And that's another thing Michael won't be handicapped with, an old fiend like this. He'll manage Mrs F, but the devil in hell couldn't cope with this one. His head was immediately brought up by yet another thought: God in Heaven! What if she gets wind of this? He took his handkerchief and wiped the sweat away from around his face.

He's sweating, Mrs McMullen commented to herself, and he's a right to, it's his sins oozing out of him. He's got a nerve to put his face in the church door. There should be some law about Protestants being allowed in the church; they should be made to sit separate like. She looked towards the altar. She wished the priest would put a move on, he was talking too much. They would find out what it was all about before long, especially her grandson. That poor lad had taken on a packet, he must be mad. If she had had anything to say in the matter it would never have come about . . . a cripple like her. Well, God worked in strange ways. There had been that talk of them going off on a holiday together, hadn't there, when they weren't even engaged; and people knew what happened on holidays. Well, Sarah Flannagan had paid in advance for that sinful thinking . . . Aw, would the priest never finish? She was dying for a cup of tea and a drop of something in it – her legs were playing her up, like cramp she had, from the back of her heels up to her buttocks . . . Aw, there they were coming from the altar, and not afore time. It was a disgrace it was, dressed in white and walking like that, like some drunk. It was a wonder Michael wasn't ashamed to be seen with her. Aye, she supposed, her face was all right, but that didn't make up for that dot-and-carry-one gait of hers . . . Aw, and look at those two behind, the long and the short of it. Well, we get what we deserve, God sees to that. And she's going to get Fanny McBride's grandson, and good luck to her, she deserves no better. But of the two it's him that should be pitied, for if ever there was a little upstart it's that one. Look at her now walking down there as pious-looking as a saint, and mealy-mouthed into the bargain. If ever there was a creature with a mask on it's her. The damned little spitfire. Well, he's big enough, and I hope begod he takes it out of her . . . And look at Old Flannagan there, grinning like a Cheshire cat. He's no man is that one, as soft as clarts . . . And now there was the big fellow, Mike himself, leaving her side and the pew and not giving her a hand up. Aw, well, his day would come, and it wasn't very far ahead if all rumors were right. For years she had told her daughter what he was, and what thanks had she got? Told to mind her own business. Well, it was her business. She pulled herself to her feet . . . she couldn't wait to get back to the house to get on with that particular business. There was never smoke without fire, and, as she said to herself as she walked up the aisle amid the crowd leaving the church, If I can bring a glow to the fire that's under him, God guide me.

Sarah was ready to go. She sat in the front-room dressed in a smart grey costume and a cherry-coloured hat. She looked quiet and utterly happy, and as Mary Ann stood holding her hand within her own two, she said softly, 'You look so serene.'

'I feel it . . . as if I was sort of filled with wonder.'

'Oh, I wish I was like you, Sarah.'

On this they both laughed, and Sarah said, 'Fancy saying that. Remember the fights, the rows? But it seems to me now as if they never happened, or they happened in a different life. You know what I mean?'

Mary Ann nodded her head. 'I wish you all the happiness in the world, Sarah; you know that, don't you?'

'Yes, Mary Ann.'

'And you know, Sarah?' Mary Ann squeezed her hand. 'I can say this to you now. You know, I've been a bit green about you, and I still am, because . . . well, I can see you going down the years supremely happy, no skull and hair flying between you and Michael, whereas us—' she spread out her free hand significantly, 'we're like two wild animals at times. You see, even today, on this very special day, we're not speaking.' She smiled wistfully. And Sarah could not help but laugh, as she replied, 'Well, you know something . . . as confessions seem the order of the day I might as well tell you that I'm not such a reformed individual as you think, for I've done my share of turning green. While you've been envying Michael and me for our placidness, for that's what it really is, well, I've been jealous of you and Corny many a time when you've been going at one another.'

'What!'

'It's a fact. You see, you're both so boisterous, so full of life. That's how it should be when you're young. For myself, I feel I've been pushed into something that I shouldn't have realised for years and years, some kind of acceptance that only comes with age, if you know what I mean.'

'Aw, Sarah, don't think like that. Aw, you've been wonderful, wonderful. But' – she pulled a long face – 'I'm glad you've been jealous of me, it's a sort of comfort in a way . . .'

They were both laughing again, loudly now, their two heads together. They were like this when

Lizzie found them, and she paused for a moment in the doorway before saying, 'Come on, come on, stop your carry-on the pair of you, everybody's waiting. They've all gone to the barn.'

Lizzie bustled around, gathering up Sarah's handbag, her case, her silk scarf, talking all the while to cover her feelings, to cover the fact that at this moment her son was leaving her for ever. There was no real thought for Sarah in her mind now, no affection; what was filling her mind and body was an agony that cried, Oh, Michael! . . . Michael! She had lost her husband – she felt sure of this – and she was losing her son; in a different way perhaps, but more irrevocably, she was losing her son.

'Come on, come on.' She bustled them into the hall and to Michael, where he was standing waiting for his wife, and out of the front door and down the garden path towards the car and the crowd outside the barn.

Amid the confusion and good-byes, Michael now detached himself for a moment and, going to Mary Ann, to her utter surprise, he took her face between his hands and shyly kissed her, saying hastily, 'It's been fun knowing you.'

It was too much. Before the car was out of sight she was back in the front-room, standing with her face to the wall, very much as she had done when a child, and as she had often said when standing in such a position, Oh, our Michael! our Michael! She said his name again, but in a different way. He had said, 'It's been fun knowing you.' He had said that . . . their Michael. Oh, our Michael! Our Michael!

'What's the matter with you?' Lizzie had come

quietly into the room. She had not expected to see Mary Ann there.

'Oh, nothing. I just feel I've lost our Michael.'

'You feel you've lost our Michael?' Lizzie closed her eyes and, biting on her lip, hurried from the room.

It was eight o'clock and the jollification was going with a swing in the barn . . . too much with a swing. There was too much noise, too much raucous laughter. Lizzie wished it was over. Oh God! How she wished it was over. To Lizzie's feelings now was added one of fear. She feared what she might do if she let herself go. For two solid hours she had watched that girl ogling Mike, she had watched them dance together. True it was in the lancers, and he had danced with others as well, but when he put his arm around her Lizzie felt it was with a difference. And there were others who were aware of it too. Her mother, hawk-eyed, waiting. She did not know how she hadn't sunk to the ground and dissolved in shame and tears as she watched them. That was until this feeling took possession of her, the feeling that urged her to get the girl outside, somewhere quiet, and thrash her with her hands, a stick, anything, anything.

Lizzie moved away from the barn doorway. Where was she now? She looked about her, her eyes searching the thronged floor . . . There she was. The bitch. Lizzie made no apology for the title. There she was dancing with Corny . . . But Corny didn't like her. Was he doing it to upset Mary Ann because of what happened yesterday? Oh! . . . Like a gleam of light coming into the darkness of her mind came the thought, if only she would turn to Corny. Mary Ann was young; she would get over it; it was different when you were young. But now the gleam of light faded. This dance was the ladies' choice. It was she who had asked Corny . . . Then where was Mike? She remembered now that she hadn't seen him for quite some time.

'Ma.' Lizzie turned and looked at Mary Ann. In times of stress Mary Ann nearly always substituted ma for mother. 'Yes,' she said.

'Have you seen me da?'

Lizzie shook her head. 'No; why do you ask?'

'I haven't seen him for nearly an hour.'

'Have you looked?'

'Yes, in the house and all over.'

'Is the car in the garage?'

'Yes; I looked there.'

They stood close together now, their eyes scanning the room. 'Mrs Radley's talking to me grannie,' said Mary Ann.

'I see that.'

'Ma.'

'Yes?'

They were still looking ahead.

'Me grannie's got wind of something.'

'How do you know?' The words came as a groan from Lizzie.

'She was at me, trying to stir me up, when they were dancing together. She caught hold of me as I was passing, and dug me in the ribs and said, "Look at that. How does that look to you, eh?" '

'What did you say?'

'I pretended I didn't know what she meant.'

'I . . . I don't think I can stand much more.'

Lizzie's hand was encircling her throat and she strained her neck upwards as if she was choking.

'But, Ma' – Mary Ann caught hold of her arm and said softly and rapidly, 'You won't have to. He . . . promised me yesterday it's going to be over the night.'

Lizzie's eyes darted to Mary Ann's. 'What did he say?'

'Only that . . . that it'll be finished the night.'

Lizzie now moved her head in a bewildered way, and as Mary Ann was about to say something further there was a fuddled movement in the doorway to the right of them, a gurgle of a laugh, deep and well remembered, and they both swung round to see Mike smiling at them, and to see him as drunk as they had ever seen him for years.

'Oh, no, no.' Mary Ann put her hand to her mouth. She knew her da had disposed of a good many glasses since he returned from the church, but then he could stand a good many glasses both of beer and whisky. It took a lot to make him shake on his feet. Before she had time even to think anything further Mike had shambled the few steps towards them, and, gripping Lizzie roughly by the shoulder, he cried, 'Come on, Lizzie Shaughnessy, let's trip a measure. Come on.'

'Leave go of me.' Lizzie hissed the words at him. 'Stop it! Stop showing yourself up, and leave go of me.'

'Come on, it's a weddin', girl, it's a weddin'.'

Mary Ann watched her da reel and stumble almost on to his back as her mother thrust him forcibly from her. She knew that her da was what is termed rotten drunk, which meant fighting drunk. Anything could happen now. And after he had promised, promised faithfully to finish it. Oh . . .

Mike was rocketing through the couples now, knocking them right and left with his swaying gait, causing laughter here, surprise there, and not a little uneasiness generally. And now he was thrusting Corny from Yvonne. Gripping her round the waist, he swung her into a staggering quick step. The next moment the inevitable had happened: they were both on the floor, as were the next two couples. Again the laughter was high, but only in some quarters.

When they got Yvonne to her feet her face was white. It could have been with shock or with anger, but no-one was to know, for her mother quickly took charge and, guiding her to a seat, consoled her, while Mike lay with his legs spreadeagled and his one arm flaying the air.

As Lizzie rushed from the barn into the night Mary Ann followed her, but more slowly. It was the first time that she had turned from her da when he was in drink. Before, this fact had always drew her irresistibly to him to protect him from people's censure, and always the following morning from what was even worse, censure of himself.

As she saw the pale blur of her mother running towards the road, making for the house, she stopped; she couldn't follow her, she couldn't witness her pain. She stood with her knuckles pressed tightly to her teeth and her feelings in this moment took her beyond tears . . . she felt ashamed, degraded.

The door of the barn was wrenched open

and Corny came running, making for the house. And then he saw her. Last night was forgotten. Immediately he put his arms about her and pressed her head gently to his shoulder, and they stood silent for some minutes, until Mary Ann's voice, in almost a whimper, said, 'Oh, Corny, how could he do it? And he promised to finish with her the night. He promised faithfully. He said it would be all over the night, and just look at him . . .'

'What did you say about him finishing it?' Corny was now holding her from him, peering down into her face. 'He told you he was going to finish it?'

'Yes, he promised faithfully.'

'Well then.' His voice was high and his grip tightened on her shoulders and her body jerked under the movement of his hand. 'Don't you see? This is how he's doing it . . . getting blind drunk to put her off, to . . . well, to show her his other side as it were . . . Can't you see?'

Mary Ann brought her eyes from the dim outline of Corny's face to the door of the barn. Then she whispered, 'You think that's why he's doing it?'

'Certain, because I've never seen him as blotto as this, and you know I've seen him when he's been pretty far gone and razing Burton Street.'

'Perhaps you're right. Now I come to think of it you are . . . Oh, let's get him out.' She tugged at his arm now.

'Oh no, leave him to it – for a time, anyway. Let's walk quietly round the buildings.'

'But what if he's still carrying on when Tony and Lettice come back?'

'Well, they'll understand. But the old man . . . it's him I'll be worrying about . . . I wouldn't have him upset for anything, you know that.'

Although she couldn't see his face she knew from the tone of his voice that he was grinning at her, and she said softly, 'You . . . Oh, Corny.' Then she added, 'About yesterday, you're right, I know you're right.'

Again he had his arms around her and again they were silent, until a great whoop of drunken laughter came from the barn and tore them apart, and Mary Ann cried, 'I've got to get him out, Corny.' And as she turned to go towards the door she stopped and, looking up at the dim figure at her side, exclaimed, almost in horror, 'Me grannie's in there. Aw, dear Lord, she only needed this to set her up for the rest of her life. Now he'll never live this down, never.'

When they opened the barn door there were no dancers on the floor, the band was having a rest and being entertained by the sight of the big one-armed red-headed bloke making a pass at a young girl up in the corner.

Mike's antics had drawn the attention of the whole room towards him. He had his arm around Yvonne's shoulders and he was slobbering and grimacing and yammering as only a drunken man can. Mary Ann's eyes jerked to where her grannie was sitting. Her eyes riveted on her son-in-law, she looked like a female god, a self-satisfied female god. It was as if all her prophecies were being enacted before her eyes, and not only her own eyes but also of a large audience.

Mary Ann groaned audibly and was about to make her way across the room when Corny's hand gently stayed her, and he whispered down to her, 'Hold on a tick, just a minute or so.'

It was at this moment that Mr Flannagan, self-appointed MC, declared that they would now give the young-uns a chance to show their capers and have a twist.

As the band struck up Mike pulled himself to his feet with the obvious intention that Yvonne should partner him in the twist, but apparently the proceedings were becoming too much for Miss Radley's nerves, for now and in no gentle manner she tore her hand from his, pushed him upwards away from her to allow herself to rise, and as he reeled to the side she hurried as quickly as her stilt heels could carry her around the outskirts of the dancers and made for the door, there to be joined by her flurried mother and to be confronted by Mary Ann.

'You going?' As Mary Ann, with a great effort, forced an ordinary inquiring lightness into her tone, Yvonne Radley looked down at this inter-fering, tonguey little upstart, as she thought of her and she had the desire to take her hand and slap her mouth for her. She cast her glance towards Corny and her instinct told her that here was the one she would have gone after if he'd had any prospects, her mother or no mother. As if her mother had heard her thinking and decided right away to make clear their future policy she listened to her voice saying to Mary Ann with that calmness she both envied and hated, 'Well, we'll be going now, but we'll look in tomorrow perhaps.' There followed a pause before she added, 'Your father's in high fettle, isn't he, but that always happens at weddings.

The soberest of men always let go at weddings, don't you think?'

Before Mary Ann could answer, 'But me da's not a sober man at any time,' Mrs Radley put in quickly, 'Well come on, dear, we'll just go to the house and get our things . . . and say good-bye to your mother.' She nodded at Mary Ann, her long thin face and granite jaw pushed into a smile. 'She'll be glad when it's over, weddings mean nothing but hard work. Good night. We'll be seeing you soon.'

When the door closed on them, Mary Ann looked sadly up at Corny. 'It didn't work, they'll be back.'

'No, they won't; that was a face-saver.' He nodded quickly down at her. 'You'll see. As your da said he was going to, he's put an end to it.'

'You think so?'

'Sure of it. Come on, let's go out.'

'No. Look.' She made a small movement with her hand.

Mike was no longer standing where the Radleys had left him. He was now, to Mary Ann's horror, confronting her grannie. Swaying before her, he was telling her exactly how she was feeling.

'Bustin', aren't you? Bustin' at the seams with righteousness. Haven't . . . haven't you told Liz all these years what to expect, eh? An' haven't your words come true? Aye, an' with interest. You're gloatin', aren't you? Your black beady li'l eyes are full of divilish de-light . . . Will I help you up now an' . . . an' push your creakin' bones over to Liz so's you can tell her once again how right you are . . . "He's no good. Aa've told you afore an' Aa tell you now." Come on, you rat-faced old divil; come on, an' I'll help you on your way, an' you can tell her . . .'

'Da! Da!' Mary Ann was pulling on his arm, with Corny at his other side, saying, 'Mike. Mike, come on, man . . . come on away.'

'Aw.' Mike was allowing himself to be turned from the unblinking eyes and tight-lipped face of his mother-in-law when Mrs McMullen spoke. Addressing herself solely to Mary Ann now, she said, 'You should feel at home now you've got your old job back again. And it looks as if it might be permanent . . .'

Mike almost swung Mary Ann off her feet, so quickly did he jerk around, but Corny's bulk and young strength restrained him from returning to the attack, perhaps now with more than words.

On their erratic journey towards the door they passed Mrs Flannagan. Her look held a mixture of disdain, patronising pity, and self-glorification, and the glorification covered her family. But she made no comment. Perhaps because Mr Flannagan was standing close to her side, his hand hidden in the fold of her dress. Mr Flannagan was no longer the worm that she had created in the early years of her marriage. Mr Flannagan was now a person to be contended with, so much so that when he nipped her leg she did not even turn on him, she just kept her mouth shut.

They were outside when Mike, jerking his body from right to left, freed himself from their clutching hands and cried loudly, and angrily, 'Leave over, leave me go, I'm not a child you're playin' with, I'm a man an' I make me own decisions. Do you hear that?' He was leaning towards Mary Ann, peering at the outline of her that seemed to have grown even smaller. 'I do things in me own way. You see. Well, it's over. I promised you, didn't I? But in my own way, I said, an' with no words . . . No, begod! No words on . . . on either side, 'cos you can't end with words somethin' that's never been started with words, can you now?'

As Mary Ann gazed unseeing up at Mike and felt the gust of his breath fall on her she realised that, although he was drunk, he wasn't half as drunk as he had made out to be in the barn.

'Well now, back to normal, eh? Back to normal and everybody happy. Aw God, yes, everybody happy.' There was such sadness in his tone now that she wanted to fling her arms around him and comfort him, but he was moving away, and although he was still swaying his step was much steadier than it had been.

When Mary Ann heard the little wicket gate bang shut, she knew that he had not gone to the house but into the fields. And as she felt Corny's hand groping for hers, she said sadly, 'Let's go to me ma.'

Lizzie was in the kitchen. She had been standing looking down at the fire, but she turned her head swiftly as they entered the room.

Mary Ann went to her side while Corny stood at the table.

'They came over for their clothes. Have they gone?'

Lizzie made no answer but turned her eyes towards the fire again.

'Ma.' Mary Ann was clasping Lizzie's arm with her two hands. 'Sit down for a minute. Come on, sit down; I've got something to tell you.'

'I don't want to hear anything more.' Lizzie's head drooped, yet she turned from the fire and sat down on the chair that Corny brought forward. Then raising her weary face to Mary Ann, who was now standing in front of her, she said, 'Where is he?'

'Outside.'

'Going to take them home in his condition?' Her voice was bitter.

'No, Ma, no.' Mary Ann shook her head. 'He's gone into the fields. Ma—' she stood close beside her mother, holding her hand tightly, 'he did it on purpose, it was his way of breaking it off, to show her . . . well, what he was like – in drink I mean . . . you see?'

Lizzie saw, and she lowered her head. Then raising it again she looked at Corny and, asking for confirmation, said, 'You really think so?'

It was as he nodded that Mary Ann put in, 'It was Corny who realised it first. He saw why he was doing it, and I know now it's true, because knowing how our Michael hated me da when in drink he would have done anything rather than get drunk the day. You can see that, can't you? . . .' Mary Ann now lifted Lizzie's hand up towards her breast and asked pleadingly, 'Be nice to him. Talk to him, he'll feel awful the morrow . . . will you?'

'I'll see . . .' said Lizzie slowly. Then sighing, she added, 'Your grannie'll be here until tomorrow night. After that perhaps . . . perhaps things might get back to normal . . . They might.'

'I've always wished she'd never set foot in the house, but tonight, of all nights, I wish it. And he's been for her already.'

'What! In the barn?' Lizzie's tone was sharp.

'Yes.'

'I'd better go over. You're sure he's not there?'

'No, Ma, no; he went through the bottom gate.'

As Lizzie moved across the room, she said, 'The electric blanket's on in the front-room bed—' She no longer called it Sarah's bed. 'Will you see to the bottles for upstairs?'

'All right, Ma, I'll see to them.'

When they were alone together, Corny sat down in Mike's chair to the side of the fireplace and, holding out his hand, said softly, 'Come here.'

When Mary Ann went to him he lifted her as lightly as if she had been a child and sat her on his knee, and, looking at her, he said briefly, 'Let's make our day as soon as possible, eh?'

'Our wedding? . . . But . . . but we said December.'

'I know, but there's no need to wait that long, the date wasn't fixed. We could do it in November, say about the middle.'

She waited a moment; then moving her head slowly, she said, 'All right. I'll . . . I'll go and see Father Owen and make arrangements for us to see him together. Will I?'

'Yes . . . yes, do that.'

His arms slid over one another as they pressed her to him, and she lay against him, not joyful but sad and quiet; and when his voice, close to her ear, said, 'We'll make a big go of it, us two together; we'll show 'em how it really should be done,' she turned her face into the opening of his coat and began to cry.

4

'It's not right for an old woman to be on her own. I could be taken ill or drop down dead and who would know but God himself.' Mrs McMullen shook her abundantly haired head at the sadness of it all. 'I'd be in nobody's way in the front-room there. If you could put up with strangers for two years, and after all what was Sarah but a stranger to you, then you should consider the nearest of your kith and kin, and who's nearer your kith and kin than your own mother?'

'I want my front-room for myself.' Lizzie was mixing a batter as she stood at the long table, her gaze concentrated on her moving hand.

'I've never heard anything so selfish in my life.'

'Perhaps not.'

'I'm nearly eighty.'

'I'm aware of that.'

There followed a pause, and it added significance and emphasis to Mrs McMullen's next words. 'Aw, well, you never know but that you'll be offering it to me in a very short time. With them all gone and you on your own you might be glad of company.'

As Lizzie's hands became still Mary Ann came

in from the hall. Her face looked small and pinched, and she glared at her grannie as she cried, 'The day me ma'll be entirely on her own won't matter to you very much because you'll be dead.'

'Mary Ann!' Lizzie turned sharply towards her.

'Nice, isn't it?' Mrs McMullen's head dropped downwards as she spoke. 'All ready to go to mass she is and she comes out with things like that. If any girl has taken advantage of her convent education I would say it was your daughter, Lizzie.'

'Aw, I don't care what you say about me, Grannie, you've never said a good word about me in your life and I don't expect you to start now, but let me tell you . . .' As Mary Ann advanced across the room, Mrs McMullen brought her head up sharply to meet the onslaught. 'The only way me mother would be left alone is if you come to live here. And the Lord himself knows, when that happens—'

'Mary Ann!' Lizzie had her daughter by the shoulders now, and, swinging her about, propelled her forcibly back towards the hall, and when she had her there she pushed the kitchen door closed with her foot, saying under her breath, 'As she said, you're going to mass and this is no way to—'

'Look, Ma, the old devil won't rest until she's in that room.' Mary Ann thumbed violently towards the front-room door. 'And if you want to drive me da away you let that happen.'

'She's not coming here, now or at any other time.'

'Honest?'

'Honest.' Lizzie closed her eyes. 'Don't you think I've had enough to put up with without asking for more. Be sensible, girl.'

'Yes, yes, I know.' Mary Ann took in a deep breath, then added, 'But I also know her. She'll keep on till she wears you—'

'She won't wear me down, never.'

'But what would happen if, as she says, she took bad?'

'Then she'll go to hospital, or I'd travel all the way down to Shields every day to see to her, but I won't let her come here.'

Mary Ann's tight gaze dropped from Lizzie's; then her head sank down towards her chest as she asked, quietly, 'Have . . . have you spoken to me da?'

Her mother's silence brought her head up again, and when their eyes met they held for a moment before Lizzie answered, 'It'll take a little time, but don't worry.' She put out her hand and touched Mary Ann's arm gently with her finger. 'It'll come all right now, so don't worry any more.'

'And you'll stop worrying?'

'Yes . . . yes.' Lizzie sighed. 'It takes two to make a quarrel and two to mend it, you understand?'

'Yes, Mother.'

'Go on, get yourself off or you'll miss the bus.'

Before Mary Ann turned away she asked, 'Can I bring Corny back to dinner?'

'Yes, of course . . . But I thought he went to Mrs McBride's?'

'Not every Sunday, he sometimes has it at home.'

'Well, please yourself; he's welcome, as you know.'

When Lizzie closed the door on Mary Ann she stood with her back to it for a few minutes, as if fortifying herself before returning to the kitchen.

As she entered the room she saw that her mother was sitting stiff and straight in her chair, with her index finger tapping out a slow rhythm on the wooden arm; this was always a bad sign. Lizzie picked up the bowl of batter, went into the scullery and put it in the fridge; then, returning to the kitchen, she was in the act of clearing a small side-table when her mother said, 'How long has it been going on?'

Again Lizzie's hands became still, before she answered, 'What do you mean?'

'Now, don't try to pull the wool over my eyes, because even if you did I could still see, I'm not blind. If he had humiliated me as he's done you I would send him flying. A young piece like that! Brash as they come. But he picked his own colour . . . like to like.'

'Be quiet!' Lizzie had swung round from the table but was pressing her hips into its edge, and she stood twisting her hands as if aiming to wrench them from the wrists, as she cried, 'There's nothing in it, nothing, I tell you. It's in your mind, your bad mind. You would like it to happen, wouldn't you? You've been waiting for it for years. Well, I tell you it won't happen, it's finished . . . It never started, it was nothing . . . And I should know, who better? If I was worried about it I would have done something about it, wouldn't I? Well, I've done nothing, not lifted a finger. That's just how much I was worried. Some girls are all mixed up inside and this causes them to make a dead set at older men, but it doesn't say that the older man makes anything of it other than something to laugh at, and that's how it is. For your information, that's how it is.' She bent her body from the table while still keeping her buttocks pressed against it. 'That's what happened in this case, so make out of it what you like.'

As her mother and she exchanged glances, one sceptical, the other defiant, Lizzie became aware of a movement in the scullery. She had been shouting so hard, she hadn't heard anyone come in, but as she turned away from her mother she saw from the window who it was who was going quietly out. Mike was making his exit towards the back gate, not on the paved path, but on the grass verge. Lizzie pressed her lips tightly together and her face puckered painfully. How much had he heard? Enough, she supposed, to make him creep out like that. The breath that she took into her body lifted her breasts upwards. Well, as she had said to Mary Ann, it took two to mend a quarrel. She had done her part, now the rest was up to him. He knew where he stood with her, and now she could await his reaction.

The almost silent dinner was drawing to a close when the front door bell rang. Lizzie raised her head, Mary Ann raised her head, Mrs McMullen went on scraping the remains of her pudding from her plate, and Corny, rising from the table, said, 'I'm nearest, I'll see who it is.'

Mike pushed his chair back and went to the fireplace and took his pipe from the mantelpiece.

He was standing with his back to the fire, scraping the bowl, when the muffled but recognisable voices came to him, and he stared, or rather gaped, towards the door to where Corny was standing aside to allow Mrs Radley and her daughter to enter the room.

'We were on our way to Newcastle to my cousin's for tea, but we thought we could drop in to see how you're all faring after the excitement of yesterday.'

Lizzie, her eyes wide, her mouth tight, stared at the woman. Then her gaze slowly moved to Yvonne, but the girl was not looking at her; she was looking across the room at Mike, and her brown eyes soft and moist were forgiving him for his misdemeanour of last night. Lizzie's head now moved to take in her husband's face. There was a white line around his mouth, standing out against the ruggedness of his weather-beaten complexion, and there was a look on his face she had never seen before. She likened it to that of a ship-wrecked man who, sighting the shore, felt the tide turning beneath him and knew that he was helpless against it. Deep from within her there arose the familiar prayer, but in the form of a cry, 'Holy Mary, Mother of God, pray for us sinners now and at the hour of our death!'

5

'It's good of you to see me, Father.'

'It's good to see you, Mary Ann.' The priest put out his hand tentatively and touched her cheek. 'You're looking a bit pale. Are you all right?'

'Yes, Father.'

'And everybody at home?'

'Yes, Father.'

'Ah, sit down, Mary Ann, and let's have a crack . . . It's a long time since we had a wee crack, isn't it?' The priest lent his long length towards her, and she smiled widely at him. Oh, Father Owen was nice, wasn't he? Comforting; like Mrs McBride in a way, only different. She had always been able to talk to these two people without reserve. Well, not quite without reserve to Father Owen. Whereas she could openly discuss her da's weakness with Mrs McBride, she had already tried to hide it from the priest. Not that her efforts accomplished anything in the long run, for he always got to the bottom of things.

'It was a lovely wedding, Sarah and Michael's, wasn't it?'

'Yes, Father, lovely.'

'They should be very happy . . . Have you seen them since?'

'Yes, Father. They both came over on Monday night . . . they made on they felt lonely.' She laughed. 'Michael said he missed the farm, and Sarah said she missed the house and me ma and me, but nobody believed them.'

'And I don't blame them.' They were both laughing now. 'And if I know anything, Sarah will be at the farm as much as Michael when he gets back to work. That car is a godsend . . . You know, Mr Lord is a very good man, Mary Ann.'

'I know that, Father.' She nodded at him. 'I can't imagine where we would have been without him. But yes I can . . . still in Burton Street.'

'Yes, perhaps . . . perhaps you're right, Mary Ann.' The priest paused. Then putting his head on one side, he went on, 'He's an old man, set in his ways, and the only pleasure he's got in his life is doing little things for other people. Of course, it all depends on what you call little. But he likes to help, Mary Ann, you know that?'

'Yes, Father.' She sat stiffly now, knowing what was coming.

'His intentions are always good, I'm sure of that, no matter how things appear, and you know, Mary Ann, I think it's very foolish of Corny to have turned down his offer.'

Mary Ann did not ask the priest how this piece of news had come to his knowledge. Years ago she had likened Father Owen to God, and the impression at times still held. She looked straight at him as she said, 'It's no use, Father, he won't be persuaded; he's got his own ideas about what he wants to do . . . and . . . and I'm going along with him.'

The priest's head went back now and he let out a high laugh. 'Aw, it's funny it is to hear you say you're going along with anybody, Mary Ann. The individualist of individualists following a leader. Aw, well, perhaps it's a good thing.'

After her laughter had died down, the priest waited a moment, giving her the chance to state the reason for her visit, but when she sat looking at her hands he prompted gently, 'And what were you wanting to see me about, Mary Ann?'

She raised her eyes to his without lifting her head. 'We . . . we wanted to bring our wedding forward, Father. We . . . we thought about the beginning of November instead of December.'

Father Owen stared at her, and although his eyes didn't leave her face, Mary Ann knew that he was seeing her as a whole, and the thought this prompted brought a rush of blood to her face and caused her to bring out in fluttering protest, 'No, Father . . . no, there's no reason, Father. I mean we just want to get married sooner.'

She watched the shadow pass from the priest's face and his eyes light up, and the lightness came over in his voice as he cried, 'And why not? Why not indeed!' Mary Ann did not return his smile but said soberly, 'You were going to see us one or two evenings before . . .'

'Yes, yes, that can be arranged at any time . . . Tell me, have you discussed the future between yourselves?'

'Yes, Father; yes, a bit.'

'You've talked about children?'

'Yes, Father.'

'And you yourself want children, Mary Ann . . . sincerely want them?'

'Oh, yes, Father, yes.' Now she did smile at him, her eyes and mouth stretching with the achievement she would in time accomplish. 'I'm going to have three, Father,' she said; 'two girls and a boy.'

'Oh?' The priest's long face took on a comic serious expression. His eyebrows formed points directed towards his white hair, and his voice was flat as he said, 'Three?' Then again, 'Three! You've got it all cut and dried, Mary Ann, like the rest of them. Tell me, why stop at three? That is, if the good God means you have any at all. But if He does, I ask you, why stop at three? . . . You know something?' He bent towards her again and poked out his long turkey neck as he stated firmly, 'I'm one of thirteen.'

'You are, Father? Thirteen!'

'Ah-ah. Ah-ah. Thirteen, and there wasn't a happier family living, although mind, it was a bit hectic at times.'

'Oh, your poor mother!' Mary Ann shook her head, and her lips were now pressed together to stop her laughter.

'Aw, you needn't pity her, for she was in her element. It was her vocation to have children, and she reared every one of those thirteen children with the sole help of Hannah Anne.'

'Hannah Anne?'

'Yes, Hannah Anne.' The priest looked across at the sparsely furnished room to where, on the wall, hung a large portrait of Our Lady, and he seemed to be talking to the picture rather than to Mary Ann as he went on, 'Out of all the millions of impressions that a child takes in . . . that a youth takes in, only a few come over with him into manhood, only a few remain clear-cut, the rest are vague and have to be grabbed at and pulled into the light, but a few remain clear . . . Hannah Anne remained clear.'

Mary Ann was no longer smiling, she was looking up at this old priest who she felt at this moment had gone from her; although he was talking to her, he was no longer with her, and she said no word, made no sound to prompt him onwards, but waited, and then he said, 'Mondays and Fridays, those are the days I always connect with Hannah Anne, Mondays and Fridays.' He turned his face now towards Mary Ann, but his eyes still looked unseeing as he went on, 'You see, she washed all day on Monday, and she baked all day on a Friday. She baked yuledoos on a Friday; you know what I mean, bits of dough with currants in. There were nine of us when she first came to the house, and she made nine separate yuledoos, all different sizes according to our ages. I was fourteen then and Hannah Anne fifteen. She was paid one and sixpence a week and she slept under the roof.' His head drooped slightly, and so quiet did he become that it almost seemed as if he was dozing. But Mary Ann knew he wasn't dozing. He was back in his boyhood standing in the kitchen waiting for his yuledoo from Hannah Anne, who was just a year older than himself. Then with a quick movement that almost startled her he was back with her again, and from the look on his face she knew that he was going to speak no more of Hannah Anne. But she wanted to hear more, so she said quickly, 'Did you lose sight of her, Father?'

'Lose sight of her?' There was surprise in his tone. 'No, no, she's in Felling to this day, and every time I'm that way I call.' He screwed up his face at her. 'I try to make it on a Friday for she still bakes on a Friday, but tea cakes now, and she's generous with the butter.' His chin moved outwards. 'No, Hannah Anne is still going strong. And you know something? She was twenty-seven when she married. She waited until we were all up, so to speak, and then she married, and I, Mary Ann . . . I performed the ceremony. It was my first wedding. People laugh, you know, when they hear of folks crying at weddings.' He had once again turned his eyes from her, and once again they were on the picture on the wall, and Mary Ann's heart became sore for something intangible, something that could not be spoken of, something that might have been if God had willed it; something between Hannah Anne who washed on a Monday and baked on a Friday and was just a year older than a boy of fourteen. Hannah Anne who had shown the priest how easy it was to cry at a wedding. Quite suddenly she decided to let God, and of course Corny, settle as to the size of her coming family. She put her thoughts into words by saying gently, 'I'll let things take their course, Father.'

'That's it, that's it, Mary Ann, let things take their course. It's a wise decision. Now when do I see you and Corny? Say on Tuesday evening at half past seven, how's that?'

'That will be fine, Father.'

She rose from the chair, and Father Owen, getting to his feet, said, 'Now will you have a cup of tea before you go? Miss Neilson always has the pot on the hob.'

'Thanks all the same, Father, but I've got to go to Mrs McBride's; Corny's meeting me there.' She had no desire to meet the priest's house-keeper, for she still had memories of that gaunt lady's reception of her in the past.

'Aw, you're going to Fanny's. Well, give her my regards, although it's not over two days since I last saw her. She keeps fine, doesn't she? In spite of everything, she keeps fine.' He bent his long length down towards her and grinned as he said, 'She'll take some killing that one, what do you think?'

'I think like you, she'll take some killing, Father. And I'm glad.'

'That makes two of us.'

'Good-bye, Father.'

'Good-bye, Mary Ann. Don't forget, half past seven on Tuesday night the pair of you. God bless you. Good-bye now.'

She walked up the street, crossed the road in the direction of Burton Street, and as she went her mind reiterated: Thirteen children . . . I don't think I'd want thirteen; it would wear you out, wouldn't it, thirteen. And they'd all have to be fed and clothed . . . and if the garage didn't go all right . . . Aw – she literally shook herself – what was she going on about? Thirteen children . . . But what if she did have . . . ? Aw, she was mad, daft, thinking this way. As she had said to Father Owen, let things take their course.

In a few weeks she would be married. Her step became slower. She couldn't quite take it in, but she was glad they weren't waiting until December. When the true reason for this came to her she tried to turn away from it, to bang a door in her mind shut on it, but the fact still remained clear before her, she wanted to get away from home. She wanted to get away from the sight of her da. The da who had become weak, the da who had lost his power to create wonder in her. Nothing had apparently changed since the Radleys' visit last Sunday afternoon; an onlooker might imagine that Mike Shaughnessy had made his stand last Saturday night and was abiding by it, but she knew differently. She was too close to Mike not to gauge his feelings, and she knew that before him lay a course from which he was shying. She knew, and he knew, that the only way to treat this matter was with decisive action, to openly tell the pair of them not to come back to the house again. But she also knew that it was almost impossible for her da to take such action towards a girl who was being charming to him, for he wouldn't want to be confronted with the look of feigned incredulity and the consequent reply of, 'You've got ideas about yourself, haven't you? Fancy you thinking like that; why, you're old enough to be my father.' And Mary Ann knew that was the kind of retort he would get from a girl like Yvonne Radley once she was made aware that she was wasting her time, and he wasn't strong enough to face being made to look an old fool.

She should be happy and joyful because she was to be married – she loved Corny with all her heart – yet here she was, sad to the soul of her. For the first time in her life she felt dislike and bitterness well up in her against her da; and she said to herself, If he keeps it up I won't own him, I won't, I won't!

*　　*　　*

It was Sunday afternoon again and Lizzie had all her family around her. This, she knew, should have made her the happiest woman on earth: there was Michael and Sarah looking so radiant that it brought a soft pain to her heart; there was Mary Ann, a quieter, more subdued Mary Ann these days, and Lizzie felt she liked her daughter better this way, she seemed more predictable. Yet one never knew with Mary Ann. And there was Corny, talking, talking, talking. She should be thankful for Corny, grateful to him, for she knew why he was talking. He was, in his own way, aiming to bring a lightness to the atmosphere, and she really was grateful to him. There were sides to Corny that she could not help but admire, sides that she could trace back to his grannie; one side, in particular, that made him wise . . . heart wise . . . And then there was Mike. Her husband was sitting to the side of the fireplace, smoking. He might appear at ease, but she knew that, like herself, he was on tenterhooks, he was waiting . . . If they had been on the two-o'clock bus they would have been here before now, but there was always the three-o'clock, and the four-o'clock. How many times, she wondered, had he seen her since last Sunday? During the past week he had been out only once in the evening, and then for not more than two hours. But a lot could happen in two hours. She had wanted to tackle him on his return and say 'Well?' but she had thought better of it, there might just be the chance that he hadn't been with her. Sometimes she told herself she was making a mountain out of a molehill, that there was nothing in it, only what her imagination put there. She explained the situation to herself; Mrs

Radley and her daughter were two people they had met at a holiday camp, wasn't it natural that they should pop in and see them now and again? But the answer that burst from her tortured mind was, 'Natural that they come every Sunday and her looking like that? Contriving always to expose herself in some way: showing off her bust with her low, square necklines; sitting with her legs crossed so that her skirt rode almost to her thighs.' No, she was no fool. That girl meant business . . . and her mother meant business. Once during the last few days she had said to herself, 'I'll walk out and leave him.' But then her reason told her that that was what they were waiting for. Like a double-headed cobra, they were waiting their time to strike. For a moment she saw them ensconced in her house, in her front-room, which, since Sarah's departure, had become 'her' room again.

Lizzie's mind was brought from herself by Corny speaking to her, and she turned to him and said, 'What was that, I didn't get what you said?'

'I was just sayin',' said Corny, 'that she should send this one to one of the magazines, the ones that sell round the North-East.'

'Which one is that?'

'The one called "The Northerner".'

'Oh, give over.' Mary Ann reached out to grab the sheet of paper from Corny's hand. 'Me mother hasn't heard it.'

'She hasn't?' Corny looked at Lizzie again. 'Well, it's about time she did,' he said. 'Listen to this.'

Lizzie listened as she looked at the big fellow, standing in a set pose, his arm extended as he read

what was apparently Mary Ann's latest effort at
poetry.

'The Northerner,' announced Corny in the
grandiose manner:

'I longed for spring after winter gales,
And sleet and snow and muddy feet,
But when it came it quickly passed,
And summer followed, and that was fleet.
Then Autumn brought me thoughts of wind,
Of raging, tearing, swirling air.
And, as a dreamer, I awoke
To beauty of trees dark and bare,
Of branches lashed with sleet and rain,
Of racing cloud and raging sea,
And I was bidden to rise and greet
The winter which is part of me.'

'There now. Isn't it good?'
Sarah was the first to answer. 'I think it's
grand,' she said; 'it says what it means.'
'Yes, it's quite good.' Michael pulled on his
cigarette as he lay back in the corner of the couch;
then with a brother's prerogative he added, 'But I
think it's a bit too simple, I mean to get into a
magazine or anything.'
'Simple, you say? Of course it's not too simple.'
Corny was on the defensive. 'Anyway, that's how
people want things written, so's that they can
understand them.'
'There is simple and . . . simple, old fellow.
There's the simplicity of things like "Milk
Wood" . . .'
'Aw, you and "Milk Wood". We had this out
afore, remember?' Corny now threw himself into

a chair opposite Michael. 'Because you went on about it, I read it. And you know what? It's snob stuff. He mightn't have meant it that way when he wrote it, but I'd like to bet me bottom dollar that seventy-five per cent of people who read it do so because they think it's the thing to do, sort of slumming in literature . . .'

'Slumming! "Milk Wood"? Go on, man, you don't know what you're talking about.' Michael laughed derisively.

'Don't I?' Corny pulled himself to the edge of the chair, and he spread his glance over Mary Ann, Sarah, Lizzie and Mike, who were all sitting now like people waiting to be entertained, and he went on, 'I'm tellin' you: half the people that read that kind of stuff neither understand nor like it, but they're afraid to say that they don't because they'll be looked upon as unintelligent nitwits.'

'What do you know about it, Corny?' Michael was smiling with a quiet, superior smile now, a smile that was meant to draw Corny on still further. 'Have you joined a literary society or something?'

'No, I haven't, and I wouldn't if they paid me, but I read; I read what I like not what they tell me to read in the reviews, 'cos what happens then? Some bloke quotes two lines of something out of a book and they sound wonderful and you break your bloomin' neck to go and get the book, and before you're half-way through the damn stuff you realise you're being had. All the fellow wrote in that book was those two lines, all the rest is what you or anybody else could think of. But some bloke, I mean a reviewer, for one of a dozen reasons picks on those two lines, and when you can't like the book you get the feeling there is something wrong with you up here.' He prodded his head with his forefinger. 'And you start to ask why.'

'Very good question, Corny, a very good question to ask yourself, and it's about time you did, too.'

'Give over, Michael, stop teasing.' Sarah pushed at her husband, and they both laughed and looked at Mary Ann. And Mary Ann laughed, and Lizzie smiled faintly, but Mike . . . he just kept looking at Corny, his countenance giving nothing away, not of amusement or interest, and Corny, going back into the attack, demanded of Michael, 'Come on, let's know what you've read. Have you read Steinbeck, John Steinbeck?'

'Oh, years ago.'

'What? What did you read of his?'

'Oh, I've forgotten.'

'If you had read Steinbeck, man, you wouldn't have forgotten a word of it. An' I bet you've never heard of Salinger, eh, have you?'

'Of course I've heard of him.'

'Have you read him? Have you read *The Catcher in the Rye*? . . . No, you haven't. Well, it's a marvellous book. He's a marvellous writer . . . an American.'

'You don't say!' Michael was now shaking with laughter and Corny, suddenly thrusting his hands out, gripped him by the collar and pulled him off the couch and on to the floor. At this Lizzie cried, 'Give over! Give over, the pair of you. Corny, get up. Michael, do you hear me? Stop acting like children.'

Still laughing, they broke apart, and Michael,

taking his seat again beside Sarah, looked at her as he straightened his tie and remarked in a mock serious tone, 'Her a poetess and him a literary critic . . . coo! Won't we have something to brag about? . . . 'Cos neither of them can spell!'

'Now stop it, Corny!' Lizzie clamped down on yet another attack, and Corny, putting his coat to rights, cried, 'There's many a true word said in a joke.' He was now nodding his big head at Michael, and Michael, returning the same gesture, answered solemnly, 'True, true, Victor Ludorum of the literary field. True, true. Ah! How true.'

Corny, now screwing up his eyes questioningly, asked, 'Victor Lu . . . who? Who's he? Never heard of him.'

'He was in a band, blew a cornet before he started . . .'

'Stop it, our Michael!' Mary Ann thrust out her hand towards her brother. 'Don't be so clever.'

'Well, I'm only telling him.' Michael was shaking with laughter again.

'OK, I'm willing to learn, who is he? I can't know them all, can I, and if you don't ask you never know.'

'You want your ears boxed, our Michael. Box his ears, Sarah.' Mary Ann was on her feet, and, thrusting out her hand and grabbing hold of Corny, said, 'Come on, I want to go for a walk.'

'But I want to get to the bottom . . .'

Michael was now rolling helplessly on the couch, and he clutched at Sarah as he tried to speak, and Mary Ann cast a withering glance at him and cried again, 'Come on. Do you hear, Corny?'

Corny, grinning, and scratching his head with

one hand, allowed himself to be tugged across the room, and as he passed Mike's chair Mike touched him on the sleeve, and, looking up into his face, said, with strange gentleness, 'You'll be Victor Ludorum in anything you take up; you'll master all that comes, Corny, never you fear.'

As they exchanged glances the grin slid from Corny's face. Then, still being led by Mary Ann, he went out into the hall and on into the kitchen, and there, pulling her to a stop, he said under his breath, 'What's this Victor Ludorum lark? Who is he, anyway?'

Mary Ann dropped her lids for a moment before looking up at him, saying, 'It's just a term, Corny. It's for whoever comes top of the sports at school, it's a Latin term meaning victor of the games.'

'Aah.' He stared at her for a long moment, and again he said, 'Aah.' Then, rubbing his hand across his wide mouth, he remarked, 'That's what comes of not going to a grammar school . . . Still—' his eyebrows moved up, 'we live and learn, don't we?'

'Michael didn't mean anything, you know that. He wasn't trying to be clever or anything. It's just that he's so slap-happy he doesn't know what he's saying half the time.'

'Aw, I don't take any notice of Michael.' He turned from her and walked slowly down the length of the long kitchen, and as he went he muttered, 'Victor Ludorum. Your da says I'll be Victor Ludorum in anything I take up.' He turned his head slightly and glanced down at her. 'Victor of the games, you said; master of anything, Mike said. Well! Well!'

They went out through the scullery and down the garden path that led to the road, and although he had hold of her hand and they were walking close together, she knew that he wasn't with her. This silly business had put a bee in his bonnet. She almost felt it taking shape: Victor Ludorum . . . Victor of the literary game! She wanted to go back and slap their Michael's face for him. Showing up Corny's ignorance like that. And yet . . . and yet Corny wasn't ignorant. Corny had read more than their Michael, much more.

When he turned his head towards her and said abruptly, 'I am the captain of my soul, I am the master of my fate. It's the same thing, isn't it, as this Victor Ludorum?' she remained silent. It wasn't really; one was physical, the other was mental and spiritual . . . Or was it? Was conquering your fate physical? Oh, she didn't know, it was the kind of thing that took thinking out. But Corny was waiting for an answer and he wanted her to say, yes, it was the same thing, because he intended to be master of his fate, did Corny. And so she smiled softly as she replied, 'Yes, Corny, it's the same thing exactly.'

With a sudden jerk he pulled her hand up through his arm, and with a step to which she had to trot he marched her down the road.

Already, she knew, he was Victor Ludorum.

6

The weeks that followed went with different speeds for different members of the family. For Lizzie, each day dragged, yet, overall, they seemed to move too fast and ominously towards Sundays, when the visitors would call, sometimes to stay only for an hour, sometimes to stay for as long as four or five. It all depended if they had to wait to see Mike or not. But if their visits were long or short, during them Lizzie tortured herself all the while as she watched for some signal, some look to pass between Mike and the girl which might mean the arranging of a meeting or a change of plan. Now he went out twice a week in the evenings, and with the coldness forming into ice between them, she could not break through and inquire, even in anger, where he'd spent his time.

For Mary Ann the days were moving too fast. It was only just over a fortnight before she would be married, and nothing settled yet about the garage. But perhaps Corny would clinch it this afternoon. She hoped so. Oh, she did, she did, because she didn't want to start her married life living at home. A few months ago she wouldn't have minded a jot, but not now.

She came down the stairs and into the kitchen, and Lizzie, turning and looking at her, said flatly, 'You're off then?'

'Yes, I'm meeting Corny at the garage; it might be settled this afternoon.'

'I hope so,' said Lizzie kindly.

'Thanks, Mother . . . You wouldn't like to come along with me? It's a nice day, the outing would do you good.'

'No, thanks, lass. Michael and Sarah might pop over and I wouldn't like to be out if they came.'

'All right.' She nodded. 'But don't wait tea for us, you never know how long it will take . . . that's if the business gets going.'

'Will he move out straight away if it's settled?' asked Lizzie.

'He said he would . . . he said he's going to live with his daughter. He's got nothing much left in the flat upstairs anyway, she's already seen to that . . . the daughter I mean . . . Well, I'll be off.' She kissed Lizzie's cheek. 'Bye-bye, Mother.'

'Bye-bye, dear.' Lizzie now looked Mary Ann up and down before saying, 'I like you in that coat; that particular blue suits you and it adds to your height.'

Mary Ann leaned forward and again kissed Lizzie, then hurried out without making any comment. It hurt her when her mother was kind, because she knew the effort it must take to say nice things, feeling as she did, desolate and lost, and . . . and spurned. Yes, that was the word, for her da was spurning her ma openly now.

As she went up the lane towards the main road she glanced about her. Her da would likely be walking the fields, she had heard him whistle

Simon earlier on. Not that she wanted to see him; this looking for him was only a habit. As she rounded the bend of the lane she heard Simon bark, but she could not see the dog, or Mike. Likely they were in the old barn. She looked towards the building that stood somewhere off the road on the edge of a field path, and then her gaze darted to the further end of the lane to where two people were walking with their backs to her. They were Yvonne and Mrs Radley. Her heart gave a double sickening beat and she thought bitterly, Oh, me da, having her here on the sly. It didn't lighten the accusation that the mother was with Yvonne. She was always with her; she'd be with her until something was definitely settled. That seemed the mother's self-appointed role.

When she came level with the barn she looked deliberately towards it, and there standing outside was Mike, and his gaze was brought sharply from the distance by the sight of her. She would have kept walking on but his voice, sharp and commanding, said, 'Mary Ann! Wait . . . wait.'

When he came up to her he looked down into her face before speaking, and then he said quietly, 'Again it's not what you think, they just happened to be passing and saw me.'

She returned his penetrating look as she answered derisively, 'Da, don't be so silly.' She watched the colour deepen in his face, and now he growled, 'I'll have you remember who you're talkin' to; you seem to have forgotten lately.'

His angry tone did not upset her as it once would have done, and she replied defiantly, 'Well, who's fault is that? You said they were just passing. We're miles off the beaten track. Why would they be coming this way if it was not to see you? Don't tell me they were taking a walk right from Pelaw.'

'I don't know what they were doing, but they told me just that, that they were out for a walk . . . You don't believe me?' His voice was quiet now and she hesitated a moment before replying. 'No, Da, I can't . . .' Then, her voice almost gabbling, she rushed on, 'How can I believe anything you say when you're out two nights a week or more and you never used to go, and me ma nearly demented, and you not opening your mouth to her, except to talk at her . . . Don't you see what you're doing to her? Don't you?'

'I'm doing nothing to her; it's her imagination that's doing it to her . . . and yours.'

'And mine? Then why did you say on the night of the wedding that you'd finish it if there was nothing to it? Why?'

'You can't finish what hasn't started, can you?'

'But you admitted it then . . . you did.'

Mike dropped his head and raised his hand to it, and, moving his finger across his wide brow, said tensely, 'Mary Ann, don't make me lose me temper. I've told you, I've told you more than once, there's nothing in it; but I'll be damned if I'm going to insult two nice people just to please you an' your mother and make meself out a bloody fool into the bargain. And what makes me more determined on this point is that neither of them has ever said a wrong word against you, or Lizzie. Just the reverse; they've had nothing but praise for the whole family . . .'

'Oh, be quiet, Da, be quiet.' Mary Ann was now cupping her ears with her hands, pushing her hat awry as she did so. 'You're talking like a young lad. Even Corny would laugh at that. And me . . . I'm not very old but I know that's one of the oldest of women's tricks in the world. They're clever, both of them . . . clever, and you're a fool, Da, a fool.' She stepped back from the angry glare in his eyes and the pressure of his voice as he cried, 'Mary Ann!'

'I don't care, I don't care, somebody's got to tell you. Do you know what they are?' She pressed her lips tightly together before she gave vent to the word, 'Bitches! That's what they are, a pair of bitches.' She didn't wait for his reply to this, but, turning from him, ran up the road. And it wasn't until she neared the main road that she drew to a walk. Her body was smouldering with her temper, and when, leaving the lane, she saw Yvonne and Mrs Radley waiting for the bus, it needed only this to ignite it into flame.

What would have been the outcome of the meeting had the bus not arrived at that moment is left to surmise, but the look that Mary Ann bestowed on both of them as they turned smiling faces towards her must have warned them that their tactics and polite conversation were going to be lost on this particular member of the Shaughnessy family. They mounted the bus before her and took their seats together on the right-hand side. There was a double empty seat in front of them, but she ignored this and sat next to a woman on the opposite side. The woman alighted at the next stop and Mary Ann moved up to the window and sat looking out, telling herself that if they didn't get off before her she would pass them without as much as a glance.

But they did leave the bus before her; they alighted on the outskirts of Pelaw, and for a moment she saw them standing on the pavement, from where they looked straight at her and she back at them before snapping her gaze away as the bus moved forwards.

And apparently she wasn't the only one who had looked at them through the window, for almost immediately she became aware of the voice of one of the women sitting behind her, saying, 'Did you see who that was?'

'Yes,' answered the other. 'Ma Radley and her insurance policy.' At this the two women laughed, and Mary Ann said to herself, 'Insurance policy?' They were referring to Yvonne, but insurance policy . . . she just couldn't get it. She strained her ears now to hear their conversation, but because of the noise of the bus only isolated words came to her, and these didn't make sense and could have referred to anything. But it was at the next stop that she heard something that brought her sitting upright in her seat. The woman who had first spoken said, 'Two she's had; the second's in a home, and they tell me the mother has an old bloke lined up now.'

'Two she's had,' Mary Ann repeated. That could have meant men, but the words 'The second's in a home' didn't apply to men, it applied to children, babies. She turned round quickly and looked at the women, and they brought their eyes from each other and looked back at her. She noticed that they were very nicely dressed, very respectable-looking. One of them flushed and glanced quickly at her companion; then, looking out of the window, she said, 'We're here,' and on this they both rose to their feet and left the bus.

And Mary Ann left it also. Almost as it was about to move off she jumped from the step.

'Excuse me.' She was breathless when she came to their side. 'Please' – she moved her head now – 'I know it's awful, but I was listening. I heard what you said about . . . about Mrs Radley and her daughter . . .'

'Now look here.' The taller woman pulled in her chin – an indignant motion. 'We were merely discussing something private.'

'I know, I know, but this is important to me. I wonder if you could tell me anything . . .'

'No! It's none of our business what other people do.' The indignation was righteous now. 'And you shouldn't listen to people's conversation.'

'Then you shouldn't talk about them, should you?' Mary Ann thrust her chin up at the woman. Then, reminding herself that this attitude would get her nowhere, she said in a softer one, 'I just wanted to know if—'

'You'll get no information out of me. If you want to know anything about Mrs Radley or her daughter why don't you go and ask them?'

On this the taller woman turned away and, after a quick glance at Mary Ann, her companion joined her.

Mary Ann stood on the pavement. She stood biting her thumbnail and watching the women walking away. She watched them cross the road, pass three streets and then pause before the taller woman went up a side street while the other woman continued along the main road.

Intuition was Mary Ann's second nature, and

now once again she was running. And when she came abreast of the woman she crossed over the road in front of her and waited for her approach.

'I'm sorry,' she began immediately, 'but . . . but will you help me? It's important. You see . . .' She paused, and, looking at the straight face of the other woman, she realised that only stark truth would get her anywhere, so she went on rapidly, 'Well, the old man your friend referred to is . . . is me father.'

The woman's face softened and she nipped at her lip before saying, 'Oh, lass, I'm sorry, but it's no business of mine. An' you were right, we shouldn't have said anything.'

'Oh, please, please, don't mind that. I'm so glad you did. But the Radleys . . . well, you see they are causing trouble; me ma's in a state.'

The woman shook her head in sympathy. 'I bet she is, poor soul. Look' – her voice dropped to a whisper now – 'don't stand here. I just live round the corner; come on in for a minute.' But before she moved away the woman glanced surreptitiously over her shoulder as if she expected to see her friend appear again. Then, as if by way of explanation, she said, 'I . . . I wouldn't like her to think I'm doing anything behind her back. You understand?'

'I understand,' said Mary Ann, nodding her head quickly.

Again the woman felt there was need for explanation, and as she walked quickly up the street she went on, 'She's my friend and she has a lot to say, but when it comes to the push she'll never stand by it. I know more about the Radleys than she does, but I don't let on, I just let her have her say . . . Well, here we are.' She fumbled in her bag for her key, and after opening the door she stood aside to allow Mary Ann to enter.

It was a nice house, Mary Ann decided at once, clean, spanking clean, and orderly.

'Sit down,' said the woman as she herself took off her hat and coat. 'Well now.' She took a seat opposite to Mary Ann and she poked her chin out as she said, 'You look so young, hinny, for your da to be such an old man.'

'But he's not old, not really, he's just turned forty.'

The woman now screwed up her eyes. Then, her lips pressing together, her face expressed a knowing smile. 'Forty?' she said, on a high note. 'Well, that puts a different side to it, for the man that goes to the Radleys, well, he'll never see sixty again, not by a long chalk, although, mind, he's pretty spruce. You see . . .' She wriggled her buttocks to the edge of the chair. 'How I know all this is because me daughter lives two doors from them. I get all me news from her, but I don't let on to me friend.' She nodded towards the door now as if to indicate her friend. 'I always say Peggy tells me nothing – that's me daughter – but this old boy has been going to the Radleys, as far as I understand, for the last three months or so. You see, Ma Radley wants to get her married off . . . Yvonne I mean. I always said the French name went to her head, because she was like a march hare when she left school. Our Peggy was at the same school but she was a bit older. And then she had the bairn afore she was sixteen . . . I don't mean our Peggy, I mean Yvonne, you understand?' She was smiling at Mary Ann, but Mary

Ann did not return the smile, for her face was set in a blank, fixed stare, and her mouth opened twice before she repeated, 'A baby! She had a baby?'

'Oh, aye, two, and by different fellows. That's why Ma Radley won't let her out of her sight. I've got no room for her at all . . . I mean Ma Radley, but I must admit she's had a handful with that girl.' The woman, warming to the theme, was becoming colloquial, her speech thickening with the northern inflexion as she went on, 'Then the second one she had last year. The man was married and he was made to pay for the bairn. And that one's in a home, sort of, because Ma Radley wouldn't have it in the house. But her first one was to a lad no older than herself, in fact not as old, and they couldn't do much about that. Anyway, he's skedaddled. But that one was adopted. Oh, she's been the talk of the neighbourhood, has that madam. But now I think this second business has scared her a bit because she's letting her mother hold the reins, so to speak. There's no coffee bars for her now an' coming home at two in the morning. And, of course, now it's pretty hard on her because none of the lads around here or in the factory wants her . . . except for one thing, and perhaps she's realised that twice is enough; anyway, everybody's just been waiting to see if she snaffles the old boy. Mrs Radley gave it out that he was her uncle, but it's funny that nobody round the doors heard of the uncle up till a few months ago. As for the old boy, well, he must be barmy thinking he can hold a young girl like her. But then all men of that age are barmy, aren't they?' She waited for an answer, and when none was forthcoming she made an inquiring movement with her head and said, 'And your da, hinny, he's gone on her, is he?'

'No,' Mary Ann denied firmly what she knew to be true. 'No, but she keeps . . . they keep coming to the house. My mother and father met them at a holiday camp, you see, and as far as I gather she made a set at me da . . .'

'Oh, aye, she would that, anything with trousers on. And you don't think he knows about the bairns?'

'Oh no.' Mary Ann shook her head. 'I'm sure of that.' And she was sure of that. Her da, she would swear, had no knowledge of this wonderful piece of news, and to her at the moment it was a wonderful piece of news. If he had known about her having a baby . . . in fact two babies and getting rid of them as it were, that would have finished anything before it had begun, because he himself had been brought up . . . not in a home, but in the workhouse, left at the gate when only a few weeks old, without even a name pinned on him, and had been christened after the porter who had found him, Mike Shaughnessy . . . Oh no, there would have been no affair if Mike had known about the babies. Although she did not raise her eyes towards the ceiling, her whole being was looking upwards in thanksgiving. This, she considered, was the answer to her daily prayers over the past months.

She smiled now, saying, 'It's been good of you telling me this. You don't know what it means to me, what it'll mean to me ma.'

'Oh yes I do.' The woman nodded knowingly. 'And you tell your ma, it'll stop her worrying.

He won't be such a fool when he knows the truth.'

Mary Ann rose to her feet, and although she said, 'Yes, yes, I'll do that, and thanks again,' she was already in two minds about passing her information on to her mother; she would have to think about it, talk it over with Corny. Yes, that reminded her, she was late already, she must hurry.

As she followed the woman along the passage to the front door she said again, 'You don't know how thankful I am.' And the woman, on opening the door, said, 'I can give a good guess, lass. Anyway, I hope everything turns out all right for you.' She dropped her head to one side now. 'If you're passing this way any time I'd like to hear how things turn out. Will you call in? Oh, except on a Friday.' She laughed selfconsciously. 'My friend comes round on a Friday; we have tea and go to the pictures.'

'Yes, all right. Yes, I will. Thank you.' Mary Ann was now in the street, and she looked at the woman where she stood above her on the step and said again, 'Yes, I'll drop in and tell you. Good-bye.'

'Good-bye,' said the woman; then added quickly, 'Oh, by the way, what's your name?'

Mary Ann hesitated. She realised now she had hoped to get away without revealing her name. 'Shaughnessy,' she said.

'Oh,' said the woman; 'Shaughnessy. It's an unusual name . . . Well, bye-bye and good luck.'

'Bye-bye,' said Mary Ann.

By the time she had waited for another bus

she was half-an-hour late when she reached the garage and she fully expected Corny to explode before she had time to explain what had delayed her. But Corny, standing in the wide doorway of the barn-like structure, greeted her with a smile. He did not even say, 'You're late'; what he did say was, 'It's done, clinched.' He was breathing fast.

'No!' said Mary Ann, forgetting her own news in this moment.

'Aye, it all happened like that.' He snapped his fingers. 'When I came along this morning he was still for holding out, saying the road might come through this way next year; he'd had a hint of it, he said.' And now Corny's voice fell to a whisper and he pulled her further into the garage as he went on: 'When I got here this afternoon, his daughter was on the scene and had been arguing with him like mad. It appears that they are moving to Doncaster and she told him that if he didn't give up the place, then he would just have to get somebody in to look after him because they'd be gone within a fortnight. She told him to sell when he'd the chance, because if he was coming with them the place would be left empty and go to rot – she's like a good many more, she doesn't even believe the road will come this way. But, anyway' – he let out a long breath – 'he's put his name to the paper at last, and it'll all be fixed good and proper on Monday.'

'Did he come down?' Mary Ann asked him eagerly.

At this Corny lowered his head and kicked his toe gently against an oil cask as he said, 'No, just the reverse, he pushed me up another couple of hundred.'

'Aw, Corny.'

His head came up quickly. 'Look, I'm telling you, even at that it's a clinch. Just you wait, give me a couple of years.'

'But that'll make it four thousand.'

'I know, but I can manage it . . . I mean I've got just about enough to put down. And look, Mary Ann, it's worth it.' He pulled her now from the shelter of the garage and on to the rough, gravelled front, where stood two petrol pumps, and beyond into the road, and pointing to the side of the main garage he said proudly, 'There, look at it, our house.'

It was as if he was showing her something she hadn't seen before; and she was looking at it now as if it wasn't a place she had seen before. There it stood, a red brick building, the lower part given over to what appeared like a shop window, with a space behind it big enough to hold a car, and about the same amount of space to the side which was blocked now by two garage doors looking badly in need of a coat of paint. Above this was the house, their future home. She knew it had four rooms, a bathroom and a lavatory, but she had never seen them. She slipped her hand through his arm and, squeezing it, said, 'When can we go up?'

Corny looked down at her and said softly, 'He'll be out by Wednesday – his daughter's insisted on that – so we can get the place done up, at least as much as we can do in a week. But it'll be enough to start with, eh?' His voice had dropped to a whisper and she nodded back at him and answered as quietly, 'Yes, yes, it'll be enough to start with.' Their arms pressed close together, he said, 'Come on, I want to go and tell me grannie, and then we'll go home and tell Mike and your ma, eh?'

It was as they rode into Jarrow on the bus that she told him about the episode with the woman, and the knowledge she had come by.

Corny was wide-eyed as he looked down at her, and there was almost a touch of awe in his voice as he said, 'You were right about her, what she meant to do, I mean. If she's done it twice she could do it again, and with a fellow like Mike and how he feels about bairns . . . well. But now this'll clinch it, he'll get her measure now. But how are you going to tell him?'

'I don't know,' Mary Ann said, and she didn't. 'But,' she went on, 'I don't think I'll tell me ma yet, for somehow I imagine she would feel worse about it than ever. She'd likely get frightened that he might be more sympathetic towards her simply because she's had the two babies. I don't think he would, but me ma doesn't think like me, I know that.'

'Why not tell me grannie?' said Corny. 'She might come up with some idea of how to use it, I mean the information. She's wise, is me grannie, about these things; she's had a lot of experience you know.'

'I know,' said Mary Ann. And yes, she thought, if anybody could tell me how to go about this it would be Mrs McBride.

'Name of God!' said Fanny. 'That should put the kibosh on it. Two bairns you say? God Almighty! She's got a nerve has that one, whoever she is. But I should say it was more the mother to be feared than the girl, although she couldn't do any damage without the daughter. Well now.' She looked across the table to where sat Mary Ann and Corny, side by side, and she said, 'It takes some thinking about, this. You ask me what you should do. Well, as I see it at the moment it's this way, and I'm speaking now with my knowledge of Mike. Now were you to put this to him gently, and give him time to think, begod, it might have the opposite effect altogether and put him in sympathy with her. You never know men . . . oh no, you never know men, even the best of them. And another thing: if she's given time she'll like explain the whole thing away with a wet eye; there's nothing like tears for turning a man's opinion, even against himself and his better judgement.' She moved her big head on her thick neck. 'No, as I see it, you've got to use surprise tactics . . . drop it like a thunderbolt when they're both there.'

'Both there!' Mary Ann, her eyebrows raised, glanced at Corny. 'You mean tell her, or tell me da, in front of her?'

'Nothing short of it, as I see it. You've got to blow the lid off it with no lead up. An' you can do it in an easy, diplomatic sort of way.'

'I can?' Mary Ann again glanced at Corny before looking back at Mrs McBride.

'Aye . . . aye, when they're here together you can just sort of inquire how the bairns are. You see?'

Mary Ann saw – oh, she saw – but she also saw she wasn't up to this task, and she said rapidly, 'Oh no, Mrs McBride, not in front of them both,

I couldn't. I could tell me da or . . . or I think I could go to her and tell her what I know, but . . . but to say it in front of them both . . . I . . . I couldn't.'

'Well now, please yourself. You've asked for my advice and I've given it to you. But do whatever you think is best.'

'She's right.' Corny was nodding down at Mary Ann. 'You go to Mike and tell him and give him time to think and he'll soften; in spite of him being brought up in a home – in fact that's what'll make him soften towards her, the very thing, and the Lord knows what the offshot will be. Then if you go to the girl she might call your bluff, and as me grannie says' – he nodded in Fanny's direction without looking at her – 'tears can have a knockout effect especially if they're from a VP like she is . . . VP has nothing to do with important persons, in this case it stands for voluptuous piece.' He grinned at her, but she wasn't to be drawn into smiling at his quip.

'But . . . but, Corny, I just couldn't.'

'There's another way,' said Fanny. 'You could tell your mother and perhaps she would do it . . . Aw' – she screwed up her face dismissing the idea – 'but then it might look like spite comin' from Lizzie, and Mike being a man might hold it against her, you never know. They keep worms in their minds for years, men do.'

Mary Ann looked from one to the other now, her face wearing a sadness, and her voice matching her expression, she said, 'It's me wedding day a week come Saturday, and now I've got this to tackle.'

Corny made no comment, he just continued to

look at her tenderly, but Fanny, pulling herself up from the table, stated flatly, 'That's life, Mary Ann, that's life.' And going to the hob, she picked up a huge brown teapot, from which she refilled their cups, but in silence now, and in silence they drank.

7

It was again Sunday, and judging from Mary Ann's feelings it could have been the day of doom. She was still doubting very much whether the bombshell method, suggested by Mrs McBride, was the right course to take. Yet the alternative ways in which she could use her information all seemed to have loopholes that could lead to further complications.

She should be highly delighted about Corny's deal and the fact that she would now have a home to go to when she was married, but this big event in her life was being overshadowed and pushed into the background by the weight of the knowledge she carried.

Her preoccupied manner had not been lost on her mother either, for Lizzie had said to her, 'Are you having second thoughts about the garage?' and although she had answered immediately, and emphatically, 'No, no, I'm over the moon,' she knew her mother hadn't believed her.

Then there was Corny's mother and father. They had said to her last night, 'How do you feel about it?' whereas, if her manner had been normal, there would have been no need to put this question. Not that she minded very much what Corny's parents thought, because she hadn't taken to either of them, Mr Boyle least of all. And she knew she wasn't alone in her attitude, for Corny didn't like his father either, although he had never put his feeling into words. And with his mother he was impatient; and Mary Ann thought he had every right to be, for she never kept the house clean or her pantry well stocked, her excuse being that it was no use trying to keep a place clean where there were eight children, which also made it hopeless trying to keep any food in the house. Although Corny's mother was Mrs McBride's own daughter, they had nothing in common, except perhaps their untidiness, because that, too, was Mrs McBride's failing. But of one thing Mary Ann was sure: Corny loved his grannie. He had always shown this by spending more time in her two rooms in Mulhattan's Hall than across the water in his own home in Howden, where, incidentally, he didn't often take her. But because he was excited about getting the garage they had gone over last night.

And then this morning, her mother, pushing her own trouble aside, had taken her into the front room and said gently to her, 'Don't worry, everybody is like this before their wedding, you're up and down. At times you don't know if you should go on with it.' She wouldn't have been surprised had her mother added, 'And it would be a good thing if some of us didn't.' But what she said was, 'This time next week it'll be over and' – she had smiled wryly – 'just beginning.'

Mary Ann had wanted to take her mother's hand in hers and say, 'But, Ma, it's not that I'm worrying about, it's you, and me da and . . . and what I've got to do this afternoon, because I still don't know if it's the right way to tackle this thing.' But she hadn't spoken and Lizzie had said, 'Go up and see Tony and Lettice.' And then she had added, 'It's a pity you went to first mass; if you had gone to eleven o'clock that would have filled the morning and made the time pass until he came. You always need to be reassured by the sight of them at this time.'

Mary Ann had stared at her mother in silence; she couldn't tell her that she was barking up the wrong tree.

But now the waiting was nearly over. It was close on three o'clock, and if they had caught the two-fifteen bus they should be here at any time. She looked around the room. All the family were present, and as her glance passed from one to the other she thought, It's getting like a play every Sunday afternoon, the stage all set waiting for the first act to begin . . . or perhaps, today, the last act.

It was raining heavily outside and blowing a bit of a gale, and the big fire in the open grate was doubly welcome. If she hadn't known how he was feeling it might have appeared that her da was enjoying the blaze, at least from the way he was sitting with his legs stretched out towards the tiled hearth, his pipe in his mouth, and his head in the corner of the winged chair. She could not see his expression, but she had no need to look at his face to know that it would be tight . . . he was waiting.

Her mother was sitting back from the fire, more towards the window. She was knitting. She did not usually knit on a Sunday afternoon, she generally read. Not once did she turn her eyes towards the window, but Mary Ann knew that she, too, was waiting.

Then there was Michael and Sarah, seated as usual on the couch, their hands joined as naturally as if they were children. Looking at them, Mary Ann thought, Our Michael's changed, in this short time he's changed. He's all bubbly inside, yet relaxed. His main job, she felt, was to keep his happiness under cover, to stop himself from being too hearty. As for Sarah, her happiness formed a radiance round her. Mary Ann could almost see the light, and at the present moment it aroused just the slightest bit of envy in her. Sarah could be happy, she had nothing on her mind, nothing to worry her . . . Aw, Mary Ann Shaughnessy! Mary Ann now reprimanded herself sternly. Sarah nothing on her mind? With that handicap? Aw, well – she mentally shook her head at herself – what I meant was, her da's not in trouble, and she hasn't facing her what I have in the next hour or so.

At this moment Sarah, looking across at her, caught her eye. Michael's gaze also joined his wife's, and Mary Ann, gazing back at them, realised that they, too, were waiting, and that below their evident happiness there was anxiety.

And then there was Corny. Corny was holding the floor again. Like a master of ceremonies, he was to the forefront of the stage, and as if he knew there was a bad play to be put over he was doing his best to entertain the audience beforehand.

'Anybody can write pop songs: Lyrics they

call them. God-fathers! They've got a nerve. It's a racket, 'cos they can pinch the tune from the classics. But they daren't go pinching some bloke's verse, they've got to pay for that. So what do they do, the smart lads? Well, they hash up these so-called lyrics.' Corny now threw himself into a pose and sang in an exaggerated but tuneful tenor voice, 'I ain't loved nobody since I loved you, and, 'coo Liza, you ain't half got me in a stew.'

Even Lizzie laughed, at least she laughed with her mouth; Michael and Sarah rocked together; and Mike, turning his head, cast a quizzical glance up at the big clown. As for Mary Ann, she held her hands tightly across her mouth, and as she laughed she thought, Oh, Corny, you're sweet. It wasn't the right adjective to describe her future husband, but it described his intention, the intention of his clowning.

Corny was demanding of the entire room now, 'I'm right, though . . . it is all tripe, isn't it?'

'Oh, I wouldn't say all.' Michael came back at him. 'There are some good lyrics.'

'Tell me them then. Go on, just one.'

'Oh, I can't think of any off-hand.'

' "Trees", for instance,' said Sarah.

' "Trees"!' Corny's voice was high. 'But that's as old as the hills; it was written over thirty years ago, it's got whiskers.'

Corny's eyes were now brought round to Mike's face where Mike was once again slanting his eyes towards him, and he pushed his hand in the direction of his future father-in-law, laughing heartily as he cried, 'You know what I mean, Mike. Anyway, you haven't got whiskers.' He turned once again to Michael. 'I'm meaning the modern stuff. Granted there are plenty of decent writers, but they don't get the chance. I tell you, it's a racket. As for writing lyrics, I've made up umpteen tunes on me cornet but do you think they'd ever be taken?'

'Have you written them down?' asked Michael.

'No, I haven't.'

'Then how do you expect them to be taken? Put them down and send them up, and then if they're rejected you'll be speaking from experience; as it is you're just speaking from hearsay.'

Corny turned his gaze upwards now as he scratched the back of his head, and his mood changing with mercurial swiftness, he said seriously, 'Aye, perhaps you're right. If I could put them down . . . if. But' – he now looked at Michael – 'I can't read music.' He was grinning in a derogatory way at himself. 'I can make tunes up – I've got umpteen in me head – and can bring them through the wind, but that's as far as it gets. But anyway' – he moved his body impatiently – 'we weren't talking about tunes, we were talking about the words. Now Mary Ann there: do you think they would put any of her stuff to music?'

Michael now cast a glance in his sister's direction, and with brotherly appreciation he said, 'There's a chance, that's if she ever did anything good enough.'

'Oh!' Mary Ann's voice sounded indignant. 'Don't praise me, Michael.'

'Don't worry,' said Michael, 'I won't.' But he laughed gently at her as he spoke.

And then Corny came back at him, crying, 'She's done some good stuff. If she had any sense she'd keep sending it off, but she doesn't.' He bounced his head at her, and for a second they exchanged glances, and then he went on, 'Some of her prose is like poetry.'

'You don't say,' said Michael, with mock awe now.

'Aye, I do. It's always the same in families, it takes an outsider to see what's going on.'

'Well, that's soon going to be rectified,' said Michael. 'And then you'll be blind to all our good points, especially your wife's . . .'

As the door-bell rang and cut off Michael's voice they all looked startled. It would seem that Corny had succeeded in his efforts during the last few minutes and had made them forget what they were waiting for, but now he stopped his fooling; his part for the present was finished, but he said, 'Will I go?' And Lizzie nodded to him without raising her head. Sarah pulled herself further up into a straighter position on the couch, as did Michael, while Mike, leaning forward, knocked the doddle from the bowl of his pipe. Only Mary Ann made no move. She sat farthest from the door and to the side of her mother, and as the sound of footsteps came across the hall her heart began to race. She hardly saw the mother and daughter enter the room, for there was a mist before her eyes, and she was afraid for the moment she was going to faint, or do something equally silly. That was until she saw Corny's face. His expression soft, his eyes were looking at her over the heads of the others, saying, 'It's all right, it'll soon be over.'

'What a day!' said Mrs Radley. 'And how are you, Lizzie?'

Lizzie had not risen to greet the guests, but she

raised her eyes and, looking at Mrs Radley, answered, 'Quite well, thank you . . . I wonder that you ventured out in such weather.'

'Oh' – Mrs Radley swung her permed, blueygrey head from side to side, dismissing the weather – 'we like to get out. We must get out.' She leaned towards Lizzie now. 'We're not like you all here, we're not so fortunate as to have open land all round us; and when one loves the country, it's a great strain on the nerves being hemmed in by brick walls.'

Yvonne Radley was standing to the side of her mother; she had not addressed anyone in the room as yet. Her eyes had gone straight to Mike as soon as she came through the door. He'd had his back towards her, but now, when he turned to her, there was a defeated look about him; yet at the same time his eyes spoke of the anger he was feeling, anger at the combined attitude of his family and the obvious hostility filling the room. Getting to his feet, he said, 'Sit down.'

'Thanks . . . Mike.'

Yvonne's hesitation in saying Mike's name suggested to Mary Ann's disturbed mind an endearing familiarity. She watched her father pointing to the couch and saying to Mrs Radley, 'Sit down, won't you?' And as he spoke his angry glance was directed towards his son, for Michael, although he had risen reluctantly to his feet on their entry, had not offered his seat to the visitors.

'We are not going to stay long. We merely come with an invitation.'

Mary Ann's gaze, which had been directed towards her hands, snapped upwards now to Yvonne Radley, but the girl, a simpering expression on her face, was still looking at Mike and holding his attention as she went on, 'You see, it's my birthday on Wednesday and we'd like you to come along in the evening. We're having a little party.' She paused; then, her eyes flitting to Lizzie, she added with a girlish laugh, 'All of you I mean, of course, that's understood . . . Will you?'

Lizzie now laid down her knitting and looked across the room at this girl for a full minute before answering her. She took in once again her long legs, her high bust, her round blue eyes, her simpering expression, her hair hanging like burnished bronze on to her shoulders, and as she looked she had the fearsome urge to spring on her, grip her by the throat and bang her head against the wall. The thought was terrifying in itself and it affected her voice as she answered, 'I'm . . . I'm sorry, but I have an engagement for next Wednesday evening.'

The word engagement seemed so out of place, the excuse so evidently an excuse that it actually created a wave of embarrassment among all those present, with the exception perhaps of the Radleys themselves.

'How old will you be?' It was Corny speaking now. His voice rough-edged, his face straight, he looked directly at the girl, and she, returning his look with a searching one of her own, answered, 'Nineteen.'

'Oh, Mary Ann's got a couple of months up on you.'

'Yes . . . yes.' Yvonne smiled now across the room at Mary Ann, and Mrs Radley, following her own reasoning, put in quickly, 'Yvonne's got an aunt who is only sixteen. That's funny, isn't it?

Yvonne nineteen, with an aunt sixteen.' She beamed from one to the other.

'Would you like a cup of tea?' Although Mike's voice sounded ordinary, his whole body looked stiff and defiant as he asked the question.

'Oh, no, Mike, don't bother; we won't stay,' said Mrs Radley. 'We set out to have a nice long walk and we'll carry on. The weather doesn't deter us . . . does it, Yvonne?'

'What?' Yvonne brought her gaze from Mike's averted face, then said, 'No, no. No, we love tramping. I love open spaces.'

As Corny, the devil in him, began to whistle softly, 'Oh give me a home where the buffalo roam,' Mike turned a fiery glance on him, and Corny allowed the tune to fade slowly away, but not too slowly, then went and stood beside Mary Ann and imperceivably nudged her with his arm.

Mary Ann did not need any nudging to be reminded of what she had to do. But how? How was she to start? She became panicky when she saw Mrs Radley rise to her feet, followed by Yvonne. She had never expected them to go so soon, they had only just arrived. She couldn't do it – not in a hurry like this, anyway. She glanced at Lizzie sitting frozen-faced beside her, and it was the sight of her mother's patent unhappiness that loosened her tongue.

'Are you having many to the party?' Her voice was high and unnatural sounding, and she was conscious of everyone turning their eyes towards her, for never had she addressed either of the Radleys since their first visit.

'Well, no.' Again the simpering attitude from Yvonne. 'Only friends, close friends.'

Mary Ann gathered saliva into her dry mouth and swallowed deeply before she said, 'But you'll be having the children . . . the babies?'

There, it was done. The fuse was lit.

From the time the match is put to a fuse until the actual explosion takes place there is a period of comparative silence. This silence now filled the room; and as all eyes were once more turned towards her she had the desire to scream and break it. She saw the mother and daughter exchange a startled glance; then they were looking at her again, their eyes seeming to be spurting red lights towards her. The knowledge of exposure had been in their flicking glance, and it brought trembling power to her, and she said now, addressing Yvonne pointedly, 'Oh, of course, you mightn't be able to bring your eldest, him being adopted, but the baby you could; they'll let you have him from the home for the day, won't they?'

'Yo-u! . . . yo-u!' Yvonne took two rapid steps forward, but was checked from advancing farther by her mother crying, 'Stop it, Yvonne!' Mrs Radley had gripped her daughter's arm and now, turning her white-strained face towards Mary Ann, she said, 'I don't know what you mean?'

'I think you do,' said Mary Ann, her voice more normal sounding now; 'and so does she. Or would you like me to explain further?'

Yvonne Radley, pulling herself from her mother's grasp, gripped the head of the couch and, leaning forward over Sarah towards Mary Ann, hissed, 'You swine! You prying, sneaky little swine.' And now her tone was no longer recognisable, nor yet her expression. 'You think you're smart, don't you? You pampered, under-sized little brat you. For two pins I'd . . .'

'You'd what?' said Corny.

'Yvonne! Yvonne! Stop it.' Mrs Radley was now pulling at her daughter's arm, and the girl, angered with frustration and disappointment, burst into tears. Her wide, heavily painted mouth agape, she spluttered, 'I'll . . . I'll get me own back on you, you'll see, you little upstart you. I hated you from the minute I clapped eyes on you . . . you . . .'

'Come away, come on.' Mrs Radley's voice, piercing now, seemed to verge on hysteria, as she cried to Mary Ann, 'You haven't heard the last of this, miss, oh no. Oh no, not by a long chalk. You'll hear more of this; up for defamation of character, you'll see. You'll see, you nasty minded little—.' Mrs Radley used a term which no-one, judging from her previous refined manner, would have dreamt she ever knew – 'That's what you are, nothing else, a nasty minded little—. Come on. Come on. You'll not stay here another minute.' She pulled her daughter through the doorway into the hall, and nobody in the room made a move to follow them and let them out of the house.

The feeling of apprehension and worry which had filled Mary Ann since hearing Mrs McBride's suggested method on how best to deal with the information concerning the Radleys was nothing compared with the terror filling her as she looked at her da. She was unaware of the others look-ing at her, their expressions all different. There was admiration in Michael's and Sarah's eyes; there was love and concern in Corny's; there was

a look of amazement, mixed with pity and incredulity on her mother's face; but she saw none
of these, she only saw Mike's face filled with
black anger; it seemed to ooze from him. She
fancied she could smell it, and her mind gabbled:
He must have been in love with her. It was serious
then. Oh dear Lord. As she watched him coming
slowly and heavily towards her, she trembled with
this new fear, fear of her da and what he was
going to do to her. Now he was towering over
her, his body stretched, his muscles hard and his
one fist clenched. His jaw moved a number of
times before his mouth opened to speak; then he
said in a terrible tone, terrible because it was
quiet, 'You think you've done something clever,
don't you, Little Miss Fix-it? You've torn out
somebody's innards and held them up for in-
spection. She had sinned, hadn't she? not once,
but twice, so you, the good Catholic little miss,
must—'

'Mike!' It was Lizzie's voice, commanding,
loud, and it brought Mike's head swinging
towards her, and, his voice no longer quiet now,
he barked, 'You! . . . You! I'm warning you. You
be quiet. It's you who started this, you and your
fancies. And you see what you've brought her to,
because she did it for you. She's turned into a
sneaking little righteous ferret. So do what you've
been doing for many a week, keep your mouth
shut.'

And Lizzie kept her mouth shut, tight now, in a
proud, bitter line.

Mike was again looking at Mary Ann, and,
his tone dropping once more, he addressed her,
saying, 'You're not out of the wood yet, me girl;

389

marriage won't make you immune from emotions. Well, now' – he pushed his shoulders back even further – 'you intended to fix it for her, didn't you? Well, perhaps you have. Perhaps you've done just that . . . the lot of you, among you.' He flicked his eyes around the room before again levelling them on Mary Ann and going on: 'There's an emotion you know very little about as yet, me girl. It's called compassion, an' it can do very odd things, especially with an . . . old . . . man' – he stressed the old – 'an' a young lass saddled with two bairns.' He paused now, and into the pause Mary Ann whimpered, 'You wouldn't, Da, you wouldn't. Oh, I'm sorry, for what I did, but you wouldn't, you wouldn't.'

'Wouldn't I? Well, just you wait and see, me girl. I'm going to finish what you and your mother started. It's always good policy to finish a job, isn't it?'

Mary Ann, still staring at Mike, heard her mother's sharp intake of breath, and it was as if she had leapt inside Lizzie's body and was retaliating for her, because now, of a sudden, she cried up at Mike, 'Well then, go on, go on, what's stopping you? Everybody wants to laugh out loud; they've been smothering it for weeks, so go on, and they can let it rip. You with your neck all creasy' – she pointed up at him – 'and big brown freckles on the back of your hand, which are not freckles at all, but the first signs of age coming on they say; and there's grey in your hair, but you can't see it at the back of your head, the same as you won't be able to see yourself as a doddery old man when you're left home here with the bairns while she goes . . .'

As the hand came across her face she thought that her head had left her body. She was conscious of herself screaming as she toppled backwards over something hard, then there was noise and yelling all about her.

As she felt her mother's hands raise her head from the floor the mist cleared from her eyes and she saw, standing like two giants within the open doorway, Corny and her da. They stood close together. Corny had hold of Mike's lapels, and Mike, his good arm sticking out at an angle from his body, was saying in that terrible voice again, 'Take your hands off me, boy.'

'YOU . . . You shouldn't have done that.' Corny's voice, too, was deep and unnaturally quiet, but his anger was causing him to stammer. 'If . . . if you were . . . weren't . . .'

'I told you . . . take your hands off me.'

'Corny! Corny!' Michael was now tugging at Corny's arms. 'Leave go . . . Do you hear?' With a quick, strong pull he wrenched one of Corny's hands from Mike's coat and slowly Corny relinquished the other.

Mike now, taking a step backwards, lifted his hand and straightened his collar and tie while straining his neck upwards, and as he did so he looked at the two young men confronting him, both faces, that of his son and his future son-in-law, full of dark hostility. With a movement that seemed to lift his body completely from the floor he swung round, and the next sound that came to them was the banging of the front door.

Corny shook his head as if coming out of a dream; then, turning swiftly, he went across the room to where Mary Ann was being supported by

Lizzie, with Sarah in an unwieldy position on the floor at her other side.

'Don't cr . . . cry. Don't cry.' He was still stammering.

'Lift her on to the couch,' said Lizzie in a toneless voice. 'She's hurt her hip on the side of the chair.'

Corny lifted Mary Ann from the floor as if she were a child, and, seating her on the couch and still with his arms about her, he pressed her head into his shoulder, and it was the warm comfort, the understanding pressure of his arms, that released, in full flood, the agony in her mind – the agony of the knowledge that her da had hit her. Her da! . . . Corny, Mr Lord, Mrs McBride, or even Father Owen could have struck out at her – fantastic as the assumption was, she could have stretched her imagination to see it happening – but never, never her da.

'Don't, don't cry like that. Mary Ann, do you hear me?' Lizzie's hands had turned her face from Corny's shoulder and were cupping it. 'Stop it now.'

'Oh, Ma! M . . . ma!' She was spluttering and jabbering incoherently as she had done at times when a child and her world had broken apart. But now she was no longer a child, and things, some things, were more difficult to say; the words were sticking in her gullet, 'He . . . he . . . Ma.'

'Give over, child, give over.' It was as if Lizzie, too, was seeing her as a child again; and now she said to Corny, 'Carry her up to bed, will you?'

As Corny picked her up in his arms she turned her head towards Lizzie, crying, 'Ma, he . . . he didn't mean it.'

'There now, don't fret yourself any more, go on.' Lizzie pressed Corny forward.

'He didn't, Ma, he didn't, I te . . . tell you . . . Where's he gone? Our Michael . . . our Michael, go and find him. Go on, Michael.'

'All right,' said Michael. 'Don't worry, I'll go and find him.'

From somewhere behind Mary Ann now her mother's voice, no longer toneless, said quickly, quietly and bitterly, 'You'll do no such thing, Michael. Stay where you are. He's gone. Let him go and I hope I never see him again.'

As Corny lowered Mary Ann on to the bed she held on to him, crying hysterically now, 'See . . . see, I shouldn't have done it. She said it would be all right; your grannie, she said it'd be all right, and now, look. A bombshell, she said. Fancy Mrs McBride saying that . . . A bombshell, a bombshell . . .'

8

Lizzie didn't know how much past midnight it was; she couldn't recall whether it was Saturday, Sunday or Monday; she was only aware that she had reached the crisis of her life, and she was living in that crisis. Years ago she had almost walked out on Mike and gone to her mother's, but now he hadn't almost walked out on her . . . he had walked out, he had gone completely. Why had this happened? Was she to blame? If she had laughed at the whole thing, would it ever have reached this point of torment? But she wasn't made to laugh when the vital issues of life were being undermined. She was not one of those who could follow the advice given by the wise sages in the women's magazines; these wisdom-filled females who had never touched on the experiences on which, each week, they poured out their advice; and such advice: 'Your best plan is to ignore the whole situation'; 'Welcome her to the house, treat her as if she were your daughter.' Were there women anywhere who could follow such advice?

Well, it was over, he had gone. She looked at the clock. No-one had wound it up and it had stopped at twenty-five past twelve. If he had been coming back he would have been here long before now. Yes, it was over. Then she should go up to bed, shouldn't she?

She couldn't face that bed. She didn't think she would ever lie in it again; happy or otherwise, they had shared that bed for close on twenty-five years. No, tonight of all nights she couldn't face that bed. She would stay where she was, by the fire. She leant her head back in the corner of the high chair and looked across to where Mike's chair, startlingly bare, faced her. 'Oh, Mike, Mike.' It was a wail, coming as it were from far back in the beginning of time, spiralling up through her being, choking her, strangling her with the agony of things past, good things past.

'Are you all right?' Michael's hand on her shoulder brought her upright in the chair, her own hands gripping her throat.

'I'm sorry; did I wake you?'

'No, no, I wasn't asleep.'

He was on his hunkers before her now, his eyes soft on her face. 'Go on up to bed, Mother, go on.'

'I couldn't, Michael. I'm all right here. Don't worry. You go on in to Sarah.'

'She can't sleep either.'

'It's the couch, it isn't long enough.'

'No, it isn't that.'

'Where's Corny?'

'Outside somewhere.'

Lizzie's eyes stretched slightly. 'Outside in this?' She listened for a moment to the howling of the wind and the steel-rapping of the rain on the windows. 'What's he doing out there?'

'I don't know, he just feels like that. He's upstairs one minute and outside the next. He's been like that for hours.'

'What time is it?' she asked.

'It's after one, nearly half-past I should say . . . How is she?'

'She was still asleep a short while ago.'

'That tablet has done the trick. It'll likely put her out until the morning . . . Michael.' Although Lizzie spoke her son's name she turned her face from him, and it was some seconds before she went on, 'Will . . . will you carry on the farm?'

And it was some seconds before Michael answered, 'Aw, Mother, you know I will . . . but . . . but it won't come to that . . .'

'It'll come to it all right, Michael, let's face it. This is the end.'

'He'll come to his senses. You've got to give him a chance. He was mad at the way it happened.'

'I don't want him, Michael, when he comes to his senses. Once he has spent a night with that girl nothing on God's earth could make me take him back. I can't help it, that's how I'm made. I've never wanted anybody but him in my life, and up to now it's been the same with him. But . . . but it wouldn't be any use him crawling back when his madness has cooled off. No use at all.'

Her voice was so level and conveyed such finality that Michael knew that no persuasion would make any impression on his mother's attitude. As he pulled himself up straight a noise in the yard brought him sharply round, his face to the kitchen door. And Lizzie's head came up, too, at the sound of running steps. The next minute they heard the back door open, and within seconds Corny appeared in the doorway. The water was running from his plastered hair down on to his black plastic mack. He stood gasping for a moment, wiping the rain from his face with his hand before coming farther into the room; then looking from Michael to Lizzie, he brought out, 'He's back.'

'Me father?' It was a soft question from Michael, but Lizzie made no movement.

'Where?' said Michael now.

'I saw him going up into the loft. All night I had a feeling he was somewhere round the place. I looked everywhere, but no sign of him, yet I couldn't get rid of it, the feeling. And then it was Simon who gave me the tip. You know that little bark he gives when he sees him, or smells him. Well, I heard him come out from the lower barn growling and then there was this little bark, and I stood in the shelter of the byres, and I saw the outline of him. He . . . he was swaying a bit. It could be that he's got a load on, yet I don't know. But I didn't go near him.' He jerked his head to the side. 'After what happened he wouldn't welcome the sight of me.'

'I'll get the lantern.' Michael was running across the room; then at the door he turned and said to Corny, who was about to follow him, 'Don't come. Stay with me mother.' And he cast a glance in Lizzie's direction before hurrying out of the room.

Getting to her feet, Lizzie went and stood before the fire, with her hand lifted to the mantelpiece and her head bowed. It was a stance she often took up when deeply troubled.

After some minutes of silence Corny approached the fire, but not too near to her; and holding his hand out to the warmth, he said softly, 'I feel that I'm to blame as much as anybody for what has happened, Mam. You see, when Mary Ann told me and said she didn't know what to do, I mean about letting on about what she knew, I told her that the best one to go to for advice was me grannie, and it was me grannie who suggested that she make her information into a bombshell. I can see now it was wrong, but . . . but you can always be wise after the event, can't you?' He waited a moment, and when no answer came to him he lowered his head and muttered, 'I'm sorry.'

Lizzie turned towards him now and, putting out her hand, touched his arm. 'Don't blame yourself, Corny,' she said. 'If you want to know something, I think it's just as well it happened like this. It had to come to a head sooner or later. It had to burst.'

'What'll happen now?' he asked softly. 'You'll not take it out of . . . ?'

Turning from him, Lizzie said abruptly, 'We'll just have to wait and see, Corny, won't we? We'll just have to wait and see . . .'

They were standing in silence, finding nothing more to say, when Michael came hurrying back into the kitchen. It seemed that he could not have been as far as the big barn in so short a time. He, too, was gasping with his running against the wind, but he came straight to Lizzie, where she stood on the hearthrug waiting, and straight to the point, saying, 'He's in a bad way, Mother, he's—' He shook his head slowly. 'He's never been out of the fields. He's covered with mud from head to foot and wet to the skin; the things are sticking to him. He must have been headlong in the dyke down by Fuller's Cut. He's shivering as if he had ague.' He put his wet hand on her. 'He's never been away, you understand, not farther than the fields.'

Michael watched as his words slowly brought the colour back into his mother's face. He seemed to watch the years drop away from her. Her voice had a slight tremble in it as she said to him, 'Give me my coat, will you?' Then when Michael had brought her coat from the hall and helped her into it, she asked, 'Is the lamp outside?' And when he nodded, she said, 'Don't come with me.' Then, looking from him to Corny, she added, 'Go to bed, Corny – the spare bed is ready.'

Corny said nothing, and Michael said no more, but they both watched her as she swiftly pulled the hood of her coat over her head and went out of the room.

Having picked up the lantern at the back door, Lizzie battled her way across the farmyard towards the barn. When she reached the great doors she stood for a moment to regain her breath; then, pushing open the small hatch door, she bent down and entered the barn. As she walked unsteadily towards the ladder that led to the loft, the light from the lantern, and her steps, caused a scurrying of small creatures. Then she was on the ladder, mounting it slowly, and when she reached the top Simon's wet nose greeted her before he turned and ran to the far end of the loft, where a bale of straw had been broken and on which lay a huge, huddled figure.

As the light of the lantern fell on Mike, Lizzie

paused. Her body still stiff and erect, her face still wet, she looked down on her husband, and with the exception of the empty sleeve no part of him was recognisable to her, but she was made immediately aware that the mud-covered shape was shivering from head to foot. Bending slowly over him, she touched his shoulder, and after a moment he turned his face towards her, only to turn it as quickly away again. Evidently he had not expected to see her.

It was the unguarded look in his eyes that softened the ice round Lizzie's heart, for the look reminded her of the dog they had found in Weybridge's cottage three years ago. The Weybridges were a no-good family who had lived off the beaten track about two miles over the fields, and whose debts had caused them to do a moonlight flit one night, and they had left their dog chained up in an outhouse. He was there a fortnight before Michael had found him and brought him home, and the poor creature had crawled on his belly across the length of the kitchen and laid his head across her feet. He was an old dog, and partly blind. Apparently he had been used to a woman and had immediately given to her his allegiance, and in return she had looked after him lovingly until he had died last year.

'Come on, get up,' she said softly. But Mike did not move. 'Do you hear me?' she said. 'Get on your feet.'

For answer he buried his face in the straw and muttered something which she could not hear.

Placing the lantern at a safe distance, she bent over him again, and, gripping him by the shoulder and using all her strength, she jerked him from his prone position. And now, with his head hanging, he muttered through his chattering teeth, 'Leave me be for the night, will you?'

'I'll do no such thing; get on your feet.'

'I . . . I can't. I'm finished for the time being. I'll . . . I'll be all right in the mornin'. Go on in, go on in.' He went to lie down again but her hands prevented him. 'Get up,' she said. 'Come on, get up.' Her voice was soft, pleading now, and after a moment he turned on all fours and raised himself up on to his knees, and then up to his feet.

She was appalled at the sight of him. As Michael had said, he must have fallen headlong into the muddy ditch at Fuller's Cut.

She guided his shaking form to the ladder, then on to it, and held the light aloft until he had reached the floor of the barn. Then descending quickly, once again she guided him, and when they were in the yard she put her arm about him to steady him against the wind, and with the docility of a child he allowed himself to be helped by her until they reached the back door, and there, stopping and pulling himself slowly from her grasp, he muttered, 'Are they in?'

'No, no,' she whispered hurriedly, 'they're all in bed.'

In the scullery he stopped again, and, looking down at the condition of himself, he brought out, his words rattling like pebbles against his teeth, 'I'll . . . I'll change here.'

For answer she pulled off her coat, saying briskly, 'You're going straight upstairs into a bath.'

She led the way now, quietly through the

kitchen, into the hall and up the stairs; and he followed, stepping gingerly, his limbs shaking with every step he took. But when they entered the bathroom and she had turned on the bath and pulled some warm towels from the rail, he said, without looking at her, 'Leave me be now, I can manage.'

When he felt her hesitation he added, in a tone that was more like his natural one, 'I'll be down when I'm tidied, leave me be.'

When Lizzie returned to the kitchen her own legs were shaking so she felt she must sit down before she dropped. But as she neared a chair she stopped, saying to herself, 'No, no, keep going, keep going.' She knew it would be fatal at this moment to sit down and think. If she sat down she would break down, and she didn't want that. He would need something hot, piping hot, if there weren't to be repercussions to this state he was in. How long had he been wet through to the skin? Eight . . . nine hours? And in this wind that was enough to cut through you like a sword! Hot bread and milk, she said, that will act like a poultice and . . . She looked towards the store cupboard, seeing at the back of it, hidden among the bottles of sauces, mayonnaise and pickles, a flask of whisky. It had stood there a long, long time, waiting for an emergency; and this was the emergency. She had put her foot down on Mike having whisky in the house, yet she had always kept that flask hidden there. It was strange, she thought, as her hand groped knowingly over the shelf and brought out the bottle of Johnnie Walker, strange that she herself should give him whisky . . .

It was half-an-hour later when Mike came downstairs. When she heard his soft, padded approach her body began to tremble and she went hurriedly into the scullery and brought the pan of bread and milk from the stove, and she was pouring it into a basin when he entered the room. She did not look towards him; nor did Mike look at her, but, pulling the cord of his dressing-gown tighter about him, he walked to the fire and stood, very much as she had done earlier, looking down into it, his one hand gripping the edge of the mantelpiece.

Lizzie now opened the flask of whisky and poured a generous measure into a beaker, and after adding brown sugar to it she went to the fire and, bending sideways so that no part of her touched Mike, this seemingly back-to-normal Mike, she lifted the boiling kettle from the hob and, returning to the table with it, filled the beaker. Then, the kettle in one hand, the beaker in the other, she went once again to the fireplace, placed the kettle on the hob and, with her eyes fixed on the beaker as she stirred the hot whisky and sugar, said softly, 'Drink this.'

Without moving his body Mike brought his head round and looked at her, then at the beaker. The smell that came from it was of whisky, the liquor that was forbidden in the house, forbidden because of his weakness. The hot stinging aroma swept up his nostrils and down into his body. It was too much, too much. He took his hand from the mantelpiece and pressed it over his face, digging his fingers into his scalp as if he would tear the whole façade of his features from their base, and his body crouched forward and writhed in agony as he brought out her name, 'Liz. Oh, Liz.'

As she swiftly laid her hand on his bent head she had the feeling she was touching him for the first time. She could not see her hand or his head now; the ice fast melting round her heart was flowing from her eyes, bathing her face, and refreshing her soul like spring floods on a parched land. She put her arms about him and he clung to her fiercely while a torrent was released from him, too – a torrent which checked his speech and choked him yet could not stop him repeating her name over and over. And he asked forgiveness and said what he had to say with his hand as it moved in tight pressure over her head, her shoulders and her back. How long they stood like this they didn't know, but presently Lizzie muttered chokingly, 'It'll . . . it'll be cold.' Blindly she put out her hand to the side and lifted the glass from the mantelpiece and put it to his lips; and over the brim of it they looked at each other. Once again they were survivors, once again they had swum ashore. And with this rescue Lizzie was sure of only one thing: never again would Mike sail so near the wind, and never would he sign on, so to speak, in a vessel similar to the one that he had just escaped from.

That voyage was over.

As the late dawn broke Mary Ann came out of her drugged sleep. She lay for a moment quite still, staring towards the dim lines of objects in the room. She felt awful, her head ached; and as she thought of her head aching, she realised that her face was aching too, as if she'd had toothache, and her leg felt stiff. As she put her one hand to her face and another to her hip the reason for her aches and pains crept slowly into her mind and she groaned as she turned round and half buried her face in the pillows. Closing her eyes, she went over the scene of last night. She remembered crying and shouting after her da had hit her. She remembered that she couldn't stop, and that she had kept blaming Mrs McBride for it all. That was just before her mother gave her that tablet; it must have been a sleeping tablet.

She turned on to her back again and looked towards the window. Mrs McBride wasn't to blame, she herself was to blame. When she had found out about Yvonne Radley she should have gone to her mother with the news, or, failing that, she could have got her da on the quiet and risked the consequences. She felt a wave of sickness creep over her as she thought that, whatever she had done, the result couldn't have been any worse.

But what had happened since last night? Her mother left all alone. In this moment she had no doubt but that her mother had been alone all night, for remembering the look in her da's face she knew it meant defiance and going his own road. She must get up and see her mother.

As she pulled herself into a sitting position she thought, Oh dear, I feel awful, awful, and she lay back again, her head against the bed-head, listening for a moment to the usual household sounds that the dawn brought: the muffled steps rising from the kitchen below, a door closing, Simon barking, the lowing of the cattle . . . the cattle. She lifted up her head from its resting position . . . Who'd look after the cattle, the farm as a whole? Michael, of course . . . Yes, there was Michael. Her head dropped back yet again. She must get up and find out what was going on, but oh, she felt awful.

She was pushing the bedclothes off her when there came the sound of footsteps on the landing; they were quiet, heavy and slow. Recognition of these steps brought her face round to the door. She paused with the bedclothes in her hand, one leg hanging over the side of the bed, and when the gentle almost imperceptible tap came on the door she pulled her leg back into the bed and the clothes about her and waited.

When the door opened and she saw her da enter, and he in his night things with his dressing-gown on, a cup of tea in his hand and a look on his face that she hadn't seen there for many a day, she wondered for a moment if she had died in the night, or if she was still dreaming? Or, if she was awake, was she being affected still by the sleeping tablet? She kept her eyes on him as he walked slowly to the bed. She watched him put the cup of tea on the table, then lower himself down on to the bed side. As she stared into his face the years slipped from her; she was seven again, or nine, or eleven, or thirteen, and she knew that in all the world there was no-one like her da. There had never been anyone anywhere on earth like him before and there would never be again; yet in all their past comings together she had never seen a look on his face like now. She would have said her da knew nothing about humility; her da could never be humble, but within this big-framed, virile individual who was sitting before her now was a humble man, a shamed man, who was half afraid of how his gesture might be received. She watched him bring his hand to her face, to the painful side, and when she felt his fingers touch her cheek she hunched her shoulders and cradled his hand while her arms went swiftly up around his neck.

'I'll never forgive myself.'

'Forget it, oh forget it, Da. It was nothing. I asked for it.'

'I'll never forget it to me dying day.'

She pressed him from her and she looked at him, but she couldn't see him. And she asked him a question. It didn't seem necessary but she had to ask it. She had to hear him answer it. She said, 'Is everything all right, Da?' Dimly she saw the movement of his head, and then he held her again before he answered, in a thick murmur, 'Aye, thanks be to God.'

Thanks be to God, he had said, and her da didn't believe in God – well, not the recognised God anyway . . . But thanks be to God. And she, too, from the bottom of her heart, from the core of her being to which he had given life, she, too, said, 'Thanks be to God.' But aloud she responded in her usual way. 'Oh, Da! Oh, Da!' she said.

9

'You had better go on up,' said Lizzie, 'Mr Lord will be waiting for you.'

'I will in a minute, Ma,' Mary Ann answered as she dashed through the kitchen and into the hall, calling from there, 'I just want to see the weather report.'

Lizzie smiled at Sarah where she sat in a chair to the side of the fire busily stitching, and she whispered down to her as she passed her, 'The weather report. The weather report for the third time today.' They laughed softly, exchanging glances, and then Lizzie went on into the front room, there to hear the announcer, who was seemingly talking solely to Mary Ann from the screen, telling her she had no need to worry, for he and God had conspired on her behalf to still the elements, and all would be bright and serene on the morrow.

Mary Ann turned and smiled at Lizzie as she came to her side, and she leant against her mother's shoulder, and Lizzie put her arm around her and squeezed her gently for a moment. Then, pressing her hastily away, she went and closed the front-room door and came quietly back; and, looking down at her daughter for a moment before dropping her gaze to the side, she said hesitantly, 'I've . . . I've never spoken about last Sunday, and there mightn't be any more time before tomorrow, I mean . . . I mean when we can be alone, but I want you to know' – she raised her eyes slowly – 'I want you to know how I feel . . .'

'Oh, Ma, don't talk about it, it's over.'

'I've got to talk about it, just this once; I've got to put into words that I'm grateful.' With her raised hand she hushed Mary Ann's attempt to speak, and went on, 'Perhaps it's the last thing you need ever do, in that way, for your da. I know now what it must have cost you to go through with it, because if it had gone wrong, as it could well have done, you would have blamed yourself to the end of your days. But as usual, where he is concerned, you took the right tack.'

'It wasn't me, it was Mrs Mc . . .'

'I know all about that, my dear. But Mrs McBride didn't do it. And you know something! I've got a feeling that all this just had to happen . . .' She paused, and her expression softened still further before she went on, 'I can say this to you because tomorrow you're going to be married. You've got a lot to learn, and as the years go on it'll get harder, not easier, but somehow I think you already know that . . . you've had enough experience.' She smiled a small smile that Mary Ann returned. 'But this business has opened your da out . . . I mean towards me, because he's never been the one to talk and try and get to the bottom of things; he's been afraid to, inside. And I know now that I haven't helped him much in that way; I close up like a clam. It's my nature, I suppose, and I've always told myself that I couldn't help it, but now I know it would have been better for both of us if I'd tried. Anyway' – she jerked her head – 'to cut a long story short, we've talked the last few days as we've never done in our lives before. We've gone deep into things, and the deeper we've gone the closer we've become; and as I see it, we've got you to thank for it.'

'Oh, Ma, no. No. Don't, don't go on.'

Lizzie leant forward now and kissed her daughter and they held each other tightly for a moment. Then pushing Mary Ann towards the door, Lizzie said in a voice that was not quite steady, 'Go on now, go on up. You don't want him to get annoyed, do you?'

Mary Ann made no answer to this, but, going swiftly into the hall, she grabbed up her coat from the hall-stand and went out by the front way.

The light from the cow-sheds was illuminating the yard as she hurried towards the far gate. She heard her da chastise Primrose, saying, 'Behave now, behave yourself.' Primrose was a milk chocolate, dappled, wide-eyed Jersey cow, and, unlike her eight sisters, she had a temper. Their Michael used to say that she herself was like Primrose both inside and out. She saw Michael now, his silhouette outlined against the window. He could be mistaken at a distance for her da. She made her way more slowly now, up the hill towards the brightly lit house standing on the brow, and when she entered the kitchen Lettice, wearing a large apron over her smart dress, turned to greet her. Ben was sitting to the side of the Aga stove, a small table at his hand, on which stood articles of silver that he was busily cleaning. She had never seen Ben with his hands idle. He gave her his tight smile, and Lettice, coming round the table and taking off her apron, said softly, 'Oh, I'm glad you've come, he's getting fidgety. Tony's with him now. He's had poor Ben here run off his feet all afternoon.'

'But it was only about an hour ago I got the message . . . I was coming up, anyway.'

'Well, you know what he is.' They smiled at each other, and then Lettice, leading the way into the hall, asked softly, 'Excited?' She turned and looked at Mary Ann. And Mary Ann, looking squarely back at her, said, 'No. I don't feel anything at all. It's as if I've had an injection, like after getting a tooth out, you know, just like that.'

Lettice laughed softly. 'It's the usual reaction.'

'I suppose so.' Mary Ann gave a little hick of a laugh. 'The only thing I've been concerned about today is tomorrow's weather.'

'Well, that's a good sign.' They were laughing quietly together as they entered the drawing-room.

'Oh, hello there.' Tony rose to his feet. 'Well, how goes it?'

Before Mary Ann could answer him Mr Lord turned his steely gaze on her and remarked caustically, 'Taken your time, haven't you, miss?'

'I've been busy.'

'What about a drink?' said Tony. 'A glass of sherry or something?'

'No, no thanks, Tony.' Mary Ann shook her head. 'I'm not long after having my tea.'

'Don't encourage her to drink.' Mr Lord now glared at his grandson. 'Sherry, sherry, sherry . . . I don't believe in this constant imbibing, and don't encourage her to start; she'll acquire enough bad habits after tomorrow.' Mr Lord was staring towards the blazing fire as he spoke, and Lettice, Mary Ann and Tony exchanged glances.

Looking at Mary Ann but speaking to Mr Lord, Tony said teasingly, 'I grant you she's very young, but we aren't and we need a drink.' And on this diplomatic reply he took Lettice by the hand and they went from the room, Tony winking at Mary Ann knowingly.

And now Mary Ann sat down facing Mr Lord. They looked at each other in silence for some minutes, and as she stared at her benefactor – and benefactor he had been – the odd numbness that had been filling her all day quietly dispersed and she was filled, in fact overcome, by a feeling that could be described by no other name but love. She loved this old man, really loved him. Her feelings stretched out her hands to him, and when he grasped them they still remained in silence looking at each other. When at last she spoke, she said something that was quite unrehearsed, something she had never dared to say before. She said, 'I've never had a granda . . . I mean I've never known one, either me mother's or me da's, and so inside I've always thought of you as me granda.'

The sagging muscles twitched, the lips moved, the creasy lids dropped over the eyes, then gently he drew her up from her chair and towards him, and then for only the second time in their acquaintance she found herself sitting on his knee. And as she lay with her head buried in his shoulder he talked to her. His voice no longer harsh or cutting, he said, 'You have not only been to me as a granddaughter, Mary Ann, you have also been a source of life. The day you came on to my horizon I was merely existing . . . You remember that day?' She made a slight movement but did not speak. 'And with your coming you restored my faith in human beings. Moreover, you brought me a family, because, you know, I look upon your mother and father, and Michael and Sarah now – as my family. You brought me Tony, and through Tony you brought me Lettice, which, contrary to my first opinion, has turned out to be a good thing after all . . . You've brought me all this and now you are going. Tomorrow, I could say, I am going to lose you. But no . . . no' – the bony frame moved in the chair – 'I'm not going to say that, Mary Ann, because I'll never lose you, will I?'

Her voice was cracked and high as she said, 'No, no, never.'

'There now, there now. Don't cry.' He blew his own nose violently, then added, 'I don't want to be browbeaten by Mr Cornelius Boyle for upsetting you.' This was intended to be funny, and Mary Ann smiled at him as she sat up and wiped her face. Mr Cornelius Boyle! Would he never call him Corny? No, never. That would be too much to ask. He was saying now, 'That reminds me. Look, there on the desk.' He pointed. 'There are two envelopes, go and get them.'

She slid from his knee and brought the envelopes to him, and when she put them into his hand he looked at them, then, handing one to her, he said, 'That is for you. I haven't bought you a wedding present, get what you want with it.' The envelope was addressed simply: 'To Mary Ann.' Then he handed her the other envelope, on which was written 'Mr Cornelius Boyle', saying, 'This is for Cornelius. I always believe that a man and woman should share everything, happiness, money, and troubles, so I have made you both alike. I would have given this to him himself if he had honoured me with a visit, but one must make allowances, for he is a very busy man at the moment . . . a very busy man.'

Again he was attempting to be amusing, and now Mary Ann, flinging her arms around his neck, hugged him almost boisterously, and as she hugged him she whispered softly, 'I love you, I love you.' And she did.

'Go on. Go on.' He pressed her up from him; his head was lowered, and once again he was blowing his nose; and now through his handkerchief he said, 'I'll see you tomorrow.' And then he added softly, as he lifted his misted eyes towards her, 'Look beautiful for me, Mary Ann. Look beautiful for me.'

She could say no more, she could only stare at him for a moment longer before hurrying from the room.

In the hall she stopped and wiped her face and blew her nose; and while she was busy doing this, out of the morning room came Lettice and Tony. Apparently they had been waiting for her, and without speaking they took up a position on either side of her and walked with her into the kitchen and to the back door.

And now Tony took her face in his hands, and, bending solemnly towards her, kissed her, saying, 'Be happy, Mary Ann. And you will be, you deserve it. God bless you.' And as he turned away from her, Lettice put her arms about her and muttered something like, 'Thank you, Mary Ann; I hope you'll be as happy as you've made it possible for me to be.'

She was running quite blindly down the hill, completely choked with happiness. Everybody was nice. Everybody was being kind to her. Everybody was lovely. Look what her ma had said, and Tony and Lettice. But look what Mr Lord had said. Oh, she loved him. She did, she did . . .

She went headlong into the gate and winced with pain, and as she rubbed her leg, which was still sore from contact with the chair on Sunday, she said to herself, 'Wipe your face; don't go in like that. If our Michael sees you looking like that you know what'll happen, he'll give you a lecture on the feebleness of sentiment. Even when he's wallowing in it he won't spare you. You know our Michael.'

As she entered the scullery she heard Corny's voice coming from the kitchen, saying, 'Lord, I'll never get through, and I've got to go to confession, I promised Father Owen I would.'

'You should have gone with me last night, I told you.'

He turned to her, his eyes merry, his face bright. 'Stop nagging,' he said. And now he looked at Mike, who was standing with his back to the fire. 'Coo! What it's going to be like after, man. You know, I've got cold feet.' And now his merry tone changed and he added flatly, 'And no kiddin'.' As he finished speaking he held out his hand towards Mary Ann – the action in itself had an endearment about it – then, looking at her more closely, he asked, 'What's up?'

'Nothing, nothing.' She put her hand in her

pocket. 'I've been up to the house. Mr Lord's given us our wedding present, one each.' She handed him the envelope, and Corny, looking down at it, read aloud, 'Mr Cornelius Boyle', then asked quietly, 'What's on yours?' She turned the envelope towards him and he read, 'To Mary Ann.'

'Funny, isn't it?' He glanced at Mike, and Mike nodded, saying, 'It's one of the things you'll have to get used to, Corny. We've all been through it.' And half in fun and whole in earnest, he said, 'She's been . . . ours' – he had almost said 'mine' – 'only after she's been his, and the situation will remain the same after tomorrow. You'll have to get used to taking second place, lad.'

'Oh, Da.' Mary Ann chided him with her look; then she slit open the envelope. Inside was a cheque, nothing else, and the sum on it brought her mouth agape. She looked from the cheque to Corny and back to the cheque, and she whispered, 'It's for a thousand pounds.' Then, casting her eyes first to Lizzie, and then to Mike, she repeated again, 'A thousand pounds. Ma, look . . . look, Da.' She held the cheque out stiffly to them, and they looked at it. Then Mike, raising his eyes to Corny, where he stood slightly apart, his face wearing a blank look, said, 'Open yours, Corny.'

Slowly Corny opened the envelope and he, too, drew a cheque from it and his amazement and mystification when he saw the same sum written on it elicited the exclamation of 'God Almighty!' before he added below his breath, 'Why, he's givin' me the same, the same as you.'

Mary Ann nodded at him.

'A thousand.' Corny, his eyebrows pushing

towards his hairline, shook his head; then on a higher note: 'A thousand pounds!' His head moved wider. 'Mike! Man! A thousand pounds! Two thousand atween us! Struth, I can't take it in.' He brought his eyes down to Mary Ann. Then his tone changing, he asked, 'Is it something he's up to?'

'No. No.' Mary Ann's voice sounded like a bark. 'Stop being suspicious of him. It's his kindness; he done it out of kindness and understanding. He . . . he said that a' – she could not bring herself at the moment to say husband and wife so substituted a couple – 'couple should always start off equal, that's what he said, and you go putting the wrong construction on it as usual.' Her voice was rising and was only checked by Corny lifting his hand in a very good imitation of Mike, saying, 'Enough. Enough.' As they all laughed, Mary Ann bowed her head and tried to suppress a grin. Then swiftly she raised it, and looking at Corny again she said quietly, 'But it's wonderful, isn't it?'

'Wonderful? That isn't the word. I'm simply floored.' He looked at the cheque once again. 'I've never seen a cheque for a thousand pounds, but, what's more, I just can't get over him givin' it to me. Why, you should have heard him when I was up there last time, I almost crawled out of the room. I mean I would have if I'd let myself be intimidated by him, he went for me left, right and centre. And now—' he waved the cheque, 'and now this . . . It's way . . . way beyond me.'

'You'll have to go up and thank him,' said Lizzie.

'Yes, yes,' Mary Ann nodded emphatically.

'Aye. Yes, of course,' said Corny. 'Yet' – his mouth twisted into a wry grin – 'I'll need some practice. I don't know how I'll go about it. Anyway, I can't go now, as I said I've got to go into church, so I'll do it when I come back.'

'He'll be in bed then,' said Mike.

'Well, I won't be able to do it until tomorrow after . . .' He paused and looked softly towards Mary Ann; then asked her, 'Will that be all right then?'

'Yes. He doesn't know I'm seeing you to-night, anyway. You needn't have received it until tomorrow. But look, before you go' – she held out her hand – 'come and see what the girls in the office bought us.'

Corny allowed himself to be led into the front room, which had taken on the appearance of a combined linen and china shop, and there she pointed out to him an addition to the presents; it was a fireside chair.

'Coo! That's nice.' He sat in it and stretched out his long legs. 'It was decent of them, wasn't it, and you not being there long.'

'Yes, it was. They got it at cost from the firm; it's a very good one.' She patted the back near his shoulder, and Corny, looking at her, his eyes almost on a level with hers, turned the subject by asking her quietly, 'How do you feel?'

'Aw, well. You know . . .' She gave a sheepish grin, shrugged one shoulder, then lowered her head a little. 'I don't believe it's happening to me. It's as if all this' – she waved her arm about the room – 'was for somebody else. One thing I can't take in is that it's . . . it's my last night here . . . in this house.'

'You're going to miss it.' He was staring straight-faced at her now. 'Our place is nothing like this. Even when we get it all fixed up it still won't be like this; we'll be looking out on to a main road . . . at least I hope it will be a main road. And if that comes about the fields at the back will be built on. It'll never be like this. That's what we've got to face up to.'

'I can face up to anything as long as you're there.' They stared at each other, and the time passed and neither of them made a move until Corny, putting his joined hands, which looked like one large fist, between his knees, concentrated his gaze on them as he said, 'There's something I want to say to you. I don't suppose I'll ever mention it again after we're married, and . . . and I find it difficult to say it now. And that's funny because all the time inside it's what I'm feeling . . . It's just this. I . . . I want to say thanks for having me, Mary Ann.'

'Aw. Aw, Corny.' The sound was like a painful whimper, a surprised whimper.

'I mean it.' He had raised his eyes to her again. 'All the time, inside, I'm grateful. It started a long time ago. I think it was when we walked together through Jarrow for the first time. You remember? And when his lordship' – he motioned his head towards the house on the hill – 'when he stopped the car and ordered you inside and I yelled at him. I remember the very words I used: "Aa'm as good as you lot any day. Aye, Aa am. An' Aa'll show you. By God! Aa will that." That's what I said . . . Well, I haven't shown him very much, only that I don't look upon him as God Almighty. But it was on that day that I became grateful to you inside, for you didn't want to leave me. And then you asked me to your party and we went walking after and you tried to teach me grammar' – his hand moved slowly up and gripped hers – 'and with your mother and the old fellow openly against me, and your school friends horrified at me accent, me clothes, and me scruffy look, you faced them all and stood up for me. It was that I remembered when I was in America. All the time I kept saying to meself, Who among all those fine pieces—' His mouth again gave a small, wry twist, but there was no laughter on his face as he went on – 'I said to meself, which one of them would have championed me, me as I was as a lad, for what I lacked in looks I didn't make up in charm, and I was too well aware of it. So my weapon was defiance, open defiance. Your da believed in me and that helped, but it was you, Mary Ann, you who brought me up out of the mire.'

'Oh, Corny!' The tears were once again raining down her cheeks. She had no voice with which to protest.

He rose to his feet and drew her gently into his arms, and as he bent his head and buried his face in her hair he muttered, 'So thanks, Mary Ann.'

It was too much, really too much. She wasn't used to people thanking her, and all day everybody had been thanking her: her mother, Mr Lord, Lettice, and now Corny. And what was more, she hadn't done anything, she hadn't. She knew she hadn't really done anything in her life to help anybody; she just did what she wanted to do, what pleased her. She was selfish she was. Recrimination, self-denigration, was attacking her on all sides when Corny, pushing her from him and gripping her by the shoulders, and in his now recognisable voice hissed down at her, 'But mind, I'm tellin' you, I'm not keeping this up. I've said it and that's the finish, understand?' He shook her gently, and as she laughed through her tears and he pulled her fiercely towards him again the front door bell rang.

As the sound pierced the house it also pierced Mary Ann's memory, and, clapping her hand over her mouth, she whispered between her fingers, 'Me grannie! We forgot about the bus. Oh! Oh, heavens above! Nobody thought to meet the bus.' She scampered from him into the hall, there to meet Lizzie coming out of the kitchen. Pushing her mother back into the room, she gabbled in a whisper, 'It'll be me grannie.'

It was now Lizzie's turn to put her hand to her mouth, and she turned her head over her shoulder and looked towards Mike, saying under her breath, 'I clean forgot. Oh, there'll be murder.'

'Is the room ready?' said Mike, coming forward.

'Oh yes, that's all right. But how could I forget about her coming to stay?'

'Well,' said Mike with a grin, 'that's to be understood; it'll be the first time she'll have slept under our roof.'

As the bell sounded again, a continued ring now, Corny said, 'Will I go and open it?' and Lizzie answered, 'No, no, I'll go and get it over.'

'Now don't tell me that you've been so very busy and occupied that you forgot.' The avalanche hit Lizzie as she opened the door.

'There I was in the dark, out in no-man's-land. You could fall in the ditch and not be found until you're dead. Talk about thoughtlessness!' She was in the hall now and the very hairs of her head seemed to be quivering, and as her hold-all hit the floor it was as if she had thrown it from a great height. 'Froze I am. Talk about a reception. You could be murdered on these roads. An' would that have mattered, says you.'

'Give me your coat, Gran.'

'What!' Mrs McMullen turned on her grand-daughter and glared at her; then she put her head on one side as if she hadn't heard aright. And perhaps she hadn't, because never before had she heard Mary Ann speak to her in this gentle, quiet way, nor offer to relieve her of her outdoor things. Her head straight once again, she replied, 'I'm still able to take me own coat off, thank you. And don't come all smarmy with me, for it's past the eleventh hour. It's too late now.'

Mary Ann, her face tight now, left the hall and went into the kitchen, there expecting to have a sympathetic exchange of glances with her da, and Corny. But the room was empty, until Sarah came hobbling from the scullery and towards her, saying softly, 'Corny says to tell you he's going straight back to the house after church, and Mike says to tell you' – her smile broadened here – 'that he and his son are going to the house now . . . Pronto, and they hope to get the sitting-room done tonight.'

'Oh.' Mary Ann shook her head helplessly. Then motioning it backwards, she whispered, 'She's her old self, only worse. It's going to be a lovely evening.'

'We'll go in the front room, there's plenty to do.'

'I'd forgotten clean about her coming.'

'I hadn't,' said Sarah. 'But I didn't think it was so late. Ssh! . . .' She moved forward, hoping to reach a chair before the visitor should enter the room. But this she did not accomplish, and Mrs McMullen stood surveying her erratic progress with a cold eye in a flaming face; then herself moving towards the fire, she looked at Sarah as she passed her, saying, 'Why don't you use your wheel-chair, girl?'

The question and all it implied caused Sarah's head to droop and the sight of this was too much for Mary Ann. She had prayed last night to Our Lady to give her the strength to be nice to her grannie, at least until the wedding was over, and she had started off well. She had spoken nicely to her and what had she got? Well, if she wanted it that way she could have it, wedding or no wedding. How she spoke to her was one thing, but to tell Sarah that she looked awful when she was walking, and that's what she had meant, was another. Looking boldly now at the bane of her life, she declared, 'Sarah doesn't need a chair, she's walking fine, she's getting better every day. Anyway, who would have thought this time last year that she would have been on her feet at all; and, what's more, driving a car. She . . .'

'All right, all right, madam. I thought it wouldn't be long before you started. It's well I know you and can't be taken in. Your good intentions are about as strong as a May Day wind. You're still the . . .'

'Are you ready for a cup of tea, Ma?' Lizzie

was looking towards the old woman, the tight, defensive look back on her face again, for although this woman was her mother she held thoughts akin to her daughter's concerning her.

'Well, as I haven't broken my fast since dinnertime I suppose I am ready for a cup of tea . . . and a bite of something. But if you're busy, don't stop what you're doing, for of course you must have been very busy to forget that I was coming.'

'I didn't forget you were coming, only I didn't think it was as late as it was.'

'You still have clocks.' The terrible old woman turned her gaze up to the mantelpiece; then she sighed and lay back in the chair. It was as if the first onslaught was over.

Lizzie turned to the table and began preparing her mother a meal, and Sarah, looking towards Mary Ann where she stood in a somewhat undecided manner near the door, said, 'If you'll bring me the box with your veil in, Mary Ann, I'll fix the wreath – it'll save us doing it in the morning – and now that there's nobody in you can try it on.'

'Veil? Weath? I didn't know you were going to be married in white.'

'You did, Mother.' Lizzie spoke without turning round. 'We told you a while back.'

'You didn't tell me. You talked about it over my head, and as far as I could gather you decided against it. And it would have been wiser if you had stuck to that, for she's not big enough for white . . . And as for those two sisters of his being bridesmaids . . . Huh!'

Lizzie signalled across the room to Mary Ann now, warning her with a look not to take any notice, and as she watched her daughter swelling visibly with indignation she put in quickly, 'The girls look bonny enough when they're dressed. As for Mary Ann's frock, it's lovely, and she looks lovely in it.' And on this she nodded to Mary Ann as if to stress the truth of her statement.

'Huh!' Mrs McMullen looked up at one corner of the ceiling, and then to the other, as if searching for inspiration for her invective; then turning her gaze in the direction of Sarah, she said in a conversational tone, 'White weddings and no honeymoons don't go together. What do you say? You managed a honeymoon, and under the circumstances you should have been the last one to tackle it . . . You know what I mean?'

Sarah knew what she meant only too well, and in this moment she fully understood Mary Ann's hate of her grannie, for she was a dreadful old woman, cruel.

'We don't want a honeymoon.' Mary Ann's voice, in spite of Lizzie's silent, imploring gaze, came barking across the kitchen now. 'I could have a honeymoon, as you call it, if I'd wanted it, but I don't want to waste money staying in some strange hotel. We'll have a honeymoon all right, but we'll have it in our own home.'

'All right, all right, madam, stop your bawling; I can make a remark, can't I? But no, I should have learned by now I can't open me mouth in this house. My God!' Mrs McMullen shook her head sadly. 'If you can't act like a human being the night afore your wedding you never will be able to . . . I hold out no hope for your future happiness if this is how you mean to start off. Anyway, truth to tell, now that we're on, I might as well say that I've never held out much hope for you in that direction, so you have it, not with the partner you've picked. Bairns and a scrubbing brush, that's your future. As I can read anything I can read that.'

'Mother! Now look' – Lizzie was standing above the old lady, her face white and strained, her forefinger wagging violently – 'if you're going to stay the night, and I hope you are, you've got to keep a civil tongue in your head.'

'Me! A civil—'

'You, yes. A civil tongue in your head. There's nobody starts these things only you. Now I'm warning you.'

'Oh, I only needed this . . .' Mrs McMullen closed her eyes. 'That's all I needed, you to start on me. Anyway, I hope I've got it in me to understand, 'cos I saw the minute I entered the door you were all het up. And is it any wonder? If everything I hear is true . . . if only half I hear is true, it's understandable that your nerves are all of a frazzle . . . Tell me. Are you still being visited by the Radleys, or are the visits going the other way now? For by what I hear . . .'

Mary Ann seemed to shoot across the room to her mother's side, and from there she glared at her grannie and, leaning threateningly towards the old woman, cried at her, 'You know what I wish? You know what I wish?' Her voice dropping suddenly, she added through her clenched teeth, 'I wish you would drop down dead, you old—'

'Mary Ann!' Lizzie, seizing her by the shoulders, pushed her towards the hall, then into the front room, and there she put her arms around her and held her as once more she burst into tears, angry tears now, bitter tears; and looking up at her mother, Mary Ann stammered, 'Oh . . . on the night be . . . before me wedding she's made me say a thing like th . . . that. It was awful, I know, but it's true, Ma, it's true. But f . . . fancy me saying it.' She was crying loudly now, and Lizzie hushed her and rocked her as if she was a little girl, the little girl who had many, many times wished her grannie dead. And now Mary Ann, raising her head again, spluttered, 'Scrub . . . scrubbing brushes and b . . . bairns, that's what she said, that's all Corny can give me, scrubbing brushes and b . . . bairns.'

'One scrubbing brush,' said Lizzie with a faint smile.

'What, Ma?' She was sniffing loudly now.

'Bairns, and a scrubbing brush,' Lizzie explained, 'just one scrubbing brush.'

'Oh.' Mary Ann slowly began to glean the funny side of it all, and weakly she returned Lizzie's smile. And Lizzie, stroking her hair back from her wet brow, said softly, 'There's worse things than bairns and a scrubbing brush, if you're happy with the man that provides both.'

10

'But, Mrs McBride, you've got to come to the church; Corny would go mad.'

'Now look, me lass, I proffered to come over here so that I could see to things when you had all gone, and have everything nice and ready when you come back.'

'But everything is ready, and Jonesy and his wife are staying behind, it's all arranged. What's got into you?' Mary Ann's high tone dropped. 'It won't be me wedding if you're not there. And I'm telling you, he'll go mad.'

'Huh! He'll know nothing about it. He'll be so taken up wondering if you're going to come or not. They're all like that at the last minute.'

'But why? It's always been understood you'd be there.'

Fanny turned from Mary Ann and walked down the length of the large barn, and as she walked she moved her head to the right, and the left, looking at the tables set as yet with only crockery and flowers, and, going to the top table, she gazed at the two chairs, bigger than the rest, like two thrones awaiting their occupants. Then turning and facing Mary Ann, who had followed her, she said, on a deep sigh, 'Well, knowing you, you won't stop till you get to the bottom of it, so it's like this, plain and simple, I'm not going to go into the church and disgrace you both in me old togs.'

Mary Ann's mouth opened and shut like that of a dying fish, and then she brought out, 'But, you've got new clothes . . . you were getting new clothes.'

'Aye, so I thought.' Mrs McBride examined the skin on the back of her large, wrinkled hands. Then she repeated quietly, 'Aye, so I thought, right until just a week ago when it was too late to do anything about it. You see' – she lifted her eyes to Mary Ann – 'our Florrie said she would get me a couple of clubs, enough to get me a coat and hat and be shod decent, and I waited and waited, never thinking but that she would get them for me. And then over she comes at the last minute, on Wednesday night it was, saying she can't get any more, for the whole crowd of them want so much of this and that, and she had gone over her credit, far over . . . Aw, suppose it wasn't too late even then. If I had dropped a word to our Phil he would have been down from Newcastle like a shot and rigged me out – he's wanted to do it time and time again – but as I said, what do I want new clothes for, I'm never out of the door except to go to early mass on a Sunday, and along to the shop. If I got new clothes, I've always said to him, what would I do with them? They'd just hang there and rot.'

'But Corny would have . . . he would have seen to everything.'

'I know, lass. Don't I know he would have seen

to everything . . . and beggared himself still further. I've had to put me foot down afore where that 'un's concerned, and I'm keeping it down from now on that he's a married man, for, refuse how I may, he's left me something every week; come back and pushed it under the door he has after we've gone for each other hell for leather. Oh, I know Corny would have me rigged out like a duchess, but, Mary Ann' – she moved her head slowly – 'I'm an independent spirit, I've never asked anybody for anythin' in me life. Why don't you get supplementary? they say. You've earned it, they say; it isn't charity, it's yours by rights, they say. Huh! . . . I know what's mine by rights, so I'm not goin' after any supplementary an' havin' a man comin' to me house checking on what I've got and sayin' to me, "With all those children scattered all over the country you shouldn't be wantin' supplementary, now should you?" Aw, I know. No, Mary Ann, what I can't have I've always made it a point of doin' without. And so there you have it. So you just keep quiet, me dear, and no-one will be any the wiser but that I was in church. I can say to them here that I'm comin' in the last car, an' at that time I won't be around.'

'No. No.' Mary Ann shook not only her head but her whole body. 'You're coming, and not in the last car. I tell you Corny'll go mad. And don't think he won't miss you; he'll be standing in the front of the church and he'll see everybody, and it'll upset him if he doesn't catch sight of you.'

'Nonsense, nonsense. There's only one thing that would upset him this day and that would be if you didn't arrive. Why . . . do you think he'll say, "Hold your hand a minute, hold everything, I must go and find me grannie"?' Fanny let out a bellow of a laugh at her own joke, and Mary Ann laughed too. Then stopping abruptly, she said, 'You're coming, clothes or no clothes,' and, turning from her, she ran down the barn, out across the sunlit farmyard, up the path and into the back door, where the buzz of noise came at her like a blow. The house was full. She had never seen so many people in it. Sarah met her, saying, 'Where have you been? Mam's looking all over for you. It's time you were getting ready.'

'Where's me da?'

'With my dad in the front room, I think. And Corny's father and the lads are there . . . What's the matter?'

'I'll tell you in a minute.' Mary Ann made her way through the kitchen which was packed to capacity. People were standing, and sitting, and talking, and she heard the tail end of Mrs Flannagan's voice saying in high, refined tones, 'And he thinks the world of her. He must do, mustn't he, to buy her a car after setting her up in a bungalow.'

Some section of her mind told Mary Ann that Mrs Flannagan had heard of Mr Lord's generous wedding present to herself and Corny and was proving to somebody that it was nothing compared with what he had given to Sarah. She could smile at this.

The front room seemed full of men of all ages.

'Da . . . Da.' She tugged at his arm.

'Aren't you away upstairs getting ready?' Mike looked tenderly down at her, and she answered, 'I want you a minute.'

431

As she went into the hall, followed by Mike, Mrs McMullen came out of the kitchen and made her way to the front room, remarking in passing, to no-one in particular, 'Common as muck, the lot of them.'

Her grannie, Mary Ann knew, was referring to Corny's mother and father and the squad of children, and although she would have died rather than agree with anything her grannie said, she did think they could behave a bit better than they did. Corny's father was useless with regards to keeping his tribe in order, and his mother wasn't much better; she just shouted and the lads just laughed at her.

'What is it?' asked Mike.

'Come outside a minute.' She took his hand and drew him through the front door and round the corner of the house. And there she said hastily, 'It's Mrs McBride. You know what, she's not coming to the wedding because she has no new clothes.'

'Not comin' . . . No new clothes! But didn't they see to that?'

She told him briefly what had happened, and when she had finished he stood looking down at her with his face screwed up. 'Hell for a tale that,' he said. 'Well, to my mind she must be at your weddin'. What do you think?'

'I think the same, Da. She's always been in my life . . . I mean she's closer . . . well, than most people. But apart from that, Corny . . . he'll go mad if she's not there. You know, Da' – her voice sank to a whisper and she glanced about her in case any of Corny's family should be within hearing distance – 'Corny doesn't care two hoots for any of them except her. He loves her.'

'Aye, aye, I think you're right. In fact, I know you are . . . What time is it?' He looked at his watch. 'Ten past eleven . . . You leave this to me. Where is she?'

'In the barn, Da.' Her eyes were bright as she whispered, 'you'll take her in . . . get her a coat and things?'

'Yes, just that . . .' Pausing, he patted her playfully on the cheek. 'You knew I would, didn't you?'

'I hoped so, Da. But . . . you'll be back in time?'

'I'll be back, never fear. You go upstairs and get dressed, that's the main thing. It won't take me two shakes of a lamb's tail to get into me togs, so go on now an' leave it to me.'

'Thanks, Da.' She reached up and kissed him; then added, 'You might have a job getting her to agree.'

'She'll agree . . . go on now.'

She turned from him and ran into the house, and Lizzie, meeting her in the hall, said, 'Where've you been? Look at the time. Go on up, it's time you were starting . . . Where's your da?'

'Here a minute.' Mary Ann took her mother by the hand and led her upstairs, and briefly she put her in the picture. And Lizzie said, 'Oh dear. But yes, I see she's got to be there, but . . . but will he have time, will he be back in time? He's got to put a new suit on and you know what he's like with a new suit.'

'It'll be all right, Ma.'

'Well I hope so . . . Come on, off with your things and let's get started.'

433

As Mary Ann went to pull her jumper over her head there came a tap on the door, and when Lizzie, her tongue clicking impatiently, opened it, she gave a cry of surprise that turned Mary Ann about, and, her arms still in her jumper, she, too, exclaimed aloud, for there stood Sarah; at one side of her was her father, at the other, Mr Boyle.

'She's made it,' said Mr Flannagan proudly. 'We wanted to carry her up, but no. "One at a time," she said, and she's made all sixteen of them.'

Sarah, her face flushed to a deep pink with the exertion of her effort and the triumph over herself, shambled into the room and, flopping into the chair, looked at Mary Ann and laughed as she said, 'I always intended to do it . . . to help you dress like you did me.'

'Aw, Sarah.' Mary Ann put her hand gently on Sarah's head, and as she did so Lizzie exclaimed, 'Well now, well now, we want to get started.' This remark was directed towards the men, and as she was about to close the door on them Mr Boyle turned a red-faced grin on her, and under his breath he said, 'No disrespect, Lizzie, but—' He paused here and his eyes flashed to Mr Flannagan, then to Mary Ann, who had turned towards him, then back to Lizzie before he added, 'Has anybody thought of shooting your mother?'

Lizzie forcibly prevented herself from laughing, but from Mary Ann there came a high, gleeful sound and she cried in no small voice, 'Oh, I have, Mr Boyle.' She had always addressed him as Mr Boyle and couldn't see herself ever calling him anything else. She had never liked him; in fact if she had asked herself the question she would have answered that she disliked him, but now in a flash she saw him in a different light. He might booze, swear, and not bring his money home, but there, beneath the skin, she saw Corny.

Lizzie prevented him from taking a step into the room as Mary Ann cried, 'We'll get together later and fix up something, eh?'

'Right. Right, Mary Ann, that's a deal.'

'And count me in.' It was little Mr Flannagan now piping up his face alight with merriment.

Lizzie slammed the door on the two men and, turning to the laughing girls, she said indignantly, 'Really! Really!' But in spite of the reprimand, Mary Ann saw that her mother had her work cut out to stop herself laughing aloud.

'And you!' said Lizzie. 'Standing there with no jumper on.'

'Eeh!' Mary Ann looked down at herself. 'So I was. What are things coming to?' The two girls giggled. Then Mary Ann, about to divest herself further, turned to Lizzie and exclaimed, 'Queenie and Nancy. Who's seeing to them?'

'Their mother. She'll put them right.'

'But will she?' Mary Ann's eyebrows moved up. 'If she sees to them as she does every day I'm going to have two beautiful bridesmaids.'

'She can do things all right when she puts her mind to it, and I've seen them and they're very sweet. Now don't bother about them; get your things off and let's get started.'

As Lizzie moved towards the wardrobe she had to pass the window, and Mary Ann's bedroom window overlooked the farmyard. Lizzie looked at the farmyard so many times a day that now she didn't see it, and she had glanced through the window and reached the wardrobe before she dived back to the window again and there a long-drawn-out 'Ooh!' escaped her.

'What is it?' asked Mary Ann and Sarah together.

'The boys, they're on the silage in their new clothes and their father and your grannie are going at it.'

Mary Ann came to the window and looked down on Corny's two youngest brothers, the nine-year-old twins, who had evidently been enjoying themselves. The silage was kept in a yard apart from the main one, and the boys with long pronged forks in their hands stood now in the opening between the two yards, and even from this distance she could see that their boots were filthy and their clothes bespattered. They had only once before been at the farm and everybody remembered their visit. The open spaces seemed to have a maddening effect on them, for they had raced like wild horses from one place to the other. She brought her eyes from them to their father. She could see that he was smiling, but she could also see that he was wagging a large forefinger in her grannie's face and the forefinger, denying the smile, spelled out to Mary Ann, 'Now look here, old lady, you mind your business and I'll mind mine.'

As Lizzie opened the window and called down to her mother, Mrs McMullen's voice came high and clear on the crisp, sun-filled air, saying, 'Disgrace, that's what they are; like young pigs on the wrong side of the fence.'

'Oh, look!' As the exclamation was drawn from Mary Ann she pulled her mother back from the window and whispered urgently, 'Mr Lord, Tony and Lettice . . . coming down the hill.'

'Oh no!' Lizzie lifted her hand to her head. 'They'll run into that, and if my mother corners Mr Lord . . . Oh, why isn't Mike here! And where's Michael in all this?' She turned and looked at Sarah as if she were responsible for Michael's non-appearance in the yard. Then Mary Ann put in, 'Look, Ma, you go on down, I'll manage. And I've got Sarah. Go on, see to things. Don't let me grannie meet him, not out there. And if he sees the twins like that, he'll be so wild, and . . . and it'll look bad for Corny. Oh go on, Ma.'

'Aw. Dear, dear.' Lizzie hesitated only for a moment then hurried from the room, and Mary Ann and Sarah looked at each other. Then Mary Ann, going to her dressing-table, sat down and through the mirror said to Sarah, 'Me wedding day. I just can't believe it's me wedding day.' She gave a wry smile. 'All these little things happening, just like any other day, or more so, and yet I don't feel the same as on other days. I've . . . I've got a racing feeling inside . . . You know what I mean?'

Sarah nodded through the mirror.

'I don't know whether I want to race to the church or race away from it.' They both giggled at this, then Mary Ann went on, but seriously now, 'For a while last night I felt wonderful, not a bit afraid or anything. When we stood outside, just before he went, and the moon was shining and everything was so quiet, it was then I felt wonderful, happier than I'd ever been in my life. I had a sort of safe feeling with it. I felt as long as

I was with Corny everything would always be all right . . . You know?'

Again Sarah nodded through the mirror. 'Yes, I know. And it's the right feeling. If you feel like that nothing much can touch you.'

'You think so?'

'I know so.'

Mary Ann, staring hard at Sarah now, saw that she was looking at a woman, that Sarah had grown up, leaving her still a child. She said thoughtfully, 'But the feeling didn't stay, for as soon as I woke this morning I felt frightened, in fact I wished it wasn't going to happen, and I wanted to be some place quiet and think and try to get a nice feeling inside.' She spread out her hands. 'But look at it. Everything's happened that could. And people coming far too early; his mother was to bring the girls at half-past ten and what did she do but bring the whole bang lot of them with her . . . and at ten o'clock. Of course there was one person delighted . . . me grannie, for she was running out of targets.'

As if in answer to this jibe Mrs McMullen's voice came penetratingly through the floor, and Mary Ann put her hands over her ears and, swinging round and facing Sarah, her eyes dancing, whispered, 'What do you bet, when Father Owen says "If anyone knows of any impediment, etc.," she doesn't get to her feet and shout, "Any impediment! I can give you a round dozen . . . Now you just listen to me." ' Mary Ann had mimicked her grannie's voice, and now the two girls, hands clasped, threw back their heads and laughed, high, gleeful laughter. But in Mary

438

Ann's case it spoke plainly of nervous strain and tension.

It was here, this was the moment. This was the joyous moment . . . At least, it should have been joyous but she still felt frightened. She was too young to be married. She should never have said she would do it. Her legs would give way when she was walking down the aisle. And all those people behind her outside the church door, how had they known? Mrs McBride. Yes, Mrs McBride. They couldn't get the car near the kerb, and the voices from all over the crowd shouting, 'Eeh! Look, Mary Ann. Hello, Mary Ann. Mary Ann. Oo! Oo!' She had kept her head down but had lifted it to look at a woman as she entered the church door, for the woman had said, and somewhat sadly, 'Aw, hinny, you won't be Mary Ann Shaughnessy for much longer now.'

And she wouldn't be Mary Ann Shaughnessy for much longer. She hadn't thought about that before, she was going to lose her name. She liked her name. MARY ANN SHAUGHNESSY. In a short while she would be Mary Ann Boyle. It sounded awful . . . Mary Ann Boyle. Oh no, she didn't want to be Mary Ann Boyle.

'Are you all right?' Mike was looking down at her, gently drawing her hand through his arm. She looked up at him blinking. She was hot and sweating; her make-up must look awful, and she wanted to cry . . . Don't be so silly. She blinked rapidly and saw Mike's face, then all of him. He looked grand, did her da. His new suit fitted him to a 'T'. They stared at each other oblivious for the moment of the bustle about them. Somebody was whispering to the bridesmaids, 'Hold them like this, don't let them droop.' That would be the posies. The organ was rumbling overhead, waiting for the signal, and in this moment there came to Mary Ann the strange idea that she was inside her da, right inside of him, thinking his thoughts, feeling his feeelings, and he, too, wanted to cry. She turned her eyes from him. It was awful, awful. She was going to be married, she should be joyful. What was the matter with her, anyway? MARY ANN BOYLE. Oh, she didn't like that name. She would never be Mary Ann Boyle whatever happened, she wouldn't. Inside herself she would always be Mary Ann Shaughnessy. She would remain Mary Ann Shaughnessy for ever. She wanted to tell her da that she would never be anybody but Mary Ann Shaughnessy. She would always keep his name. But . . . but what was she talking about, for Shaughnessy wasn't his name, not really . . . Anyway, what was in a name?

Mike squeezed her hand and, bending his head sideways down to her, whispered, 'You'll be all right. Don't worry. Do you know something?' He waited.

'What, Da?' Her lips were trembling and she spoke without turning her head.

'You look very beautiful.'

'Oh, Da.' She pressed his arm to her.

'And . . . and I'll love you till the day I die. Never forget that.'

Ooh! Oh, he shouldn't have said that, he shouldn't, it was too much. She would burst, she would cry.

There was a movement in front of them; some-one said, 'Ready?'

There was bustle behind; a second later the organ swelled into loud chords and she was walking forward out of the dim vestibule, round by the holy water font, in which she had dipped her fingers from the time she could reach it, to the top of the central aisle. The wish was strong in her now that they could go down the side aisle and that she could be married at the altar of the Holy Family, for they had always been part of her family . . . Where had all the people come from? The church was almost full. Her high-heeled shoes slipped just the tiniest bit on the grating and she felt the heat from the pipes coming up under her dress. She had loved to stand over the grating in the cold weather and get her legs warm. Sometimes the boiler went wrong and the church was as cold as death, but today the boiler was all right, Father Owen had seen to that. The church was warm, the atmosphere was warm, the people's faces, those turned towards her, were warm. She didn't look at them but she could feel their warmth. But when she approached her own people she looked at them. Her mother, oh, her mother looked bonny, lovely, young, even though her eyes were sad; and there was Sarah, bright-faced, happy-looking Sarah; and Lettice and Tony. Tony was looking full at her and she exchanged a direct glance with him, which said something, which meant something, but which in this moment she couldn't decipher. Then there was Mrs Flannagan, proud, pinched-faced, but smiling Mrs Flannagan, kind at last; and now the face of her grannie . . . Oh! Why had she to look at her grannie, why at this moment had she to look at her grannie, for belated maternal love and benevolence had not touched her grannie's countenance. It was the same as she had always seen it. But there was another face, a face really showing love and benevolence . . . and pride: the face of Mr Lord. His eyes were on her, pale-blue misty eyes, but piercing into her, sending her a message, and she answered it, sending him her love and gratitude for as long as he might need it.

Then on the other side of the aisle were Corny's people. His mother and father, their faces full of smiling good-will . . . Why had she never liked them? – because they were really likeable. What did it matter if she didn't keep her house clean? And there were all Corny's relations filling three pews . . . Corny had said they would fill three pews. But in the very first seat of the first pew was a face whose beam spread itself over all of them. It was topped by a blue velour hat of unspotted newness, it was the wrinkled, battered face, the wise face of her friend, Fanny McBride, and the knowledgeable eyes held Mary Ann's for more than a second until they seemed to usher her gaze to the front, to where, on the altar steps, stood Father Owen, kind, loving, understanding Father Owen . . . They had said to her, 'Why do you want to be married in Jarrow Church? You're nearer to Pelaw.' But Jarrow had always been her church, and Father Owen was her priest. Father Owen knew all about her, everything, the good and the bad. Now Father Owen's gaze drew her eyes with his and they travelled past their Michael, tall and handsome, a young edition of her father, to someone else, tall . . . and handsome. For Corny in this moment looked handsome to her. His red hair was lying for once

in well-brushed order, his deep-set dark eyes
were warm and shining, his wide-lipped mouth
was gentle. She wished he wasn't so tall, she
wished she wasn't so small, she wished . . .
she wished . . .

'MARY ANN . . . MARY ANN.'

It was as if he was calling her name.

'MARY ANN, OH, MARY ANN.'

Mike let her go. She felt the moment of release
as if he had thrust her from him. She was by
herself, getting nearer to Corny. She was close to
him now, and as she looked at him for a moment
his eyes blotted out everything about her. Gently
their message sank into her and she felt it lift her
round to face the priest.

GOOD-BYE, MARY ANN SHAUGHNESSY.

Good-bye, Mary Ann Shaughnessy.

Good-bye, Mary Ann.

Good-bye.

Good-bye.

'Wilt thou take this woman . . . ?'

MARY ANN'S ANGELS

Catherine Cookson

CORGI BOOKS

MARY ANN'S ANGELS

Catherine Cookson

CORGI BOOKS

**To Mam
My Mother-in-law**

1

'If he can talk, why doesn't he, Rose Mary Boyle?'

''Cos he doesn't want to, Annabel Morton.'

The two six-year-olds stared at each other, eyes wide, nostrils dilated. Their lips spread away from their teeth, they had all the appearance of two caged circus animals dressed up in human guise for the occasion.

'My mam says he's dumb.'

'Your mam's barmy.'

Again, wide eyes, quivering nostrils and stretched lips, and a waiting period, during which the subject of their conversation, one hand held firmly in that of his twin, gazed alternately at the two combatants. He was fair-haired, round-faced, with dark blue eyes, and his expression was puzzling, for it could have been described as vacant, yet again it could have been described as calculating.

'He spoke the day, an' if your ears hadn't been full of muck, you'd have heard him.'

The fray was reopened. Rose Mary turned to her brother and bounced her head towards him, whereupon he stared back at her for a moment, then looked towards their opponent again.

'He made a funny sound, that's all he did, when he was eating his dinner.'

'He didn't make a funny sound, he said "HOT".'

'He didn't, he said "ugh!" Like a pig makes.'

Rose Mary's right, and working arm, throwing itself instinctively outwards, almost lifted David from the ground, and by the time he had relinquished his hold of her hand and regained his balance, with her help, Annabel Morton had put a considerable distance between them. And from this distance she made a stand. 'Dumb David!' she called. Then added, 'And Rose Mary, pain-in-the-neck Boyle.' And if this wasn't enough she went as far as to mis-spell Boyle. 'B-O-I-L!' she screamed at the limit of her lungs.

'Now, now, now.' There loomed over Annabel the tall, thin figure of her teacher, Miss Plum.

Rose Mary, her hand again holding David's, watched Miss Plum as she reprimanded that awful Annabel Morton. Oh, she hoped she got kept in the morrow. Oh, she did. And Miss Plum was nice, after all she was nice. Oh, she was.

Now Miss Plum was advancing towards her, and Rose Mary greeted her with uplifted face, over which was spread a smile, the like that had in the past been called angelic . . . by people viewing it for the first time. Miss Plum had never made that mistake. She looked down on Rose Mary now and, her finger wagging near her nose, she said, 'I don't want to hear, Rose Mary, I don't want to hear. And you should be on your way home.'

'But Miss Pl—'

'No, not another word. Away with you now.'

Rose Mary turned round abruptly, and her twin had his eyes wrenched from Miss Plum and was jerked into step by his sister's side, and only because she was grasping his hand firmly could he keep up with her. His legs were plump, and although he was older than his sister by five minutes his speed was geared to about half hers. But of necessity, perhaps out of instinctive urge for preservation, he had learned to put on a brake against her speed. He did it now by throwing himself backwards and resting on his heels.

Rose Mary came to a stop. She looked at him and said, 'Miss Plum! Four-eyed, goggle-mug Plum. Her head's like Lees's clock.' Whereupon David laughed a high appreciative laugh, for as everybody in Felling knew, even the works in Lees's clock were made of wood.

Rose Mary now joined her laugh to her brother's. Then pulling him to her side, she walked at a slower pace down Stewart Terrace, and as she walked, her whole mien sober now, she thought, 'It must be made of wood else she'd be able to make him talk. There must be something that would make him talk, more than one – unintelligible to others – word at a time. Yes, there must be something. But what?'

When she felt a sharp tug on her hand she realised she had almost passed the point where they crossed over to get the bus, but David hadn't. She looked at him in admiration, a grin splitting her pert face. 'There, you see,' she addressed an adversary known only to herself. 'He's all right, you see. I nearly didn't cross over, but he was all there.' She jerked her head at the adversary then gripping David's hand more tightly, she crossed over the road and went towards the bus stop.

The bus conductor, assisting them upwards with a hand on each of their shoulders, said, 'Come on, you Siamese twins you. And don't you have so much to say, young fellow-me-lad.' He pushed David playfully in the back. 'And now I want none of your cheek,' he admonished him with a very thick index finger as David hoisted himself on to a seat.

David grinned broadly at the conductor, and Rose Mary, handing him their passes, said, 'You back then?'

'Well, if I'm not,' said the conductor, straightening up, 'somebody's havin' a fine game.' Then bending down to her again, he asked under his breath, 'No talkie-talkie?'

Rose Mary shook her head.

'Shame.'

They both now looked at David.

'Aw well.' The conductor ruffled David's hair. 'Don't you worry, young chap, you're all there.'

When the conductor had passed down the bus Rose Mary and David exchanged glances, and to her glance Rose Mary added a small inclination of the head. The bus conductor was a nice man, he knew that their David was all there.

The bus stopped on the long, bare, main road, bare that is except for traffic, and right at the top end of their side road. Rose Mary and David stood gazing at the conductor where he stood on the platform until he was lost to their sight, then hand in hand they ran up the lane that lay between two fields, and to home.

The first sight they got of home was of two petrol-pumps, around which lay a curved line of whitewashed stones. The line was terminated at each end by green tubs which were now full of wallflowers, and to the right-hand side of the pumps and some distance behind them, there stood their home. Their wonderful, wonderful home. At least it was to Rose Mary; David, as yet, had not expressed any views about it.

The house itself was perched on top of what looked like a shop, because the front of the ground floor was taken up by a large plate-glass window and was actually the showroom to the garage. But at present it was empty. Next to the house was a low building with a door and one window, and above the door was a board which read simply: FELL GARAGE: C. BOYLE, Proprietor. Below this, above the door frame, was another slim board with the single word 'OFFICE' written on it. To the side of the office was a large barn-like structure, the garage itself, and inside, and leaving it looking almost empty, were three cars. One car stood on its own, a 1950 Rover, which was polished to a gleaming sheen. The other cars were undergoing repairs, and under each of them someone was at work.

'Hello, Dad.' Rose Mary, still pulling David with her, dashed up to the man who was lying on his back half underneath the first car, and for answer, Corny kicked one leg in the air, and when they knelt down on the ground by his side to get a better look at him his muffled yell came at them, 'Get up out of that, you'll be all oil. Get up with you.'

By the time he had edged himself from

underneath the car, they were on their feet, grinning at him.

'Hello there.' He looked down on them. 'Had a nice day?'

'Ah-ha.' Rose Mary jerked her chin up at him, then brought her head down to a level position and a soberness to her face, before adding, 'Well, except for Annabel Morton. She's a pig.'

'Oh. What's she done now?' Corny was wiping his greasy hands with a mutton cloth.

'Here.' His daughter beckoned his distant head down to hers, and when his ear was level with her mouth, she whispered, 'She said he couldn't talk.'

As Corny straightened himself up and looked down at his daughter, who was his wife in miniature, he wanted to say, 'Well, she's right, isn't she?' but that would never do, so he said, 'She doesn't know what she's talking about.'

'An' I told her, an' I told her that.'

'And what did she say?'

Rose Mary, picking up David's hand, now turned him about, and glancing over her shoulder at her father, said flatly, 'She called me pain-in-the-neck Boyle.'

There came a great roar of laughter, but not from her dad. It came from behind the other car, and she yelled at it, 'Aw, you Jimmy!' before dashing out of the garage, along the cement walk, around the back of the house – no going in the front way, except for company – and up the stairs, still dragging David with her. And from here she shouted, 'Mam. Mam. We're here, Mam.'

'Is that my angels?'

As they burst on to the top landing, Mary Ann

came out of the kitchen and, stooping over them, enfolded them in her arms, hugging them to her.

'Oh, Mam.' Rose Mary sniffed. 'You been bakin'? What you been bakin'?'

'Apple tarts, scones, tea-cakes.'

'Ooh! Mam. Coo, I'm hungry, starvin'. So's David.'

Mary Ann, still on her hunkers, looked at her son, and, a smile seeping from her face, she said to him quietly, 'Are you hungry, David?'

The light in the depths of David's eyes deepened, his round, button-shaped mouth spread wide as he stared back at his mother.

'Say, "Yes, Mam".'

For answer David made a sound in his throat and fell against her, and, putting her hand on the back of his head she pressed it to her, and over it she looked at her daughter. And Rose Mary returned her glance, soft with understanding.

Now Mary Ann, pushing them both before her, said, 'Go and get your playthings on. Hang your coats up. And Rose Mary . . .' When her daughter turned towards her she said slowly, 'Rose Mary, let David take his own things off and put his playthings on.'

'But Mam . . .'

'Rose Mary, now do as I say, that's a good girl. Go on now, and I'll butter a tea-cake to keep you going until teatime.'

When they had gone into their room Mary Ann stood looking down at her hands. They were working one against the other, making a harsh sound; the action made her separate them as·if she was throwing something off.

She was in the kitchen again when her

daughter's voice came to her from the little room across the landing, saying, 'I hate Miss Plum, Mam.'

'I thought you liked Miss Plum, I thought she was your favourite teacher?'

'She's not, I hate her. She's a pig.'

'Now I've told you about calling people pigs, haven't I?'

'Well, she is, Mam.'

'What did she do?'

'She wouldn't let me talk.'

Mary Ann, about to lay the tea cloth over the table under the window, put her hand over her mouth to suppress her laughter. It was as if she had gone back down the years and was listening to herself.

'Mam.'

'Yes?'

'David drew a lovely donkey the day, with me on its back.'

'Oh, that's wonderful. Have you brought it home?'

'No. Miss Plum said it was good, and she pinned it on the wall.'

'Oh, that's marvellous.' Mary Ann swung the cloth across the table, then paused and looked down, over the garden behind the garage, on to the waste land, and she thought, 'I'm blessed. I'm doubly blessed. He'll talk one day. Please God, he'll talk one day.'

'We're ready.' They were standing in the doorway when she turned round to them.

'Come and have your tea-cakes.'

'Can't we take them out with us?'

'Yes, if you like . . . Did David change himself?'

Rose Mary's brows went upwards, and her eyelids came down slowly twice before she said, 'I helped button him up, that's all.'

Mary Ann handed them the tea-cakes, and they turned from her and ran across the landing and down the back stairs, and as she listened to Rose Mary, her voice high now, talking to her brother telling him what games they were going to play, she was back in the surgery this time last week looking at the doctor across the desk. He was smiling complacently and telling her in effect to do the same. 'Not to worry, not to worry,' he said. 'Half his trouble, I think, is his sister. He doesn't talk because there's no real necessity, she's always done it for him. But don't worry, he's not mental, or anything like that. He'll likely start all of a sudden, and then you won't be able to keep him quiet.' And he had added that he didn't see much point at present in separating them.

Separate them? As if she would ever dream of separating them; it would be like cutting off one of their arms. Separate them, indeed. If David's power of speech would come only by separating them, then he would remain dumb. On that point she was firm. No matter what Corny said . . .

It was half-past five when Corny came upstairs. The seven years during which he had been the owner of a garage, a married man and the father of two children had aged him. The boy, Corny, was no more. The man, Corny, was a six-foot-two, tough-looking individual, with a pair of fine, deep blue eyes in an otherwise plain face. But his plain features were given a particular charm when he smiled or grinned. To Mary Ann he was still irresistible, yet there were times when even their

Creator could not have been blamed for having his doubts as to their love for each other.

'Anything new?' She mashed the tea as she spoke.

'Thompson's satisfied with the repairs.'

'Did he pay you?'

'Yes, in cash, and gave me ten bob extra.'

'Oh, good.' She turned and smiled at him.

'Hungry?'

'So, so.'

'Give them a shout.'

Corny went to the window and, opening it, called, 'Tea up.'

The thin voice of Rose Mary came back to him, crying, 'Wait a minute, Dad, he's nearly finished.'

'What are they up to over there?'

'They were digging a hole when I last looked,' said Mary Ann.

'Digging a hole?' said Corny, screwing up his eyes. 'They're piling up stones on top of something . . . Come along this minute. Do you hear me?'

'Comin', comin'.'

A few minutes later, as they came scampering up the stairs, Mary Ann called to them, 'Go and wash your hands first, and take your coats off.'

Tea was poured out and Corny was seated at the head of the little table when the children entered the room. 'What were you up to over there?' He smiled at Rose Mary as he spoke.

'David made a grave,' she said, hitching herself on to her seat.

Mary Ann turned swiftly from the stove and looked at her daughter. 'A grave?' she said. 'What for?'

'To bury Annabel Morton and Miss Plum in.'

'Rose Mary!' There was a strong reprimand in Mary Ann's voice. 'How could you.'

'But I didn't, Mam, he did it hisself.'

'He couldn't do it himself, child.' Mary Ann leaned across the table and addressed her daughter pointedly, and Rose Mary, her lips now trembling, said, 'But he did, Mam.' Then turning to David, she said, 'Didn't you, David?'

David smiled at her; he smiled at his mother; then smiled at his father. And Corny, holding his son's gaze, said quietly, 'You dug a grave, David?'

David remained staring, unblinking.

'You dug a grave, David, and put Miss Plum and Annabel Morton in?'

Still the unblinking stare, which left Corny baffled and not a little annoyed. Turning to his daughter, he now asked her quietly, 'How do you know it was Miss Plum and this Annabel Morton?'

"Cos he took a picture out of my book, the Bantam family, where the mammy wears glasses like Miss Plum.'

'And he put that in the hole?' asked Corny, still quietly.

Rose Mary nodded.

'And what did he put in for . . . for Annabel Morton?'

'A bit out of the funnies, "The One Tooth Terror", 'cos Annabel Morton's got stick-out teeth with a band on.'

Corny put his elbow on the table and rubbed his hand hard over his face before again looking at his daughter and saying, 'And who told him to dig the grave and bury the pictures in it?'

'I didn't, Dad.'

'Rose Mary!' The name was a threat now, and Rose Mary's lips trembled visibly, and she said again in a tiny squeaking voice, 'I didn't, Dad, I'm tellin' the truth I am. He thought it all up for hisself, he did.'

'You're going to instruction for confession on Thursday, Rose Mary; what will you tell Father Carey?'

'Not that, Dad, not that, 'cos I didn't.'

'Well, how did you know it was a grave?'

'I don't know, Dad, I don't know.' The tears were on her lashes now.

'Corny.' Mary Ann's voice was low, and it, too, was trembling, but Corny, without looking at her, waved her to silence and went on, 'Did he tell you it was Miss Plum and Annabel Morton?'

'No, Dad.'

'You just knew?'

'Yes, Dad.'

'How?'

''Cos he dug a long hole and put the pictures in the bottom and covered them up, like when they put people in the ground in Longfields.'

'Have you ever seen anyone being put in the ground in Longfields?'

'Corny.' Mary Ann's voice was high now, but still he waved her to silence.

'Yes, and everybody was cryin' . . .'

Corny lowered his eyes, then said, 'And you didn't tell David to do this?'

'No, Dad. I was diggin' my garden, putting in the seeds you gave me, when I saw him diggin' a long hole. Then he ran back to the shed where all our old books an' things are and he came back with the pictures.'

Once more Corny and David were looking at each other. David's lips were closed, gently closed, his eyes were dark and bright, and if he hadn't been a six-year-old child, a retarded six-year-old child, a supposedly retarded six-year-old child to Corny's mind, he would have sworn that there was a twinkle of amusement in the eyes gazing innocently into his. He rose from the table, pushing his chair back, and went out of the room, and Mary Ann, looking from one to the other of the children, said quickly, 'Get on with your teas. No chatter now, get on with your teas.' And then she followed her husband.

Corny was expecting her, for when she went into the bedroom he rounded on her immediately, and with his arm extended down towards her he wagged his hand in her face, saying, 'It's as I've said before, that little bloke's laughing at us, he's having us on a string.'

'Stop talking about your son as that bloke, will you, Corny; it's as if he didn't belong to you.'

'Look, I'm not going to be made a fool of by a nipper of six, no matter what you say. As I said before, if he was on his own for a time he would talk all right. Send him to the farm for a few weeks and he'll come back yelling his head off.'

'No, no; they can't be separated, they mustn't be separated. And the doctor said so. It's inhuman. I don't know how you can stand there and say such a thing. He's your son, but the way you talk you'd imagine he didn't belong to you.'

'He's my son all right, and I want him as a son, and not as the shadow of Rose Mary. If he can think up that grave business and put the teacher and the Morton child into it because they had upset Rose Mary, he's got it up top all right. The only reason he's not talking is because he finds it easier not to. And mark you this.' His finger was jabbing at her again. 'He thinks it funnier not to . . . That bloke . . . All right, all right, all right, THAT CHILD. Well, that child is laughing up his sleeve at us, let me tell you.'

'Don't be so silly. A child of six . . . Huh!'

'Six, you say. Sometimes I think he's sixty. I believe he's an old soul in a young body.'

'Oh, Corny.' Mary Ann's voice was derisive now, and she closed her eyes giving emphasis to her opinion on this particular subject. 'You've been reading again.'

'Never mind about reading, I mean what I say, and as I've said before, if those two are separated that boy'll talk, and that's just what I'm . . .'

'Well, you try it.' Mary Ann drew herself up to the limit of her five feet as she interrupted him, and, her face now red and straight, she said under her breath, 'You separate them and you know what I'll do . . . I'll go home.'

As soon as it was out she knew she had made a grave mistake. In her husband were a number of sensitive spots, which she had learnt it was better to by-pass, and now she had jumped on one with both feet, and she watched the pain she had caused, tightening his muscles and bringing his mouth to that hard line which she hated.

'This is your home, Mary Ann, I've told you before. These four rooms are your home. You chose them with your eyes open. The place that you've just referred to is the house where your parents live, the home of your children's grandparents, but this . . .' He took his fist and brought it down with a bang on the corner post of the wooden bed. 'This is your home.'

'Oh, Corny.' It was a faint whisper. 'I'm sorry. You know I didn't mean it.'

'You've said it before.'

'But I didn't mean it. I never mean it.' She moved close to him and leant her head against his unyielding chest, and, putting her arms about him, she said, 'I'm sorry. Hold . . . hold me tight.'

It was a few minutes before Corny responded to the plea in her voice. Then, his arm going about her, he said stiffly, 'I'll get you a better house, never you fear. One of these days I'll build you a house, and right here. But in the meantime, don't look down on this . . .'

'Oh, Corny.' She had her head strained back gazing up at him and protesting, 'I don't, I don't. Oh that's not fair, you know I don't.'

'I don't know you don't, I know nothing of the sort, because you're always breaking your neck to visit the farm.'

'Well, so are you. Look at the Sundays I've wanted to stay put, but it's been you who's said, "Let's go over. If we don't they'll wonder. And they want to see the bairns!" You've said that time and again.'

'I've said it because I knew you wanted to go. All right, let's forget it.' He took her elfin face between his two big hands, and after gazing at it for a moment he said below his breath, 'Oh, Mary Ann.' Then pulling her close to him, he moved his hand over her hair, saying, 'Aw, I want to give you things . . . the lot, and it irks me when I go to the farm and everybody looks prosperous. Your da and ma, Michael and Sarah, Tony and Lettice.'

'Aw, now, Corny, that's not fair.' She was bristling again. 'It isn't all clover for Tony and Lettice living with Mr Lord. As for me ma and da looking prosperous. Well, after the way they've struggled. And as for our Michael and Sarah, we could have had a better place than them if . . .' Mary Ann suddenly found her words cut off by Corny's hand being placed firmly but gently across her mouth.

'I'll say it for you.' Corny was speaking slowly. 'If I'd taken the old man's offer and let him set me up with the Baxter garage, we'd have been on easy street. That's what you were getting at, isn't it? But I've told you before I'd rather eat bread and dripping and be me own boss. I'm daft I know, do-lally-tap, up the pole, the lot, I know, but that's the way I'm made. And again I say, you knew what you were taking on, didn't you?'

He took his hand slowly away from her mouth, and with his arms by his sides now he stood looking at her, and she at him. Then she smiled up at him, a loving little smile, as she said, 'And I've told you this afore, Corny Boyle. You're a big pig-headed, stubborn, conceited lump of . . .'

'You forgot the bumptious . . .'

Suddenly they were laughing, and he grabbed her up and swung her round as if she, too, was a child.

'Eeh! stop it, man, you'll have the things over.' She thumped him on the chest, and as he plonked her down on the side of the bed there came to them from directly below the wailing note of a trombone.

464

The sound seemed to prevent Mary Ann from overbalancing. Looking up at Corny, she screwed her face up as she exclaimed, 'Oh no! No!'

'Look.' He bent his long length down to her. 'It's only for half-an-hour. I told him he could after he had finished the job and before the bairns had gone to bed. And think back, Mary Ann, think back. Remember when I hadn't any place to practise me cornet, who took pity on me?' He flicked her chin with his forefinger and thumb.

'But that's a dreadful sound, he knows nothing about it.'

'So was my cornet.'

'Aw, it wasn't.' She pushed him aside as she got to her feet. 'You could always play, you were a natural. But Jimmy. Why doesn't he stick to his guitar, he isn't bad at that?'

'They're trying to make the group different, introducing a trombone and a flute into it.'

'Well, why didn't he pick the flute?' She put her fingers in her ears as a shrill wobbling note penetrated the floor-boards. 'Oh, let's get into the other room. Not that it will be much better there.'

As they entered the kitchen Rose Mary turned excitedly from the table, crying, 'Jimmy's playing his horn, Mam.'

'Yes, dear, I can hear. Have you finished your tea?'

'Nearly, Mam. David wants some cheese.'

'David can't have any cheese, I've told you it upset his stomach before. He's got an egg and . . .' She bent over her son and looked down into the empty egg-cup, saying, 'Oh, you've eaten your egg, that's a good boy. But where's the shell?' She turned her eyes to her daughter, and Rose Mary, looking down at her plate, said quietly, 'I think he threw it in the fire, he sometimes does. But he'd like some cheese, he's still hungry.'

'Now, Rose Mary, don't keep it up. I've told you he can't have any cheese.'

'I've had some cheese.'

'Oh.' Mary Ann closed her eyes and, refusing to be drawn into a fruitless argument, took her seat at the table, only to bring her shoulders hunching up and her head down as an extra long wail from the trombone filled the room.

When it died away and she straightened herself up it was to see her daughter convulsed with laughter. David, too, was laughing, his deep, throaty, infectious chuckle. She was feigning annoyance, saying, 'It's all right for you to laugh,' when she saw Corny standing behind David's chair. He was motioning to her with his head, and so, quietly, she rose from the table and walked to his side and stood behind the children, and following her husband's eyes her gaze was directed to the pocket in her son's corduroy breeches. The pocket was distended, showing the top of a brown egg.

As they exchanged glances, she wanted to laugh, but it was no laughing matter. This wasn't the first time that food had been stuffed into her son's pockets, or up his jumper; it had even found its way into the chest of drawers. She was about to lift her hand to touch David when a warning movement from Corny stopped her. The movement said, leave this to me. Quietly she walked to her seat and Corny, taking his seat, drew his son's attention to him by saying, 'David.'

466

David turned his laughing face towards his father.

'Did you eat the egg that Mam give you for your tea?'

The smile slid from David's face, the eyes widened into innocence, the moist lips parted, and he bestowed on his father a look which said he didn't understand.

'Dad. Dad, he tried . . .'

'Rose Mary!' Without moving a muscle of his face Corny's eyes slid to his daughter. 'Remember what I told you about telling lies. Now be quiet.' The eyes turned on his son once again. 'Where's the egg you had for tea, David?'

Still no movement from David. Still the innocent look. Now Corny held out his hand. He laid it on the table in front of his son and said quietly, 'Give it to me.'

David's eyelids didn't flicker, but his small hand moved down towards his trouser pocket, then came upwards again, holding the egg. It took up a position about eight inches above Corny's hand, and there remained absolutely still.

'Give me the egg, David.' Corny's voice was quiet and level.

And David gave his father the egg, his little fist pressed into the softly-boiled egg crushing the shell. As the yolk dripped on to Corny's fingers he smacked at his son's hand, knocking the crushed egg flying across the table, to splatter itself over the stove. Then almost in one movement he had David dangling by the breeches as if he was a hold-all, and with his free hand he lathered his behind.

David's screams now rent the air and vied with

the screeches of the trombone and the crying of Rose Mary as she yelled, 'Oh, Dad, don't. Oh don't hit David. Don't. Don't.'

Mary Ann wanted to say the same thing, 'Don't hit David. Don't,' but David had to be smacked. Quickly, she thrust Rose Mary from the room, saying, 'Stay there . . . Now stay.' And turning to Corny, she cried, 'That's enough. That's enough.'

After the first slap of anger she knew that Corny hadn't belaboured David as he could have done. It was only during these past few months that he had smacked his son, and although she knew it had to be done and the boy deserved it the process tore her to shreds.

She wanted to go to David now and gather him up from the big chair where he was crouched and into her arms, and pet him and mother him, but that would never do. She took him by the hand and drew him to his feet, saying, 'Go into the bathroom and get your things off.'

Outside the door, Rose Mary was waiting. She exchanged a look with her mother; then, putting her arms about her brother, she almost carried him, still sobbing, to the bathroom.

When Mary Ann returned to the room Corny said immediately, 'Now don't say to me that I shouldn't have done that.' She looked at him and saw that his face was white and strained, she saw that he was upset more than usual, and she could understand this. The defiance of his son, the indignity of the egg being squashed on to his fingers, and having to thrash the child had upset him, for he loved the boy. About his feelings for his son, she had once analysed them to herself by saying that he was crazy about Rose Mary but he loved David.

Everything seemed to have changed this last year, to have got worse over the past few months. At times she thought it was as Corny said, David had it all up top and he was trying something on. And this was borne out by the incident just now, for even she had to admit it appeared calculated.

Another blast from the trombone penetrating the room, she flew to the window, thrust it open and, leaning out, she cried, 'Jimmy! Jimmy, will you stop that racket!'

'What, Mrs Boyle . . . Eh?'

She was now looking down on the long lugubrious face of Corny's young assistant, Jimmy McFarlane. Jimmy was seventeen. He was car mad, motor-cycle mad and group mad, in fact Mary Ann would say Jimmy was mad altogether, but he was a hard worker, likeable and good-tempered. Apart from all that, he was all they could afford in the way of help.

'Sorry, Mrs Boyle, is it disturbin' you? Is the bairns abed?'

'They're just going, Jimmy, but . . . but give it a rest for tonight at any rate, will you?'

'OK, Mrs Boyle.' Jimmy's voice did not show his disappointment, and he added, 'The boss there?'

'What is it?' Mary Ann had moved aside and Corny was hanging out of the window now.

'Had an American in a few minutes ago. Great big whopper of a car . . . A Chevrolet. Twelve gallons of petrol and shots and oil, an' he gave me half-a-crown. Could do with some of those every hour, couldn't we, boss?'

'I'll say.'

'He was tickled to death by me trombone, he laughed like a looney. He laughed all the time, even when I wasn't playing it. He must have thought I looked funny or summat, eh?'

'Well, as long as he gave you a tip, that's everything,' said Corny. 'I'll be down in a minute.'

'OK, boss.'

After he had closed the window, Corny went straight into the scullery and returned with a floor cloth with which he began to wipe the mess from the stove.

'Corny. Please. Leave it, I'll see to it.'

Abruptly he stopped rubbing with the cloth, and without turning his head said, 'I want to clean this up.'

Standing back from him, Mary Ann looked at his ham-fisted actions with the cloth. There were depths in this husband of hers she couldn't fathom, there were facets of his thinking that she couldn't follow at times. There were things he did that wouldn't make sense to other people, like him wanting to clean up the mess his son had made. She said gently, 'I'm going to wash them; will you come in?'

He went on rubbing for a moment. Then nodding towards the stove, he said, 'I'll be in.'

When he had the room to himself, and the egg and shell gathered on to the floor cloth, he stood with it in his hand looking down at it for a long moment. Life was odd, painful and frightening at times.

2

Mary Ann liked Sundays. There were two kinds in
her life, the winter Sundays and the summer
Sundays. She didn't know which she liked best.
Perhaps the winter Sundays, when Corny lay in
bed until eight o'clock and she snuggled up in his
arms and they talked about things they never got
round to during the week. Then before the clock
had finished striking eight, the twins would burst
into the room – Rose Mary had her orders that
they weren't to come in before eight o'clock on a
Sunday, on a winter Sunday, because Dad liked
a lie in.

On the summer Sundays, Corny rose at six and
brought her a cup of tea before he went off to
early Mass in Felling, and as soon as the door had
closed on him the children would scamper into
the bed and snuggle down, one each side of her, at
least for a while. Eight o'clock on a summer
Sunday morning usually found the bed turned
into a rough house, and on such mornings Mary
Ann became a girl again, a child, as she laughed
and tumbled and giggled with her children. Sometimes she was up and had the breakfast ready for
Corny's return, but more often she was struggling

to bring herself back to the point of being a mother, with a mother's responsibility, when he returned.

But this summer Sunday morning Mary Ann was up and had Corny's breakfast ready on his return. Moreover, the children were dressed and both standing to the side of the breakfast table, straining their faces against the window-pane to catch a sight of the car coming along the road.

'He's a long time,' Rose Mary commented, then added, 'can I start on a piece of toast, Mam?'

'No, you can't. You'll wait till your dad comes in.'

'I'm hungry, I could eat a horse. David's hungry an' all.'

'Rose Mary!'

Rose Mary gave her shoulders a little shake, then turned from the window, and, moving the spoon that was set near her cereal bowl, she said, 'I hope old Father Doughty doesn't take our Mass this mornin', 'cos he keeps on and on. He yammers.'

'Rose Mary, you're not to talk like that.'

'Well, Mam, he does.'

'Well, if he does, it's for your own good. And you should listen and pay heed to what he says.'

'I pay heed to Father Carey. I like Father Carey. Father Carey never frightens me.'

Mary Ann turned from the sideboard and looked at her daughter; then asked quietly, 'Are you frightened of Father Doughty?'

Rose Mary now took up her spoon and whirled it round her empty bowl saying, 'Sometimes. He was on about the Holy Ghost last Sunday and the sin of pride. Annabel Morton said he was gettin' at me 'cos I'm stuck up. I'm not stuck up, am I, Mam?'

'I should hope not. What have you to be stuck up about?'

'Well, it's because we've got a garage and it's me dad's.'

'Oh,' Mary Ann nodded and turned her head back to the cutlery drawer. 'But I thought you said you weren't stuck up.'

'Well, just a little bit. About me dad I am.' The spoon whirled more quickly now. Then it stopped abruptly, and Rose Mary, turning to her mother said, 'What's the Holy Ghost like, Mam?'

'What?'

'I mean, what's he like? Is he like God? Or is he like Jesus?'

Mary Ann made a great play of separating the knives and forks in the drawer. Then, turning her head slightly towards her daughter but not looking at her, she said, 'God and Jesus and the Holy Ghost are all the same, they all look alike.'

'Oh no they don't.'

Mary Ann's eyes were now brought sharply towards her daughter, to see a face that was almost a replica of her own, except for the eyes that were like Corny's, tilted pointedly upwards towards her. 'Jesus is Jesus, and I know what Jesus looks like 'cos I have pictures of him. An' I know who God looks like. But not the Holy Ghost.'

Mary Ann's voice was very small when, looking down at her daughter, she said, 'You know who God looks like? Who?'

'Me granda Shaughnessy. He's big like him, and nice and kind.'

Mary Ann turned towards the drawer again before closing her eyes and putting her hand over her brow. Her da like God. Oh, she wanted to laugh. She wished Corny was here . . . he would have enjoyed that. Big, and nice, and kind. Well, and wasn't he all three? But for her da to take on the resemblance of God. Oh dear! Oh dear!

'Aha!' The sound came from David who was still looking out of the window, and Rose Mary turned towards him, crying, 'It's me dad.'

Both the children now waved frantically out of the window, and Corny waved back to them.

The minute he entered the room they flew to him, and he lifted one up in each arm, to be admonished by Mary Ann, crying, 'Now don't crush their clothes, they're all ready for Mass.'

'Dad. Dad, who said seven o'clock?'

'Father Doughty.'

'Oh, then Father Carey will say eight, and Father Doughty will say nine, and Father Carey will say ten. Oh goodie!' She flung her arms around his neck and pressed her face against his, and David following suit, entwined his arms on top of hers and pressed his cheek against the other side of his father's face.

The business of Friday night was a thing of the past; it was Sunday and 'family day'.

Although the pattern of Sunday differed from winter to summer it had only been what Mary Ann thought of as 'family day' since Jimmy had been taken on, because Jimmy came at eight o'clock on the summer Sunday mornings and stayed till ten, and, if required, he would come back again at two and stay as long as Corny wanted him. Jimmy was saving up for a motor-bike and Sunday work being time and a half he didn't mind how long he stayed. And when he was kept on on Sunday afternoon it meant they could all go to the farm together.

'Sit yourselves up,' Mary Ann said, 'and make a start. I'll take Jimmy's down.'

Before she left the room they had all started on their cereal. When David had emptied his bowl he pushed it away from him, and Corny, looking down on his son, asked quietly, 'Would you like some more, David?'

David looked brightly back into Corny's face and gave a small shake of his head, and Corny, putting his spoon gently down on to the table, took hold of his son's hand and said quietly, 'Say . . . no . . . thank . . . you . . . Dad.' He spaced the words.

David looked back at his father, and Rose Mary, her spoon poised halfway to her mouth, looked at David.

'Go on, say it,' urged Corny, still softly. 'No, thank you. Just say it. No . . . thank . . . you.'

David's eyes darkened. The mischievous smile lurked in the back of them. He slanted his eyes now to Rose Mary, and Rose Mary, looking quickly at her father, said, 'He wants to say no thank you, Dad. He means, no thank you, don't you, David?' She pushed her face close against his, and David smiled widely at her and nodded his head briskly, and Corny, picking up his spoon again, started eating.

Rose Mary stood with one hand in Mary Ann's while with the other she clutched at David's. She wasn't feeling very happy; it wasn't going to be a very nice Sunday. It hadn't been a very nice Sunday from the beginning, because her mother had got out of bed early, and then her dad had been vexed at breakfast time because David wouldn't say No thank you, and now they were going into Felling by bus.

Her mam had snapped at her when she asked her why her dad couldn't run them in in the car. She couldn't see why he couldn't close up the garage for a little while, just a little while, it didn't take long to get into Felling by car. And what was worse, worse for her mam anyway, was that she had to go all the way to Jarrow by bus. She didn't like it when her mam went to Jarrow Church, but she only went to Jarrow Church when she was visiting Greatgran McBride, killing two birds with one stone, she called it. She herself liked to visit Greatgran McBride, and so did David. They loved going to Greatgran McBride's. They didn't mind the smell.

'Mam, couldn't you leave going to Greatgran McBride's until this afternoon?'

'Don't you want to go to the farm this afternoon?'

'Yes, but I'd like to go to Greatgran McBride's an' all. Dad could run us there afore we went to the farm.'

'Dad can't do any such thing, so stop it. And don't you start on that when we get home. I'm going to see Greatgran McBride because she isn't well and she can't be bothered with children around.'

'She always says she loves to—'

'You're not going today.'

There was a short silence before Rose Mary

suggested, 'Couldn't we come on after Mass? We could meet you an' we could all come back together. I could get the bus; I've done it afore.'

'Do you want me to get annoyed with you, Rose Mary?'

'No, Mam.' The voice was very small.

'Well, then, do as you're told. What's the matter with you this morning?'

'I think it might be Father Doughty an' I don't like—'

'You know it'll be Father Carey. And not another word now, here's the bus, and behave yourself.'

Twenty minutes later, Rose Mary, still holding David by the hand, entered St Patrick's Church. Inside the doorway she reached up and dipped her fingers in the holy-water font, and David followed suit; then one after the other they genuflected to the main altar. This done, they walked down the aisle until they came to the fifth pew from the front. This was one of the pews allotted to their class. Again they genuflected one after the other, then Rose Mary entered the pew first. One foot on the wooden kneeler, one on the floor, she was making her way to where sat her school pals, Jane Leonard and Katie Eastman, when she became aware that she was alone, at least, in-as-much as the other half of her was not immediately behind her. She turned swiftly, to see David standing in the aisle looking up at Miss Plum. Miss Plum had David by one hand and David was hanging on to the end of the pew with the other. Swiftly, Rose Mary made the return journey to the aisle, and Miss Plum, bending down to her and answering her look, which said plainly, 'Now what are you up to with our David?' whispered, 'I'm putting David with the boys on the other side.'

'But, Miss Plum, he won't go.'

A low hissing whisper now from Miss Plum. 'He'll go if you tell him to, Rose Mary.'

A whisper now from Rose Mary. 'But I've told him afore, Miss Plum.'

'Go and sit down, Rose Mary, and leave David to me.'

Rose Mary stared up into Miss Plum's face. Then she looked at David, and David looked at her. Whereupon David, after a moment, turned his gaze towards Miss Plum again and made a sound that was much too loud for church. The sound might have been interpreted as, 'Gert yer!' But, of course, David never said any such thing. He just made a sound of protest, but it was enough to put Miss Plum into action. In one swift movement she unloosened his fingers from the end of the pew and, inserting both her hands under his armpits, she whisked him across the aisle, plonked him none too gently on the wooden pew, then sat down beside him.

David made no more protesting sounds. He gazed up at the straight profile of his teacher, stared at her for a moment with his mouth open, then bent forward, to see beyond her waist, to find out what Rose Mary was up to in all this. He was now further surprised to see his sister, miles away from him, kneeling, with her chin on the pew rail staring towards the high altar. His brows gathered, the corners of his eyes puckered up. He was very puzzled. Rose Mary wasn't doing anything. He gave a wriggle with his bottom to bring him farther forward, when a hand, that almost covered the whole of his chest, pushed him backwards on the seat, making him overbalance and bump his head and bring his legs abruptly up to his eye level.

When Rose Mary, from the corner of her eye, saw Miss Plum push their David and knock his head against the pew, she almost jumped up and shouted out loud, but, being in church, she had to restrain her actions and content herself with her thoughts. She hated Miss Plum, she did, she did. And David wouldn't know anything about the Mass. He wouldn't understand what Father Carey was saying, and he wouldn't be able to sing the hymn inside hisself like he did when he was with her . . . Wait till she got home, she would tell her dad about Miss Plum. Just wait. She would get him to come to the school the morrow and let her have it. Plum, Plum, Plum. She hoped a big plum stone would stick in her gullet and she would die. She did, she did. In the name of the Father, and of the Son, and of the Holy Ghost. Amen.

Father Carey was kneeling on the altar steps. 'Our Father Who art in heaven, hallowed be Thy name.' She had taken their David across there all because of Annabel Morton, 'cos last Sunday when Annabel Morton had punched their David under her coat so nobody could see, David had kicked her and made her shout out . . . 'An' forgive us our trespasses, as we forgive them that trespass against us.' Miss Plum had blamed her and she wouldn't believe about Annabel Morton punching David and she had been nasty all the week. Oh, she did hate Miss Plum. Their poor David havin' to sit there all by hisself, all through the Mass, and it would go on for hours and hours. Father Carey was talking slow, he was taking his time, he always did. 'I believe in God the Father Almighty, Creator of Heaven and Earth.' If her dad wouldn't come down and go for Miss Plum the morrow she knew who would. Her Grandad Shaughnessy would. He would soon tell her where she got off. Yes, that's who would give it to her, her Grandad Shaughnessy. 'I believe in the Holy Ghost, the Holy Catholic Church.' And Father Carey would likely go on about the Holy Ghost and the Trinity this morning; when he started his sermon he forgot to stop, although he made you laugh at times. Oh, she wished the Mass was over. She slanted her eyes to the left, but she couldn't see anything, only the bowed heads of the other three girls who were filling up the pew now. If she raised her chin and stuck it on the arm rest she had a view of Miss Plum, but there was no sign of David. Poor David was somewhere down on the kneeler yon side of Miss Plum. Well, it would serve Miss Plum right if he started to scream.

Rose Mary brought her head slowly forward and she looked to where the priest was mounting the steps towards the altar. But she wasn't interested at all in what Father Carey was doing, for forming a big question mark in her mind was the word WHY? . . . WHY? . . . Why hadn't he screamed? Why wasn't their David screaming? He always screamed when he was separated from her? Perhaps Miss Plum was holding his mouth. She jerked round so quickly in the direction of her teacher that she overbalanced and fell across the calves of the girl next to her.

When a hand came down and righted her more

quickly than she had fallen, she caught a fleeting glimpse of its owner, and now, staring wide-eyed towards the altar again, she wondered how on earth Miss Watson had got behind her. Miss Watson was the headmistress. Miss Watson usually sat at the back of the church in solitary state.

As the Mass went on the awful thought of Miss Watson behind her kept Rose Mary's gaze fixed on the altar, except when she was getting on or off her seat to stand or kneel, when her head would accidentally turn to the left. But she might as well have kept it straight, for all she could see past the bodies of her schoolmates was the tall, full figure of Miss Plum. No sight, and what was more puzzling still, no sound of their David . . .

The Mass over at last, Rose Mary came out of the pew in line with the others, genuflected deeply, then looked towards Miss Plum. But Miss Plum's profile was cast in marble, in fact her whole body seemed stone-like. A push from behind and Rose Mary was forced to go up the aisle, and she daren't look round, for there at the top stood Miss Watson. She bowed her head as she passed Miss Watson as if she, too, demanded adoration.

Outside, she waited, her eyes glued on the church door. All the girls had come out first, and now came the boys . . . but not their David, and not Miss Plum. The grown-ups appeared in a long straggling line, and among them was Miss Watson, but still no sign of Miss Plum. Rose Mary could stand it no longer. Sidling back into the church, she looked down the aisle, and there, standing next to Miss Plum and opposite Father

Carey, was their David, looking as if nothing had happened. The priest was smiling, and Miss Plum was smiling, and they were talking in whispers. When they turned, David turned, and they all came up the aisle towards her. And when they reached her Miss Plum looked down on her and said, 'David's been a very good boy, and he's going to sit with me every Sunday.'

Rose Mary sent a sweeping glance from Miss Plum to David, then from David to Father Carey, and back to Miss Plum. She was opening her mouth to protest when the priest said, 'Isn't that a great favour, David, eh?' He had his hand on David's head. 'Sitting next to your teacher. My, My. Everybody else in the class will be jealous.' He now looked at Miss Plum, and Miss Plum at him, and they smiled at each other. And then Miss Plum said, 'Goodbye, Father.' She said it like Annabel Morton said things when she was sucking up to somebody. Then she went out of the church.

Rose Mary, now grasping David's hand, looked at the priest, and said softly, 'Father.'

'Yes, Rose Mary.' He bent his head towards her.

'Father, our David doesn't like being by hisself.'

'But he hasn't been by his – himself, he's been sitting next to Miss Plum, and liked it.'

'He doesn't like it, Father.'

'Now, now, Rose Mary. David's getting a big boy and he must sit with the big boys, mustn't you, David?' The young priest turned towards David, and David grinned at him.

Rose Mary contemplated the priest. She liked Father Carey, she did, he was lovely, but he just didn't understand the situation. She now jerked her chin up towards him, and whispered, 'Father.' The word was in the form of a request that he should lend her his ear, and this he did, literally putting it near her mouth, and what he heard was, 'He can't talk without me, Father.'

Now it was Rose Mary's turn to lend him her ear and into it he whispered, 'But he doesn't talk now, Rose Mary.'

Now the exchange was made again, and what he heard this time was, 'He does to me, Father.'

Again a movement of heads and a whisper, 'But we want him to talk to everybody, don't we, Rose Mary?'

'Yes, Father . . . oh yes, Father. But . . .'

The priest whisked his ear away, straightened up and said, 'We'll have to pray to our Lady about it.'

'But I have, Father, an' she hasn't done anything . . . Perhaps if you asked her, Father.'

'Yes, yes, I'll ask her.' Father Carey drew his fingers down his nose.

'When?' She could talk now quite openly because their David didn't know what it was all about.

'Oh, at Mass in the morning.'

'The first Mass, Father?'

Father Carey's eyebrows moved slightly upwards and he hesitated slightly before saying, 'Yes. Yes, the first Mass.'

'Could you make it the half-past eight one, Father?'

The priest's eyebrows rose farther; then his head dropped forward as if he was tired, and he looked at Rose Mary for a moment before saying slowly, 'Well, if you would like it that way, all right. Yes, I'll do it at the second Mass.'

'Thank you, Father.' She bestowed on him her nice smile, the one that had earned the unwarranted title of angelic, then she finished: 'An' now we'd better get home, 'cos me mam worries if we're late. We'll have to run, I think.'

'That's it, run along. Good-bye, David.' The priest patted David's head. 'Good-bye, Rose Mary.' He chucked her under the chin; then with a hand on each of them he pressed them towards the church door, and then for a moment he watched them running down the street, and he shook his head as he thought, dear, dear. It was as Miss Plum said, she had her work cut out with that little lady. It was also true that the boy would make little progress as long as he had a mouthpiece in his sister. And what a mouthpiece, she'd talk the hind leg off a donkey. He re-entered the church, laughing.

Rose Mary walked down the street and away from the church in silence, and the unusualness of this procedure caused David to trip over his feet as he gazed at his sister instead of looking where he was going. Then, of a sudden, he was pulled to a stop, and Rose Mary, bending towards him, said under her breath, 'Father Carey's going to tell Our Lady to ask God to make you speak the morrow mornin', he's goin' to tell her at the half-past eight. And you will, won't you, David?'

David's eyes darkened, and shone, his smile widened and he nodded his head once.

Rose Mary sighed. Then she, too, smiled. That was that then. Everything was taken care of. If things went right he should be talking just when they reached their classroom.

Getting on the bus, Rose Mary reminded David, in no small voice now, that it being Sunday they'd have Yorkshire pudding and if he liked he could have his with milk and sugar before his dinner; then she went on to explain what there would be for the dinner, not forgetting to pay stress on the delectability of the pudding. Following this she gave him a decription of what there was likely to be for tea at Gran Shaughnessy's. By the time they alighted from the bus the other occupants had no doubt in their minds but that Rose Mary and David Boyle had a mother who was a wonderful cook, a father who could supply unstintingly the necessities to further his wife's art and grandparents who apparently lived like lords. And this was as it should be, otherwise she would have indeed wasted her breath.

3

Lizzie Shaughnessy looked at her daughter from under her lowered lids. When they were alone like this it was always hard to believe that her Mary Ann was a married woman and the mother of twins, for she still looked so young and child-like herself. It was her small stature that tended towards this impression, she thought.

Lizzie knew that her daughter was worried and she was waiting for her to unburden herself, and she knew the substance of her worry: it was the child. She joined on another ounce of wool to her knitting, then said, 'Do you know what they're going to do with Peter?'

'Send him to boarding school,' Mary Ann said.

Lizzie slowly put her knitting on to her lap and, turning her head right round to Mary Ann, said, 'Who told you?'

'Nobody, but I guessed it would come. I remember years ago Tony saying that Mr Lord had a school all mapped out for the boy.'

'But neither Tony nor Lettice wants to send him away to school.'

'I know that, but he'll go all the same; they'll

send him because that's what Mr Lord wants. He always gets what he wants.'

'Not always,' said Lizzie quietly. And to this Mary Ann made no rejoinder, for she knew that one of the great disappointments in her mother's life, and Mr Lord's, was when his grandson and herself hadn't made a match of it.

'The old man will be the one who will miss him most,' Lizzie went on. 'But it amazes me that he can put up with the boy; he's so noisy and boisterous and he never stops talking . . .'

Mary Ann got up from her chair and walked to the sitting-room window, and Lizzie said softly, 'I'm sorry, I wasn't meaning to make comparisons. You know that, oh you know that.'

'Of course I do, Ma.' Mary Ann looked at her mother over her shoulder. 'It's all right. Don't be silly; I didn't take it to myself, it's just that . . .' She spread out her hands, and then came back to her seat and sat down before ending, 'I just can't understand it. He's not deaf, he's certainly not dim, and yet he can't talk.'

'He will. Be patient, he will . . . You . . . you wouldn't consider leaving him with us?'

'Corny's been at you, hasn't he?'

'No. No.' Lizzie shook her head vigorously.

'Oh, don't tell me, Ma. I bet my bottom dollar he has. He thinks that if they were separated, even for a short time, it would make David talk. It wouldn't. And Rose Mary wouldn't be able to bear it. Neither would David, they're inseparable. At any rate, the doctor himself said it wouldn't be any use separating them.'

'You could give it a trial.' Lizzie had her eyes fixed on her knitting now.

'No, Ma, no. I wouldn't have one worry then, I'd have two, for I just don't know what the effect would be on Rose Mary, because she just lives and breathes for that boy.'

'Yes, that's your trouble.' Lizzie was now looking straight at her daughter. 'That's the trouble, she lives and breathes for him.'

'Oh, Ma, don't you start.'

'All right, all right. We'll say no more. Anyway, here they come . . . And don't look like that else they'll know something has happened. Come on, cheer up.' She rose from her seat and put her hand on Mary Ann's shoulder, adding under her breath, 'It'll be all right; it'll come out all right, you'll see.'

'Gran, Gran, Peter's got new riding breeches. Look!' Rose Mary dashed into the room, followed by a dark-haired, dark-eyed, pale-faced boy of seven.

'Have you all wiped your feet?' was Lizzie's greeting to them.

'Yes, Granma,' cried Rose Mary. 'An' David has, an' all.'

'An' I have too, Granshan.'

This quaint combination of the beginning of her name with the courtesy title of Gran attached had been given to her by Tony's son from the time he could talk. To him she had become Granshan, and now it was an accepted title and no-one laughed at it any more.

Following Peter, Sarah hobbled into the room. She was still on sticks, still crippled with polio as she would be all her days, but moving more agilely than she had done nearly seven years ago, when she had stood for the first time since her illness at the altar to be married. Behind her came Michael, refraining, as always, from helping her except by his love, which still seemed to hallow them both, and behind Michael, and looking just an older edition of him, came Mike.

Mike's red hair was now liberally streaked with grey. He had put on a little more weight, but he still looked a fine strapping figure of a man, and the hook, which for a long time had been a substitute for his left hand, was now replaced by thin steel fingers that seemed to move of their own volition.

Mike, now turning a laughing face over his shoulder, asked of Corny who was in the hall, 'You wiped your feet?'

'No,' said Corny, coming to the room door. 'I never wipe my feet; it's a stand I've made against all house-proud women, never to wipe my feet.'

'You know better,' said Lizzie, nodding across the room at him. Then she cried at the throng about her, 'I don't know what you all want in here when the tea's laid and you should be sitting down.'

'Am I to stay to tea, Granshan?'

Lizzie looked down on the boy and said, 'Of course, Peter, but you'd better tell your mother, hadn't you?'

'Oh, she knows.' He wagged his head at her. 'I told her you'd likely invite me.'

In his disarming way he joined in the roar that followed, and when Michael cuffed him playfully on the head the boy turned on him with doubled-up fists, and there ensued a sparring match, which David and Rose Mary applauded, jumping and shouting around them. It was the fact of David shouting that brought Corny's and Mary Ann's hands together, because the boy was actually making an intelligible sound which could almost be interpreted as 'Go on, Peter. Go on, Peter.'

Mary Ann's head drooped slightly and she made a small groaning sound as her mother's voice brought the sparring to an end with a sharp command of, 'Now give over. Do you hear me, Michael, stop it. If you want any rough-house stuff, get you outside, the lot of you. Come on now.'

Michael collapsed on the couch, and this was the signal for the three children to storm over him, and Lizzie, turning to the rest, commanded, 'Get yourselves into the other room and seated . . . I'll see to these.'

Five minutes later they were all seated round the well-laden tea table. There had been a little confusion over the seating in the first place as Rose Mary wanted to sit next to Peter, and Peter evidently wanted to sit next to Rose Mary, but David not only wanted to sit next to Rose Mary, he also wanted to sit next to Peter, so in the end David sat between Peter and Rose Mary and the tea got under way.

It was in the middle of tea, when Corny and Mary Ann between them were giving their version of Jimmy's trombone playing, that Peter suddenly said, 'I'd jolly well like to hear him. They've got a band at school, but it's just whistles and things. Perhaps Father will bring me over tomorrow when he comes to see you, and I'll hear him play then, eh, Uncle Corny?'

'Tony . . . your father's coming to see me tomorrow, Peter?' Corny looked down the table towards the boy, and Peter, his head cocked on one side, said, 'Yes, he said he was. He wants a new car, and you're going to buy it for him.'

'Oh?'

All eyes were on Corny. This was a good bit of news. It meant business, yet the elders at the table knew that Corny wasn't taking it like that. To get an order from Tony, who was the grandson of Mr Lord, Mr Lord who had for so long been Mary Ann's mentor and who was still finding ways and means of handing out help to her, would not meet with Corny's approval, even if it meant badly needed business.

Mike's voice broke the immediate silence at the table, saying, 'You've spilt the beans, young fellow, haven't you?'

Peter looked towards the man, whom, in his own mind, he considered one of his family, and said, with something less than his usual exuberance, 'Yes, Granpa Shan, I have . . . Father will be vexed.' He now turned his gaze down the table towards Corny and said, 'I'm sorry, Uncle Corny. I wasn't supposed to know, I just overheard Father telling Mother . . . I'll get it in the neck now, I suppose.' The statement, said in such a polite tone, was too much even for Corny. He laughed, and the tension was broken as he said, 'And you deserve to get it in the neck too, me lad.'

'You won't give me away to Father?' Peter was leaning over his plate as he looked down towards Corny, and Corny, narrowing his eyes at the young culprit, said, 'What's it worth?'

This remark brought Peter upright. He looked first towards Rose Mary's bright face, then towards David's penetrating stare, and, his agile mind working overtime, he returned his gaze to Corny and said, 'Let's say I'll help to clean one of your cars for you during the holidays . . . that's if I can stay to dinner.'

They were all laughing and all talking at once, and Sarah, leaning across the corner of the table towards Mary Ann, said, 'He'll either grow up to be Foreign Minister, or a confidence trickster,' whereupon they both laughed louder still.

But behind her laughter a little nagging voice was saying to Mary Ann: If only David had said that; and he could have, he could be as cute as Peter any day, if only he could break through the skin that was covering his speech.

If only. If only. If only there was some way . . . But not separating them as Corny wanted, and now her mother. No, not that way.

4

It was half-past ten in the morning and a beautiful day; cars were spinning thick and fast over all the roads in England, and the North had more than its share of traffic. There were people going on their holidays to the Lake District, to Scotland, to Wales. There were foreigners in cars who were discovering that the North of England had more to show than pits and docks. Yet Corny, who had been in the garage since half-past six that morning, had sold exactly four gallons of petrol.

It couldn't go on, he had just told himself as he sat in his little office looking at his ledger. Last week he had cleared seventeen pounds, and he'd had Jimmy to pay out of that, and then there had been the building society repayments, insurance, and the usual sum to be put by for rates, and what did that leave for living? They had dipped into their savings so often, the money they had banked from Mr Lord's generous wedding present to them both, until it was now very near the bottom of the barrel. Mary Ann worked miracles, but at times there was a fear in him that she would get tired of working miracles. She was young, they were both young, and they weren't seeing much of life, only hard work and struggling. This was what both his parents and hers had had in their young days, but the young of today were supposed to be having it easy, making so much money in fact that they didn't know what to do with it, or themselves. And it was a fact in some cases. There was his brother, Dan, twenty-four years old, not a thought in his head but beer and women, and yet he never picked up less than thirty quid from his lorry driving; forty-five quid some weeks he had told him, and just for dumping clay, not even stepping a foot out of his cab.

Life at this moment appeared very unfair. Why, Corny asked himself, couldn't he get a break? Nobody worked harder, tried harder. It was funny how your life could be altered by one man's vote in a committee room. When he had bought the garage seven years ago he had been sure that the council would widen the lane and make it into a main connecting road between Felling and Turnstile point, but one man's vote had potched the whole thing . . . But not quite. It was the 'not quite' that had kept him hanging on, for there had been rumours that the council had ideas for this little bottle-neck. Some said they were going to buy the land near the old turnstile for a building estate. Another rumour was that they were going to build a comprehensive school just across the road in what was known as Weaver's field.

During the first couple of years he had sustained himself on the rumours. He seemed to have been very young then, even gullible, now he knew he was no longer young inside, and certainly not gullible. No rumour affected him any more; yet at the same time he kept hanging on, and hoping.

He rose from the stool and walked out into the bright sunshine. Everything looked neat and tidy. Nobody, he assured himself, had a prettier garage. The red flowers against the white stones, the cement drive-in all scrubbed clean, not a spot of oil to be seen – perhaps that was a bad sign, he should leave the oily patches, it would bear out the old saying: where there was dirt there was money. He turned and looked into the big garage. It, too, was too tidy, too bare. He hadn't a thing in for repairs. The garage held nothing now but his old Rover and some cardboard adverts for tyres.

As he stared down the long, empty space Jimmy came from out of the shadows with a broom in his hand, and, leaning on it and looking towards Corny, he said quizzically, 'Well, that's that. What next, boss? . . . There's a bird's nest in the chimney, I could go and tidy that up . . .'

'Now I'm having none of that . . . an' you mind.' Corny's voice came as a growl, and Jimmy, the smile sliding from his face, said, 'I was only kiddin', boss. I meant nowt, honest.'

'Well, let's hope you didn't. I've told you afore, if you don't like it here there's plenty of other jobs you can get. I'm not stopping you. You knew the terms when you started.'

'Aye. Aye. I know. An' it's all right with me. I like it here, I've told you, 'cos I've learned more with you than I would have done in a big garage, stuck on one job . . . It's only, well . . .' Jimmy didn't go on to explain that he got bored when there were no jobs in but said, with a touch of excitement, 'Look, what about me takin' that monstrosity out there to bits and buryin' it, eh?'

He walked past Corny, and Corny slowly followed him to the edge of the garage, and they looked towards his piece of spare land that bordered the garden and where stood a car. Three nights ago someone had driven a car there and left it. The first indication Corny had of this was when he opened up the next morning, and the sight of the dumped car almost brought his temper to boiling point. They just wanted to start that; let that get round and before he knew where he was he'd be swamped. They had started that game up near the cemetery, and there were two graveyards up there now. He couldn't understand how he'd slept through someone driving a car down the side of the building, because a car had only to pass down the road in the night and it would wake him, and he would say to himself, 'It couldn't come down in the daytime, could it.'

He had been on the point of taking a hammer and doing what Jimmy suggested they should do now, break the thing up and bury it, but the twins had caused him to change his mind, at least temporarily, for Rose Mary had begged him to let them have it to play with, and strangely, Mary Ann had backed her up, saying, 'It would give them something to do now that they were on holiday, and might stop her pestering to be taken to the sands at Whitley Bay or Shields.' So Corny had been persuaded against his will to leave the car as it was. He had siphoned out what petrol there remained in the tank, cleared the water and oil out, and left the children with a gigantic toy, hoping that their interest might lag within a few days and he would then dispose of it. But the few days had passed and their interest, far from waning, had increased.

From where he stood he could see the pair of them, Rose Mary in the driving seat with David bobbing up and down beside her, driving to far-off places he had no doubt, places as far away as their Greatgran McBride's in Jarrow. He smiled quietly to himself as he thought they were like him in that way, he had always wanted to go to his Grannie McBride, for his grannie's cluttered un-tidy house had been more of home to him than his real home; and it had been her dominant, loud, yet wise personality that had kept him steady . . . Yes, undoubtedly, the pair of them would be off in the car to their Greatgran McBride's.

'No go, boss?'

Corny gave a huh! of a laugh as he turned to Jimmy and said, 'What do you think? Go down there and tell them you're going to smash it up and there'll be blue murder.'

'Well, what'll I do?' Jimmy was looking straight up into Corny's face, and Corny surveyed him for a full minute before answering, 'Well now, what would you like to do?'

On this question the corner of Jimmy's mouth was drawn in, and he looked downwards at his feet as if considering. Then, his eyes flicking upwards again, he glanced at Corny and they both laughed.

'Well, mind, just until the missus comes in. I'll give you the tip when I see her coming up the road, for she's threatened to leave me if she hears any more of your efforts.'

Jimmy's mouth split his face, and on a loud laugh, he said, 'Aw! I can see her doing that, boss. But ta, I'll stop the minute you give me the nod.'

Less than a minute later the too quiet air of the garage and the immediate vicinity was broken by the anguished, hesitant wails of the trombone.

The sound had no effect on Corny one way or the other. He had practised his cornet so much as a lad that he now seemed immune to the awful wailing wind practice evoked. Although when he stopped to think about it the boy was learning, and fast, in spite of the quivering screeches and wrong notes.

He was in the office again when he heard a car approaching the garage and almost instantly he was outside, rubbing his hands with a cloth as if he had just come off a grimy job. The car might pass, yet again it might stop. He had noticed before that the sight of someone about the place induced people to stop, but apparently this car needed no inducement, for it swirled on to the drive and braked almost at his feet.

Jimmy's American.

Corny recognised the Chevrolet and the driver, inasmuch as the latter's nationality was indicated by his dress, particularly his hat.

'Hello, there.' The man was getting out of the car.

'Good morning, sir.'

The man was tall, as tall as Corny himself, and broad with it. Like most Americans, he looked well dressed and, as Corny thought, finished off. He was a man who could have been forty, or fifty, there was no telling. He was clean-shaven, with deep brown eyes and a straight-lipped mouth. His face had an all-over pleasantness, and his manner was decidedly so. Without moving his feet he leaned his body back and looked up through the empty garage, and, his face slipping into a wide grin, he said, 'The youngster's at it again?'

'Oh yes. He's gone on the trombone. I let him have a go at it . . .' He just stopped himself from adding 'when we're not busy'. Instead he said, 'They're forming a new group and he's mad to learn.'

'He's not your boy?'

'Oh no. No.' Corny turned his head to one side, but his eyes still held those of the American. 'Give us a chance.'

'Of course, of course.' The American's hand came out and pushed him familiarly in the shoulder. 'You in your middle twenties I should say, and him nearing his twenties.' His laugh was deep now. 'You would have to have started early.'

'You're saying!'

'Well now.' He looked towards his car. 'I want it filled, and do you think you could give her a wash?'

'Certainly, sir.'

'Not very busy this morning?'

'No, not yet; it's early in the day. A lot of my customers work on a Saturday morning, you know, and they . . . they bring them in later.'

'Yes, yes.'

As Corny filled the tank with petrol the American walked to one end of the building, then to the other. He stood looking for a moment at the children climbing over the car. Then coming back, he walked into the empty garage, and when he came out again he stood at Corny's side and said, 'Happen you don't have a car for hire, do you?'

'No. No, sir. I'm sorry, I don't run hire cars.'

'It's a pity. I wanted this one looked over, I've been running her hard for weeks and I've got the idea she's blown a gasket. I'm staying in Newcastle, but I want a car to get me back and forwards until this one is put right . . . You've a car of your own, of course?'

'Only the old Rover, sir.'

'Oh, that one in there? She looks in spanking condition.' He walked away from Corny again and into the garage, and Corny, getting the hose to wash the Chevrolet down, thought, 'That's what I want, a car for hire. I've said it afore. Look what I'm losing now, and it isn't the first time.'

'Do you mind if I try her?'

'What's that, sir?' Corny went to the opening of the garage. The American had the Rover's door open and was bending forward examining her inside, and, straightening up, he called again, 'Do you mind if I try her?'

'Not in the least, sir. But she's an old car and everything will be different.'

The American had his back bent again, and he swung his head round to Corny and his mouth twisted as he said, 'I was in England during the war, and after, I bet I've driven her mother.'

They exchanged smiles, and then the American seated himself behind the wheel. 'Can I take her along the road?'

'Do as you like, sir.' Corny stood aside and looked at the man in the car as he handled the gear lever and moved his feet, getting the feel of her.

'OK?' He nodded towards Corny, and Corny

nodded back to him, saying, 'OK, sir,' and the next minute Fanny, as Mary Ann had christened the car after Mrs McBride, moved quietly out of the garage, and Corny watched the back of her disappearing down the road.

He would have to take her right to the end before he turned, he thought, but that bloke knew what he was doing, he was driving her as if along a white line. She looked good from the back, as she did from the front, dignified, solid. He wasn't ashamed of Fanny, not for himself he wasn't.

Well, he'd better get on cleaning this one down. He was a nice chap was the American. No big talk. Well, not as yet, but you could usually tell from the start . . . Lord, this was a car . . . and look at the boot, nearly as big as a Mini.

He had almost finished hosing the car down before the American returned. He brought the Rover on to the drive and, getting out, came towards Corny and said, 'You wouldn't think of letting her out for a day or two?'

'The Rover? To you?' Corny's mouth was slightly agape.

'Yes, she's a fine old girl. You wouldn't mind?'

'Mind? Why should I mind, when you are leaving this one?' He thumbed towards the Chevrolet.

'Yes, I see what you mean, but, you know, I consider that many a wreck of a Rover is a sight more reliable than some of the new models that are going about now.'

'You're right there, sir; you're right there.'

'Well then, if you would hire her to me you could go over this one.' He pointed towards his car.

'If it suits you, sir, it suits me.'

'That's settled then.'

An extra loud wail from Jimmy's trombone reverberated round the garage at this moment. It went high and shrill, then on a succession of stumbling notes fell away and left the American with his head back, his mouth wide open, and laughing heartily, very like, Corny thought, Mike laughed.

'You know.' He began to dry his eyes. 'I've thought a lot about that young chappie since I saw him last, and I always couple his face with the trombone . . . No offence meant. It's a kind of face that goes with a trombone, don't you think, long an' lugubrious.'

'Yes, I suppose so, looking at it like that.' Corny, too, was laughing.

'Will you stop that noise, Jimmy!'

The voice not only hit Jimmy, but startled the two men, and they turned and looked to where Mary Ann was standing at the far end of the garage. She had come in by the back door and the children were with her.

'Coo, Mrs Boyle, I thought you was out.'

'Which means I suppose that every time I leave the house you play that thing. Now I'm warning you, Jimmy, if I hear it again I'll take it from you and I'll put a hammer to it . . . Mind, I mean it.'

'Aw, Mrs Boyle . . .'

Mary Ann turned hastily away, taking the children with her, and Jimmy came slowly down the garage, the trombone dangling from his hand. The American began to chuckle. Then, looking at Corny, he said softly, 'That was Mrs Boyle?'

'You're right; that was Mrs Boyle,' said Corny, below his breath.

The American shook his head. 'She looks like a young girl, a young teenager, no more. But there's one thing sure, no matter what she looks like, she acts like a woman.'

'And you're right there, too, sir.' Corny jerked his head at the American. 'She acts like a woman all right, and all the time.'

The American laughed again; then said, 'Well now, about you letting me have your old girl. Oh, make no mistake about it, I'm referring to the car.' His head went back and again he was laughing, and Corny with him, while Jimmy stood looking at them both from inside the garage.

'It's up to you, sir.'

'All right, it's up to me, and I'll settle for a charge when I pick up my car. You won't be out of pocket, don't you worry. You won't know at this stage how long it's going to take you to do her, but I'll look in tomorrow, eh?'

'Do that, sir. If there's nothing very serious I should have her ready by then.'

'Oh, there's no hurry. I'll enjoy driving the old lady.'

'Corny.'

The American now looked over Corny's shoulder to where a petite young girl – this was how he saw Mary Ann – was standing at the door of the house. Corny, following the American's gaze, turned to see Mary Ann, and Mary Ann, her head drooping slightly, said quickly, 'Oh, I'm sorry, I didn't know you were busy. I just came to tell you . . .' Her voice trailed off.

The American was smiling towards Mary Ann,

and Corny, motioning towards her with his hand, said, 'This is my wife, sir.' Whereupon, with characteristic friendliness, the American held out his hand as he walked towards her, saying, 'The name's Blenkinsop.'

'How do you do, Mr Blenkinsop.' Mary Ann smiled up at the American and liked what she saw. And now Corny said, 'Mr Blenkinsop's taking our car for a day or so while I do his.'

'Our c . . . car?' Her mouth opened wide and she looked towards the Chevrolet. Then she turned her gaze towards Corny, and he said, 'Mr Blenkinsop knows she's an oldun but he's driven Rovers before.'

'Oh.' Mary Ann gave a small smile, but she still couldn't see how a man who drove this great chrome and cream machine could even bear to get into their old Rover.

At this moment Rose Mary and David put in an appearance. They came tearing out of the garage, and when they reached Mary Ann, Rose Mary didn't take in the presence of the American for a moment before she said, 'You wouldn't break up Jimmy's trombone, would you, Mam? I told him you were only funnin'.'

Mary Ann looked at the American; she looked at Corny; then, shaking her head, she looked at her daughter and said, 'I'm not funning, and you go back and tell Jimmy that I'm not funning.'

There was a pause before she added, 'He's practising the trombone and he makes a dreadful racket.' She was addressing the American now, and she was surprised when he let out a deep rumbling laugh as he said, 'I know.' Then, the smile slipping from his face, he asked her in all seriousness, 'You don't think he's funny?'

'Funny! Making that noise?' Mary Ann screwed up her face. 'No, I don't.'

'Well! Well! Well! It just goes to show. You know, Mrs Boyle, he's the only thing that's given me a belly laugh since I came to England. Plays, musical comedies, the lot, I've seen them all and I've never had a good laugh until I saw that boy's face as he sat blowing that trombone. As I was just saying to your husband, he's got a face for the trombone.'

Mary Ann smiled. She smiled with her mouth closed, and she looked at Corny as she did so. Then looking back at the American, she said, 'The difference is, you don't have to live above the racket.'

'I wouldn't mind.'

'You wouldn't?'

'No.'

'Well, there's a pair of you.' She nodded to Corny. 'He doesn't mind it at all, but I really can't stand it, it gets on my nerves.'

The American now lowered his head and moved it from side to side, looking at Corny as he remarked, 'It's as I said, she acts like a woman. They're unpredictable.' He turned his head now towards Mary Ann and smiled broadly, then added, 'Well now, I must be off. I've got a lunch appointment for one o'clock . . . Here.' He beckoned to the children. Then, putting his hand in his pocket and pulling out his wallet, he flicked a pound note from a bundle and handed it to Rose Mary, saying, 'Split that between you and get some pop and candy.'

'Oh, thank you.'

Before Rose Mary had finished speaking, Mary Ann said, 'Oh, sir, no; that's too much.' She took the note from Rose Mary, whose fingers were reluctant to release it, and she handed it back to Mr Blenkinsop, and he, his face looking blank, now asked rather sharply, 'What's the matter? Don't they have ice-creams or candies or such?'

'Yes, yes, but this is too—'

'Nonsense.' His tone was sharp, and he turned abruptly from her and, speaking to Corny in the same manner, he said, 'Well, I'll be off. See you tomorrow.'

Mr Blenkinsop got in the Rover and started her up; then, leaning out of the window, he said, 'How's she off for petrol?'

'She's full.'

'That's good. See you.'

'Yes. See you, sir.' Corny smiled at Mr Blenkinsop, then raised his hand and stood watching the car going down the road before turning to Mary Ann.

Mary Ann, with the pound note still in her hand, held it towards him, saying, 'He must be rolling, and he must be bats or a bit eccentric to go off in ours.'

'What do you mean, bats or a bit eccentric, there's nothing wrong with our car?'

'No, I'm not saying there is, but you know what I mean. Look at it compared with that.' She pointed to the Chevrolet.

'You're just going by externals. Let me tell you that the engine in the Rover will still be going when this one's on the scrap heap.'

'Yes, yes, I suppose so, but it's the looks of the

thing. Anyway,' she sighed, 'he seems a nice enough man.'

'Nice enough?' said Corny, walking towards the car. 'He's a godsend.'

'I wonder what he's doing round these parts,' said Mary Ann.

'I don't know,' said Corny, 'but I hope he stays.'

'Can we keep it, Mam?'

'What?' Mary Ann looked down at her daughter, then said, 'Oh yes. Yes, you may, but you're not going to spend it all, either of you. You can have half-a-crown each, and the rest goes in your boxes.'

'Oh, splash!' said Rose Mary. 'I know what I'm going to buy. Can we go into Felling this afternoon, Mam?'

'I suppose so.' Mary Ann turned abruptly towards Corny, saying, 'By the way, what did he mean, I act like a woman?'

Corny brought his head from under the bonnet of the car and, laughing towards her, said, 'He took you for a young girl, a real young girl, and then when he heard you going for Jimmy he said you acted like a woman.'

'Well, I should hope I do act like a woman. What did he expect me to act like, a chimpanzee?'

There was a splutter of a laugh from the garage doorway, and Mary Ann turned her head towards Jimmy. But she had to turn it away again quickly before she, too, laughed. It would never do to let Jimmy think she was softening up.

'Don't stand there with your mouth open.' Corny was shouting towards Jimmy now. 'We've got a job in.'

'That!' said Jimmy, moving slowly towards the big cream car. 'The American's?'

'Yes, the American's.'

'An' she's in for repair?'

'She's in for repair,' said Corny.

'And it all happened when you were concentrating on your trombone, Jimmy.' This last, said quietly, but with telling emphasis, was from Mary Ann, as she stood at the corner of the building, and, making a deep obeisance with her head, she moved slowly from their view.

Corny and Jimmy exchanged glances; then Jimmy, jerking his head upwards, muttered under his breath, 'It's as that American says, she acts like a woman, boss.'

'Go on, get on with it.'

And Jimmy got on with it. But after a while he said, 'You know what, boss? That has something.'

'What has?' asked Corny from where he was sitting in the pit under the car. 'What you talking about?'

'What the American said: she acts like a woman. It's a punch line, boss. Could make a pop Da-da-da-da-da-daa. She acts like a woo . . . man.' He sang the words, and Corny, stopping in the process of unscrewing a nut, closed his eyes, bit on his lip and grinned before bawling, 'I'll act like a man if I come up there to you. Get on with it.'

5

Mary Ann was sitting at the corner of her dressing-table. She had a pencil in her hand and a sheet of paper in front of her, and she sat looking through the curtains over the road in front of the garage, over the fence and to the far side of Weaver's field, where four men had been moving up and down for a long time, at least all the time she had been sitting here. The far side of Weaver's field was a long way off and she couldn't see what they were doing. But she wasn't very interested; they were only a focal point for her eyes, for her mind was on composing a song.

Last week, after the American had been and left his car, Corny had come upstairs and said, 'You know, Jimmy's all there, in this music line, I mean.' And she had turned on him scornfully, saying, 'Music line! You don't put the word music to the sounds he makes.' And to this he had replied, 'Well, he's got ideas. Things strike him that wouldn't strike me.'

'I should hope so,' she had said indignantly; then had added, 'He's a nice enough lad, but he's a nit-wit in some ways.'

'He's no nit-wit,' Corny had protested. 'You've

got him scared, and that's how he acts with you. You don't know Jimmy. I tell you he's a nice lad, and he's got it up top.'

'All right,' she had said. 'He's a nice lad, but what's struck him that's so brilliant?'

'The title of a song,' Corny had said. 'The Amer . . . Mr Blenkinsop said you acted like a woman, you remember? Well, Jimmy said it was a good title for a song, and the more I've been thinking about it the more I agree with him. She acts like a woman. It's like the titles they're having now, the things that are catching on and get into the Top Twenty. So why don't you have a shot at writing the lyrics?'

'What! Write lyrics to, She acts like a woman? Don't be silly.'

'Oh, all right, all right. It was only a suggestion. You're always talking about wishing you had something to do, something to occupy your mind at times. And I've told you you should take up your writing again now that you've got time on your hands, with them both away at school. Anyway it was just an idea. Take it or leave it.'

He had turned from her and stalked out, and she had looked at the door and exclaimed, 'She acts like a woman!' But the words had stuck with her and she had begun to think less scornfully about them when, following Mr Blenkinsop's return and his generous payment for the hire of the car and the repairs Corny had done, there had been no further work in of any sort for four days.

This morning, their Michael had brought the tractor over and ordered some spares, but they couldn't keep going on family support. It was this that prompted the thought, yet again: if only she could earn some money at home.

Years ago when Corny's hopes were sinking with regard to the prospect of the road, she had started to write furiously, sending off short stories and poems here and there, but they all found their way back to her with 'The editor regrets'. At the end of a year of hard trying she had to face up to the fact that they would have been better off if she hadn't tried at all, for she had spent much-needed money on postage, paper and a second-hand type-writer.

But this idea of writing ballads, not that she thought the words to some of the pop songs deserved the name of ballad, might have something in it. She had always been good at jingles. But that wasn't enough these days. For a song to really catch on it had to be, well, off-beat.

She had thought that if she could get the tune first she could put the words to it, so she had hummed herself dry for a couple of mornings until she realised that she wasn't any good at original tune building, because most of the songs she was singing in her head were snatches and mixtures of those she heard on the radio and television. So she decided that she would have to stick to the words, and for the last three days she had written hundreds of words, all unknown to Corny. Oh, she wasn't going to let him in on this, although he had given her the lead. She had her own ideas about what she was going to do.

She knew what she wanted. She wanted something with a meaning, something appertaining to life as it was lived to-day, something a bit larger than life, nothing milk and water, or soppy-doppy; that would never go down to-day. It must be virile and about love, and understandable to the teenager, and to her mother and grand-mother.

She had almost beaten her head against the wall and given up the whole thing, and then this morning, lying in bed, the words 'She acts like a woman' going over and over in her mind, there came to her an idea. But she couldn't do anything about it until she got Corny downstairs and the children out to play. Now she had con-veyed her idea in rough rhyme, and it read like this:

SHE ACTS LIKE A WOMAN

SHE ACTS LIKE A WOMAN.
Man, I'm telling you,
SHE ACTS LIKE A WOMAN.
She pelted me with everything,
And then she tore her hair.

SHE ACTS LIKE A WOMAN.
I'd given her my lot,
I was finished, broke,
And then she spoke of love,

SHE ACTS LIKE A WOMAN.
Me, she said,
Me, she wanted,
Not diamonds, mink, or drink,
SHE ACTS LIKE A WOMAN.

I just spread my hands,
What was I to do?
You tell me.
SHE ACTS LIKE A WOMAN.

Early morning, there she stood,
No make-up, face like mud,
And her big eyes raining tears,
And fears.
SHE ACTS LIKE A WOMAN.

Then something moved in here,
Like daylight,
And I could see,
She only wanted me.
SHE ACTS LIKE A WOMAN.

The lead singer would sing the verse, then the
rest of the group would come in with 'She acts
like a woman', and do those falsetto bits. Again
she read the words out aloud. As it stood, and for
what it was, it wasn't bad, she decided. But then,
it must have a tune and she wasn't going to send
it away to one of those music companies; they
might pinch the idea. These things happened. No,
it must be set to a tune first, and the only person
she could approach who dealt in tunes was . . .
Jimmy.

She didn't relish the idea of putting her plan to
Jimmy. Still, he was in a group and perhaps one of
them could knock up a tune. Of course, if they
made the tune up they'd have to share the profits.
Well, she supposed half a loaf was better than no
bread, and the way things were going down below
they'd be lucky if they got half a loaf.

She got slowly to her feet, still staring across the field. She could see her song in the Top Twenty. Young housewife makes the Pop grade, Mary Ann Boyle – she wished it could have been Shaughnessy – jumps from number 19 to number 4 . . . No, number 2, with her 'She acts like a woman'.

What were they doing over there, those men? Ploughing? Oh no; they could never grow anything in that field, it was full of boulders and outcrops of rock. Her mind, coming down from the heights of fame, concentrated now on the moving figures. What were they doing going up and down? Then screwing her eyes up and peering hard, she realised they were measuring something, measuring the ground.

She took the stairs two at a time.

'Corny! Corny!' She dashed into the office, only to find it empty, then ran into the garage, still calling, and Corny, from the top end, came towards her hurriedly, saying, 'What's up? What's up? The bairns?'

'No, no.' She shook her head vigorously. 'There's something going on in Weaver's field.'

'Going on? What?'

'I don't know. I saw them out of the bedroom window, men with a theodolite. They looked like surveyors measuring the ground.'

He stared down at her for a moment, then repeated her words again, 'Measuring the ground?'

'Yes. Come up and have a look.'

They both ran upstairs now and stood at the bedroom window, and after a moment Corny said, 'Aye, that's what they're doing all right. But it's yon side, and what for?'

'Perhaps they've been round this side and we

haven't heard them. They could have been, you know; they could have been at yon side of the hedge and we wouldn't have seen or heard them.'

'They could that,' said Corny. 'But why? . . . Anyway, whatever they're going to do, you bet your life they'll do at yon side, they wouldn't come over here.'

'Aw, don't sound like that.' She sought his hand and gripped it.

'Well, it always happens, doesn't it? Look at Riley. He's made a little packet out of the buildings going up at yon side, and he's got a new lot of pumps set up now. I actually see my hands turning green when I pass the place.'

She leant her head against him and remained quiet. She, too, turned green when she passed Riley's garage. His garage had been no better than theirs when he started, at least not as good – Riley never kept the place like Corny did – but because of a new estate over there and the factories sprouting up, he had got on like a house on fire. And now Riley acted as if he had been born to the purple; his wife had her own car, and the ordinary schools weren't good enough for the children; two of them were at the Convent, and the young one at a private school . . . Would they ever be able to send Rose Mary to the Convent and David . . . ? Her thinking stopped as to where they would send David, and, straightening herself abruptly, she said, 'Why don't you take a run round that way and make a few enquiries?'

'It's not a bad idea. But no matter what I find out it won't be that they're going to build this end of the field, for this part's so rock-strewn it even frightens off the speculators.'

'Well, go and see.'

'Aye, yes, there's no harm in having a look.'

He was on the point of turning away from her when he paused, and, gripping her chin in his big hand, he bent down and kissed her, then hurried out of the room.

Mary Ann didn't follow him. There had been a sadness about the kiss and she wanted to cry. The kiss had said, 'I'm sorry for the way things have turned out, that my dream was a bubble. I'm sorry for all the things I've deprived you of, I'm sorry for you having to put on that don't-care attitude, and this is the way I want it, when you go to the farm.'

'Blast! blast!' The ghost of the old impatient, demanding, I'll-fix-it Mary Ann, came surging up, and she beat the flat of her hand on the dressing-table. Why? Why? He worked like a trojan, he tried every avenue, he was honest . . . perhaps too honest. But could you be too honest? There was more fiddling in cars than there was in the Hallé Orchestra, and he could have been in on that lucrative racket. Three times he had been approached last year, and from different sources, but he would have none of it. You're a mug, they had said. He had nearly hit one of them who wanted to rent 'this forgotten dump', as he had called it, for a place to transform his stolen cars.

Slowly now, she picked up the paper on which she had been writing from the dressing-table. In the excitement of the moment she had forgotten about it. It was a wonder Corny hadn't seen it. At one time he always picked up the pieces of paper lying around, knowing that she had been scribbling.

She heard the Rover start up and saw Corny driving into the lane. After the car had disappeared from view she looked at the sheet of paper in her hand. This would be a good opportunity to tackle Jimmy and see what he thought about the idea.

She was halfway across the room when she stopped. Would he think she was daft? Well, the only way to find out would be to show him what she had written, and she'd better do it now, for Corny wouldn't be long away.

She ran down the back stairs, and when she reached the yard she saw, over the low wall, the children playing in the old car. She waved to them, but they were too engrossed to notice her. She went through the gate, down the path between the beans and potatoes, over a piece of rough ground, to the small door that led into the garage.

'Jimmy!'

Jimmy was sitting on an upturned drum, stranding a length of wire. He raised his head and looked towards her, and said, 'Aye, Mrs Boyle.' Then he threw down the wire and came hurrying to her. He liked the boss's wife, although at times when she had her dander up she scared him a bit, but they got on fine. That was until he started practising. Still, he understood, 'cos his mother was the same. She was good-hearted, was the boss's wife, not stingy on the grub. He wished his mother cooked like she did. Cor, the stuff his mother hashed up . . .

'Aye, Mrs Boyle, you want me?' He smiled broadly at her.

Mary Ann smiled back at him, and she

swallowed twice before she said, 'I'd like your advice on something, Jimmy.'

'. . . My advice, Mrs . . .'

'Yes. Yes.' She shook her head, and her smile widened. 'And don't look so surprised.' They both laughed sheepishly now, and Mary Ann, taking the folded sheet of paper from her apron pocket, said, in a voice that held a warning, 'Now, don't you make game, Jimmy, at what I'm going to tell you, but . . . but I've written some words for a song.'

She watched Jimmy's long face stretch to an even longer length, and, perhaps because of the tone of her voice, all he said was, 'Aye.' He knew she wrote things, the boss had told him, the boss said she was good at it, but a song. He never imagined her writing a song. He thought she was against pop. He said quickly now, 'Pop? Pop, is it?'

'Well, sort of. I wondered what you would think of it. Whether you would think it was worth setting to a tune. You know what I mean.'

'Aye, aye.' He nodded, then held out his hand, and she placed the sheet of paper in it.

'She acts like a woman. Coo! 'cos I said that?' He dug his finger towards the paper. ' 'Cos I said that was a good title you've made this up?' He sounded excited; he looked excited; his large mouth was showing all his uneven teeth.

'Yes.' She nodded at him. 'Mr Boyle' – she always gave Corny his title when speaking to his employee – 'Mr Boyle thought it was a very good title.'

'Aye, I think it is an' all, but . . . but you know, it wasn't me who said it in the first place, it was that American, and it just struck me like . . .'

Time was going on and she didn't want Corny to come back while they were talking. 'Read it,' she said. She watched Jimmy's eyebrows move upwards as his eyes flicked over the lines, and at one stage he flashed her a look and a wide grin.

When his eyes reached the bottom of the page he took them to the top again and said slowly, 'She acts like a woman.'

'Well, what do you think?'

'Ee! I think it's great. It's got it, you know, the kind they want. Could I take it and show it to Duke? He's the one that got our group up. He's good at tunes. He can read music an' all; he learned the piano from when he was six. I'll swear he'll like this, 'cos it's got the bull-itch.'

Mary Ann opened her mouth and closed it again before she repeated, 'Bull-itch? What do you mean, bull-itch?'

'Well, you know.' Jimmy tossed his head. 'A girl after a fellow.'

'Oh, Jimmy.'

'Well, that's what they say, Mrs Boyle. When it's t'other way round they call it the bitchy-itch, an' this 'as really got both.'

'Oh, Jimmy. And you think that the words give that impression?'

'Oh aye. An' they're great. But I didn't know you wrote this stuff, Mrs Boyle. I bet Duke'll make somethin' of it.'

'Oh, if only he could, Jimmy. And then we'll get together and see about getting it recorded and trying for the Top Twenty.'

She could have sworn that Jimmy's face

dropped half its length again. 'Top Twenty?' His voice was high in his head. 'But, Mrs Boyle, you don't get into the Top Twenty unless you've got a manager and things, like the Beatles, and we're just startin' so to speak. Well, I mean, I am; I'm the worst, among the players, that is.' He lowered his head.

'What do the others do?' asked Mary Ann, flatly now.

'Well, Duke can play most things a bit; Barny, he plays the drums; and Poodle, he's best on the cornet. But he's on the flute now, and Dave has the guitar.'

'What do you call yourselves?' asked Mary Ann.

'Oh, nowt yet. We've been thinkin' about it, but we've not come up with anythin' yet, not anythin' catchy. You want somethin' different, you do, don't you?'

'Yes,' said Mary Ann. 'I'll think up something.'

'Aw.' Jimmy's face was straight now. 'Duke'll want to see to that; he's good on thinkin' up titles and things.'

There was a pause; then Mary Ann said, 'You'll have to bring Duke along to see me.'

'Aye, I will,' said Jimmy. 'He'll be tickled, I think.'

'Jimmy.'

'Aye, Mrs Boyle.'

'I don't want you to say anything to Mr Boyle about this.'

'No?'

'No. It might come to nothing, you see.'

Jimmy looked puzzled, then said, 'Well, even if it doesn't, it'll still be a bit of fun.'

Mary Ann wanted to say that at this stage she wasn't out for fun, she was out for money, but she was afraid Jimmy wouldn't understand, so all she said was, 'Don't speak of it to Mr Boyle till I tell you, will you not?'

'OK, Mrs Boyle, just as you say.'

'And when you bring Duke along, tell him not to say anything either.'

'Will do, Mrs Boyle, will do.'

'Thanks, Jimmy.' She smiled at him. And he smiled at her; then watched her go out through the little door.

Well, would you believe that, her writin' things like that. He looked down at the paper and read under his breath: 'I'd given her my lot. I was finished, broke and then she spoke of love. She acts like a woman.' He lifted his head and looked towards the door again. It was as Duke was always sayin', you never could tell . . .

6

Rose Mary, from her position on top of the car, saw her mother come out of the garage and go into their back yard, and she called to her 'O-Oo, Mam!' but her mother didn't turn round. Perhaps she hadn't called loud enough.

Oh, it was hot. She clambered down from the roof, saying to David, 'I'm going to lie in the grass, it's too hot. Come on.'

When they were both lying in the grass, she said, 'I wish we could go to the sands at Shields. If Greatgran McBride lived in Shields instead of Greatgran McMullen we would go more often. I don't like Greatgran McMullen, do you?' She turned her head and looked at David, and David, looking skywards, shook his head.

She wished it wasn't so hot; she wished she had an ice-cream. She wished they could go on a holiday. Peter had gone on a holiday. He was going to come and play with them when he came back, but that would be a long time, nearly three weeks. He had said the other day that he would rather stay here and play on the car. He liked playing with them . . . Oh, it was hot. They had only broken up for the holidays three days ago and she wished she was back at school . . . No, she didn't, 'cos last week had been awful. Miss Plum had been awful right from the Monday following the Sunday when she had taken their David to sit beside her. Nothing had gone right from then. And Father Carey had messed things up an' all. She had gone to school on the Monday knowing that something would happen because Father Carey was a good pray-er. And things did happen, but not the way she wanted them to, because they had hardly got in the classroom before Miss Plum collared their David and put him in the front seat right under her nose, and David didn't let a squeak out of him. He usually squawked when anybody took him away from her, but he didn't squawk at Miss Plum. She waited all morning for him to squawk, or do something. It was nearly dinner-time before she realised that Miss Plum had got at Father Carey before she had, and that he was doing it her way.

Oh, it was hot. Oh, it was. And she hated Miss Plum, oh, she did. And she didn't like Father Carey very much either. Ee! She would get wrong for thinking like that. Well, she couldn't help it. She had thought it without thinkin'. And she hadn't made her first confession yet, so she wouldn't have to tell it, so that was all right.

Her mam said when she was a little girl she took all her troubles to Father Owen and he sorted them out for her. She wished she could go and see Father Owen, but he lived far away in Jarrow.

Aw, it was hot.

'Come on.' She pulled herself up and put out her hand. 'I'm goin' in for a drink.'

She was too hot to do any shouting on the back stairs, and she was in the kitchen before she opened her mouth. And then she closed it quickly because her ma and da were talking, dark talking. She knew she hadn't to interrupt when they were dark talking. They dark talked at night-time when she was in bed, and if she tried hard enough she could hear what they said. Usually, it made her sad, or just sorry like. And now the tones of their voices told her they were dark talking again. Her ma looked sad and her da's face was straight, and her da was saying, 'Sort of winded me like, to see him sitting there talking to Riley and the car standing near the pumps. I thought he liked what I did to the car and I just charged him the minimum. I didn't put a penny extra on because he was an American, and he seemed over the moon at the time. But that's over a week ago; and when he didn't show up this week I thought he had gone on. But there he was, at Riley's garage.'

Rose Mary watched her mother look down towards her feet, and she wanted to say to her, 'Can I have a drink, Mam?' But she didn't, 'cos her mam was taking no notice of her.

'What's he doing in these parts, anyway?' said Mary Ann now.

'I don't know, I didn't like to probe. And a funny thing, unless I'm vastly mistaken, the car he had to-day, although it was a cream one, wasn't the same one as he brought here the other day.'

'But he can't have two cars like that?'

'A fellow like him could have three, or half-a-dozen.'

'But how could you tell the difference when you were just passing?'

'Oh, you notice things quick when you're deal-ing with cars. This one hadn't so much chrome on, but it was as big. I noticed, too, that the boot was open a bit and the end of a long, narrow case was sticking out, like the end of a golf bag, only it couldn't have been a golf bag 'cos that boot would take ten golf bags. Anyway, it looked chock-a-block, as if he was all packed up to go . . . so, that's that.'

'And you didn't find out about the men in the field?'

'No, I stopped before I got to Riley's and tried to find a place over the hedge to look through, but it's a tangled mess down there. But I did ask a scavenger, but he could tell me nothing. And well, after I passed the garage I didn't bother, the wind seemed knocked out of me. It was a funny feeling. I mean about the American. I really thought as long as he was in these parts he would come here.'

The silence that fell on the kitchen was too much for Rose Mary, and besides she had that sorry feeling seeing her dad and her mam with their heads bent and she wanted to cry. She said softly, 'We're dry, Mam; can we have a fizzy drink? Lemon?'

'What? Oh yes. Just a minute.' Mary Ann turned away and went into the scullery, and Rose Mary went and stood close against her father's leg, and, taking his limp fingers in hers, she looked up at him, and said, 'I hate that American.'

'Rose Mary!' His voice was sharp now. 'You're not to say such things. Mr Blenkinsop was very kind to you.'

'Well, I don't want him to be kind, I hate him. An' David hates him an' all. Don't you, David?'

She looked to where David was stretched out on the floor, and David turned his head lazily towards her and moved it downwards.

'Stop it!' Corny now bent down, and his face close to hers, he said, 'Now look, Rose Mary. You don't have to hate everybody that doesn't do what you want them to do, understand? And David doesn't hate the . . . Mr Blenkinsop. Who bought you the ice-cream and lollies last week? Mr Blenkinsop gave you that money, and don't forget it.'

There came to them now a distant tingling sound, and Mary Ann called from the scullery, 'That's the phone, I think.' And when she came into the kitchen with the two glasses of fizzy lemon water, Corny was gone. As she handed one glass to Rose Mary and one to David, Rose Mary said, 'I do hate that American.'

'You heard what your father said to you, didn't you?'

'Well, he's buying his petrol from Riley's.'

'He can buy his petrol anywhere he likes.'

'Our petrol's better than Riley's.'

Mary Ann closed her eyes and turned away.

'It is.'

'Rose Mary!'

'If I had that pound note I'd give it him back.'

'Rose Mary!'

'Mary Ann!'

Hearing Corny's voice calling up the front stairs, Mary Ann hurried out of the room and on to the landing, and, looking down at him, she said, 'What is it?'

'Prepare yourself.'

'What's happened? What's the matter now?'

'Michael's just phoned. Your grannie's on her way here.'

'Me grannie coming here!'

'So Michael thinks.'

'But why? Is she at the farm?'

'No, she was there on Sunday. But Michael was driving back from Jarrow and at the traffic lights he happened to glance up at the bus, and there she was sitting, and, as he said, you couldn't mistake the old girl. Busby an' all.'

'But how does he know she's coming here?'

'Well, she was on the Gateshead bus, and she doesn't get that one to go to the farm, so he put two and two together and got off at the first telephone box and broke the news. He thought you would like to be prepared.'

'Oh no. I only wanted this . . . But why is she coming, and at this time in the day? It must be two years since she was here.'

'Well, get the bairns changed.' Corny's voice was soft now, soothing. 'And put your armour on, and smile.'

'Aw, Corny.' Mary Ann's voice, too, was low, but it had a desperate sound. Her grannie. The last person she wanted to see at any time. 'Corny, look.' Her voice was rapid. 'What about me taking them out for the day? You could tell her we've gone to the sands.'

'It's no use. From the time Michael phoned, the bus could be at the bottom of the road by now, and you could just run into her, even if you were ready . . . Stick it out; you're a match for her.'

'Not any longer, I haven't got the energy.'

'Wait till you see her, it'll inject you with new life.' He smiled up at her, then turned away, and she stood for a moment looking down the stairs, before moving swiftly back in the room.

'Hurry up and finish your drinks,' she said, 'and come on into the bathroom.'

'We goin' to have a bath again, Mam? We had one last—'

'I only want you to wash your face and hands and put on your blue print, the one with the smocking.'

'We going to the sands?'

'No.' Mary Ann called now from the landing. 'Your great-gran's coming.'

'Me great-gran?' Rose Mary was running out of the room on to the landing, and David was behind her now. 'Which one?'

'McMullen.'

'Aw, not her, Mam.'

'Yes, her. Come on now.' Mary Ann pulled them both into the bathroom. 'Get your things off and you wash your face and hands, I'll see to David.'

David had never been washed and changed so rapidly in his life. When he was attired in clean pants and tee-shirt he stood watching his mother jumping out of one dress into another, and then, with Rose Mary, he was hustled back into the living-room and ordered to sit. He sat, and Rose Mary sat, and while they waited they watched their mother flying round the room, pushing their toys into the bottom of the cupboard, tidying up the magazines, putting a bit of polish on the table, even rubbing a wash leather over the lower panes of the window, and she had only cleaned the window yesterday. At last Rose Mary was forced to volunteer, 'Perhaps she's fallen down, Mam?'

Oh, if only she had. Mary Ann groaned inside. If only she had fallen into the ditch and broken her leg. How gladly she would call the ambulance and see her whisked away. But her grannie wouldn't fall into a ditch and break her leg. Nothing adverse would happen to her grannie; her grannie would live to torment her family until she was a hundred, perhaps a hundred and ten. She could never see her grannie dying. Her grannie was like all the evil in the world. As long as there were people there would be evil. As long as there was a Shaughnessy left there would be Grannie McMullen to torment them.

'Mary Ann! You've got a visitor.' It was Corny's voice from the bottom of the stairs, and Mary Ann, turning about, walked across the room. But she paused near Rose Mary's chair to say, 'Now mind, behave yourself. I don't want any repeat of that Sunday at the farm. You remember?'

Her words were like an echo from the past, like an echo of Lizzie saying to her, 'Now mind yourself, don't cheek your grannie, I'm warning you.' She opened the door and went on to the landing and said, 'Who is it?' Then she made a suitable pause before adding, 'Oh, hello, Gran.'

Mrs McMullen was coming unassisted up the steep stairs, and when she reached the top she stood panting slightly, looking at Mary Ann, and Mary Ann looked at her.

Ever since she first remembered seeing her grannie she hadn't seemed to change by one wrinkle or hair. Her hair was still black and abundant, and as always supported a large hat, a black straw to-day. Her small, dark eyes still held their calculating devilish gleam. The skin of her face was covered with the tracery of lines not detectable unless under close scrutiny, so she looked much younger than her seventy-six years. She was wearing this morning an up-to-date light-weight grey check coat which yelled aloud in comparison to the hair style and hat adorning it.

'It's warm to-day,' said Mary Ann.

'Warm! It's bakin', if you ask me. And the walk from the bus doesn't make it any better. I would have thought that after being stuck miles from civilisation afore you married you would have plumped for some place nearer the town. But I suppose beggars can't be choosers . . . Aw, let me sit down, off me feet.'

'Let your grannie sit down.' Mary Ann was nodding towards Rose Mary, and Rose Mary, sliding off the dining-room chair, stood to one side, and as Mary Ann watched her grannie seat herself she thought, 'Beggars can't be choosers. Oh, what I'd like to say to her.'

'I'll get you a cup of tea.' Mary Ann moved towards the scullery now, and Mrs McMullen, without turning her head, said, 'There's time enough for that; I'll have something cold if it's not too much trouble . . . Well now.' Mrs McMullen put her hands up slowly to her hat and withdrew the pin, and as she did so she looked at the children. First at Rose Mary, then at David, then to Rose Mary again, and she said, 'You underweight?'

'What?'

Rose Mary screwed up her face at her great-grandmother.

'I said are you underweight? And don't say "What?" Say, "What, Great-gran?" Do you get weighed at school?'

'Yes.'

'Didn't they tell you you were underweight?'

'No . . . no, Great-gran.'

'Well, if my eyes don't deceive me, that's what they should have done.'

'I've brought you a lemon drink.'

'Oh . . . thanks. I was just saying to her' – Mrs McMullen nodded to her great-grandchild – 'she looks underweight. Anything wrong with her?'

'No, no, nothing. She's as healthy as an ox.' Mary Ann was determined that nothing that this old devil said would make her rise.

She watched the old woman take a long drink from the glass, then put her hand in her pocket and bring out a folded white handkerchief with which she wiped her mouth. And then she watched her turn her attention to David. 'Hello there,' she said.

David looked back at this funny old woman. He looked deep into her eyes, and his own darkened and he grinned. He grinned widely at her.

'He not talking yet?'

Mary Ann hesitated for a long moment before saying, 'He's making progress.'

'Is he talking or isn't he?'

Steady, steady. Metaphorically speaking, Mary Ann gripped her own shoulder. 'He can say certain words. The teacher's very pleased with him, isn't she, Rose Mary?'

'Yes, yes, he's Miss Plum's favourite. She takes him to the front of the class and she pins up his drawings.'

'They only have to do that with idiots.'

The words had been muttered below her breath but they were clear to Mary Ann, if not to the children. As Rose Mary asked, 'What did you say, Great-gran?' Mary Ann had to turn away. She went into the scullery, and as her mother had done many many times in her life, and for the same reason, she stood leaning against the draining-board gripping its edge. She longed, in this moment, for Lizzie's support, and she realised that this was only the second time that she had battled with her grannie on her own; there had always been someone to check her tongue, or even her hand. On her grannie's only other visit here two years ago, she'd had the support of their Michael and Sarah, but now she was on her own, and she didn't trust herself. How long would she stay? Would she stay for dinner? Very likely. But Corny would be here then, and Corny could manage her somehow. She had found she couldn't rile him, consequently she didn't get at him. She was even pleasant to him; the nasty things she had to say she said behind his back.

She almost jumped back into the kitchen as she heard her grannie say, 'Be quiet, child. Give him a chance, let him answer for himself.'

'I was only sayin' —'

'I know what you were saying.' Mrs McMullen now turned her head up towards Mary Ann. 'This one' – she thumbed Rose Mary – 'is the spit of you, you know, she doesn't know when to stop. I don't think you'll get him talkin' as long as he's got the answers ready made for him.'

Mary Ann forced herself not to bow her head,

and not to lower her eyes from her grannie's. It was galling to think that this dreadful old woman was advocating the same remedy for David's impediment as Corny and her mother. Mrs McMullen now turned her eyes away from Mary Ann, saying with a sigh, 'Aw well, it's your own business. And you'd never take advice, as long as I can remember . . . I think I'll take me coat off, it's enough to roast you in here. I'd open the window.'

'The window's open.' Mary Ann took her grannie's coat and went out of the rom with it, and laid it on the bed in the bedroom. And now she stood leaning against the bed-rail trying to calm herself before returning to the room. The old devil, the wicked old devil. And she was wicked – vicious and wicked. On the bedroom chimney-breast hung a portrait of Corny and her on their wedding day, and her mind was lifted to the moment when they were walking down from the altar and her grannie stole the picture by falling into the aisle in a faint; and in that moment, that wonderful, wonderful moment when all her feelings should have been good, and her thoughts even holy, she had wished, as she saw them carrying her grannie away down the aisle, that she'd peg out. Yes, such was the effect her grannie had on her that on the altar steps she had wished a thing like that.

When she returned to the kitchen it was to hear Mrs McMullen saying to Rose Mary, 'But how many in a week, how many cars does he work on in a week?' and Rose Mary replying, 'Oh, lots, dozens.'

'Does he get much work in?' Mrs McMullen's

gimlet eyes met Mary Ann's as she came across the room.

'Who? Corny?' Her voice was high, airy. 'Oh yes, he gets plenty of work in.'

'Well!' The word was said on a long, exhaling breath. 'It must be his off time, for what I could see when I passed the garage was space, empty space, and the floor as clean as a whistle . . . Why doesn't he sell up? I heard your father on about him having an offer.'

'Oh yes, yes, he's had offers, but he doesn't want to sell up, we're quite content here.'

Her da on about them having an offer. Her grannie must have been saying something to her mother and her da had made it up on the spur of the moment about them having an offer. That's what he would do. Good for her da.

Mary Ann said now, as she brought the tray to the delf-rack and took down some cups and saucers, 'We did consider one offer we had, but then it's so good for the children out here, plenty of fresh air and space, and the house is comfortable.'

'You can't live on fresh air and space. As for comfort . . .' Mrs McMullen looked round the room. 'You want something bigger than this with them growing, you couldn't swing a cat in it.'

'Well, we don't happen to have a . . .' Mary Ann abruptly checked her words, and, so hard did she grip the cup in her hand that she wouldn't have been surprised if it had splintered into fragments. There, her grannie had won. She put the sugar basin and milk jug quietly on to the tray and took it to the table under the window before saying, 'It suits us. I'm happy here. We're all happy here.'

'Your mother doesn't seem to think so.'

'What!' Mary Ann swung round and looked at the back of her grannie's head. 'My mother would never say I was unhappy. She couldn't say it, because I'm not unhappy.'

'She doesn't have to say it. She happens to be my daughter, I know what she's thinking, I know how she views the set-up.'

Mary Ann again went into the scullery and again she was holding the draining-board, and she bit on her lip now, almost drawing blood. It was at this moment that Rose Mary joined her and, clutching her dress at the waist, she looked up at her. Her ma was upset, her ma was nearly crying. She hated her great-gran, she was an awful great-gran. She whispered now, brokenly, 'Don't cry Mam. Aw, don't cry, Mam.'

'I'm not crying.' Mary Ann had brought her face down to her daughter's as she whispered, 'Go back into the room and be nice. Go on. Go on now for me.'

'Aw, but, Mam.'

'Go on.'

Rose Mary dutifully went into the room and took her seat again, but she did not look at her great-grandmother.

'What are you doing at school?'

When silence greeted Mrs McMullen's question, David turned his bright gaze on his sister, and when she didn't answer he moved quickly to her and shook her arm, and for the first time in her life she pushed off his hand, and Mrs McMullen, quick to notice the action, said, 'You needn't be nasty to him, he was only telling you to answer in the only way he knew.'

Now Rose Mary was looking at her great-grandmother and, the spirit of her mother rising in her, she said, 'I don't like you.'

'Ah-ha! Here we go again, another generation of 'em. So you don't like me? Well, I'll not lose any sleep over that.'

'I like me Great-gran McBride.'

Mrs McMullen's face darkened visibly. 'Oh, you do, do you? And I hope you like her beautiful house, and her smell.'

'Yes, yes, I do. And David does an' all. We like goin' there, I'd go there all the time. I like me Great-gran McBride.'

'Rose Mary!' Mary Ann was speaking quietly from the scullery door, and Rose Mary, now unable to control her tears, slid to her feet, crying, 'Well, I do like me Great-gran McBride, I do, Mam. You know I do.'

'Yes, I know, but now be quiet. Behave yourself, and stop it.'

'I don't like her, I don't, Mam.' Rose Mary, her arm outstretched, was pointing at Mrs McMullen.

'Rose Mary!' As Mary Ann advanced towards her, Rose Mary backed towards the door staring at her great-grandmother all the while, and as she groped behind her and found the handle she bounced her head towards the old lady, saying, 'I'll never like you 'cos you're nasty.' Then, turning about, she ran out of the room and down the stairs.

She'd find her dad, she would, and tell him. Her great-gran was awful, she was a pig, she'd made her mam cry, she'd tell her dad and he would go up and give her one for making her mam cry.

She ran to the garage, but she couldn't see her dad. But through the tears she saw a big car standing in the mouth of the garage and another car at the top end with Jimmy working on it. She ran out of the garage again and went towards the office, but she stopped just outside the door. Somebody was talking to her dad, and she recognised his voice. It was that nasty American who bought his petrol from Riley's.

'Rose Mary!' It was her mother's voice coming from the stairs. She looked round before running again. She wasn't going to go upstairs and sit with her great-gran, she wasn't. She hated her great-gran. She would hide. Yes, that's what she would do, she would hide. She looked wildly round her. And then she saw a good hiding-place and darted towards it . . .

7

In the office, Corny leant against his desk, mostly for support, as he stared down at the American sitting in the one seat provided. 'I can't quite take it in,' he said.

Mr Blenkinsop smiled with one corner of his mouth higher than the other. 'Give yourself time,' he replied. 'Give yourself time.'

'May I ask what made you change your mind, I mean to build your factory at this side instead of yon side?'

'You may, and I'll tell you. But it won't do you any good. I mean it won't help you any further, for you've already reached the stage when you know that it's best in the long run to play fair.'

Corny screwed up his eyes as he surveyed Mr Blenkinsop. He had always played fair in business, but he wondered where he came in the American's plan in this line, but he waited.

'As I told you, my father built up Blenkinsop's from making boxes in a house yard, with my three brothers and six sisters all rounded up to help in the process, cutting, nailing, getting orders, delivering. It was before the last war and things were bad. I was just a youngster, but my father thought I had what it took to sell, and so I was put on to do the rounds going from door to door in the better-class neighbourhood of our town, showing them samples of our fancy-made boxes to put their Christmas presents in, the kind of presents that we kids only dreamed of. From the beginning it was, as our father said, small profit and quick return. "Put into your work", he said, "more than you expect to get back in clear cash and the profits will mount up for you." You know, that took a bit of working out to us boys whose only thought was to make money, and fast, but after a time we understood that if you make your product good enough it will sell itself a thousandfold, and in the end your profits will be high . . . Well, after the war the business went like a house on fire. We were all in it, those of us who were left. Three died in the war, my three brothers, but the girls and their husbands still carry on their end of it, and our father's maxim still holds good.'

Corny shook his head, but he still did not quite follow, and the American knew this, and he lit a cigarette and offered Corny one before he went on, 'It's like this. I have two cars. I brought one to you, and I took one to Mr Riley. I knew exactly what was wrong with each; in fact, the same was wrong in both cases. Mr Riley charged me almost fifty per cent more than you did, and he bodged the job, at least his mechanics did. I guessed he'd put on twenty per cent in any case, me being an American and rolling. They think we are all rolling. But to pile on fifty per cent . . . Oh no. No. So I made a call on Mr Riley this morning and told him I thought he had slightly overcharged me. He was, what you call, I think, shirty. In any case, Mr Riley thought he'd got it all in the pan. He knew I had bought this whole piece of land a month ago, and as he said, only a fool would think of building this end, for just look at the stuff they would have to move, rock going deep. Well, he got a little surprise this morning when I told him it was on this end I had decided to put my factory, at least the main gates of it. My storehouses will now back on to the far road, there will be main gates leading to the main road, and another at the far end of this road leading to your Gateshead, but I'm putting my main building towards the end of your road, here . . . Oh no' – he raised his hand and waved it back and forward – 'not entirely to help you, but because it is advantageous, as I see it, to my plan. As I've told you, seeing the material we're dealing with I don't want petrol stores too near to the works, but I want them near enough to be convenient for the lorries and cars, and from the first I saw I had the choice of two petrol stations, and I've made it. The fifty per cent supercharge finally decided me which of the two men I preferred to deal with. That's how I do business. I look over the ground first – panning for gold dust my father used to call it. Always look for the gold and the dirt will drop through the riddle, he would say . . . Well.' Mr Blenkinsop surveyed Corny. 'There it is.'

'Well, sir, I'm . . . flabbergasted.'

'Oh.' The American put his head back. 'That's a wonderful word, flabbergasted.' He rose to his feet. 'We'll do business together, young man.' He put his hand on Corny's shoulder, much as a father would, and said quietly, 'You leave this to me now. You'll need money for more pumps; we'll want a lot of petrol because our fleet of lorries won't be small. There'll be a great many private cars, too, as nearly all the workers in England have cars now; it isn't an American prerogative any longer.' He smiled. 'How much land did you say you had to the side of you, I mean your own?'

'Just over three-quarters of an acre. It runs back for about four hundred feet though; it's a narrow strip.'

'Good, you'll need every bit of it. You'll want workshops and a place for garaging cars. That's a good idea.' He made for the door now. Then, turning abruptly, he said, 'What's kept you here for seven years, in this dead end?'

'Hope. Hoping for the road going through; hoping for a day like this . . . someone like you, sir.'

'Well, all I can say is that I admire your tenacity; it would have daunted many a stronger man. You know, you with your knowledge of cars would likely have made a much better living working in one of the big garages.'

'I know that, sir, but I've always wanted to be my own boss.'

The American surveyed him with a long, penetrating glance, then, punching him gently on the shoulder, he said, 'You'll always be your own boss, son. Never you fear that. But now . . .' He stepped out of the door, saying, 'I've got a mixed weekend before me, business and pleasure. I'm off to Doncaster to see a cousin of mine, who'll be on the board of the new concern. Also, I hope to persuade him to be my general manager. I should be back on Monday, and then we will get round the table and talk about ways and means.' He took two steps forward and half-glanced over his shoulder and said, 'You wouldn't like me to buy you out?'

Corny stopped behind him. He could see only a part of the American's profile; he didn't know what expression was on his face, whether this was a test or not; but he said immediately, 'No, sir, I wouldn't like you to buy me out. I don't want anybody to buy me out; I want to work my business up.'

'Good.' Mr Blenkinsop moved on again towards the garage, saying, 'And I haven't the slightest doubt that our arrangement will go well.'

'Nor me, sir. I've always liked working with Americans.'

Mr Blenkinsop stopped and turned fully round now. 'You've worked with Americans before?'

'Yes, I was in America for close on a year, just outside New York.'

'Well, I'll be jiggered. And you never opened your mouth about it?'

'Well, sir, I didn't think it would be of any interest to you; you must meet thousands of people who have been in America.'

'Yes, and they always start by telling me just that. What were you doing over there?'

'Oh, I first of all worked on the ground floor in Flavors.'

'Flavors! The car people?'

'Yes. And then I did a bit in the office, and got into the showrooms.'

'All in under a year?' Mr Blenkinsop's eyes were

now slits of disbelief, and Corny, lowering his head, said, 'It was influence, sir.'

'Ah! Ah! I see. But why didn't you stay on?'

'Well, just as I said a minute ago, I wanted to be me own boss, go on my own road. I wouldn't turn down help, but I didn't want to be carried, and in this particular case I wasn't being carried for meself; it was . . . well, it's a long story, sir, but it was because of my wife. There's an old gentleman – he's the owner of the farm her father manages. He's very fond of her, and between you and me he wanted to get me out of her way; he had other ideas for her.'

The American's head went back and he let out a bellow of a laugh. 'And you beat him to it by coming back. Good for you. You know' – his chin was forward once more – 'I wouldn't like to come up against you in a fight, business or otherwise. I've an idea I'd lose.'

'Aw, sir.' Corny, laughing too, now, moved his head from side to side.

'Well, anyway, I'm glad to know you've been to America. But tell me, did you like it there?'

'Oh yes, sir. I liked it, and the people, but I was missing Mary Ann . . . my wife.'

'The one that acts like a woman?' Again there was laughter. 'Well, you did right to come back. Now I'd better be off. And you go and tell your wife the good news . . . Well, I hope you consider it good news.'

Corny opened the car door for Mr Blenkinsop. Then, closing it, and bending down, he said, 'Quite truthfully, sir, I'm dazed.'

'You won't remain in that state long. I'm speaking from experience. You'll take the breaks good and bad, in your stride. You'll see.' They smiled at each other. Corny straightened up, then watched the car backing out of the garage. He followed it as it turned out of the drive, and he answered Mr Blenkinsop's wave with a lift of his big arm.

Lord! Lord! Could he believe it? Could he? That his luck had changed at last? He had the desire to drop down on his knees and give humble thanks, but, instead, he turned round and pelted back across the drive, through the house door and up the stairs, and bursting into the room, he came to a dead stop. Aw, lor, he'd forgotten about old bitterguts! But why not spill the good news into her lap as a way of repayment for all she had put Mary Ann through for marrying him, and before that? 'Mary Ann!' He shouted as if she were on a fell top, and she came to the scullery door wide-eyed, saying, 'What's wrong?'

It was funny, he thought, that whenever they shouted at each other they always thought there was something wrong. In a few strides he was across the little kitchen, and, his arms under her armpits, he hoisted her upwards as if she was a child, and before the amazed gaze of her grannie he swung her around, then set her to the floor. But, still holding her with one hand, he bent and lifted David on to his shoulders, and, like this, he looked down at Mrs McMullen and cried, 'Behold! You see a successful man, Gran.'

'You gone barmy?'

'Yes, I've gone barmy.'

'Well, it's either that or you're drunk.'

'I'm both. I'm barmy and I'm drunk.' He pressed Mary Ann to his side until she almost cried out with the pressure on her ribs. Something has happened, something good. But what? The road? She looked up at him and said in awe-filled tones, 'Corny. The road . . . the road's going through?'

He looked down at her, and, still shouting, he said, 'No, not the road . . . the American.'

She tried to pull away from him. 'The American? What you talking about?'

'He's building a factory right at our door, this side of the field, and Bob Quinton's got the job. But he's contracting me to supply all the petrol, and much more, oh, much more, cars, garaging, repairs . . . the lot . . . the lot. What do you think of that?' He was not looking at Mary Ann now but bending towards Mrs McMullen, and that undauntable dame looked back at him and said, 'I wouldn't count me chickens afore they are hatched; there's many a hen sat on a nest of pot eggs.'

'Oh, you're the world's little hopeful, aren't you, Gran?' He was still bending towards her, with David holding on to his hair with his fists to save himself from slipping, and Mary Ann, now pulling away from him, stood with her hands joined under her chin, and, forgetting about her grannie, forgetting about everything but Corny and the American, she said, 'Oh, Corny! Oh, Corny! Thank God. Thank God.'

'Humility. Humility. Thanking God. You must be cracking up.'

'Gran!' Mary Ann looked towards the set-faced old woman. 'You couldn't upset me if you tried. Go on. Think up the worst that's in you, and I'll fling my arms around you and hug you.'

Mary Ann was surprised at her own words, as was Mrs McMullen. The old lady was evidently taken aback for a moment, but only for a moment, before she said, 'I wouldn't do any such thing. I'm an old woman and the shock might be the finish of me; for you to show me any affection would be more than me heart could stand, the last straw in fact.'

Corny and Mary Ann looked at each other; then they laughed, and Corny, reaching out an arm, pulled Mary Ann once more into his embrace, and said, 'I would like to take you out this minute and give you a slap-up meal. What've you got in? What's for dinner? All of a sudden, I'm ravenous.'

'Some ham and salad and a steamed pud, that's all. But we'll have a drink, eh? Go on. Put him down.' She laughed up at David, who laughed back at her. Then, pulling herself from Corny, she ran towards the scullery, but paused at the door to call over her shoulder, 'Go and bring Rose Mary.'

'Rose Mary? Aw, where is she?' Corny looked about him.

'Oh, she went downstairs a little while ago, about ten minutes ago. She'll likely be in the old car.'

Corny took his son from his shoulder and put him on the floor, and he didn't enquire why Rose Mary had gone out without David, for he fancied he knew the reason. The old girl had likely upset her, as she had done her mother so many times in the years gone by.

He ran down the back stairs and looked towards the old car and called, 'Rose Mary! Rose

Mary!' And when he didn't receive an answer he went into the garage and there saw Jimmy at the far end. Oh, he would have to tell Jimmy the news. Oh, yes, he must tell Jimmy.

It took a full five minutes to tell Jimmy, and all the time Jimmy, bashing one fist against the other, could only say, 'Ee, boss! Coo, boss! No, boss! You don't say, boss!'

Then as Corny bent his long length to go out of the top door to the back of the garage again, Jimmy called to him, 'Does that mean I'll get a rise, boss.'

Twisting round, Corny grinned at him. 'It could,' he said. 'It just could.'

'Good-oh, boss.'

Corny now ran across the field towards the old car. He wanted to hold his daughter, to throw her sky-high and cry, 'We're going places, my Rose Mary, we're going places. And you're going to a good school, me girl.' He wanted to get into his car and fly to the farm and yell to Mike, 'I've done it, Mike. It's come, Mike.' And Mike would understand, and he would thump him on the back. And Michael would thump him on the back, and Sarah would hold his hands and say, 'I'm glad for you both.' . . . But what would Lizzie say? Perhaps Lizzie wouldn't be so pleased, because her eyes had always said to her daughter, 'Well, I told you so.' And then there was Mr Lord. Mr Lord, who had offered him the bribe of Baxter's up-to-date garage, not to help him personally but so that he would be able to afford to keep his wife in the way that Mr Lord thought she should be kept, the way she would have been kept if she had married his grandson, the way

Lettice was kept now. Aw, he would go to him and say . . . What would he say? He stopped at the end of the field. He would say nothing; he would just let time speak for him; he had a long way to go yet but the road was going through. Oh boy, yes. A different road to what he thought, but, nevertheless, a road.

'Rose Mary!' he shouted towards the car; and again 'Rose Mary!' She was hiding from him, the little monkey.

When he got to the car he saw at a glance she wasn't there. He returned to the garage, calling all the way, 'Rose Mary! Rose Mary!'

'Jimmy.'

'Yes, boss?'

'You seen Rose Mary?'

'No, boss, not since the pair of them were on the old car.'

Corny stood at the opening of the garage, looking about him, and spoke over his shoulder to Jimmy, saying, 'That was some time ago. She's been upstairs since, and came down.'

'Where's David?' Jimmy had come to his side now.

'Oh, he's upstairs; their great-grandmother's come. She upset Rose Mary and she came downstairs. She must be hiding somewhere.'

'But where could she be hiding, boss?'

Corny looked at Jimmy. He looked at him for about ten seconds before swinging round. Yes, where could she be hiding? He now ran round to the back of the house and opened the coalhouse door, and the doors of the two store-houses; then, dashing up the back stairs, he burst into the kitchen, saying, 'Has she come in?'

'Rose Mary?' Mary Ann turned from the table. 'No, I told you, she's out.'

'She's not about anywhere.'

'But she must be somewhere.' Mary Ann moved slowly towards Corny and stared up into his face as he said, 'I've looked everywhere.'

'Perhaps . . . perhaps she's gone for a walk up the road.' Her voice was small.

She'd never go up the road without him. Corny slowly drooped his head in the direction of David, who was standing stiffly staring at them, his eyes wide, his mouth slightly open.

'Take the car,' said Mary Ann quietly, 'and go to both ends of the road.'

'Yes, yes.' Corny nodded quickly, and as quickly turned about and went out of the room and down the stairs.

As Mary Ann looked towards her grannie, thinking, 'It's her fault; she's to blame; she scared her, as she did me for years,' David made a sound. It was high, and it sounded like Romary. Mary Ann, moving swiftly towards him, caught him to her, and he clutched at her dress, crying again, higher this time, on the verge of a scream, 'Romary!'

'It's all right, darling.' Mary Ann lifted him into her arms. 'Daddy's gone to fetch Rose Mary. It's all right; it's all right.'

'Romary.'

Mary Ann stared into the eyes of her son, glistening now with tears. Romary he had said. It wasn't a far cry to Rose Mary. She pressed him closer to her.

'She wants her backside smacked.'

Mary Ann hitched David to one side in her arms

so that she could confront her grannie squarely. 'She doesn't want her backside smacked, and she's not going to get her backside smacked, wherever she is.'

'That's right, break her neck with softness. It's been done before.' The old woman's gimlet eyes raked Mary Ann up and down.

'How I bring up my children is my business . . .'

'Oh, now, don't start. You were acting like an angel coming down by parachute a minute ago, and now you're getting back to normal.'

'Look, Gran. I don't want to fight with you.'

'Who's fightin', I ask you? Who starts the fights?'

'As far back as I remember, you have.'

'Well, I like that. I like that. I come here, all this way in the baking heat, and that's what I get. Well, I should have known. I've had so much experience, I should have known.' The big, bushy head was moving in wide sweeps now, and Mrs McMullen, pulling herself to her feet, said, 'Get me me coat.'

Mary Ann didn't say, 'Aw, Gran, don't be silly. Stay and have a bite of dinner.' No. She put David down and marched out of the room, and returned a minute later with the coat in her hand. She did not attempt to help her grannie on with it; she just handed it to her, for she couldn't bear to touch her.

'There.' Mrs McMullen pulled on the coat. 'Wonderful, isn't it? The kindness of people. I'm going out the way I came, without a bite or sup, except for a drop of watery lemonade. I've got a long journey ahead of me afore I reach home, and I could collapse on the way . . . But that would suit you, wouldn't it? Wouldn't that suit you, if I collapsed on the way?'

'You won't collapse on the way, not you, Gran. If I know you, you'll stop at some café and fill your kite.'

Mrs McMullen stared at her grand-daughter. Begod, if she had the power she would strike her dead this moment. God forgive her for the thought, but she would. But on second thoughts, perhaps not dead, but dumb. She would have her dumb, like her son, so that she could talk at her and watch her burning herself up with frustration. If there was anybody in this world she hated more than another, it was this flesh of her own flesh. But there was little or none of her in this madam; she was all Shaughnessy; from her toes to the top of her head, she was all Shaughnessy . . . Mike Shaughnessy.

Mrs McMullen now passed her grand-daughter in silence. Her head held high, her body erect, she went out of the room and, unaided, down the dim stairs.

Mary Ann sat down and dropped her face into her hands for a moment. Why was it that her grannie could make her feel so bad, so wicked? She felt capable of saying the most dreadful things when her grannie started on her. And everything had been lovely for those few minutes, with Corny's great news. Well, she straightened up, she wasn't going to let the old cat dampen this day. No, she wasn't. When they found Rose Mary they would celebrate; in some way they would celebrate, even with only ham and steamed pudding.

'Come on,' she said, rising and holding out her

hand to David, who had been standing strangely still on the middle of the hearth rug. His stillness now got through to her, and she bent to him swiftly, saying, 'It's all right. It's all right. Rose Mary's only hiding. Come on, we'll find her.'

Ten minutes later, with David still by the hand, she was standing on the drive-way when Corny brought the car back, and she looked at him, and he looked at her and shook his head. And it was a moment before he said, 'Not a sign of her anywhere. I . . . I met the old girl halfway down the road and gave her a lift to the bus. She's black in the face with temper. You go for her?'

'Me go for her? You should have heard what she said. But don't bother about her, what's happened to Rose Mary?'

'You tell me. Why did she run out?'

'Because me grannie was at her an' all. She was saying . . . Oh . . .' She put her fingers to her lips. 'I know where she is.' She pressed her head back into her shoulders as she stared at Corny. 'She's gone to your grannie's.'

'Me grannie's?'

'Yes, I bet that's where she's gone. That's how it started. Me grannie was needling her, and I heard her say she liked her Great-gran McBride, and me grannie said did she like her house and the smell an' all? Then Rose Mary said she didn't like her, and she ran out.'

'But how would she get there, all that way?'

'She'd go on the bus, of course; she knows her way.'

'Has she any money?'

'She could have taken it out of her pig, the bottom's loose.'

'Well, did she?'

'I don't know, Corny; I haven't looked.' Mary Ann's voice was high now, and agitated.

'Well, we'd better look, hadn't we?' He dashed from her and up the stairs, and when Mary Ann caught up with him he had the pig in his hand and the bottom was intact.

'She might have had some coppers in her pocket,' Mary Ann said as she stared down at the pig. Then she added, 'Oh, why had this to happen on such a day, too? Oh, Corny, suppose she's not at your grannie's.'

He gripped her hand. 'She's bound to be there. Look, I'll slip down; it won't take long. If she went by bus she'd just be there by now.'

'Roo Marry!'

The scream startled them both. Then it came again, 'Roo Marry!' Not Romary but two distinct words now, Roo Marry.

They flew down the stairs, and there stood David on the drive, his body stiff, his mouth wide, ejecting the two words 'Roo Marry!'

Corny hoisted him up into his arms, saying, 'All right, all right. It's all right, David. Rose Mary will soon be here.'

'Roo Marry! Roo Marry!'

Corny turned his strained face towards Mary Ann. 'Rose Mary. He's saying Rose Mary.'

'Yes, yes.' She put her hands up to her son's face and cupped it, saying, 'Don't cry, David. Don't cry. Rose Mary's only gone for a walk.'

'Roo Marry! Roo Marry!' Now there followed some syllables in quick succession, unintelligible. Then again, 'Roo Marry!'

'Put him down and get to your grannie's.'

Corny put David down, and Mary Ann took hold of the child's hand. Then, as Corny strode towards the car, he was stopped in his stride by a yell that said 'Da-ad! Da-ad!' And he turned to see his son tugging his hand from Mary Ann's and stretching out his arm to him. Retracing his steps, he took the child's outstretched hand, saying, 'I'll take him with me.'

Long after the car had disappeared from her view, Mary Ann stood on the drive. She was possessed of a strange feeling, as if she had lost everybody belonging to her. David had wanted to go with his dad. And he had said dad. In his own way he had said dad. He was talking. The wonder of it did not touch her in this moment, because Rose Mary was lost, really lost . . . Don't be silly. She actually shook herself, and swung round and went into the house. But in a moment she was downstairs again and sitting in the office with the phone in her hand.

It was Mike who answered her. 'Hello there,' he said.

'It's me, Da. Tell me. Has Rose Mary come over there?'

'Rose Mary?' She could almost see her father's puckered brows. 'No. What's happened?'

'Oh, so much, I don't know where to begin. Only we can't find Rose Mary. Corny's gone down to Gran McBride's. You see, me grannie came this morning . . .'

'Oh my God!'

'Yes, as you say, oh my God! She was in fine fettle, and she taunted Rose Mary about something, and Rose Mary told her she didn't like her and she liked Grannie McBride, and then she ran out, and we think she may have made her way down there.'

'God above! What mischief will that bloody woman cause next? Somebody should shoot her. Look, I'll come over. Have you looked everywhere round the place?'

'Yes, Da, we've looked everywhere. And don't come over yet; wait until Corny comes back. I'll ring you then; he might have found her.'

'But what if he doesn't? What will you do then?'

'I don't know.'

'Now look. If when Corny comes back he hasn't got her, you get on to the police straight away.'

'The police! But she might just be round about . . .'

'Listen to me, girl. If Corny hasn't got her, get on to the police, and don't waste a minute. Look, I think I'll come over.'

'All right, Da.'

Mary Ann rang off, then sat looking out of the window to the side of her. This should have been a wonderful day, a marvellous day, but her grannie had to turn up, that evil genie, her grannie. Corny had made it at last; they should be rejoicing. And look what had happened. But she didn't really care about anything, about the garage, or the factory, or anything . . . if only Rose Mary would come back.

'Would you like a cigarette, Mrs Boyle?' Jimmy was standing in the doorway, a grubby packet extended in his hand, and, shaking her head, she said softly, 'No thanks, Jimmy.'

'She'll turn up, never you fear, Mrs Boyle.

She's cute, and she's got a tongue in her head all right.'

'Yes, Jimmy, she's got a tongue in her head. And she'll talk to anyone. That's what I'm afraid of.' It had come upon her suddenly, this fear; as she had said to Jimmy, she'd talk to anyone. Oh my God! She got off the seat and pushed past Jimmy; she wanted air. You heard of such dreadful things happening. That child, just a few months ago, taken away by that dreadful man. Oh God in Heaven! Holy Mary, Mother of God, pray for us sinners now and at the hour of our death. Amen. Protect her. Oh, please, please. It won't matter about the garage, or money or anything, only protect her . . . Here she was back to her childhood again, bargaining with the denizens of heaven. It was ridiculous, ridiculous. God helped those who helped themselves. She had learned that . . . She must do something, but what? She had got to stay here until Corny returned. And then her da might come any minute. But she just couldn't stand about. She turned swiftly to Jimmy, saying, 'I'm going up the road, to the crossroads. Tell Mr Boyle if he comes back, I won't be long.'

She was gone about twenty minutes, and when she returned there was the car on the drive and Corny standing near the office door with David by his side. Some part of her mind registered the fact in this moment that her son didn't rush to her, and she was hurt. The secret core in her was already crying. She stood in front of Corny and again he shook his head, then said, 'She's never seen hilt nor hair of her, and I've stopped the car about twenty times and asked here and there.'

'I phoned the farm; me da's coming over.'

'I phoned an' all, from Jarrow.'

Corny, his face bleached-looking, turned from her and went into the office and picked up the phone, and coming on his heels, she stood close to him and whispered, 'What are you going to do?'

'Phone the police.'

A few minutes later he put the phone down, saying, 'They'll be here shortly.' Then, rubbing his hand over his drained face, he walked out on to the drive, and he looked about him before he said, 'I didn't think about it at the time when I was taking her to the bus, but now I wonder why I didn't throttle that old girl. Somebody's going to one of these days. I never really understood how you felt about her.' He looked down at Mary Ann. 'But I do now. My God! I do now.'

8

The search was organised; the police cars were roaming the district. Mary Ann was walking the streets of Felling; Michael was doing Jarrow; Jimmy was stopping odd cars on the main road to enquire if anyone had seen a little girl in a blue dress, while Corny traversed the fields and ditches, and the by-lanes right to the old stone quarry four miles away and back to the garage, all the while humping David with him. As he came at a trot into the driveway carrying David on one arm, he heard the phone ring, but when he reached the office and lifted up the receiver the operator asked for his number.

He went out on to the drive again, David still by his side, and rubbed his sweating face with his hand. Where was Mike? Mike was supposed to stay put. 'Mike!' he called. 'Mike!' Then, going round to the back, he saw Mike's unmistakable figure in the far distance walking by the side of the deep drain.

Corny shook his head; they had done all that. He should have stayed here and waited for the phone. He had asked him to do just that because Jimmy was better on the road, and he himself was quicker on his pins over the fields, even handicapped as he was with the child. 'Mike!' he shouted. 'Mike!'

Mike was breathing hard when he reached the old car, and he called from there, 'You've got news?'

Corny shook his head, and Mike's pace slowed. 'The phone's been ringing,' said Corny when Mike reached him.

'Oh! Oh well, I was about for ages, I just couldn't stay put, man. I thought of the ditch over there. It's covered with ferns in places.'

'We've been all round there, I've told you.' Corny turned away and Mike's chin went upwards at the tone of his voice, and then he lowered it again. This wasn't the time to take umbrage at a man's tone, not the state he must be in. For himself he was back to the time when Mary Ann had run away from the convent in the south and had been reported seen in the company of an old man. Those hours had nearly driven him to complete madness.

Around to the front of the garage again they went, David still hanging on to his father's hand. There, Corny stood, leaning for a moment against the wall. He felt exhausted both in mind and body; too much had happened too quickly in the last few hours. He couldn't ever remember feeling like this in his life before, weak, trembling all over inside.

'Da-ad.'

David repeated the word and tugged twice at Corny's hand, before Corny looked at him, saying, 'Yes. Yes, what is it, David?'

'Roo Mary . . . Lost?' The word lost was quite distinct.

Corny continued to look at his son for a moment. Then, lifting his eyes to Mike, he said, wearily, 'I've always said part them and he'd talk. But God, I'd rather he remained dumb for life than this had to happen before he did it.'

Mike said nothing but looked down at his grandson, to the little face swollen with crying. Lizzie, like Corny, had always maintained that the boy would talk if he hadn't Rose Mary to do it for him, and they had been right. He could talk all right, stumbling as yet, but, nevertheless, he had been shocked into speech.

Corny, now pulling himself from the wall, said, 'If only that damned old witch hadn't put in an appearance this morning. With the news Mr Blenkinsop brought me I should be on top of the world. I was for about five minutes.'

'You will be again,' said Mike. 'Never you fear.'

'That depends.' Corny looked his father-in-law straight in the eye.

Again Mike made no answer, but he thought, 'Aye, that depends.'

Corny slowly moved towards the office with David at his side, and Mike, walking on his other side, looked towards the ground as he said, 'I don't think there's a woman anywhere who's caused as much havoc as that one. You know . . . and this is the truth . . . twice . . . twice I've thought seriously of doing her in.' He turned his head to the side and met Corny's full gaze. 'It's a fact. When I think, and I've often thought that I could have been hung for her, I get frightened, but not like I used to, because she can't make me rise now as she could a few years ago. And I'm positive that's why she came here to-day, just to get Mary Ann on the raw, because when she came to us on Sunday she got no satisfaction. Peter was at the tea-table, and Peter in his polite, gentlemanly way is a match for her. And we were all laughing our heads off and not taking a pennorth of notice of her. She didn't like it. She couldn't make anybody rise. Everybody was too happy for her. But she couldn't go a week without finding a target, so she came back to the old firm. Who better than her grand-daughter? God, I wish she had dropped down dead on the way.'

'I endorse that. By, I do!' Corny shook his head. Then, drawing in a deep breath and looking down at David, he said, 'Are you hungry?'

'NO-t.'

'You're not hungry?'

'No-t, Da-ad.'

'Would you like some milk?'

'No-t.'

'Say, no, David.'

'No-oo.'

'That's a good boy.' Corny turned and looked at Mike, and their glances said, 'Would you believe it?'

Now David, crossing his legs, pulled at Corny's hand and said quite distinctly, 'Lav, Da-ad.'

'Well, you know where it is, don't you? You can go by yourself . . . Go on.'

David went, and as Corny and Mike watched him running round the corner of the building, the phone rang. Within a second Corny was in the office and had the receiver to his ear. 'Yes?'

'Mr Boyle?'

'Yes, Mr Boyle here.'

'It's Blenkinsop.'

'Oh, hello, Mr Blenkinsop.'

'I don't know how to begin, for I suppose you're nearly all mad at that end . . . You'd never believe it, but . . . but I've got her here.'

Corny closed his eyes and, gripping Mike's arm tightly, he wetted his lips, then said, 'You did say you've got her there, Mr Blenkinsop?'

'Yes. Yes, I've got her here all right. She gave me the shock of my life. I stopped at an hotel for a drink and when I came out, there she was, sitting as calm as you like in the front of the car.'

'In the front of the car?' Corny repeated slowly as he cast his eyes towards Mike. 'How did she get there?'

'Well, as far as I can gather she was hiding from someone, great-grandmother or someone, so she says, and she climbed into the boot, as the lid was partly open. At this moment I feel I should pray to somebody in thanks that the lid was open and wouldn't close tight because of some gear I had in there. She says she fell asleep because it was hot, but woke up once the car got going and did a lot of knocking, and, by the look of her face, a lot of crying, and then she fell asleep again. Apparently she found no difficulty in lifting the lid up once the car had stopped. One thing I can't understand and that is how she slept in there at all, especially when the car was moving.'

'Oh, she's been used to sleeping on journeys since she was a baby. They both have, her and David.'

'Well, boy, am I dazed. But you . . . you must be frantic.'

'You can say that again. The whole place is

alerted. The police, the lot. But I never thought of you, not once.'

'Well, who would? I tell you, she gave me a scare sitting there; I thought I was seeing things. Look. Here she is; have a word with her.'

Corny bowed his head and closed his eyes and listened.

'It's me, Dad.'

'Hello, Rose Mary.' His voice was trembling.

'I didn't mean to do it, Dad, but I wanted to hide from great-gran. I didn't want to go back upstairs, 'cos she was horrible, and so I climbed into the boot, like it was the old car. The lid was open a bit but it was hot. When the car started going I tried to push the lid up, and I shouted, but it was noisy. Are you all right, Dad?'

'Yes, yes, I'm all right, Rose Mary. We only wondered where you were.'

'And David? Is he wanting me?'

'David's all right, too.'

'And me ma. Did she cry?'

'Yes, yes, because she couldn't find you, but she'll be all right now.'

'I'm sorry, Dad.'

'It's all right. It's all right, Rose Mary.'

'Mr Blenkinsop has been trying to get on the phone a lot.'

'Has he? We've been out and about.'

'I'm going to have some dinner now and then I'm coming back . . . You're not mad at me, Dad, are you?'

'No, no, I'm not mad at you.'

'You sound funny.'

'And so do you.'

He heard her give a little laugh. Then he said, 'Let me speak to Mr Blenkinsop again.'

'Ta-rah, Dad.'

'Bye-bye, Rose Mary.'

'Well now.' It was Mr Blenkinsop speaking again. 'If it's all right with you, as she says she'll have some dinner, and then I'll make the return journey as quickly as possible.'

'I'm sorry, sir, if this has spoiled your trip.'

'Oh, don't be sorry about that. I'm sorry for scaring the daylights out of you. And if I know anything you're still in a state of shock; I know how I would feel . . . I tell you what though. We're just about twenty miles out of Doncaster; I wonder if you'd mind if I ran in and told my cousin . . . I was going to spend the night with him and his family – I think I told you – and if I explain things they'll understand, because I won't make the return journey back to them until tomorrow.'

'Yes, yes, you go ahead and do that. I'm sorry it's putting you out.'

'Oh, not at all. Just that being so near, it would be better to explain in person, rather than phoning.'

Mr Blenkinsop laughed his merry laugh. 'What a day! What a day! I'm just thinking; I brought you a bit of good news and then I took all the good out of it.'

'It wasn't your fault, sir.'

'Well, I'm glad you look at it like that. I'll be back as quickly as I can, and that should be shortly after six.'

'Right, sir.'

'Here she is to say another good-bye.'

Corny heard Rose Mary take a number of sharp

breaths. 'Bye-bye again, Dad. Tell David I won't be long. And me mam.'

'Bye-bye, dear.'

He listened until the receiver clicked, then put the phone down and turned and looked at Mike. Mike was leaning against the stanchion of the door, wiping his face and neck with a coloured handkerchief. Corny sat staring at him. He felt very weak as if he had just got over a bout of flu or some such thing.

'Well!' said Mike, still rubbing at his face.

'Aye, well,' said Corny. 'I just can't take it in. I feel so sick with relief I could vomit.'

The corner of Mike's mouth turned up as he said, 'Well, before you give yourself that pleasure you'd better get on to the police.'

'Aye, yes.' Corny picked up the phone again.

'Aw, I'm glad to hear that,' said the officer-in-charge. 'Right glad.'

'I'm sorry to have put you to so much trouble.'

'Oh, don't bother about that. As long as she's OK, that's everything. I'll start calling them off now.'

'Thank you very much. Good-bye.'

Corny walked past Mike and looked up at the sky. He still felt bewildered.

'What are you going to do now?'

'Go and find Mary Ann,' said Corny. 'She seemed to think she might have gone to some of her playmates. I'll go round Felling, and when I pick her up I'll go and find Michael. That's if the police haven't contacted him beforehand . . . You'll stay here?'

'Oh aye, I'll stay here. I feel like yourself, a bit sick with relief.'

'Da-ad be-en.'

The two men turned to where David was running across the cement towards them, and when the boy threw himself against Corny's legs, Corny looked down at him but didn't speak, and Mike, after a moment, said softly, 'Aren't you going to tell him?'

Corny looked at Mike now and he said slowly, 'I've only got till six o'clock.'

'What d'you mean?'

Corny, now speaking under his breath, muttered, 'The minute she comes back he'll close up like a clam; she hasn't been away long enough.'

'Aw man, my God, be thankful.' Mike's voice was indignant.

'I am, I am, Mike. Thankful! You just don't know how thankful, but this' – he motioned his head down to the side of him – 'I wanted to hear him . . . You know what?' He moved his lips soundlessly. 'More than anything in life I wanted to hear him . . . I wanted this garage to be successful as you know. For seven years I've hung on, but if I had to choose, well, I know what I would have chosen . . . His state has come between me and sleep for months now. I've told Mary Ann that if . . .' He looked down at David again, at the wide eyes staring up at him, and, looking back at Mike, he began to speak enigmatically, saying, 'If what has happened the day could have been made to happen, you know what I mean, one one place, one the other, just for a short time, it would have worked. I've told her till I'm sick, but she wouldn't have it. But I've been proved right, haven't I? You see for yourself.'

'Yes, I see. And Lizzie's always said the same thing. But be thankful, lad, be thankful. He won't close up.'

'I wish I could bet on that. She'll be so full of talk that he'll just stand and gape.'

'Ssh, man! Ssh!' Mike turned away with a jerk of his head towards David, and Corny, now looking down at his son's strained face, and trembling lips, said, 'Rose Mary is coming back, David.'

'Ro-se Ma-ry,' the child's lips stretched wide, and then he again said, on a high note, 'Ro-se Ma-ry.' The name was clear-cut now.

'Yes, Rose Mary is coming back. You remember the American man, Mr Blenkinsop?'

David nodded his head, and Corny repeated, 'You remember the American man, Mr Blenkinsop?'

'Ya.'

'Yes,' said Corny.

'Ye-as,' said David.

'Well, Rose Mary was hiding in the boot of his car, and he drove away and she couldn't get out . . . What do you think of that?'

The light in David's eyes deepened, his mouth stretched wider, and then he laughed.

'I'm going to pick up Mam now. Do you want to come?'

'Ye-as,' said David.

'Go on, then, get into the car.' Now Corny, turning to Mike, said, 'If she should phone in tell her I'll wait outside the school. That's the best place.'

'Good enough,' said Mike. 'Get yourself off.'

Corny brought the car out of the garage and

stopped it when he neared Mike, and, looking at David sitting on the seat beside him, he said, 'Say good-bye to Granda.'

'Bye, Gran . . . da.'

'Good-bye, son.'

Corny, with his face close to Mike, looked him in the eyes and said, softly, 'You know, it's in me to wish that she wasn't coming back to-night or to-morrow.'

'Corny! Corny, don't be like that!' Mike's voice was harsh.

'She's safe so I'm content. And I say again, give me another day, perhaps two, and I'd have no fears after that. But just you wait until to-night, it'll be a clam again, you'll see.'

'Aw, go on now. Go on and stop thinking such nonsense.' Mike stepped back and waved Corny away, and as he watched him driving into the road he thought, 'That's a nice attitude to take! There'll be skull and hair flying if he talks like that to her.' But after a moment of considering he turned in the direction of the office, asking himself what he would have felt like if Michael had, to all intents and purposes, been dumb? Pretty much like Corny was feeling now, because he knew, in a strange sort of way, that he and Corny were built on similar lines and that their reactions, in the main, were very much alike.

'Look, have a drop of brandy.' Corny was on his hunkers before Mary Ann, where she sat in a straight-backed chair in the kitchen.

'No, I'm all right. I'm all right; it's just the reaction; it's just that I can't stop shaking.'

'I'll get you a drop of brandy . . . You keep it in

as a medicine, and this is a time when medicine is needed.' Corny went to the cupboard and, reaching to the back of the top shelf, brought out a half-bottle of brandy, and, pouring a measure into a cup, he took it to her. Placing it in her hand, he said gently, 'There now, sup it up.'

'I don't like brandy.'

'It doesn't matter what you like, get it down you. Come on.' He guided the cup to her lips, and when she sipped at it she shuddered. Then, looking at him, she said, 'What time did he say he'd be back?'

'Something after six.'

'And it's just on five.' She raised her eyes to the clock. Then, stretching out her hand, she put the cup on the table near where David was standing looking out of the window, waiting for a glimpse of the car that would bring Rose Mary back, but the movement of her hand caught his attention and he turned from the window and, looking from the cup to Mary Ann, he said distinctly, 'Sup?'

There was a quick exchange of glances between Corny and Mary Ann, and, smiling now, she said, 'No, David, it's nasty.' Then again she was looking at Corny, the smile gone, as she said, 'I can't believe it. I just can't believe it. I won't be able to really take it in until I see her.'

Corny made no answer to this. He was looking towards David, where the boy was again gazing out of the window, and he said softly, 'I always told you, didn't I? Get them apart for a while . . .'

'It wasn't that, it wasn't that.' Mary Ann was on her feet. 'It was the shock.'

'Aye, you're right. But if she had come back right away there would have been no chit-chat, not like now . . . As it is, I'm a bit afraid that as soon as she puts her face in the door he'll close . . .'

At this moment they heard a knocking on the staircase door and Jimmy's voice calling, 'The phone's going, boss. You're wanted on the phone.'

As Corny made swiftly for the door Mary Ann was on his heels, and she was still close behind him when he entered the office, and when, with his hand on the phone, he turned and looked at her, he said quietly, 'It's all right, it's all right, there's nothing to worry about now.'

She shook her head as she watched him lift the phone to his ear. 'Hello. Oh, it's you, Mr Blenkinsop. Hello there, everything all right?' Although he wasn't looking at Mary Ann he felt her body stiffen, and when Mr Blenkinsop's voice came to him, saying, 'Oh yes, as right as rain,' he cast a quick glance at her and smiled reassuringly, then listened to Mr Blenkinsop going on, 'It's just that I thought I'd better phone you as I've not been able to get away from my cousin's yet. You see he has four sons and there was quite a drought of female company around here, and they've got her now up in the train-room. I've had two unsuccessful attempts at getting her away; not that she seems very eager to leave them. They've gone right overboard for her. Their verdict is she's cute. This is quite unanimous, from Ian who is three, to Donald who is ten. So, as it is, it's going to be nearer nine when I arrive . . . I hope you're not mad.'

'No, Mr Blenkinsop. That's OK, as long as she's all right.'

'All right? I'll say she's all right. Can you hear that hullabaloo?' He stopped speaking, and Corny hadn't to strain his ears to hear the excited shrieks and the sound of running feet. Then Mr Blenkinsop's voice came again, saying, 'They've just come in like a herd of buffalo.'

Corny turned his eyes to Mary Ann again. There was an anxious look on her face, but he smiled at her and wrinkled his nose before turning his attention to the phone again as Mr Blenkinsop's voice said, 'Just a minute. There's a conclave going on, they want to ask you something. Just a minute, will you?'

As Corny waited he put his hand over the mouthpiece and said under his breath, 'She's having the time of her life.'

'He hasn't left there yet?'

'No, there's four children, boys, and apparently they've got a train set. They're kicking up a racket.' As he looked at her strained face he said, 'It's all right, it's all right, there's nothing to worry about.'

'Hello. Yes . . . yes, I'm here.'

'Look, I don't know how to put this but they're all around me here, the four of them . . . and their mother and the father an' all. Well . . . well, it's like this, they want me to say will you let Rose Mary stay the night?'

'. . . Stay the night?' Corny put his hand out quickly to stop Mary Ann grabbing the phone, and he shook his head vigorously at her and pressed the receiver closer to his ear to hear Mr Blenkinsop say, 'You know, if you could agree to this it would save me a return journey to-morrow because Dave, my cousin here, and me, well we could get through our business tonight and I'd make an early start in the morning. But that's up to you. I know that you and your lady are bound to want her back, but there it is.' There was a pause which Corny did not fill, and then Mr Blenkinsop's voice came again, saying, 'Would you like to speak to her? Here she is.'

'Hello, Dad.'

'Hello, Rose Mary. Are you all right?'

'Oh yes, Dad. It's lovely here. They've got a big house and garden, an' a train-room, and they're all boys.' Her next words were drowned in the high laughter of children.

'Don't you want to come back to David?' As Corny listened to her answer he held out his free arm, stiffly holding Mary Ann at a distance from the phone.

'Oh yes, Dad. Yes, I wish David was here. And you, and me mam. Is me mam all right?'

'Yes, she's fine. And would you like to stay there until the morrow?'

'No! no!' Mary Ann's voice hissed at him as he heard Rose Mary say, 'Yes, Dad, if it's all right with you and me mam.'

'Yes, it's all right with us, dear. You have a good time and enjoy yourself, and then you can tell us all about it to-morrow. Well, good-bye now.'

'Bye-bye, Dad. Bye-bye.'

As Mary Ann rushed out of the office he listened to Mr Blenkinsop saying, 'We'll take care of her. She's made a great impression here. I think you'd better prepare yourself for the visit of four stalwart youths in the future.'

Corny gave a weak laugh, then said, 'Well, until to-morrow morning, Mr Blenkinsop.'

'Yes, until to-morrow morning. I'll bring her back safe and sound, never fear. Good-bye now.'

'Good-bye.' Corny put down the phone and tried to tell himself that he was disappointed that she wasn't coming back tonight. And then Mary Ann appeared in the doorway again.

'You shouldn't have done it.'

'What could I have done?'

'You could have told him that I was nearly out of my mind and I wanted her back.'

'Well, she's coming back. It's only a few more hours, and the man asked me as a favour.'

'Oh yes, you'd have to grant him a favour, knowing how I felt, knowing that I was waiting every minute. You know . . .' She strained her face up to him. 'You're glad, aren't you, you're glad that she's not coming back to-night because it'll keep them apart a little longer. You're glad.'

'Now don't go on like that. Don't be silly.'

'I'm not being silly. I know what's in your mind; you've been preening yourself, ever since I got in, about him talking, that it would never have happened if they hadn't been separated. You were frightened of her coming back in case he wouldn't keep up the effort.'

'All right, all right.' He was shouting now. 'Yes I was, and I still am. And yes, I'm glad that she's not coming back until to-morrow morning. It'll give him a chance, for he damn well hadn't a chance before. She not only talked for him, she thought for him, and lived for him; she lived his life, he hadn't any of his own . . . I'll tell you this. He's been a new being this afternoon. And I'll tell you something else, I wish they had invited her for a week.'

There was a long, long silence, during which they stared at each other. Then Mary Ann, her voice low and bitter, said, 'I hate you. Oh how I hate you!' Then she turned slowly from him, leaving him leaning against the little desk, his head back, his eyes closed, his teeth grating the skin on his lip.

I hate you! Mary Ann had said that to him. Oh, how I hate you!

'Da-ad.' Corny opened his eyes and looked down to where David was standing in the open doorway, his face troubled, and he said, 'Yes, son. What is it?'

'Ma-am.' There followed a pause before David, his mouth wide open now, emitted the word, 'Cry.'

Corny considered his son. The child had seen his mother cry, yet he hadn't gone to her, he had come to him. He reached out and took his hand. Then, hoisting him up on to the desk, he looked straight at him as he said, 'Mam's crying because Rose Mary is not coming back until to-morrow.'

David's eyes remained unblinking.

'You're not going to cry because Rose Mary isn't coming back until to-morrow, are you?'

The eyes still unblinking, the expression didn't change, and then David slowly shook his head.

'Say, No, Dad.'

'No, Da-ad.'

'That's a good boy. I'm going to mend a car. Are you coming to help me?'

Again David moved his head, nodding now, and again Corny prompted him. 'Say, Yes, Dad.'

'Yes, Da-ad.'

'Come on then.' He lifted him down, and they walked out of the office side by side and into the garage, and as he went Corny thought, 'I'll give her a little while to cool off and then I'll go up.'

9

If Corny hadn't heard the car slow up and thought it was someone wanting petrol he would never have gone on to the drive at that moment and seen her going.

The occupants of the car decided not to stop after all, and it was speeding away to the right of the garage. But, going down the road to the left, Corny stared at the back of Mary Ann. Mary Ann carrying a case. He stood petrified for a moment, one hand raised in mid-air in an appealing gesture. God Almighty! She wouldn't. No, she wouldn't do that without saying a word. She was near the bend of the road when he sprang forward and yelled, 'Mary Ann!' When there was no pause in her step he stopped at the end of the line of white bricks edging the roadway, and now, his voice high and angry, he yelled, 'Do you hear? Mary Ann!'

Taking great loping strides, he raced towards her, and again he shouted, 'Mary Ann! Wait a minute, Mary Ann!' It wasn't until he saw her hasten her step that he stopped again, and after a moment of grim silence he yelled, 'If you go, you go. Only remember this. You come back on your own, I'll not fetch you. I'm telling you.' Her step didn't falter, and the next minute she was lost to his sight round the bend.

The anger seeped out of him. He felt as if his life was seeping out of him, draining down from his veins into the ground. How long he stood still he didn't know, and he wasn't conscious of turning about and walking back to the garage. He didn't come to himself until he saw David standing with his back to the petrol pump. She hadn't even come to see the child. She was bats about the boy, she was bats about them both. Why hadn't she taken him with her? Perhaps because she knew that he wouldn't have let him go. And she was right there. He wouldn't have let the boy go with her.

'Ma-am . . .'

Corny looked down at the small, trembling lips, and he forced himself to speak calmly, saying, 'Mam's gone to Gran's.'

'Gra-an's?'

'Your Grannie Shaughnessy has got a bad head, she's not very well. Can you go upstairs and set the tray for your supper, do you think? Your Bunny tray with the mug and the plate. Then wash yourself.'

The boy was looking up at him, his eyes wide and deep, with that knowing look in their depths. Then he said, 'Yes, Da-ad,' and went slowly towards the house. And Corny turned about and went into the office and dropped into his chair. He felt weak again and, something more, he felt frightened; this kind of thing happened to other fellows, to other couples, but it couldn't happen to them. He had loved her since he was a boy, and she had loved him from when she was ten. She had loved and championed him since he could remember. She had stood by him through all the hard times. And there had been hard times; there had been weeks when they both had to pull their belts in in order that their children got their full share of food, and during these times both had resisted gobbling up food when they went to the farm on a Sunday and sat down to the laden table. No-one must know how things really stood. They would get by. It was she who had always said that. 'We'll get by,' she'd said. 'We'll have a break, you'll see. It'll come . . .' And it had come; it had come to-day, like a bolt from the blue. And with it the break in his family had come too.

But it just couldn't happen to him and Mary Ann. They had made a pact at the beginning, never to go to sleep on a row, and they never had. Well, there was always a first time, and by the looks of things that first time was now, because she had no intention of coming back to-day; she had taken a case with her. He dropped his head on to his hands. And all because he hadn't said the word that would bring Rose Mary back to-night. What were a few more hours of separation if it was going to loosen her son's tongue? Couldn't she see it? No; because she didn't want to see it. She didn't want them separated for a minute from each other, or from her. She had once said they were as close as the Blessed Trinity, and on that occasion he had asked where he came in in the divine scheme of things, and she had laughingly replied, 'We'll make you Joseph.' But he was no Joseph, he was no foster-father. David was his son, and he had carried a deep secret ache, a yearning to hear his voice. And now he was hearing it, but he was going to pay dearly apparently for that pleasure.

He heard a car come on to the drive and it brought him to his feet, and when he reached the office door, there, scrambling out from a dilapidated Austin, was Jimmy and his pals. Corny had never seen this lot before. He had seen other pals of Jimmy's, but they hadn't been so freakish as the boys now confronting him. These looked like a combination of The Rolling Stones and The Pretty Things, and Jimmy looked the odd man out, because he appeared the only male thing among them. At any other time Corny would have hooted inside, he would have chipped this lot and stood being chipped in return, but not to-night. His face was straight as he looked at Jimmy and asked, 'Well?'

'I just popped in, Boss – we was passing like – just to see if Rose Mary was back.'

'No, she's not back. She's staying with Mr Blenkinsop's friends until the morning. He's bringing her back then.'

'Oh.' Jimmy now turned and nodded towards his four long-haired companions, who were all surveying Corny with a blank, scrutinising stare.

'The missus all right?' Jimmy glanced up at the house-window as he spoke, and Corny, after a moment, said, 'Yes. Yes, she's all right.'

'Busy, is she?'

'No.' Corny screwed up his eyes in enquiry. 'She's got a headache; she's lying down. Do you want something?'

'No, no, boss. I was just wondering, after all the excitement of the day, how she was farin'. And we was just passing like I said. Well, fellas,' he turned towards the four, 'let's get crackin'.'

The four boys piled back into the car. Not one of them had spoken, but Jimmy, now taking his seat beside the driver, put his hand out of the window and passed it over the rust-encrusted chrome framing the door and, smiling broadly, said, 'She goes.'

'You're lucky.' Corny nodded to him but did not grin, as he would have done at another time when making a scathing remark, even if it was justified, and Jimmy's long face lengthened even further, his mouth dropped, and his eyebrows twitched. He sensed there was something not quite right. The boss was off-hand, summat was up. 'Be seeing you the mornin',' he said.

For answer, Corny merely nodded his head, and as the car swung out of the driveway he went into the office . . .

Again he was sitting with his head in his hands when the phone rang. He stared at it for a moment. He knew who it would be . . . Mike. Slowly he reached out and, lifting up the receiver, said, 'Yes.'

'Corny.'

He had been wrong; it wasn't her da, it was her ma.

Lizzie's voice sounded very low, as if she didn't want to be overheard. 'I'm sorry about this, Corny.'

He didn't speak. What was there to say?

'Are you there?'

'Yes, I'm here, Mam.'

'I want you to know that I'm with you in this.'

He widened his eyes at the phone.

'I've always said if they were separated, even for a short time, it would give him a chance. I've told her I think you're right. But . . . but, on the other hand, she's been worried nearly out of her mind and it mightn't have been the right time to have done it.'

'What other chance would I have had? You tell me.'

'I don't know, but, as I said, I'm with you. I can't tell her that, you understand, not at present. She's in an awful state, Corny . . . What are you going to do?'

'Me?'

'Yes, you. Who else?'

'I'm going to do nothing, Mam. She walked out on me, she didn't even come and see the boy. I ran down the road after her, yelling me head off, but she wouldn't stop. I wouldn't even have known she had gone, it was just by chance I saw her. So what am I going to do? I'm going to do nothing.'

'Oh dear. Corny. Corny. You know what she is; she's as stubborn as a mule.'

'Well, there's more than one mule.'

'That's going to get neither of you anywhere. And you've got to think of the children.'

'It strikes me you can think of the children too much. In one way I mean. The children shouldn't come before each other. Whatever has got to be done with the children should be a combined effort.'

'Well, you didn't make it much of a combined effort from what I hear, Corny. You told that man that Rose Mary could stay until to-morrow morning, and didn't give her the chance to say a word.'

'Well, what harm was there in it? Just a few more hours. And if she had been unhappy then I would have whisked her back like a shot; I would have gone out there for her myself; but by the sound of her she was having the time of her life. And at this end David wasn't worrying. That is what really upset madam, David wasn't really worrying. What was more, he was talking.'

'He'll worry if she doesn't come back soon . . . I mean Mary Ann not Rose Mary.'

'I think he's worrying already, he's trying not to cry.' Corny's voice was flat now.

'Would Mike come over and get him?'

'No, Mam, no thank you.' His voice was no longer flat. 'The boy stays with me. If she wants him she's got to come back home . . . Home I said, Mam. This is her home, Mam.'

'I know that, I know that well enough, Corny. And don't shout.'

'Where is she?'

'She's gone down to the bottom field to see Mike.'

There followed a short silence. And then Lizzie spoke again, saying, 'It seems terrible for this to happen, and on a day when you've got such wonderful news.'

'Oh, she told you that, did she?'

'Yes, she told me. I'm so glad, Corny, I'm delighted for you. If only this business was cleared up.'

'Well, there's a way to end it. She knows what to do. She walked down the road, she can walk up it again.'

'Don't be so stubborn, Corny. Get in the car and come over.'

'Not on your life.'

'Very well, there's no use talking any more, is there?' Lizzie's voice was cut off abruptly, and Corny, taking the phone from his ear, stared at it for a moment before putting it on the stand.

Go over there. Beg her to come back. Say he was sorry. For what? For acting rationally, sensibly?

He marched upstairs and into the kitchen. David had put his mug and plate on the tray but was now standing looking out of the window. He turned an eager face to Corny on his entry, then looked towards the table and the tray, and Corny said, 'By, that's clever of you! Are you hungry?'

David nodded his head; then before Corny had time to prompt him, he said, 'Yes, Da-ad.'

'You'd like some cheese, wouldn't you?'

David now grinned at him and nodded as he said, 'Yes, Da-ad, cheese.' He thrust his lips out on the word and Corny was forced to smile. Cheese upset his stomach; it brought him out in a rash; but that was before he could say cheese. He would see what effect it had on him now.

He was cutting a thin slice of cheese from the three-cornered piece when he heard the distant tinkle of the phone ringing again. 'You eat that,' he said quickly, placing the cheese on a piece of bread. Then he patted David on the head and hurried out.

This time it was Mike on the phone, and without any preamble he began, 'Now what in the name of God is all this about? What do you think the pair of you are up to?'

Corny, staring out of the little office-window, passed his teeth tightly over each other before saying, with forced calmness, 'Well, I'm glad you said the pair of us and didn't just put the lot on me.'

'That's as it may be.' Mike's voice was rough. 'But this I'm going to say to you, and you alone. What the hell were you at to let her come away?'

'Now look you here, Mike. I don't happen to have sentries posted at each corner of the house to let me know her movements; I didn't even know she was going until I saw the back of her going down the road . . .'

'Well, why didn't you bring her back?'

'Look, I shouted and shouted to her, and the harder I shouted the quicker she walked.'

'You had legs, hadn't you? You could have run after her.'

There was a long pause following this. Then Corny, his voice low, very low now, said, 'Yes, I had legs, and I could have run. And I could have picked her up bodily and carried her back. That's what you mean, isn't it? Well, now, you put yourself in my position, Mike. Liz walks out on you; you run after her; you call to her, and she takes not a damned bit of notice of you. What would you have done? She's got a case in her hand; she's leaving you and your son . . . and, this is the point, Mike, she's going home.'

'Oh, I get your point all right. But what do you mean, home? That's her home.'

'Aye, it should be, but she's never looked on this as home; she's always looked on your place, the farm, as home. And there she was, case in hand . . . going home. Think a minute. What would you have done, eh?'

'Well.' Mike's voice faltered now. 'Most girls

look upon their parents' place as home. Look at Michael here. Never away, even when he's finished work. That's nothing.'

'It mightn't be nothing to you, but it's something to me. She knew what she was taking on when she married me. This was the only home I could give her until I could get a better, and now, when the prospects of doing just that are looking large, this happens.'

'You're a pair of hot-headed fools.' Mike's voice was calmer now. 'Look, get into the car and come over.'

'No, not on your life, Mike. If there's any coming over she's going to do it. She can get cool in the stew she got hot in.'

'Man!' Mike's voice was rising again. 'She's upset. More than upset, she looks awful. You know for a fact yourself she just lives for those bairns.'

'Yes,' shouted Corny now. 'I know for a fact she just lives for those bairns. She's lived for them so much she's almost forgotten that I've got a share in them. If she'd done what I'd asked months ago and let you have David for a few days this would never have happened. But no. No, she couldn't bear either of them out of her sight. She made on it was because she didn't want them separated, they mustn't be separated, but the real truth of the matter is that she couldn't bear to let one of them go, not even for a night. All this could have been avoided if she had acted sensibly.'

'It's all right saying if . . . if . . . the thing's done. But you can't stick all the blame for what's happened to-day on her. The one to blame is that blasted old she-devil. If she hadn't come along Rose Mary would have been home this minute and nothing like this would have happened. The trouble that old bitch causes stuns me when I think about it.'

There was silence again between them. Then Mike's voice, coming very low, with a plea in it, said, 'When you shut up the garage come on over. Come on, man. Drop in as if nothing had happened.'

Slowly Corny put the receiver back on to its stand. Then looking at it, he muttered, 'Aw no, Mike. Aw no. You don't get me going crawling, not in this way, you don't. I've just to start that and I'm finished.'

10

Mary Ann stood at the window of the room that had been hers from a child. She had never thought she would spend a night here again, at least not alone, unless something had happened to Corny. Well, something had happened to Corny.

She stood with her arms crossed over her breast, her hands on her shoulders, hugging herself in her misery. There was a moon shining somewhere. The light was picking out the farm buildings; the whole landscape looked peaceful, and beautiful, but she did not feel the peace, nor see the beauty. She was looking back to the eternity that she had lived through, from the minute she had come back home yesterday.

She had never for a moment thought that he would let her go. Although she had been flaming with temper against him, the sensible, reasonable part of her was waiting for him to convince her that he was right. When she heard his voice calling to her along the road she had felt a wave of relief pass over her; she wouldn't have to go through with it. He would come dashing up and grip her by the shoulders and shake her, and go for her hell for leather. He would say, 'Did you mean what you said about hating me?' And after a time she would say, 'How could I? How could I ever hate you, whatever you did?'

All this had been going on in the reasonable, sensible part of her, but on the surface she was still seething, still going to show him. After he had called her name for a second time and she heard his footsteps pounding along the road behind her she quickened her stride and told herself she wasn't going to make this easy for him. Then she was near the bend and his footsteps stopped, and his voice came to her again, saying, 'If you go, you go. Only remember this, you come back on your own, I'll not fetch you.' That forced her pride up and she couldn't stop walking, not even when she was round the bend, although her step was much slower.

When she was on the bus she just couldn't believe that she was doing this thing, that she was walking out on him, walking out on David. But David wasn't hers any more, he was his. He had claimed David as something apart from Rose Mary.

Her temper had disappeared and she was almost in a state of collapse when she reached the farm. The shock of Rose Mary's disappearance was telling in full force and it had been some time before she had given her mother a coherent picture of what had happened. And then, later, she was further bemused and hurt when Lizzie, of all people, took Corny's side in the matter, because her mother had always had reservations about Corny, but in this case she seemed whole-heartedly for him.

It was only her da's reactions that had soothed

her. He didn't blame her, he understood. After talking to Corny on the phone he had put his arm about her and said, 'Don't you worry, he'll be along later,' and she hadn't answered, 'I don't want him to come along later. I don't care if I never see him again,' which would have been the expected reaction to a quarrel such as theirs. She had said nothing, she had just waited. She had waited, and waited, and when ten o'clock came, her mother had said, 'Go to bed; things will clear themselves to-morrow.'

The clock on the landing struck three. She wondered if he was asleep, or was he, too, looking out into the night. She remembered their pact, never to go to sleep on a quarrel. She had the urge to get dressed and fly across the fields, cutting the main roads, by-passing Felling, and running up the lane to the house and hammering on the door. But no, no, if she did that, that would be the end of her, he'd be top dog for life.

By eleven o'clock the following morning the bitterness was high in Mary Ann again. Her da, Michael, and her mother were in the kitchen. It was coffee time, and their Michael, forgetting that she was no longer an impulsive child but the mother of two six-year-old children, was leading off at her, 'You know yourself you were always ram-stam, pell-mell, you never stopped to think. Now I know Corny as well as anybody, and if you're going to sit here waiting till he comes crawling back you're going to have corns on your backside.'

'Oh, shut up, our Michael. What do you know about it?'

'I know this much. I think Corny's right. I also know that you haven't changed very much over the years. Oppose you in anything and whoof! The balloon goes up.'

'That's enough,' Mike said sharply, his hand raised. He looked towards Michael as he spoke and made a warning motion with his head.

During the heated conversation Lizzie had said nothing; she just sat sipping her coffee. And so it was she who first heard the car draw up in the roadway. This was nothing unusual, but the next moment a faint and high-pitched cry of 'Mam! Mam!' brought her eyes wide, and her head turned to the others, and she cried to Mike, who was now consoling Mary Ann with the theory that Corny was waiting for Rose Mary to arrive and then he'd bring them both across, 'Quiet a minute! Listen!' And as they listened there came the call again, nearer now, and the next minute the back door burst open and Rose Mary came flying through the scullery and into the kitchen, and as she threw herself at Mary Ann, Mike cried, 'Well, what did I tell you? It was as I said.' His face was beaming. Then breaking in on his grand-daughter's babbling, he cried, 'Where's your dad? Has he gone on the farm?'

'Me Dad?' Rose Mary turned her face over her shoulder. 'No, Grandad; me dad's back home. Mr Blenkinsop brought me. He's looking in the cow byres, waitin'.'

Mary Ann rose to her feet, and, looking down at Rose Mary, she said quietly, 'Mr Blenkinsop? Why did he bring you here, not home?'

'Me dad asked him, Mam. He did take me home, and me dad said would he drop me over.'

Rose Mary now glanced about her quickly, and added, 'Where's David? Where is he, Mam?'

'David?' There was a quick exchange of glances among the elders, and then Mary Ann said, 'Didn't you see David when you went home?'

Rose Mary screwed up her face as she looked up at her mother, and her voice dropped to a low pitch when she said, 'No, Mam. David wasn't there. I just got out of the car and me dad said hello and . . . and kissed me; then he asked Mr Blenkinsop to bring me over 'cos you were here, and I thought David was with you . . . Isn't he, Mam?'

Mary Ann stood with her head back for a moment, looking over the heads of the others. Her fists were pressed between her breasts, trying to stop this new pain from going deep into the core of her. He had split them up, deliberately split them up, giving her Rose Mary and keeping David; he had not only split the twins, he had split her and him apart, he had rent the family in two. Oh God! She drooped her head slowly now as she heard Mike say, 'I'd better go and see this man.'

'No . . . No, leave this to me.' She walked stiffly towards the door, and when Rose Mary made to accompany her she said, 'Stay with your grannie, I'll be with you in a minute.'

She found the American, as she thought of him, talking to Jonesy in the middle of the yard. When she came up to them Jonesy moved away and she said, 'Mr Blenkinsop?'

'Yes, ma'am. Well.' He moved his head from side to side. 'I don't know how to start my apologies. You must have been worried stiff yesterday.'

'Yes, yes I was, Mr Blenkinsop.'

'Well, she's back safe and sound and she's had the time of her life. She floored them all, they went overboard for her, hook, line, and sinker . . .' His voice trailed away as he stared down at this pocket-sized young woman. There was something here he couldn't get straight. He was quick to sum people up; he had summed her husband up and found him an honest, straight-forward young fellow, and also a man who had, you could say, taken to him, but she was a different kettle of fish. She wasn't for him in some ways. The antipathy came to him even though her voice was polite. And there was something else he couldn't get straightened out; the young fellow's attitude had been very strained this morning, he hadn't greeted his daughter with the reception due to her, in fact he had been slightly off-hand. He bent his long length towards Mary Ann and asked her quietly, 'Did you mind me keeping the child overnight?'

Mary Ann took a long breath. This man was to be a benefactor, he could make Corny or leave him standing where he was. She should be careful how she answered him about this. But no, she would tell him the truth. 'Yes, I did mind, Mr Blenkinsop. I was nearly demented when Rose Mary was lost and . . . and naturally I wanted her back, but . . . but my husband saw it otherwise. You see, my son hasn't been able to talk, and it's been my husband's theory that he would talk if he was separated from his sister. I've always been against it. Well . . .' She swallowed again. 'My husband saw your invitation as a means of keeping them separated for a longer period to . . . to

592

give the boy a chance, as he said. I didn't see it that way. I . . . I was very upset.'

Mr Blenkinsop straightened up and his face was very solemn as he said, 'Yes, ma'am. Yes, I can see your point. I can see that you'd be upset. Oh yes.' He did not add that he could also see her husband's side of it. It was no use upsetting her still further. 'I'm very sorry that I've been the instigator of your worries. I can assure you I wouldn't have enlarged upon them for the world. If only I had known I would have whipped her back here like greased lightning.'

Mary Ann's face softened, and she said now, 'Thanks. I feel you would have, too.'

'I would that. Yes, I would that.'

They stood looking at each other for a moment. Then Mr Blenkinsop said, 'Well, I must be on my way, but I'll be seeing you shortly.'

'Would you like to stay and have a cup of coffee?'

'No, no thank you, not at the moment. But in the future we'll have odd cups of coffee together no doubt, when the work gets under way.' As he turned towards the car he stopped and said, 'You're pleased about the factory going up?'

'Yes, oh yes, Mr Blenkinsop; I'm very pleased.'

'Good, good.' When he reached the car, he looked over it and said, 'Nice little farm you've got here.'

'Yes, it's a very nice farm.'

'I'd like to come and have a look round some time.'

'You'd be very welcome.'

'Goodbye, Mrs Boyle. Please accept my apologies for all this trouble.'

'It's quite all right, Mr Blenkinsop.' They nodded to each other, and then she watched him drive away, before slowly walking out of the yard and through the garden to the farmhouse again. As she entered the house Rose Mary's voice came to her, laughter-filled and excited, saying, 'Yes, Grandma, I'd have liked to have stayed if David had been there, but I couldn't without David, could I?'

Mary Ann paused in the scullery. She leant against the table and looked down at it. How was she going to explain the situation to Rose Mary? How to tell her that she had to stay here while David remained at home? How? She could put her off for a few hours, but in the end, come this evening, when she knew she wasn't going home she'd have to explain to her in some way . . . Oh God! Why had this to happen to her, to them all?

11

But before Mary Ann was called upon to explain the situation to Rose Mary she had to explain it to someone else – to Mr Lord.

It happened round about teatime that Rose Mary came running into the house calling, 'Mam! Mam!'

'What is it?' Mary Ann came out of the front room, where she had been sitting alone, leaving Lizzie busy in the kitchen. Lizzie had refused her offer of help, and this, more than anything else since she had come home yesterday, had made her feel, and for the first time in her life, a stranger, a visitor in her home. She had gone into the front room and made a valiant effort not to cry. She had met Rose Mary in the hall, and again she said, 'What is it?'

Rose Mary was gasping with her running. 'It's Mr Lord, Mam. He says you've got to go up.'

'Didn't I tell you not to go anywhere near the house? I told you, didn't I? I told you to keep in the yard.'

'But I was in the yard, in the far yard, and Mr Ben, he waved me up the hill. And when I went up he took me in to Mr Lord, and Mr Lord asked if you were still here.'

Mary Ann lowered her head, then walked slowly into the kitchen and spoke to her mother.

Lizzie was setting the table. She had her back to Mary Ann, and she kept it like that as Mary Ann said, 'He knows I'm here; he wants me to go up.'

'You should know by now that you can't keep much from him, and you'd better not try to hide anything from him when you see him.'

'It's none of his business.'

Now Lizzie did turn round, and her look was hard on her daughter as she said, 'Your life has always been his business, and I'm surprised you have forgotten that.'

Again Mary Ann hung her head, and as she did so she became aware of Rose Mary standing to the side of her, her face troubled, her eyes darting between them.

As she turned away, walking slowly towards the door, Rose Mary said, 'Can I come with you, Mam?'

'No, stay where you are.'

'Are we going home when you come back?'

Mary Ann didn't answer, but as she went out of the back door she heard her mother's voice speaking soothingly to Rose Mary.

Mary Ann entered Mr Lord's house by the back door, as she always did, and found Ben sitting at the table, preparing his master's tea, buttering thin slices of brown bread, which he would proceed to roll into little pipes. His veined, bony hands had a perpetual shake about them now; he was the same age as his master but he appeared much older; Ben was running down fast. Mary

Ann was quick to notice this, and for a moment she forgot her own troubles and the interview that lay before her, and she spoke softly as she said, 'Hello, Ben. How are you?'

'Middling, just middling.'

'Is Mrs Rice off to-day?'

'They're always off. Time off, time off, that's all they think of.'

'Shall I take the tray in for you?'

'No, no, I can manage.' He looked up at her and, his voice dropping, he said, 'He's waitin'.'

'Very well.' She paused a moment longer and added, 'You should stop all this; there's no need for it.' She waved her hand over the tray. 'There's plenty of others to do this; you should have a rest.'

'I'll have all the rest I need shortly.'

'Oh, Ben, don't say that.'

'Go on, go on. I told you he's waitin'.'

As she went through the hall, with its deep-piled red carpet hushing her step, she wondered what he would do without Ben. Ben had been his right arm, also his whipping post, and his outlet; he'd pine without Ben.

She knocked gently on the drawing-room door, and when she was bidden to enter, the scene was as it always remained in her mind. This room never changed; this was Mr Lord's room. Tony and Lettice had their own sitting-room. It was modernly furnished and very nice, but this room . . . this room had beauty, and dignity, and it was a setting for the figure sitting in the high-backed chair. There was no beauty about Mr Lord, except that which accompanies age, but there was dignity. It was in his every moment, every look, every glance, whether harsh or soft.

He turned his head towards Mary Ann. Giving her no greeting, he said, without preamble, 'You have to be sent for now?'

She did not answer, but walked to the seat opposite to him and, sitting down, said quietly, 'How are you?'

'I'm very well. How are you?'

'All right.'

'Then if you're all right you should make your face match your mood.'

She stared at him; she had never been able to hide anything from him. She turned her gaze to the side now and looked out of the window; then looking back at him, she said, 'Have you heard from Tony and Lettice?'

'Yes, I had a letter this morning. They're enjoying their holiday very much.'

'And Peter?'

'I understand that he, too, is enjoying himself.'

'You will miss him.'

'You have to get used to missing people.'

'Yes . . . yes, I suppose so.' You have to get used to missing people. Would she ever get used to missing Corny? How was it going to end? What was she going to do? . . .

'Well. Now, you've made all the polite enquiries that are necessary to this meeting, you can tell me why you came yesterday and spent the night alone, without either your husband or children?'

She kept her gaze lowered. It was no use saying who told you I came yesterday. Ben was also Mr Lord's scout; nothing escaped Ben. He might be old and doddery, but his mind was as alert as his master's. From his kitchen window he looked down on to the farm, and on to the road that led to the farm. Few people came or went without Ben's knowledge.

'Have you and Cornelius quarrelled?'

She still kept her head lowered; she still made no sound.

'Look at me!' Mr Lord's voice was now harsh and commanding. 'Tell me what this is all about?'

She did not look at him, but as she used to do when a child, she pressed her joined hands betweeen her knees and rocked herself slightly as she said, 'Rose Mary got lost yesterday. Me grannie came to visit us and upset her. She hid in the boot of a car belonging to an American, a Mr Blenkinsop. He didn't discover she was there for a long time. We were all searching when Mr Blenkinsop phoned to say he had found her and he took her to some friends of his. They live in Doncaster. Then, later, he phoned to ask if she could stay the night.' She paused here before going on. 'I wanted her brought back straight-away, but Corny said it was all right and she could stay.'

'Well, well, go on. He said it was all right; he wouldn't have said that if it wasn't all right. Did he know this man?'

'Yes.'

'Well then, there would seem little to worry about. But I take it that you didn't like the fact that Rose Mary wasn't coming back right away and so you got into a paddy.'

'It isn't as simple as that. You see . . .' She now looked him full in the face. 'Corny has always said that David would talk if they were separated. I

599

have always been against it, and when I came home yesterday, I mean after searching for Rose Mary, he was full of the fact that the boy was talking. It must have been the shock of Rose Mary being lost, and Corny said he would have a better chance if they were kept apart a little longer. I thought it was cruel; I still think it is cruel.'

Mr Lord pressed his head back against the chair and screwed his pale-blue eyes up to pin-points. His lips moved from his teeth and he kept his mouth open awhile before he said, 'You mean to say that is the reason you left Cornelius?'

'It sounds so simple saying it, but it wasn't like that.'

'Stick to the point, child.' He still thought of her as a child. 'Your husband wants his son to talk; he feels that if he is separated from his sister he will talk. The opportunity presents itself, and no-one is going to be any the worse for the experiment, and you mean to say that you took umbrage at this and came home, and stayed the night away from him, purposely . . . You mean to tell me that this is what it was all about?'

'I tell you it isn't as simple as all that . . .'

'It is as simple as all that.' He leant towards her. Then moving his index finger slowly at her, he said, 'Now, if you know what's good for you, you will get down to the farm quickly, get your things on and make for home.'

Mary Ann straightened herself up. 'No, no, I can't.'

'You mean you're going to remain stubborn.'

'I mean I can't; he saw me coming away and he didn't stop me.'

'Well, I should say that is something in his

favour. I uphold his action . . . But tell me. How did Rose Mary come here? Did she come by herself?'

'No, he . . . he sent her with . . . with the American. When Mr Blenkinsop took her home he asked him to bring her here.'

Mr Lord leant back in his chair again, and after a moment he said, 'Do you realise, Mary Ann, that this is serious? Situations like this lead to explosions. Now, you do as I tell you.' He did not say take my advice; this was an order. 'Get yourself away home this very minute, and try to remember that you're not dealing with a silly boy, but a strong-willed man. I've reason to know the strength of Mr Cornelius Boyle. Twice in my life I've come up against it. Because he cares for you deeply you might bend his will, but don't try to bend it too far. For, if you do, you'll break yourself and your little family . . . Come here.' He held out his hand and she rose slowly and went to him, and when she stood by his side he took hold of her arm, and looking up at her, he said, 'Don't destroy something good. And you have something good in your marriage. As you know, he wasn't the one I wanted for you, but one learns that one is sometimes wrong. Cornelius is the man for you. Now promise me,' he said, 'you'll go home.'

Mary Ann moved her head from side to side. She pulled in her bottom lip, then uttered under her breath, 'I can't, I can't.'

With a surprisingly strong and swift movement she was thrust aside, and, his voice angry now, he cried at her, 'You're a little fool! Now, I'm warning you. Start learning now before it's too late. If you make him swallow his pride you'll regret it to your dying day, but you'll gain if you swallow yours. Have sense . . . Go on, get away, get out of my sight.'

She got out of his sight. Slowly she closed the door after her and walked through the hall and to the kitchen. There Ben raised his eyes but not his head, and neither of them spoke.

She did not immediately return to the farm-house but went up a by-lane and stood leaning against a five-barred gate that led into the long field. Her whole being ached. She wanted to cry and cry and cry; she felt lonely, lost and fright-ened. But she couldn't go back. He had let her come away when he could easily have stopped her if he had wanted to. If he had cared enough he could have stopped her. She had been in paddies before and he had talked her out of them, coaxed her out of them. He had always brought her round, sometimes none too gently. Once he had slapped her behind, as he would a child, because he said she was acting like one. That had made her more wild still. They hadn't spoken for a whole day then, but come night time and in bed his hand had sought hers and she had left it there within his big palm.

But she couldn't go back, she couldn't, because what he had done to her was cruel. She had nearly been demented when Rose Mary was missing, and no matter how much stock he had put on his theory of David talking if they were separated, he should have forgone that, knowing the state she was in, knowing how she longed to see Rose Mary again and to feel that she was really safe. But all he could think about was that he had been right, and David was talking. She was glad, oh yes, she was glad that David was talking; and now once he had started he would go on. There had been no need to keep them apart; no matter what he said there had been no need to do what he had done. He had been cruel, cruel, and she couldn't go back, not . . . not unless he came for her.

12

But Corny did not come for her, and now it was Tuesday and the situation had become terrifying. Her da had been over to the house; Michael had been over to the house; and when they had come back neither of them had said a word, and she had been too proud to ask what had transpired.

Then today her mother had been over. She hadn't known she was going; it was the last thing on earth she thought her mother would do, to go and talk to Corny. Now Lizzie was sitting with a cup of tea in her hand and she looked down at it as she said, 'You'll have to make the first move.'

'What if I don't?'

'Well, that's up to you; it's your life.'

'Why should I be the one to make the first move?'

'Because you're in the wrong.'

'Oh, Ma!' Mary Ann was on her feet. 'You're another one. Everybody's taken his part, everybody. It's fantastic. Nobody sees my side of it and what I went through, what agony I went through when Rose Mary was lost.'

'We know all about that.' Lizzie took a sip from her cup. 'But that's beside the point now; the whole issue, to my mind, is the fact that you've always been against the twins being separated even for a few hours. Now, if you'd only been sensible about that, this whole business would never have happened. And another thing, Corny was absolutely right, the child's really talking. Four days they've been separated and he's chatter- - ing away like a magpie.' Lizzie now leaned towards Mary Ann and repeated, 'Chattering. It's like a small miracle to hear him. And that alone should make you realise that you've been in the wrong, girl.'

'All right, all right.' Mary Ann flung her arm wide. 'He's proved his point, he's right. But that's just the outside of things; there was the way this was done, and the time it was done and how I felt. Isn't that to be taken into consideration?'

'You're not the only one who's felt like this; I nearly went mad when you were lost, remember. All mothers feel like this.'

'Aw, you're just twisting it, you won't go deeper. And another thing.' Mary Ann bounced her head towards Lizzie now. 'You don't want me here. Oh I know, I can tell, but don't worry, you won't have to put up with me much longer, I can get a job anytime.'

Lizzie, ignoring the first part of Mary Ann's small tirade, said quietly, 'And you'll let Rose Mary go back home?'

'No, I won't.'

'Who's keeping them separated now? And that child's fretting. She's hardly eaten a peck in two days; she's got to go back to that boy, not because of him but for her own sake. David's not worry-ing so much. He asked for her, but that's all. He's as bright as a cricket. Do you know where he was when I got there? Under a car with Corny, and thick with oil, and as happy as a sandboy.'

Mary Ann walked towards the window. She wanted to say sarcastically: was Corny as happy as a sandboy too? But she couldn't mention his name. Her mother hadn't said anything about Corny. She was acting like her da, and their Michael, in this. They were all for him. Yes, even her da now. It was fantastic; everybody was for Corny and against her. She swung round from the window, saying, 'Well, I'm not crawling back, Ma, no matter what you say or any of you. As I said, I'll get a job.'

As she stumped past her mother on her way across the room to the hall, Lizzie said quietly, 'Don't be such a fool, girl. The trouble with you is that you have done the manoeuvring and fixing all your life, so much so, until you've come to think that things have to be done your way or not at all.'

'Oh, Ma!' Mary Ann turned an accusing face on Lizzie.

'You can say Oh, Ma! like that, but it's true. Now you've come up against something you can't have fixed on your terms. Corny's a man; he's not your da, or Mr Lord, or Tony, he's your husband; and he has his rights, and I'm warning you. You try to make him crawl and you'll regret it all your days.'

Mary Ann banged the door after her. Her ma had said practically the same words as Mr Lord. What was the matter with everybody? They were treating her like someone who had committed a crime. She had rights too. Or hadn't she any right to rights? The equality of the sexes. That made you laugh . . . Bunkum! It was all right on paper, but when it was put into action, look what happened. Everybody took the man's side, even her mother . . . She couldn't get over that. She could understand her da in a way, him being a man, but her mother! She was for him, up to the neck and beyond. Everybody was for him and against her.

Then the next morning Fanny came.

Mike ushered her in, unexpectedly, through the back door, crying, 'Liz! Liz! Look at this stupid, fat old bitch walking all the way up from the bus. Hadn't the sense to let us know she was coming, and we could have picked her up . . . Get in there with you.'

Mary Ann was entering the kitchen from the hall, and she saw her mother rush down the long room and greet Fanny at the scullery door, saying, 'Oh, hello there, Fan. Why didn't you tell us?'

'Now, why would I, Lizzie? I've a pair of pins on me yet; and when the doctor said it would do me good to lose some of me fat, do a bit more walking, I said to him, "Now where the hell do you think I'm going to walk . . . round and round the block?" "No," he said; "get yourself out for a day or so. Take a dander into the country, a bus ride, and then a wee stroll." I thought to meself at the time that's Mike and Liz getting at him . . . did you get at him?'

Lizzie and Mike were laughing loudly, and they both shook their heads, and Mike said, 'No, we didn't get at him. But we wish we had thought of it, if it would have brought you out more often. There, sit yourself down.'

He helped her to lower her great fat body into a chair while saying to Rose Mary, 'Let her be now. Let her get her puff.'

Rose Mary, moving aside, looked towards her mother and cried, 'Me Great-gran!'

Fanny turned her eyes and looked across the room now towards Mary Ann and said, 'That's just in case you can't see me, Mary Ann, just in case.'

Mary Ann smiled and came forward and, standing by her friend's side, she said simply, 'Hello.'

'Hello, hinny.' Fanny patted her hand; then asked, 'How are you keepin'?'

'All right.'

'Good, good.' Fanny nodded her head.

Her questions and attitude as yet gave Mary Ann no indication that she knew anything about . . . the trouble, yet it took an event of importance to get Fanny away from the fortress of her home in Mulhattan's Hall, that almost derelict, smelly dark house, divided into flats, one consisting of two rooms in which Fanny had lived since she was married, in which she had brought into the world twelve children, all of whom had gone from her now, some not to return, although they were still living. Jarrow Council had not got down yet to demolishing Burton Street and Mulhattan's Hall, but they would surely come to it before they finished the new Jarrow, and Mary Ann often hoped that Fanny would die before that day, for surely if she didn't she would go when Mulhattan's Hall went.

'Here,' said Lizzie; 'drink that up.'

'And what's this?'

'Don't ask the road you know, get it down

608

you,' said Lizzie, speaking brusquely to this old friend of hers; and Fanny, sniffing at the glass, smiled and, looking sideways at Lizzie, said, 'Brandy, I'm glad I came.' Then, putting the glass to her lips, she threw off the drink at one go, gave a slight shudder, then placed the glass back in Lizzie's hand, saying, 'Thanks, lass.'

'Look,' put in Mike. 'Now that you've got this far and we're in this lovely weather why don't you stay for a day or two?'

'Mike, I'm getting the four o'clock bus back. I've said it and that's what I'm going to do. But thanks all the same for the invitation.'

'You're a cantankerous old bitch still.' He pushed her head none too gently with the flat of his hand, and she retaliated by bringing her hand across his thigh with a resounding wallop. 'There,' she said. 'An' there's more where that comes from. Now get yourself away about your business with your female family, go on.'

All except Mary Ann were laughing now, and as Mike made for the door he replied, 'Me family's not all females; there's a definite male element in it, and I'm expecting two results of his efforts at any minute now.'

'Aw, the poor animals, they don't get away with much, like ourselves. What do you say, Lizzie?'

Lizzie smiled gently as she said, 'I'd say, give me your hat and coat now that you've got your breath and get yourself settled in the big chair there.' She pointed to Mike's leather chair at the side of the fireplace. 'Then you'll have a cup of tea and a bite that'll put you over till dinner time.'

If Mary Ann at first had wondered what had

brought her friend to the farm, half-an-hour later she was in no doubt whatever, because, of all the topics touched upon, Corny's name or that of David had not been mentioned, and when her mother, holding her hand out towards Rose Mary, said, 'I'm going to the dairy, I want some cream. Come along with me,' Mary Ann knew that Mrs McBride was being given the opportunity to voice the real reason for her visit.

Mary Ann was standing at the long kitchen table in the centre of the room preparing a salad, and Fanny was looking at her from out of the depths of the leather chair, and for a full minute after being left alone neither of them spoke, until Fanny said abruptly, 'I don't blame you, lass. Don't think that.'

Mary Ann turned her head swiftly over her shoulder and looked at this fat, kindly, wise, bigoted, obstinate and sometimes harsh old woman, and after a pause she asked, 'How did you find out?'

'Oh, bad news has the speed of light. I read that somewhere, and it's true. It was last night, comin' out of confession, I met Jimmy's mother. She's got a mouth on her like a whale. She didn't know the real rights of the case, she said, but she said you were gone to your mother's because she was ill, and you had taken the girl with you, leavin' the boy behind you. She thought it was a funny thing to do as Jimmy had said you couldn't separate the two with a pair of pliers. What did I think of it, she said. Was it all right between them; they weren't splitting up or anything? I said to her, when I heard that the Holy family was splitting up then I'd know for sure that my grandson and his wife were following suit . . . But I was worried sick, lass, sick to the soul of me. I knew that something must have happened for you to separate the children, an' so I went along this mornin'.'

Mary Ann was standing with her buttocks pressed against the back of the table. She moved her head in small jerks before she said, 'You've been home already to-day?'

'Aye, I got there around half-past nine, and, when I got to the bottom of things, let him take what I gave him.'

Mary Ann stared at Mrs McBride, her lower lip hanging loose. Corny was the pride and joy of this old woman's heart. In Mrs McBride's eyes Corny was all that a man should be, physically, mentally and morally. Her standards might not be those of Olympus but they were high, and she knew what went to make a good man, and she had always considered that her grandson, Corny, had all the ingredients for the pattern in her mind. Yet here she was, against Corny, and the first one to be so.

Everybody had been against her. They had said: You're a fool. It's your temper. It's your stubbornness. You can't have everything your own way, and you've got to realise that. But nobody, up till now, had said that Corny was at fault. Yet here was his grannie shouting him down.

'I told him he was a big, empty-headed nowt, and he didn't know which side his bread was buttered, and that if you never went back to him he was only gettin' what he deserved.'

'Oh, Mrs McBride!' It was a mere whisper, and Mary Ann's head drooped as she spoke.

'Well!' Fanny was sitting upright now, as upright as her fat would allow. 'When he told me what it was all about I nearly went straight through the roof. A man! I said. You call yourself a man, and you take the pip at a thing like that. Just because she expresses her opinion you go off the deep end?'

Mary Ann raised her head slightly. 'I . . . I said things I shouldn't have, Mrs McBride; he's . . . he's not altogether to blame. I . . . I said I hated him.'

'Aw!' Mrs McBride pushed her fat round in the chair until she was half-turned away from Mary Ann, and, looking into the empty fireplace, she thrust her arm out and flapped her hand towards Mary Ann as she cried, 'Aw, if a man is going to let his wife walk out on him because she says she hates him, then every other house in the land would be empty. I've never heard anything so childish in me life. Hate him! I'd like a penny for every time I've said I hated McBride. And mind . . .' She twisted herself round again in Mary Ann's direction, and, her arm again extended and her fingers wagging, she said, 'I always acccompanied me words with something concrete, the frying pan, the flat iron, a bottle, anything that came to hand. You know me big black broth pan, the one I can hardly lift off the hob when it's full? I can just about manage it when it's empty. Well, I remember the day as if it was yesterday that I hurled it at his head, and I used those very words to give it God speed: I hate you. And I didn't say them plain and unadorned, if you get what I mean; I always made me remarks to McBride a bit flowery. Begod!' She moved her triple chins from one shoulder to the other. 'If that pan had found its target that particular day it would have been good-bye to McBride twenty years earlier. Aw! Me aim was poor that time. An' it was likely because I was carryin'. I gave birth to me twins three days later. One of them died, the other one is Georgie, you know.'

Mary Ann wanted to smile; she wanted to laugh; she wanted to cry; oh, how she wanted to cry.

'Come here,' said Fanny gently. 'Come here.' And Mary Ann went to her, and Fanny put her arms round her waist and said, 'I'm upset to me very soul. He's as near to me as the blood pumping out of me heart, but at the same time I'm not for him. No, begod! The way I see it, he was given a pot of gold and he's acted as if it was a holey bucket picked up off a midden. He let you walk away . . . just like that.' She made a slow gliding movement with her hand.

'B . . . b . . . but, Mrs McBride . . .'

'Oh, I don't blame you for walkin' out, I don't blame you not a jot, lass. You've got to make a stand with them or your life's simply hell. Even when you do make a stand it isn't easy, but if you let them walk over you you might as well go straight to the priest and arrange for a requiem to be said, because your time's short. You can bank on that.'

Mary Ann stood quietly now, fondling the creased and not over-clean hand as she asked, 'How was he? And David?'

'Oh, a bit peakish-looking about the gills. They all get very sorry for themselves. He'd been having his work cut out getting the breakfast ready; the place was strewn with dishes. Hell's cure to you, I said. You're just gettin' what you deserve. But David, he was sprightly. He speaks now. I got the gliff of me life.'

Mary Ann's hands stopped moving over Mrs McBride. 'It was about that that all the trouble started.'

'About David talkin', you mean?'

'Yes, Corny had said that if they were separated David would talk . . . Well he's been proved right, hasn't he?'

'Nonsense, nonsense. It was the scare he got when Rose Mary was lost that made him talk, not the separation.'

'Yes. I know. But Corny thought that if they came together too quickly that David wouldn't make any more effort. And I can see his point, I can, Mrs McBride, but—'

'Now don't you go soft, girl. No matter what points you see, don't you go soft, because you'll have to pay for it in the end. He's a big, ignorant, empty-headed nowt, as I told him, an' I should know because he's inherited a lot of meself.' She nodded at Mary Ann, and Mary Ann was forced to smile just the slightest.

It was funny about people. They never acted as you expected them to. She had really been afraid of Mrs McBride finding out and going for her, and yet here she was taking her part. She bent down swiftly and kissed the flabby, wrinkled face, and Fanny held her and said, 'There now. There now. Now don't cry, he's not worth it. Although it's meself that's sayin' it, he's not worth it.'

At the same time, deep in her heart, Fanny was praying, 'God forgive me. God forgive me for every word I've uttered against him in these last few minutes.'

It was the evening of the same day, when Mary Ann was in the bathroom bathing Rose Mary, when she heard the car stop in the lane outside the front door. Rose Mary, too, heard it, and she looked up at her mother and said, 'There's a car, Mam.'

Mary Ann's heart began to pound and she had trouble in controlling her voice as she said, 'Come on, get out and get dried.'

'Mam.' Rose Mary hugged the towel around her. 'Do you think it'll be me . . . ?'

'Get dried and put your nightie on. Here, sit on the cracket and give me your feet.' She rubbed Rose Mary's feet vigorously; she rubbed her back, and her chest. She had put her nightdress on and combed her hair when the bathroom door was pushed open and Lizzie stood there, saying, 'You'd better come down; there's an assortment down there wanting to see you.'

Mary Ann's eyes widened. 'An assortment? Who? What?'

'Well, come and see for yourself. Five of them, headed by that Jimmy from the garage.'

A cold wave of disappointment swept through her, making her shiver.

'What do they want?' she said.

'You, apparently.'

'Me! What do they want with me?'

'You'd better come down and see.'

'Can I come, Mam?'

'No, stay where you are. Go and get into bed.'

'But, Mam.'

'Get into bed, Rose Mary.'

She turned from her daughter and passed her mother; then ran down the stairs and to the front door. And it was as Lizzie had said, it was an assortment that stood on the front lawn facing her.

She knew for certain that Jimmy was a boy, but she had first of all to guess at the sex of the other four. True they were wearing trousers, but there ended any indication of their maleness, for they were also wearing an assortment of blouses, one with a ruffle at the neck; their hair was long and ranged from startling blond to tow colour, from dead brown to a horrible ginger. There wasn't a hair to be seen on their faces, nor yet on what skin was showing of their arms. The sight of them repulsed Mary Ann and made her stomach heave. She turned her attention pointedly to Jimmy, and noticed in this moment that although his hair, too, was longish, his maleness stood out from that of his pals like a sore finger.

Jimmy grinned at her. 'Hello, Mrs Boyle,' he said.

'What do you want, Jimmy?' Mary Ann's tone was curt.

'Aw, I just thought I'd pop along and see you. You know, about . . . about the lines you did. You know.'

'Oh!' Mary Ann closed her eyes for a moment and wet her lips. She had forgotten about the lines. She wanted to say, 'Look, I'm not interested any more,' but Jimmy's bright expression prevented her from flattening him with such a remark.

'These are me pals . . . the Group. This is Duke.'

He thumbed towards the repulsive, red-haired individual. 'He runs us and he's good at tunes. I was tellin' you.' He nodded twice, then thumbed towards the next boy. 'This is Barney. He's on the drums.' Barney was the tow-haired one. He was also the one with the ruffle. He opened his mouth wide and smiled at Mary Ann. She had never seen such a big mouth on a boy before. It seemed to split his face in two. She turned her eyes to the next boy as Jimmy said, 'This is Poodle Patter. We call him that 'cos he's good at ad lib, small talk you know, keeping things goin'. Aren't you, Poodle?'

Poodle jerked his head at Mary Ann, and a ripple passed over his face. It was an expression of self-satisfaction and had no connection whatever with a pleased-to-meet-you expression.

Mary Ann stared at Poodle, at his startlingly blond hair, and she had to stop her nose from wrinkling in this case.

'And he's Dave.' Jimmy thumbed towards the back of the group, where stood the brown-haired individual. He had small merry eyes and a thin mouth, and he nodded to Mary Ann and said, 'Wat-cher!'

'Dave plays the guitar, and he can do the mouth-organ.'

Jimmy jerked his head towards Dave, and Dave jerked his head back at him, and they exchanged grins.

Mary Ann was tired; she was weary with worry; she was sick at this moment with disappointment; she had thought, oh, she had thought that Corny had come for her; and now she was sick in another way as she looked at these four boys. Jimmy didn't make her sick, he only irritated her. She said to him, 'Look, Jimmy, I'm very busy. What do you want?'

Jimmy's long face lengthened; his eyebrows went up and his lower lip went down, and he said, 'Well, like I said, about your lyrics. Duke's put a tune to them.'

'Oh!'

'Haven't you, Duke?'

Duke now stepped forward. He had an insolent walk; he had an insolent look; and he spread his look all over Mary Ann before he said, 'It was ropey in parts.'

'What was?'

'Well, that stuff that you did. The title's all right, and the punch line, "She acts like a woman", but the bit about not wantin' diamonds and mink, well, that isn't with it, not the day. They don't expect them things. A drink, aye, but not the other jollop.'

'No?' The syllable sounded aggressive, even to Mary Ann herself.

'No! Not the teenagers don't. Who's going to buy them furs an' rings and things, eh? Unless a fellow hits the jackpot he can just scramble by by hisself.' Duke now wrinkled his nose as if from a bad smell. 'Aw, it's old fashioned. Ten years, even twenty behind the times. But I've left in about the rings. But they don't talk like you wrote it any more; still the way I've worked it, it'll come over.'

'Thank you.'

'The pleasure's mine.'

Mary Ann's jaws tightened. They don't talk like you wrote it any more. How old did he think she was, forty?

'Well, how do they talk?' The aggressive note was still there.

'Huh!' Duke laughed, then slanted his eyes around his mates, and they all joined in, with the exception of Jimmy, for Jimmy was looking at the bad weather signs coming from Mrs Boyle. He knew Mrs Boyle's bad weather signs.

'Want me to tell you?'

Before Mary Ann could answer Jimmy put in, 'Aw, give over Duke. You know you like it; you said it had it, especially that line.'

'Oh aye, I've just said, that's a punch line: "She acts like a woman." But the rest . . . aw, it's old men's stuff . . . Bob Hope, Bing Crosby.'

'Well, there's nothing more to be said, is there?' Mary Ann had a great desire to reach out and slap his face. She turned quickly away. But as she did so Jimmy put his hand out towards her, saying, 'Aw, Mrs Boyle, that's just him. Don't take any notice; he's always like this. But he likes it, he does.' He turned his head over his shoulder and said to Duke, 'Come off it, Duke, an' tell her you think it's good. We all think it's good.' He swung his gaze over the rest of them, and the other three boys nodded and spoke together, and the gist was that they thought the lyrics fine and with it, just a word had needed altering here and there.

'You see.' Jimmy nodded at Mary Ann. 'Would you like to hear it?'

'No, Jimmy.' Mary Ann's tone was modified now, and she added swiftly, 'I'm . . . I'm busy.'

'Aw, come on, Mrs Boyle; that's what we've come out for, to let you hear it. And then if you think it's all right we was goin' to try it out at "The Well" on Saturday night. An' you never know, there's always scouts hanging round an' they might pick it up.'

Mary Ann looked from Jimmy to Duke, and back to Jimmy, and she said, stiffly now, 'That wasn't my idea; I thought it could be sent away to—'

'You do what you like, missus,' Duke put in, shaking his head vigorously, 'but if you send it away that's the last you'll hear of it, until you recognise snatches of the tune on the telly and hear your words all mixed up. You send it away if you like, but it's as Jimmy says, there are scouts kickin' around, on the look-out for punch lines, an' you've got one here, "She acts like a woman". It's got a two-fold attraction; it'll appeal to the old dames over twenty, and make the young 'uns think they're grown up. See what I mean?' Duke was speaking ordinarily now, and Mary Ann nodded and said, flatly, 'Yes, I suppose you're right.' But she wished they would get themselves away. She was still feeling sick with disappointment. She wanted to be alone and cry. Oh, how she wanted to cry at this minute. What was she standing here for anyway? As long as she remained they wouldn't budge. She was turning round when Jimmy pleaded, 'Will you listen to it, then?' His face was one big appeal, and before Mary Ann could answer, and without taking his eyes off her, he said, 'Get the kit out.'

The four boys stared at Mary Ann for a minute, then turned nonchalantly about and went towards the car, and Mary Ann, looking helplessly at Jimmy, said, 'Where are they going to do it?'

'Why, here.' Jimmy spread his hands. 'We can play anywhere.'

Mary Ann cast a glance over her shoulder. There was only her mother in the house; her da and their Michael were still on the farm; they were having a bit of trouble getting a cow to calve. If they had been indoors she would have said a firm no to any demonstration, but now she just stood and looked at Jimmy, then from him to where the boys were hauling their instruments out of the car.

Jimmy brought his attention back to her when he said, softly, 'I miss you back at the house, Mrs Boyle.'

She looked at his straight face and it was all she could do not to burst into tears right there.

'It isn't the same.'

'Be quiet, Jimmy.'

It was no use trying to hoodwink Jimmy by telling him she was staying with her mother because she was sick, or some such tale, for behind Jimmy's comic expression Mary Ann now felt, as Corny had always pointed out, there was a serious side, a knowing side. Jimmy wasn't as soppy as he made himself out to be. Even a few minutes ago, when he had pointed to Duke as the leader of the group, she felt that whatever brains were needed to guide this odd assortment it was he who supplied them.

The boys came back up the path, and one of them handed a guitar to Jimmy; then, grouping themselves, they faced her and, seemingly picking up an invisible sign, they all started together. There followed a blast of sound, a combination of instruments and voices that was deafening.

SHE ACTS LIKE A WOMAN
SHE ACTS LIKE A WOMAN

Mary Ann screwed up her face against the noise. She watched the fair-haired boy, Poodle Patter as Jimmy had called him, his head back, wobbling on the last word: WOOMA . . . AN. This was followed by a number of chords, and then they all started again.

MAN, I'M TELLING YOU.
SHE ACTS LIKE A WOMAN.

SHE PELTED ME WITH THINGS,
AND THEN SHE TORE HER HAIR.

SHE ACTS LIKE A WOMAN.

I'VE GIVEN HER MY LOT,
NOW I WAS FINISHED, BROKE,
AND THEN SHE SPOKE OF LOVE.

SHE ACTS LIKE A WOMAN.

ME, SHE SAID, SHE WANTED,
NOT RINGS OR THINGS.

SHE ACTS LIKE A WOMAN.

MAN, I JUST SPREAD MY HANDS.
WHAT WAS I TO DO?
YOU TELL ME,
WHAT WAS I TO DO?
EARLY MORNING THERE SHE STOOD,
NO MAKE-UP FACE LIKE MUD,

BIG EYES RAINING TEARS AND FEARS.

SHE ACTS LIKE A WOMAN.

*THEN, MAN, SOMETHING MOVED IN
    HERE,
LIKE DAYLIGHT,
AND I COULD SEE SHE ONLY WANTED
    M-EE.*

SHE ACTS LIKE A WOOO-MA-AN.

As the voices trailed off the last word and all
the hands crashed out the last note, Mary Ann
gaped at the five boys, and they stood in silence
waiting. For a brief second she forgot her misery.
It had sounded grand, excellent, as good as
anything that was on the pops. He was clever.
She looked directly at Duke and said what she
thought.

'I think you've made a splendid job of it, the
way you've arranged the words and brought out
that line. I think it's grand.'

All the faces before her were expanding now
into wide, pleased grins. Even Duke's cockiness
was lost under the outward sign of his pleasure,
when, at that moment, round the corner of the
house, came Mike. He came like a bolt of
thunder.

'What the hell do you think you're up to!
What's this?'

After the words had crashed about them they
all turned and looked at the big fellow who was
coming towards them, his step slower now, his
face showing an expression of sheer incredulity.

They stood silent as he eyed them from head to toe, one after the other. Then, his voice exploding again, he cried, 'What the hell are you lot doing here? Who's dug you up?'

'Da . . . Da, this is Jimmy. You know Jimmy.'

Mike turned his eyes towards Jimmy; then returned them slowly back to the other four as Mary Ann went on hastily, 'They are Jimmy's Group; they've . . .' She paused. How to say they had set some of her words to music; this wasn't the time. 'They had a tune they thought I . . . I would like to hear.'

'THEY . . . HAD . . . A . . . TUNE they thought you'd like to hear? Have you gone barmy, girl? You call that noise a tune? It's nearly put the finishing touches to Freda.'

'Then Freda isn't with it, is she, Mister?' This was Duke speaking. His tone was insolent and brought Mike swinging round to him. 'Freda's more with it than you, young fellow, if that is what you are, which I doubt very much. Freda's only a cow, a sick cow at the present moment, but I wouldn't swap her for the lot of you.'

The four boys stared back at Mike, their faces expressionless. It was a tense moment, until the fair-haired boy, Poodle Patter, asked quietly, 'What she sick with, Mister?'

'She's trying to calve, but you lot wouldn't understand anything about that, being neither one thing nor the other.'

Again there was a silence, during which Mary Ann's hand went out towards Mike. But she didn't touch him; she was afraid she might explode something here, for she could see him tearing his one arm from her grasp and knocking them down like ninepins.

'You'd be surprised.' This calm rejoinder came from Duke. 'As me dad says, ministers wear frocks but they still manage to be fathers.'

Mike and Duke surveyed each other for a moment. Then Mike, his lips hardly moving, said, 'Get yourselves out! An' quick.'

For answer, Duke lifted one shoulder and turned about, and the others followed suit, Jimmy coming up in the rear. As they neared the gate Poodle stopped, swung round, and, his face wearing a most innocent expression, addressed Mike, calling up the path to him, 'Can you tell me, Mister, if the caps are put on the milk bottles after the cows lay them, or do they all come through sealed up?'

Mary Ann's two hands now flashed out and caught Mike's sleeve, and she begged softly under her breath, 'Da! Da! Don't, please.'

Outside the gate and standing near the car, Duke turned again and looked up towards Mike, and he called in a loud voice now, 'If you'd started anything, old 'un, you'd have come off second best, an' if you hadn't been a cripple with only one hand I wouldn't have let you get away with half what you did. But don't try it on again.'

Mary Ann leant back and hung on to Mike now, and as she did so Lizzie and Michael appeared at the other side of him, and Lizzie said, tersely, 'Let them go. Let them go. Come on, get yourself inside.' They pulled him around and almost dragged him indoors.

Neither of them had said a word to Mary Ann,

and she stood leaning against the stanchion of the door, looking at the car, waiting for it to go, and as she watched she saw Jimmy spring out and come up to the path again. And this brought her agitatedly from the doorway and hastily towards him, crying under her breath, 'Get yourself away; get them out of this.'

'All right, all right, Mrs Boyle; they'll do nothin'. I'm sorry. I'm sorry about all this, but you see I didn't only come about the tune, there . . . there was something else. It was . . . well, I won't be seeing you again, I don't suppose. That's what I meant to say first of all.'

Mary Ann shook her head, and the boy went on, 'You see, I'm leavin'.'

Mary Ann forced herself to say, 'I'm sorry,' and was about to add yet again, 'Get yourself and that crowd away,' when Jimmy put in, 'So am I, but with the boss s . . . sellin' up . . .'

'What! What did you say?' She put her hand out towards him as if she was going to grab the lapel of his coat. Then she closed her fist and pressed it into her other hand and almost whimpered, 'Selling up. What do you mean?'

'Well, that's what I came about. You see, I think the boss is goner sell out to Mr Blenkinsop. He wouldn't sell out to Riley, 'cos he doesn't like Mr Riley, does he? But . . . but I think he'll sell out to the American. And I wouldn't want to stay if the boss wasn't there, so I'm lookin' out for another job . . .'

'Who . . . who told you this?'

'Oh. Well, you know me; I keep me ears open, Mrs Boyle.' He stared at her, his long face unsmiling. 'It's awful back there without you. An' I don't think the boss can stick it, that's why he's goin' I suppose.'

There was a loud concerted call from the car now, and Jimmy said, 'I'll have to be off, but . . . but that's really what I came about. Bye, Mrs Boyle.'

She nodded at him and then said under her breath, 'Good-bye, Jimmy.'

She watched the car move away in a cloud of black smoke from the exhaust, and when it was out of sight she still stood where Jimmy had left her. It was many, many years since she had experienced the feeling of utter despair, and then it had been her da who had evoked that feeling in her. Yet she could recall that her despair in the past had always been threaded with hope, hope that something nice would happen to her da. And nice things had happened to her da. Bad things had also happened to him, but in the main they were nice things that had happened. He stood where he was to-day because of the nice things she had wished and prayed would happen to him. She had always worked at her wishing and her praying – she had never let God get on with it alone – and so her da had made good.

But now she had reached a point in her existence where the main issue was not somebody else's life but her own; she could see her life disintegrating, crumbling away before her eyes. How had it started? How had this situation come about? How did all such situations come about but by little things piling on little things. One stick, one straw, one piece of wood, all entwined; another stick, another straw, another piece of wood, and soon you had a little dam; and a little dam grew with every layer until it stretched across the river of your life and you were cut off, cut off from the other part of you, that part of you that held your heart, and, in her case, cut off from her own flesh and blood, from her son. But the son, in this moment, was a secondary loss; it was the father she was thinking about; Corny was going to sell up. He had stood fast from the beginning; he had bought the garage in the face of opposition. Everybody had said he had been done. Four thousand for a place like that! He must have been bonkers, was the general opinion. Oh yes, it would be a good thing if the road went through, but would it go through? Corny had held on, held on to the threadbare hope of the road going through. And the road hadn't gone through, yet still he had held on. Something would turn up, something; he knew it would. She could feel him stroking her hair in the darkness of the night, talking faith into himself, recharging himself for another day. 'You'll see, Mary Ann, you'll see. Something 'll turn up, and then I'll make it all up to you. I'll buy you the biggest car you ever saw. I'll have the house rebuilt; you'll have so many new clothes that Lettice will think she's a rag-woman.' Corny, in the dark of the night, talking faith into himself and her. And now he was going to sell up. He couldn't, he couldn't.

'What's come over you?'

Mary Ann turned and looked up the path to where Michael was standing in the doorway, so like his father that he could be his younger brother. She did not answer him but walked towards him, her face grim with the defiance his tone had evoked in her.

'How in the name of God have you got yourself mixed up with that lot?'

'I'm not mixed up with that lot; I've never seen them in my life before, except Jimmy.'

She glared at him as she passed him, and she was going across the hall when his voice came to her, softly now, saying, 'You take my advice and get yourself off home this very minute. Don't be such a blasted little fool.'

'You mind your own business, our Michael. You're so blooming smug you make me sick.'

'And you're so blooming pig-headed you're messing up your life. Corny is right in the stand he's taking. Everybody is with him.'

She was at the foot of the stairs now, and she turned to face him, crying, 'I don't care if the whole world is with him. I don't need your sympathy or anybody else's. I stand on my own feet. And you mind your own business and gather all your forces to run your own life. You're not dead yet; you may have a long way to go, so don't crow.'

She was at the top of the stairs when Michael's voice came from the foot, crying at her, 'Who's crowing? Be your age, and stop acting like little Mary Ann Shaughnessy.'

As Mary Ann burst into her room she heard her mother's voice crying, 'Michael!' and his voice trailing away, saying, 'Aw well, somebody's got to . . .'

And then she was brought to a stop by the sight of Rose Mary standing near the window. She was looking straight at her, her face tear-stained and her lips trembling. 'I saw Jimmy, Mam,' she said.

'Get into bed. I told you to get into bed.'

'I want to go back home, Mam.'

'Get into bed, Rose Mary.'

'I want our David, Mam, and me dad. I miss them. I miss our David, Mam.'

'Rose Mary, what did I say?'

'Could I just go over the morrow and—?'

Mary Ann's hand came none too gently across Rose Mary's buttocks, and Rose Mary let out a loud cry, and when the hand came again she let out another. A minute later the door burst open and there stood Lizzie.

'You've got no need to take it out of the child. Michael was right; you've got to come to your senses. And don't you smack her again; she's done nothing. The only thing she wants is to go home to her father and her brother.'

'She happens to be my child, Mother.' Mary Ann always addressed Lizzie as mother in times of stress. 'And I'll do what I like with her, as you did with me.'

'Well, you smack her again if you dare!' Lizzie's face was dark with temper, and Mary Ann's equally so as she snapped back, 'I'll smack her when I like. She happens to be mine, and I'll thank you not to interfere. And I'd better inform you now that this is the last night you'll have to give me shelter; I'm going to find a place for us both to-morrow.'

'You're mad, girl, that's what you are, mad. It's a pity Corny didn't use his hands on you and beat sense into you. He's slipped up somewhere.'

The door banged and Mary Ann turned slowly

round to see her daughter sitting up in bed, her face puckered, her arms held out towards her, and, rushing to her, she hugged her to her breast. Then throwing herself on the bed, she cradled the child in her arms and they both cried together.

13

The following morning Mary Ann went to Newcastle, and she took Rose Mary with her. Lizzie had shed tears in front of her before she left the house, saying, 'Don't be silly, lass, don't be silly. We've all said things we're sorry for, but it's just because we're all concerned for you.'

She had replied to her mother, 'It's all right, it's all right, I know.' She had sounded very subdued, and she was very subdued. Inside, she felt lifeless, half dead. She left Lizzie with the impression that she was going after a job, and she was, but it wasn't the real reason for her visit to Newcastle.

First, she must go and see Mr Quinton. It was many years since she had seen Bob Quinton. At different periods in her life he had loomed large, and when he appeared on her horizon it had always spelt trouble, mostly for her da, because her da had thought Mr Quinton wanted her ma, and he had at one time. But all that was in the past. She was going to Mr Quinton now to ask him how she could get in touch with Mr Blenkinsop.

Mary Ann was not shown into Mr Quinton's presence immediately. The girl in the enquiries office wanted to know her business, and when she said it was private, the girl stared at her, then she took her time before she lifted the receiver and began to speak.

Mary Ann's spirits were so low at this moment that she couldn't take offence.

When the girl stopped speaking she looked up at Mary Ann and said, 'Miss Taylor will see if he's in; you had better take a seat.'

Mary Ann had hardly sat herself down and pulled Rose Mary's coat straight when the phone rang again, and the girl, looking up, said, 'He'll see you.'

It was almost at the same moment that Mary Ann heard a remembered voice coming from the adjoining room. The intersecting door was opened by a woman, and, behind her, appeared Mr Quinton. 'Well, hello, Mary Ann.' He held out his hand as he crossed towards her.

'Hello, Mr Quinton.'

'Oh, it is good to see you. It's years since I clapped eyes on you.' He held on to her hand. 'And this, I bet, is Rose Mary. When was it I last saw her?' He bent down to Rose Mary. 'When was it when I last saw you?' He chucked her under the chin. 'At your christening, I think.'

'That's right,' said Mary Ann.

'Come on, come on in.' He pushed them both before him, past the staring young lady at the desk, and the smiling elderly secretary, through the secretary's office and into a third room.

'Sit yourself down.' He stood back from her and looked at her. 'You haven't altered a scrap. You know, you never age, Mary Ann.'

'Aw, I wish you were speaking the truth.' She

moved her head sadly. 'I feel an old woman at this moment.'

'Old woman? Nonsense.' He waved his hand at her and pulled his chair from behind the desk to the side of it, so that he was near to her, and he sat looking at her hard before he asked quietly, 'How's Lizzie?'

'Oh, she's fine.'

'And Mike?'

'He's fine, too.'

'And how's that big fellow of yours?'

Mary Ann's face became stiff for a moment, and then she said, 'Oh, he's quite well.'

Bob Quinton stared at her; then he looked at the child and smiled widely, and put out his hand once again and chucked her chin. And Rose Mary giggled just a little bit.

'Mr Quinton, I've come to ask you if you could give me Mr Blenkinsop's address. I . . . I understand you're going to build this factory for him?'

'Yes, I am, I'm very pleased to say.' He bent his body in a deep bow towards her. 'It's a very big contract.'

'Yes.' Mary Ann nodded.

'And you want his address?'

'Yes, please. If you would.'

Bob Quinton narrowed his eyes at Mary Ann. There was something here that wasn't quite right. He had heard from Blenkinsop that he was putting the petrol side of the business in young Boyle's hands. He had intended to pay him a visit this very morning and congratulate him, yet here was his wife looking for Mr Blenkinsop on the side. Why hadn't she asked Corny for the address? Mary Ann was a fixer; she had fixed so many people's lives that at one time he had attributed to her special powers. But the powers she had possessed were of innocence, the power attached to love, the great love that she bore her father. Yet the Mary Ann sitting before him now looked deflated, sort of lost. She didn't look possessed of any special power. He glanced at the child again; then, getting to his feet, he said, 'What about a cup of coffee, eh? You'd like one?'

'I would, thank you.' Mary Ann nodded at him.

'And milk for this lady?' He tugged gently at Rose Mary's hair.

'If you please,' said Mary Ann.

'Come along. No, I don't mean you.' He flapped his hand at Mary Ann. 'I mean this young lady. She'll have to go and help Mrs Morton fetch it.'

He pulled open the office door and said, 'Mrs Morton, do you think you could take this young lady over to Simpson's and bring a tray of coffee?' Then leaning over towards his secretary, he said softly, 'I would ask Miss Jennings to do it but I don't think I can trust her to bring the coffee and the child both back safely. What do you say?'

Mrs Morton gave him a tight smile. Then, holding her hand out to Rose Mary, she said, 'Come along, my dear.'

Rose Mary hesitated and looked through the door towards her mother. And when she saw Mary Ann nod her head she gave her hand to the secretary.

Back in the room, Bob Quinton resumed his seat, and, bending towards Mary Ann, one elbow on his knee, he held out his hand, palm upwards, saying, 'Come on, spit it out. What's the trouble?'

'Oh,' Mary Ann looked away from him. 'Corny. Corny and I have had a bit of a disagreement.'

'Corny?' Although he had wondered why she hadn't asked Corny for Mr Blenkinsop's address he hadn't, for a moment, thought the trouble was with him. Her da again, yes, because Mike, being Mike, was unpredictable. There had been some talk years ago about him carrying on with a young girl. But Mary Ann having trouble with Corny. Why? He understood they were crazy about each other. He remembered Corny from far back when, as a boy, Mary Ann had championed him. Surely nothing could go wrong between those two. But things did go wrong between people who loved each other. He had only to look at his own life. He said gently, 'You and Corny . . . I can't take that in, Mary Ann.'

'Nor can I.' There were tears in her eyes.

'A woman?'

'Oh no, no!' She sounded for a moment like the old spirited Mary Ann, and he smiled at her, then said, 'What then?'

'Oh, it started with the children.'

'The children?'

She nodded. Then, haltingly, she gave him a brief outline of what had happened, and finished with, 'I heard yesterday he's going to sell out to Mr Blenkinsop, and he mustn't do it, Mr Quinton, he mustn't. He's worked and slaved, he's lived just to make the place pay, and now it's in his hands and it's going to be a big thing he's going to sell up.'

'Well, you know, Mary Ann, I think the cure lies with you. You could stop all this by going back.'

Mary Ann straightened her shoulders and leant her back against the chair, and then she said sadly, 'He doesn't want me any more. If he had wanted me badly he would have come and fetched me.'

'Aw! Aw! Mary Ann.' Bob Quinton rose to his feet and flapped his hands in the air as if wafting flies away. 'A woman's point of view again. Aw! Aw! Mary Ann. The medieval approach . . . is that what you want?'

'No. No, you misunderstand me.'

'No, I don't. I don't. But you, above all people, I would have thought would have tackled this situation with reason. You, who have patched up so many lives, are now quite willing to sit back and watch your own be smashed up on an issue of chivalry, because that's what it amounts to.'

'Oh no, it doesn't, Mr Quinton.' Mary Ann shook her head widely. 'You're misconstruing everything; in fact, you're just like all the others.'

'What, has your da said something similar, and your mother?'

'Everybody has.'

'Well, I think they're right. But look; the time's going on and the child will be back in a moment. What do you want to see Mr Blenkinsop for? To ask him not to buy Corny out?'

'Yes, that's it.'

'Well, have you thought of the possibility that if he doesn't sell to him he'll sell to someone else?'

'Yes, I have. But . . . but if Mr Blenkinsop makes it clear that he doesn't want to buy and that he won't give the business to anyone else if Corny goes then there'll be no point, will there, because he won't get very much for it as it stands, just what we paid. And we've hardly paid anything off the mortgage – you don't in fact the first few years, do you?'

A slow smile spread across Bob Quinton's face, and he moved his head from side to side as he said, 'I'm glad to see that little scheming brain of yours can still work. And now it's my turn to act fairy godmother in a small way, because I'm meeting Mr Blenkinsop in exactly' – he looked down at his watch – 'twenty-five minutes from now. He's picking me up and we're going round the site. You know, I intended to look in on you today . . . Ah, here they come with the coffee.' He went swiftly towards the door and took the tray from his secretary. 'And cakes! Who likes cakes with cream on?'

'I do.'

Bob Quinton looked down towards Rose Mary as his secretary said, 'She picked them.'

'Well, she'll have to eat them,' said Bob, laughing.

'I can't eat all the six. Anyway, Mam only lets me have one.' Rose Mary smiled towards her mother. Then, still looking at her, she added, 'But I could take one in a bag for David, couldn't I, Mam?'

'Rose Mary!' said Mary Ann chidingly, and Rose Mary bowed her head.

It was half an hour later, and Mary Ann was sitting in the same chair, looking at Mr Blenkinsop, and Mr Blenkinsop was looking at her, and a heavy silence had fallen on them. They had the office to themselves, for Bob Quinton had thoughtfully conducted Rose Mary to the next room.

Mr Blenkinsop now blinked rapidly, placed his hands together as if in prayer, then rubbed the palms one against the other before he said, 'How did you come to know that I was going to buy your husband out?'

'Jimmy . . . our boy, he came round last night to the farm and told me. He . . . he thought I should know.'

'Jimmy.' Mr Blenkinsop's lips were pursed, then again he said, 'Jimmy.' And now his eyes rolled back and he inspected a corner of the ceiling for a long moment before saying, 'Well, well!' Then, rising from his chair, he walked about the room. When he came to a standstill, he said, 'And you don't want your husband to sell?'

'No.' She screwed her head round. 'He's worked so hard, and he's doing it because . . . well, of what I told you . . . the trouble between us.'

'He's a fool.'

'What!'

Mr Blenkinsop walked round to face Mary Ann. 'I said he's a fool. He shouldn't put up with this situation; he should have gone to the farm and picked you up and taken you home and spanked you.'

'You think he should?' Mary Ann smiled a weak smile.

'I do.'

'You don't think I should have gone crawling back?'

'He shouldn't have given you time to do anything; he should have followed you straightaway, got you by the scruff of the neck and yanked you home.' He was smiling as he spoke, and Mary Ann, swallowing deeply, said, 'You know, Mr Blenkinsop, you're the only one who has said that, except . . . except his grannie. Everybody else seems to think that I should have gone back on my own.'

'We . . . ell.' He drew out the word. 'Perhaps I'm used to dealing with American women, but under the same circumstances if their man hadn't come haring after them and grabbed them up and yanked them home . . . We . . . ell.'

'That's what a man would do if he cared for a woman, wouldn't he, Mr Blenkinsop?'

'Yes. Yes.' Mr Blenkinsop suddenly stopped in his walking again. Then, thrusting his neck out and bringing his head down, he said, 'Ah, no. Hold it a minute. Don't let's jump to conclusions. I'm saying that's what men should do, but we're talking about your man, and if he didn't do that then there's a very good reason for it. I've a very high opinion of your husband, Mrs Boyle. I haven't known him very long but I take him to be a man of his word, a man of strong character, an honest man. Now a man with these characteristics doesn't stay put for nothing. Is there something more in it than what you've told me, eh?'

Mary Ann lowered her head. 'Perhaps. It's a long story. It's got to do with the children. You see, he's always maintained that David would talk if they were separated, I think I told you. He's been on like this for a couple of years now. And Rose Mary getting lost proved him right, and we quarrelled, and I said something to him I shouldn't have done. It's that I think that has prevented him from coming to me.'

'Ah, well now, if you know that you've put a stumbling block in the way of him coming for you, it's up to you to remove it, isn't it? Fair's fair.'

Mary Ann rose to her feet and, going to the desk and picking up her bag and gloves, said, 'About the business of buying him out, is anything signed yet?'

There was a long pause before Mr Blenkinsop said, 'No, no, not yet.'

'Could . . . could you be persuaded to change your mind and say you don't want it, I mean say that you are not going to buy the place after all?'

'Well, seeing that he wants to sell, if I don't buy somebody else will, and that wouldn't suit my plans.'

Mary Ann turned towards him but didn't look at him as she said, 'You . . . you could say that if he sold out to anyone else you would stick to your original plan and put the buildings on the west side, Riley's side.'

Mr Blenkinsop's head went back and he laughed a loud laugh. Then, mopping his eyes, he said, 'You should have been in business, Mrs Boyle, but . . . leave it to me . . . Mind, I'm not promising anything.' He wagged his finger at her.

'Thank you.'

'Well now, come along, I can drop you off at the end of the farm lane. How's that?'

Mary Ann should have said, 'No, thank you, I've got other business to do in Newcastle,' there was a job to be found, but she was tired and weary and so utterly, utterly miserable that she said, 'I'll be glad of a lift.'

It was about twenty minutes later that Mr Blenkinsop halted the car at the end of the farm lane and watched Bob Quinton assist Mary Ann and Rose Mary to alight, and after the good-byes were said and Bob Quinton was once more seated beside him he drove off.

Mr Blenkinsop drove in silence for some minutes before saying, 'Well!'

'Yes, well,' replied Bob Quinton.

'What's all this about, do you know?'

'About you buying Corny out?'

'Yes.'

'I only know what she told me, that you're going to buy the garage and run it in your own company.'

'Well! Well! Well!' The car took an S-bend, and when they were on the straight again Mr Blenkinsop said, 'When I go back to the States I'm going to tell this story like that play that is running, you know, "A funny thing happened to me on the way to . . ." I'd better say on the way to a little garage tucked up a side-lane. Because, you know, I don't know a blasted thing about me going to buy him out.'

'You don't?' Bob Quinton turned fully round in his seat.

'No, not a thing; it's all news to me. I did say to him jokingly, when I first told him of my plans, "You wouldn't like to sell out?" and he said flatly and firmly no.'

'Well, I'll be jiggered. But she said the boy, Jimmy, or some such name, the boy who works there, he came and told her last night.'

'Yes, that's what she told me too. Well! It

would appear that Jimmy knows more about my business than I do myself. Perhaps he's thought-reading, perhaps I do want to buy the garage. I don't know. But we'll find out when we meet Mr Boyle, eh?' Mr Blenkinsop glanced with a merry twinkle in his eye at Bob Quinton, and, together, they laughed.

A few minutes later they drew up outside the garage and Corny came to meet them.

During the last few days Corny had averaged a loss of a pound a day weight, this was due more to worry than to the scrappy meals he had prepared for himself. And only an hour ago he had decided he couldn't go through another day, more important still, another night of this. Whether she came back or not he would have to see her, talk to her before this thing got absolutely out of hand. There was a fear in him that it was already out of hand, the situation had galloped ahead, dragging them both with it. He had been saying to himself during the last two days what Mike had been saying to him from the beginning: why hadn't he stopped her, grabbed her up, brought her back and shaken some sense into her? But he had let her go; he had played the big fellow, the master of his house, the master of his fate who couldn't be . . . the master of his wife, the big fellow who couldn't keep his family together. He had reached the stage where he was telling himself that he had been to blame from the beginning, that he should never have suggested the twins being separated. Yet the truth in him refuted this, and he knew that he had done right, and the proof of this was now dashing round the place chattering twenty-to-the-dozen. Further proof was, his son had seemed to come alive before his eyes; he was no longer the shadow of his sister, he was an individual; the buried assertiveness that had at times erupted in temper was now verbal. There was no longer any fear of the boy being submerged by Rose Mary . . . She could come back at any minute . . . any minute.

Last night he had sat in the screaming loneliness of the kitchen and wondered what Mary Ann was doing, but whatever she was doing, he imagined she would be doing it in more comfort than if she were here. She had never really considered this her home. That fact had slipped out time and time again. In her mind, home was still the farm, with its big kitchen, and roaring fire, and well-laden table, and its sitting-room, comfortable, yet elegant in the way her mother had arranged things. It seemed ironic to him that it had to be at the moment when he had prospects of giving her a replica of her childhood home that she should walk out on him.

He hadn't fallen asleep until after three o'clock, and he had been awakened at six by a hammering on the door. It was a motorist requiring petrol. That was another funny thing; he'd never had so much work in for months as he had in the last few days. Nor had so many cars passed up and down the road; it was as if the word had gone round. He had been thankful in a way that he had been kept busy during the day, yet all the while under his ribs was this great tearing ache.

A car coming on to the drive brought him out of the garage, and he now walked towards where Mr Blenkinsop was getting out of it on one side, and Mr Quinton the other. He nodded to each but did not smile.

'Hello, Corny.'

'Hello, Mr Quinton.'

'It's a long time since we met.'

'Yes, it is that.' Corny jerked his head, while wiping his hands on a piece of clean rag. He brought his gaze from Bob Quinton and looked at Mr Blenkinsop. The American had him fixed with a hard stare. He returned the stare for a moment; then said, 'Anything wrong, sir?'

'Well, that's acording to how you look at it. Can I have a chat with you?'

Corny's eyes narrowed just the slightest. 'Yes, certainly.' He turned and went towards the office, the two men following. When they were inside there wasn't much room. Corny indicated that Mr Blenkinsop should take the one seat, but Mr Blenkinsop waved it aside, and, coming to the point straight away, said, 'What's this about you wanting to sell out?'

'Sell out? Me wanting to sell out?' The whole of Corny's face was puckered. 'I don't know what you're getting at, sir.'

Mr Blenkinsop flashed a glance towards Bob Quinton, and the two men smiled, and Bob said, 'Curiouser and curiouser.'

'You've said it,' said Mr Blenkinsop. 'Curiouser and curiouser.'

'Who said I was going to sell out? And who am I going to sell to?'

'I was informed this morning that you were selling out to me.'

'You! . . . I don't get it.'

'Well, to be quite frank, Mr Boyle, neither do I,

so I'd better put you in the picture as much as I can see of it . . . I had a visit from your wife this morning.'

Corny's mouth opened the slightest, then closed again. He made no comment and waited for Mr Blenkinsop to continue.

'She came to ask me not to buy you out.'

Corny's head moved from side to side, and then he said, 'I don't understand. There's been no talk of you buying me out, has there?'

'No, not to my knowledge, but she had been told that you were going to sell out to me, and apparently this upset her. She knows how much stock you lay on the place and how hard you've worked and she didn't want me to reap the benefit.' Mr Blenkinsop laughed.

'But I don't see how. I've never said any such thing to her.' His head drooped. 'I suppose it's no news to you that there's a bit of trouble between us?'

'No, it's no news,' said Mr Blenkinsop flatly.

'Well, how did she get this idea?' Corny looked from Mr Blenkinsop to Bob Quinton.

'Well, as far as I can gather,' said Mr Blenkinsop, 'it came from you. You told your assistant, Jimmy, that you were going to sell out, and he goes and tells your wife.'

'Jimmy!'

'Yes, Jimmy.'

'He went and told her that?'

Almost before he was finished speaking Corny was out of the office door, and the two men looked at each other as they heard him bellowing, 'Jimmy! Jimmy! Here a minute . . . in the office.'

As Corny re-entered the office Jimmy came on

his heels. He stood in the doorway, covered with oil and grease. You could say he was covered in it from his head to his feet. He, too, had a piece of rag in his hands, which he kept twisting round and round. He looked at the American and his grin widened; he looked at the strange man; then he looked at Corny, and from his boss's expression he knew that there was . . . summat up.

'You've been to the farm to . . . to see Mrs Boyle,' said Corny now.

'Aw, that.' The grin spread over Jimmy's face and he said, 'Well, I took the lads. You see, one of the fellows had set the piece she did, I mean Mrs Boyle, to a tune.'

'What are you talking about now?' said Corny roughly.

Jimmy again glanced from one to the other, then went on. 'Just what I said. I went to the farm with the lads because of the piece Mrs Boyle had written, the pop piece.' He stopped, and again his glance flicked over the three men. And then he gabbled on, 'She had the idea that if she wrote a pop piece it could bring in some money, and it could you know. It still could, it's good. Duke, our Group leader, he says it's good; he says she's got the idea. We're going to play it on Saturday night at "The Well". She got the idea because of what you said . . . sir.' He nodded at the American. 'You said she acts like a woman, you remember? An' I said to the boss here it was a good line, and so she worked on it and she said not to tell you.' He was nodding at Corny now, and Corny said quickly, 'Stop jabbering, Jimmy; that's not what I want to know. What else did you tell Mrs Boyle when you saw her?'

The silly expression slid from Jimmy's face, and it was with a straight countenance that he said, 'Nowt.'

'Did you tell her that I was going to sell out, that Mr Blenkinsop was wanting to buy me out?'

Jimmy now looked down at his feet. Then he looked at his hands and began to pull the rag apart. Next he looked at the men, one after the other; but not at their faces, his glance was directed somewhere at waist level. At last, after a gulp in his throat, he said, 'Well, I . . . I did say that.'

'But what for?'

Jimmy's head now came up quickly and, staring with a straight face at Corny, he said, 'I thought it would bring her back, that's what. She knows what stock you put on the place. I thought she'd come haring back straightaway. She's miserable, an' you're as miserable as sin, an' it's awful workin' here like this, so, well I got wonderin' what I could do, an' I just thought up that. But it didn't work. But . . . but how did you know about it?' His glance swept the other men again, and he chewed on his lip as the explanation came to him, even before Corny said, 'She went to Mr Blenkinsop here and asked him not to go through with it.'

'Cor! I never thought she'd do that; I just thought she'd pack up an' grab Rose Mary and come haring back. I expected her to be here when I got in this mornin' . . . I'm sorry, boss.' He was looking with a sideward glance at Corny, and Corny's voice was low as he said, 'All right, Jimmy, you tried. I won't forget it. Go on.'

The three now looked at each other for a moment; then Corny turned away and stood gazing out of the window while Mr Blenkinsop said, 'I wouldn't mind a factory full of that type.'

'Nor me,' said Bob Quinton. 'It rather gives the lie to the thoughtless modern youth; at least, that they are all tarred with the same brush.'

There followed another silence. Then Mr Blenkinsop said, 'You know, I feel very guilty about the situation; I feel I'm the cause of it.'

'No, sir, don't think that.' Corny turned towards him. 'This started long before you came on the scene, and now it's up to me to put an end to it.'

'You're going to fetch her?' asked Bob quietly.

'Yes, I would have done it before if I hadn't been so pig-headed. You climb up so far in your own estimation and it's a devil of a job to get down again.' He looked from one to the other. 'If you'll excuse me I want to get the boy ready; I'll take him with me.'

'You go ahead.' Mr Blenkinsop nodded at him and patted his shoulder as he went out of the office, and then he looked at Bob Quinton and they raised their eyebrows at each other, and Bob said under his breath, 'It's a pity he's been driven to do this.'

'What? Go for her?'

'Yes; it won't do her any good in the future making him climb down.'

'I know what you mean.' Mr Blenkinsop nodded. 'Pity she couldn't have met him halfway.'

Bob Quinton jerked his chin upwards and, nodding at Mr Blenkinsop, he said, 'That's an idea. That-is-an-idea.'

'What do you mean?'

'Just a minute, I'll tell you.' He put his head out of the door in time to see Corny taking David into the house and he called to him, 'Do you mind if I use your phone?'

'Go ahead,' Corny shouted back.

The next minute Bob was dialling the farm number. The phone had been switched to Mike's office in the yard and it was Michael who answered.

'Hello, Michael,' said Bob. 'This is Quinton here. Remember me?'

'Of course, of course.'

'Look, I'm in a bit of a hurry. Is Mary Ann anywhere about?'

'She's over in the house.'

'Could you get her for me? Or switch over to the house? You are on the phone in the house, aren't you?'

'Yes, yes, I'll do that. Hold on a minute.'

It was some seconds later when Mary Ann said, 'Hello, Mr Quinton.'

'Listen, Mary Ann. There's no time for polite cross-talk. I'm at the garage and as usual you're getting your way, Corny is coming over for you . . . Are you there?'

'Yes.' Mary Ann's voice was scarcely audible.

'As I said, you've got your way. I only hope you don't live to regret it; no man likes to come crawling on his knees.' Bob Quinton jerked his head towards Mr Blenkinsop as he spoke, and Mr Blenkinsop jerked his head back at him.

'Oh. Oh, I don't want him to come crawling on his knees, I don't. Believe me, I don't.'

'Well, you can't do much to stop him now; he's practically on his way; he's gone upstairs to have a wash and get the boy ready, and that shouldn't take him more than fifteen minutes.'

'I . . . I could . . .'

'What?'

'I . . . I don't know. Oh, I want to come home, Mr Quinton, I want to come home.'

'Well then, what about doing it now?'

'But we'd likely miss each other. Anyway it wouldn't make much difference now because he'd think I'd only done it because you'd told me to. But . . . but I was going to come, I really was, I was going to come back after dinner.'

'Look, listen to me. It's twenty-past twelve. There's the Gateshead bus if I'm not mistaken, passes along the main road around half-past. You and Rose Mary could sprint up that road in five minutes. It's only a fifteen-minute run in the bus to the bottom of the road here. It would be extraordinary if just as you were getting off the bus you should see the car coming down the lane. What about it?'

'Yes, yes.' She was gasping as if she was already running. 'Yes, I'll do that and . . . and even if I miss him I'll be there when he gets back. Thanks, thanks, Mr Quinton.'

'You did the same for me once. I always like to pay my debts. Get going, Mary Ann. Presto!' He put down the receiver, then passed his hand over the top of his head, and, looking at Mr Blenkinsop, he said, 'And she did, you know. She fixed my life for me years ago, and I have never forgotten it . . . Well now, what we've got to do is to try to delay the laddie a little if he comes down within the next fifteen minutes. Have you time on your hands?'

'I've time for this,' said Mr Blenkinsop, 'all the time that's needed . . .'

Upstairs, Corny was saying, 'Wash your ears. Wash them well now; get all the dirt out.'

'Washed 'em, Da-ad, clean.'

'Run and get your pants, then, the grey ones. And your blue shirt.'

'Clean sand-ams, Da-ad?'

'Yes, and your clean sandals.'

Corny scrubbed at the grease on his arms. The sink was in a mess; there was no hot water; he had let the back-boiler go out last night. He thickened his hands with scouring powder. It was like the thing. No hot water when he wanted to get the grease off, and she would go mad when she saw the state of the sink, of the bathroom, of the whole house. He stopped the rubbing of his hands for a second. What had he been thinking of? Why had he been so damned stubborn? He knew her; he knew she hadn't meant what she had said; he knew quite well that she'd had no real intention of walking out on him, that she had expected him to prevent her. Why hadn't he? Just why hadn't he? Looking back now over the interminable space of time since he stood on the road calling after her, he saw himself on that day as a stubborn, pig-headed, high and mighty individual. He saw himself on that day as a man still young, but he felt young no longer; the last few days had laid the years on him.

'Da-ad.' David stood in the doorway, dressed in his clean clothes, and he looked from Corny down to his feet, and Corny said, 'That's fine . . . fine.'

'Goin' ride, Da-ad?'

'Yes,' said Corny. 'We're going to see your

mam and Rose Mary.' Corny did not look at his son when he gave him this news, but after a moment, during which David made no sound, he turned his head sharply. There stood the boy, his face awash with tears. The silent crying tore at Corny as no loud bellowing could have, and when, within the next moment, David had rushed to him and buried his face in his thigh he wiped a hand quickly, then placed it gently on the boy's head. This was only the second time he had seen David cry since that first wild outburst of grief when Rose Mary was lost, and it had been a similar crying, a silent, compressed crying, an adult sort of crying. There came to his mind the look he used to see in the boy's eyes when he was defiant, the look that had made him say, 'That fellow knows what he's up to; he's having me on.' He realised, as he stroked his son's hair, that there was a depth in this child, an understanding that was beyond his years. Perhaps it had matured because it had not been diluted by speech.

He bent to him now and said, 'Come on. Come on. You don't want your mam to see you with your face all red, do you?'

David shook his head, then gave a little smile.

It was a full fifteen minutes later when they came down the stairs together, and Corny was not a little surprised to see that Mr Blenkinsop and Bob Quinton were still about the place. But Mr Blenkinsop gave an explanation for this immediately.

'You don't mind?' he said. 'We've been looking at the spare piece of land, getting ideas . . . you don't mind?'

'Mind!' Corny shook his head.

'We would like to tell you what we think could be done, subject to your approval, of course. But that'll come later, eh?'

'Yes, if you don't mind.'

Mr Blenkinsop now stood directly in front of Corny and said, 'How about to-morrow morning? . . . Is that all right with you, Mr Quinton?' He looked at Bob Quinton; and Bob nodded, then said, 'Hold on a minute. I'd better look and see.' And then he proceeded to take a book from his pocket and study it.

Corny's eyes flicked from one to the other. They were blocking his path into the garage and the car. He didn't want to be brusque, or off-hand, but they knew where he was going, so why must they fiddle on.

'Yes, that'll do me fine,' said Bob Quinton, glancing at Mr Blenkinsop, and Mr Blenkinsop, turning his attention again to Corny, said, 'All right, will eleven suit you?'

'Any time, any time,' said Corny. 'I'll be here.'

'Well now, that's settled. And now you're wanting to be off.'

'If you don't mind.'

'And we'd better be making a move, too. What about lunch? Have you any arrangements?' Mr Blenkinsop moved slowly from Corny's path, and as Corny hurried into the garage he heard Bob Quinton say, 'Nothing in particular, but you come and lunch with me. I have found a favourite place and . . .'

Their voices trailed away and Corny pulled open the car door and lifted David up on to the seat. A minute later he was behind the wheel and had driven the car to the garage opening. But there he stopped. You just wouldn't believe it, he said to himself; you'd just think they were doing it on purpose, for there was Mr Blenkinsop's car right across his path and his engine had stalled. He put his head out of the window and called, 'Anything wrong?'

'No, no.' Mr Blenkinsop shouted back to him. 'She's just being contrary. Sorry to hold you up. She'll get going in a minute; she has these spasms.'

Corny sat gripping the wheel. If he had to get out and see to that car he would go bonkers.

For three long, long minutes he sat waiting. Then with an exclamation he thrust open the door and went towards the big low car, and just as he reached it and bent his head down to Mr Blenkinsop's the engine started with a roar.

Mr Blenkinsop was very apologetic. 'It's a long time since she's done it; I'll have to get you to have a look at the plugs.'

'They were all right last week.'

'Oh yes, I forgot you did her over. Well, it's something; she's as temperamental as a thoroughbred foal. I've always said cars have personalities. I believe it, I do.'

Mr Blenkinsop had turned his head towards Bob Quinton, and it seemed to Corny that Bob Quinton was enjoying Mr Blenkinsop's predicament, for he was trying not to laugh.

'Ah, well, I'd better get out of your road before she has another tantrum. Sorry about all this.' Mr Blenkinsop again smiled at Corny, and Corny straightening himself, managed to say evenly, 'That's all right.'

He got into the Rover again and the next minute he was driving on to the road. The

American's car, he noticed through his driving mirror, was again stationary. Well, it could remain stationary until he came back. But whatever was wrong with it, it didn't seem to be upsetting Mr Blenkinsop very much for he was laughing his head off. Americans were odd – he had thought that when he was over there years ago – nice but odd, unpredictable like.

He turned his eyes now down to David, and the boy looked up at him, and they smiled.

When he rounded the bend he saw in the distance the bus pulling to a stop at the bottom of the road. He saw two people alight, a mother and child; he saw the conductor bend down and speak to the child; and it didn't dawn on him who the woman and child were until the car had almost reached them.

Mary Ann! Mary Ann had come back on her own . . . Aw, Mary Ann.

He stopped the car and stared at her through the windscreen. She was some yards away and she, too, had stopped and was staring towards him. Then the next minute, as if activated by the same spring, they moved. Corny out of the car, and she towards him. They were both conscious of the children's high-pitched, delighted screams, but at this moment they were something apart, something separate from themselves. Eye holding eye they stared at each other as they moved closer, and when his arms came out she flung herself into them pressing herself against his hard, bony body, crying, 'Oh, Corny! Oh, Corny!'

'Mary Ann. Mary Ann.' His voice was as broken as hers. He put his face down and buried it in her hair.

'I'm sorry. I'm sorry. Oh, Corny, I'm sorry.'

'So am I. So am I.'

'I shouldn't have done it. I shouldn't. I never meant it. I never meant to leave you; I must have been barmy . . . I had to come; I couldn't stand it any longer.' She lifted her streaming face upwards and simulated surprise as he said, softly, 'I was coming for you.'

'You were?'

He nodded at her, then said under his breath, 'I've nearly been round the bend.'

'So have I . . . Oh, I've missed you. Oh Corny! Corny . . . And home . . . and everything. Oh, I wanted to be home, Corny. I . . . I never want to see the farm again . . . Well, not for weeks.'

With a sudden movement he pressed her to him again; then said, 'Let's get back.'

They came out of their world to see Rose Mary and David standing, hand in hand, looking at them.

Both of the children now recognised that the gate into their parents' world was open again and, with a bound, they dashed to them, Rose Mary towards Corny, who hoisted her up into the air, and David towards his mother. Mary Ann lifted the boy into her arms, and he hugged her neck, and when Mary Ann heard him say, 'Oh, Mam . . . Mam,' the words as distinct as Rose Mary would have said them, she experienced a feeling of deep remorse and guilt.

Corny had been right. Her son was talking, and it was she herself who had prevented him from talking. She herself, who prayed each night that God would give him speech, had kept the seal pressed tightly on his lips; and the seal had been

Rose Mary. And she had done it, as she knew now, not so much because she couldn't bear the thought of the twins being separated, but because she couldn't bear the thought of herself being separated from either of them. It was funny, the things that had to happen to you before you could be made to see your real motives.

'Oh, Dad, Dad.' Rose Mary was moving her hands over Corny's face. 'Oh, I've missed you, Dad. And our David. Oh, I have.'

As the child's voice broke, Corny said briskly, 'Come on, let's get back home.' He put her down on the ground and put his arm out and drew Mary Ann to him; and she put David down, and together they went to the car, the children following.

A few minutes later they were back on the drive, and as they piled out, Jimmy came running down the length of the garage. The grin was splitting his face as he stopped in front of Mary Ann, and with his head on one side he said, 'Ee! But I'm glad to see you back, Mrs Boyle.'

'I'm glad to be back, Jimmy.'

Mary Ann's voice was very subdued and slightly dignified. He jerked his head at her twice. Then looking towards Rose Mary, he said, 'Hello there, young 'un.'

'Hello, Jimmy.' Rose Mary ran to him and clasped his greasy sleeve, and he cried at her, 'Look, you'll get all muck and oil and then your ma'll skelp me.'

'She wouldn't . . . Oh, lovely! We're home.' Rose Mary gave a leap in the air, then swung round and grabbed David with such force that he almost fell over backwards; then she herself almost fell over backwards, metaphorically speaking, when her brother said to her, 'Give over.' Rose Mary stood still looking at him; then glancing towards her mother and father, she cried, 'He said give over. Did you hear him, Mam? A big word, give over, he said. David can talk proper, Mam.'

'Yes,' said Mary Ann, avoiding looking at Corny. Then she turned away and walked towards the house, and Corny followed her. And when Rose Mary, pulling David by the hand, came scrambling behind her father he turned, and, bending to them, said under his breath, 'Stay out to play for a while.'

'But, Dad, we've got our good things on.'

'It's all right. Just for a little bit. Don't get mucked up. I'll give you a shout in a minute.'

David pulled his hand from Rose Mary's and, turning about, ran back to where Jimmy stood. But Rose Mary continued to look at her dad. She wanted to go upstairs and get out of her good things; she had been in them far too long. Anyway, her dad should know that she couldn't play in her good things.

'But, Dad, it won't take a minute.'

'Rose Mary! Stay out until I call, you understand?'

'Yes, Dad.' Rose Mary remained still as Corny walked away from her and into the house; and as she stood, it came to her that their David had gone off on his own. She turned quickly about and watched David following Jimmy into the garage. He hadn't shouted to her to come on, or anything.

A funny little feeling came over Rose Mary. She

couldn't understand it. All she could do was associate it with the feeling she got when Miss Plum, after being nice to her, turned nasty. The feeling spurted her now towards the garage. She was back home with her mam and dad and their David, and their David couldn't get along without her . . .

Upstairs, in the kitchen, Corny sat in the big chair with Mary Ann curled up in his arms, very like a child herself. There was a tenderness between them, a new tentative tenderness, a tenderness that made them humble and honest. Mary Ann moved her finger slowly round the shirt button on his chest and looked at it as she said, 'It's taught me a lesson. I don't think I'll ever need another.'

'You're not the only one.'

'Talk about purgatory. If purgatory is anything like this last few days I'm going to make sure that I'm not going to be a candidate for it. And you know,' she glanced up at him, 'they were awful. Everyone of them, they were all against me.'

'Don't be silly.'

'I'm not, Corny. It's true; even me da.'

'Your da against you!' Corny jerked his head up and laughed.

'I'm telling you. As for my mother, I wouldn't have believed it. Even after she came to see you she made you out to be the golden boy.'

Again Corny laughed. 'Well, that's a change,' he said.

'You should have seen the send-off she gave me when I came away. She was crying all over me. They all were, or nearly so. They were glad to see the back of me.'

'Now, don't you be silly.' He took her chin in his hands and moved her head slowly back and forward. 'They took the attitude they did because they knew I'm no use without you.'

She lowered her lids, then muttered, 'You mean, they knew I was no use without you.'

'Well, let's say forty-nine, fifty-one. But I know this much; they were all upset and they did their best to put things right. But it took Jimmy to do the thinking.'

'Jimmy?' She screwed up her eyes at him.

'Yes. That tale about me selling out seemed to do the trick, didn't it?'

Mary Ann pulled herself upwards from him with a jerk and, with her two hands flat on his chest, she stared at him as she said, 'You mean to say that was all a put-up job, you sent Jimmy?'

'Oh no, no, no! Don't let's start. Now, let's get this right . . . right from the beginning, from the word go. I knew nothing about it until an hour ago.'

Mary Ann was making small movements with her head. Then she asked softly, 'You weren't going to sell out to Mr Blenkinsop?'

'No, I never dreamt of it. Now ask yourself, as if I would, getting this far, after all this struggle. No, it was his idea. He thought . . . well . . .' Corny lowered his head and shook it. 'He thought it might bring you back and try to prevent me doing anything silly.'

Mary Ann brought one hand from Corny's chest and put it across her mouth. 'And I went to Mr Blenkinsop and . . . and asked him not to buy you out, and . . . Oh! Oh! I didn't only see him, I . . . I first went to Bob Quinton. Oh, what will they think? They'll think I'm batty.'

'They'll think nothing of the kind; they've been here.'

'No!'

'Yes. Now don't get het up. They wanted to know what it was all about. And that's how I found out that Jimmy had been to you with this tale.'

'Oh, wait till I see him.'

'Now, now.' He took hold of her by the shoulders and shook her gently. 'Think, just think, if he hadn't given you that yarn we might have gone on and on. There's no telling. Anything could have happened . . . Mary Ann.' He bent his head towards her. 'I just don't want to think about it; it frightens me; it frightens me still. I'm just going to be thankful that you're back.' He smiled softly at her; then added slowly, 'And take mighty good care in the future – you don't leave this house without me unless I have a chain attached to you.'

He held her tightly; and as he stroked her hair he said, 'And you won't go for Jimmy?'

She moved her face against him, and after a moment she said, 'Fancy him thinking all that up.'

'I've always told you that that lad has a head on his shoulders. There's a lot goes on behind that silly-looking face of his. And he's loyal, and that means a great deal these days. When things get going I'll see he's all right . . . You know, I could have kissed him this morning when he owned up to telling you that tale, and to know you still cared enough about me to stop me doing something silly.'

Mary Ann gazed into his face, her own face serious now, as she said, 'I've never stopped caring . . . Corny, promise me, promise me that if I ever forget about this time and what's happened and I try to do anything stupid again, you'll shake the life out of me, or box my ears.'

'Box your ears?' He pulled his chin in. 'You try anything on, me lady, and I won't stop at boxing your ears; I'll take me grannie's advice and I'll black your eyes. "You should have blacked her eyes," she said.'

'What! your grannie . . . she said that?'

'She did. And much more.'

'But, Corny, she . . . she was the only one who was on my side; she called you worse than dirt; she . . . Oh . . . Oh!' Mary Ann bit on her lip to try and prevent herself from laughing. 'The crafty old fox!'

'Ee! me grannie.' There was a look of wonderment on Corny's face. 'She's wise, you know.'

They began to laugh, their bodies pressed tight again, rocking backwards and forwards. They laughed, but their laughter was not merry; it was the kind of laughter one laughs after getting a fright, the laughter that gushes forth when the danger is passed.

14

They'd had a meal; Mary Ann had cleaned up the house; she was now going to bake something nice for their tea; but before she started she felt she must have a word with Jimmy. She had just put the bread-board and cooking utensils on the table near the window when she saw him crossing the yard with some pieces of wood in his arms. Quickly she tapped on the window and motioned to him that she wanted to see him. In a minute she was down the back stairs and in the yard, and there he was, waiting for her at the gate. She walked up to him slowly and looked at him for a second or so before saying, 'You should take up writing short stories, Jimmy.'

'Me! Short stories, Mrs Boyle? I couldn't write, me spellin's terrible.'

'That doesn't stop you telling the tale, does it?' She looked up at him from under her eyelids.

'Aw, that. Eeh! Well, I thought you would never come back. You see.' He stooped and placed the wood against the railings; then, straightening up but still keeping his head bent, he gazed at his feet as he said, 'You see, me mam and dad were separated for nearly a year once. Me mam always said it started over nothin', and neither of them would give in. Both of them were at work, you see, and me dad was on the night shift and we hardly ever saw him. Ships that passed in the night, he said they were. And they had a row, and she walked out. There was only me at home, 'cos me only sister, she's married. It was awful being in the house and nobody there, I mean no woman. I never forget that year, and so I felt a bit worried like about . . . about the boss and you.'

'Aw, Jimmy, I'm sorry. I didn't know. But I'm glad you got worried about us. Thanks . . . thanks a lot.' She put out her hands and clasped his arms, bringing the colour flooding over his long face, and for a moment he was definitely embarrassed. Then, his natural humour coming to his aid, he slanted his gaze at her as he asked, 'It'll be all right for me to play me trombone then, Mrs Boyle?'

She gave him a sharp push as she laughed. 'You! That's blackmail. Go on with you.'

He was chuckling as he stooped to pick up the wood, and she looked down at him and said, 'I might stand for your trombone wailing, but I'll never stand for you having long hair like that crowd of yours.'

'Aw.' He straightened and jerked his head back. 'Funny thing about that. Your dad got under Duke's skin a bit. My! I thought for a minute there was goin' to be a bust-up, but after we got back Duke began to talk about breakin' the barrier with a new gimmick, and he came up with the idea of shavin' their heads.'

'No!' Mary Ann was covering her face with her hands.

'Aye, it's a fact. He's thinking of shaving up the sides and just leavin' a rim over the top here' – he demonstrated to her – 'like a comb, you know, and callin' us "The Cocks".'

'The Cocks!' squeaked Mary Ann, still laughing.

'Aye, that's what he says.'

'Why not shave the lot off and call yourself "The Men"? That would break the sound barrier, at least among all the long-haired loonies . . . THE MEN!' She wagged her finger up and down. 'And underneath you could have "Versus the rest".'

'Ee! you can think quick, can't you, Mrs Boyle? That isn't half bad. "The men . . . versus the rest". I'll tell him, I'll tell him what you said.'

'You do, Jimmy. Tell him I'll put words to all his tunes if they all get their hair cut.'

'Aye, I will.'

'Jim-my!'

'Ee! That's the boss bellowin'. I'll get it in the neck.' He turned from her and ran with the wood towards the back door of the garage, and, as he neared it, Rose Mary emerged and, seeing Mary Ann, came swiftly towards her, crying, 'Mam! Mam! Wait a minute.'

'Yes, dear?' Mary Ann held out her arm and put it round Rose Mary and hugged her to her side as she looked down and listened to her saying, 'Mam, it's our David. He won't do anythin'.'

'Do anything? What do you mean?'

'Well, he won't play with me.'

'Nonsense.' Mary Ann pressed Rose Mary from her. 'David won't play with you? Of course he will. Where is he?'

'He's with me dad, under the car.'

'Under the car?'

'He wanted me to get under but I wouldn't, and me dad said I hadn't to anyway. Me dad told David to go and play on the old car with me, but he wouldn't. He waited till me dad got under the car and he crawled under with him. And they were laughin' . . . and Jimmy an' all.'

Taking Rose Mary's hand, Mary Ann said, 'Come on,' and with something of her old sprightliness, she marched towards the garage. David under a car! Thick with oil and grease! She had enough of that when she had Corny's things to see to.

Halfway up the garage, she saw Corny's legs sticking out from beneath a car, and next to the legs were those of David. His buttocks, too, were also in sight as he was lying on his stomach.

When she stood over the two pairs of legs she said, softly, 'David, aren't you going to play with Rose Mary?'

She waited for a moment, and when no reply came she said sharply, 'David!'

There was a wriggle of the buttocks and David emerged, rolled on to his back, stared up at her and said, by way of enquiry, 'Mam?'

Mary Ann looked down at her grease- and oil-smeared son. She wanted to grab him by the shoulders, yank him upstairs, take his clothes off and put him in the bath. She kept her voice calm as she said, 'Aren't you going to play with Rose Mary on the old car?'

'No, Mam. Helpin' Da-ad.' He held up one hand to her, and in it was a spanner.

Corny's voice now came from under the car,

saying, 'Give it me here, the big one, the one with the wide handle. Then go and play with Rose Mary.'

'No, Da-ad.' David was again lying on his stomach, only his heels visible now, and his muffled voice came to Mary Ann and Rose Mary, saying, 'No, Da-ad, don't want to. This spinner?'

Mary Ann waited for Corny to say something. He had stopped tapping with the hammer. She could imagine him lying on his back, his eyes tightly closed, biting on his lip as he realised a new situation had arisen, a new situation that she would have to face. And not only herself but Rose Mary also. Her little daughter would need to be helped to face it, helped to watch calmly this severed part of her making his own decisions, choosing his own pleasures, living his own life. She gripped Rose Mary's hand tightly as she called in a light voice, her words addressed to her son but their meaning meant for her husband, 'It's all right. Rose Mary's coming upstairs to help me bake something nice for tea . . . aren't you, Rose Mary?' She looked down into her daughter's straight face. Then, bending swiftly down, she called under the car in a jocular fashion, 'But don't either of you dare to come up those stairs in that condition; I'll bring a bucket of hot water down for you to get the thick of it off.'

'We hear.' Following on Corny's laughing answer, David now piped in, 'We hear. We hear, Mam.'

Mary Ann moved away and drew Rose Mary with her, but all the way down the garage Rose Mary walked with her head turned over her shoulder, looking back at the car and David's feet, and she didn't speak until they reached the kitchen, not until Mary Ann said, 'Go and get your cooking apron, and your board and rolling-pin, and you can make some tea-cakes, eh?' And then, her lip quivering, she looked at her mother and said, 'But, Mam, David doesn't want to play with me any more. Now he can talk he doesn't want to play with me any more.'

'Of course, he does, dear. He's just new-fangled with the idea of helping your dad. That'll wear off. We'll go to the sands to-morrow if it's fine and, you'll see, he'll be like he was before. Go on now and get your things out and help me, because, you know, you're a big girl; you're six, and you should help me.'

'Yes, Mam.'

Mary Ann went to the table and made great play of setting about her cooking. New-fangled because he was helping his dad. Things would be like they were before. No. She was confronted with the stark truth that things would never be like they were before, for David had become Corny's; of his own choice, the boy had taken his father. As, years ago, she had taken her father and left her mother to their Michael, now David had taken Corny and left her to Rose Mary. Oh, she knew there would be times when he needed her, like there had been times when she had needed her mother, but it would never really be the same again. They might always be a close-knit unit, but within the unit one of her angels would fight his twin, and herself, for his independence. It was only in this moment that she realised that David was like neither Corny nor her; he was like her da, like Mike. He had been slow to talk, but now he had started he would have his way and fight for the right to have it.

'Mam, will I put some lemon peel in me tea-cakes?'

Mary Ann turned smilingly towards Rose Mary, saying, 'Yes, yes, that's an idea; David likes lemon peel, doesn't he?'

'Yes, Mam. Mam, will I make my tea-cakes just for David and me?'

'Yes, you do that, I'll make some for your dad and you make some for David. That's a good idea.'

Rose Mary smiled, then said, 'Don't say I've made them until he's eaten one, then he'll get a gliff, eh?'

'All right. And make them so nice he won't believe you've made them.'

'Yes, and he'll want me to make them every day. He'll keep me at it, and I won't be able to have any play or anything.'

'Well, if he does,' said Mary Ann, measuring the flour into a bowl, 'you'll just have to say, "Now look, I'll make them for you twice a week, but that's all, because I want to play sometime." You'll have to be firm.'

'Yes, I will.' Rose Mary clattered her dishes on to the board, and after a pause she said, 'But I wouldn't mind baking tea-cakes for David every day. I wouldn't mind, Mam.'

'It wouldn't be good for him,' said Mary Ann. 'You won't have to give him all his own way.'

'No, I won't.'

Mary Ann turned to glance at her daughter. She was busily arranging her little rolling-pin and cutter, her knife and her basin, and as she did so she said, as if to herself, 'But I wouldn't mind. I wouldn't mind, not really.'

Mary Ann turned her head slowly round and looked out of the window. David, almost with one blow, had cut the cord that had held them together. He had flung it aside and darted away, as it were, leaving Rose Mary holding one end in her hand, reluctant to let go, bewildered at being severed from her root.

The plait of joy and sorrow that went to make up life was so closely entwined that you could hardly disentangle the strands. She wanted to gather her daughter into her arms and try to explain things to her, but she knew it did not lie in her power to do this; only unfolding years and life itself could explain, within a little, the independence of a spirit.

15

It was Sunday again and, outwardly, life had returned to normal; not that Corny's frequent diving upstairs was his normal procedure. Sometimes Mary Ann had never seen him from breakfast until lunch time, except when she took his coffee down, but now it seemed he didn't want to let her out of his sight. He came upstairs on any little pretext just to look at her, to make sure she was really there. It was a similar pattern to the first month after they were married.

But it was almost two o'clock now and Corny hadn't got back for his dinner. There had been a breakdown along the road and he had been called to see to it. She went into the front room and looked out of the window. She couldn't keep the children waiting much longer; yet Corny liked them all to sit down together, especially for a Sunday dinner. And she had made a lovely dinner . . . roast pork, and all the trimmings, and a lemon meringue pie for after. Rose Mary came into the room now, accompanied by David, and asked, 'Is me dad comin', Mam?'

'I can't see him yet.'

'Oh, I'm hungry.'

'Me an' all,' said David.

They were standing one on each side of her, and she put her arms around them and pressed them tightly to her. And they both gripped her round the waist, joining her in the circle of their arms.

She smiled softly as she looked down on them. Oh, she was lucky . . . lucky. She must never forget that. No, she never would, she assured herself. She thanked God for her angels and that everything in her life was all right again . . . But not quite.

It being Sunday, and Jimmy content to stay on duty, they should have all been going to the farm, but there had been no mention of the farm to-day. Corny had remembered what she had said: 'I never want to see the farm again. Well, not for weeks and weeks.' And so he had not brought up the subject. Yet here she was, and had been all day, wishing she was going to see her ma and da and their Michael and Sarah, and sit round the big table and have a marvellous tea – that she hadn't had to get ready – and laugh . . . above all, laugh.

What was the matter with her that she could change her mind so quickly? A couple of days ago she had been glad to see the last of them. Did that include her da?

She bowed her head and released her hold on the children, and turning away, went into the kitchen.

She had just looked into the oven to see that everything hadn't been kizzened up, when Jimmy's voice came from the bottom of the stairs, calling, 'Mrs Boyle!'

She hurried to the landing and looked down on him. 'Yes, Jimmy.'

'The boss has just phoned from the crossroads to tell you he'll be back in ten minutes.'

'Thanks, Jimmy.'

'That's givin' you time to dish up; he wants it on the table.' Jimmy laughed, and she laughed back. Funny, how she had come to like Jimmy. Before, he had simply been a daft youngster, but now she saw him in a different light altogether. She asked him now, 'Will you have any room for a bite when I put it out?'

'Corners everywhere, Mrs Boyle.'

She flapped her hand at him and said, 'All right, I'll give you a knock when it's ready.'

'Ta, ta, Mrs Boyle . . .'

Twenty minutes later Corny was washed and sitting at the table and doing justice to Mary Ann's cooking, and every now and again he would look at her and smile with some part of his face. Then he would look at the children. He caused Rose Mary to laugh and almost choke when he winked at her.

After Mary Ann had thumped her on the back and made her drink some water, Rose Mary, her face streaming, said, 'It was a piece of scrancham, my best bit, it was all nice and crackly . . . Can I have another piece, Mam?'

'Yes, but mind how you eat it. Don't go and choke yourself this time.'

After Mary Ann had helped Rose Mary to the pork rind she said to David, 'You want some too, David?'

'No, Mam.' David looked up at her; then immediately followed this by asking, 'Goin' farm, 'safter-noon?'

Mary Ann resumed her seat, and David looked

from her to his father, and Corny, after glancing at Mary Ann's downcast eyes looked towards his plate, and said, 'No, not this afternoon. But we might take a dander down to your Great-gran McBride's.'

Corny now said softly to Mary Ann, 'All right?'

'Yes,' she replied, but there was little enthusiasm in her voice. Not that she didn't like going to Fanny's, but free Sundays had always been reserved for the farm. She told herself that if she was strong enough she would say to Corny now, 'We'll go to the farm.' But it was early yet to face her family and the hostility they might still be feeling towards her; and this included Mr Lord. She felt as if she had been thrust out by them all. The feeling touched on the primitive. As, in the dark past, some erring member of a tribe was cast aside, so had her family treated her . . . or so she felt; and the feeling wasn't lessened by the knowledge that it was all her own fault . . .

Dinner over, the dishes washed, the kitchen tidy, Mary Ann set about getting the children ready before she saw to herself.

In the bedroom Corny was changing his shirt. He was in the act of pulling it over his head when he heard a car come on to the drive. His ear was like a thermometer where cars were concerned. He looked at himself in the mirror. When the cars began coming on to the garage drive thick and fast he felt his temperature would go up so high he'd blow his top. He was grinning at himself in pleasurable anticipation of this happening when he swung round on the sound of a well-known voice coming from the stairs, crying, 'Anybody in?'

It was Mike. He was through the door and on to the landing in a second, but not before Mary Ann, half dressed, with the children coming behind her.

They all stood on the landing looking down the stairs. Corny was exclaiming loudly, as were both the children, but Mary Ann remained quiet. She watched her father coming towards her, followed by her mother, and behind her mother slowly came Sarah, and behind Sarah, as always, Michael.

The hard knot came struggling up from her chest and lodged itself in her throat, and when her da put his arms round her shoulders she felt it would choke her. But when her mother, smiling gently at her, bent and kissed her, it bolted out from her mouth in the form of an agonised sob.

'Oh, there, there, child.' Lizzie enfolded her as if indeed she was still a child, and she sounded very much like it at this moment, so much so that the twins stopped their gabbling and gazed at their mother. Then Rose Mary, tears suddenly spouting from her eyes, darted towards her, crying, 'Oh, Mam! Mam!' And David stood stiffly by, his lips quivering.

'Aw, Mary Ann,' Sarah lumbered towards her. 'Don't . . . don't cry like that. We just had to come. I'm sorry if it's upset you.'

Mary Ann, gasping and sniffing now, put her hand out to Sarah and shook her head wildly as she spluttered, 'It hasn't. It hasn't; it's just . . . Oh!' Her glance flashed from one to the other of this, her family, and she spread her arms wide as if to enfold them all. 'It's just that I'm so glad to see you.'

Corny was standing by her side now, holding her, and he looked at her family, endorsing her sentiments, saying briefly, 'Me an' all.'

'Well,' said Michael, who always had a levelling influence on any disturbance, 'I don't like buses with standing room only. We're almost crushed to death in here, so if I'm not going to be offered a seat I'm going down into the garage to find an empty car . . . And it's about time we were offered a cup of tea, if you ask me, we must have been here three minutes flat.'

'Go on with you.' Corny pushed Michael in the back and into the kitchen, and Lizzie, following Sarah into the bedroom to take off their outdoor things, shouted, 'I'll see to it, Mary Ann, although it isn't fifteen minutes since they all had tea.'

The children, returning to normal, followed their father and uncle. This left Mary Ann on the landing with Mike. Again he put his arm around her shoulders and, pressing her tightly to him, asked under his breath, 'How's things?'

Shyly she glanced up at him. 'Fine, Da.'

'Sure?'

'Yes. Better than before, I think. I've learned a lesson.'

'Don't we all?' He moved his head slowly above hers. 'I've been sick over the last couple of days wondering, and your mother has an' all, and the others.' He was referring to Michael and Sarah. 'The house hasn't been the same; it was like something hanging over us.'

Mary Ann moved slowly from the protection of his arm and went into the front room, and he followed her, and when they were quite alone he said, 'You won't hold it against us for the way we went on? We only acted for your own good; we knew that you would never be happy away from him.'

'I know, Dad, I know.' Her head was drooping. 'It seemed hard to bear at the time because nobody seemed to see my side of it, but now, looking back, I realise I hadn't much on my side, except temper.'

'Oh, you weren't all to blame. Oh no.' Mike jerked his head. 'The big fellow's as stubborn as a mule. But, as I said, we knew that, separated, you would both wither . . . You know, lass.' He took her chin in his one hand. 'In a way, it's the pattern of Lizzie's and my life all over again; except' – he wrinkled his nose and added quizzically – 'except for my weakness, for I can't ever see you havin' to cart Corny home mortal drunk.'

'Ah, Da, don't, don't.' She turned her eyes away from him, and he said, 'Aw, I can face the truth now, but as I was saying, the pattern of your life is much the same as ours. I knew I was no good without Liz, and he knows he wouldn't be any good without you; we're two of a kind, Corny and me. There's only one woman for us. There might be little side slips, occasioned by glandular disturbances in the difficult years.' He pushed her gently and laughed, and caused her to laugh, too, and say, 'Oh, Da . . . Da, you're awful. Anyway' – her smile broadened – 'when Corny reaches his glandular disturbance I'll be ready and—'

Mary Ann's voice was suddenly cut off by the sound of a band playing; at least it sounded like a band, and it wasn't coming from the wireless in the next room; it was coming from outside, from down below on the drive. She almost jumped towards the window, Mike with her, and together they stood staring down at the four instrumentalists.

'In the name of God!' said Mike, then continued to gaze downwards with his mouth open. Now glancing at Mary Ann, he added, 'Did you ever see anything like them in all your born days?'

Mary Ann put her fingers across her mouth. 'They've shaved off their hair, nearly all of it.'

'Shaved off their . . . !' Mike narrowed his eyes as he peered downwards. 'You mean to say that's the blasted lot that came to our place the other night?'

Mary Ann nodded. 'He said they might; Jimmy said they might . . . Corny! Corny!' she called now over her shoulder, and almost before she had finished calling his name Corny was in the room, accompanied by Lizzie and Michael.

'What's all the racket?'

'Look at this.'

'Aw,' Corny leaned over her and looked down on to the drive. 'This is going a bit too far. I'll tear Jimmy apart; you see if I don't.'

'Corny!' Mary Ann gripped his arm as he turned to go. 'Don't . . . don't say anything to him, because . . . well, he only tried to help me. You see,' she spread a quick glance round the rest of them now and said, 'I . . . I wrote some words and one of them set them to music; that's . . . that's what they came to let me hear the other night.'

'Well I never! Hitting the pops!' Mike was grinning now, his attitude entirely different from what it had been a moment ago. 'And you wrote the words?' There was pride in his voice.

'Yes, Da.'

'What are they?' asked Michael.

'Oh, I've forgotten; I've got them written down in the other room.'

'Well, go and get them,' said Mike now, 'and we'll all join in. Listen to it! It's as good as you hear on "Juke Box Jury". I'm telling you that. Anyway, it's got a tune. What you call it?'

Mary Ann turned as she reached the door. 'She Acts Like a Woman.'

'She acts like a woman?' Lizzie was looking quizzically at Mary Ann, who, her face very red now, said, 'It . . . it was something Mr Blenkinsop said about me; well . . . about me going for Jimmy practising his trombone.' She looked down and tried to stop herself laughing. 'He said I acted like a woman.'

'Well, I never!' said Lizzie. 'And you turned it into a song?'

'Sort of.'

'Well, go on and get the words,' said Mike, pushing Mary Ann out of the door.

It was plain that Mike was tickled and amused at the situation. But Corny wasn't amused; he didn't mind Jimmy practising now and again, but that was different from having that queer-looking squad doing a rehearsal on his drive, and a car might draw up at any minute. He turned from the others, who were now crowded round the window, and, running swiftly downstairs, he went past the instrumentalists and made straight for Jimmy, who was standing well away from the group and inside the garage.

Jimmy seemed to be expecting him, and he didn't give him time to start before getting in,

'Now look boss, it isn't my fault; I didn't ask them here. I told them not to start, but you might as well talk to the wall.'

'*SHE ACTS LIKE A WOMAN.*'

The group had become vocal; the voices soared now, and Corny, without speaking, turned and looked towards the performers. They had looked funny enough with their hair on, but now they looked ridiculous; their scalps bare except for a fringe of hair running from the top of the brow to the nape of the neck, they appeared to him like relics of a prehistoric tribe.

'*SHE ACTS LIKE A WOMAN.*'

'Look!' shouted Corny above the falsetto pitch. 'Drop it a minute.'

Duke, his fringe of red hair making him look more odd than the rest, glanced towards Corny and said, 'Why?'

'Because I say so,' shouted Corny.

'You don't like it?'

'Look,' Corny said, 'we won't talk about liking or disliking anything at the moment. What I want to point out is that this isn't the place for practising.'

Duke stared at Corny, and his eyes narrowed as he said, 'I thought you were all right; Jimmy said you didn't mind.'

'I don't mind Jimmy practisin' when he's got nothing else to do, but he'll certainly not do it on the main drive.'

'Aw.' Duke's head nodded backwards. 'See

what you mean. But do you like it? It's the thing your missus wrote. I had to alter bits here and there you know . . .'

Corny rubbed his hand hard across his face, then said patiently, 'It was very good of you to take it up, but look, go to the back.' He pointed to the garage. 'Go and play it there; you won't be in anybody's way there; then perhaps I'll tell you what I think of it.'

'It's very kind of you, I'm sure.' This cocky comment came from Poodle and brought Corny flashing round to say, 'Now look, me young cock-a-doodle or whatever you're supposed to be; mind what you say and how you say it. Now' – he spread his hands out indicating the lot of them – 'get yourselves through there before I change me mind.'

The four boys went past him and into the garage; their steps were slow, and the glances they bestowed on him told him they were quite indifferent to anything his mind might do.

'For two pins!'

'Corny!' Mary Ann touched his sleeve, and he turned quickly to her. 'I'm sorry.'

Now he gave a forced laugh. 'What's there to be sorry about? But you see' – his voice dropped – 'I couldn't have them on the drive, could I?'

'No, no, of course not.' She agreed wholly with him. 'But I'm sorry that I ever thought about writing that bloomin' stuff.'

'Don't you be sorry.' He grinned widely at her. 'They've made something out of it; they're going to play out at the back. Come on upstairs and let's have a look at the words and see how it goes.'

'You're sure you don't mind?' Her voice was

very small, and he became quite still as he looked at her, and after a moment he said, 'I mind nothing, nothing at all as long as you're with me.'

'Oh, Corny.' Their hands held and gripped painfully for a moment; then they were out on the drive, their hands still joined, running towards the front door. But when about three steps from it, Mary Ann pulled them to a stop and on a groan, she said, 'Oh no! Oh no!'

'What is it?'

'Look down there. Am I seeing things or is that me grannie?'

'Good God! It's her all right.'

'Oh, Corny. To-day of all days. And remember what happened when she was here last. Oh, Corny!'

'Look. Go upstairs and warn the others. I'll hold her off for a minute; I'll go and meet her.'

Mary Ann seemed glued to the ground, until he pushed her, saying, 'Go on, go on. You're not the only one who's going to welcome this visit . . . think of Mike.'

The next minute Mary Ann was racing up the stairs.

'Ma! Da!' She burst into the kitchen where they were all gathered now, and, after swallowing deeply, she brought out, 'Me grannie! She's coming up the road.'

'What?' Lizzie, the teapot in her hand, swung round, 'No!'

'It is. It is. Corny's gone to meet her.'

Mike turned slowly from the window and looked at Lizzie, and Lizzie, looking straight back at him, said, 'She must have gone to the house and found nobody there.'

Mike moved farther from the window. He didn't speak, only lowered his lids and rubbed his teeth across each other, making a sound that wasn't quite a grind.

'How she can come back here after the things I said to her the other day I don't know.' Mary Ann was shaking her head when Mike said, 'The one that can snub that woman won't be from this earth, lass; he'll have to be from another planet, with powers greater than any we can dream of; that woman's got a hide like a herd of rhinoceroses pressed together.'

'Laugh at her.'

They all turned their eyes towards Sarah, and she smiled her beautiful smile, saying, 'It's about the only thing, failing a man from another planet, that will make a dent in the rhinoceros's hide.' She was looking at Mike as she spoke.

'You're right. You're right.' Mike nodded his head at her. 'As always, Sarah, you're right. And that's what we'll do, eh?' He looked from one to the other now with the eagerness of a boy, finally letting his eyes come to rest on Mary Ann, and he added, 'What do you say?'

'You know me.' Mary Ann gave a quizzical smile. 'I'll promise God's honour, and then she's only to open her mouth and say something nasty about Corny, the bairns, or . . . well, any one of you.' She spread her arms wide. 'You know me.'

They all looked at her; there was a chuckle here and there, then they were all laughing, and at the height of it the group outside suddenly blared forth 'She acts like a Woman'. But even this combination couldn't drown Mrs McMullen's voice as she came up the stairs.

No-one went towards the door, and when Corny thrust it open and ushered the old woman in he did so with a flourish. 'Look!' he cried. 'It's Gran. I saw her coming up the road . . .'

'All right. All right,' Mrs McMullen interrupted him sharply. 'Don't go on. I don't need any introduction, they know me now. No need to act like a circus master.' She moved forward, her glance sweeping over the crowded room. 'Looks like a cattle market,' she said. 'Still, it doesn't take many to fill this place. Let's sit down.'

It was Michael who brought a chair towards her, and when she was seated she looked directly at Lizzie, saying, 'You could have told me, couldn't you, you were all going out jaunting? It would have saved me legs. But I'm of no importance; I'm young enough to trek the God-forsaken road.'

'I didn't see any need to tell you we were going out, Mother; I didn't know you were coming.'

'You know if I'm coming any day I come on a Sunday.'

'It must be five weeks since you came; do you expect me to wait in for you?'

'No, I don't; I don't expect any consideration from anybody, so I'm not disappointed when I don't get it . . . What's that racket out there?' She turned her head sharply towards the window. 'What is it?'

'It's a group.' Corny now walked past her and looked down into the yard before turning to her and saying, 'They're playing a thing of Mary Ann's; she wrote the words. It'll likely get into the Top Twenty.' He winked at Mike, who was standing to the side of him.

'Am I going to get a drink of tea?' Mrs

McMullen was again looking at her daughter – she was adept at turning conversations into side channels when the subject wasn't pleasing to her, and any achievement of her grand-daughter's was certainly not pleasing to her.

'Well, give yourself a chance to get your hat and coat off; the tea's all ready, just waiting for you.'

Lizzie accompanied this with small shakes of her head that spoke plainly of her irritation, and Mrs McMullen, after raising her eyebrows, folded her hands on her lap and bowed her head, and her whole attitude said, There now. Would you believe it? Would you believe that anybody could speak to me in such a fashion after asking them a civil question?

Then her head was brought up quickly by a concerted drawn-out wail and she cried, 'Stop that lot! Who are they, anyway? And why do you let them carry on here?' She pulled herself to her feet and moved a few steps to the window and glared down on to the group, and its open-mouthed audience of Rose Mary and David.

All those standing behind her mingled their glances knowingly. Mrs McMullen remained silent for a moment; then, turning her head over her shoulder, she looked at Corny and asked, 'What are they?'

'What do you mean, Gran, what are they?'

'Just what I said: what are they? They're not human beings; don't tell me that; they look like something Doctor Who left lying around.'

There was a splutter of laughter from Michael and Sarah, and Mary Ann, too, had her work cut out not to bellow, but on principle she wouldn't laugh at anything her grannie said.

'What are they singing? She . . . what?'

' "She acts like a woman",' said Corny, his grin wide now. 'It's the title of the song Mary Ann wrote. Look, the words are here.' He looked about him, and Mike, picking up the sheet of paper from the table, handed it to him with an exchange of glances.

'Look.' Corny thrust the paper in front of Mrs McMullen. 'Read them; then you'll be able to sing with the group.'

Mrs McMullen's look should have withered Corny. She grabbed the paper from his hand and, holding it well from her as if it smelt, she read aloud, 'She acts like a Woman. Man, I'm telling you she acts like a woman.' Then only her muttering was heard until she came to the end. And now, handing the sheet back to Corny, she stared at him a moment blankly before emitting one word, 'Edifying!' She turned about and resumed her seat; then repeated, 'Edifying. Very edifying, I must say. But I'm not surprised; nothing could surprise me.'

Mary Ann's face looked tight now, and Corny was signalling to her above the head of her grannie when that old lady explained the reason for her visit. She did it in clipped, precise tones, talking rapidly.

'Well, I didn't come here to read trash, or to look at four imbeciles; nor yet to listen to that awful wailing. I came to tell you me news.'

Her statement, and the way she issued it, had the power to catch and hold all their attention.

'I've won a car,' said Mrs McMullen flatly.

There was a long pause before anybody spoke; then Lizzie said, 'A car, Mother?'

'Yes; you're not deaf, are you? I said a car. An' don't look so surprised. Why shouldn't I win a car? There's no law against an elderly person winning a car, is there?'

'No, no, of course not.' Lizzie's voice was sharp. 'I was only surprised that you had won a car. But I'm glad, I'm glad.'

'You won a car, Gran?' Corny was standing in front of the old lady. 'What make is it?'

'They call it a Wolseley.'

'A Wolseley!' The expanse of Corny's face widened.

'Do I have to repeat everything? A Wolseley.'

Corny now looked towards Mary Ann; then to Lizzie; then his glance flashed to Mike, Michael and Sarah, before coming to rest on Mrs McMullen's unblinking eyes again. Now he asked, 'How did you win it, Gran? Bingo?'

'I don't go to bingo, I'll have you understand. No, I won it with a couplet for Pieman's Pies. A good couplet that had a real rhyme in it, and sense: "Don't buy a pig-in-a-poke, buy a pig in a pie, Pieman's pie".'

Now the old lady's eyes flicked for a moment in Mary Ann's direction, and Mary Ann caught their malevolent gleam. Oh, she was an old bitch. Yes, that's what she was, an old bitch. A couplet that rhymed, with sense in it. 'Don't buy a pig-in-a-poke, buy a pig in a pie'. But fancy her of all women writing a couplet of any kind! She herself had sent in slogans for years; slogans for corn flakes, sauce, soap, boot polish, the lot, and what had she got? Nothing; not even a consolation prize. Yet here, this old tyke could win a car. There was no justice. It wouldn't have mattered if anyone else in the world had won a car with a couplet except her grannie, because her grannie was the least deserving of luck.

'And that's not all.' Mrs McMullen's head was now swaying like a golliwog's.

'Don't tell me you've won the chauffeur and all.' This was from Michael, and his grandmother turned her head swiftly in his direction and said, 'No. No, I didn't win a chauffeur, but I won a fortnight's holiday in Spain.'

Nobody spoke; nobody moved. It would have to be her, thought Sarah. Why couldn't it have been my mam and dad? What use will she make of a car, or a fortnight in Spain?

Mike thought that the truest saying in the world was that the devil looked after his own.

Lizzie thought, 'What is this going to mean?'

And Mary Ann thought, 'I just can't believe it. It isn't fair.' And some small section of her mind took up her childhood attitude and asked what God was about anyway, for in dealing out prizes to this old witch he had certainly slipped up.

Corny, still standing in front of the old lady, said, 'A fortnight in Spain? That's hard lines all round.'

'Hard lines all round? What do you mean?' Mrs McMullen picked him up even before he fell.

'Well, I mean you not being able to go to Spain, or use the car.'

'What makes you think that I'm not going to use the car or go to Spain?'

Corny opened his mouth, straightened his shoulders, blinked his eyes, then closed his mouth as he continued to look at this amazing old woman. And she, staring back at him with her round dark eyes, said, 'I'm going to use me car all right.'

'But you'll have to get somebody to drive it,' Michael put in.

'There'll be plenty to drive it, falling over themselves to drive it. Oh, I'm not worried about that. They'll break their necks for free jaunts.'

'But where are you going to keep it?' asked Michael.

Mrs McMullen now looked back at Corny, and for a moment he thought she was going to say, 'In your garage,' but she didn't.

'Outside the front door,' she said. 'Like everybody else in the street.'

'A Wolseley outside the front door!' There was a shocked note in Corny's voice at the thought of a Wolseley being left out in all weathers.

'Why not? There's not a garage within half-a-mile of my street, and there's cars dotted all over the place. I've had an old wreck near my window for two years. And the Baileys across the road have just got a cover for theirs. Well, I can get a cover for mine.'

A silence fell on the room again. Corny turned away. He didn't look at anyone, not even at Mary Ann, for the thought in his mind was: a Wolseley, a new Wolseley, standing outside a front door, subject to hail, rain and shine. It was too much for him.

'Did you win them both together, I mean the car, and the trip abroad?' asked Michael now.

'Yes, I did. It depended on how many points the judges gave you for the correct answers to the puzzle and the couplet, an' I got the highest.'

'What are you going to do about Spain?' Michael had more sense than to say, 'You can't go to Spain, Gran.'

'I'm going.'

'Don't be silly.' Lizzie seemed to come alive at last. She swung round, grabbed up the teapot, went to the little tea table, and began pouring out the tea.

'That's a nice attitude to take, isn't it? I'm not in me grave yet.'

Again Lizzie swung round, the teapot still in her hand. 'I didn't suggest you were in your grave; but I do maintain that you're too old to go off to Spain on your own.'

'Who said I was goin' on me own?'

Lizzie stood still now; they all stood still and waited.

'It's for two people.'

Lizzie took in a deep breath, but didn't say anything.

'I suppose you think I can't get anybody to go with me.'

'Well, I wouldn't bank on it,' said Lizzie now. 'Who's going to go traipsing off to Spain with . . . ?' She just stopped herself from saying 'with an old woman'. But Mrs McMullen supplied the missing words. 'Go on,' she said. 'Who's going to go traipsing off to Spain with an old woman like me? . . . And who should I ask but you, me own daughter?'

'Me!' Lizzie gaped at her mother. Then thrusting her arm backwards, she put the teapot on the edge of the table. It was only Mike's hand, moving swiftly towards it, that stopped it from toppling off.

'Now look here, Mother. Now get this into your head right away—'

'All right, all right, don't start. But I'm just putting it to you. Who's got more right to have a share of me success than me daughter? And on the other hand, whose duty is it to see to me but me daughter's? And there's a third thing. I remember years ago, years and years ago when you were young and bonny you saying how you'd like to go to Spain. You wanted to meet a Spaniard in those days. You thought the contrast with your fairness and his darkness would look well. Aye, and it would have. An' it's not too late; your life's not over yet. And if anyone deserves a holiday, it's you. A real holiday . . . a real one.'

There was a movement behind the old woman as Mike went quietly out of the room, and now Lizzie, bending down to her mother, hissed at her, 'Look. Now look, Mother. Don't you start on any of your underground tactics, because they won't work. I'm not going to Spain with you, now let that sink right in, and say no more about it, not another word.' With this, Lizzie straightened herself up, glared at her mother for a moment; then she too went out of the room.

It was at this moment that the group down below, after having stopped, struck up again, and Mrs McMullen, turning towards Michael with ill-concealed fury, cried, 'Shut that blasted window or I'll throw something out on that lot!'

'The window's closed, Gran,' said Michael quietly.

'Well, it doesn't seem like it.' She looked round from one to the other. Then, turning her gimlet eyes towards the window again, she said, 'You can't expect noise or anything else to be kept out of this little mousehole; it's a tunnel for wind and weather.'

Corny planted himself deliberately in front of Mary Ann and swung her round and pushed her out of the door; and when she was on the landing she stood with her face cupped in her hands. She would hit her, she would. The wicked old . . . ! She wasn't really stumped for words – they were all there in her mind – but she wasn't in the habit of voicing swear words.

She walked slowly across the little landing towards the bedroom door; then came to an abrupt halt. The door was open and in the reflection of the wardrobe mirror she saw her ma and da. Mike had his arms around Lizzie and she had her arms around him. Mary Ann didn't turn away. Years ago she had joyed in watching such reunions between her parents – it meant that everything was all right – and as she looked at them the anger died in her. Mike's voice came to her softly now, saying, 'I wouldn't mind, Liz. You can; it's up to you.'

'Don't be silly, man. When I travel I'll travel with you or not at all. As for the Spaniard . . . I got him years ago.'

Mary Ann turned away, and as she did so the kitchen door opened and Corny came on to the landing. 'All right?' he whispered down to her.

She nodded and pointed towards the bedroom, and after catching a glimpse of Mike with Lizzie in his arms, Corny turned quickly away.

Taking Mary Ann into the sitting-room, he said quietly, 'Your world all right now?'

She nodded and dropped her head slowly on to his breast. Then she muttered, 'Why couldn't I have won that car and the trip abroad instead of that old devil? I would have loved you to have had a Wolseley.'

'Look.' He took her by the shoulders and brought his face down to hers. 'I don't want a Wolseley; I've got everything. I'll be so busy in a little while that I won't know where to put meself. As for money . . . well' – he moved his head slowly – 'there won't be any more worries about that. Yet all that is on the side; the main thing is I've got you. You've always been all I wanted; you'll go on being all I want. I want you to get that in your head. Make it stick. You understand?'

Mary Ann's eyes were moist as she gazed up into his face. He hadn't mentioned the children, just her. She buried her head again, and he held her tightly. Then after a moment he said, 'Do you know what? I know a way we could get her car.'

She screwed up her face and he bent his head and touched her nose lightly with his lips as he said, 'You could bring her to live here and I could garage—'

'Oh, you!' She punched at him with her two fists.

'Well, it's a way. I mean we'd be sure of the car. And just think . . . a Wolseley!'

'Corny Boyle.' Again she was punching at him as he laughed. 'Do you want me stark staring mad?'

His arms enfolding her once more, he rocked her backwards and forwards. 'I want you any way . . . any way, Mary Ann Boyle. As long as you . . .'

He released one arm and, throwing it dramatically upwards, thrust back his head and bellowed, 'ACT LIKE A WOMAN.'

'Oh, Corny! Corny! Oh, you're daft.' She was shaking with her laughter.

'Come on,' he said, hugging her to his side. 'We'd better get next door and see the end of Dame McMullen's pantomime.'

When they reached the landing, there was Mike and Lizzie coming towards the kitchen door, and Corny, taking up another dramatic pose, cried in an undertone, 'United we stand, divided we fall. Forward, the Shaughnessy McBoyles!' And on this he thrust open the door and, with an exaggerated bow, he ushered each of them into the room. Mike followed Lizzie. Both were laughing. Mary Ann, following Mike, caught at his hand, and her other hand she placed in Corny's. She was happy . . . happy.

'Mam! Mam!'

'Ma-am!'

But when she heard her children call she released her hold on her father and husband, and, running back to the top of the stairs, she spread her arms wide to her angels. And as she held them she thought that it was odd but during the last few telling days, although she had not forgotten about her angels, they had been thrust into the background, and she had thought only of their father.

And that's how it should be at times; and that's how it must be . . . in the future.

MARY ANN AND BILL

Catherine Cookson

CORGI BOOKS

To Foster and Rose Mary.
A generation does not
divide us.

Contents

1

WORDS

Mary Ann sat in the living-room above the garage and looked at her children, and she wondered, and not for the first time, why it was possible that you could be driven almost demented by those you loved most; if it wasn't Corny, it was one of the twins driving her to the point where she wanted to break things.

When the great stroke of luck had befallen them a few months earlier she had thought that all was set fair now for peace, plenty and pleasure. She couldn't have been more mistaken.

Peace, with that noise going on across the road! What had once been fields overlaid by a wide canopy of sky that she could look into from the bedroom window, was now a contorted mass of scaffolding and buildings in the process of erection. Even to the side of the house, on the spare bit of land, there was hammering and battering and clanking going on all hours of the day; and whereas, at one time, they were lucky to get half-a-dozen customers for petrol during the day, now the custom was so thick they never seemed to close.

This white elephant of a garage, off the beaten track from the main road, which they had supported for seven years in the hope that the road would be extended to take them in had never materialised. Instead, Mr Blenkinsop, the American, had. And Mr Blenkinsop had transformed Green Lane and Boyle's garage into a place where the last thing one expected now was peace.

As for plenty, Corny had always said that when his ship came in he'd build her a fine house on this very spot, or anywhere else she liked; they'd get a spanking new car; they'd take a holiday, not a fortnight, but a month, and abroad, and it would be first-class for them from beginning to end; no mediocre boarding-houses for Mrs Mary Ann Boyle. These were the things he had promised her just before he went to sleep at nights, and she forgot about them the next day, knowing they were but dreams. Yet when the miracle happened and he could have built them a house, bought a smashing car, especially as he was in the business, and taken them for a holiday, what had happened? He couldn't leave the garage; he had to be here at Mr Blenkinsop's beck and call. As for the house, that would have to wait; let Mr Blenkinsop get the factory up first and let him get the garage premises extended on the spare land, and then he would think about a house. As for the holiday, well, she could take a week off if she liked, but he couldn't come along . . . So much for plenty.

And pleasure? Oh! pleasure. She had never had less pleasure in her life than during these last few months. Corny was so tired when he came upstairs he couldn't even look at the television. As for going out, say to Newcastle, to the pictures, even that was a thing of the past since the miracle had happened.

All she seemed to do now was to cook more because there was always somebody popping in for lunch. Mr Blenkinsop and his cousin Dan from Doncaster, who was now in charge of the works, and other big pots who were interested in the new factory. She had liked doing it at first because she liked being told she was a smashing cook, but she found you could weary of praise when a mountain of dishes kept you going well into the afternoon; and a box of chocolates and a bunch of flowers failed to soothe you since they couldn't wipe up.

And besides the peace, plenty and pleasure, there were the twins. She had always considered she could manage the twins. Even during all those long years when David hadn't been able to speak and his dumbness made him obstinate she had been able to cope with him, but since he had begun to talk six months ago she had found him almost unmanageable. He would lapse into long aggravating silences, during which no-one could get a word out of him; but when he did talk the substance of his conversation was such as to make you wonder how on earth he had come by his knowledge, and sometimes create in you a desire to brain him for his precociousness, and at other times to laugh until you cried at his patter.

But this evening she felt no way inclined to laugh at her small son. Anyway, he was in one of his obstinate moods and she could also say that so was she herself. She was fed up to the teeth with this day and all its happenings; from early morning she had been on the go. She had made arrangements to go and get her hair done when Corny had phoned up to say that Mr Dan Blenkinsop had just come in from Doncaster; how about a cuppa? And she had made a cuppa, and over it Mr Blenkinsop had been so talkative and charming that the time had gone by and now it was too late for her to keep her appointment in Felling, and her hair looked like nothing on earth, and Corny had accepted the invitation of Mr Blenkinsop for them all to go to Doncaster tomorrow . . . Well, she wasn't going. She would just tell Corny and he could phone and call it off; she wasn't going looking a mess like this. In any case it was he who accepted the invitation and not her. He had jumped at it like a schoolboy, saying, 'Oh, that'll be grand, a day out. And the twins will be over the moon to see the boys.'

She had memories of the last time the twins and Mr Daniel Blenkinsop's four sons had met. Neither the house nor the garage had returned to order for a week afterwards.

But in the meantime she would use the promised trip – about which their father had already informed them – as a means of making the children come clean regarding why David had been kept in at school.

'You tell me what he's been up to, Rose Mary, or there'll be no trip to Doncaster tomorrow for anybody.'

Rose Mary lowered her eyes from her mother's face and slid them towards her brother, but David had his gaze fixed intently on the mantelpiece and, because it meant he had to look over the top of his mother's head, his chin was up and out, and Rose Mary knew from experience it was a bad sign. Their David never talked when he pushed his chin out, no matter what he was looking at. There was a vague yearning in the back of her mind for the time past when their David couldn't talk at all. Everything had been lovely then. She had looked after him and talked for him, and he yelled if he couldn't be with her, but now the tables were turned so completely that he yelled if she insisted on being with him. The only thing their David wanted to do now was to muck about with cars, and get all greased up. He didn't play any more. She didn't see why she kept sticking up for him, she didn't. But when she saw her mother's hand jerk forward suddenly and grip David by the shoulders and heard her voice angry sounding as she cried, 'Don't put on that defiant air with me! I warn you, you'll go straight to bed. That's after you get a jolly good smacked backside,' she shouted as loudly, 'Aw, Mam, don't. Don't bray him. He'll tell you.'

Rose Mary was hanging on to her mother's arm now, and, her lips trembling and her voice full of tears, she looked at her brother and cried, 'Well, tell her you! If you don't I will, 'cos I'm not goin' to not go to Doncaster the morrow through you. See! 'Cos you won't play with me if we don't go, so tell her.'

Both Mary Ann and Rose Mary now concentrated their gaze on David; and David stared back into his mother's eyes and remained mute, and Mary Ann had her work cut out not to box his ears instantly.

Aiming to keep in command of the situation, Mary Ann turned her eyes slowly away from her son's penetrating stare, and looking at her daughter, said, 'Well, it's up to you.'

Rose Mary swallowed; then, her head drooping on to her chest, she whispered, 'He swore.'

'SWORE!' Mary Ann again looked at her son. 'You swore? Who did you swear at?'

Rose Mary once more supplied the information. 'At Miss Plum.'

'You didn't, David; you didn't swear at Miss Plum!' Mary Ann was really shocked.

David's round face stretched slightly as he pulled his lower lip downwards and pushed his arched eyebrows towards the rim of his ginger hair.

'What did you say?' Mary Ann's voice was tight, and when the only response she got was the further pulling down of his lip and the further pushing up of his eyebrows she put the question to Rose Mary, 'What did he say?'

Rose Mary blinked, then bit on the nail of her middle finger before she said, 'Lots.'

'Lots! You mean he swore more than once?'

'Ah-ha.'

Mary Ann closed her eyes for a moment. She knew this would happen some time or another. The boy spent too much time down in that garage and with the workmen on the site, and knowing some of the adjectives used by the workmen, she trembled to think which one of them he had levelled at his teacher.

'Go on, tell me,' she said. She addressed her daughter.

Rose Mary nipped at her lower lip; then,

wagging her head from side to side, she cast a glance at her brother, who was now staring straight at her, and said, 'Fumblegillgoozle.'

'Fumble-gill- . . . ? But that's not a word. I mean, that's not swearing.'

The twins now exchanged a deep look which Mary Ann could not interpret, and she said, 'Well, it isn't. It's a made-up word, isn't it?'

'Yes. Yes, Mam; but Miss Plum said that he said it like swearin'.'

Mary Ann hadn't a doubt but that her son could put the inflection on fumble-gill-goozle to make it sound like swearing. He was learning words, he was fascinated by words, and he had a way with his inflection. 'Is that all he said?'

'No, Mam.' Again the brother and sister exchanged a deep glance before Rose Mary, continuing with the betrayal, whispered, 'Antimacassar.'

Again Mary Ann closed her eyes, this time to prevent herself from laughing outright. When she opened them she looked directly at her son and said, 'Antimacassar and fumblegillgoozle aren't swear words. But it all depends how you use them, and you know that, don't you, dear?'

'Yes, Mam.' It was the first time he had spoken since he had come into the house, and the sound of his own voice was like an ice breaker cleaving a way through his imposed silence, for now he added rapidly, 'I don't like Miss Plum, Mam. She's big. And I don't like her hands. And when she bends over you you can see right down her throat, and she'd had onions. And she marked me sums wrong and they weren't wrong; and she gave

Tony Gibbs ten, and he's a fool. Tony Gibbs is a fool. An' I told her I'm not sittin' next to her at mass on Sunday any more. I told her I'm goin' to sit with Rose Mary . . .'

'Yes, yes, he did, Mam. He told Miss Plum that.'

Rose Mary's face was alight with her pleasure. For many months now she had been deprived of her twin's company in so many ways, and to be separated from him in church was to her the last straw. It had been Miss Plum's idea to keep them apart, hoping that the separation might go some way towards enabling David to break the dominance of his sister. Undoubtedly this strategy had helped towards David's independence, but now there was nobody more aware than David that he did not need Miss Plum's help, or that of anyone else for that matter, to make him talk.

'You cheeked Miss Plum, David?'

'No, no, I just told her.'

'You must have cheeked her.' Mary Ann was bending towards him. 'What else did you say?'

David looked up into his mother's face. His eyes were twinkling now, and the corner of his mouth was moving up into a quirk, when Rose Mary spluttered, he spluttered too, until Mary Ann said sharply, 'Stop it! Stop it, the both of you. Now I want to know what else you said.'

They stopped their giggling and David lapsed into his silence again and Rose Mary said, '. . . Gordon Bennett, Mam, and Blimey Riley.'

Mary Ann swallowed deeply. Gordon Bennett

was a saying that Jimmy down below in the garage often resorted to. He didn't swear much in front of the children but his intonation when he said 'Gordon Bennett!' spoke volumes. And Blimey Riley. Well, that was one Corny often came out with when he was exasperated. He would exclaim between gritted teeth 'Bl-i-mey, Riley!' and it certainly sounded more like swearing than swearing. So, in a way, David had sworn.

Poor Miss Plum; she had her sympathy. She had thirty-eight in her class and she needed only two or three Davids to drive her round the bend. She said now sternly, 'Miss Plum had every right to keep you in, and if I had been her I would have given you the ruler across your knuckles.' She looked from one straight face to the other. 'And don't think you're out of the wood yet. Wait till I tell your father about this. Now go and get yourselves washed and then come back and have your tea. And there's no play for you until I say so, understand?'

They stared at her for a moment longer, then as if governed by the same impulse they turned together and went out of the room, and as they passed through the door she cried after them, 'What is that you said, David?'

She was on the landing now looking down at her son. She took him by the shoulders again and shook him. 'Tell me what you said.'

When she paused for a moment and his head stopped bobbing, he spluttered, 'Rub-rubber guts.'

Mary Ann drew in a deep breath that seemed to swell her small body to twice its size, and she twisted him round and grabbed him by the collar and thrust him into the bedroom to the accompanying pleas of Rose Mary, crying, 'Oh, no, Mam! Oh, no! Don't, don't Mam. Don't bray him.'

With one hand she thrust Rose Mary back on to the landing, then, standing with her back to the bedroom door, she swiftly stripped down David's short pants and laid the imprint of her hand four times across his buttocks. And then she released him and, panting, stood looking down at him.

She was looking now not at a cheeky little devil, but at a little boy with the tears squeezing from under his tightly closed lids, and she had the desire to grab him up into her arms and soothe him and pet him and say, 'There, there! I'm sorry, darling, I'm sorry.' But no; Master David had to be taught a lesson. Rubber guts, indeed!

When she turned and hurried from the room she almost fell over Rose Mary, and she yelled at her, 'Get into that bathroom and get yourself washed! You're as bad as he is. Wait till your father comes in. There's going to be a change in this house; you see if there isn't.'

'Oh, Mam, Mam, you shouldn't; you shouldn't have hit our David. I'll tell me da of you. I will. I will.'

Now Rose Mary found herself lifted by the collar and thrust into the bathroom and her dress whipped up and her knickers whipped down, and she screamed open murder as Mary Ann's hand contacted her rounded buttocks. And when it was over she sat on the floor and looked up at Mary Ann and cried between her gasping, 'I don't love you. I don't love you. I'm going away. I'm going away to Gran's. And I'll take our David with me. I will, I will. I don't love you.'

Mary Ann went out, banging the bathroom door after her; and on the landing once more she put her hand up and cupped her face. 'I don't love you. I don't love you.' The words were like a knife going into her. Although she knew it was a momentary spasm, and one she had indulged in many a time herself, it had the power to send her spirits into the depths.

She was just going into the kitchen when Corny came bounding up the stairs. 'What's the matter? I could hear her screaming downstairs. What's up?'

Mary Ann sat down on a chair and looked up at her tall, homely-looking red-haired husband, and what she said was, 'Oh, Corny!'

Dropping on his hunkers, Corny gathered her hands into his and gazed into her twisted face as he asked softly, 'What is it, love? What's the matter? What's happened?'

'I . . . I don't know whether to laugh or cry. I . . . I think I'll cry . . . I've . . . I've had to skelp both their behinds.'

'Well, it won't be the first time. But what's it about, anyway?'

'He's . . . he's had one of his defiant moods on. They were kept in at school. He's been swearing at Miss Plum.'

'No!' He sat back on his hunkers; then grinned, 'Swearing? What did he say?'

'Antimacassar.' She watched him droop his head on to his chest, and when his eyes, wide and merry, came up to meet hers, she said, 'And fumblegillgoozle.'

713

'. . . Fumble-what?'

'That's what I said, fumble-what. It's one he's made up. Fumble-gill-goozle. Have you ever heard anything like it?'

He shook his head.

'But that isn't the worst . . . Gordon Bennett.'

'Oh, no!'

'Yes, Gordon Bennett. And you can imagine the emphasis he would put on it. And wait for it, Mr Boyle.' She inclined her head towards him. 'Blimey, Riley!'

He took one of his hands from hers and covered his mouth to smother his laughter; then his shoulders began to shake.

'And he called me rubber guts.'

The next minute his arms were around her and their heads were together.

After a moment she pressed herself away from him and, looking into his face, she said, 'We can laugh, but, you know, it's serious. He's got this thing about words; you never know what he's coming out with next. And I've told you he spends far too much time down in the garage, and on the site, and you can't put a gag in men's mouths.'

'Well, he doesn't hear anything really bad down in the garage. There's only Jimmy there; he might come out with a damn and an occasional bloody.'

'It's plenty.'

'Aw.' He rose to his feet. 'If he hears nothing worse than that he won't come to much harm.'

'He does hear worse than that on the site.'

'Well, I can't tie him up, and I can't keep my eye on him all the time, we've just got to let things

take their course. He's a lad, Mary Ann. You see'
– he turned to her again – 'all his life, not being
able to talk, he was cut off. To him it must feel
as if he'd been born just six months ago, and
from the minute he found his voice, he's been
experimenting. Let him be and don't worry. Come
on, up you get.' He pulled her to her feet, then
ended, 'It's a break you need. Tomorrow's a day
out; it'll do you good.'

She looked up at him, saying coolly, 'A day out
you said? Who for? The Blenkinsop boys?'

'Oh, it won't be a repeat of the time they were
here. There's plenty of room up their place. That
big field beyond. And then there's the ponies and
what not. Once you get there you won't see them
or ours until we're coming back. I've got a feeling
it's going to be a good day . . . Come on, let me
inject you with that feeling, Mrs Boyle.' Swiftly he
picked her up in his arms and kissed her hard, and
when he put her down again he said, 'There,
how's that? Feel the difference?' And when she
replied, 'Not that you'd notice,' he said, 'You
know, the trouble with you, Mrs Boyle, is you're
growing old.'

She didn't laugh with him or retaliate in any
way but, going into the scullery to start the
tea, she thought, 'Yes, I am growing old. I'm
twenty-seven.' And the train of thought caught a
grievance that was in her mind a lot of late,
that asked her what had she done with her
life? What was she doing with her life? The
answer came as before, nothing, except cooking
and cleaning, and washing and shopping, and
worrying, and waiting for Corny to come up from
the garage so she would have company; then

watching him going to sleep watching the telly. Then awakening to it all over again the following morning.

Yes; she was twenty-seven, and she was getting old.

2

THE DAY OUT

Rose Mary looked up unsmiling into her mother's face. Although she loved her mother again this morning she wasn't really kind with her, because she hadn't said she was sorry about braying them last night.

They had an arrangement regarding clearing the air after incidents like last night. Whoever was at fault was to be the one to say sorry, and then everybody was kind again. There was no doubt in Rose Mary's mind that her mam was at fault for braying them, because, she reasoned, Miss Plum had punished David for swearing, or for sounding like swearing, and it was awful for her mam to lather into him again.

When Mary Ann said, 'Now, let either of you get a mark on your clothes and you're for it. Do you hear me?' she said stiffly, 'Yes, Mam.'

'Do you hear me, David?'

'. . . Yes, Mam.'

'Well, remember it. Now go downstairs, but don't you move away from the garage drive. And don't go into the garage. Understand?'

They both looked at her silently, then turned and walked slowly away.

The scene outside was most unusually quiet today. There were no cranes and grabs clanking across the road; no sound of men's voices shouting; no lorries churning up the mud in the lane; and for once no car standing at the petrol tanks opposite the wide space that led into the hangar-like shed that constituted the workshop and garage.

Bringing her eyes to David, who was standing with his hands thrust deep into his pockets, Rose Mary now said, 'She never said she was sorry.'

He returned her glance and wagged his head twice before saying, 'I don't care.'

'Neither do I.'

'I know some more words.' He slanted his eyes at her.

'Eeh! our David. You'd better not. Mam'll give it to you . . . What are they?' She leant her head towards him, and he grinned at her, then whispered, 'Skinnymalink.'

'Oh, that's not a word; I know that one.'

He jerked his head; then said, 'Well, you don't know skilligalee.'

'Eeh! skilligalee.' She whispered the word back at him. 'Where did you get it?'

'One of the men.' His chin was jerking again.

'Is it a bad swear?'

'Ah-ha.'

'Eeh! our David. Mam'll tan you purple if she hears it.'

He grinned at her again, then walked jauntily towards the opening of the garage, and Rose Mary followed him. And there they both stopped and looked into the dim interior where Jimmy was standing talking to a shock-haired, tight-trousered young man, whom they recognised as Poodle-Patter, the nickname given to one of the group with which Jimmy played.

As David went to move forward Rose Mary pulled him back, saying, 'Don't go in; Mam'll be down in a minute, and you know what she said.'

'I'm not going in; I'm just going to the office door.'

'Eeh! our David.' Rose Mary remained where she was, but David moved forward, and at the office door he stopped and cocked his ear to hear Jimmy say, 'Yes, I know I could get more money at Baxter's but I don't want to go, man.'

'You must be barmy.' Poodle-Patter dug Jimmy in the chest with his fist. 'Five quid a week more and you're turning your nose up at it.'

'I'm not turning me nose up at it, man. It's just that I'm well set here. I'm all right.'

'How long is it since you had a rise?'

'Couple of months since.'

'How much?'

'Ten bob.'

'Ten bob!' Poodle-Patter's nose crinkled in scorn. Then leaning towards Jimmy, he said, 'You want to come with us in the car, don't you?'

'You know I do.'

'Well then you'll have to do something about it. Duke's got his eye on this mini-bus. He can get it for two hundred if we put the money down flat, I told you, but if it's spread over it'll mean another thirty quid on it, and as Duke says somebody's got to take the responsibility of the never-never and he's not going to. He's been done afore, you remember? It's cash and equal shares: forty quid each, then we'll all have a say in it.'

'Forty quid?' Jimmy's voice was scornful. 'I couldn't raise forty shillings at the minute, and you know it. Look here, Poodle.' He now dug his finger into Poodle's chest. 'You an' Duke an' the rest talkin' about responsibilities, well, I've got responsibilities; and to me mam. There's only one wage comin' into our house, and that's mine; and there's three of us to keep on it, with Theresa still at school. You can tell Duke from me he can buy his blasted car and count me out.'

'Ah, don't get ratty, man; you know we wouldn't do anything without you. Anyway, you're necessary to our lot and we know it; there's not one of us knows owt about a car, we'd have to pay God knows what for repairs. You've kept The Duchess going over the last year when she should have been on the scrap heap. I don't know how you've done it. I said so to Dave and Barny. "I don't know how Jimmy does it," I said. Look.' Poodle-Patter moved nearer to Jimmy, his voice wheedling now, 'I'm not asking you to do anything out of line, I'm only saying make a move. Everybody should make a move, and you've been in this dump long enough. And it isn't as if you're not sure of a job. I tell you, Baxter's are wantin' somebody like you, a bloke with experience. And that's the basic they're paying, fifteen quid a week. Will you think on it?'

'Look!' Jimmy bowed his head while thrusting his fist out towards Poodle, and Poodle, playfully gripping it between his hands, wagged it, saying, 'That's a boy! That's a boy! Sleep on it. There's no real hurry, not really; The Duchess has carried us a good many trips, she'll carry us a few more. I'll tell Duke you're considering it. Look, I must be off. See you, fellow.'

Poodle now punched Jimmy once more in the chest, then turned swiftly towards the garage opening, and when he passed Rose Mary he put his hand out and chucked her chin, saying, 'O-o-oh! hello there, gorgeous.'

Rose Mary blinked her eyes and tossed her head. She wasn't displeased with the title of gorgeous. All Jimmy's band called her gorgeous, but Jimmy didn't because he knew her dad wouldn't have let him.

As she saw David move further into the garage she whispered hoarsely, 'No, our David! Mam'll be down in a second; you'll only get wrong.'

David didn't appear to hear her, for he walked towards Jimmy, who was now standing with his two hands on the bonnet of a car, his head bent forward as if he was thinking deeply, and he looked up at him for some seconds before he said, 'Jimmy.'

'Oh; hello there.' Jimmy straightened himself up, then grinned down at the small boy. 'By, you look smashin'. I never knew you looked like that; it must be 'cos you've been washed.'

David did not grin back at his friend but considered him seriously for a moment before saying, 'You wouldn't leave here, would you, Jimmy?'

'Leave here? . . . Aw.' Jimmy jerked his chin to the side. Then looking down slantwise at David, he said, 'Trust you to hear things you shouldn't. You've got lugs on you like a cuddy.'

'But you wouldn't, would you, Jimmy?'

'No.'

'But you'd get five pounds more at Baxter's.'

'Aye, I'd get five pounds more at Baxter's, so what?'

'Why . . . why don't you ask Dad for more money?'

'Look.' Jimmy dropped on to his hunkers and, his face level with David's, he was about to put his hands on his shoulders when he stopped himself and exclaimed, 'Eeh! I just need to do that and I'll have your mam knock the daylights out of me.' He rubbed the palms of his oily hands together and said, slowly now, 'Your dad gave me a rise just a while ago. That's the second in six months, and who knows, maybe I'll get another one shortly. I'm satisfied, so what is there to worry about?'

David stared unblinkingly into the long, kindly face. Although Jimmy neither came upstairs for meals nor slept in their house he considered him part of his family; he liked him next to his mam and dad. He didn't place Rose Mary in his list of affections; because Rose Mary was already inside of him, part of himself. He might fight with her, tease her and torment her, but he also listened to her and considered her views and demands as if they were issuing from his own brain. He asked now quietly, 'Will they put you out of the band if you don't help to buy the car?'

Jimmy put his head on one side and began to chuckle; then he shook it slowly before he said, 'You know, you're a rum customer. You know what I think? I think you've been here afore. Me mother always says that some folks have been here afore. She says that they couldn't know what to do at an early age unless they had learned it in another life.' He drooped his head to the other side, adding, 'You don't know what I'm on about do you? But to answer your question. Aye, very likely if I don't fork out they might . . .'

At this moment there came the toot-toot of a motor-horn and Jimmy, stretching his long length upwards, exclaimed, as he smiled at David, 'Ah, here we go again,' then went out towards the petrol pumps and the customer.

David was once more standing beside Rose Mary when Mary Ann and Corny appeared on the drive. He watched his father walk slowly towards Jimmy, then stand waiting while Jimmy took the money from the driver, saying, 'A pound and sixpence.'

The man in the car handing Jimmy two pound notes, said, 'I'm sorry I haven't any less,' and Jimmy replied, 'That's all right, Sir, I'll get you the change.'

Within seconds he came back from the office and, looking at Corny, said, 'I haven't got it in the till; can you change it, boss?'

'No, not a pound note,' said Corny, then bending towards the man in the car, he said, 'We'll call it straight.' He nodded towards Jimmy, and Jimmy handed the man the pound note back again.

'That's very kind of you.' The driver smiled up at Corny, saying, 'I'll have to remember to call this way when I'm coming back and do the same again.'

They all laughed now.

As the car drove away Mary Ann said to no-one in particular, 'That's the third time to my knowledge you've run out of change in a fortnight. Oh! Oh!' She raised her hand, 'It's only sixpence I know. It was only threepence before, and a shilling before that. But what's a shilling? And what's sixpence? And what's threepence in a fortnight? Only one and nine. But there's fifty-two weeks in a year. Cut those by half, and you have twenty-six one and ninepences. At least.' She turned round now and confronted both Corny and Jimmy.

There was a grin on Jimmy's face but he remained silent.

There was a grin on Corny's face too, and he said airily, 'Yes, twenty-six one and ninepences up the flue . . . But, Mrs Boyle.' He walked towards her, then took her arm and led her into the garage towards their car. 'Did you hear what that gentleman said? I'll call this way when I'm coming back. Now. He's no fool, and he knows I'm no fool; I'm not going to do that every time he calls in. But the impression is made, the good impression. He'll tell his friends. He won't say they'll get cheaper petrol here, or that this garage bloke doesn't care about money; he'll say, "Go to Boyle's, you'll get service. It's a good garage." Aw, to heck!' He pulled open the car door. 'What does it matter? We needn't worry about the coppers any longer. Get yourself in, woman.' He slapped at her bottom. 'Aren't I always telling you "them days are gone"? Come on you two.' He yanked the children into the back of the car, and as he started her up he said in grave, dignified tones, 'Remember, Mrs Boyle, you're married to a man with a bank balance that is getting blacker and blacker every week. Twenty-six one and ninepences . . . Rabbit feed!'

When she dug him in the ribs he laughed; then pushing his head out of the window, he called to Jimmy, saying, 'Now, you'll lock up at six and see everything's OK before you leave . . . right?'

'Don't you worry, boss. Have a nice time.'

And Mary Ann called, 'And don't forget to turn the gas off. I've left it in the oven for you, a pie; it just needs warming. Half-an-hour.'

'Right-o, Mrs Boyle. Thanks. Thanks . . . Bye-bye, nippers.' He waved to the children, and they waved to him.

As the car swung into the road Mary Ann sat back and sighed. It was nice after all to get away for a day, away from the honk-honks, the smell of petrol and the irritations, which were still present even when the banging and noise had ceased. She sighed again. She would enjoy today. Yes, she would enjoy today. And it went without saying that the twins would; they loved the Blenkinsop horde. She was about to turn to them when the unusual quiet that prevailed in the back of the car was forced on her notice and she nipped at her lips to suppress her smile. The events of last night were evidently still with them and they were expecting her to say she was sorry. Well, they could expect. Rubber guts, indeed!

Corny, too, noticing the absence of chatter remarked under his breath, 'No talkie-talkie from backie-backie' and she replied softly and in the same idiom, 'Coventry. Waiting for sorry-sorry, but no feely like it.'

When Rose Mary saw her mam and dad laughing quietly together she felt slightly peeved; she hadn't been able to make out what they were talking about. She wanted to lean over and say,

'What you laughing at, Mam?' She always liked to be in on a joke. But she wasn't kind with her mam. Yet she was still kind with her dad, so she could talk to him.

She leaned towards Corny now and said, 'Do you know Annabel Morton, Dad?'

'Annabel Morton? No.' His head went up as if he was thinking. 'Never heard of her in me life.'

'Oh, Dad!' Rose Mary pushed him in the back. 'You do know Annabel Morton. I'm always talking about Annabel Morton. She's a beast, and she's Miss Plum's favourite. You do know Annabel Morton.'

'Oh . . . h! that Annabel Morton. Oh yes, I know that stinker. She's dreadful; she's terrible; she's horrible; she's . . .'

'Dad! you're takin' the micky.'

'Oh, no, I'm not; I'm just agreeing with all you've said about that Annabel Morton. What's she done now . . . that Annabel Morton?'

'Well, yesterday dinner-time, after we came out of the hall, Patricia Gibbs was telling me about the girl who lives next door to her and who's going to be married in a long white dress with a train, and a wreath and veil and everything, and she's going to marry a priest.'

Mary Ann's head, on the point of jerking round, stopped abruptly and she continued to gaze ahead while she waited and left the sorting of this one to Corny.

'Oh, she's going to marry a priest, is she? Is she a Catholic?'

'No; she said she wasn't, but she's going to marry a priest.'

'It'll be a minister she's going to marry.'

'No, no, I said that, 'cos I know they're called ministers, and misters, but she said no, he was a priest and she was going to marry him.'

'Oh, I think she made a mistake,' said Corny. 'It wouldn't be—'

'It wasn't a mistake, Dad. And as we were talkin' about it Annabel Morton had her lugs cocked and she said Patricia Gibbs was barmy and she'd picked a barmy one to tell it to, and she meant me, and I slapped her face for her.'

After a short pause Corny said, 'In a way, I think Annabel Morton was right this time. I think Patricia Gibbs is a bit barmy if she says that the girl is going to marry a priest.'

There was another short silence before Rose Mary said, 'Well, why can't priests marry, Dad?'

Corny was saved from trying to explain a situation that was beyond his understanding by his son saying, ''Cos they can't marry people, women, you nit, they can only marry nuns.'

The car seemed to do a side-step. In the middle of a splutter Mary Ann cried, 'Careful!' Then with her head down she said, 'Look where you're going.'

'They don't marry nuns. Eeh! our David. Nuns can't marry; they're angels.'

There was a short silence now as David tried to digest this. Then he put the question to his father's back. 'They're not, Dad, are they? Nuns aren't angels. They've got legs, haven't they?'

The car took another erratic course before Corny replied thickly, 'Well, angels could have legs . . . Speaking of legs—' Corny now aimed to direct the conversation into safer channels. 'Did you bring your football boots?'

'No, Dad.'

'Well, you won't have any toes left in your shoes when Brian and Rex get that ball going.'

'Do you think we'll see Susan and Diana?' asked Rose Mary now.

'Perhaps,' said Corny. 'We'll see Susan, anyway.'

'Well, we didn't last time; she was away on the complement.'

'Continent.'

'Yes, Dad; that's what I said, complement.'

Another short pause before Rose Mary stated, 'I like Susan; she's nice. She said I'm going to be tall like you, Dad. I want to be tall, I don't want to be little.'

'Stabbed in the back.' Mary Ann muttered the words below her breath, and Corny muttered back, 'Better give in and get it over.'

'Susan says when you're tall you can . . .'

Mary Ann turned around and surveyed her offspring, looking first at Rose Mary, then at David, then back to Rose Mary again. She said quietly, 'I'm sorry.'

Rose Mary wriggled her bottom on the seat, drew her lower lip right into her mouth, drooped her head, then wagged it from side to side before raising it sideways and glancing at David.

David's reactions had not been so obvious. All he did was to sit on his hands and lower his lids.

Then, again as if released by one spring, they were standing up and their arms were about Mary Ann's neck and they were laughing as they cried, 'Oh, Mam! Mam!'

'There now. There now. You'll choke me. Sit down. Sit down.'

David sat back on the seat, but Rose Mary lingered. Her mouth rubbing against Mary Ann's ear, she whispered, 'I was only having you on, Mam. I don't care how big I am.'

Mary Ann kissed the face so like her own; and when she was settled in her seat again she looked at Corny, whose amused glance flashed to hers, and she thought, as she had done often as a child, It's going to be a lovely day, beautiful.

The Dan Blenkinsops lived in an old house on the outskirts of Doncaster. It had the added attraction of a tennis court, a paddock and a strip of woodland.

Dan and Ida Blenkinsop had six children, four boys and two girls. Tommy, the youngest, was eight; Rex was ten; Brian, eleven; and Roland, thirteen; then there was Susan, fifteen, and Diana, nineteen.

Mary Ann had met all the family with the exception of Diana, and she was looking forward to meeting Mr Blenkinsop's eldest daughter, for she would likely see a great deal of her in the future as she was going to act as secretary to her father who was now in the position of managing director of the English side of Blenkinsop's Packing Company.

Mary Ann was now sitting in the corner of a luxurious couch which was upholstered in pale blue satin and bore the imprint of grubby hands and, even worse, dirty feet. She looked about her at the lovely pieces of furniture, all, to her mind, ill-treated; cups and glasses standing on the grand piano; a conglomeration of boys' implements, all of a destructive nature ranging from catapults to guns, and including a bow and arrow, lay piled on what was evidently an antique desk. The Chinese carpet showed the tread of dirty shoes all over it, and from where she sat she could see into the hall and to the bottom of the stairs where a long coloured scarf hung like a limp flag from the banisters. She could see shoes lying jumbled on the parquet floor, and coats and sweaters heaped on a chair.

Mary Ann smiled to herself. It took all sorts to make a world. And in this world of the Blenkinsops there was evidently no discipline but a lot of fun. Also, she sensed there was a lot of money squandered needlessly. Yet, she had to admit, the children didn't act spoilt. They were very good-mannered and charming – that's when they were forced to stand, or to sit still for a moment, but most of the time they seemed to be bounding, jumping or rushing somewhere, yelling, shouting and calling as they went. And their mother wasn't in the least affected by it.

Mary Ann now watched Mrs Blenkinsop come into the room. She never seemed to hurry. She was tall and rather graceful, with black hair and black eyes, in sharp contrast to her husband who was very fair, and, incidentally, much shorter than his wife.

Mrs Blenkinsop came straight towards Mary Ann, saying, 'Diana's coming; you've got to pin her down when you can.' She sank on to the couch, adding, 'She's making the best of the time left to her. She loves riding; she's never stopped all the holidays. Ah.' She turned her face towards Mary Ann, 'But they're only young once, aren't they?'

She was speaking as if to an equal, and quite suddenly Mary Ann again felt old, like she had done last night. Mrs Blenkinsop must be forty if she was a day, but her words seemed to imply that they were both of a similar age and frivolity was past them.

Mr Blenkinsop now came across the room, walking with Corny. He was saying, 'Well, the main office is ready and that's all that matters at present. Get the brain working and the body will take care of itself.' He laughed his hearty laugh, adding, 'Anyway, from Monday next that'll be my headquarters and . . .' He paused and looked towards the door and, his voice rising, he added, 'And that of my able secretary, Miss Diana Blenkinsop.'

From the very first sight of the tall, leggy, blonde-headed, extremely modern-looking Diana, Mary Ann experienced a feeling of apprehension, even danger, for there arose in her immediately the fighting protective feeling that she had lived with, and acted on, during the years of her childhood . . . and after. The feeling had centred then around her father, but now it wasn't her father who was bringing it to the fore, but her husband.

She looked at Corny standing in front of the girl who was almost his height, and his ordinary looking face, which at times appeared handsome to her, was, she imagined, looking its most attractive at this moment. The girl, she noted, had almond-shaped, wide-spaced blue eyes and she was using them unblinkingly on Corny. It wasn't until her father drew her attention away by saying, 'And this is Mrs Boyle,' that she turned from him.

Mary Ann didn't stand up. She was at a disadvantage sitting down, but she knew she would be dwarfed still further if she got to her feet.

'This is Diana. Now you two will be bumping into each other pretty often, I'm sure, so the sooner you get acquainted the better.'

Diana lowered herself down on to the arm of the couch, and Mary Ann was forced to put her head well back to look up at her, and she made herself speak pleasantly to the disdainful-looking madam, as she had already dubbed her.

'Will this be your first post as secretary?'

'No.' The voice was cool, matching the whole appearance. 'I've been with Kent, the solicitor, for three months . . .'

'Oh, and then she was with Broadbent's.' It was her mother speaking now. 'She was there for nearly six months, weren't you, dear?' It was as if Mrs Blenkinsop was emphasising that her daughter wasn't without experience.

'You're going to find it a change from a solicitor's.' They all looked at Corny. He was seated opposite the couch and he was looking directly at Diana Blenkinsop, and she looked back at him as she asked pointedly, 'What way, different?'

'Oh.' He jerked his head. 'Well, a bit rougher, I should say. There are nearly two hundred chaps knocking around there and you'll be the only female. Oh, of course, except Mary Ann.' He now looked towards Mary Ann, and she looked back at him. Oh, of course, except Mary Ann, he had said. She wasn't a female; she was just some gender that passed unnoticed among two hundred men.

'Oh, we're not worried about Diana.' Mrs Blenkinsop was walking towards the french windows. 'She can take care of herself.' She cast a smiling glance back to her daughter before going on to the terrace and calling, 'Roland. Brian. Lunch. Bring them in . . . lunch.'

Mr Blenkinsop now seated himself beside Mary Ann and began to talk to her. She had a feeling that he was trying to be kind, going out of his way to be kind. When she looked at him she thought he was in much the same position as herself, being small. Perhaps he was being kind because he knew what it felt like to be confronted by the big types, either male or female.

His effort was checked by the avalanche of his four boys and their sister, Susan, together with her own two. They all came into the room yelling at the top of their voices; even Rose Mary and David. She wanted to check them but resisted. And then Rose Mary had hold of her hands, gabbling, 'Oh, Mam! Mam, you must come and see them. They're beautiful, lovely, aren't they, David?'

'Oh yes. Come and see them, Mam, will you, 'cos they're super.'

She smiled her bewilderment not only from one to the other, but also to the group of Blenkinsops, who were all around the couch now, and they explained in a chorus, 'The puppies . . . The Grip's had puppies.'

Fancy calling a dog, a female dog, The Grip; yet she remembered her one and only encounter with the family's bull terrier, and the name, she imagined, wasn't entirely inappropriate, although they had assured her The Grip was as gentle as a kitten . . . with people. With other dogs it was a different matter, they explained. Apparently, she had earned her title from her power to hang on to any four-footed creature which earned her dislike. But now The Grip had had puppies. It was odd that anything so fierce was capable of motherhood. Mary Ann widened her eyes and showed pleased surprise and assured them that she would love to see The Grip's puppies.

'But not before lunch,' said Mrs Blenkinsop emphatically, as she shooed the children into the hall, with orders to wash.

A few minutes later they were all in the dining-room, and Mary Ann was both impressed and saddened by the quality of the silver and china used, and the chips and cracks in the latter. And she was almost horrified at the toe and heel indentations on the legs of the period table and chairs. It was all right being free and easy, she thought, but the condition of this beautiful furniture almost amounted to vandalism. But, as her dad was always saying, it took all kinds.

The lunch, she considered, was very ordinary, and the food would have been completely dull if it hadn't been enlivened with wine. She took note that Corny allowed his glass to be filled up three times, and also that the two Blenkinsop girls and Roland were allowed wine, and the boy was only thirteen. By the end of the lunch she told herself this was an entirely different way of living from her own; nevertheless, she preferred her own every time.

The children's demands that they should go to see the puppies cut short any lingering over coffee, and Mary Ann wasn't displeased that they should get outside, because she was finding herself irritated by Diana Blenkinsop's supercilious attitude, and more so because it seemed lost on Corny, for he was talking to her as if he had known her all his life; and she had even condescended to laugh at something he said.

But one thing Mary Ann told herself as she walked down the garden by Mr Blenkinsop's side, nodding politely as he talked without really paying much attention to what he was saying, was that when they left here she must say nothing detrimental about Diana Blenkinsop. She must keep her spleen to herself; all the books told you that you got off on the wrong foot when you showed your jealousy. Not that she was jealous. Oh no; it was only that Corny had seemingly found Diana Blenkinsop attractive, and if she should voice the opposite view about her it would only show her less attractive by comparison . . . That's what all the books said.

They came to the paddock and the stables, and here, in a wire-netting enclosure, were The Grip and her six offspring.

The barking and yapping of the young puppies was overlaid by the exclamations of admiration from the children.

Mr Blenkinsop stooped down and picked up one of the puppies and, putting it into Rose Mary's arms, said, 'There. What does he feel like?'

'Oh, Mam! Mam!' Rose Mary was laughing hysterically as she strained her face away from the puppy's tongue and endeavoured to hang on to his wriggling body.

'She may drop it,' said Mary Ann anxiously, and Mr Blenkinsop said, 'It's all right, I've got him. But she mustn't drop this one because he's the prize pup. Thirty-five guineas' worth there. He goes tomorrow.'

'Thirty-five guineas!' Corny was making appreciative movements with his head.

'Yes. It seems a lot,' said Mr Blenkinsop, 'but she's a thoroughbred. And what's more, I'm going to be out of pocket by the time they all go. You have no idea . . . I'm telling you you've no idea what it takes to feed these youngsters. But, thank goodness, they'll all be gone by the end of the month, with the exception of Bill there.' He pointed to where David was scratching the tummy of one of the pups who was lying on its back. 'He's the runt.'

'What's the matter with him?' Mary Ann asked politely.

'Oh, nothing really, except that his chest is too broad. It's supposed to be broad – these brindles are noted for their chests, but they've got to have legs to support them, like this one here.' He took the puppy from Rose Mary's arms and held it up. 'You see, his front legs are as straight as broom shanks, but when Bill there grows, his weight will make him bandy. But he's full of life. He's a lad, is Bill.'

'Dad!' Amid the hubbub David's voice went unheard. 'Dad! Dad!' He tugged at his father's sleeve.

'Yes, what is it?' Corny bent over David, and David looked up into his father's eyes, then down at the puppy lying on its back. 'Aw-w! I don't know about that.' Corny straightened up; then looked at Mary Ann and said under his breath, 'He's after a pup.'

Mary Ann gave him one telling look. A pup indeed! she had enough to put up with without a dog going mad round the house. Oh, no! She was about to turn away in the hope of drawing her offspring with her when David's voice hit her, crying loudly, 'Mam! Mam!' And she looked down at him and said under her breath, 'No, David.'

But Rose Mary had picked up the scent now. Standing close to Mary Ann she caressed her hand and looked up at her pleadingly, saying, 'Couldn't we, Mam? Couldn't we?'

'No! And that's final. And stop it.' Mary Ann was hissing now.

It would seem that Mr Blenkinsop had not heard any of the exchanges, at least he gave a good imitation of being unaware of what was going on, for, stooping down, he picked up the now bounding puppy and, bringing it over the wire, held it in front of Mary Ann and said, engagingly, 'Can I make you a present of him?'

'WH . . . !' Mary Ann swallowed, blinked her eyes, glanced wildly around her, then was forced to take the puppy into her arms, and her acceptance or refusal was drowned by the shrieks of delight from both Rose Mary and David, and these were echoed by the entire male side of the Blenkinsop family.

'Oh good. I'm glad you're going to have Bill,' cried Roland; and Brian, endorsing his brother's words, said, 'We wondered what would happen to him. We wouldn't be able to keep him, you see, not with The Grip. Sort of mother and son, you know.'

And so Mary Ann, who didn't want a dog, who had never really been fond of dogs, well, not since she was a child, who felt herself cramped and restricted in the confines of her four small rooms, and whose life at the moment seemed full of drudgery and empty of anything creative, was now to be saddled with a dog, and, of all breeds, a bull terrier, which type was known for its ferocity. She'd go mad. And this, without taking into account the future, in which Diana Blenkinsop portended to move large. But with eleven people all milling around, all expounding in different ways on Bill's virtues, what could you do but just smile. She was still smiling when Diana, staring her straight in the face, said, 'Runts are always unpredictable, but the best of luck.' Whereupon, Mary Ann had an almost uncontrollable desire to reach up and slap her face. Eeh! she'd be glad when she was home.

It was a quarter to one when Corny was roused from a deep sleep by a small hand on his face and a voice whispering, 'Dad! Dad!'

'Yes . . . yes. What is it?'

'It's Bill, Dad. He's howling. He's crying.'

'Look, Rose Mary!' Corny too was whispering hoarsely now. 'Go on back to bed.'

'But he misses his mam, Dad. And it's the first night. Could we not bring him up . . . ?'

'No! Definitely no. Get back to bed.'

'But, Dad.'

'Look. Do you want your backside skelped? Go on; you'll wake your mam, and David.'

'David's awake, Dad; he's on the landing, top of the stairs.'

'Oh my God!' The words were muttered thickly as Corny dragged himself out of bed, and, pushing Rose Mary before him, he groped his way out of the dark room and on to the darker landing.

'David!'

'Yes, Dad.'

'Get yourself back into bed this instant.'

There was no movement from the head of the stairs.

'Do you hear me?' Corny felt his son groping his way across the landing; then he followed him into the small room and switched on the light, and, looking from one to the other, he said, 'Bill's not coming upstairs. That was agreed last night. Now, wasn't it? He's got to sleep downstairs. You know what your mother said; you were lucky that she brought him. Now don't press your luck, and get back into bed, both of you!'

The last three words were like the crack of a whip. With a lift of his hand he hoisted David into the upper bunk, and without another word he switched off the light and groped his way back into his own room again.

Corny hadn't slept side by side with Mary Ann for eight years not to know when she was asleep or awake, even if she was silent. As he wriggled himself down under the clothes he said, 'Don't say it,' and for answer she replied very quietly, 'I'm going to say it. You evaded the issue when we came to bed by very conveniently going straight to sleep, but I saw you giving Mr Blenkinsop the wink to pass the puppy on to me. You wanted that dog as much as they did, and you saw the only way to get it was to put me on the spot. Well now, you got your way and what are you going to do about it? Just listen to him.'

For a moment they lay and listened to the heart-rending howls that came up through the floor boards from the garage where Bill was ensconced in a blanket-lined wash-basket. Corny, making no reference to the duplicity of which he was accused, grunted, 'He'll get used to it.'

'But what are we going to do until he does? He's been like that for the last two hours.'

'You've been awake all that time?' He turned quickly and drew her into his arms, where she lay unyielding against him.

'I'm sorry, love; I'm sorry. But . . . but they wanted him. Yes, yes, I know I did an' all. I've always wanted a dog about the place, and he's cute. You'll get to like him. He's cute.' He squeezed her.

'O-o-o-o! Ow'll! Wow! Wow! WO-OW-OOO!'

'Oh my God!' Corny pulled the clothes over their heads, and as Mary Ann pushed them back again she remarked coolly, 'You'll get used to it.'

'Now, look; don't take that attitude. Very likely I will get used to it. I'll have to, won't I? But don't be snooty and so damn self-righteous.'

Corny turned round on to his other side again and again put his head under the bed-clothes . . .

At half-past two, dragging on his trousers with such ferocity that he pulled off the brace belt, he went from the room and down the stairs and, unlocking the garage, grabbed up the yapping pup and marched upstairs with it to the kitchen where, dragging a cushion from a chair, he put it inside the fender, near the oven, and plonked the now quiet animal into the middle of it. Bending down close to it, he growled, 'Now, another word out of you, just one more peep, and out of the window you go.'

Bill stared up at Corny with his small round eyes, then he opened his mouth and yawned widely. He understood. The first round had been won.

Mary Ann arose at half-past six. She didn't always get up so early, and after the night she'd had she needed extra rest, but something told her that she should rise. Perhaps it was the small scufflings from behind the wall to the right of her.

When she entered the kitchen she stopped dead, absolutely dead, and so did Bill.

Bill was in the middle of disembowelling the armchair; he was covered all over with kapok, and he gave two delicate sneezes to rid his nose of the fluff adhering to it; then he jumped down from the chair and bounded towards her. Mary Ann let him jump around her feet as she leant against the door, with one hand on the knob and the other across her mouth. Inside the fender was the remains of a cushion; on the hearth rug was what had once been a tea towel; the woollen hand-knitted tea-cosy that she had bought from the bazaar just a few weeks ago had almost returned to its original state of unknitted wool. Great lengths of it stretched from one corner of the room to the other, and the legs of a chair had taken on the appearance of a loom. All that was left of the tea cosy was the pink woollen rose that had adorned the top. And pervading this chaos was a peculiar smell. It was what her da had been wont to call a widdle scent. He had said that animals didn't smell, they just gave off a widdle scent.

Widdle scent! Three puddles and two mounds of dark matter, the result, no doubt, of the extra mince with which the children had fed him.

'Get away!' Her voice was almost a thin scream. She slapped her hand so hard on his rump that he was bowled over sideways. But Bill was a friendly, forgiving chap, and he showed it by again jumping up at her. For this show of affection he found himself being lifted by the scruff of the neck and thrown into the scullery and the door banged on him. Well, well; that's what a fellow got for simply passing the time until people turned up.

Mary Ann now stalked into the bedroom, and when she ripped the bedclothes from her husband he sat bolt upright, spluttering, 'W . . . what . . . What is it? what's the matter?'

'Would you mind coming into the kitchen.'

'Aw, Lord!' Corny flopped back on to the bed again. 'He's wet. All right, he's wet. I'll wipe it up.'

'Corny!'

He opened his eyes, there was a danger signal in that note. He got out of the bed and followed Mary Ann out of the room and into the kitchen. There he took one look then closed his eyes tightly and muttered deeply and thickly, 'Oh, Christopher Columbus!'

When he opened his eyes again she was standing a yard from him, the tears glazing her cheeks, and he went to her and said softly, 'I'm sorry, love, I'm sorry. I'll keep him downstairs. I promise.'

'Have . . . have you seen the chair?'

He looked towards the disembowelled chair. Then drooping his head, he said, 'I'll get you another. This very day, I'll get you another, a better one.'

'It's . . . it's one of a pair. It's spoilt the pair.' Her whole face was trembling.

'I'll get you a pair. It doesn't matter about that, but . . . but I'll kill him for this, see if I don't. Where is he?'

Corny would have had to be deaf not to know where Bill was, and he made for the scullery door, only to stop before opening it and say, 'I'd better get my things on first.'

A few minutes later, carrying Bill by the scruff of the neck, he took him downstairs and thrust him into the basket in the garage, and, holding him there, he addressed him. 'Look here. The quicker you learn to put up with this the better for all concerned. This is your home. Now understand that, this basket, this place.' He beat the side of the basket with his hand and rolled his head to indicate the garage.

Bill, sitting on his hindquarters, now thrust out the tip of a very pink tongue, and, lifting his right front paw, he wagged it at Corny, and Corny rubbing his hand across his brow, said, 'Aw, man, it's no use; you won't last a week at this rate, she won't put up with it. And I don't blame her. Look, if I'd had any idea of what you were going to do upstairs you could have yelled your lungs out; and you will the night.'

The paw was still flapping at him, and after raising his eyes heavenwards and shaking his head he took it and said, 'All right, all right. But I'm warning you. You've got to stay mum if you want to last out here.'

3

LIKE MOTHER LIKE DAUGHTER

This was the third time Rose Mary had been to confession. She had been frightened the first time, but she wasn't any more. Father Carey was nice, but she wouldn't like to go to Father Doughty. Eeh! no. They said he gave you awful penances like standing on your head and walking on glass in your bare feet, but Father Carey just said, 'Say one Our Father and three Hail Mary's.' She liked Father Carey. She was trying to explain to him now a particular kind of sin; the sin of telling her mother she didn't love her while all the time she loved her a lot, heaps and heaps.

'Why do you keep telling your mother you don't love her?' The priest's voice was very soothing.

''Cos of Bill.'

'Bill?'

'Our dog.'

'OO-h!'

'Mam says we've got to get rid of him.'

'She doesn't like Bill?'

'No; 'cos he tore up the chair and the tea-towels,

and he howls all night, and he makes widdles and dollops all over the place if he's let upstairs.'

The priest cleared his throat and it was some seconds before he was able to say, 'Well, you must train your dog.'

'He doesn't want to be trained, Father; he jumps all over you and licks you. He's nice, Father.'

There was another silence before the priest said, 'What kind of a dog is he?'

'He's a bull terrier, Father.' Rose Mary thought the priest groaned. 'Father.' She craned her face up to the dark mesh that separated her from the faint outline of the hand that was cupping the youthful cheek of Father Carey. 'Will you pray that she'll like him, Father, make something happen sort of that she'll like him?'

The hand moved on the face and she could see the mouth now, the lips moving one over the other; then the priest said, 'You want a miracle.'

Rose Mary's eyebrows, stretching upwards, seemed to make her grow taller because she was now seeing Father Carey's whole head as she exclaimed on a high note, 'Oh yes, please, Father. Oh yes! That would do it, a miracle.'

The priest's voice was hurried now and slightly stern and very dampening as he said, 'You've got to pray awfully hard for miracles, awfully hard; they're not easily come by; you've got to work at them. What you'll have to do is to be very good and please your mother and keep the dog out of her way for a time while you train it.'

'Yes, Father.' Her voice was meek but some part of her mind was answering him in a different tone altogether, saying, 'Ah, man, we've done all that.'

'Now, for your penance say one "Our Father" and three "Hail Mary's", and be a good girl.'

It was dismissal, but she knelt on; and then she said, 'But I haven't said me act of contrition, Father.'

Her eyebrows again moved upwards because she thought she heard the priest saying, 'Oh, lord!' Like that, like their David said sometimes, not holy-like at all.

'Make a good act of contrition.'

'Oh, my God, I am very sorry that I have sinned against Thee because Thou art so good and by the help of Thy Holy Grace I'll never sin again. In the name of the Father, SonHolyGhostAmen. Ta-rah, Father.'

'Good night, my child.' The priest was coughing badly now.

She left the confessional with her head bowed, her hands joined, and she acted holy all the way to the rail of Our Lady's altar. And there she said her penance; and there, very much as her mother had done not so many years ago, she laid her problems before the Holy Family, and not only the problem of the dog, but the problem that was really, in a way, more important.

She would like to have told Father Carey about this other problem but it was a jumbled confused mass of impressions in her mind; there was nothing clear cut about it as there was about Bill. Bill either went or he stayed; yet this other problem, in a way, was also about going and staying, and it concerned her mam and dad and . . . her. She always thought of Diana Blenkinsop as her. She didn't like Diana Blenkinsop, and this troubled her too because she liked all the other Blenkinsops, all the boys and Susan, and Mr Blenkinsop and Mrs . . . Well, she liked Mrs Blenkinsop a little bit, not a lot, but she hated Diana, 'cos Diana made her da laugh, and that made her mam angry, proper angry.

Diana Blenkinsop was always coming to the garage for this and that. She hadn't seen her herself because she was at school, but she had heard her mam asking her dad at night why she had to leave her office so often. She had asked did Diana want her dad to sharpen her pencils for her. That could have been funny but it wasn't; it was sort of frightening. And now, even when she tried to explain this problem to Our Lady, who was holding Jesus and looking down on her, she found she couldn't formulate her fears into words; all she could say was, 'Please, Holy Mary, will you make me mam happy again and laughin' like, like she was a while back.'

David was waiting for her outside of the church. He was kicking his toecaps alternately against the kerb. She said to him immediately, 'Did you ask him to do something about Bill?'

He looked sideways at her before drooping his head; then he replied briefly, 'No.'

'Oh, our David . . . you!' She walked away, and he followed her, just a step behind, and she said over her shoulder, 'You're no help, are you? Yet what will you do if she won't let us keep him?' She slowed her step and they walked together now, glancing at each other.

'Father Carey says we want a miracle. He's going to try.'

'Don't be daft.'

'I'm not daft, our David. That's what he said. But he said we'll have to work at it.'

'How?'

She shrugged her shoulders. 'Train Bill.'

'Train Bill!' he repeated scornfully; then added, 'You know what Dad said.'

Yes, she knew what her dad had said: anybody who could train Bill would qualify for a lion tamer. Not that Bill was like a lion, he was just playful, slap-happy like. She said now, 'I hope he hasn't yapped all day.'

'Some hope.'

'You're some help, our David.' Her voice was high. 'You do nothing about anything, never.'

'I do so.'

They were standing confronting each other in the middle of the street now. 'I do something about lots of things you don't know about.'

'Like what?'

'Never you mind.'

'Tuppence you don't fight.' They turned their heads quickly and looked at the man who was passing them with a broad grin on his face, and they both walked away, Rose Mary remarking, 'Cheeky thing.'

They were unusually quiet on the bus journey home, but it wasn't their nice conductor so there were no remarks made, and once they got off at the end of the road they ran all the way up the lane.

This time last year the lane had been bordered by hedges; now there was no hedge on the left side and the area appeared to be a moving mass of men and machinery. Just before they reached the white stones that edged the garage drive the buzzer went and all around them became black with men hurrying towards cars and motor-bikes.

They both ran into the garage, as they always did, to say 'Hello!' to Corny and to see how Bill was faring, but tonight their steps were checked at the entrance, for there stood their dad leaning nonchalantly against the side of a car talking to Diana Blenkinsop. They were looking at each other and smiling, and Rose Mary turned away as Corny put his head back and laughed; then she turned quickly back again as she realised there was no excited yapping or bounding body tripping them up. David must have sensed this at the same time because he called loudly to Corny, saying, 'Dad! Dad! where's Bill?'

'Oh.' Corny straightened his back; then pointing, he said, 'He's out the back in the woodshed; he's been under my feet and nearly driven me mad.' He jerked his head in the direction of the far end of the garage.

The children stared at him for a moment, then transferred their gaze to Diana Blenkinsop, and she, looking down at them, said, 'Hello there. Had a nice day?'

When neither of them answered, Corny said, 'You're being spoken to. Miss Blenkinsop was asking you a question.' His voice and face were stiff.

'Yes,' said Rose Mary.

'Yes,' said David. Then together they walked away down the garage.

'Hello there, nippers.' They both turned their heads in the direction of a car that was standing over the repair well, and they called back to the figure squatting underneath, 'Hello, Jimmy, we're going to see Bill.'

'Oh, Bill. Coo! he's been a devil the day.'

They said nothing to this but went through the small door that led on to open ground and across it to the shed.

Bill's whining faded away as they unlatched the door, and then they were almost smothered with shavings.

'Oh, Bill! Bill!' Rose Mary turned her face away from the licking tongue and David, falling back on to his heels, cried, 'Hold it! Hold it!' Then, oblivious of the dirt, they were both kneeling on the floor, holding the dog between them, and Bill quivered his pleasure from his nose to the extreme tip of his tail.

When eventually they got to their feet and ran back to the garage Bill was bounding between them, barking joyously now. As they neared the small door David stopped and, grabbing at Bill's collar, said, 'You go and ask Mam for a piece for me and I'll take him down into the field.'

Rose Mary's face puckered. This wasn't fair; yet it would be more unfair to take Bill back into the garage and have him getting wrong, so she cried, 'Well, don't go far away mind, 'cos if you do I won't bring you any. Just the first field.'

He was running from her now, with Bill at his heels, and Rose Mary, too, ran into the garage. But once through the door she stopped, for her mother was in the garage. She was standing some yards away from her father and Diana Blenkinsop, but Diana was talking to her. She was smiling as she said, 'It's patience that's needed. You've got to have a way with animals, they need handling. With some you've got to take a firm hand. I think Bill's one of the latter.'

There was a slight pause before Mary Ann said, in a voice that sounded cool and thin to Rose Mary, 'And he's not the only one.'

There was a funny silence in the garage now and all of a sudden her mother turned towards her, as if she had known all the time she was there, and grabbing her hand, took her through the small door again, across the open ground and through the gate into their back yard, and she never let loose of her hand until they reached the landing. Then quite suddenly she stopped and leant against the wall and put her two hands over her face.

'Oh, Mam. Mam.' Rose Mary had her arms around her waist now. 'Don't cry. Oh, don't cry. Please, please, Mam.'

Mary Ann stumbled blindly into the kitchen and, sitting down in the armchair, turned her face into the corner of it.

'Oh, Mam.' Rose Mary was stroking her hair. 'I hate Diana Blenkinsop, I do, I do. I hope she dies. I'll scratch her face for her so I will.'

Mary Ann raised her head, her eyes still closed, and she gulped in her throat a number of times before she said, 'Be quiet. Be quiet.' She did not say, 'How do you know I'm crying because of Diana Blenkinsop?' This was her child, flesh of her flesh, brain of her brain. She herself hadn't to be told when, as a child, she had watched her mother suffer.

She was about to get to her feet when the sound of Corny's quick heavy tread came to them, and she muttered under her breath, 'Go on out to play; don't hang around. Do you hear? Go out to play.'

Rose Mary was going out of the kitchen as her father burst in. He banged the door behind him and stood against it and he looked to where Mary Ann was taking the table-cloth from the sideboard drawer. It was some seconds before he spoke, and this alone was evidence of his anger.

'Now look, we've got to have this out.'

Mary Ann spread the cloth over the table, stroking down the edges, then turned to the sideboard again to get the cutlery. And now he was standing behind her. 'Listen to me.' When his hand came on her shoulder and he swung her round she sprang from him, her face dark with anger as she cried, 'Yes, I'll listen to you. But what are you going to tell me; that I've got a vivid imagination? That it's all in my mind?'

'You insulted her.'

'WHAT! I INSULTED HER! . . . All right then, I insulted her. Now perhaps it'll get through that thick skin of hers that it isn't a done thing to throw herself at a married man.'

'Aw, don't be so ridiculous, woman.'

'Ridiculous am I? She's been down below—' she thumbed the floor – 'She's been down below three times today to my knowledge.'

'Her father sent her. He wanted some papers, consumption of petrol . . .'

'Consumption, me grannie's aunt! Every day last week she was in the garage. Every time I went down I saw her there. Consumption of petrol! Papers! Huh! They've got a phone attached from the main office to yours, haven't they? Look, Corny.' Her voice suddenly dropped. 'You're no fool, and you know I'm no fool. If this had been happening to somebody else you'd say that girl wants a kick in the backside, that's what you'd say. You would say she's taking advantage of her father's position; you'd say she's a supercilious big-headed madam. And there's something else you would say. You would say she's sex mad.'

Corny's face was a dull red – it seemed to have caught alight from his hair – and his voice had a blustering note as he answered, 'All right, all right. Say she's all that, say you've hit the nail on the head, now what about me? It takes two to make a deal. What kind of a fool do you take me for?'

'A big one.' Her voice was quiet and bitter. 'Somebody's going to get hurt before this play is over and it won't be Miss Diana Blenkinsop. You'll be just one of the male heads she's cracked in passing. She's out for scalps. She's the same type as her mother; I can imagine the same thing happening years ago . . .'

'Aw, for God's sake!' He put his hand up to his brow. 'It's Mrs Blenkinsop now.'

'No, it isn't Mrs Blenkinsop now. We'll stick to her daughter; that's quite enough to be going on with.'

They were staring at each other in bitter, painful silence. Then Corny, his head moving in small jerks and his body seeming to slump, said quietly, 'Ah, Mary Ann, what's happened? Look.' He moved a step nearer to her. 'You know how I feel. God in Heaven, woman, there's never been anybody in my life but you. You know in your heart all this is bunkum; there's only you for me, ever . . . ever.'

She gulped in her throat but her eyes held his steadily as she said, 'Yes, I know there's only me for you; and you know I'm safely tucked away in these four small rooms, cooking, cleaning, washing, looking after the children. I'm for you up here, but downstairs you're having your fun. All right, all right.' She lifted her head. 'It could be innocent on your side, but I know girls, and I'm telling you, that girl is in deadly earnest. And in your heart of hearts you know it too.'

She drew in a deep breath now before adding, 'We've talked about this in the past, haven't we, about men going off on the side and coming back and being forgiven? And women doing the same thing. And we've agreed that neither of us could tolerate that; neither of us could take back the soiled article, because that's what it is. The old-fashioned term of the woman being soiled still held good for us.' She moved away from him back to the sideboard, and from there she said, 'It's up to you.'

His body seemed on the point of exploding with the rising tide of anger as he stalked to the door, and from there he turned and bawled at her, 'Aye, it's up to me! And I'm not going to jeopardise all I've worked for to pander to your jealous whims. If you had any blooming sense, woman, you would realise that although Mr Rodney Blenkinsop put me on my feet I've still got to depend on Dan Blenkinsop. He could just as easily contract with Riley's on the other side of the field for his petrol, or Baxter's. They're breaking their necks to get in, Baxter's are. There's nothing signed or sealed and you know that. Rodney Blenkinsop said he'd do this and he'd do that for me, but there's no contract. Dan Blenkinsop could back out the morrow; he could make some excuse to Mr Rodney about it. He's in America, and it's a long way off, and I could be flat on my face before he comes back, and it would all be because my wife wouldn't allow me to speak to an attractive young lass. That's the trouble, isn't it? Because she's tall and elegant and attractive you can't bear it. Well, you might have something more to bear than that afore you've finished. You say it's up to me, and it is, and I'm telling you straight, I'm not jeopardising my future, all our futures, because you're bitchy. If she comes into the place I'm speaking to her; I say, if she comes in; it's ten-to-one she's along in the office now telling her father about the reception she got from you. And this could be the beginning of the end, Mrs Boyle, 'cos families are funny things, especially fathers and daughters, and he thinks the sun shines out of her. Now you really have something to worry about.'

The kitchen door banged; the bottom door banged; and Mary Ann hadn't moved. For years she had prayed that some day Corny would have a break. She had seen the break as the road going through. They had bought the place eight years ago on the supposition that the by-road was going to connect the two main roads, one in and one out of the town, and thereby making the garage a thriving one. But the council had put paid to that scheme and they had merely existed for years, until the American, Mr Blenkinsop, had come on the scene and had seen the waste land across the road as a site for his factory. And after testing Corny as to his honesty, with regard to a repair bill, he had decided to build the main gates facing the garage, and to make use of his petrol station and the spare land for garaging and lorry repairs. They had looked upon it as a sort of miracle. Now she was learning that miracles have their drawbacks, for she knew that she would give ten years of her life if the clock could be turned back for six months and Mr Blenkinsop had decided to build his gates facing on to Riley's garage on the further road . . .

Downstairs in the office Corny sat on the high stool, his elbows on the desk, his hand cupping his forehead. What had happened to her? This was crazy, crazy. They should be on top of the world. Instead . . .

'Good night, boss; I'm away.'

'Oh, good night, Jimmy. Is it that time?'

'Not me usual, but I asked you, you know. We're going to Blyth to play for a dance. I told you, you know.'

'Oh aye.' Corny nodded.

'I'll make up for it.' Jimmy hesitated in the doorway.

'Oh, that's all right, Jimmy. Go on, go on, enjoy yourself.'

'Thank you, boss . . . Boss.' Jimmy's long body was bent forward a little.

'Yes, Jimmy?'

Jimmy lowered his head, then he rubbed his none too clean hands over his hair and said, 'Aw, it doesn't matter. Good night, boss.'

'Good night, Jimmy.'

Corny got to his feet and went into the garage, and as he did so a car came on to the drive. The driver wanted five gallons of petrol. When he went back into the office for change he pulled open the till, took out the silver and his hand moved to the side where a short while ago he had seen a ten shilling note. Now there were only pound notes. He picked up four half-crowns from the silver till and went out on to the drive.

Once more in the office he pulled the till open and looked at it. There had been a ten shilling note there just before he went upstairs. He had been checking the takings when he saw Diana crossing the drive. He had purposely gone out of the office and into the garage because he didn't want her coming in here. He didn't admit to himself the place was too small to hold both of them without coming into contact, and he feared contact with her. No petrol had been sold while he was talking to her, nor when Mary Ann came on the scene. How long had he been upstairs? Five minutes, ten minutes, not more. But Jimmy could have filled a tank during that time. Well, he could soon check on that.

He went out and looked at the registers on the tanks and when he returned the number corresponded with the amounts he had put in the book earlier.

Here was another problem.

Again he dropped his elbows on the desk and supported his head. There were only two people had access to this till, Jimmy and himself.

Jimmy had been with him since he was a nipper and he had never done this before. But there was always a first time, there was always a circumstance that pressed you just a little bit too much, and the group's car was the circumstance in Jimmy's case. But pinching from him! He had only noticed the deficiencies during the past three weeks, but it could have been going on for months, even years; not notes, but a bit of silver here and there. But now apparently he was getting reckless. Or, on the other hand – Corny's jaw tightened – he might be thinking that his boss's mind was preoccupied with other things and would be above noticing the cash desk. Aye, that was likely it. What had he wanted to say to him before he left? He'd a guilty look on his face; perhaps he had wanted to own up.

Well, there were two courses he could take. He could tackle him with it and perhaps give him the sack, or take temptation out of his way by getting a cash register in. But if he did the latter he still wouldn't be able to trust him.

Aw, God above, what with one thing and another life wasn't worth living. Why was it things had turned out like this? He had thought that when his break came he would be on top of the world; and he wasn't on top of the world, the world was on top of him.

4

SUNDAY AFTERNOON

Sunday's pattern ran along set lines. Corny went to first Mass; the children went to ten o'clock, often accompanied by Mary Ann, after she had prepared a cold lunch to come back to.

The afternoon pattern varied slightly. Either they went to the farm or the children's grandparents visited them, or they all went to Michael's and Sarah's. Sometimes if the day was very fine the combined family would take a run out to the coast, but once a week they all met, and today Mike and Lizzie Shaughnessy were coming. Michael and Sarah would have acompanied them but they were on holiday.

At lunch Rose Mary tried to break the unhappy silence, but only succeeded in creating more tension when she remarked, 'Me granda loves Bill 'cos he's like me granda, somehow, is Bill.'

This remark had brought her mother's wrath on her and Mary Ann had exclaimed on a high note, 'Don't be ridiculous, Rose Mary. And don't dare say any such thing when your granda arrives.'

Yet when the silence fell on them again and

there was only the sound of their eating and the scraping of cutlery on the plates she thought that, in a strange way, Rose Mary was right; that dog was like her father, not in looks, because it was an ugly beast, and her father, although nearing fifty, was still a handsome-looking man, but the animal had traits very like those in her da. Once he had set his mind on a thing nothing or no-one would turn him away from it.

In the dog's case it was bent on making this room its headquarters. Three times this morning she had pushed him downstairs; the last time she had almost thrown him down.

At two o'clock they stood before her, all scrubbed and clean, wearing their Sunday best, and she looked from one to the other as she said, 'Now, you get messed up before your granda and grandma comes and see what I'll do.' She wagged her finger, first at Rose Mary, and then at David. 'Let him out of that shed if you dare. Mind I'm warning you.'

As they stared back at her she read their minds. 'She's cruel. Mam's cruel.'

The phone ringing broke their concentration; the phone was connected with the office downstairs and Corny was downstairs. Mary Ann hesitated a moment before picking it up, and then his voice came to her.

'Your mother's just phoned. She says Gran's arrived; she'll have to bring her along.'

Mary Ann closed her eyes.

'Are you there?'

She forced herself to say, 'Yes.' Where did he think she was?

'Look, honey.' His voice was low. 'This has got to stop.'

She glanced round at the children. They were both still looking at her, and she motioned them away with her hand, and as they went out of the door she said stiffly into the phone, 'I didn't start it.'

'Well, neither did I. Look, love, I tell you there's not a thing in it. Believe me . . . Look, your mam and dad's coming; they'll smell a rat if we go on like this.'

'Is that all you're afraid of?'

The shout he gave into the phone made her pull her head sharply back.

'I'm afraid of nothing. I've told you I've done nothing to be afraid of. You'd drive a man mad. I'm tellin' you mind, if you go on like this you'll get what you're askin' for.'

When she heard the phone being banged down she put the receiver back and put her hand up to her lips to stop their trembling. She had her head bowed as she went on to the landing but she brought it up with a jerk when she saw the two of them standing looking at her. The next minute they were on her. Their arms about her, their heads buried in her waist, they enfolded her in silent sympathy, and she had to bite tight on her lips to stop herself from breaking down.

'Come on. Come on.' She ruffled their heads; then exclaimed, 'Aw, now look what I've gone and done, and me going for you to keep tidy.' She looked down into their faces, and they stared back at her. Then she said brokenly, 'Come on, I'll tidy you up,' and, still clinging to her, they went into the bedroom. And as she combed their hair she thought, They're so big a part of me, there's nothing I think that they don't sense and she pulled them towards her again and kissed them one after the other. And then she was crying softly, and Rose Mary was crying softly, and David was blinking hard and sucking his bottom lip right into his mouth.

'If you wanted a dog, why didn't you get a dog, not an ugly beast like that?' Gran was addressing Mary Ann pointedly, and Mary Ann, as always, was praying that she be given the power to answer her grandmother civilly. This woman who had been the torment of her da's life, the thorn in the side of her mother, and the constant pinprick – and that was putting it mildly – in her own.

Grandma McMullen never seemed to get any older. Her well-preserved body, her jet black hair piled high on her head, her thick-skinned face and round black eyes looked ageless. Mary Ann could never imagine her dying, although she wished it every time they met; but this, she knew, was the vainest of all her wishes.

She replied to her now, 'I didn't want the dog; I didn't bring it here.'

'Oh! Oh!' Mrs McMullen swung her head widely, taking in her daughter, Lizzie and her son-in-law Mike, and Corny, and then she appealed to an invisible figure standing somewhere near the window. 'Did you hear that? The world is coming to an end; somebody's got one over on her at last . . .'

As Mary Ann went into the scullery, Lizzie rose to her feet, saying, 'You're in one of your good moods today, aren't you, Mother?' Then she went hastily towards the door between the kitchen and scullery and closed it and, coming towards her mother again, ended, 'Now I warned you before we came away, no-one's got to put up with your tongue.'

Mrs McMullen slowly bowed her head, then brought it up sideways and again she appealed to the imaginary figure near the window, 'Well! Do you hear that?' she said. 'Do you hear that? It's come to something when you can't open your mouth. Look.' She now confronted her daughter with a hard black stare. 'I was meaning to be funny. Hasn't anybody got a sense of humour around here?'

'You could have fooled me.'

'What!' The old lady turned and glared at her son-in-law's back as it moved towards the door leading out on to the landing, and as Mike went through it she said in no small voice, 'Yes, I could have fooled you; it wouldn't take much to do that.'

Lizzie almost sprang towards the other door now and, banging it closed, she cried under her breath, 'Now that's finished it. Now I warned you; this is the last time you come out with us.'

Mrs McMullen stared at her daughter again. Then, her head wagging and her mouth working as if she was chewing on gum, she said, 'You were glad enough to come in me car.'

'Oh, my goodness!' Lizzie put her hand to her head and was about to turn from her mother but confronted her again, crying, 'Your reasoning has always been a mystery to me, Mother. It still is. We've got a car of our own; we didn't need yours to come in. You got Fred Tyler to bring you to the farm today so that Corny could look it over.'

'No such thing. Who told you that?'

'Fred Tyler told me that, if you want to know. You told him it would be a free ride as he wanted to visit his folks in Felling.'

'He's a liar.'

'Oh well, that's all right then, he's a liar and you don't want Corny to look her over.' She glanced swiftly at Corny, and Corny who had remained silent all this while looked at Gran, and Gran looked at him, and after a moment she said, 'I'll pay you; I don't want you to do it for nothing. But those other beggars in Shields, they sting me to death. They sent me in a bill for seven pounds. Where am I going to find seven pounds?'

Before Corny could answer, Lizzie said, 'You shouldn't be keeping the car, you can't afford to run it. You know you can't. You should have sold it the minute you won it. Now it's going to rack and ruin standing outside your front door. What do you want with a car, anyway, at your age?'

'It's my car and I'll keep it as long as I like, and I'll thank you to mind your own business. As for age; if you had half as much life in you as I have you'd be more spry than you are now.'

As Lizzie looked down on her mother she wondered how, during all these long years of torment, she had prevented herself from striking her; for most of her life she'd had this kind of thing to deal with. Age had not softened her mother or changed her, except for the worst.

'What's wrong with her?' asked Corny flatly now.

'I don't know. That's what you'll have to find

out. She goes pink-pink-pink-pink, like that. Fred Tayler says he thinks it's just due to verberration.'

'Verberration? You mean vibration.'

'I mean verberration. That's what he said. I'm not daft.'

No, she wasn't daft, not her. Corny, looking down on Mrs McMullen, hardened his heart enough to say, 'If it's anything big I won't be able to tackle her; I've got too much in.'

'How can it be anything big, it was new only a few months ago.'

'Lots of things go wrong with new cars.'

'Not with this one. You said it was one of the best.'

'So it is. But still things can go wrong. And I'm telling you, if it's anything that's going to take time you'll have to get it fixed elsewhere.'

He felt mean acting like this, but once he started doing her repairs she'd never be off the door. When she had won the car he had offered to buy it from her, but no; and now it was being ruined standing out in all weathers and had depreciated by hundreds already. He turned abruptly and went out.

On the drive he found Mike. He was standing quietly smoking and looking towards the chaotic jumble of machinery on the other side of the road; he grinned at him and said, 'I suppose you know by now why she came. She's after you for free repairs. If you once start she'll have you at it.'

'She'll not. I told her, if it's anything big she can take it elsewhere.'

'Aw, she's a crafty old bitch if ever there was one.' Mike squared his teeth on the stem of his pipe, then turned and walked with Corny towards the Wolseley. But before Corny lifted the bonnet he said, 'I'd better put on a set of overalls else I'll get me head in me hands.'

When he returned and began to tap various parts of the car engine, Mike stood watching him in silence for a few minutes, then he asked casually, 'What's up, Corny?'

Corny's eyes flicked towards Mike; then he turned his attention again to the car. You couldn't keep much from Mike; in any case, the feeling between himself and Mary Ann was sticking out like a sore thumb.

'Serious?' asked Mike quietly.

'Could be.' There was a pause before Corny straightened himself and, looking at Mike, said, 'She's mad.'

Mike was smiling tolerantly. 'Haven't noticed it up to now. Quick-tempered like. Takes after her male parent' – his smile widened – 'but mad? Well—' he shook his head – 'what's made her mad, Corny?'

'Come in here a minute.' Corny led the way into his office, where, having closed the door, he confronted Mike and said plainly, 'She thinks I'm gone on somebody else.'

They stared at each other. They were both about the same height, touching six foot two, and they could have been father and son in that their hair was almost the same hue of red. But whereas Corny's body was thin and sinewy, Mike's was heavily built.

Mike took the pipe from his mouth and tapped it against the palm of his hand, but still kept his eyes on Corny as he asked quietly, 'Well, are you?'

Corny tossed his head. It was an impatient gesture, and it was some seconds before he said 'Look; it's like this, Mike.' He now went on to explain how Diana Blenkinsop came into the picture, and when he had finished there was a long pause before Mike said, 'Well, as I see it, she's got a point, Corny. Oh! Oh!' he held up his hand. 'Hold your horses; don't go down me throat. I've been through this meself, you remember?' His mouth moved up at one corner. 'It nearly spoilt your wedding. I don't need to go through all that again, do I? But I'm just telling you I know how you feel . . .'

'But Mike, man, I don't really feel anything for her, not really. She's nice to natter to, she gives you a sort of kick . . . Well . . .' Again he tossed his head. 'When anybody seeks you out it gives you a kick whether it's man, woman or child. You know that yourself.'

'Aye, as you say, I know that meself; but I'm going to say this to you, Corny. It's a dangerous game to play. But for Mary Ann confronting me with the truth about that little bitch who had almost hypnotised me, well I don't know where I'd be the day. It was a sort of madness. At least it was in my case; I was clawing my way back to youth, willing my dreams to take shape in the daylight. Aw, lad, I know all about it. But in your case you haven't reached that stage yet; you're young. But young or not, this could be serious. You know, Mary Ann's nature is like a fiddle string, the slightest touch and it vibrates. God forgive me, but I made it vibrate more than enough when she was young. I was a heart scald to her, and she doesn't want to go through that again, Corny, not in any way.'

Corny sat slowly down on the high stool and he bowed his head as he said, 'You know how I feel about her. I don't need to put it into words; you know the whole story. Ever since I was an ignorant nipper, a loud-mouth lout, she has stood by me, defended me, and I could have loved her for that alone, but I loved her for herself. I still do. God, she knows it. But Mike, that doesn't mean to say I daren't look at another lass.'

'No, no, it doesn't; of course it doesn't . . . What does she look like, this Diana Blenkinsop?'

Corny raised his eyebrows and smiled wryly. 'The lot. Straight off the front of a magazine. Long legs, no bust, flaxen hair down her back, blue eyes, red lips, and five foot ten.'

Mike took the flat of his hand and flapped it against his brow as he said, 'And you wonder why she's up in the air. Why man, you know she hates being small, and for you to look at anybody an inch taller would be enough, but five foot ten, and all that thrown in, aw, Corny, that isn't playing the game.'

'Well,' Corny got up from the seat and his voice was serious, 'game or no game, Mike, I've got to be civil to her; she's Dan Blenkinsop's daughter and he's in charge here while Mr Rodney's in America. Even when he's back Dan'll still be in charge. As I tried to explain to Mary Ann, at this stage he could make me or break me.'

'And so you've got to suck up to his daughter.'

'NO!' The word was a bark. 'And don't use that expression to me, Mike. I suck up to nobody; never have. If I'd been that way inclined I'd be further on the day, I suppose.'

'I'm sorry, Corny.' Mike put his hand on Corny's shoulder. 'I shouldn't have put it like that, it was too raw. But you feel you've got to be nice to her?'

Corny's face was sullen and his lips were tight as he said, 'I feel I haven't got to do as me wife says and tell her to stay to hell out of the garage, and when she brings a message from her father I haven't got to say to her, "Look I don't want anything by hand, use the phone." '

'Aye. Aye, I know it's awkward, but remember, Corny, Mary Ann's got her side to it. Anyway, we all run into patches like this, and they pass.'

'Patches! They're more than patches that hit me. My life is either as dull as ditch water with nothing happening, or everything's coming at me from all sides at once. I've got another thing on my mind and all . . . Jimmy.'

'Jimmy?'

'Aye, he's helping himself to bits of cash.' He nodded towards the till.

'Jimmy! I can't believe that; he's a good lad. I would have said he's as straight as a die.'

'So would I, staked me life on it; but he's after a car. That gang of his want a new van to hold them and their instruments, and naturally he's expected to pig in. If he was on his own he likely could, but with his mother to see to money's tight. I've given him two ten bob rises this year, I can't give him any more at the present. I've promised him I'll put him on a better basis at the end of the year. I'll know where I stand then. The factory should be up and if I get my way I'll be under contract to Blenkinsop, Mr Rodney, not Dan, and then to hell with them all. But in the meantime

I'm not putting Jimmy's money up and then not being able to pull it down again if things don't go the way they should.'

'Aye, I see your point, but I wouldn't have believed it about Jimmy if you hadn't told me yourself. You've got proof?'

'Well, there's ten shilling notes been slipping away once or twice a week. I haven't kept tag on the silver, the Lord knows how much of that's gone . . . Aw come on.' He moved towards the door. 'I'd better see to the old faggot's machine.'

As they went on to the drive again the children came tearing round the end of the garage, with Bill on their heels, and Rose Mary cried, 'Granda! Granda! Look at him jumping. Up Bill! Up Bill!' She held her hand brow high and Bill leapt at it, but when he dropped to the ground again he fell on his side and rolled on to his back, and Mike laughed and Corny was forced to smile. 'It's his legs,' he said . . . 'they just won't hold that chest of his. That's why we got him. He was the runt. But runt or not, he's a thoroughbred, he's a good dog, Mike.'

Mike, looking at Bill, nodded, saying, 'Yes, he looks a fine fellow. I wouldn't like him to get a hold of my leg when he's a few months older. Just look at those jaws.'

As the children dashed away again with Bill tearing after them, Corny said, 'She hates the sight of him.'

'Well, you can't say he's a pretty dog; women like something nice to look at.'

'Nice to look at!' Corny jerked his chin. 'That dog's got character.' He now turned and grinned widely at Mike and there was a chuckle in his voice as he said, 'I'll say he has. Oh lad, if you could have seen the kitchen on that first night you would have thought a ship load of rats had been at it.' He gave a deep gurgle. 'She nearly went daft. Mind, I could have killed him meself, but after, when I thought about it, I had to laugh. He reminded me of Joe. Do you remember the dog I had as a lad? I used to bring him to me grannie's.'

'Oh, Joe. Oh yes, I remember you and Joe. Didn't you nearly break Fanny's neck with him once?'

'Yes, I had him on a piece of rope and there was a kid from upstairs came in. She had a cat in her arms and Joe dived and hurled me across the room, and he took me grannie's legs from under her, and she grabbed at the tablecloth as she went down. She had just put out four plates of stew. Oh, I never forget that night.' He was laughing loudly. 'I can see her, to this day, sitting on the floor covered in it, and Joe, flat out under the table, looking at her. Eeh! my, we had to run. And I daren't show me face in the door for days after . . . But it might have killed her, the fall she took.'

They were both laughing now.

'It would take more than that to kill Fanny,' said Mike. 'By the way, how is she?'

'Oh, grand. I saw her last week. She's got a new lease of life. Going to bingo now.'

'No!'

'Aye; she had won thirty-six bob and she was standing treats as it was thirty-six thousand. You know her.'

'Oh aye, I know Fanny. I wish there were more like her . . .'

It was about half-an-hour later when Lizzie put her head out of the window and called, 'Tea's ready!' and Mike called back, 'Coming!' Then looking at Corny, who was still tinkering with the engine, he said, 'I would leave that and let her get on with it, we'd better not keep them waiting, we don't want any more black looks.' Then turning round, he called, 'Rose Mary! David! Come on; tea up.'

'Granda! Dad!' Rose Mary came running up to the car. 'Have you seen Bill?'

Corny brought his head up so quickly from the engine that it bumped the top of the bonnet, and, rubbing it, he screwed up his face as he said, 'Have we seen Bill? You're asking me when you've had him all afternoon?'

'Well, he was with us a minute ago and now he's gone.' She looked over the road and called, 'Is he there, David?' and David came running and shouting, 'No, I can't see him.'

'Where had you him last?' asked Mike, and Rose Mary answered, 'Down in the field, Granda. We came round the back way and on to the drive, and we thought he'd be here.'

'Oh Lord!' Corny covered his face with one hand, then, oblivious of the grease on it, he pushed it upwards through his hair and said, 'Take ten to one he's upstairs.'

'No.' Mike moved quickly now towards the door of the house, saying, 'I'm going to enjoy this.'

'You'll be the only one then,' said Corny, pulling off his overalls and throwing them into the front of the garage.

When he reached the stairs he expected to find Mary Ann at the top with the dog by the scruff of the neck, but there was no-one to be seen, not even Mike or the children.

On entering the kitchen he stood within the door taking in the scene. Bill was seated inside the fender, his rump to the stove that housed a back boiler and was comfortably warm. His mouth was wide open, his tongue lolling out of one side, and with his small round black eyes he was appraising the company, one after the other.

Lizzie stood staring down at him. Mary Ann, too, stood staring at him, but from the distance of the scullery doorway, her mouth grim, one hand on her hip, her pose alone spelling battle. The children stood close to Mike by the side of the table, their attention riveted on Bill.

And Mrs McMullen. Well, Mrs McMullen sat in the big chair to the side of the fireplace and she glared at Bill, and her look seemed to bring his eyes to focus finally on her, and as they stared at each other she passed sentence. 'Dogs like him want puttin' down when they're young,' she said; 'they're a dangerous breed, they can't be trusted with children. Once they get their teeth in they hang on. Killed a bairn they did. It was in the papers not so long ago. Just give him another couple of months, and you won't be able to do anything with him, you'll find yourself in Court with a summons and a hospital bill to pay for somebody's leg, that is if he hasn't finished them off.'

'He could be trained,' said Lizzie.

'What, to finish them off?' laughed Mike.

Lizzie ignored this and, looking at her mother, said, 'Give him a chance, he's only a puppy.'

'Puppy! He's as big as a house end now, what'll he be like when he's fully grown? This poky room won't hold him. It doesn't hold much now, but wait till he's reached his size . . .'

'Then we'll move into a bigger house to accommodate him.'

They now all looked at Corny as he moved past Mary Ann and went into the scullery to wash his hands.

'Oh, you're all going to break eggs with a big stick. You're a long time moving into your bigger houses.'

As the kettle boiled Mary Ann went to the gas stove and from there she heard Corny mutter over the sink, 'Break eggs with a big stick, the old buzzard!'

If only everything had been all right, Mary Ann knew that at this minute she would have been standing close to his side and he would have made her giggle. She also knew that she would even have taken Bill's part, simply because her grannie didn't like him.

As she made the tea Corny stood drying his hands watching her, and when she went to pass him to get the tea stand from the cupboard he suddenly caught her by the arm, and they stared at each other for a moment; then quickly his mouth dropped on hers, hard, possessively. When he looked at her again her eyes were gushing tears and he put his arms about her, whispering, 'Don't. Don't. Don't let her see you crying, for God's sake; that'll give her too much satisfaction.

Go on. Go on.' He pushed her towards the sink. 'See to your face, I'll take the tea in.'

As he passed her with the tray he put out his free hand and touched her hair, and this did not help to ease her crying.

'You didn't tell me what was wrong with her, the car?' Gran greeted him as he entered the room again, and he said, 'It was a hole in the exhaust; I've done what I can.'

'How much will it be?'

'I'll send me bill in,' he said.

'Well, don't forget,' she answered.

It would just serve her damn well right if he did send a bill in. And wouldn't she get a shock? He could imagine her coming storming up here, raising the roof on him.

The talk was falsely animated during the meal. It was Corny who kept the conversation going, and in this he was aided by Mike.

Mary Ann, from her place at the bottom of the table, poured out the tea, and from her seat, if she cast her eyes to the right, she could see Bill. He had settled down by the stove with his head lying on his front paws. He looked utterly relaxed. She found herself wishing she could like him; she wished she could put up with him for everybody's sake, especially now that her grannie couldn't stand him. There must be something good about the beast if her grannie didn't like him.

There was always a climax when Mrs McMullen visited her relations. It came earlier than usual during this visit, just as tea was finished.

It should happen that Bill had found the stove slightly too warm for his thin coat and had moved from the inside of the fender to the outside, and this brought him to the foot of 'Gran's chair'. When she left the table and went to sit down there was Bill. He was not impeding her; she could have sat down and not even touched him, but that wasn't Gran's way. Taking her foot, she gave him a sharp dig in the ribs. The result was surprising but, as she herself had stated earlier, predictable.

Bill had been happy today, as he had never been since he had left his mother. He was in a warm place which was permeated with nice smells. He had discovered he was very fond of biscuits, not the broken biscuits that you got with your dinner, but biscuits with chocolate on them. He knew he was going to develop a real taste for biscuits with chocolate on them. Chocolate had a particular smell and there was a strong smell of chocolate in this room. He knew that if he waited long enough and quietly enough he would be rewarded. That was, until the thing hit him in the ribs. His reaction to the pain was for his jaws to spring open, then snap closed, and to give vent to a cry that was part yelp, part yap and part growl, and all the time he felt the pain he jumped madly around the room dodging under one object after another.

'There! There! What did I tell you? He's dangerous. He went for me.'

'He did no such thing!' Lizzie was yelling at her mother. 'You asked for it.'

'I asked for what?'

'You should have left him alone.'

'Don't chase him, let up,' cried Corny.

'Look, stop it!' Mary Ann was shouting at the twins now. 'You'll have the things off the table.'

'Here he is! Here he is!' Mike reached down

behind the couch and grabbed at Bill's collar, and, pulling him up, he thrust him wriggling and squirming into David's arms and David, now looking fearfully up at his mother, said, 'He didn't do it. He didn't start it, Mam, it was Gran. She kicked him. I saw her; she kicked him.'

'I did nothing of the sort, boy. Well! would you believe it?'

'Yes, you did, Gran, I saw you.' Rose Mary was now standing by David's side confronting the old woman, and Mrs McMullen, looking from one to the other of her great-grand-children, didn't know which she disliked most, or whether her dislike for them was greater than that for their mother. But that couldn't possibly be. Nevertheless, she knew that there was a time when it was advisable to retreat, and so with great dignity she sat down in her chair again and, her chin moving upwards, she made a statement, which was sinisterly prophetic in this case.

'Every dog has his day,' she said.

David stared at her; then grinning he said flippantly, 'Aye, and a bitch has two afternoons.'

Such a reply coming from her great-grandson not only brought Mrs McMullen's eyebrows almost up to her hairline but also created an amazed silence in the room, and an assortment of astounded expressions.

Still holding on to the wriggling dog, David now looked apprehensively from one face to the other. He'd get wrong, he knew he would. He felt a little afraid, until all of a sudden there came a sound like an explosion. It was his granda and his dad bursting out laughing together. His granda had his hand on his dad's shoulder and he was roaring. And his grandma too, she was laughing with her head down and her face covered. But his mam wasn't laughing. The next minute she had hold of his collar and was pushing him and Bill outside while Rose Mary came after them shouting, 'No Mam. No Mam.'

On the landing, Mary Ann looked down at her son and hissed under her breath, 'David! where on earth did you hear that?'

'It . . . it wasn't swearin', Mam.'

Mary Ann swallowed deeply. 'It was a kind of swearing.'

At this David shook his head and glanced at Rose Mary, and Rose Mary said, 'Not really, Mam, not proper swearin'.'

'Who told you it?'

David blinked and hitched Bill further up into his arms and had to avoid his licking tongue before he said, 'Nobody, Mam; I just heard it.'

'Where?'

David glanced at Rose Mary again, then looked down but didn't answer, and Mary Ann wanted to take him by the shoulders and shake him. But that meant shaking that animal too and then anything might happen. 'Where?' she repeated.

It was Rose Mary who answered for him. 'Jimmy. Jimmy says that, Mam.'

Mary Ann straightened herself up. Jimmy? Well, wait until she saw him tomorrow. 'Take that animal downstairs and lock him up,' she said.

Neither of them moved. They were looking up at her, blinking all the while.

'You heard what I said.'

'She kicked him, Mam. He wouldn't have done anything if she hadn't have kicked him.' As David spoke the door opened and Corny and Mike came on to the landing. They were still laughing. Mary Ann did not look at them but at the children and repeated, 'Take him downstairs.'

They both glanced at their father and grandfather, then went slowly down the stairs, and Mary Ann turned and looked at these two whom she loved so deeply that the feeling often brought nothing but pain, and she saw them now as a couple of boys. They were leaning against each other and she hissed at them under her breath, 'Stop it! D'you hear? Stop it!'

Mike now put his hand out towards her, spluttering, 'And a bitch has two afternoons.'

As she saw their laughter mounting she pushed them towards the bedroom, and once inside she cried, 'If you must act like bairns do it in here.'

'She . . . she wants her hat and coat,' Mike gasped; 'she's going . . . we're going. We're going out on a wave. We always go out on a wave when she's about.'

She picked up her grannie's coat and went out and into the kitchen, there to be met by the standing figure of Mrs McMullen.

Mary Ann didn't hand her grannie her hat and coat; instead, she handed them to her mother, and it was Lizzie who went to help the old lady into her things, only to be repulsed with the words, 'Thank you! I can see to meself.'

And that was all Mrs McMullen said until they reached the bottom of the stairs, and there, turning and looking straight into Mary Ann's face, she remarked, 'They're a credit to you. They're a pair you could take anywhere. You must be proud of them.'

The pressure of her mother's fingers on her arm stilled her retort, and Lizzie, bending down, kissed her and whispered, 'I'll ring you later.'

When her da kissed her his eyes were still wet and gleaming, but he said nothing more, he just patted her cheek and went towards the car.

She did not wait to see them off but returned upstairs, and a few minutes later Corny entered the room. He came straight towards her, the twinkle deep in his eye, but he did not repeat the joke; instead, he picked her up in his arms as he had been wont to do and sat down with her in the big chair, and when he pressed her face into his neck her body began to shake, but not with laughter; she was picking up where she had left off in the scullery earlier on.

5

GETTING ACQUAINTED

'Now Rose Mary, if I've told you once I've told you a hundred times, he can't come upstairs; he's all right where he is.'

'But listen to him, Mam, he's yelling the place down. He's lonely. He likes people, he does; he only cries when he's by hisself . . .'

Mary Ann had turned her head away, but now she brought her gaze down to her daughter again as she said patiently, 'He's a puppy, Rose Mary, he's got to learn. He won't learn if you give in to him.'

Rose Mary's lips trembled as she muttered, 'I worry all day 'bout him, shut up in there in the dark. I'm frightened of the dark, you know I am, Mam, and he—'

'Rose Mary!' It came on a high note, but when she saw her daughter's face crumpling into tears she knew that this would continue all the way to school, and all during Miss Plum's questioning, and she was forced to compromise. 'Look,' she said; 'you can go and let him out. He can run round behind the garage, but see that the lane gate is closed, for mind' – she bent down towards her daughter – 'if he gets out on the road among all those lorries he could be killed.'

'Yes, I know, Mam. All right, Mam, I'll fasten the gate tight.' Swiftly now Rose Mary's arms came up and hugged her mother around the neck. 'Thanks, Mam . . . Ta. I'll tell our David.'

David was standing in grim silence at the bottom of the stairs waiting for her, and she dashed at him, whispering hoarsely, 'Mam says we can let him out and he can run in the back.'

'She did?'

'Yes. Come on, hurry, 'cos we'll miss the bus else.'

They raced round the side of the building, through the wooden gate that was laced with wire netting, and to the woodshed, and when they released Bill he showed his thanks by bounding around them until David grabbed his collar and, pressing on his hindquarters to keep him still, said, 'Now look; you behave yourself and we'll take you out the night, eh?' He wanted to rub his face against the dog but refrained. But Rose Mary, dropping on to her hunkers, cupped the long snout in her hands, and as she bent to kiss it the slobbering tongue covered her face in one stroke from chin to brow, and she almost fell over laughing.

When they ran to the gate Bill galloped with them, but when he realised he wasn't going to be allowed through he stood up on his hind legs against the wire netting and howled. He howled and he howled until gradually he tired and then he reduced his howling to a whimper before turning forlornly away to investigate the open area.

He found it a place of little interest, except for the wooden walls of the garage out of which a number of quaint smells oozed, none of them very alluring. The investigation over, he returned to the gate and discovered that if he kept to one side of it he could see occasional activity on a small patch of road fronting the garage. It was as he lay gazing in this direction, and bored to extinction, that he saw coming towards him an apparition which brought his body springing upwards. When the apparition reached the other side of the gate and pressed its nose against the wire netting and so touched his, the effect was like an electric shock. It shot up his bony muzzle, along his spine and right to the end of his tail, where it recharged itself and retraced its path.

Bill hadn't seen one of his own kind since he had left his family, and now he was being confronted by a female. That she wasn't of his own breed, nor yet could lay claim to being a thoroughbred didn't trouble him. He couldn't have cared less that she wasn't a simple cross between a poodle and a terrier, and that obvious other breeds could be detected in her ancestry; to him she was the most fascinating creature he had encountered so far in his young life, and urges, entirely new to him, were acting like crossed wires under his coat, for ripples of delight were darting off at tangents through every part of his body.

He said a breathless, 'Hello,' and she answered with a cool, 'Hello'. And then she indicated by turning her back on his and taking a few steps from the gate that she wouldn't mind if he accompanied her.

There was nothing Bill wanted more at this

moment than to accompany this witch, and when she returned to the gate, squatted, and gave him absolute proof of her feeling for him, there arose in him a blind fury against the barrier between them, and nothing or no-one was going to prevent him from breaking it down. To this end he got his teeth into the bottom strand of the wire netting and he pulled, and he tugged and he bit while the temptress walked up and down on the other side of the gate giving him encouragement in the way she knew best.

When Bill had made a hole big enough to get his head through the lady walked away again, and when she realised he wasn't following she stood looking at him in some disappointment; then, like many another lady before her, she suddenly got fed up with the whole business and trotted off.

Bill, now working with intensified fury, enlarged the hole, and with a wriggle he was through. Like lightning he was on the garage drive, then on the road, and across it. He pulled up once to sniff at what was left of a thorn bush, which confirmed that she had passed this way, and then he was running amidst the tangle of building material, cranes, grabs and lorries . . .

Mary Ann was feeling somewhat better this morning, though not exactly light in heart; she would never feel like that again until Miss Blenkinsop decided to take a position elsewhere, and as things stood she couldn't see her doing that. But last night Corny had been his old self and he had assured her that in the whole wide world she was the only one that mattered to him, and she believed him. But that was last night, in the darkness, with her head buried on his chest; this morning, in the stark light of day, and the time approaching ten minutes to nine when Miss Blenkinsop would be arriving, bringing her car on the drive with a flourish and pulling up, with a screech of brakes, at the garage door, she wasn't so sure. Anyway madam would be disappointed this morning, for it would be Jimmy who would take her car and park it in the garage, because Corny had gone into Shields on business.

Even knowing that she wouldn't witness Corny greeting Diana Blenkinsop as he did most mornings, Mary Ann found herself standing to the side of the front room window which overlooked the drive. She wondered what madam would be wearing this morning; perhaps a mini skirt. No, she wouldn't dare wear a mini skirt, not with her height.

The drive was empty of cars and people, and after a moment Mary Ann's gaze was drawn across the road and to a section practically opposite the window, where last week they had started to excavate the land prior to building an underground car park beneath one of the factory shops. The excavations had reached the point where the hole was about twenty feet deep. On the edge of it a grab was working. At present it was stationary. Her eyes were passing over it when they were brought leaping back to take in a black and white figure standing on top of the grab itself.

Bill! No, it couldn't be, he was in the yard. But . . . but there was only one Bill, there could only be one Bill hereabouts and that was him. He had got out. Then something happened that caused her to push up the window and yell at the top of her voice, 'Stop it! Stop it!'

As she ran down the stairs she could still see the wide grin on the grab operator's face as he leant from the cab pointing out the dog to his mates, and even before he pulled the lever gently to set the grab in motion Mary Ann had known what he was about to do.

When she reached the driveway she saw the grab swinging into mid-air, with the petrified dog clinging with its two front paws to one of the supporting chains, while its hind legs slithered here and there on the muddy surface of the lid. The operator was doing it for a laugh. If he opened the grab the dog would fall between the lips, but he was just having a laugh and the men on the rim were guffawing loudly.

'Stop it! Stop it this minute!' She was below the cab now yelling up at the man. 'You cruel, sadistic devil, you! Stop it, I tell you.'

'What do you say, missus?'

The grin was wider now.

'You heard what I said. You'll hear of this. That's my dog.'

'He's all right; he's just havin' an obstacle put in his way, he's after a bitch. He's all right.' The man flapped his hand at her.

'You'll be far from all right when my husband finishes with you.'

'Oh aye? Just make the appointment then, missus, just make the appointment. Tell him any time.'

'Stop that thing.'

'I'd better not, missus. Better get it to the

bottom, break his neck else. Would you like his neck broke?'

When the grab hit the bottom of the hole she watched Bill fall off into the mud, then make an attempt to crawl out of it. But the harder he paddled the more he stuck.

'Oh, you're a horrible swine. That's what you are, a horrible swine.' There were tears in her voice as she yelled, not only at the crane man now but at the men standing further along the rim. Then before anyone knew what she was up to she was slipping and sliding down the wet clay face of the hole.

Mary Ann wasn't aware of the scene behind her now, but a man in a trilby hat and leather jacket had come up to the crane demanding, 'What's this? What's up?'

'Aw, it was just a joke.'

'A joke?' The man bawled: 'What's that woman doing down there? What's this anyway?'

'The dog was on the grab,' one of the men put in sheepishly, 'and Sam let him down.'

'You did what!' The man looked up at the operator.

'He's not hurt. He was just sitting there and I set it moving.'

The two men stared at one another for a moment; then the man in the trilby hat said, 'I'll bloody well set you moving after this.' Then going over the rim himself, he reached Mary Ann just as she fell flat on her face in the quagmire with Bill in her arms.

When he pulled her to her feet he said, 'Give him here.' But Bill refused to be parted from Mary Ann. His whole body quivering, he clung on to the shoulder of her dress and as the man's hands came on him he made a pitiful sound and Mary Ann gasped, 'It's all right, I can manage him.'

'Look; you'll have to let me help you; you can't walk in this.' Without further words he put his arm around her waist and lifted her sucking feet from out of the mud, and like a mother carrying a child on her hip he bore her to the far side of the hole where the ground was comparatively dry, then mounted a ladder that had been laid against the sloping ground.

When he reached the rim he put her on her feet and steadied her, saying, 'There, there; you're all right.'

'Th-thank you.'

''Struth! we're in a mess.' He knocked lumps of mud from his jacket, then added, 'Somebody'll pay for this. Come on.'

As they walked back around the perimeter of the hole he said, 'You're Mrs Boyle, aren't you? Used to be Shaughnessy?'

'Yes. Yes, that's right.'

'You don't remember me? Aw well, it's not the time to press an introduction. You'd better get yourself into the house and get that stuff off you, and him.' He nodded towards Bill who was still clinging tenaciously to Mary Ann's shoulder.

Mary Ann looked at her rescuer. She didn't remember ever having seen him before; but then his face was all bespattered and his clothes were in a similar plight to her own, which made her say, 'I think you need cleaning up an' all. Would you like to come inside? You're about the same build as . . . as my husband, you could have a change of clothes if you like.'

'Well, that's very nice of you. I wouldn't mind getting out of this clobber at the moment.'

When they came to the grab the operator was busily at work, as were his mates, and the man muttered, 'I'll see to them later.'

There were two other people who had witnessed the incident, Jimmy and Diana Blenkinsop. Jimmy, his long face stretched even to a greater length, said, 'Eeh! Mrs Boyle, you shouldn't have gone down there.'

Diana Blenkinsop gave a little laugh, and she said, 'You have got yourself into a mess, haven't you? He would have got out on his own you know; he comes of a very tenacious breed.'

'AND SO DO I!' said Mary Ann, pausing slightly before marching across the road, followed by the man.

When they reached the drive he said under his breath, 'Friend of yours?'

'What do you think?' She glanced sideways at him, and he grinned back at her, and the grin stirred a faint memory in her mind. She had seen him before but she couldn't place him.

After scraping their feet on the scraper let into the wall, she led the way upstairs, and on the landing she pointed to a door, saying, 'That's the bathroom. There's plenty of hot water. I'll bring you some clean clothes as soon as I get the thick off.'

'Don't hurry.' He was grinning again. 'And I think you'd better start on the bold boy first; if you let him down he'll leave you some trade marks.'

'Yes, you're right.' She laughed at the man. She liked his voice, his easy manner. He was nice.

In the scullery, when she attempted to put Bill into the sink he dug his claws into her shoulder again and hung on to her, and she stroked his muddy head with her equally muddy hand and said, 'It's all right. It's all right, I won't hurt you.'

When finally she had him standing in the sink he sat down quite suddenly as if his legs would no longer support him, and when he looked up at her and made a little whining sound she laughed again and said, 'It's all right, I'm not going to drown you.'

When he was clean she put him inside the fender and, pressing him firmly downwards, commanded sternly, 'Now stay. Stay. I'll be back.' Then she scrambled into the bedroom, whipped some clean things for herself out of the wardrobe, together with a shirt and old trousers and a coat of Corny's, and going to the bathroom door called, 'I'm leaving the things outside.'

The voice came to her cheerily, 'Right-o. Thanks. Thanks a lot. I could stay in here all day.'

As she heard the swish of water she smiled and hurried into the scullery again, and there she stripped her clothes off, washed her face, legs and arms in the sink, and got into her clean clothes; and she was in the kitchen again before a tap came on the door.

When he entered the room she looked at him and laughed with him as he said, 'All made to measure. Would you believe it? Except that your man's a bit longer in the leg than me, we must be of a size.'

'You are.' She nodded at him. 'Would you like a drink of something, I've got the kettle on?'

'Now that's very nice of you, but I should be

getting back, that lot will be having a holiday knowing I'm out of the way for five minutes . . . On the other hand, they'll be expecting me to blow me top and are likely playing wary, so yes, thanks, I'll take that drink.'

He sat down by the side of the table and as she went into the scullery he called to her, 'His nibs has settled down all right, not a peep out of him.'

'I think he's still suffering from shock,' she called back.

'Well, aye, it would be a shock to the poor little beggar to find himself whisked into mid-air like that. That Fred Tyler's an empty-headed nowt, if ever there was one. If it had been his mother on top of the grab he would have done the same. By the way, don't you remember me?'

She came to the scullery door and stared at him. Yes, yes, she had seen him somewhere before. He was a very attractive looking fellow; black hair, deep brown eyes, squarish face, well built.

'Fillimore Street. You know, behind Burton Street and Mulhattan's Hall. We used to live next to the Scallans, the daughter who married Jack McBride. They were Salvationists, and old Fanny nearly went barmy.'

'Murgatroyd!' Mary Ann was pointing at him, her finger wagging. 'Yes, yes, of course, Murgatroyd. Johnny Murgatroyd, of course.'

'I used to chase you round the back lanes and try to scare the wits out of you.'

She laughed widely as she recalled the big lanky fellow swooping down on her from the street corner when she was returning from school; especially would he swoop on St Patrick's Day, because she was green and he was blue.

She brought the cups of coffee to the table, and as she sat down she said, 'Well, well, after all these years, and you've got to rescue me as an introduction.'

'Aye,' he said; 'funny that. Pity the TV cameras hadn't been there, it would have caused a laugh him going down on the grab,' he nodded towards Bill, 'and the three of us then slithering on our bellies.' He jerked his head at her and paused before saying, 'You should make up a song about that an' all.'

Her eyes widened, but before she could say anything he said, 'Oh, I know quite a lot about you; I thought that song you made up for Duke and them was really fine.'

'You know Duke?'

'We live next door to him in Jarrow.'

'It's a small world.' She shook her head.

'You've said it. By!' he said, 'they're a lot, that group. I don't know why Jimmy strings along with them. Me mother's threatened to get the polis time and time again. They come back from a do on a Saturday night – or a Sunday morning – and start raising the place. Drums, guitars, mouth organs, the lot.'

'You live with your mother?' Her head was bowed enquiringly towards him. 'You're not married?'

For reply he jerked his chin upwards; then running his hand through his hair he said, 'Nearly came off two years ago, but she changed her mind.'

'I'm sorry.'

'Oh, don't be.' He was grinning again. 'She's got a bairn now and she goes about like something the cat dragged in. Talk about counting your blessings; it nearly made me go to church the last time I saw her . . .'

They were laughing uproariously when the door opened and they both turned and looked at Corny.

Mary Ann got to her feet, saying, 'You've missed it all. This is Johnny Murgatroyd. He . . .'

Corny came forward, saying, 'Jimmy's told me something of it. It was very good of you.' His voice had a slightly stiff note to it.

Johnny Murgatroyd was on his feet now, his hand extended. 'Oh, that's all right. It was a sort of re-introduction. We know each other; brought up back to back so to speak. I used to chase her when she was a nipper.'

'Oh, yes.' Corny gave a weak smile; then looked from the fellow's coat to his trousers; and Mary Ann said, 'We were covered from head to foot in slime. I've lent him your things. That's all right, isn't it?'

'Oh aye. Yes, yes.' He nodded his head airily; then looking towards the fireplace, he asked, 'How did he get out?'

'Don't ask me; I haven't had time to investigate that yet. But there's one thing certain, it's frightened the life out of him.'

Corny was on his hunkers by the fender and he stroked Bill's back, saying, 'All right old chap?' but Bill made no move towards him.

'He's shivering.' He looked up at Mary Ann.

'I had to wash him and, as I said, he got an awful shock and I think he's still frightened.'

'Well, I'd better be on me way.'

They both turned towards Johnny Murgatroyd.

'If you could give me a sheet of paper to put round my old duds I'd be grateful.' He smiled at Mary Ann and added, 'Then I'll see to somebody taking over from me and dash home and make a change and let you have your things back.' He nodded at Corny now, and Corny said, 'Oh, there's no hurry.'

'Good job we're much of a build.' Johnny's engaging grin widened, and Corny said, 'Aye, it is.' He stared at the man, he was about an inch shorter than himself but of a thicker build and good looking in a sort of way. He was the kind of fellow that women would fall over their feet for.

'Many thanks. I'm grateful.'

'You're welcome,' said Corny.

'I'll pop in again and have a word with you, if that's all right.' He looked at Mary Ann, and Mary Ann resisted looking towards Corny before saying, 'Yes, yes, of course, Johnny.'

Five minutes later, after seeing their visitor away, they returned upstairs, and Mary Ann said, 'You didn't mind me lending him your things?'

'No, no, of course not.'

She stared at him. 'But I couldn't do anything else, he was in such a mess, and I would never have got out of there but for him.'

'Oh, I suppose somebody would have dragged you out. They would have sent down the grab again.'

As he turned away she looked at his back, and then she nipped on her lip to stop herself from smiling and forced herself to say casually, 'Yes, I suppose so, but he seemed the only one who wanted to. It was nice meeting him again after all this time.'

'Yes, yes, very nice I should say.' He was talking from the scullery now. 'And he's going to drop in again. Never waited to be asked. Bit fresh, if you ask me. Going to make you pay for the rescue.'

'Well, that's an attitude to take.' She was looking at him from the doorway as he poured himself out some coffee, and her control went by the board. 'You've got room to talk, haven't you? You can laugh and joke with whom you choose, but because you came in and found me laughing with a man that's all wrong. And after he had done me a great service. I don't think your lady friend has ever done you a service, but then,' she closed her eyes and bobbed her head, 'I may be mistaken.'

She had turned into the kitchen again and like a flash he was after her.

Pulling her round to him, he ground out under his breath, 'Now look you here. We straightened me out last night, now I'm going to straighten you out . . . before it goes any further. Johnny Murgatroyd is a womaniser. That is the first time I've met him to speak to, but I've heard quite a lot about him. He was going to be married a while ago but the lass found out he was keeping a woman in Wallsend, and apparently she wasn't the first, and she won't be the last; so Mrs Boyle, take heed to what I'm saying. No more tête-à-têtes with Mr Johnny Murgatroyd.'

'You're hurting my shoulders.'

'I'll hurt more than your shoulders if I've got to tell you about this again, I'll skelp your lug for you.'

'Just you try it on.'

'Don't tempt me.'

She watched him stalk from the room; then she sat down on the chair near the fireplace, and again she was biting on her lip. But now she let the smile spread over her face. It filled her eyes and sank into her being, filling her with a warmth.

A movement to the side of her brought her eyes to Bill. He was on his feet, and slowly stepping over the fender he put his two front paws on her knees and leapt up on to her lap, and there, laying his muzzle between her breasts, he gazed up at her. And she looked back at him. Then after a moment she said to herself, 'Well, well, who would have thought it?' and her arms went round him and she hugged him to her.

6

What's Good For The Goose

'It is, our David. It is because of the miracle
Father Carey made.'

'Don't be daft.'

'I'm not, our David, I'm not daft. I told you I
told Father Carey in confession and he said it
wanted a miracle, and he made it. Mam was going
to throw Bill out. You know she was. She wasn't
going to let us keep him, and now she has him all
the time and he won't leave her, and she's trainin'
him herself. It couldn't have happened if Father
Carey hadn't . . .'

They had just got off the bus in Felling and were
walking up Stuart Crescent making for Carlisle
Street where the school was, and David, jumping
into the gutter and kicking at a pebble, said, 'It's
'cos Mam got him out of the hole and he was
frightened and she was nice to him, that's why.'

''Tisn't. He was frightened of the dark and
being tied up and being by hisself. But that didn't
make him keep with Mam all the time, like now.
You don't believe anything, our David, like you
used to. It is a miracle, so!'

David glanced at her and grinned, but she didn't grin back at him. Since he had begun to talk he had moved further and further away from her. At first he had been all for their dad. He was still for their dad; but now he was for other people too, like Jimmy. He was always trailing round after Jimmy. Yet there were odd times when he wanted to be near her, and he would look at her and grin, like he was doing now, and she would feel happy. Only she couldn't feel happy this morning; she had too much on her mind. She said sudddenly, 'Do you like Diana Blenkinsop?'

When his reply came with startling suddenness she was in the gutter beside him. 'You don't? Why?'

David kicked another pebble, then started to dribble it along the roadway. Why didn't he like Diana Blenkinsop? When the answer came to him he turned his head and gave it to Rose Mary: ''Cos me mam doesn't like her.'

'Oh, David.' She was running by his side now. She didn't like Diana Blenkinsop because her dad liked Diana Blenkinsop. And David didn't like Diana Blenkinsop because her mam didn't like Diana Blenkinsop. You see, it was all the same. She said now, 'They were talking about her again last night.'

'I know.' He kept his gaze concentrated on his dribbling feet; the stone veered off into the middle of the road and as he went to follow it Rose Mary grabbed him, crying, 'Eeh no! The cars.' And they returned to the pavement and for a while walked in sedate silence.

When they came in sight of the school gate

Rose Mary's step slowed and she said, 'There's that Annabel Morton talkin' to Patricia Gibbs. Patricia promised to bring me a book full of pictures, but she only promised so's she could get you to carry it back.'

David's glance was slanted at her again, his eyebrows showing a surprised lift in their middle, and she nodded at him and said, 'She's gone on you.'

'Polony!'

'It isn't polony, she's sucking up. She wants to be asked to tea, but she's not me best friend and I'm not goin' to.'

Annabel Morton was nearly eight and a big girl for her age, and, as Sarah Flannagan had hated Mary Ann as a child, so Annabel Morton hated Mary Ann's daughter, and the feeling was reciprocated in full. When Annabel's voice, addressing no-one in particular, said, 'Somebody stinks,' Rose Mary turned on her like a flash of lightning, crying, 'You! You don't know what you're talking about. Scent doesn't stink, it smells. It's scent, me mam's.'

'It's scent, me mam's,' mimicked Annabel to her solitary listener. 'But it still stinks, doesn't it?'

'You're a pig!' Rose Mary did not yell this statement, she hissed it under her breath and she embroidered it by adding, 'If you lift a pig up by its tail its eyes'll drop out. Mind somebody doesn't do that to you.'

This would take some beating, and at the moment Annabel could find nothing with which to match it, and so Rose Mary, having won the first round of the day, put on her swanky walk, which wobbled her buttocks, which in turn swung her short skirt from side to side. The result was entertaining, or annoying; it all depended on the frame of mind of the onlooker . . .

It was in the middle of the morning, after they had had their milk, that they started to paint. Rose Mary liked the painting lesson, she was good at it. The whole class were doing a mural of history. It was depicting Bonnie Prince Charlie and Flora Macdonald. Each table was doing a section, and then they would put it together and it would fill one wall of the classroom. Rose Mary and Patricia Gibbs and her brother, Tony, were doing the water section with the boat on it. Rose Mary had just mixed up a beautiful deep blue for the water under the boat when Patricia dug her in the ribs with her elbow, at the same time withdrawing from under her painting board a big flat book.

They both looked about the room to ascertain the whereabouts of Miss Plum and saw that they were safe, for she was at the far end showing Cissie Trent what to do. Cissie Trent was dim and took a lot of showing. Patricia quickly flicked over the pages and pointed to a coloured plate and looked at Rose Mary, and Rose Mary looked at the picture. For a moment she couldn't make out what it was. And then she saw it was all about a man and a woman; the woman had hardly anything on the top of her, and the man had long hair right past his shoulders. He was lying on a kind of bed thing and the woman was bending over him with a knife in her hand. Eeh! it looked awful. She looked at Patricia and Patricia looked at her and, her eyes round and bright, she whispered, 'She's going to cut his hair off. It's called Samson and De-lie-la-la.'

'. . . Sam . . . son and De-lie-la-la?' Rose Mary's lips moved widely over the name. 'What's she doing?'

'I told you: she's going to cut his hair off.'

'Eeh! what for?'

'So's he won't be able to do anything.'

'What is he going to do?'

'Things.'

'What things? . . . Like what things? Playing a group?'

That explanation was as good as any for Patricia, and she nodded as she smiled, 'Yes. Ah-ha.'

Rose Mary considered a moment before saying, 'But that's daft. How can cutting his hair off stop him playing in a . . .'

They both felt the hot breath on their necks and turned startled eyes towards the face of Annabel Morton. But Annabel was looking down at the picture. Then she looked from one to the other, and she said, 'Mushrooms.'

The word was like a sentence of death to both of them. Mushrooms was the word in current use in the classroom to express deep astonishment, amazement or horror. The book was whipped from sight and pushed under Rose Mary's drawing board, and they both attacked their painting with such energy that they were panting when Miss Plum loomed up before them.

'Which of you is hiding a book?'

Patricia looked at Rose Mary, but Rose Mary was staring at Miss Plum.

'Come on. Come on, hand it over.'

Still Rose Mary didn't move.

'Rose Mary! Have you got that book?'

Rose Mary's fingers groped under the pad and she pulled out the book and handed it up to Miss Plum. She had done this without taking her startled gaze from the teacher.

Miss Plum now flicked over the pages of the book, her eyes jerking from one art plate to another, and when her eyes came to rest on Bacchus in his gross nudity sporting with equally bare frolicking females she swallowed deeply; then looking at the children again she said, 'Who owns this book?'

'I do, Miss,' said Patricia.

'Where did you get it?'

'From home, Miss. It's . . . it's me brother's. I took a loan of it.'

Again Miss Plum swallowed, twice this time, before saying, 'When you go home tonight tell your mother, not your brother, that I have this book, Patricia; and tell her I would like to see her . . . But anyway I will give you a note.'

'Yes, Miss.'

'Now get on with your work, both of you, and I'll deal with you later.'

They both resumed their painting, but with less energy now; and after a while Rose Mary in a tear-filled voice, whispered, 'You've got me wrong, Patricia Gibbs.'

'Well, you wanted to see it.'

'No I didn't; I didn't ask to see your nasty book.'

' 'Tisn't nasty.'

'Yes, it is. She had no clothes on her . . .' She dare not pronounce the word breast.

' 'Tisn't nasty,' repeated Patricia. 'Our John says it's art. He goes to the art classes at night, he should know.' Her voice sank lower. 'Miss Plum's a nit . . .'

The result of this little episode was that Rose Mary was met at the gate by Annabel; tactics vary very little with the years. Annabel did what Sarah Flannagan used to do to Mary Ann. She allowed Rose Mary to pass, then fired her dart. 'Dirty pictures,' she said. And when Rose Mary flung round to confront her she repeated loudly and with a defiant thrusting out of her chin, 'DIRTY PICTURES!'

What could one say to this? You couldn't give the answer 'I'm not,' nor could you give the answer, 'They weren't,' because in the back of her mind she felt they were.

David was waiting for her at the corner of the railings. He knew all about it, all the class knew about it. Rose Mary thought the whole school knew about it, and soon everybody who went to church would know about it.

She was crying when they got on the bus and their special conductor said, 'Aye, aye! What's this? Got the cane?'

Rose Mary shook her head, then lowered it.

'Well, this is a change; I've never seen you bubbling afore. Something serious happened the day? You set the school on fire?'

Setting the school on fire would have been nothing to the heinous crime for which she was being blamed.

'What's she done?' The conductor was now addressing David pointedly, and David, after glancing at Rose Mary, craned his neck up, indicating that what he had to say must be whispered, and when the conductor put his ear down to him he said, in a voice that was threaded with what might be termed glee, 'She was looking at mucky pictures.'

The conductor's head jerked up. 'Good God! You don't say?'

'I wasn't.' Rose Mary hadn't heard what David had said, but the conductor's reactions told her as plainly as if he had shouted it. She now dug David in the arm with her fist, crying, 'I wasn't, our David.' Then looking up at the conductor, she said, 'I didn't. They were in a book, in Patricia Gibbs's book. She was just showing me.'

'Oh!' The conductor was trying hard to keep his face straight. He pushed his cap on to the back of his head and said, 'And the teacher caught you at it?'

Rose Mary nodded.

'Too bad! Too bad!' With his knee he gently nudged David's hip, and this caused David to bow his head and put his hand tightly across his mouth.

Rose Mary was still protesting her innocence not only to the conductor and their David now and the man and woman who were sitting behind them and who were very interested in the tragedy, but also to the two men who were sitting on the other side of the bus.

When she alighted from the bus she imagined that everybody in it suddenly burst out laughing. But then it might only be the funny noise the wheels were making; anyway, she continued to cry and protest at intervals until she reached the house, the kitchen and Mary Ann . . .

'It's all right. It's all right,' said Mary Ann. 'Now let's get this straight . . . And you David,' she reached out and pushed David to one side, 'take that grin off your face and stop sniggering, it's nothing to laugh at. Now tell me all about it.' She sat down on the chair and drew Rose Mary on to her knee, and Rose Mary told her and finished, 'I only saw that one, Mam, honest, the one with the man and woman called Sam-son and De-lie-la-la. She hadn't much clothes on and he had long hair, and that was all.'

Mary Ann took a firm hold on her face muscles and forbade herself to smile. 'Well, now, Samson and De-lie-la- I mean Delilah. She's called Delilah. Say Delilah.'

'De-lie-la-ha.'

'. . . It's all right. Don't worry, you'll get it. Well, that isn't a dirty picture.'

'It isn't, Mam?'

'No, no; it's a great picture, it's very famous. There's a story about Samson and Delilah.'

So Mary Ann told Rose Mary, and David, the story of Samson and Delilah, and she ended with, 'All his strength was in his hair, you see. Once he was without his hair, Delilah knew that he wouldn't be able to do anything, win battles and things like that, all his strength would go, all his power, and so she cut off his hair.'

'And did it, Mam? I mean, didn't he fight any more battles after, and things?'

'No, no, he didn't.' She didn't go on to explain the gory details of what happened to Samson after this, she left it at that. Instead, she said, 'There, you weren't looking at a mucky picture, you were looking at a great picture. And when you go back to school tomorrow you can tell Annabel Morton that. And if Miss Plum says anything more to you about it you tell her what I've said, that Samson and Delilah is a great picture and there's nothing to be ashamed of in looking at it.'

'Yes, Mam.' Rose Mary's voice was small. She couldn't see herself telling Miss Plum that, but she was comforted nevertheless. And wait until she saw that Annabel Morton, just wait.

'Go on now and get washed and then have your tea. Afterwards you can take Bill out and have a scamper.'

'Has he been out today, Mam?' asked David now, as he rolled Bill on to his back on the mat.

'I took him down the road at dinner-time and left him in the yard a while after, but that's all. He could do with a run. Go on now and get washed, tea's ready.'

They both now ran out of the room, leaving the door open and calling to Bill; and Mary Ann went into the scullery while Bill stood on the mat looking first one way, and then the other, finally he walked towards the scullery.

7

MATERIAL AND IMAGINATION

The idea came to Mary Ann a fortnight after the
incident of the grab. She sat down, as she usually
did after she had finished washing the dinner
dishes, with a cup of tea and a book. Sometimes
she gave herself fifteen minutes, sometimes half-
an-hour, it all depended on her interest in what
she was reading. There was no chance to read
once the children were home, and this was the
only time of day when there seemed to be an
interval between the chores. But the pattern over
the last two weeks had changed, for as soon as she
sat down Bill moved from the fireplace and took
up his position on her lap. She was amused at the
dog's sudden devotion to her, and not at all
displeased, although she still protested to Corny,
'I don't want the thing up here, but he's quiet and
behaving himself – at least at present, but should
he start again . . . well.' And to the children, when
they grumbled, 'He doesn't want to stay out,
Mam; he'll come if you'll come,' she would say,
'Don't be so silly. Put his lead on and take him
over the fields. He's got to have a run, and I can't

take him out all the time. And don't tug him. And tell him to heel, and sit, and when he does it pat his head.'

When she talked to them like this they would stare at her in a disconcerting way and she always had to busy herself in order not to laugh in front of them, because the transference of Bill's affection from them to herself was really funny when she came to think of it. And now here he was on her lap again, and every time she lifted the book up he would push his muzzle in front of it and open his mouth and laugh at her.

Mary Ann was convinced that he was laughing; his lolling tongue, the light in his eyes, the way his dewlaps quivered, he couldn't be doing anything else but laughing.

She had got into the habit over the last few afternoons of talking to him. 'I'd like to read if you don't mind,' she said to him. 'Oh, you do? Well, do you know this is the only time of the day I have to myself? . . . What do I want time to myself for? . . . Don't ask such a silly question. Oh, you know it's a silly question, do you, and you're sorry.' She put her head on one side and surveyed him; then touching his muzzle with her finger she said, 'You know you are the ugliest thing I've ever seen in my life, at least the ugliest dog, but you've got something . . . What? I don't know, you tell me. We've all got something, you say? Oh yes, very likely . . . How do you see us, Bill, eh? What do you call us in your mind? Big he, and little she? Angel one, and angel two?'

She laughed at the description of her family and Bill wriggled on her knee, then let his front paws go slack around her hips and placed his muzzle in his favourite position, the hollow of her breasts, and she stroked his head and stared at him, and he stared back at her.

How long they remained like this she wasn't sure but when she next spoke aloud she said, 'It's an idea. Why not? It's worth trying; dafter things than that have been known to succeed. I've seen nothing like it in any of the papers. There's Dorfy of course. She writes dialect pieces in the Shields Gazette, but this would be from a dog's point of view, how he sees us. I could make it funny. Yes, if I tried I could make it funny . . . Ooh, I'm sorry.' She had jumped up so quickly that Bill found himself sprawling on the floor and she stooped down and soothed his rumpled feelings. Then looking into his eyes again she said, 'It would be funny, wouldn't it, if it came off.' And now there came into her mind the picture of Diana Blenkinsop.

Diana Blenkinsop, and life from the viewpoint of a dog would appear to have no connection whatever, but in Mary Ann's mind they were closely linked.

During the next three weeks the house was like a simmering kettle, on the point of boiling but never reaching it.

Mary Ann was in a state of suppressed excitement. She was hugging a secret to herself, and if things worked out, as she prayed they would, that would show them. When her thoughts took this line she saw the picture of Corny and Diana Blenkinsop standing together. Twice in the last week she had seen Diana come out of Corny's office; once she had seen their heads together under the bonnet of her car. She was the type, Mary Ann decided, that would go to any lengths to get what she wanted, even to messing up the engine of her car.

She had written, and written, and re-written three five hundred word snippets about Bill, supposedly his outlook on life, and last Monday she had sent them to the editor of the *Newcastle Courier*. Now the sight of the postman coming along the road would drive her down the stairs to meet him at the door, but here it was Friday and she had received no reply, not even an acknowledgement. But then, she hadn't received the stuff back either, so perhaps no news was good news . . .

Corny's life over the last three weeks had been one of irritation. First in his mind was the fact that Mary Ann was playing up. She was up to something, he could tell. He only hoped to God it wasn't anything against Diana Blenkinsop, but knowing to what limits she had gone to put things right for her father, one such effort incidentally, resulting in him losing one hand, he was more than a little worried as to what lengths she would go with regards to himself. And then there was Jimmy. For two pins he would give him the sack, but where would he get another like him. Jimmy could turn a car inside out. He was a good worker; give him a job and he stuck at it until it was finished, but the quality didn't make up for being light fingered. Two ten shilling notes had gone from the till this week. The second one he had marked, but when later he had asked Jimmy if he had change for a pound note on him, and Jimmy had given him a ten shilling note and ten shillings worth of silver, it hadn't been the marked note. He was cute was Jimmy; and that was the worst type of thief, a cute one.

And then there was Mr Blenkinsop. He had come into the garage yesterday and looked around for quite a while before he said, 'You all right, Corny?' and he'd replied, 'Yes, I'm all right. What makes you think I'm not?'

'The little lady all right, Mary Ann?'

'Yes, yes, she's all right.'

Then Mr Blenkinsop had jerked his head and said, 'Oh, I was just wondering.'

He didn't ask him what was making him wonder, he daren't. Had he noticed that his daughter was never away from the garage? Even lunch times now she would come in. She said it was the quickest way to the hill beyond; she sunbathed there when it was fine. She'd even brought her lunch twice or thrice and had it out there. He wished to God she hadn't come to work here. Nothing had been the same since. He was all mixed up inside. He kept telling himself that the next time she put her nose in the door he would ignore her, but when he heard her say 'Cor-ny!' in that particular way she had, he found himself looking at her and smiling at her, and saying, 'Yes. Yes. Yes.' He agreed with every damn thing she said.

But yesterday she had said, 'I wonder what you would be like in a fight, Corny?' and he had said, 'Fight? Who should I fight?'

She had shrugged her shoulders. 'I was just wondering.'

'You don't wonder things like that without a reason.' He had stopped smiling at her, but she had continued to smile at him; then walking away she said, 'Do you know that our handsome ganger is upstairs?'

He made himself utter a small 'Huh!' when she turned and confronted him, then shook his head and said, 'Well, what would you like to make of that? She's known Johnny Murgatroyd since they were bairns.' He had then nodded his head in a cautionary fashion towards her as he said, 'You're a starter, Diana, aren't you?'

'What do you mean, a starter?'

'You know what I mean all right. They could say the same about you. You're in here with me, but you're not going to lose your good name because of that, are you?'

'I might.' She walked a step towards him. 'Perhaps I have already.'

He gulped in his throat, rubbed his hands with an imaginary piece of rag, then said, 'You want your backside smacked, that's what you want. Go on outside and do your sunbathing.'

'You're trying to make me out a child, Cor-ny, aren't you?' she said. 'But you know I'm not. We both know I'm not, so . . .' She tossed her blonde head backwards and her hair jumped from her shoulders as if it was alive. 'We've got to face up to these things. But there's plenty of time, it'll grow on you. I'm in no hurry.'

She went out through the small door in the back wall of the garage, and Corny went to a car, lifted the bonnet and bent over the engine with his hands gripping the framework. My God! What was he to do? She was a little bitch. No, she was a big bitch; a long-legged, beautiful, attractive big bitch. He hated her. No. No, he didn't, he . . .

His head went further down over the engine. He wouldn't even allow himself to think the word . . .

And the children? Rose Mary was unhappy for a number of reasons. Their David didn't want to play with her at all. Even when they came home from school he didn't want to play with her like he used to. He would yell at her and say, 'I'm going with the cars.' She didn't want to go into the garage with the cars but she wanted to be near David. And she wanted to be near Bill, but Bill, after ten or fifteen minutes' romping, would make straight for the house and upstairs and their mam. She was glad that Bill liked her mam because now they could keep him. But he just liked her mam and he didn't like her. Well, if he liked her he didn't want to stay with her, he just wanted to stay with her mam. She couldn't understand it.

And then there was her dad. He used to come and play with them when they were in bed. If he was late coming upstairs he would always come into the room and have a game with them. That was, up till lately. Now, even if she kept awake until he came in, he would just kiss her and say good night and God bless, and that was all.

And her mam. Her mam was worried and she knew what her mam was worried about 'cos she had seen her standing to the side of the curtains looking down on to the drive, watching her dad and Diana Blenkinsop. Yet her mam hadn't cried these last few weeks. Of the two, it was her dad she was more worried about. Her dad . . . and Diana Blenkinsop . . .

And David. David, too, had his worries. David's worries were deep; they were things not to be talked about. You didn't think too much about them but you did something to try to get them to go away. His worries were concerned, first with Jimmy, secondly with his dad. About Jimmy he was doing something definite; with regard to the problem of his dad he was working something out.

In a way it was David who had inherited his mother's ingenuity.

8

BEN

The phone rang about quarter-to-seven. It was Lizzie. 'Is that you, Mary Ann?' she said.

'Yes, Mam.'

'I've got some rather sad news for you. Ben is going fast. Tony's just been down, and he says that Ben asked for you, just as if you were in the house. "Where's Mary Ann?" he said. He's rambling a little, but I wondered whether you'd like to come and see him.'

'Oh, yes, Mam, yes. I didn't know he was ill.'

'He's only been bad since Tuesday. But he's a good age, you know.'

'What's Mr Lord going to do without him?'

'That's what we're all asking, lass. But he's got Tony and Lettice.'

'I know, I know, but they're not Ben; Ben's been with him nearly all his life.'

'Can you come?'

'Yes, Mam, yes, of course. I was just going to get them ready for bed but Corny will see to them, he's just downstairs.'

'All right, dear. We'll expect you in an hour or so.'

'Bye-bye, Mam.'

'Bye-bye, dear.'

She had put the phone down before she realised that Corny wouldn't be able to run her over, somebody must be here with the children. She could have asked her da to pick her up; but it didn't matter, she'd get the bus.

She ran downstairs and into the office where Corny was sitting at the desk. She forgot for the moment that there was any coldness between them and she said, 'Ben . . . Ben's dying. Mam's just phoned, he'd like to see me. Will you put the children to bed?'

He was on his feet looking down at her and he shook his head, saying, 'Aw, poor old Ben. But still he's getting on, it's to be expected . . . He asked for you?'

'Mam said so.'

'Well, get yourself away. But look—' He put out his hand towards her and she turned as she was going through the door. 'I won't be able to run you over. Are they coming for you?'

'I forgot to ask Dad.'

'I'll get on to them.'

'No, no, it doesn't matter. He could be busy or anything; I'll get the bus at the corner. If I hurry I'll get the ten past seven.' She was running up the stairs again.

Five minutes later, when she came down, Corny was waiting for her on the drive. 'Get your Dad to bring you back mind.'

'Oh, he'll do that.' She looked up at him. 'Don't let them stay up late, will you?'

'Leave that to me.' He nodded at her.

'And . . . and Bill; don't leave him on his own upstairs, will you not? He might start tearing the place up again.'

He smiled wryly at her, then said, 'We couldn't risk that could we?' They stared at each other for a moment; then as she turned away he said to her quietly, 'Forgotten something?' She paused, then looked down at her handbag before saying, 'No I don't think so.'

'Well, if that's how you want it, it's up to you.'

She walked away from him with a quick light step, the only thing about her that was light at the moment.

Whenever they left each other for any length of time she always kissed him, and he her; it might only be a peck on the cheek but it was a symbol that they were close – kind, as Rose Mary would have said.

The sketches she had been writing around Bill during the last three weeks had provided tangents for her thoughts along which to escape from the thing that was filling her mind; the thing that was making her sad deep inside, and not a little fearful. Her impetuous battling character was not coming to her aid over the business of Corny's attraction for Diana Blenkinsop, and no matter what excuse he gave about having to be civil to the girl because of her father she knew it was just an excuse, and she knew that he knew it too. He was attracted to Diana Blenkinsop.

She had always felt she knew more about the workings of a man's mind than she did of a woman's. This was likely, because since she was a small child she had dissected her father's character, sorting out his good points from his bad ones, but loving him all the while. But in her husband's case her reaction to the dissection was different. She had worked and schemed to turn her father's eye and thoughts away from another woman and back to her mother, but she couldn't do that with regard to her husband. She knew that she would never work or scheme to keep Corny, not when there was another woman involved. He would have to stay with her because he loved her, because he found her more attractive than any other woman. He would have to stay with her because her love for him alone would satisfy him. This was one time she could not fight.

She was lost in her thinking and did not notice the car, which had just flashed by, come to a stop until it backed towards her.

'Hello there. Waiting for the bus?'

'Oh, hello, Johnny. Yes, yes, I'm going home; I mean to my mother's.' She still couldn't get out of the habit of thinking of the farm as her home, although Corny had impressed upon her that she had one home now and it was where he lived.

'Get in then; I'll run you along.'

'Oh, no, no, Johnny; the bus will be here in a minute, it's due. I won't take you out of your way.'

'You won't take me out of my way. I'm at a loose end, you'll be doing me a kindness. Come on, get in.'

She stood looking down at him. Corny didn't like this man, he liked him as little as she did Diana Blenkinsop. He'd be wild if he knew she had taken a lift from him, but it seemed silly not to, and he'd get her there in a quarter of the time.

When he leant forward and pushed open the door she could do nothing but slide into the seat beside him. He looked different tonight, very smart, handsome in fact. He was wearing a shirt and tie that the adverts would have described as impeccable, and his light grey suit looked expensive. He had told her that he sometimes picked up fifty pounds a week when bonuses were good. He had been foreman at Quinton's for five years and Bob Quinton thought very highly of him. Johnny wasn't bashful about himself. His car, too, was a good one, and she knew it would take something to run. The way he looked now he had no connection with the ganger on the site.

'Why didn't your hubby run you along?'

When she explained he said, 'Oh, oh, I see.' Then added, 'You know, I'll like meeting your mam and dad again. I wonder whether they'll remember me?' He grinned at her.

She had been going to say to him, 'Will you drop me at the end of the road,' but when, in his mind's eye, he was already seeing himself talking to her parents she couldn't do anything else but allow him to drive her up to the farm.

Lizzie was waiting on the lawn for her. She had been expecting to see her hurrying along the road; remembering that the children couldn't be left alone she had phoned the house to say that Mike would come and pick Mary Ann up, but Corny had said she had been gone sometime and would already be on the bus. But here she was getting out of a car with a man.

Mary Ann kissed Lizzie, then said, 'Do you know who this is, Mam?'

Lizzie looked at the man before her. Her face was straight. She shook her head and said, 'Yes, and no. I feel I should know you.'

'Johnny Murgatroyd.'

'Murgatroyd. Oh yes.' Lizzie smiled now. 'Of course, of course. But you've changed somewhat since those days.'

'I . . . I told you about him getting me and Bill out of the mud, you remember?'

'Yes, you did. Come on.' Lizzie led the way into the house and Mike got up from his seat and put down his pipe and took Mary Ann in his arms and kissed her; then looking across the big farm kitchen to where the man was standing just inside the door, he said, 'Hello.'

'You don't remember me either?' Johnny came forward.

'Yes, yes, I do, Johnny Murgatroyd.'

Johnny turned round and looked from one to the other. 'Recognised at last. No more an orphan. Daddy! Daddy! I've come home.'

They all laughed. 'Oh, you'd take some forgetting.' Mike jerked his head. 'You were a bit of a devil if I remember. How have you come here?' He looked at Mary Ann and Mary Ann said, 'I was waiting for the bus, Da, and . . . and Johnny was passing and he gave me a lift.'

'Oh, I see. Sit down, sit down.'

Johnny Murgatroyd sat down, and he looked at Mike. Mike had said, You'll take some forgetting; well, and so would he. He had a vivid memory of battling, boozing Mike Shaughnessy. Who would have imagined that he would have settled down and had all this? A farm, and a grand house. It's funny how some people fell on their feet. Well, he'd have a grand house one day, just wait and see. Great oaks from little acorns grow.

'Will you have a cup of tea before you go up?' Lizzie was looking at Mary Ann.

'No, Mam; it's no time since I had a meal, I'll go now. But perhaps Johnny here would like one?'

'I never say no to a cuppa.' He was laughing up at Lizzie.

'Thanks for the lift, Johnny, I'll be seeing you.'

'You will. Oh, you will.' He nodded at her, and she went out and through the familiar farmyard and up the hill to the house where lived Mr Lord, the man who had shaped all their destinies . . . with her help.

She went in the back way as she always did, and it was strange not to see Ben, either in the kitchen or coming from the hall.

Tony met her and kissed her on the cheek. Whenever he did this she was made to wonder how different her life would have been if she had married him as Mr Lord had schemed she should. But it had been Corny who had filled her horizon since the day she had championed the raggy, tousled-haired individual against Mr Lord himself. And Tony had married Lettice, a divorcee, and they were both happy, ideally happy. It shone out of their faces whenever she saw them together. And now, as Lettice came towards her, the look was still there, which made her feel a little sad, even a little jealous.

'Hello, my dear,' Lettice kissed her warmly, then asked, 'Are you going into the drawing-room first?'

'Is there time? I mean, how is Ben now?'

'Oh, he's dozing, he keeps waking up at intervals. Just go and say hello first.'

Mr Lord was sitting, as usual, in his winged chair; during the day he would face the window and look on to the garden, but in the evening he would seat himself to the side of the big open fire.

He did not turn his head when she entered the room. His hands, in characteristic pose, were resting on the arms of the chair, but tonight his chin wasn't up and out, it was bent deep into his chest. She reached him before she said, 'Hello.' She had always greeted him with 'Hello'. He brought his head round to her and a faint light of pleasure came into his pale, watery, blue eyes.

'Hello, my dear,' he said; then he shook his head slowly and said, 'Sad night, sad night.'

'Yes.'

'Sit close to me, here.' He pointed to his knee, and she brought a stool from one side of the fireplace and sat where he had bidden her.

'Part of me will go with him.'

She made no answer to this. She knew it was so.

'A great part.' He stared at her for a moment before he said, 'I have bullied him all his life, shouted, ranted and bullied him, and if we lived for another fifty years together I would continue to do so; it was my way with him. He understood it and never murmured.'

There was a great lump in her throat as she said, 'You were his life, you were all he had and ever wanted; he was never hurt by anything you said or did.'

He moved his head slowly, then said, 'He wasn't a poor man, I'm generous in my way; he could have left me years ago . . . I wish I had gone before him. But it won't be long anyway before we're together again.'

'Oh.' Her voice broke as she whispered, 'Oh, don't say that. And . . . and it's better this way. If he had been left alone he would have had no-one, not really, because there was only you in his life, whereas you've got' – she paused – 'all of us.'

He raised his head and looked at her, then put out his long, thin, blue-veined hand and cupped her chin, 'Yes, I've got all of you. But the only one I really ever wanted was you. You know that, child, don't you?'

She was crying openly now and she took his hand and pressed it to her cheek, and he said, 'There, there. Go on, go on up. Twice today he has spoken your name. I know he would like to see you.'

She rose to her feet without further words and went out into the hall. The drawing-room door was open and through it she saw Lettice and Tony standing together. When they turned and saw her they came swiftly to her and Lettice put her arm around her shoulders and said, 'Don't cry, don't upset yourself. Would you like a drink, a sherry, before you go up?'

'No; no, thanks.' Mary Ann wiped her face with her handkerchief, then said, 'I'd better go now.'

'Yes, do,' said Lettice, 'and get it over with, and I'll make some coffee.' She nodded to Tony and he walked up the stairs by Mary Ann's side, and when they entered Ben's room a nurse rose from the side of the bed and, coming towards them, said, 'He's awake.'

Mary Ann went forward and stood gazing down on Ben. He looked a very, very old man, much older than his eighty years. She bent over him and said softly, 'Hello, Ben.'

His thin wrinkled lips moved in a semblance of a smile. Ben had rarely smiled. He had in a way grumbled at others, herself included, as much as his master had grumbled at him. He had never shown any affection towards her. At first he had shown open hostility and jealousy, because from a child she had inveigled herself into his master's good books by being what he considered perky and cheeky, whereas his life-long service elicited nothing but the whiplash of a tongue that was for ever expressing the bitterness of life.

'Mary . . . Mary Ann.'

'Yes, Ben.'

His lips mouthed words that were soundless; then again they moved and he said, 'See to him, he needs you, master needs you.'

'Yes, Ben. Don't worry, I'll see to him.' She did not say that his master had his grandson and his grandson's wife to see to him, for she knew that she, and she alone, could fill the void that Ben would leave in Mr Lord's life. Even when he had been given a great grandson the boy had not taken her place; and that was very strange when you came to think about it.

'Good girl.'

The tears were flowing down her face again. When she felt the rustle of the nurse's skirt at her side she bent down and kissed the hollow cheek, and Ben closed his eyes.

Tony led her from the room and down the stairs, and in the drawing-room Lettice was waiting, and she said, 'There, sit down and have your coffee.'

'It's . . . it's awful. Death is awful.'

'It's got to come to us all,' said Tony solemnly. 'But poor old Ben's done nothing but work all his days, yet we couldn't stop him.'

'He wouldn't have lived to this age if we'd been able to,' said Lettice. 'Work was his life, working for grandad.'

'There aren't many left like him,' said Tony. 'They don't make them any more.'

No, thought Mary Ann, they didn't make Bens any more, not men who were willing to give their lives to others; it was every man for himself these days. The world of Ben and Mr Lord was passing; it had almost gone. It would vanish entirely, at least from their sphere, when Mr Lord died, but she prayed that that wouldn't be for a long time yet.

After a while she asked, 'How's Peter?'

'Oh, fine. We had a letter from him this morning,' said Lettice. 'I say fine, but he has his troubles.' She smiled. 'He informs us that he doesn't like the new sports master. His name is Mr Tollett, and they have nicknamed him Tightrope Tollett. I can't see the connection but likely they can. How are the twins?'

'Oh, they're grand.'

'I hear you've got a dog,' said Tony now, grinning slyly.

'Yes,' said Mary Ann, 'a bull terrier.'

'So I heard. You pick the breeds.'

'I didn't pick him.'

'I understand he created a little disorder in the kitchen.'

'A little disorder is right,' said Mary Ann. 'If I'd had a gun I would have shot him on the spot. Well,' she rose to her feet, 'I'd better be going; I've left Corny to see to them and they play him up.'

'Are you going to look in on grandad again?' asked Lettice.

'Yes, just to say good night . . .'

Ten minutes later Mary Ann entered the farm kitchen again and stopped just within the door and looked to where Johnny Murgatroyd was still sitting at the table. He called across the room to her, 'You haven't been long.'

As she walked towards her mother she said to him, 'You needn't have waited.'

'Oh, I had nothing better to do.'

'How did you find him?' said Lizzie.

'Very low; they don't think he'll last the night.'

'Poor old Ben,' said Mike. 'He was a good man . . . a good man.' He knocked out the dottle from his pipe on the hob of the fire. 'The old fellow's going to be lost. Things won't be the same.'

Lizzie said now, 'You'll have to pop over and see Mr Lord more often. In spite of Tony and Lettice he'll miss Ben greatly.'

'Yes,' said Mary Ann, 'I mean to. And now,' she fastened the top button of her coat, 'I'd better get back.'

'Aren't you going to have something to drink?' said Lizzie.

'No; no thanks, Mam, I've just had a cup of coffee with Lettice and Tony.'

As they all went through the hall to the front door Mary Ann said, 'You'll phone me when it happens?'

'Yes, of course, dear,' said Lizzie.

On the drive Johnny held out his hand to Mike, saying, 'Well, it's been nice meeting up with you again, and you, Mrs S.'

'It's been nice seeing you, Johnny, and talking about old times,' said Lizzie. 'Any time you're passing you must look in.'

'Yes, yes, I will. I won't need another invitation, and don't forget you asked me.'

She laughed at him; then looked at Mary Ann whose face was straight and she said, 'Don't worry, dear.'

As they drove along the lane, Johnny aiming to be sympathetic, said, 'It's a pity about the old fellow but we've all got to go some time. Your dad tells me he's eighty. Well, he's had a good run for his money.'

Mary Ann made no answer to this. Good run for his money. We've all to go some time. All trite expressions meaning nothing. Death was a frightful thing; it was the final of all final things. She knew she shouldn't think like this. Her religion should help her, for wasn't there a life after death, but she couldn't see it. She often thought about death and the fact that it was so final worried her, but it was a thing you couldn't talk about. People didn't want to talk about death. If you talked about death you were classed as morbid. And if you told the priest of your thoughts in confession all you got was you must pray for faith. Lord I believe, help thou my unbelief. At times she got all churned up inside with one thing and another. She thought too much . . . 'What did you say, Johnny?'

'You were miles away. I was saying that I bet

you a quid you don't know who I'm taking out the morrow.'

'Now why should I?' she smiled slightly at him. 'I don't know anybody you know.'

'But you do. You know this one all right.'

Her thoughts took her back to Burton Street and the surrounding district. Who did she know there that he knew? The only person who was in her life from that district was Sarah, who was now her sister-in-law. 'You've got me puzzled,' she said; 'I still don't know anyone that you know.'

'Think hard.'

She thought hard, then said, 'I give up.'

'What about Miss Blenkinsop?'

Her surprise lifted her around on the seat and she exclaimed loudly, 'What! You and Diana Blenkinsop? You're joking.'

'No, no, I'm not joking.' His tone was slightly huffed. 'Why should I be joking?' He gave a swift glance at her. 'Because she's the boss's daughter and I'm a ganger? Do I look like a ganger?' He took one hand from the wheel and draped it down the front of himself.

'No, no, I didn't mean that.' But she had meant that.

'I'm going places, Mary Ann.'

'I've no doubt of that, Johnny.' Her smile had widened.

'Do you know something?'

'What?'

'You should be thanking me for telling you, it'll get her out of your hair.'

'What do you mean?' Her body had jerked round again.

'Oh, oh, you know what I mean.'

'I don't.'

'Now, now, Mary Ann, don't let us hide our heads in the sand; you know for a fact that she's got her sights set on your man. Everybody on the job knows it.'

She felt she wanted to be sick, literally sick. She swallowed deeply and took in a great intake of breath before she forced herself to say on an airy note, 'Well, I don't care what they know on the job, it's of no importance. She can have her sights set at any angle, she'll only be wasting her time.'

'Oh, I'm glad you're not worried.'

'I'm not worried.' She sounded cool, confident, and he glanced quickly at her, the corner of his mouth turned upwards. 'Still, I think, me taking her over should help you to be less worried than not being worried, if you get what I mean.'

She remained quiet, thinking. Yes, indeed, this would make her less worried, this would show Corny what kind of girl he was almost going overboard for. The only snag was it couldn't last because when Mr and Mrs Blenkinsop got wind of it there'd be an explosion, because beneath all their camaraderie they were snobbish, especially Mrs Blenkinsop; she kept open house but she vetted the entrants. Mary Ann felt there had been more than a touch of condescension about the invitation that was extended to themselves; it was a sort of boss's wife being nice to an employee's family, attitude. But Corny was no employee of Mr Blenkinsop.

When they reached the road opposite the garage Corny was serving petrol and he jerked his head up and became quite still as he looked at Mary Ann getting out of the car and the face that was grinning at her from the window. When Johnny Murgatroyd waved to him he made no response but turned and attended to the customer.

A few minutes later he mounted the stairs, telling himself to go carefully.

Mary Ann was in the bedroom with the children and he had to wait a full ten minutes before she came into the kitchen. Her face was not showing sorrow for Ben, nor yet mischievous elation at being driven up to the door by Johnny Murgatroyd; it had a sort of neutral look that took some of the wind out of his sails. He watched her pat Bill and say, 'Down! Down!' before he forced himself to say calmly, 'How did you find him?'

'He won't last the night.'

In an ordinary way he would have said, 'I'm sorry about that,' but instead he said, 'Where did you pick that one up?'

She turned and looked at him over her shoulder. 'You mean Johnny?'

'Well, he didn't look like Cliff Michelmore, or Danny Blanchflower, or the Shah of Persia.'

She had a desire to burst out laughing, and she turned her head away and replied coolly, 'I didn't pick him up, he picked me up while I was waiting for the bus.'

He screwed his face up and peered at her back. 'You mean when you were going?'

She turned to him and inclined her head slowly downwards, giving emphasis to his words as she repeated them, 'Yes, when I was going.'

'Then he must have waited for you?'

'Yes, he waited for me, and me dad saw nothing immoral in it; neither did Mam.'

'You mean he took you right to the farm?'

'He took me right to the farm. Isn't it awful, scandalous?' She shook her head in mock horror at herself, and he said quickly, 'Now, you can drop that. And if you've got any sense you'll drop him. And the next time he offers to give you a lift you'll tell him what to do.'

'But perhaps I haven't got any sense, Corny, perhaps I'm like you.'

'Oh, my God!' He put his hand to his brow and turned from her and leaned his shoulder against the mantlepiece. Then pulling himself upwards again he shouted at her, 'Look! I don't let myself be seen around the town in a car with someone that's notorious, and he is notorious. No decent girl would be seen within a mile of him.'

'Really! you surprise me.'

'I'm warning you.' He took a step forward, his teeth grinding against each other. 'You'd better not go too far.'

Quite suddenly the jocularity was ripped from her tone and she cried back at him, 'You telling me not to go too far! You telling me you wouldn't be seen in the town with anyone like him! No. No, you wouldn't be seen around the town with Miss Blenkinsop because there's no need, you have the privacy of the garage, and the office, haven't you?'

There was a silence that only waited to be shattered, then he cried, 'You're mad, that's what you are, mad. And you'll get what you're asking for.' He marched towards the door, pulled it open, then turned and shouted, 'There'll be nobody but yourself to blame when I walk out. Now remember that. It won't be Diana who has caused it, but you, you and your rotten, jealous mind.'

When the lower door banged the house shook.

In the bedroom the children lay in their bunks perfectly still. Rose Mary was in the bottom bunk and she stared upwards, waiting for David to make a move, and when he didn't she got out of the bunk and, standing on tiptoes, touched his shoulder. But he gave no sign. His face was almost covered by the blanket, and when she pulled it down his eyes were wide open, and they stared at each other.

9

ROSE MARY'S SICKNESS

The following morning the postman brought Mary Ann a letter and she wanted to cry, 'Look! look! would you believe it.' It was from the editor of the *Newcastle Courier* and it said simply, 'Dear Mrs Boyle, I am very interested in your doggy sketches and if you would care to call on me at three o'clock on Monday afternoon we could discuss their publication, subject to alteration and cutting. Yours sincerely, Albert Newman.'

At eleven o'clock her mother phoned to say Ben had died half-an-hour earlier. She didn't know when the funeral would be, likely about Wednesday, and, of course, she would be going? Yes, said Mary Ann, she'd be there.

'Are you coming over tomorrow?' Lizzie had asked, and Mary Ann answered, 'I think we'll leave it this week, Mam.' There was a long pause before Lizzie had replied, 'All right, just as you say.'

Sunday was a long nightmare with Corny working frantically down below in the garage; the children haunting her, not wanting to leave her for a minute, even David; and Bill having another spasm of tearing up everything in sight, until she cried, 'Take him out and keep him out. And keep yourselves out too.'

And they had dragged Bill out and gone into the field behind the house and sat in the derelict car, but they hadn't played.

And so came Monday.

Rose Mary said she felt sick and didn't think she could go to school. 'You're going,' said Mary Ann. She remembered back to the days when she had been so concerned about her father that she had made herself sick and used it as pretence to be off school.

'If she says she's sick, she's sick.' Corny was standing on the landing and he looked through the open door into the bedroom, and Mary Ann looked back at him and said nothing.

'You can't send her to school if she's sick.'

'Very well; she's sick and she needn't go to school.'

Her attitude was infuriating to him, he wanted to break things.

So Rose Mary didn't go to school, but Mary Ann saw that she stayed in bed all morning. She also saw that the enforced inactivity was almost driving her daughter wild, so she allowed her to get up for lunch, and after it, when she asked if she could take Bill out for a walk, Mary Ann said, 'Yes, and tell your father I'm going into town to do some shopping.'

Rose Mary stared at her, her eyes wide.

'Do as I tell you. Take Bill. Put his lead on.'

Bill showed great reluctance, as always, to being moved out of the kitchen, and Mary Ann had to carry him downstairs. Then hurrying back and into the bedroom she made her face up, put on her best suit and hat, looked at herself critically in the mirror, then went out with only a handbag.

Corny noticed this as she crossed the drive; she was carrying no shopping bag and she had on her best clothes. He wanted to dash after her and demand where she was going. He almost called to her, but Jimmy checked him.

'Boss!'

'What is it now?'

Jimmy looked down towards his feet, rubbing his hands together. 'There's something I want to say.'

'Oh, aye.' Corny narrowed his eyes at the young fellow.

'I'm sorry, but . . . but . . . but I've just got to.'

'Well, whatever it is, you needn't take a week about it. Come on into the office; it's about time you had it off your chest.'

Jimmy's head came up and he stared at his boss striding towards the office, then he followed him. There was nothing much escaped the boss.

'Well, say your piece.' Corny sat himself down on the high stool and looked at the figures in the open book before him, and Jimmy stood just within the door and again he looked down, and now he said, 'I want to give me notice in.'

'What?'

'I'm sorry, boss, but I think it's best.'

'Oh you do, do you? And why do you want to give your notice in?'

'Well, we all need a change now and again.' Jimmy grinned sheepishly.

'More money, I suppose?'

'Aye, more money, boss.'

'You're not getting enough here and not making enough on the side?'

Jimmy stared at him, then said, 'Well the tips are few and far between.'

Corny was on the point of saying, 'Well, I'm not referring to your tips, I'm referring to your light fingers,' but perhaps it was better to let things be this way. He'd never get another like Jimmy for work, but then he'd never get another who would help himself to the takings; he'd see to that before anyone else started. But he couldn't resist one thrust. 'I suppose you've got nearly enough to stand your share in the car by now?'

'Well, not quite, boss, not quite.'

'Oh well, you've still got time, haven't you?' Corny got up from the seat and walked past Jimmy, keeping his eyes on him all the time, and Jimmy returned his stare unblinking. So that was it, he knew. He had known all along.

When Corny reached the drive again his thoughts reverted to Mary Ann. Where was she off to, dressed up like that? Where? WHERE? It couldn't be Murgatroyd. The funeral? No, no, it would be too soon for that. She didn't know yet anyway; and she wouldn't go in that cocky red hat. But perhaps she was going home for something. He would get on to the farm and have a word with Mike, not Lizzie. No; Mike understood things.

Mike answered from the milking parlour. No, Mary Ann wasn't coming there, not to his knowledge.

'What do you think about Johnny Murgatroyd?'

Corny asked, and Mike replied, 'Johnny? Oh, Johnny's all right. A bit of a lad I understand, but there's no harm in him. Why do you ask? ... Oh, because he brought her home? Oh, don't worry about that, lad. Anyway, as far as I've been able to gather there's only one fellow in her life, and also, I was given to understand, there was only one lass in yours. Does that still hold, Corny?'

'Of course, it does, Mike. I've told you.'

'Is that dame still paying her daily visits?'

There was a pause before Corny said, 'I can't tell her to clear out.'

'You could, you know. And it would clear matters up quicker than a dose of salts.'

'It's easier said than done.'

'You have no idea at all where she might be going?'

'Not in the wide world. I'll tap Lizzie, and if I hear anything I'll give you a ring.'

'Don't let on I've phoned you, Mike.'

'No, no; I can keep me big mouth shut when it's necessary. Goodbye, lad, and don't worry.'

'Goodbye, Mike.'

And then he found out where she was, who she was all dolled up for, at least he imagined he had. He was directing the backing of a lorry out of the drive when he heard one of the men on the site shout, 'Where's the boss?' And another, on a laugh, saying, 'Which one?'

'Murgatroyd.'

'Oh, he's gone into Newcastle. A bit of special business I understand.' There was another laugh. 'Swinburne's taken over. He's at yon side of number three shed; they're digging out there.'

This news had an opposite effect on Corny to

838

what might have been expected. His rage seeped away and of a sudden he felt tired and very much alone. He went upstairs and into the kitchen and sat down at the table and, putting his elbows on it, he rested his head in his hands. Well, he had asked for it, and he was getting it. Being Mary Ann she would take nothing lying down. He had threatened to walk out on her but it looked like she wasn't going to give him the chance. How had all this come about? . . .

Rose Mary, in her childish way, was wondering the same thing. Why weren't they all happy like they used to be? Why wasn't everything nice and lovely? The answer was Diana Blenkinsop. She threw the ball for Bill and he fetched it. She threw it again and he fetched it; but the third time she threw it he turned and walked in the direction of the house and she had to run after him and put his lead on.

He was always wanting to be in the house and near her mam. When she had asked for an explanation from her father concerning Bill's change of face he had said that Bill likely felt safer in the house since he had got the fright on the grab, and as it was their mam who had got him out of the hole, he had become attached to her.

She wished she had been the one who had got him out of the hole, and then he wouldn't have wanted to leave her. Everybody was leaving her, their David, and Bill, and now . . . She wouldn't let her thoughts travel any further along this frightening road. She walked the length of the field, then looked to the top of it where it adjoined the garage, where the men were building the big workshop. As she started up the field someone waved to her from the foot of the scaffolding and after a moment she waved back.

Then she was away, dashing up the field, dragging Bill with her.

'Hello, Rose Mary.' Mr Blenkinsop looked down on her as she stood panting. 'Why aren't you at school?'

'I was sick and couldn't go.'

'Oh, I'm sorry to hear that. Are you better now?'

'Yes, thank you.'

'Eating too many sweets I suppose?' He bent down to her, smiling into her face, but she didn't smile back as she said, 'No, I didn't have any sweets, I didn't want any.'

He straightened up and surveyed her for a moment. This wasn't the Rose Mary Boyle that he had come to know. He was well schooled in childish ailments, and the look on her face wasn't derived from a tummy upset, if he was any judge. Tummy upsets were soon forgotten when children got out into the open air, especially with a dog. He'd had a feeling recently that things weren't as harmonious as they might be in the little house above the garage. He began to walk away from the building and down the field, and Rose Mary walked with him. Mr Blenkinsop knew it wasn't good tactics to quiz children, but very often it was the only way anyone could get information. He said, 'I haven't seen your mother for days, how is she?'

There was a pause before Rose Mary answered, 'Not very well. She's gone into Newcastle; she's got her best things on.'

She looked up at him and he looked down at

840

her again, and she answered the question in his eyes by saying, 'She doesn't put her best things on except for something special.'

He nodded his head slowly at her. 'And what's this special thing your mother's gone into Newcastle for . . . with her best things on?' He nodded his head slowly at her.

'I don't know.'

'You don't know?'

'No, and me dad doesn't know. She just said for me to tell him that she was going shopping and she didn't take a basket, and she never goes shopping in her best things.'

They had stopped and were holding each other's gaze. 'You have no idea why she went into Newcastle?' He bent his head slightly downwards now and she answered, 'I think I have.'

'Can you tell me?' His voice was very low.

'It's . . . it's because me dad's going to leave us.'

He straightened up, his shoulders back, his chin tucked into his neck, and it was a full minute before he said, 'Your dad . . . your father's going to leave you?'

'He said he was on Friday night.'

He gave a little laugh now, then drew in a long breath before exclaiming, 'O . . . h! mothers and fathers always argue and have little fights and say they're going to leave each other, but they never do. I shouldn't worry.'

'Mr Blenkinsop.'

'Yes, what is it?' He was bending over her again, his face full of sympathy, and he watched her lips moving around the words 'Would you' like a deaf-mute straining to talk. It wasn't until he said, 'Tell me. Come along, you can tell me what's troubling you. I won't tell anyone, I promise,' that she startled him by saying, 'Would . . . would you send your Diana away, please?'

He was standing straight again, his eyes screwed up. His mind was working furiously; a voice inside him was bawling 'No, no, this can't be.' Yet in an odd way he knew, he had known it all along. But he said to her quietly, 'Why do you want me to send Diana away, Rose Mary?'

'Because . . .' She closed her eyes now and bent her head.

'Come on, tell me.' He put his fingers under her chin and raised her head, and she said, 'Because she's going to take me dad away.'

'God Almighty!' It was a deep oath. If she'd broken up this happy family, he'd break her neck; as much as he loved her he'd break her neck. She was like her mother. How could women be such devils. And how could men love them for being devils.

He knew that all good-looking men were a challenge to his wife and must be brought to her feet, but once there she let them go. Some of them, he remembered with shame for her, had crawled away broken. Time had taught him to understand his wife; for her to be entirely happy she must have these little diversions, these diversions that kept her ego balanced. She had said to him, 'At heart I'm a one man woman, and men are fools if they can't see that. It's up to them.'

Diana had had boys fluttering round her since she was ten. She had already been engaged and broken it off, but she had never tried, as far as he knew anyway, to capture a married man. Boyle was a big, attractive-looking fellow in his way, an honest fellow too. It was his honesty that had decided his cousin, Rodney, to build the plant on this side of the spare land. He was no empty-headed fool was young Boyle, but on the other hand he was the type that if he reached Diana's feet and she kicked him, he'd break. Self-esteem would see to that.

Well, whatever he had to do, he must do it warily, for his daughter, he knew, was as head-strong as an unbroken colt, and a jerk on the reins at this stage might send her off, dragging Boyle with her.

He put his hand on Rose Mary's head and, bringing his face close to hers, said, 'Now you're not to worry any more. Do you hear me? Everything's going to be all right.'

'You'll send her away?'

'I don't know what I'm going to do yet. This is just between you and me. You won't tell anyone will you what you've told me?'

'Oh, no. But our David knows.'

'He does?'

'Yes.'

'But he doesn't know that you were going to tell me?'

'Oh, no.'

'Well then, you go on home, and remember not a word to anybody. Not even to David. Promise?'

'Promise.' She made a cross on the yoke of her dress somewhere in the region of her heart and he patted her head again and said, 'Go on now.' And she turned from him, Bill pulling her into a run as she went towards home. And Mr Blenkinsop walked slowly up the field towards the building, and again he said deep, in his throat, 'God Almighty!'

10

FAME AND FORTUNE

Meanwhile Mary Ann was in Newcastle sitting in an office opposite a small bald-headed man. Mr Newman was smiling broadly at Mary Ann as he said, 'I have found them very refreshing, very amusing, something different.'

'Thank you.'

'Have you done much of this kind of thing?'

'I've been scribbling all my life but I've never had anything published.'

'Well, it's about time you did, isn't it?'

She smiled back at him and said, 'You're very kind.'

'Oh, we can't afford to be kind in this business, Mrs Boyle. If work hasn't merit it doesn't get published on sympathy, or because', he poked his head forward, 'you happen to know the editor.'

They were laughing.

'Have you any more of these ready?'

'I've got another three.' She opened her bag and handed him an envelope, and he said, 'Good. Good,' and as he pulled the scripts out he added, 'The main thing is will you be able to keep up this kind of humour; you know humorous stuff is the most difficult to write.'

'It's always come easy to me. Well, what I mean is, I can write something funny where I could never write an essay or descriptive stuff.'

'You never know what you can do until you try. By the way, I was thinking that it would be a good idea just to sign these articles "Bill", no name or anything. You see they're supposed to be written by him. Well, what do you think about that?'

What did she think about it? Not much. It was half the pleasure, all the pleasure in fact to see one's name in print, and, let's face it, for other people to see your name in print.

He said on a thin laugh, 'I know how you feel about this, but take my advice and let them be written by Bill, the bull terrier, and they'll likely catch on, much more so than if they were written by Mrs Mary Boyle.'

'Mary Ann Boyle.'

He inclined his head towards her, 'Mrs Mary Ann Boyle. Well, you see?'

Yes, she saw, and she smiled back at him.

'I like the way you started the first one. It got me reading straight away.' He picked up one of the scripts from the table and read:

'There is a tide in the affairs of men which, taken at the flood, leads on to fortune. So said some fellow. And there is a day in the span of a dog which decides what kind of dog's life he's going to have.

'Most kids know to some extent where they'll be for the first few years, but a dog knows, as

soon as he stops sucking out he goes, so
naturally he goes on sucking as long as the skin
of his belly will stand it. I did, I was the biggest
sucker in the business.'

He looked across at Mary Ann and said, 'It's
fresh. I mean fresh, you know which kind?'

'Yes, yes, I know which kind.' She was laughing
again.

He turned over a couple of pages and pointed,
saying, 'This bit where you bring him home and
he names you all: Big he, Little she, Angel one
and Angel two. Where did you get the idea from?'

'Oh, it was the day he got hung up on the grab
and the craneman dropped him into the hole. You
know, it's in the third one.'

'Oh yes, I had a good laugh over that one. I
passed it on to my assistant and he said you had a
wonderful imagination.'

She shook her head slowly. 'It actually
happened, just as I put it down.'

'You're joking?'

'No, no, I'm not.'

'And from hating his guts you took to him as it
says here?'

'Yes, that's how it happened.'

'And you mean to say the one about him getting
you up in the middle of the night and then finding
the place in shreds in the morning is true?'

'Yes, honest, everything.'

'Well, well, but nobody will believe it. This Bill
must be a lad.'

'He is, but since the business of the grab he
won't leave me. And the second one, that one
you've got in your hand,' she pointed, 'that's

about him getting into our bed in the middle of the night, and Corny, my husband, waking up and finding a black wet muzzle an inch from his face; if it had been a hand grenade he couldn't have moved faster. Poor Bill didn't know what had hit him.'

Mr Newman was laughing again, then he said, 'I may have to tighten things up here and there, do you mind?'

'No, not at all. I'm only too pleased that you like them.'

'Oh, I like them all right. I only hope that they catch on. You can never tell. I aim to print one each Saturday for a few weeks. It would be very nice if the younger generation scrambled for the paper to find out what Bill had been up to during the week, wouldn't it?'

She shook her head slowly. 'It would be marvellous.'

'Well, now, down to basic facts. How about ten guineas.'

'Ten guineas?' Her brows puckered slightly, and at this he said, 'For each publication,' and as her face cleared he laughed and added, 'Oh, we're not as bad as that.'

'I'd be very grateful for ten guineas.'

He rose to his feet and, holding out his hand, said, 'Let's hope this is the beginning of a long and successful series concerning one Bill, a bull terrier.'

'I hope so, too . . .'

When she was outside she walked in a daze until she reached the bottom of Northumberland Street, and there she thought, I'll phone him and tell him. She knew it would be better this way, because under the circumstances she couldn't go back and look at him and say 'I'm going to do a series for *The Courier*,' not with this other thing between them. And also, on the phone she wouldn't see his face, or witness his reactions, and so there was a chance she would remain calm.

When she heard his voice she said, 'It's me, Corny.'

'Oh!'

'I'm . . . I'm in Newcastle.'

'So you're in Newcastle?'

She closed her eyes. 'I . . . I thought I would phone you, I've something to tell you.'

There was a short silence, and then his voice came rasping at her, 'Oh, you have, have you? And you haven't the courage to face me. Whose idea was it that you should phone it? Is he holding your hand . . . breathing down your neck?' The last was almost a yell and she took the earphone away from her face and stared at it in utter perplexity for a moment, until his voice came at her again, louder now, 'If you're there, Mr Murgatroyd, let me tell you this . . .'

She didn't hear his next words for his voice was so loud it blurred the line and she mouthed to herself, 'Murgatroyd! Murgatroyd! He must be barmy.'

When the line became silent again she said, 'Are you finished?' and the answer she got was, 'Go to hell!'

When she heard the receiver being banged down she leant against the wall of the kiosk. Well, if she wanted her own back she was certainly getting it. But she didn't want her own back, not in this way.

It was as she was passing the station on the way to the bus terminus that a lorry drew up alongside the kerb and a voice hailed her, 'Hi, there!'

When she turned round and saw Johnny's grinning face looking down at her she said aloud, 'Oh, no! No!'

'You going back home?'

She ran across the pavement and to the door of the cab and, looking up at him, she said, 'Yes, I'm going back but not with you.'

'What's up?' His face was straight.

'Nothing. Nothing.'

'There must be something for you to jump the gun like that. I haven't asked you to go back with me, but I was going to.' The grin almost reappeared and then, getting down from the cab, he said, 'What is it?'

'Look, Johnny, just leave me and get back.'

'No, no, I'm not going back.' He thrust his hands into his pockets. 'I want to know what's up. It concerns me doesn't it?'

'Look, Johnny, it's like this,' she said breathlessly. 'I came in this afternoon to meet the editor of the *Newcastle Courier* and I didn't tell Corny because, well, well we had a bit of a row. But just a minute ago I phoned him and', she put her hand up to her brow, 'he nearly bawled my head off; he . . . he thinks I'm here with you.'

'Huh! you're kiddin'. What gave him that idea?'

'You know as much as I do about that.'

'He must be do-lally.'

'I think we're all going do-lally.'

He laughed at her now. 'All right,' he said. 'I wouldn't embarrass you for the world . . . Mrs

Boyle. I'll tell you what I'll do. I'll go straight to the garage when I get back and . . .'

'Oh no! No!'

'Now look.' He lifted his hand and patted her shoulder gently. 'Leave this to me. I'm the soul of tact. I am. I am. I'll do it innocently; I'll tell him exactly what I came into Newcastle for, it's in the back there.' He pointed to an odd-shaped piece of machinery in the lorry. 'I'll do it when he's filling me up. I'll ask after you and the children and when you get home he'll be eating out of your hand. Now go and have a cup of tea. Don't get the next bus, give me time.'

'Oh, Johnny.' Her shoulders drooped. 'What a mess!'

'We all find ourselves in it some time or other. The only consolation I can offer you is you're not alone. Go on now, have a cuppa. Be seeing you.' He pulled himself up into the cab and she walked away and did as he advised and went into a café and had a cup of tea.

Corny didn't exactly eat out of her hand when she arrived home. He looked at her as she crossed the drive going towards the front door, then turned away, and it was a full fifteen minutes before he came upstairs and stood inside the kitchen with his back to the door and watched her as she stood cutting bread at the side table. After gulping deep in his throat he muttered, 'I'm sorry about this afternoon.'

She didn't move, nor speak, but when she felt him standing behind her she began to tremble.

'I'm sorry I went on like that.'

Still she didn't answer. She piled the bread on

the plate now and when she went to move away he touched her lightly on the arm, saying quietly, 'What was it you wanted to tell me?'

'Nothing.'

'Come on now.' He pulled her round to him, but she held the plate in both hands, and it kept them apart.

'You didn't get dressed up and go into Newcastle and then go into a phone box and call me for nothing. I said I'm sorry. In a way . . . well, you should be glad I'm jealous of him.'

She didn't speak or look at him as he took the plate from her hands and put it on the table, but when he went to put his arms around her she drew back from him, and his brows gathered and his teeth met tightly for a moment. But he forced himself to repeat quietly, 'Come on, tell me what it is.'

She looked at him now and, her voice cool, she said, 'I've had some articles accepted by *The Courier*. The editor asked to see them this afternoon.'

'You have?' His expression was one of surprise and pleasure and he repeated, 'You have. And by *The Courier*! Lord, that's a good start. Well, well.' He nodded his head to her. 'I've told you all along you'd do it. And to get into *The Courier* is something. By, I'd say it is. What are they about?'

'Bill.'

'What!' His cheeks were pushing his eyes into deep hollows; his whole face was screwed up with astonishment. 'Bill? You've written articles on Bill?'

'Yes, on Bill.'

'What about?'

'Oh!' She turned to the table. 'Just the things he does.'

'Well I never!' His voice sounded a little flat now. 'Are they funny like?'

'You'll have to judge for yourself when you read them.'

'I will. Yes,' he nodded at her again, 'I'll read them after tea. By the way, what are they giving you?'

'Ten guineas.'

'Each?' His voice was high.

'Yes,' she paused, then added, 'He's got six. If they take on I'll be doing them every week.'

Into the silence that now fell on them Jimmy's voice came from the bottom of the stairs, calling, 'Are you there, boss?' and when Corny went on to the landing Jimmy looked up at him and said, 'Bloke's asking for you.'

'All right, I'll be down.' Corny looked back towards the kitchen but he didn't return to it; he went slowly down the stairs, and at the bottom he paused for a moment. Ten guineas a time. It would make her feel independent of him. He didn't like it, he didn't like it at all. It was a thing he had about money. He never wanted her to have anything in that line but what he provided.

11

THE WILL

Ben was buried on Wednesday. It was the first
time Mary Ann had been to a cremation, and
although the disposal seemed more final than
burying, there was a greater sense of peace about
the whole thing than if they had stood round an
open grave. She'd always had a horror of graves
and coffins, but this way of going was clean
somehow.

As the curtains glided on silent rails and
covered up the last move Ben's earthly body was
to experience, she fancied she saw him young
again. Yet she had never even seen a picture of
Ben when he was young. His back had been
bent the first time she had clapped eyes on him
when he had opened the door to her that morning
in the far, far past, the morning she had gone
in search of . . . 'the Lord' to beg him to give
her da a job. It was Ben who had tried to
throw her out of the house; it was Ben who had
been jealous of her; but it was Ben who had, in
his own strange way, come to depend on her
because he realised that through her, and only

her, would his master know life again.

She walked with Corny out of the little chapel. They followed behind Tony and Lettice. Then came her mother and father, and Michael and Sarah. Sarah always came last so that her shambling walk would not impede others. Mr Lord was not at the funeral, it would have been too much for him.

Tony, looking at Mary Ann, now said, 'Will you come back to the house?'

'If you don't mind, Tony, I'd rather go home. I'll—'

'He asked for you. There's a will to be read and he asked us all to be there.'

She glanced at Corny but his look was non-committal. It said, 'It's up to you.'

'It won't take long.' It was Mike speaking to her now. 'And you could do with a cup of tea. There's nothing to rush for anyway. The children will be all right with Jimmy when they get back from school.'

When they reached the house they took their coats off in the hall, then filed into the drawing-room. The day was very warm, almost like a June day, not one in early September, but Mr Lord was sitting close to the fire.

Mary Ann went straight to him. She did not, as usual, say, 'Hello,' nor did he speak to her, but when she put her hand on his he took it and held it gently, and she sat down by his side.

When they were all seated Lettice served the tea that the daily woman had brought in; then she tried, with the help of Tony, to make conversation, but found it rather difficult with Mr Lord sitting silent, and Mary Ann having little to say either.

It was almost twenty minutes later when the trolley was removed, Mr Lord looked at Tony and said, 'Will you bring me that letter from the desk?' And when the letter was in his hand he looked at it, then at the assembled company and said, 'This is Ben's will. I don't know what it holds, only that it wasn't drawn up by a solicitor. He wrote it out himself about five or six years ago and had it witnessed by my gardener and his wife, then he put it into my keeping, and he didn't mention it from that day.' He paused and swallowed and his Adam's apple sent ripples down the loose skin of his neck. 'I will get my grandson to read it to you. Whatever it holds, his wishes will be carried out to the letter.'

Tony split the long envelope open with a paper knife, then drew out a single foolscap sheet, and after unfolding it he scanned the heading, then looked from one to the other before he began to read. 'This is my last will and testament and I make it on the first day of December, nineteen hundred and sixty-two. My estate is invested in three building societies and up to date the total is nine thousand three hundred and twenty-five pounds, and God willing it may grow. I'm in my right mind and I wish to dispose of it as follows: I wish to leave one thousand pounds to Peter Brown, my master's great-grandson. This to be kept in trust for him until the age of sixteen, because at sixteen I think a boy needs a lot of things, which are mostly not good for him, at least so he is told, but by the age of twenty-one when it appears right and proper he should have these things very often the taste for them has gone.

'When I say I leave nothing to my young master, Mr Tony Brown, I am sure he will understand, because he has all he needs and more. To his wife, Madam Lettice, I leave my grateful thanks for the kindness and consideration she has shewn me since she has become mistress of this house. Never did I think I could tolerate a woman running my master's house but I found that my young master's wife was an exception.

'To my master, I leave the memory of my utter devotion. There has been no-one in my life for fifty-two years other than himself; he knows this.

'To Michael Shaughnessy, farmer on my master's estate, I leave the sum of three hundred pounds because here was a man big enough and bold enough to overcome the dirty deals life has a habit of dealing out.'

At this point Tony raised his eyes and smiled towards Mike, and Mike, his eyes wide, his lips apart, his head moving slightly, looked back at him in amazement. Then Tony resumed his reading.

'Now I come to the main recipient of my estate, namely Mary Ann Shaughnessy. Although she is now Mrs Mary Ann Boyle I still think of her as Mary Ann Shaughnessy. After the above commitments have been met I wish her to have whatever is left. I do this because, when, as a loving, cheeky, fearless child, she came into my master's life, he became alive again. She turned him from an embittered man, upon whom I, with all my devotion, was unable to make any impression, into a human being once more. You will forgive me, Master, for stating this so plainly, but you and I know it to be true. It was this child, this Mary Ann Shaughnessy, who melted the ice around your heart.

'There is another reason, Mary Ann, why I want you to have and enjoy the money I have worked for, but which brought me no comfort, no pleasure. It is because right from the first you were kind to me, and concerned for me, even when you feared me, so I . . .'

Tony's words were cut off by the sound of choked, painful sobbing. Mary Ann was bent forward, her face buried in her hands.

'There now, there now.' Lizzie was at one side of her and Lettice at the other. The men were on their feet, with the exception of Mr Lord. Mr Lord's face was turned towards the fire and his jaw bones showed white under his blue-veined skin.

Lettice now led Mary Ann into her room and there Mary Ann dropped on to the couch, her face still covered with her hands, and her sobbing increased until it racked her whole body.

When Corny came to her side he put his hands on her shoulders and, shaking her gently, said, 'Come on now, give over, stop it.' But his attention only seemed to make her worse.

Now Tony came on the scene. He had a glass in his hand and, bending over the back of the couch, he coaxed her: 'Come on. Come on, dear, drink this.'

But Mary Ann continued to sob and he handed the glass to Lizzie, saying, 'Make her drink it; I must get back to grandfather, he's upset.'

'Mary Ann, stop it! Do you hear?' Corny had

pushed Lizzie aside almost roughly and was once more gripping Mary Ann's shoulders, and Lizzie, her voice steely now, said, 'Don't Corny, don't. Let her cry it out. She needs to cry.' She looked at him full in the face, then more gently she said, 'Leave her for a while, she'll be all right.'

He straightened up and stared at her, at this woman who had never wanted him for her daughter. They had always been good friends, but he often wondered what went on under Lizzie's poised and tactful exterior.

He walked slowly out of the room and closed the door behind him, and when he looked across the wide hall there was Mike standing at the bottom of the stairs, his elbow resting on the balustrade. Corny went up to him and Mike said, 'It was the shock; it was a shock to me an' all. Three hundred pounds!' He shook his head slowly. 'Fancy old Ben thinking of me.' Then taking a deep breath he added, 'This is going to make a difference, isn't it? It's a small fortune she's got. Nearly eight thousand pounds I should imagine by the time it's all worked out. Of course, there'll be death duties to pay.' He stared at Corny now. 'You don't look very happy about it, lad.'

Corny stared back at Mike. He could speak the truth to his father-in-law; they were brothers under the skin. He said bluntly, 'No, I'm not happy about it. What do you think it'll do to her?'

'Do to her? Well, knowing Mary Ann, not much.'

'Huh!' Corny tossed his head. 'You think so? Well I see it differently.'

'What do you mean?'

'Oh, nothing.' He brought his shoulders hunching up cupping his head. The action looked as if he was retreating from something, and Mike said, 'Don't be daft, man; money will make no difference to Mary Ann. You should know that.'

Corny turned slowly towards him and quietly he asked him, 'How would you have felt if it had been left to Lizzie?'

Mike opened his mouth to speak, then closed it again. Aye, how would he have felt if it had been left to Lizzie? It would have made her independent of him. It didn't do for a woman to have money, at least not more than the man she was married to. He stared back into Corny's eyes and said, 'Aye, I see what you mean.'

12

SAMSON AGAIN

On the Thursday night, David leant over his bunk and, looking down on to Rose Mary, whispered, 'We could cut it off.'

'What?' she whispered back at him.

'Her hair.'

'Whose?'

'Don't be goofy, you know whose, Diana Blenkinsop's.'

Rose Mary was sitting bolt upright now, her face only inches from her brother's hanging upside down in mid air, and she said, 'Eeh! our David, that's wicked. Whatever gave you that idea?'

'Mam.'

'Mam?'

'Yes, 'bout Samson.'

'Samson?'

'Don't be so mutton-nappered. You remember, she told us the story about Samson. When he had his hair cut off he couldn't do nothin'.'

'But Samson was a man.'

'It's all the same. And she would look different

with her hair off, all like that.' He took one hand from the edge of the bunk and traced his finger in a jagged line around his neck, and Rose Mary exclaimed on a horrified note, 'Eeh! you dursen't.'

'I dare.'

And as she stared at him she knew he dared.

'They're still not kind,' he said.

'I asked Mr Blenkinsop to send her away.'

David swung himself down from the bunk and, crouching on the floor at her side, exclaimed incredulously, 'When?'

'Last Monday, when I pretended I was sick.' She crimped her face at him. 'I only wanted to stay off so I could see Mr Blenkinsop.'

'And what did he say?'

'He said I hadn't to worry; he would see to it.'

'Well, he hasn't, has he?'

She shook her head slowly, and he stared back at her through the dim light, looking deep into her eyes and appealing to her to solve this problem, as he had been wont to do, but inarticulately, before he could speak; and she answered the look in his eyes by whispering very low, 'I'll die if she takes me dad away.'

As he continued to stare at her, his mind registered the death-like process they would go through if Diana Blenkinsop did take their dad away. At the end of his thinking he added to himself, And Jimmy and all. But he comforted himself on this point. Jimmy wouldn't go; he could stop that, he would see to that the morrow.

Rose Mary broke into his thoughts now, saying, 'But you couldn't reach.'

'If the sun's shining and it's hot like it was the day, she'll go down and lie on the bank sun bathing. She lies with her hair all out at the back. The men on the scaffolding were watchin' her the day, and laughin'.'

'But you've got to go to school.'

'I could have a headache.'

Again they were staring at each other. Then Rose Mary whispered, 'But me mam won't stand for me being off again, I can't say I'm sick again.'

'I'll do it on me own.'

'Eeh! no, our David, I should be with you.'

'I'll be all right.' He nodded at her. 'If it's sunny in the mornin' I'll say me head's bad.'

The door opening suddenly brought both their heads towards the light and their mother.

'What are you doing out of bed?'

'I've . . . I've got a bad head.'

'You didn't say anything about a bad head when you came to bed. Go on, get up.' She hoisted him up into the bunk, then tucked the clothes around him and said, 'Go to sleep and your headache will be gone when you wake up.' Then she tucked Rose Mary in again and, going towards the door, said, 'Now no more talking. Get yourselves to sleep.'

Back in the living-room she sat down near the fire. Bill was lying on the mat, and when he rose and went to climb on to her knee she said, 'No, no!' But he stood with his front paws on her lap looking at her and again she said, 'No!' and on this he dropped his heavy body down and lay by the side of her chair.

There was a magazine lying on the little table to the side of her. She picked it up, then put it down again. She couldn't read, she couldn't settle to anything. She felt that she was moving into a world of delirium. She still wanted to cry when she thought of Ben and what he had done for her, but she mustn't start that again.

Last night she had cried until she fell asleep, and this morning she had felt terrible; and the feeling wasn't caused by her crying alone but by Corny's attitude to this great slice of luck that had befallen her. He wasn't pleased that Ben had left her the money, in fact he was angry. She had wanted to say to him, 'But we'll share it, we've shared everything'; yet she didn't because they weren't sharing everything as of old. She couldn't share even the surface of his affection with Diana Blenkinsop.

The odd thing about the money was that she hadn't brought up the subject to him, or he to her. She had hardly seen him since this morning. He had come up to dinner and eaten it in silence and then had gone straight down again. The same had happened at teatime. And now it was almost nine o'clock and he was still downstairs. He would have to come up some time and he'd have to talk about it some time.

It was half-an-hour later when he entered the room. She had his supper ready on the table and she said to him, 'Tea or coffee?'

'Tea,' he answered.

That was all, just 'Tea'. When she had made the tea and they were seated at the table she said quietly, 'Tony phoned. He . . . he wants me to go to Newcastle on Monday to see the bank manager and Mr Lord's solicitor.'

He had a piece of cold ham poised before his

mouth when, turning his head slightly towards her, he said flatly, 'Well, what about it?'

'O . . . oh!' She was on her feet, her hands gripping the edge of the table. 'You're wild, aren't you? You're wild because Ben left me that money.'

He put the ham in his mouth and chewed on it before he replied grimly, 'The word isn't wild, I just think it's a mistake you being left it. It was hard enough living with you before, but God knows what it'll be like now with fame and fortune hitting you at one go.'

Her face slowly stretched in amazement as she looked at him and she repeated, 'What did you say?'

'You heard me.'

'Yes, I heard you. It was hard enough living with me before. Well! Well! now I'm learning something. Hard enough living with me . . .' Her voice rose almost to a squeak.

'Yes, yes, it was if you want to know, because for years I've had to contend with your home. This was never your home, as I've told you before. This was just a little shack that I provided for you, it wasn't home, you never referred to it as home. But the farm was home, wasn't it? Then your mother never wanting me to have you, because I was just a mechanic, and she's never let me forget it.'

'Oh! Corny Boyle. How can you sit there and spit out such lies. Mam's been wonderful to you; she's been . . .'

'Oh yes, she's been wonderful to me, like Tony has, the great Mr Lord's grandson, the man you should have married, the man your mother wanted you to marry, the man Mr Lord created for you. Aye, created.' He raised his hand high in the air. 'And did he not prepare you for such an elevated station by sending you to a convent and giving you big ideas . . . Oh aye, they're all wonderful.'

Mary Ann stepped back from the table still keeping her eyes on him. She had never imagined for a moment he thought like this, but all these things must have been fermenting in his mind for years.

He had stopped his eating and was staring down at his plate, and she had the urge to run to him and put her arms about him and say 'Oh, you silly billy! You're jealous, and you haven't got one real reason in the world to be jealous of me. As for the money, take the lot, put it in the business, do what you like with it, it doesn't matter. What matters is that everything should be all right between us, that we should be . . . kind.' But she smothered the urge; nothing had changed, there was still Diana Blenkinsop.

She turned away and went into the kitchen and stood looking out of the small window and watched the lights of the cars flashing by on the main road half a mile away.

After a while she heard him pushing his chair back, and then his voice came from the scullery door, saying, 'I'm sorry. You enjoy your money. Take the holiday you've always been on about. I'm off to bed, I'm tired.'

She made no response by word or movement. He had said he was sorry in a voice that was still full of bitterness. 'Take a holiday,' he had said. Well, perhaps she would do that. She would take the children and go away some place. It would give him time to think and sort himself out. On the other hand it might give him time to throw himself into the waiting arms of Diana Blenkinsop. Well, if that's what he wanted then he must have it. She could see no greater purgatory in life than living with someone who didn't really want you.

13

Mr Blenkinsop's Strategy

On Friday morning Mr Blenkinsop arrived at the office not at nine o'clock, but nearer ten, because he hadn't come from Newcastle, where he stayed during the week, but from his home in Doncaster.

Last night, unknown to his daughter, he had returned home because he wanted to talk to his wife privately, and urgently.

During the journey he had rehearsed what he was going to say to her. He would begin with: 'Now look here, Ida, you've been against her going to America.' And doubtless she would come back at him immediately and he would let her have her say because he, too, hadn't taken to the idea when his cousin, Rodney, first suggested that Diana should go out to Detroit. The idea was that mixing business with pleasure she would take up a post in the factory out there with a view to coming back and acting as manageress over the women's department. Recently, however, he had changed his views about this matter and had put it to his wife that it might be a good thing for their daughter to have this experience. But Ida wouldn't hear of it. The family would be broken up soon enough, she had protested; she wasn't going to force any member to leave it.

Yet how would she react when she learnt that the member in question could be preparing to fly from the nest at any moment. He wasn't considering Corny's power of resistance, because few men, he imagined, could resist anyone as luscious as his daughter, especially a man who had been married for seven or eight years. It was a crucial time in marriage; there was a great deal of truth in the seven year itch. Moreover, he knew that when Diana set her mind on anything she would have it, even if when she got it she smashed it into smithereens, as she had done with many a toy she had craved for as a child. Now her toys were men.

But when Mr Blenkinsop reached home he found his wife knew all about the business. At least that was the impression he got as soon as he entered the house. She was entertaining three friends to tea. From the drawing-room window she had seen him getting out of his car on the drive and had met him in the hall, saying rapidly under her breath, 'I expected you. Say nothing about it though when you come in; Florence and Kate are here. Jessie Reeves popped in unexpectedly. I'm wondering if she knows anything; Kate gave me a funny look when she came in. The Reeveses were out Chalford way on Sunday too. They might have seen them, but say nothing.' She turned from him and led the way back into the drawing-room and, a little mystified, he followed her.

Chalford! it wasn't likely Boyle took her to Chalford on Sunday.

He greeted the three ladies, talked with them, joked with them and half-an-hour later saw them to their cars. Yet again he was obstructed from having any private conversation with his wife by his family descending on him and demanding to know what had brought him back on a Thursday night.

'It's my house. I can come back any time I like.' He pushed at the boys' heads, hugged Susan to him, then demanded to know what was happening to their homework; and eventually he returned to the drawing-room and closed the door. Looking at his wife he let out a long slow breath and said, 'Well!'

'Yes, indeed.' Ida Blenkinsop draped one arm over the head of the couch and lifted her slim legs up on to it before adding, 'You can exclaim, well! Of all the people she could take up with! When I think of her turning her nose up at Reg Foster, and Brian, and Charles. And look what Charles will be one of these days, he's nearly reached three thousand now. The trouble with this one is, he looks all right, too all right I understand, but what he'll sound like is another thing, and how he'll act is yet another.'

Dan Blenkinsop stood with his back to the fire, his hands in his pockets, looking at his wife. He was puzzled and becoming more puzzled every moment. He said now, 'How did you get to know?'

'Well, Kate ran into them on Sunday. She thought nothing of it; they were on the bridge looking at the water near Chalford. She saw them getting into this big car and thought, Oh! But then on Wednesday she was with John in

Newcastle and there they met them again, and John recognised the fellow. He says he is well over thirty and a womaniser. He worked on a building in Newcastle that John designed . . .'

'What! Look, Ida.' Dan screwed up his eyes and flapped his hand in front of his face in an effort to check her flow. 'Look, stop a minute and tell me who you're talking about.'

'Who I'm talking about?' She swung her legs off the couch. 'Diana, of course, and your ganger.'

'My ganger?' He stepped off the Chinese hearthrug and moved towards her, his chin thrust out enquiringly, and he repeated, 'My ganger?'

'Yes, a man called Murgatroyd. John Murgatroyd.'

There was a chair near the head of the couch and Dan lowered himself on to it; then bending towards his wife he said, 'You mean that Diana's going out with Murgatroyd, the ganger?'

'What do you think I've been talking about. And' – she spread out her hands widely – 'what's brought you back tonight? I thought that's what you'd come about.'

Dan took his handkerchief from his pocket and wiped his brow.

'It wasn't that?'

He now looked up under his lids at his wife and said slowly, 'It was about Diana, but not with Murgatroyd. You mean to say she's been going out with Johnny Murgatroyd?'

'You know him?' She shook her head. 'Of course you know him; what am I talking about? But what is he like? He's just an ordinary workman isn't he? And why have you come if not about that. Is anything else wrong?'

Again he mopped his brow as he said patiently, 'Not wrong; I would say a little complicated. I came out tonight, dear, to suggest that it would be as well if you changed your mind about her going to America. You know she wanted to go, but you were so dead against it she allowed herself to be persuaded.'

'Now don't rub it in, Dan.' Ida Blenkinsop turned her face away, and her husband said quickly, 'I'm not rubbing it in, but I think it would be the best thing under the circumstances, because I've got something else to tell you.'

Her face was towards him again, her eyes wide with enquiry.

'She's causing havoc in the Boyle family.'

'You mean with him . . . Corny?'

'Yes, with him, Corny.'

'You're joking. That's as bad as the ganger.'

'It might appear so on the surface. To my mind it's much worse. The ganger happens to be single; Corny's got a wife and two children, and even the children are aware of the situation.'

'Oh Dan!' She had risen to her feet. 'You're exaggerating.' Her tone was airy.

Dan now got to his feet and, his voice patient no longer, he snapped, 'I'm not exaggerating, Ida, and I'm really concerned, not for our daughter but for the Boyle family. I tell you the children know. That little girl came to me, and you know what she said? She asked me if I would send Diana away because she didn't want to lose her daddy.'

'Good gracious! I've never heard of such a thing. That's precociousness. She's like her mother that child . . .'

'Ida! you've got to face up to this. If Diana doesn't go haywire with Boyle she'll go it with Murgatroyd. But I want to see that she doesn't go it with young Boyle. That's a nice family and I would never forgive myself if she broke it up. But I know what you're thinking. Oh, yes I do. You would rather she amused herself in that direction than go for Murgatroyd, because you think she's safe with Boyle, him being married, whereas she could get tied up with . . . the ganger, and then you'd have to bury your head in the sand. Now from tomorrow night I'm going to tell her she's finished down there at the factory. I'm going to tell her I've heard from Rodney and he's renewed his invitation for her to go out to him. I'm going to get through to Rodney tonight and explain things, and there'll be a letter for her from him early next week endorsing all I've said.'

Ida Blenkinsop put her hand up to her cheek and walked across the room to the window, where she stood for a few minutes before coming back. Then looking at her husband she said, 'What if she meets a Boyle or a Murgatroyd out there?'

'We'll have to take our chance on that. But there's one thing I'm determined on, she's not going to break up the Boyle family to afford herself a little amusement, and as long as she's within walking distance of him, or driving distance for that matter, she'll see him as a challenge.'

'It's his wife's fault.' Ida Blenkinsop jerked her chin to the side. 'She should look after her man and see that he doesn't stray. Little women are all alike; they're all tongue and no talent. I could never stand little women, not really.'

As he took her arm and smiled at her and said, 'Come on, let's have something to eat, I'm hungry,' he was thinking: And neither can your daughter, for he now sensed that Diana's hunting of Corny was as much to vex his wife as to satisfy her craving for male adulation.

It was about twenty past ten on the Friday morning when Mr Blenkinsop came into the garage. Corny was at the far door and when he saw him he felt the muscles of his stomach tense. Diana had left the garage only a few minutes earlier. He had been in the pit under the car and he had caught sight of her legs first, long, slim, brown . . . and bare. She was wearing a mini skirt but he couldn't see the bottom of it, only the length of her legs.

When she bent down and her face came on a level with his he couldn't look at it for a moment, yet when he looked away his eyes were drawn to her thighs, which were partly exposed and within inches of his hands.

'Good morning.' That was all she had said but she could make it sound like the opening bars of an overture. She was wearing a scent that wiped out the smell of the petrol and oil. She looked fresh, young, and beautiful, so beautiful that he ached as he looked at her. He wetted his lips and said, 'Hello, there.'

'Busy?'

'No, this is a new form of exercise; they say it prevents you from getting old.'

She laughed softly. 'You're the type that'll never grow old, Corny.'

'Nice of you to say so, but you see before you a man literally prone with age.'

She laughed softly. 'When you feel like that it's a sure sign you need a change.'

'I'm inclined to agree with you.'

'It's a beautiful day.'

'I hadn't really noticed, not until a minute ago.' He wasn't used to paying compliments and the thought that he had done so brought the blood rushing to his face, but when she laughed out loud he knew a moment's fear in case the sound carried upwards and into the house.

'Do you know something?'

'What?'

'You're very, very nice, Mr Cornelius Boyle.'

He lowered his eyes for a moment, looked at the spanner in his right hand, moved his lips outwards, then drew them in tight between his teeth before he replied, 'And you know something?'

'What?'

'You are more than nice, Miss Diana Blenkinsop, much, much more than nice.' He dare not allow himself to look into her eyes; his gaze was fixed on her hair where it fell over her shoulders and rested on the points of her small breasts.

'Dad! Dad! where's Jimmy?'

He blinked quickly, his body jerked as if he had been dreaming and, turning his head, he looked at the face of his son peering at him from yon side of the car, and he said, 'He . . . he's about somewhere. In . . . in the yard, I think.'

David did not say 'All right, Dad', and run off; he still knelt on the edge of the well, his head inclined to one shoulder, and he gazed at his dad then at the other face beyond his dad.

'Well, I must be off. I'm looking for Father. He hasn't turned up yet; I thought he might be wandering around the works.'

'I haven't seen him.'

Her face became still; her eyes looked into his. 'We'll meet again.' Her smile showed all her teeth, like a telly advert. When her face lifted from his he watched her body unfold, he watched her legs as they walked away, then he turned again slowly on to his back and lay gasping for a moment.

What was going to be the outcome of it? They were nearing some point of revelation. He knew it and she knew it. Dear God, what was he going to do? Mary Ann. Oh, Mary Ann. He wanted help. He thought of Mike, but Mike could do nothing more. There was no alternative only his own reserves, and God knew they were pretty weak at the moment.

'Dad!'

He had forgotten about David and he turned his head towards him, saying, 'You still there, what do you want?'

'Can I help you?'

'No, no. I thought you had a bad head?'

'I have.'

'Well, go out in the fresh air.'

'Yes, Dad.'

After David moved away he lay until he felt his stomach heaving as if he were going to be sick, and he crawled from under the car and went to the back gate and took in great draughts of fresh air. As she said, it was a beautiful morning, like a summer's day; the world was bright, she was

bright and beautiful and young, so young . . .
Mary Ann was young, yet Mary Ann was like
a child compared with her, because Diana had
knowledge that Mary Ann had no notion of.
Diana had a knowledge of men, what they
wanted, what they needed. She was like a woman
made out of history, all the Salomes, all the
Cleopatras, all the essence of all the women who
had made love their business.

It was as he turned into the garage again that he
saw Mr Blenkinsop at the far door.

'Hello, there. Can I have a word with you,
Corny?'

Mr Blenkinsop was looking at him in an odd
way and the sweat began to run down from his
oxters and soak his shirt.

'Yes, yes,' he nodded his head quickly. 'Would
you like to come into the office?' He led the
way into his office and there he said, 'Take a
seat.'

Mr Blenkinsop sat down on the only chair, but
Corny did not perch himself on the high stool
but stood with his back to his desk and pressed
his hips against it as if for support, and as he
looked at Mr Blenkinsop's bent head his sweating
increased, and he ran a finger round the neck of
his overalls. Then Mr Blenkinsop raised his head
and said, 'I don't like to probe into a man's
private life but this is one time when I'm forced
to. I want to ask you what you know about
Johnny Murgatroyd?'

The question came as such a surprise that
Corny gaped for a moment, then said, 'Johnny?
Johnny Murgatroyd?'

'Yes.'

'Well, as you say, a man's private life is his own, but one hears things. What has he been up to?'

'It's not what he's been up to but what he might be up to.' The words were slow and meaningful, yet Corny didn't get the gist of them until a thought struck him. Was he trying to tell him something about Mary Ann and Murgatroyd? The thought brought him from the desk and he stretched himself upwards before he said, 'What do you want to say, Mr Blenkinsop?'

'Well, it's rather a delicate matter, Corny. I . . .'

Corny felt himself bridling. He'd say it was a delicate matter; and what damn business was it of his anyway. He said stiffly, 'My wife's known Jimmy Murgatroyd since they were children together. They lived next door to each other so to speak.'

'Oh, I didn't know that, but one hears things you know. Do you think there's any truth in the rumour that he's had a number of women, not girls, women, if you follow me?'

'Yes, I follow you.' Corny nodded at him slowly. 'But as I said, and as you said, the man's life's his own, it's nobody's business except his and those concerned.'

'Quite right, quite right.' Mr Blenkinsop made a movement that expressed his understanding, and then he said, 'I agree with you, a man's life is his own and he can do what he likes with it, until it impinges on your daughter's life and then one sees it differently.'

Corny had been standing straight, almost rigid, and now he brought his head down. It moved lower and lower and his eyes held Mr Blenkinsop's for a full minute before he said, 'Murgatroyd and Diana?'

'Yes, Murgatroyd and Diana.'

Now his shoulders were moving upwards again, taking his head with them, and he made a sound like a laugh as he said, 'No, no, you've been listening to rumours, Mr Blenkinsop. Diana going with Murgatroyd? Never!'

The laughing sound he made increased. There was an assurance about it until Mr Blenkinsop, getting to his feet, said, 'I haven't been listening to rumours, Corny; I only wish I had. She's going around with him. She was at a dance last Saturday night with him. I went to the house where she is staying. They're very nice people, he calls for her there. She was out with him all day on Sunday and she didn't get back until turned one o'clock on Monday morning. She's seen him every night this week and has never been in before twelve. Mrs Foster, the woman she's staying with, was glad I called. She's been a little worried, not because she knows anything against Murgatroyd but because she thinks he's too old for her and', he pursed his lips, 'not quite her class.'

Corny was leaning against the edge of the desk again. He was staring down at his feet. Again he was feeling sick but it was a different kind of sickness now. It was a sickness bred of shame, self-recrimination, and the feeling that only a man gets when he knows he's been made a fool of, when he's been taken for a ride, a long, long ride; when he's been used, laughed at.

Johnny Murgatroyd, the scum of the earth. And where sex was concerned he was the scum of the earth. Her father had said that she was out with him until one o'clock in the morning. Well, no-one could be out with a man like Johnny Murgatroyd and not know what it was all about. Oh, God! He was so sick, sick to the core of him. And not ten minutes ago she had looked into his eyes and promised him anything he had in mind to ask. Or had she? Had it just been his imagination? NO. NO. It had not been his imagination. He had been neither drunk nor daft these past weeks, but one thing he had been, and that was besotted by a cheap sexy slut.

Mr Blenkinsop had been talking for some minutes and he hadn't heard him and he brought his attention back to him again to hear him say, 'Rodney wanted her to go to America and I think the only way to nip this in the bud is to send her packing, so to speak. Of course, her mother and I will miss her terribly but we can't stand by and let her ruin her life. And you know young girls are very headstrong; when they get it into their head they're in love they imagine they'll die if they don't get their way. Yet with a girl like Diana she'll be in and out of love, if I know anything, for a good many years to come . . . I hope you didn't mind me asking about Murgatroyd, but if there's nothing you really know against him, well, that's that.'

Corny found his voice to say, 'I only know he's unmarried and women seem to like him.'

'Oh yes, yes.' Mr Blenkinsop was walking out of the office now and he smiled over his shoulder at Corny and said, 'There's no doubt about that. He's a very, very presentable man, but I don't want him,' his voice dropped and he repeated, 'I don't want him for a son-in-law, you understand?'

Corny understood. He also hoped in this moment that Mr Blenkinsop would get him for a son-in-law. He hoped that Murgatroyd would in some way manage to marry Diana Blenkinsop, and by God it would serve her right.

'Well, I must get off now, but thanks, Corny. You really don't mind me having asked you about him?'

'Oh no, not at all.'

'Thanks. Good-bye.'

'Good-bye, Mr Blenkinsop.'

He returned to the office, and now he did sit on his stool and he supported his slumped shoulders by crossing his arms on the desk. And in this moment he felt so low, so belittled there was no hole so small that he couldn't have crawled into.

Mary Ann opened the sideboard drawer and took out a pair of binoculars. They had originally been used by some naval man but now looked very much the worse for wear. She had picked them up in a second-hand shop about two years ago, around the time that Corny was taking an interest in bird life to while away the time between passing motorists. He had said to her one day, 'You wouldn't believe it but I've seen ten differnt kinds of birds on the spare land this morning. I couldn't make out half of them, only to see that they were different. You can't get near enough to them. What you want are field glasses when looking at birds.'

She had said, 'I'll get you a book on the different types of birds; you can get them in that small series.' She hadn't thought about the glasses until she had seen them lying among some junk in a dirty-looking shop in a back street in Newcastle. She had been amazed that she had been asked three pounds for them, but she had paid it, and Corny had had a lot of fun out of the glasses. That was until the stroke of luck came, and he had never touched the glasses since. But she had. She had used these glasses day after day over the past weeks, round about dinnertime, because it was at dinnertime that Diana Blenkinsop sauntered over the spare land. When it was fine she had her lunch out there on the knoll; even when it was raining she would saunter down the field, past the derelict old car that the children played with, down to where the land rose to form the knoll, and where, Mary Ann knew, the men, as they sat munching their bait, would be able to see her plainly standing silhouetted against the sky.

As time went on it was a compelling urge that made her take up the field glasses. She always seemed to know the time when the figure would appear from the side of the half-erected car park. This sprang from the same instinct that told her when Diana Blenkinsop was down in the garage. She seemed to be able to smell her there. The feeling would bring her to a stop in the middle of some job and carry her to the front room, to the side of the window, and as sure as life a few minutes later she would see the tall, lithe figure sauntering across the drive.

She stood now to the side of the scullery window and lifted the glasses to her eyes. Yes, there she was already ensconced, and she must have had her lunch because she was sunbathing.

She was lying spreadeagled like a body being sacrificed to the sun.

She was brazen, utterly brazen. Mary Ann's lips tightened. She looked all legs, bare legs. Oh, men! Couldn't Corny see what she was?

Her attention was now brought from the knoll to the derelict car and the figure that had just emerged from the shelter of it. It was David. When she realised that her son was going towards Diana Blenkinsop there entered into her a deeper note of bitterness. Even children were attracted to her. Not Rose Mary. No. No female would be. When she saw David drop on to the ground she screwed up her eyes and re-focused the glasses. What on earth was he doing? He was crawling, up the side of the knoll, right behind the prone figure.

What . . . on . . . earth . . . was he up to? Perhaps he was playing a game? He was going to give her a fright.

When he was within less than an arm's length of Diana Blenkinsop she saw him stop, and then her heart almost ceased to beat when his hand, holding something in it from which the sun glinted as if from steel, moved towards the head lying on the grass.

She gripped the glasses tightly to her face as she cried, 'David! David! Don't! Don't!' The next minute she saw Diana Blenkinsop spring to her feet and hold her head. Then David turned and ran down the hill, and Diana after him.

Now she herself was flying down the back stairs, through the yard and on to the open space behind the garage, there to see Diana Blenkinsop belabouring David about the head and shoulders.

No tigress could have covered the distance quicker and, tearing her son from the enraged girl, she cried, 'You! You great big useless hussy, take that!'

She'd had to reach up some distance to deliver the blow, but such was its force that it made Diana Blenkinsop reel backwards and she stood for a moment cupping her face before she cried, 'How dare you! HOW DARE YOU!'

'You say how dare I? You have the nerve to say how dare I? And you beating my son?'

'Beating your son?' Diana Blenkinsop was spitting the words at Mary Ann now. 'Yes, and I'll beat him again. Just look. See what he's done.' She lifted the front of her hair to show a jagged line about six inches from the bottom and two inches in width. 'He was cutting my hair off, the horrible little tyke.' She was glaring down at David, and David, from the shelter of his mother's waist, slanted his eyes up to her and clung tighter to Mary Ann.

'Whatever he did, you've got no right to lay hands on him; you should have come to me.'

'Come to you!' The words held deep scorn. 'And what would you have done? You can't control any member of your family from your dog upwards. Your children take no more notice of you than your husband does.'

Mary Ann found difficulty in breathing, and her words came as a hissed whisper through her trembling lips. 'You cheap, loose individual, you!'

There was a slight pause before Diana said, 'You had better be careful, but whatever I am, I can lay no claim to commonness.' Her lip curled on the word. 'There's a difference, Mrs Boyle.'

At this point she raised her eyes from Mary Ann's face to the small garage door and her head wagged slightly as she watched Corny come and stand beside his wife. He was looking at her as he had never looked at her before and he said quietly, 'Yes as you say, Diana, there is a difference between cheap and common, yet some folks can be both.'

As Diana stared into the face that was almost on a level with her own, she knew that her power over this man was gone. He had likely heard about Johnny. Oh well, what did it matter. The sea was teeming with such fish. She said to him, 'Your son tried to cut my hair off.'

Corny cast a swift glance down at David; then looking back at her, he said, 'Did he now!'

'Yes, he did now.' She mimicked his inflexion, then added, 'And your wife struck me.'

'Oh, she did, did she?' Now he looked down at Mary Ann. But Mary Ann did not return his glance; she was staring at the girl, sensing something had happened, even before this incident, between her and Corny.

'Yes, she did. She's keeping true to type, the back street type.'

Corny took a step from Mary Ann's side as he said grimly, 'I'll have you remember it's my wife you're talking about.'

'Oh, la-la! Aren't we becoming loyal all of a sudden! You must have lost your amnesia. How does it feel to remember you've got a wife?'

Corny's arms were stiff by his sides, his muscles tense, his finger nails digging into his palms. He was getting all he had asked for, and more. God, how could he have been so blind! Could it be that just over an hour ago there was some part of him that had loved this hussy. Aye, he'd have to admit it, some part of him had loved her; not in the way he loved Mary Ann but in a way that was like a craving for drugs, or drink. And now there was nobody in the wide world he hated as he did her.

He watched her coming nearer to him, her eyes fixed scornfully on his. She passed him without a word, but when she came to Mary Ann she paused slightly, and looking down at her, said, 'I should give him back his trousers, it might help him to find out whether he's a man or not.'

Mary Ann was in front of him, hanging on to his upraised arm. The trembling of his body went through hers. She did not look up at his face but kept her eyes fixed on the arm she was holding, yet she knew that he was watching the figure moving towards the small door in the garage. When she felt he could see her no longer she released her hold, but still not looking at him she said under her breath, 'You'd better come upstairs . . . and you an' all.' She put out her hand and pulled David towards her, and with him by her side she walked slowly forward. But she had covered more than half of the open space before she heard the crunch of Corny's steps behind her.

In the kitchen she was glad to sit down; every bone in her body was shaking. She did not know whether it was with anger or relief; anger at the things that girl had said, or relief at the knowledge that whatever had been between her and Corny was finished, dead.

When she saw Corny enter the room, she bowed her head against the look on his face. The thing might be dead but she felt he was suffering the loss as if of a beloved one . . . It wasn't over yet then.

She had to do something to ease the embarrassment between them so she pulled David towards her, and, her voice trembling, she asked him, 'Tell me, what made you do it?'

David stood before her with his head bent. When he raised his eyes he didn't look at her, but at his father who was standing with his elbows resting on the mantelpiece, his back towards them, and he said, 'Because of Samson.'

'Samson!' Mary Ann gazed at her son in perplexity. Then she asked, 'Which Samson?'

'The Samson you told me and Rose Mary about with the long hair.'

Mary Ann shook her head slightly and waited.

'Well, you said that when his hair was cut he couldn't do anything, he was no use. You said everything was in his hair, an' I thought' – he glanced quickly at his father's back again, then ended on a high cracked note, 'I thought she couldn't do anything if her hair . . .'

When his voice broke he screwed up his eyes tightly and the tears welled from between his lashes, and Mary Ann drew him into her arms and held him for a moment. Then rising from her chair, she took him by the hand and into the bathroom, and before she washed his face she held him again, and kissed him and murmured over him, 'Oh David. David.' And he cried now with his eyes open and whispered, 'He won't go, will he, Mam? Dad won't go?' And she whispered back, 'No, no. Don't worry; you've made it all right.'

Whether he had or not, at least he had been the

means of proving to her that Diana Blenkinsop was gone. But the question now was, had her effect on Corny been such that their life, as it had once been, was a thing so dead that it could never be revived?

14

THE ETHICS OF STEALING

It was just after three o'clock when David approached Jimmy for the second time that day, 'Are you still busy?' he said to him.

'Aye,' said Jimmy, without looking at him.

'I told you I've got somethin' to show you.'

'And I told you I don't want to see it.'

David stood looking at Jimmy's bent body; he was cleaning an engine that was jacked upon a low platform.

'It won't take five minutes, Jimmy.'

'I told you I haven't got five minutes. And what if your dad comes and finds me away from my job?' He straightened up and looked down on the small boy, and David looked back at him and said, 'But you're goin' the night.'

'Aye, I'm goin' the night, and a bloomin' good job an' all.'

David now turned from him and went to the door of the shed and looked into the yard, then coming back he whispered, 'Will you not go away until I come back, I mean into the garage, I've got something for you?'

'I'll be here for the next half hour or so,' said Jimmy flatly.

Jimmy watched the boy run out of the shed and across the yard, and he shook his head and muttered to himself, 'Who would believe it, eh, who would believe it?'

In less than five minutes David was back in the shed, and when he closed the door Jimmy shouted at him, 'Leave that open, I want to see.'

'Just for a minute, Jimmy. I'll switch the light on.'

He now came and stood in front of Jimmy. He was holding in his hands a cocoa tin with a lid on it and he held it out, saying, 'It's for you, for the car, so you won't have to go.'

Jimmy bent his thin bony body over David and he said one word, 'Eh?'

'You wanted money for the car, for your share. I haven't got it all but there's a lot, and me pocket money an' all. I only kept sixpence back of me pocket money and put the other one and six in.'

'Chree-ist!' exclaimed Jimmy. 'Don't tell me you've been taking it for me?' He was showing not only his teeth but his gums, and his face looked comical, but he didn't feel comical. He knew the kid had been pinching for weeks now and he knew that when the boss twigged the money was missing he would get the blame of it. He had wanted to tip the boss the wink, but he found he couldn't. How could you tell him his own bairn was a thief? He couldn't do it, he liked the boss. The only thing he could do was to leave and let him find out for himself. The boss was always easy with money, and he had been very easy these past few months when it had been flooding in, and he himself could have made quite a bit on the side but he wasn't given that way. But he would never have guessed in a month of Sundays that the young 'un was taking it for him, for the car. He remembered the day Poodle Patter had come into the garage and tried to persuade him to go to Baxter's. The kid had been listening then. Crikey! what was he to do now? He dropped on to an upturned wooden box and, looking at David, said, 'Aw man, you're daft, barmy, clean barmy.'

With the change in Jimmy's attitude David's face brightened and he pulled the lid off the tin and emptied the contents on to the bench. There were ten shilling notes, pound notes, and one five-pound note.

Jimmy closed his eyes, then put his hand over them, and when he heard David say excitedly, 'There's nearly ten pounds. You won't have to go now, will you?' he looked at the boy and said slowly, 'David man, don't you know you've been stealin'? Don't you know you'll get something for your corner for this.'

'It isn't lock-up stealing Jimmy, not real stealing, it's just from Dad, and he's got lots of money, and he doesn't bother about change, you know he doesn't. He said, "What's sixpence?" '

'Aye, he might have said what's sixpence, man, but look, these are not just sixpences, there's a fiver. When, in the name of God, did you take that?'

'Just a while back.'

'Oh crikey!'

'You won't go now, Jimmy, will you?'

Jimmy looked down into the round face that

was wearing an almost angelic expression and he was lost for words. This here kid was a corker. You never knew what he was going to get up to next, but to pinch for him! It put a different complexion on the whole thing. He'd have to do something about it.

He gathered up the money and put it back into the tin and, gazing down at David, he said, 'Now look; I've got a little job I want you to do for me. Now will you stay here and do it until I come back?'

'Aye, Jimmy, I'll do it for you, but', he paused, 'you won't leave, will you?'

Jimmy looked back into the now solemn countenance, and he jerked his head and rubbed his lips with his tongue before saying, 'We'll see. We'll see. Only you stick at this job. Now take that bit of glass paper and get a polish on this rod. I want to see me face in it. Right?'

'Right, Jimmy.'

Corny was in the office. The till was open and he was looking at the contents. He slanted his eyes towards Jimmy as he stood at the door but he didn't speak, and Jimmy said, 'Could I have a word with you, boss?'

Still Corny didn't answer. There was a five-pound note missing from the till. He wanted to turn on this lad and say, 'Hand it over before I knock it out of you!' but in another hour or so he would be gone and that would be that. And, by damn, he'd see that the new one who was starting on Monday didn't grease his fingers at his expense.

Jimmy didn't know how to begin, and the boss wasn't being very helpful. He looked in a bit of a stew. Well that to-do at dinnertime with that piece and the missus was enough to put anybody in a stew, but he didn't think the missus would be troubled any more by Miss Blenkinsop, and that was a good thing. He had been sorry for the missus lately, and he couldn't for the life of him understand the boss. He said now, 'There was a reason, boss, why I wanted to leave.'

'I've no doubt about that.' Corny's voice was cold.

Coo! he was in a stew. And now having to tell him what his lad had been up to was a bit thick, but there was no other way out of it. 'You . . . I don't know whether you've noticed anything about the takings, boss, but . . . but there's been money going.'

Corny slid from the stool and stared at Jimmy and he said, 'Aye, aye, Jimmy, there's been money going. But it's rather late in the day isn't it to give me an explanation?'

As Jimmy stared back into Corny's eyes, he realised the thing he had feared, the thing he was leaving for had already happened; the boss had known about it all along and thought it was him. Aw, crikey! He wagged his head from side to side, then thrusting the tin towards Corny, he said, 'It's all in there. But . . . but it wasn't me that took it.'

Corny looked at the cocoa tin, then lifted the lid. Following this he turned out the contents on to the desk and picked up the five-pound note. Slowly now he turned round and looked at Jimmy, then he said, 'Well, if you didn't take it, who did? The fairies? There's only you and me dealing with money here.'

Jimmy bowed his head. 'You remember Poodle

Patter coming and tryin' to get me to go a share in the car for the band, boss?'

Corny made no response and Jimmy went on, 'He was at me to go to Baxter's for more money, and to get rid of him I said I would think about it. Well, there was somebody listening and they thought up a way to get the money for me.' He lifted his head and looked at Corny and said simply, 'Young David.'

Corny stared at him. He stared and he continued to stare until Jimmy said, 'I'm sorry, boss.'

'Our David!' It was a mere whisper, and Jimmy nodded his head once. 'You mean he's been stealing from the—' he thumbed the till, 'all this time, under my nose?'

Jimmy said nothing until Corny asked, 'How long have you known about this?'

'Oh,' Jimmy wagged his head in characteristic fashion, 'it was the week you got Bill I think. Aye, about that time, because he remembered you telling me to tell the man to keep the change. You said, "What's sixpence." I saw him at it through the window the first time, but I thought I was mistaken until the next time he came in an' I watched him.'

'But why didn't you tell me, Jimmy?' Corny's voice had risen now.

'Aw, boss, ask yourself. Anyway, I tried twice but both times you were in a bit of a stew about something and I thought I'd better not make matters worse.'

'You know what you are, Jimmy, you're a fool, that's what you are, you're a long, lanky fool!' Corny was shouting now. 'I've known this money's been going all the time, but I thought it was you.'

'Aye.' Jimmy jerked his head. 'I know that.'

'Well, you didn't think I was so green as not to miss pound notes and ten shilling notes going out of the till, did you?'

'Well, you didn't say nowt, boss. Anyway,' he now hunched his shoulders up, 'I couldn't give him away; he sort of, well likes me and trails after me. Aw, I just couldn't, so I thought it was better to clear out an' you find out for yourself. But then, well he brings me the tin and tells me he's done it for me so's I won't go.'

'Oh, my God!' Corny sat down heavily on the stool and, leaning his elbow on the desk, he supported his head. He'd go barmy. After a moment he looked at Jimmy and said, 'You know I don't want you to go, don't you?'

'I don't want to go either boss.'

'You've got fixed up at Baxter's.'

'Aye, I start on Monday.'

'Could you back out?'

Jimmy looked down towards his boots, then said, 'Aye, I could, but then you've got the other fellow startin' Monday.'

'Oh, that can be fixed,' said Corny. 'We've said for some time we could do with another hand. And he's young and I won't have time to see to him myself and train him. How about it?'

'Suits me, boss.' Jimmy was grinning slightly, and Corny got off the stool and went towards him and again he said, 'You're a fool, Jimmy. No matter who it is – now you listen to me, man, woman or child – don't you take the rap for anybody, not for a thing like that, for stealing.'

He drew in a long breath, then putting his hand out and gripping Jimmy's shoulder he said, 'Nevertheless, thanks. And I won't forget you for this. Now where is he?'

'I set him cleaning a rod in the shed. You won't come down too hard on him, will you?'

'You leave it to me. This one lesson he's got to learn and the hard way.'

As Jimmy walked quickly by Corny's side he asked, under his breath, 'Where's Mrs Boyle?'

For answer Corny said, 'It'll be all over by the time she gets downstairs.'

David stopped rubbing the rod as soon as he caught sight of his father. Jimmy wasn't there, there was just his dad, and when he saw the look on his face he began to tremble.

'So you've been stealing from me?' Corny was towering over him.

'N . . . not pro . . . proper stealing, Dad.' It was as if he had gone back six months and was learning to pronounce his words again.

'There's only one form of stealing. If you take something that doesn't belong to you that's stealing, proper stealing.'

'I . . . I d-didn't want J-J-Jimmy to go, D-Dad.'

'Jimmy could have asked me for the money. If Jimmy had wanted a share in that car he could have got the money. He didn't want you to steal for him.'

'You said it di-didn't matter, Dad.'

'What didn't matter?'

'Mo-money.'

Corny remembered faintly saying, 'What's money for but to go round.'

'You knew it mattered, didn't you? If it didn't

matter why did you do it on the sly? Why did you go to the office when I wasn't there and take money out of the till if it didn't matter? You knew it was stealing. You wouldn't go upstairs and open your mother's purse and take money out, would you?'

David was past answering. He was staring at Corny, his eyes stretched to their limit.

'Take your pants down.'

'N-n-no, Dad, P-please, Dad.'

'You'll take your pants down, or I will.'

'M-Mam!'

'Your mother isn't here and if she was that wouldn't stop me from braying you. Come on.' He made a grab at him and in a second he had pulled the short trousers down over David's hips, but even before he had swung him round and over his knee David had started to holla, and when Corny's hand descended on his buttocks for the first time he let out a high piercing scream.

Ten times Corny's hand contacted his son's buttocks and it must have been around the sixth ear-splitting scream that Rose Mary entered the drive.

She knew that noise, she knew who cried like that. She ran to the garage and was borne in the direction of the hullabaloo, and she was just rushing through the small door when she saw her mother coming from the yard. She was running like mad towards the repair shed.

'Corny! what are you doing? Leave him go!'

When Mary Ann went to grab her son from her husband's hands he thrust her aside, and as he stood David on his feet he cried at her, 'Now don't start until you know what it's all about.'

'I don't care what it's all about; there's no need to murder him.'

'I wasn't murdering him, I was twanking his backside. And he's lucky to get off with just that. Do you know what he's been doing?'

Mary Ann said nothing, she just stared at her son. His face was scarlet and awash with tears, and from his face she looked to his thin bare legs and the side of his buttocks that outdid his face in colour.

'He's been stealing. This is the one that's been taking the money from the till, and all the while I thought it was Jimmy.'

Mary Ann couldn't speak for a moment, then she whispered, 'Oh, no! Oh, no!'

'Oh, yes.'

'David! you couldn't.'

Now David did a very strange thing. He did not run to his mother where he knew he would find comfort, but he turned to the man who had been thrashing him, and laying his head against his waist he put his arms around his hips and choked as he spluttered, 'Oh! Oh! Oh! Dad.'

Corny swallowed deeply, wet his lips, then bending down he pulled up the trousers and fastened them round his son's waist.

Rose Mary had been standing at her mother's side, absolutely too shocked to utter a word. Their mam smacked their bottoms sometimes, but . . . but she had never seen anybody get smacked like her dad had smacked David. He said David had stolen money. Eeh! it was a lie because David never did anything without telling her. He would not even steal without telling her. But then David wouldn't steal; he knew it was a sin, and he'd have to go to confession and tell Father Carey. Their dad was awful. She didn't love their dad. Poor, poor David. Her feelings now lifted her in a jump to her brother's side, and David did another surprising thing. With the flat of one hand he pushed her away, and whether it was with surprise or whether she tripped over one of the jutting pieces of wood that supported the engine on the bench, she fell backwards. And now she let out a howl.

She howled until she reached the kitchen and Mary Ann, taking her by the shoulders, shook her gently, saying, 'Now stop it. You weren't hurt; stop it, I tell you.'

'He . . . he pushed me, our David pushed me.'

'He didn't mean to, he was upset.'

'Dad said he stole. He's tellin' lies, isn't he?'

'If your dad said he stole, then he stole. And that's what he's been thrashed for. Now go to the bathroom and don't pester him or question him because he's upset. Run the bath for me.'

'Have . . . have we to go to bed, Mam?'

'No, I'm just going to give David a bath, then he'll feel better.' She did not add, 'It might ease the pain of his bottom.'

As Rose Mary went slowly out of the kitchen Corny came in and stood near the table, but he didn't look at Mary Ann as he gave her the explanation for David stealing the money. When he had finished there was a pause, and then she said, 'You'll have to make it up to Jimmy somehow.'

'Yes, yes, I intend to.'

He now said, 'I can't understand how he could do it under my nose.'

Mary Ann went into the scullery and put the kettle on the gas and she stood near the stove for a moment and turned her face towards the kitchen door. She wanted to shout out, 'It shouldn't surprise you; anybody could have walked off with the garage these past few weeks and I doubt if you would have noticed.' But of course she didn't. That was over, over and done with; except that the corpse was still lying between them and nothing would be the same again until it was removed. And the only way to remove such a corpse was to talk about it, and that was going to be very difficult for them both.

15

PATTERNS OF LIFE

'It's a wonder you're not struck down dead, Rose Mary Boyle. Eeh! I just don't know how you can. Like me mam says, if you got paid for being a liar you'd own the world.'

'I'm not a liar, Annabel Morton, and I'm not like you, thank goodness; I'm not a common, ignorant, big-mouthed pig!'

'No, of course, you're not, you're a common, ignorant big-mouthed idiot, that's what you are.'

'What is this?' The cool voice of Miss Plum brought Annabel Morton round to face their teacher, and Miss Plum raised her head and said, 'School hasn't begun yet and you've started.'

Rose Mary warmed suddenly to her teacher. 'She's always on, Miss Plum, she never lets up. She's always at me and our David, isn't she, David?'

David made no response. He was still in a way suffering from the effect of Friday, having his ears boxed by Diana Blenkinsop, then being thrashed almost within an inch of his life, at least that's what Rose Mary had told him had happened. But in any case the effects of the thrashing had caused him to be sick on Saturday, really sick; nervous tummy, his mam had called it. Then on Sunday his Grannie McMullen had come. She had heard about him trying to cut somebody's hair off. His grannie heard everything; she was the devil's mam, their Rose Mary said, and he could believe it. She hadn't heard about the money he had taken, and for that at least he was thankful. But she had heard about all the money his mam was getting because Ben had died. She had wanted to know what his mam was going to do with it and his mam had said they were going to have a bungalow built at the bottom of the field.

If he had known his mother was going to get all that money he would never have taken any from the till because yesterday she had given Jimmy the money he wanted for his share in the car.

The money was making things exciting and he felt he was missing a lot having to come to school; and here was Miss Plum at them already. Well, if she wasn't at them she soon would be; he could tell by the look on her face and the way she had shut up their Rose Mary.

And Miss Plum had shut up Rose Mary, she had shut her up with one word, 'ENOUGH!' Then after a pause she turned to Annabel Morton and said, 'You are not to call people liars, Annabel.'

'Yes, Miss Plum,' said Annabel meekly, before adding, 'But she is, Miss Plum. Do you know what she said? She said her mam's been left a fortune an' she's going to build a bungalow and going to give their house to Jimmy, who works in the garage. And she said her mother's a writer and she gets lots of money from the *New-castle Courier* . . .'

'Well, she does, you! She does.' Rose Mary was poking her chin out at the unbelieving individual.

'That's enough.' Miss Plum's voice was stern now. 'And Annabel is quite right this time, you are lying, and you've got to . . .'

Miss Plum was utterly amazed as Rose Mary slapped at her skirt and dared to say, 'You! you're as bad as she is. It's true . . . 'tis!'

'Don't do that!' Miss Plum had caught the hand and slapped it twice. 'You're a naughty girl, Rose Mary; I'll take you to the . . . Oooh!'

Miss Plum couldn't believe it was happening. Only the pain in her shin where David's hard toecap had kicked her proved to her that it had happened. Rose Mary Boyle had slapped at her and David Boyle had kicked her. 'Well!' She seemed to swell to twice her height and twice her breadth. As her hands went out to descend on them they turned and fled.

David was now racing across the school yard in and out of the children with Rose Mary hanging on to his hand, but just as they reached the gate he pulled her to a skidding stop. And there he turned and looked at the sea of faces mostly on his eye level, except the enraged countenance of Miss Plum. And it was to her he shouted one word, 'HELL!'

Then running again, almost flying, they scampered up the road and they didn't seem to draw breath until they reached the bus stop, and there Rose Mary, gasping, stared at her brother, at their David, who had sworn a terrible word at Miss Plum. She, herself, had slapped at Miss

Plum's dress but their David had kicked Miss Plum, he had kicked her on the shin and made her yell; and then he had said that word.

Quite suddenly the enormity of this crime and its penalty, of which she would be called upon to share, was too much for her and she burst out crying.

David stood looking at her helplessly. He didn't feel at all repentant, at least not yet. After a moment he said, 'Here's the bus.'

She was still crying as they boarded the bus. It was their nice conductor and he said, 'Hello. What's up with you two? It isn't ten minutes ago I dropped you. This day's flashed by.'

They didn't answer, and when they were seated he came up to them and, bending down, said, 'What's happened this time?' And Rose Mary, sniffing and gulping, said, 'She called me a liar, Annabel Morton, and the teacher came and she took her part and . . . and I said, I wasn't a liar and I put my hand out, like that.' She tapped the conductor's coat. 'And she slapped my hand.' She paused and cast a glance at David, but David was looking down at his finger nail as it intently cleaned its opposite number, and raising her face further to the conductor she whispered, 'He kicked her.'

'He did!' The conductor's voice was laden with awe. 'Go on.'

Rose Mary closed her eyes and nodded her head and went to impart something even worse, placing her mouth near his ear, she whispered, 'He swore.'

He brought his face fully round to hers, trying to shut the laughter out of it by stretching his eyes and keeping his lips firm; then he said, 'He swore, did he?' Now his mouth was near her ear. 'What did he say?'

'. . . Hell.'

'HELL!' The conductor straightened up and cast a glance at the interested passengers around them, and his look warned them not to titter.

'By! He's done it now, hasn't he?' The conductor looked at David's bowed head. 'Once upon a time he never opened his mouth, did he? And now, by, he's not only opened it, he's using it, isn't he?' He was talking as if David wasn't there, and Rose Mary nodded at him, then said, 'We'll get wrong.'

'Oh, I wouldn't worry.' The conductor jerked his head now.

'But we will; we'll be taken to the priest.' She turned her head swiftly to look at the man behind her who had made a funny noise, but the man's face was straight.

'What do you think he'll give you?'

'Who?'

'The priest, when you're taken to him?'

'Likely a whole decade of the Rosary, I usually only get one Our Father and three Hail Marys.'

Now the conductor turned abruptly away, saying, 'Fares, please. Fares, please,' as he went down the bus.

He was a long time down the bus because everybody was talking to him, and some people were laughing. Rose Mary thought she would never laugh again.

When they stood on the platform waiting for the bus to stop the conductor put his hand on David's head and said, 'You'll do, young 'un, you'll do,' and David grinned weakly at him. He felt he stood well in the conductor's estimation. For a moment he wished the bus conductor was his dad, at least for the next hour or so.

When they entered the lane Rose Mary started crying again, and once more he took hold of her hand, a thing he hadn't done, except when he pulled her out of the school yard, for a long, long time.

When they came in sight of the garage he drew her to a stop and they stared at each other. Rose Mary was frightened. He was frightened, but he wasn't crying. When she said to him, 'We'll get wrong,' he made no reply, and they walked on again.

It had never entered their heads to run anywhere else but home.

When Mary Ann, having made the bed and tidied the room, went to adjust the curtains she imagined she was seeing things when she saw them hand in hand walking slowly across the drive towards the front door. She pressed her face near the window for a moment; then she turned and flew down the stairs, and as she opened the door Corny was approaching them from the garage, and they both asked the same thing in different ways: 'What's the matter? Why have you come home?'

'Mi . . . Miss Plum, Mam.'

'Miss Plum! What's she done?'

'She wouldn't believe us.'

Mary Ann bent down towards Rose Mary. 'She wouldn't believe you? What did you tell her?'

'About everything in the school yard. Annabel Morton called me a liar, and a pig, and then she

906

told Miss Plum what I'd said and Miss Plum said I was lying an' all. And I didn't mean to slap her, Mam, I didn't; I just touched her skirt like that.' She flicked at her mother's hand now. 'And she slapped me, she slapped me twice. And then David . . .' She turned and looked at her brother, but David was looking up at Corny, staring up at him, fear in his eyes again, and Corny said, 'Yes, well? What did David do?'

Rose Mary waited for David to go on with the tale, but David remained mute and she said, 'He only did it because she slapped me, Mam, that's why.'

'All right, all right,' said Mary Ann patiently, 'but tell me what he did.'

'He . . . he kicked her, and he said . . .'

'You kicked Miss Plum?' Mary Ann was confronting her son, and David looked at her unblinking but said nothing.

'How could you, David.'

'He only did it because she was hitting me, Mam.'

Mary Ann took in a deep breath and Corny let out a slow one, and then Mary Ann asked of her daughter, 'What else did he do?'

Rose Mary's head drooped slightly to the side, her eyes filled with tears again, she blinked and gulped but couldn't bring herself to repeat the terrible thing their David had said to Miss Plum, and so Corny, looking at his son, asked him quietly, 'What else did you do, David?' And David looked back at his father and said briefly, 'Swore.'

Corny moved his tongue round his mouth as if he were trying to erase a substance that was sticking to his teeth, and then he asked, 'What did you say?'

There was quite a pause before David said, 'Hell!'

'. . . Hell?'

'Uh-huh!'

'Why?' Corny felt he had to pursue this, and seriously, but David went mute again, and Rose Mary, now that the worst was over, quickly took up the story. 'He grabbed me by the hand and pulled me away from Miss Plum and it was as we were going through the gate he turned back and he shouted it at her.'

Both Corny and Mary Ann saw the scene vividly in their minds, and simultaneously they turned away and Mary Ann said, 'Come along, come upstairs.'

They had hardly entered the room when the phone rang and, Corny picking it up, said, 'Yes?' and Jimmy answered. 'It's the schoolmistress. She wants to know are the bairns back.'

'Put her on.' Corny now looked at Mary Ann and she reached out and took the phone from him; then with her other hand she waved the children out of the room, whispering, 'Go into the sitting-room, I'll be there in a minute.'

'Mrs Boyle?'

'Yes, this is Mrs Boyle.'

'Have the children returned home?'

'Yes, they've just got in, Miss Swatland.' Mary Ann's voice was stiff.

'I suppose they've given you their version of the incident?'

'Yes, Miss Swatland.'

'They were very naughty you know, Mrs Boyle.

908

Of course, being twins it's understandable that they'll defend each other, but in this case they were very, very naughty. Do you know that David kicked Miss Plum?'

'I understand that he did.'

'And that Rose Mary slapped her?'

'I don't think Rose Mary slapped her. She made a movement with her hand at her skirt; there's quite a difference.'

There was a short silence on the line now, then Miss Swatland said, 'Rose Mary has a vivid imagination, Mrs Boyle. This isn't a bad thing unless it gets out of hand and then there's a very thin line between imagination and lies.'

'Rose Mary wasn't telling lies, Miss Swatland.'

There was a gentle laugh on the other end of the line. 'Oh, Mrs Boyle you don't know what Rose Mary says at school, what she said today. I understand she said you had come into a fortune, and you were giving your garage boy your house and building a bungalow, besides which you were writing for *The Courier*, and on and on.'

'Which are all true, Miss Swatland.'

There was a longer pause now, and the sound of whispering came to Mary Ann and she glanced at Corny and inclined her head towards him.

Miss Swatland was speaking again. 'Well, you must admit, Mrs Boyle, such things don't happen in the usual course of events, and when a child relates them one is apt to think they are exaggerating, to say the least. Miss Plum wasn't to know of your good fortune.'

'Miss Plum could have thought there may have been some truth in the child's prattle. It isn't unheard of for people to win the pools, is it,

although I haven't won the pools. And I think
when a child is using her imagination, even when
there isn't any truth as a basis, it doesn't help her
to be told she is a liar.'

'Miss Plum has a lot of small children to cope
with, Mrs Boyle . . .'

'I'm quite well aware of that. Well, she'll have
two less in the future, Miss Swatland, because I'm
going to take the children away.'

'Oh, that is up to you, Mrs Boyle.'

'Yes, it's up to me, Miss Swatland. Good day.'

'Good day, Mrs Boyle.'

Mary Ann put the phone down and looked up
at Corny, and Corny said, 'Take them away? But
where will you send them?'

'Her to the Convent, and him to St Joseph's
Preparatory.'

As he turned away from her and walked towards the window she said quietly, 'We can do it
between us.' Then going swiftly to the sideboard
drawer, she took from her bag an envelope and
went to his side and handed it to him, saying,
'That's for you. You won't be able to actually get
the money until it goes through probate, but it's
just to let you know that it's yours.'

'What is it?'

'Open it and see.'

He looked at her a full minute before he did as
she bade him, then when he saw the solicitor's
letter he bit on his lip and handed it back to her,
saying, 'I can't take it.'

'Corny! Look at me.'

He looked at her.

'We . . . we've always shared everything and I
won't spend another penny of the money unless

you take half. I mean it. That's to go straight into your personal account when it comes through. It's not going into the business, it's for you to do as you like with. I don't want you to put any of it towards the bungalow, and I won't, that's to come out of the business. You always intended to build a house, didn't you?'

He had his head bowed deep on his chest and he said, 'Mary Ann.'

She didn't answer him, she waited, but he seemed incapable of going on. When she saw his jaw bones working and the knuckles shining white through his clenched fists she turned away and said, 'What about us going down to Fanny's this afternoon. We've never been for ages.'

It was still a while before he answered, and then he said briefly, 'Aye.'

'The . . . the children would love it, and there's something I want to give her.'

Again she went to her bag and took out another envelope, and as she looked at it she said, 'It's wonderful to be able to do things you've dreamed about.'

He half turned his head towards her, his eyes still cast down, and she looked towards him and said, 'It's fifty pounds. They gave me an advance. Oh, I'm dying to see her face when she . . .'

'Oh, God!'

She watched him swing himself round from the window and go to the chair by the fireside and, dropping into it, bury his face in his hands, and when he muttered thickly, 'Coals of fire,' she could say nothing, only stand by the table and press her hands flat on it and look down on them and wait.

Corny squeezed his face between his hard palms. She was going to give his grannie fifty pounds. Nobody, not one of her ten sons and daughters she had alive, or any of her offspring, had ever given her fifty shillings, except perhaps himself – he had always seen to his grannie – but Mary Ann was going to give her fifty pounds; only she would have thought about giving her fifty pounds; only she would have thought about saying I'll not spend a penny of my money unless you take half. And he had been such a blind and bloody fool that he had let his thoughts and feelings slide from her. For weeks now there had been superimposed on her a pair of long, brown legs and a face that he had thought beautiful. In this moment he couldn't imagine what had possessed him not to see through the slut the moment he clapped eyes on her, but the point was he hadn't. Instead some part of him had gone down before her like dry grass before a fire.

For days now he had been consumed with shame, yet he kept telling himself that nothing had happened, not really. He hadn't been with her, he hadn't kissed her, he hadn't even touched her. That was funny. He had never once touched her hand, yet he was feeling as guilty as if he had gone the whole hog, and he knew why, oh aye, he knew why, because deep in his heart he had wanted to. Mary Ann had sensed this and nothing would be right between them until he could tell her, until he could own up.

'Mary . . . Mary Ann.'

'Yes.'

'I'm . . . Oh, God, Mary Ann, I'm sorry.' He gazed up at her, his voice low and thick. 'Oh, God,

Mary Ann, I am, I am. To the very heart of me I'm sorry. As long as I live I'll never hurt you again.' His eyes were tightly closed now, screwed deep into their sockets, and when her arms went round him and he pulled her on to his knee, she held his head tightly against her and for a moment she couldn't believe that the shaking of his body was caused by his crying. Corny crying. She had first met him when she was seven and he had been in her life since and she had never known him to cry.

The tears were raining from her own eyes now, dropping down her cheeks and on to his hair, and she moved her face in it and tried to stop him talking. Some of his words she couldn't catch, they were so thick and broken and mumbled, but others she picked out and hugged to her heart, such as 'Nothing happened, nothing, ever. Believe me, believe me – never touched her – not her hand. Like madness – As long as I live I swear to you I'll never hurt you again . . . never in that way. Oh, Mary Ann. Why? Why?'

'It's all right, it's all right.' She held his head more tightly and rocked him as she repeated, 'It's all right. It's all over now, it's all right,' and while she rocked him she thought of the time just before she got married when her da had become fascinated by that young girl, and after she herself had exposed the girl for what she was her da had struck her, and then he had gone out into the night and the storm, and her mother had thought he had gone for good, but in the early dawn Michael had found him in the barn, exhausted, and her mother had taken the lantern and gone to him. It was odd, she thought, how patterns of life were repeated.

16

FANNY

The children bounced on the back seat of the
chair chanting, 'Great . . . gran . . . Mac . . .
Bride's!' and each time they bounced Bill fell
against one or the other, until he felt forced to
protest.

Mary Ann, screwing up her face against his
howling, turned round and, dragging him up,
hoisted him over the seat on to her knee.

'Ah, Mam, he was all right.'

Mary Ann looked over her shoulder at Rose
Mary and said, 'He sounded all right, didn't he? A
little more of that and he would have been sick.'

Bill settled down quietly on her knee, and the
children took up their chant again, and Corny
drove in silence. He felt washed out, drained, but
quiet inside. The turmoil had gone.

Mary Ann, too, felt quiet inside, spent. She had
to talk to the children but all the while her mind
was on other things. She thought in a way it was
a good thing they were going to Fanny's. Life
became normal when in Fanny's company.

Most of the Jarrow that they passed through

wasn't familiar any longer. New blocks of flats, new squares, new roads; soon even Burton Street and Mulhattan's Hall would be gone. As a child she had longed to get away from the poverty of this district, from the meanness of Burton Street and the cramping quarters of Mulhattan's Hall where there were five two-roomed flats and privacy was a thing you could only dream of. Yet now, as the car drew towards the house, she thought, Once they pull it down that'll be the end of Jarrow – at least for me. And, what was more serious, once they pulled it down it certainly would be the end of Jarrow for the Hall's oldest occupant.

Fanny spied them from the window and she was at the door to greet them in her characteristic fashion.

'In the name of God, has your place been burned down! It's no use coming here for lodgings, I can't put you up . . . Hello, me bairns. Good God Almighty! what's this you've brought?' She pointed to the dog and Rose Mary shouted, 'Can't you see, Great-gran, it's a dog.'

'It's Bill. I told you about him, Great-gran,' said David. 'You know.'

Fanny bent towards David and, digging him in the chest with her finger, said, 'Aye, you told me about a dog, but you wouldn't call him a dog, would you? Snakes alive! I've never seen anything so ugly in me life. Get your things off, get your things off all of you, the kettle's on. How are you, lass?' She bent and kissed Mary Ann. Then looking at her grandson, she said, 'It's no use askin' you how you are, you're never anythin' but all right.' She paused now and added, 'There's always a first time. What's the matter with you? Have you got a cold?'

Corny stretched his face and rubbed at his eyes, saying, 'Yes, I've got a bit of a snifter.'

'It looks like it an' all. Well, you keep it to yourself, I don't want any of it. Well, sit yourselves down, can't you. Go on.'

When they were all seated she looked from one to the other and said, 'You might have given me a bit of warnin', to descend on me like this. You're not exactly manna from heaven, an' I haven't a thing in for tea.'

'Well, if you don't want us we can go.'

She took her hand and pushed at Corny's head. 'You'll go soon enough if I have any of your old buck.'

'How you keeping, Fanny?' Mary Ann now asked, and Fanny, lowering her flabby body down on to a straight-backed chair, said, 'Aw, well, lass, you know by rights I should be dead. Sometimes I think I am and they've forgotten to screw me down. Look, what's he up to, sniffing over there?' She pointed to Bill who was investigating beneath the bed in the far corner of the room.

'It's likely the last two months' washing attracting his attention,' said Corny.

'Mind it, you. I don't put me dirty washing under the bed.' She nodded straight-faced at him. 'All my dirty washing goes on the line, outside.'

They were all laughing together now and Mary Ann thought, Oh, it's good to be with Fanny.

'And what have me bonnie bairns been doin'?' Fanny embraced the two standing before her, and Rose Mary, laughing up at her, said, 'Oh, lots and lots, Great-gran.'

'Such as what?'

Oh. Rose Mary looked at David, then glanced back at her mother, and when she finally looked at Fanny again she was nipping her lower lip, and Fanny said, 'Oh, it's like that, is it?'

'It's like that,' said Mary Ann. 'We won't go into it now, it's too painful.'

'Aw.' Fanny nodded her head while she cast a glance down on the averted eyes of her great-grandson, and, bending down to him, she whispered, 'What you been up to this time, young fellow me lad? You murdered somebody?'

When David's head began to swing and his lips to work one against the other, Mary Ann put in, 'I might as well tell you. They both ran away from school this morning.'

'You're jokin'!'

'I'm not joking, Fanny; they're both very wicked. You won't believe what I'm going to tell you, but Rose Mary there slapped her teacher, and David, well he not only kicked her in the shins but swore at her. Now I bet you won't believe that of your great-grandchildren.'

Fanny, dropping her gaze to the two lowered heads, said, 'Never in this wide world, I wouldn't believe it if the Lord himself came down and said, "Fanny McBride, if you don't take my word for it you'll go to hell." '

Rose Mary's head came up with a jerk. 'That's what he said, Great-gran. It's true, it is, it's true. He did, he said that word to Miss Plum.'

'Hell? Never!'

'He did, didn't you, David?'

There was pride in Rose Mary's tone now, and Fanny, pulling herself to her feet and pressing her forearm over her great sagging breasts, turned away, saying, 'This is too much. It's the biggest surprise of me life. I'm away to get the cups, I must have a sup of tea to get over that shock . . . Mary Ann, can you help me a minute?'

Mary Ann reached the scullery just seconds after Fanny and found her standing near the shallow stone sink over which there was no tap. Fanny motioned her to close the door. Then her body shaking all over, she gave way to her laughter, and Mary Ann, standing close to her, laughed with her.

'He told her to go to hell?'

'As far as I can gather.'

'And he kicked her shins?'

'Yes, oh yes. The headmistress was on the phone a minute or so after they got in.'

'He's a lad; he's going to be a handful.'

'You're telling me, Fanny.'

Fanny dried her eyes; then patting Mary Ann on the cheek she said, 'Aw, it's good to see you, lass. I had the blues this mornin'. You know, I get them every now and again, but they were of a very dark hue the day, and I lay thinkin', Tuesday, what'm I gona do with meself all day. But I said a little prayer and left it to Him, and here you all are, lass. But tell me,' she bent her face close to Mary Ann, 'is everything all right?'

There was a pause before Mary Ann said, 'Yes, Fanny.'

'There's been somethin' up, hasn't there?'

Mary Ann now lowered her head and said in a whisper, 'Yes, Fanny.'

'I knew it. When he popped in last weekend there was somethin' about him. It's gone now. I looked at his face when he came in at the door and I knew it was gone. But he's been in trouble, hasn't he?'

Mary Ann turned her face away as she said, 'You could call it that, Fanny.'

'Money?'

'Oh, no, Fanny.'

'Not the business then?' Fanny's eyebrows moved upwards.

'No.'

There was a longer pause before Fanny whispered, 'You're not tellin' me that my Corny would ever look at . . .'

'Fanny.' Mary Ann gripped the old woman's hands. 'I'll pop in some time towards the weekend, when I'm down for my shopping, and tell you about it, eh?'

Fanny's head moved stiffly and she said, 'Aye, lass, do that, do that.' Then, turning to the rack where the cups hung, she asked in a louder tone, 'What brought you down the day anyway?'

Now her tone lighter and louder, Mary Ann answered, 'Well, we wanted to see you.'

'I'm flattered I'm sure, but is that all? I've never seen the gang of you on a Tuesday afore in me life.'

'I had a present for you and I wanted to give it to you myself.'

Fanny turned round with four cups in her hand and she said, 'A present for me? Well now; why do you have to bring me a present on a Tuesday afternoon, it isn't me birthday? And it's neither a feast, fast, or day of obligation as far as I can gather, and it's weeks off Christmas. Why a present?'

'Must there be a reason why I want to give you a present?' Mary Ann poked her face at Fanny across the table. 'I just want to give you a present, that's all. Here, give me those.' She took the cups from Fanny's hands and placed them on the saucers on the tray, and as she did so she said, 'You could do with some new ones.'

'Aye, I could that. Those that aren't cracked or chipped haven't a handle to support them. Aw, but what does it matter? Go on, I want to see this present you've brought me.'

She stopped just within the kitchen and, nodding towards Bill where he lay on the floor by the side of the bed, she said, 'I'm glad of one thing, it's not him.'

As she went to the hob to lift up the teapot that was for ever stewing there she said, 'Well, come on, where's that present.' And when she turned round, the teapot in her hand, Mary Ann handed her the envelope.

Fanny put the teapot on the table, then with her two hands she felt all round the envelope, and the thickness of it, and she looked at Mary Ann, then at Corny, and from him to the children, and they all looked at her, waiting for her reactions.

'Well, go on, open it.' Mary Ann could have been back twelve years in the past, bringing her friend a present on her birthday, or at Christmas, and saying to her, 'Well go on, open it!'

Fanny put her finger under the flap but had some difficulty in splitting open the long brown envelope, and when at last the jagged edges sprang apart she stared at the money.

Slowly she withdrew the notes. They were five pound notes and were held together by an elastic band, and her mouth dropped into a huge gape as she flicked the edge of them one after the other. They appeared to her as a never-ending stream. She lifted her eyes and looked at Mary Ann. Her expression didn't show pleasure, and you couldn't say she looked surprised, not just surprised; amazed, yes. She now looked at Corny and said, 'What is this?' Then, her eyes blinking a little and the suspicion of a smile reaching her lips, she said, 'You won the pools?'

'No.' Corny shook his head. 'Mary Ann's come into some money.'

Fanny now looked at Mary Ann again and she said, 'You've come into money, lass? From where?'

'You remember Ben, Fanny, you know who used to look after Mr Lord.'

'Aye.'

'Well, he died, and . . . and he left me nearly all his money, over eight thousand pounds.'

'Eight thousand pounds!' It was only a whisper from Fanny now, and Corny, sensing the flood of emotion that was rising in his grannie, hoped to check it by saying, 'Aye, and she's throwing it about right, left and centre; she's thrown half of it my way.'

'Half of it?' Fanny turned her attention to Corny now, but her eyes seemed glazed and out of focus. 'Well, aye, that's understandable. But me. All this?'

'It isn't that much, Fanny, it's only fifty pounds.' Mary Ann's voice was soft, and Fanny now looked at her and her lips trembled before she brought out, 'Fifty you say? Only fifty pounds. Lass, do you realise that I've never had fifty pounds in me hand in me life afore. I've . . . I've never seen fifty pounds all at once in me life afore. And . . . and what am I going to do with it?'

'Light the fire with it if you like, Fanny,' Mary Ann was smiling gently.

Fanny put the envelope down on to the table and, turning from them, her shoulders hunched, she went towards the scullery again, only to be stopped by Corny saying, 'Come on now, none of that.'

A moment ago Fanny's body had been shaking with laughter, now it was shaking with her sobbing.

When Corny sat her down in her chair, Mary Ann put her arms around her shoulders and, her own voice near tears too, she said, 'Oh, Fanny, look. I wanted to make you happy, not to see you bubble. Come on now, come on.'

But the more Mary Ann persuaded, the more Fanny cried, difficult, hard crying, crying that was wrenched up from far below her brusque, jocular, life hardened exterior.

Now the children were standing at her knees, Rose Mary with the tears running down her face and David with his tongue probing one cheek after the other in an effort not to join her.

While this was all going on Bill had been lying quietly enough on the old clippie mat by the side of Fanny's bed. He liked this room. There were smells here quite different from those at home; there was a spice about the smells here that reminded him of the morning he had met that girl, the one who had led him to the grab, and of the one solitary lamp-post he had yet encountered.

From under the bed there was wafted to him at

the present moment the musty, stingy, yet bracing aroma that had attracted him as soon as he entered the room. They had said he hadn't to go near it, but it was drawing him, inching him towards it. He turned one fishy eye in the direction of his people. They were all gathered round a chair, nobody was looking at him. The smell said, 'Come on; it's now or never.' And so, without rising, he wriggled forward and there it was, the source of this delight. It was soft and deep and warm. He pushed his nose into it. It gave him a tickly feeling that urged him to play, so he took a mouthful of it and shook it. But when it fell over his head he didn't care much for that, so he wriggled to get from under it, but the more he wriggled the more it enfolded him. This was too much of a good thing. If he didn't do something about it he'd be smothered, so, biting and scrambling, he fought until he was free.

He had reached the other side of the bed and brought the thing with him. He was in the open now, and knew how to deal with it. The smell was more exciting in the open, it was sending shivers all over him. When he saw all the feathers floating about him he growled his delight, and dashing round the bed he dragged the old eiderdown with him.

'Look. Look what he's got, Dad. Bill!'

'Oh, godfathers! Here, you rattlesnake you, give that to me.'

'Don't pull it, Corny, don't pull it, it'll only make him worse.'

'In the name of God! how did he get hold of that.'

'You shouldn't leave such things under the bed.'

Corny was yelling at Fanny now, and she, getting to her feet, flapped her hands here and there to ward off the rain of feathers.

'Corny! Corny, I'm telling you, don't pull it. I'll get him. Leave it, just leave it; you're making him worse. And you let go, David.'

Bill had never had such a game in his life. He growled his delight; he knew the more he pulled the more feathers he could raise; and his people were enjoying it too. Like all his breed he loved to give pleasure to humans, if not to his own species, so he pulled and he pulled.

'Let me get behind him.' Mary Ann was yelling at the top of her voice. 'Leave go, Rose Mary. Are you all mad? Do you hear me, the lot of you! Don't pull it!'

When at last it got through to the children and Corny that they were only adding havoc to chaos, Bill had sole possession of the tattered eiderdown again and they could hardly see each other through the cloud of feathers.

They drew the down up their nostrils then sneezed it out. When they opened their mouths to speak they swallowed feathers. They were all spluttering and coughing and flapping their hands as if they were warding off a swarm of bees.

After sneezing violently, Mary Ann cried, 'Leave . . . leave him to me. Now, now just keep quiet and leave him to me.' Then she moved slowly towards Bill who was at the far side of the table, quiet now, stretched out to his full length with his front paws lying on the edge of the eiderdown and his blunt snout resting between them.

'Bill. Bill darling. Go . . . od boy. Give it to

mother. That's a go-od boy. Bestest boy in the worldie world.' She was almost crooning as she approached him, and Bill looked at her lovingly. Here was his best pal, here was the one he liked best of the lot. Here was someone who understood him, who talked with him and played with him when the others weren't around. Well now he would give her a game like she had never had before.

When he up and dashed from her, dragging the eiderdown with him, she threw herself full length on it, and the result was disastrous. Pulled to an abrupt stop his never very steady legs gave way and he overbalanced and landed against Fanny's feet, and in the process of scrambling up again he dashed between them, and over she went.

Corny was standing within a yard of her, and springing forward he grabbed at her as she fell, hoping to break her fall; and luckily he did. It was also lucky for him that the old chair was behind him and he found himself almost pushed through the sagging bottom of it with Fanny's weight on top of him.

There was a moment of utter silence in the room; then it was broken by a rumble of laughter, a rumble that could only erupt from a chest as deep as Fanny's.

Corny, from his cramped, contorted position, had the wind knocked out of him, but the shaking body of his grannie raised in him a chuckle, then a laugh, then a roar. And now Rose Mary and David, each tugging at Fanny's hands, joined in with a high squealing glee.

And Mary Ann?

Mary Ann was lying on the eiderdown, her face

buried in the crook of her elbow. When she raised her head it was to look into the eyes of Bill, who was prone once more, his muzzle flat out, staring at her. She now looked about her, at the shambles the room represented, then ceilingwards, at the feathers floating and settling everywhere, then she looked at the huddle of her family in and around the battered armchair, and she joined her voice to theirs. She laughed and laughed until she felt that if she didn't stop she'd be ill. But it was cathartic laughter; it was what they needed to dispel the last of the nightmare. And it could never have come about except at Fanny's. Oh, thank God for Fanny . . . And Bill. Oh, yes. She put out her hand towards Bill and he wriggled his body forward. Oh yes, and Bill.

THE END

THE MARY ANN NOVELS
Volume 1
by Catherine Cookson

Her well-loved stories, featuring:
A GRAND MAN
THE LORD AND MARY ANN
THE DEVIL AND MARY ANN
LOVE AND MARY ANN

The eight novels featuring the popular, irrepressible Mary Ann Shaughnessy are for the first time collected into two volumes.

Volume 1 follows Mary Ann, a young girl living in poverty in a dockland tenement on Tyneside, from the ages of eight to thirteen. She is determined to bring about a better way of life for her family and, to the amazement of the gentle parish priest, Father Owen, and the rage and consternation of her arch-enemy, Sarah Flanagan, Mary Ann's tenacity eventually pays off.

Also available:

The MARY ANN novels Volume 2
featuring:
LIFE AND MARY ANN
MARRIAGE AND MARY ANN
MARY ANN'S ANGELS
MARY ANN AND BILL

0 552 14800 8

A SELECTION OF OTHER CATHERINE COOKSON
TITLES AVAILABLE FROM CORGI BOOKS

14624	2	BILL BAILEY OMNIBUS	£6.99
14609	9	THE BLIND YEARS	£5.99
14533	5	THE BONDAGE OF LOVE	£5.99
14531	9	THE BONNY DAWN	£4.99
14348	0	THE BRANDED MAN	£5.99
14156	9	THE DESERT CROP	£5.99
14705	2	THE GARMENT & SLINKY JANE	£5.99
13685	9	THE GOLDEN STRAW	£5.99
14703	6	THE HAMILTON TRILOGY	£6.99
14704	4	HANNAH MASSEY & THE FIFTEEN STREETS	£5.99
13300	0	THE HARROGATE SECRET	£5.99
14701	X	HERITAGE OF FOLLY & THE FEN TIGER	£5.99
14700	1	THE IRON FAÇADE & HOUSE OF MEN	£5.99
13303	5	THE HOUSE OF WOMEN	£5.99
13622	0	JUSTICE IS A WOMAN	£5.99
14702	8	KATE HANNIGAN & THE LONG CORRIDOR	£5.99
14569	6	THE LADY ON MY LEFT	£5.99
14699	4	THE MALLEN TRILOGY	£6.99
13684	0	THE MALTESE ANGEL	£5.99
14800	8	THE MARY ANN NOVELS VOLUME 1	£5.99
12524	5	THE MOTH	£5.99
14157	7	THE OBSESSION	£5.99
14073	2	PURE AS THE LILY	£5.99
14155	0	RILEY	£5.99
14706	0	ROONEY & THE NICE BLOKE	£5.99
14039	2	A RUTHLESS NEED	£5.99
10541	4	THE SLOW AWAKENING	£5.99
14583	1	THE SOLACE OF SIN	£5.99
14683	8	TILLY TROTTER OMNIBUS	£6.99
14038	4	THE TINKER'S GIRL	£5.99
14037	6	THE UPSTART	£5.99
12368	4	THE WHIP	£5.99
13577	1	THE WINGLESS BIRD	£5.99
13247	0	THE YEAR OF THE VIRGINS	£5.99